PRIDE

AND

AVARICE

PRIDE
AND
AVARICE

NICHOLAS
COLERIDGE

THOMAS DUNNE BOOKS
ST. MARTIN'S PRESS ✹ NEW YORK

THOMAS DUNNE BOOKS.
An imprint of St. Martin's Press.

PRIDE AND AVARICE. Copyright © 2009 by Nicholas Coleridge. All rights reserved. Printed in the United States of America. For information, address St. Martin's Press, 175 Fifth Avenue, New York, N.Y. 10010.

www.stmartins.com

Library of Congress Cataloging-in-Publication Data

Coleridge, Nicholas, 1957–
    Pride and avarice / Nicholas Coleridge.—1st U.S. ed.
        p. cm.
    ISBN 978-0-312-38262-9
    1. Rich people—England—Fiction.   2. Nouveau riche—England—Fiction.   3. Country homes—England—Fiction.   I. Title.
    PR6053.O4218P75   2010
    823'.914—dc22

                                                                                    2009039259

First published as *Deadly Sins* in Great Britain by Orion
First U.S. Edition: February 2010

10 9 8 7 6 5 4 3 2 1

Acknowledgements

I would like to thank Fiona Shackleton of Payne Hicks Beach, who advised me on divorce proceedings; Jennie Younger, Managing Director, Global Head of Communications and Marketing at Deutsche Bank, who advised on the mechanics of hostile corporate takeovers, as did Jeremy Quin, Senior Corporate Financial Advisor to HM Treasury, and his wife, Joanna Healey, Linklaters's takeover legal specialist. None of the above can be remotely blamed when I took liberties with their expert advice.

Katharine Barton, Sarah Deeks, Rebecca Cheetham and Becky Roach all typed stretches of manuscript, as well as offering penetrating insights and opinions on the characters in the story. Jean Faulkner copy-tasted the manuscript. Above all, I would like to thank my wife, Georgia, who reads every chapter as a work in progress and is always encouraging as well as giving the most perceptive advice.

My editor at Orion, Kate Mills, gave countless invaluable editing points at all stages and I owe a great deal too to Lisa Milton, Susan Lamb, Genevieve Pegg, Gaby Young, Lucie Stericker, Jade Chandler, Sophie Hutton-Squire and the team at Orion. Thanks also to Thomas Dunne and Karyn Marcus of my American publishers, Thomas Dunne Books at St Martin's Press. My legendary agent, Ed Victor, talks me up and reads my drafts faster than anyone.

1.

M iles Straker, resplendent in his favourite lightweight summer suit and myopically patterned silk tie, stepped outside onto the terrace and surveyed the scene. He took it all in, noticing everything . . . the perfection of his herbaceous borders, the David Linley garden gate in finest limed oak which stood at the head of the yew walk, the view along the Test valley, surely the finest in all Hampshire. He drew a deep breath of satisfaction, knowing that he, and he alone, had created . . . *all this,* this English arcadia . . . which only taste and energy, and advice from exactly the right people, and a very great deal of money constantly applied, could make possible.

For a moment he stood there, amidst all the activity of the lunch party preparations. Waiters and waitresses from the catering company were spreading tablecloths on the two dozen round tables in the marquee and laying out cutlery and wine glasses, and florists were arranging armfuls of flowers bought that morning at Covent Garden; two gardeners up ladders with lengths of twine, shears and a spirit level made final adjustments to the yew hedges; further glasses, for cocktails and champagne, were set-up on tables outside the orangerie for pre-lunch drinks.

He stared along the valley, spotted the cars parked on the horizon, and frowned. How very odd. They were parked up by old Silas's cottage—a couple of jeeps and two other cars, it looked like—and Silas never had visitors. Miles hoped they would soon leave. He didn't like the way the sunshine bounced off their bonnets.

Inside the tent, he saw his wife, Davina, in conversation with the event organiser examining some detail of the table setting. Miles wondered whether his wife looked quite her best in the summer dress she had put on, or whether he should send her inside to change into an alternative one.

Sensing they were being observed, Davina and the event organiser, Nico Ballantyne of Gourmand Solutions, spotted Miles on the terrace and hurried over to him. Miles often had that effect. People instinctively recognised that he was far too important and impatient to be kept waiting.

'There you are, darling,' said Davina anxiously. 'Nico and I were discussing whether it would be better to have salt flakes or salt crystals on the table. The salt cellars are red glass.'

'We rather felt crystals could be nicer,' Nico said, in a tone which left the door open for dissent, Miles being the paymaster.

Miles considered the question. 'I think flakes actually.' And so flakes it was.

Miles Straker was regarded, certainly by himself but by a good many others besides, as the most attractive and charismatic man in Hampshire. At the age of fifty-three, he was fit, handsome, socially confident, abominably smooth and, above all, rich. As Chairman and Chief Executive of Straker Communications, the public relations consultancy he had founded twenty-five years earlier, he was also widely viewed as influential. You had only to look at the roster of his clients (and he mailed out an impressive glossy brochure every year, to as many as four thousand neighbours and opinion formers, listing them all) to get the measure of his reach. His corporate clients included Britain's third largest supermarket group, second largest airline, an international luxury hotels chain, an arms dealer, an energy conglomerate, a Spanish sherry marque and, *pro bono*, the Conservative Party. In addition, he was privately retained by half a dozen Footsie 100 Chairmen and CEOs, either to enhance their public profile or else keep them out of the newspapers altogether. It was rumoured that the royal House of Saud paid Miles a stupendous annual retainer for presentational services, as did the Aga Khan Foundation. But Miles would never be drawn on these special arrangements, if they did in fact exist.

From Monday to Friday, the Strakers lived in a tall, white stucco house on a garden square in Holland Park, which they had owned for eleven years. If there was a faintly corporate feel to the place, and particularly to the large taupe-and-nutmeg coloured drawing room with its many L-shaped sofas, this was because Miles regularly used the house as somewhere in which to hold work-related receptions, which had the additional advantage of enabling him to write-off most of the expensive decoration against tax. Each morning, Miles was collected at 6:50 a.m. precisely from the house to be driven to one of the three hotel dining rooms he used for breakfast meetings with the great and the good, before being dropped at the mews house behind Charles Street, Mayfair, which was his corporate headquarters. For as long as he had been able to afford it, Miles had made a rule of maintaining an independent office above the fray, private and secretive, rather than sitting himself in the same building as his 900 London-based employees. 'I probably have the smallest office in London,' was his boast. 'There's scarcely room for the seven of us to squeeze in together: that's me, the three girls, two analysts, and my driver.' Needless to say, Miles's own senatorial office, within this toytown Regency townhouse, occupied virtually all the available space.

But it was the country house in Hampshire which he felt best reflected his stature and gravitas. Seven years after buying the place from the Heathcote-Palmers, whose ancestors had built the house almost 300 years earlier, Miles liked to imply that his own family had been settled there for rather longer than they had. This was put across in many subtle ways, such as the leather framed black and white photographs of Chawbury Manor dotted about the Holland Park house, and in the Charles Mews South office, and a tasteful engraving of Chawbury on the letterhead of the country writing paper, and the substantial conversation pieces hanging in both the country and London entrance halls, showing Miles and Davina and the four Straker children painted in oils on the terrace, framed by lavender beds and yew hedges, with the trophy house looming ostentatiously behind them.

It was generally agreed that Chawbury Manor was one of the loveliest setups in the county; not only the house itself, with its Georgian proportions and knapped-flint-and-brick Hampshire architecture, but for its crowning glory, its views. It stood at the head of a steep private valley, almost a mile long, bounded its entire length on one side by mature woodland, and on the other by rolling downland. The floor of the valley, through which the river Test meandered, was overlooked by the several raked and balustraded terraces of Chawbury Manor, and grazed over by a flock of rare Portland sheep.

From the wide top terrace, which opened out from French windows in the drawing room, the television room and from Miles's own wood-panelled study, you could see the full pitch of the valley, and it was here, when the Strakers entertained, that guests gathered for drinks before lunch or dinner, exclaiming at the view.

'Is this all you?' people would ask, staring into the distance.

And Miles replied, 'Actually it is, yes. Our predecessors used to finish at the fence just before the far wood, but fortunately the wood came up a few years ago and we were able to buy it. Which makes one feel much more secure, with all these alarming changes in planning regulations from the ghastly Michael Meacher.'

'Now tell us about that pretty little cottage? Now what's that all about?'

The cottage was a tiny flint-and-lathe labourer's hovel on the horizon, surrounded by a tumbledown barn and several other semi-derelict outbuildings, including an ancient *pigeonniere*. At such a distance from the manor, it was impossible to see the cluster of buildings very clearly, because they melded into the fold of the hill. And yet you could never look down the valley without being aware of them. The cottage acted as a picturesque eye-catcher in landscaped parkland.

'Well, as a matter of fact that's the one and only thing that isn't us. I hope it will be one day. I have an understanding with the old boy who lives there that he'll offer it to me first and to no one else.'

'So it is still lived in? It looks rather abandoned.'

'I think only about two rooms are habitable. He's a strange old character who lives there, the place is collapsing round his ears. Silas Trow, his name is, looks about a hundred and ten. It's reached by an unmade track from the Micheldever road. God knows how he manages out there. Collects his weekly GIRO and that's about it, I think.'

'What'll you do with the cottage when you get it?' people often enquired. 'It has so much potential.'

Then Miles would shrug. 'Well, Davina always says she wants it for her painting studio. We'll see. There are any number of uses we might put it to.'

In the back of Miles's mind was the prospect of one day installing one of his mistresses there, once it had been repaired, as a weekend trysting place. Too risky, too reckless, too close to home? Perhaps. But he thrived on risk. He assumed Davina had known for years about the existence of other women and long ago accepted it, but perhaps she didn't; it wasn't exactly something he could ask her.

2.

The Straker summer lunch party was held on the second Sunday in June for the sixth year in succession. Strictly speaking, it was a corporate event, and certainly every last penny of the cost was written off against tax, including several disputable elements, such as the entire annual upkeep of the garden, which would have raised questions from the Inland Revenue had it been presented to them in quite that way. Certainly the raison d'être of the party was to entertain clients and would-be-clients of Straker Communications, and the invitation list bristled with the Chairman and Chief Executives and their wives of the largest accounts, as well as more favoured and presentable marketing directors. As Miles reviewed the guest list for the final time, he saw that four senior representatives from Pendletons, the supermarket chain, had accepted to come today, including his neighbours Lord and Lady Pendleton of Longparish; James Pendleton being one of the four Pendleton brothers, family shareholders of Strakers's biggest client. Also on the guest list were the managing directors of British Regional Airways, Trent Valley Power 4 U, Eaziprint—the photocopy to digital services conglomerate—and several strategically useful executives from Unilever, Allied Domecq and Compaq. Miles doubted some of these guests would be a social asset at the party, and they were to be seated as unobtrusively as possible at the extreme edge of the tent; he was confident they would already be sufficiently flattered to be invited down to his private house, given his reputation and profile. Miles nevertheless made a point of memorising all their names, for it was a matter of pride that he should acknowledge every guest personally, and he would not tolerate name badges at Chawbury Manor.

The client side taken care of, the Strakers liked to embellish their lunchparties with as many of their more glamorous neighbours as possible, as well as acquaintances from further afield who would raise the game. So the local Conservative MP, Ridley Nairn, was there with his wife, Suzie, as were half a dozen senior Tories from Central Office for whom Miles was one of three favoured advisors. A deputy chairman of the Party, Paul Tanner, with whom he breakfasted every six weeks at The Ritz, had been invited with his third wife, Brigitte, and would sit at the top table with James and Laetitia Pendleton, along with several of their jollier and more prominent neighbours. In the interest of political balance (for Miles could never allow his company to be exclusively associated with the Conservative interest, given the way things stood), a couple of known Labour donors were invited, including the home-micro-curry tycoon, Sir Korma Gupta, whom Miles anticipated would shortly become a client.

Shortly before the arrival of the first guests, when he had satisfied himself that everything was perfectly ready, Miles mustered his wife and family in the hall for a final pep-talk. Whenever they gave a large party, he insisted all four children be present and prepared to pull their weight entertaining the guests. Today, he ran his eyes over them and grimaced. Davina at least now looked more appropriate, having changed into something pretty and flowery, and Samantha was undeniably attractive, despite the four inches of midriff on display and a sulky expression. Six foot tall, with straight blond hair and the best legs at Heathfield, Samantha at seventeen was a source of mild anxiety. She was also stunningly pretty, spoilt, petulant, and Miles's favourite child. Today, she made no secret of the fact she'd rather be up in London at her friend Hattie's party, than doing her bit at the Chawbury lunch.

'For heaven's sake, Peter, can't you put a tie on? And those chinos are grubby. You can't possibly wear them for lunch.' Miles glared at his eldest child.

Peter at twenty-three was the only one to be working for his father at Straker Communications. Not for the first time, Miles wondered whether his son was cut out for the business of public relations. But, then again, there seemed to be nothing else he had any aptitude for, so they had created a job for him in research, which kept him out of mischief.

'Surely I don't need to wear a tie, Dad? This is *Saturday lunch*. No one wears ties.'

'Nonsense. Look at Archie, he's got a tie on. In fact, one of mine if I'm not mistaken. Did you take that from my dressing room?'

'Just borrowed it, Dad. I'll put it back.'

'You'd better.' But Miles looked approvingly at the son who reminded him most of himself. Archie was quick, bright and extremely attractive to girls. He was also glib and unscrupulous but, unlike his father, had not yet learnt to conceal these attributes behind a carapace of sincerity.

'As for you, Mollie, haven't you got something less funereal to put on?' He stared critically at his plump youngest daughter, with her plain, serious face and droopy brown skirt and top. 'I thought you said you'd buy something new for today?'

'I did. This *is* new.' Mollie had travelled into Basingstoke especially, but found the shops in the High Street scarily trendy and hard-edged, and bought the first thing that looked neither obtrusive nor sexed-up, without trying it on.

'Sam, haven't *you* got something you can lend Mollie? There must be something buried in that heap of clothes on your bedroom floor?'

'*Da-ad*,' replied Samantha. 'Get real. As if she'd fit into anything of mine.'

The discussion was cut short by the crunching of tyres on gravel outside, and the arrival of the first guests.

One of Miles's great skills as a host—in fact, great skills in life— lay in his ability to greet newcomers with an overwhelming show of warmth and enthusiasm. He was a grasper of hands, a hugger of both men and women. When he shook hands with a client, he gripped their palm and held onto it for longer than was quite comfortable, while maintaining a glittering eye contact. His pleasure at meeting and re-meeting people of importance—and people of only tangential importance to his life—was remarkable, something he had first learnt, then assiduously practiced over many years. Not naturally tactile, even with his family, he had exerted himself, realising that if he could establish this first impression with conviction, it would carry him more than half the distance. The advice he gave in his professional life, for which he billed so handsomely, was strategic and clinical, but he understood the importance of 'connecting' with the world, and these extravagant greetings were their outward manifestation.

Today, he positioned himself outside on the terrace, just beyond the open drawing room door, through which the guests were being directed having first collected a glass of champagne from the line of waitresses standing with outstretched trays. So they had already passed through the flagstoned hall with its sweeping staircase and family group portrait above the fireplace, and through the drawing room with its many sofas and paint finishes, and then out again onto the terrace where the picture-perfect Straker family awaited, the six of them formed up in their ties and pretty dresses, marred only by Peter's grubby chinos, and behind them the famous long view of Chawbury valley.

It was shortly after they had all sat down for lunch, and the many waitresses from Gourmand Solutions were bringing out the first course of langoustines and scallops on multi-coloured glass plates, that Miles again became aware of activity on the horizon. Unmistakably, next to Silas Trow's cottage and the derelict barn, he could see three parked cars. Even at this distance, he could tell they were four-by-fours, Landcruisers or Cherokee Jeeps by the size of them. And there were several people poking about in the outbuildings. Miles found it perplexing. Who were they?

As lunch progressed and the waitresses served a main course of guinea fowl in a wild mushroom sauce with tiny broad beans, he found himself glancing again and again towards the cottage. Each time it was more troubling. He thought he could see two figures measuring out distances with a tape. One of the four-by-fours drove off and later returned followed by a truck from which several men clambered down and strode about purposefully. As soon as lunch was over and everyone had left, he would go over and discover what was going on.

Another of Miles's skills was being able to conduct several conversations simultaneously, so he kept up a lively discussion with Laetitia Pendleton about the English National Ballet's forthcoming programme (Laetitia was a trustee), and with her husband about the impact of Wal-Mart's recent acquisition of the Asda supermarket group, while tuning in to Paul Tanner's confident broadcast to the table that, in William Hague, the party finally had a leader with the ability to instil sufficient party discipline to win, and how their latest private doorstep polls were consistently registering a six percent uplift over Mori and YouGov. But even as Miles flattered and eavesdropped upon his neighbours and clients, he peered up at the cottage on the horizon.

It wasn't until well after five o'clock that they were shot of the final guests. Every year, it was the ones you were least happy to have in your house who lingered the longest, and wanted to engage Miles in conversation, often about work-related issues which made it difficult to cut them short. The partner of the marketing boss of Trent Valley Power 4 U—a shocking bottle-blonde with a wedge haircut and evidently the worse for drink—had mislaid her handbag in the garden and couldn't remember where, and then, having eventually located it, asked, 'Can I use your toilet?' and strode into the house for ages, instead of using the Portaloos behind the orangerie, until they worried she might have passed out in the cloakroom. Meanwhile, an adhesive couple from BRA—British Regional Airways—stood by the open door of their BMW making fatuous conversation instead of leaving, and thanking the Strakers 'for the lovely meal and we must get you over to us one day soon, I'll give you a bell next week and make a plan.' Miles shuddered. The downside of these lunches was that there were always people who didn't understand the ground rules, and wanted to reciprocate. Obviously they'd be stonewalled by the girls at the office, forever if necessary, but it was still an imposition.

Free at last of guests, and leaving the caterers dismantling tables and stacking chairs, Miles strode over to the stableyard. Although he had never so much as sat on a horse until his thirty-sixth birthday, he had recently become a keen rider. The Strakers kept half a dozen thoroughbreds at Chawbury, looked after by a pair of girl grooms from New Zealand. One of their duties was to keep the horses permanently tacked-up at weekends, in case the family should decide on a whim to go riding.

As he approached the stables, Miles saw Samantha, already changed into jodhpurs and riding boots, preparing to set out.

'Hang on, Sam, I'll join you. I want to ride over to Silas's cottage, there's something going on up there.'

Soon, father and daughter were clattering across the cobble-stones on their chestnut and bay mounts, heading past the wall of beech hedges which lined the path to the valley floor. They crossed an ornamental bridge over the Test and entered a wide, springy meadow, more than half a mile long, which Miles had decreed be kept perpetually free of nettles, thistles and ragwort. To this end, the two Chawbury groundsmen spent hours every month, circling the field on quad-bikes, zapping the smallest growth with noxious chemicals.

They were riding parallel to the river and powered up first into a canter, then a gallop. Miles experienced the near-exhilaration he always felt when crossing his own land at full pelt on his own horse, hooves thundering across his immaculate nettle-free acres. At the midpoint of the valley, he slowed and turned to catch sight of Chawbury Manor from the prospect he knew to be its finest. Ten yards ahead, Samantha's blond hair flowed behind her in the breeze, as she pushed her horse faster and faster. He felt a surge of pride that his eldest daughter was so indisputably attractive and classy . . . he felt it reflected well upon himself. As a man who had built his reputation and fortune on his ability to enhance the sur-face of every situation, Miles instinctively understood his own life in the same way. He saw himself riding his thoroughbred horse with his thoroughbred daughter, and the distant prospect of his thoroughbred house, and knew his life must be as near-perfect as it is possible for talent, money and hard work to secure.

Having ridden the floor of the valley, the ground now rose to-wards a bun-shaped knoll which overlooked Silas's cottage, and Miles and Samantha slowed to a halt. From here, they could see the whole decrepit property with its subsiding tithe barn and *pi-geonniere* missing half its roof slates, and a fetid, slime-green pond filled with the rotting branches of dead trees. The cottage itself had cascades of bramble clinging to the roof, the garden choked with bindweed. Parked across the track between cottage and barn were two four-by-fours and a builders' lorry, and men could be seen with clipboards and surveying equipment.

Miles rode down the hill, trailed by Samantha, and reined-in in front of a small group of workmen. 'Mind telling me what's going on here?' He spoke peremptorily, glaring down from his horse.

'And who's asking?' replied one of the men. He was a wiry character in his mid-forties, with a Midlands accent and suede jacket.

'Miles Straker,' replied Miles. He announced his name in a tone which implied it should mean something. 'I happen to own this valley, and I'm asking what you're all doing up here. This is private property. And where's Silas Trow?'

The wiry man replied, 'The old fellow who used to live here? Passed away several months ago, I believe.'

'Silas has *died*? No one told *me* that.' Miles felt wrong-footed, disliking the sensation of being under-informed; one of his principles in life was that he should always be better briefed than everyone else. 'And what are you doing here anyway? Isn't there a foreman or someone in charge?'

'There's no foreman, because I haven't appointed contractors yet,' replied the wiry man. 'But you can talk to me. I recently bought this place. Ross Clegg.' He shot out a palm towards Miles, who found his fingers crushed by the force of the handshake.

Now Miles was seriously confused. Was this bloke in the suede jacket really telling him he'd bought Silas's cottage, the cottage Silas had as good as promised him, more than once? Why the hell hadn't anyone informed him about this? Why hadn't he known Silas was dead? He hadn't even realised he'd been ill. As for the cottage being on the market, he hadn't heard a damn thing about it, when he was the obvious purchaser. It was true he'd been travelling a lot recently, in the States, in the Emirates, Tokyo, but that was no excuse. There were such things as faxes and telephones. His furious mind searched for scapegoats: his secretaries, his housekeeper and, above all, Davina. For heaven's sake, she spent four whole days a week down at Chawbury, didn't she? She had the whole of Monday and Friday there, as well as weekends. Why hadn't Davina known?

Ross Clegg was approaching Samantha to introduce himself. He walked with a slight limp, Miles noticed, one leg dragging behind the other as he crossed the ground. Miles also saw Ross was a more confident man than he'd initially realised; physically he wasn't much to speak about, but there was an unmistakeable presence.

Ross stuck his hand up to Samantha, towering above him on her horse, and said, 'Ross . . . Ross Clegg. And you're a very lovely sight, if you don't mind my saying so. Do you often ride by this way?'

Samantha replied in a brittle voice, 'Actually we live at Chawbury Manor. And I do often ride through our woods, when I'm home from school.'

'Looks like we're going to be neighbours then,' Ross said. 'We've got kids more or less your age, so we'll have to get you all together once we're in and settled. But that won't be for the best part of a year probably, when the builders are done and dusted.'

Miles felt a second shock of the afternoon. 'You're not building on, are you?' he asked Ross. He had a sudden vision of a hideous extension on the side of Silas's hovel, with additional bedrooms and bathrooms.

'No way, mate,' Ross replied. 'We're doing the job right and bulldozing the place. No good trying to patch up a mess like this, better to start over. That way, at least you end up with something that works for you. This will be our second new-build in five years. Dawn and I built our present property in Droitwich and learnt a lot of hard lessons in the process.'

3.

Miles spent much of the following week in the air, but this did not deter him from his mission. By Monday lunchtime, he had confirmed the intolerable news that Silas's cottage had indeed been sold from under his nose. It seemed that Silas had keeled over while buying a lottery ticket in Micheldever, been rushed to Basingstoke and North Hampshire General Hospital and never been discharged. His niece, Paula, had given the cottage to First Countryside estate agents to sell, which had stuck up a photograph in the window of their local branch at the laughably low asking price of £65,000. Miles's exasperation reached new heights. If the ruddy niece had only gone to Knight Frank or Savills, he'd have heard about it for sure, instead of instructing this backstreet auctioneers.

His next priority was to learn everything he could about Ross Clegg. By now, half his office was devoted to the task, his PAs Googling Clegg on the internet and searching the numerous syndicated databases to which Straker Communications subscribed. When Miles landed at JFK, his first act was to call the office for an update. To his dismay, Ross turned out to be Chief Executive and founder of Freeza Mart, a cash-and-carry grocery enterprise in the West Midlands. Before long, Miles's driver, Makepiece, had been dispatched to collect the statutory accounts from Companies House, which was brought back to Charles Mews South and faxed, page by page, to Miles's suite at the Four Seasons hotel on Madison and 57th Street, along with an investment report the girls had tracked down. Sitting at his desk before setting out to dinner, Miles studied every page, learning about the twenty-three edge-of-conurbation freezer centres from Coventry to Telford that Ross had established over the past sixteen years, and his plans to expand the business into the south-east with new outlets from Southampton to Basingstoke. This, presumably, was his reason for wanting a home in Hampshire. It irritated Miles that the balance sheet was so clean, with an admirably low debt ratio, and impressive annual growth in revenue and profits. The company had been listed on the AIM small-cap market two years ago. On the evidence of this report, Ross was a resourceful businessman.

By Tuesday afternoon, Miles's office had got hold of Ross's planning application, which arrived with the devastating information that it had already been approved by the local planning authority. When this was nervously explained by his senior PA, Sara White, Miles became agitated. But this was nothing to his annoyance when the details of the application, and supporting plans and elevations, disgorged from the fax. The proposed new house was grotesque—there was no other word for it—simply the naffest, least appropriate dwelling imaginable. It reminded him of an overgrown Bovis home, with a pretentious double-height pillared entrance with balcony on top, with plate glass, double-glazed French windows leading from the master bedroom suite. In front of the house was an in-and-out drop-off-point around a circle of lawn like a corporation roundabout, and a pitched roof with dormer windows set into fancy Dutch tiles.

The longer Miles scrutinised the plans, the more angry he became. It was simply unbelievable planning permission had ever been granted. The house was a monstrosity which would blemish the entire valley. Over his dead body would it get built.

He immediately launched a campaign to lobby every person and organisation of influence he could think of. The Lord Lieutenant of Hampshire was written to (Miles's letter was simultaneously posted, faxed and couriered for maximum effect), as was the High Sheriff, the Chairman of the local authority and six local County Councillors who owed him favours. Each of these blistering missives was copied to the local MP, Ridley Nairn, who received a long letter of his own for good measure, as did Paul Tanner at Conservative Central Office.

A second wave of letters was dispatched the next day, this time to English Heritage, making them made aware that a historic tithe barn was in jeopardy, with copies to SAVE Britain's Heritage and the Architectural Conservancy Trust. All these letters were worded with great cunning, and did not fail to mention Miles's connection to several public companies which supported the work of these bodies, or sponsored their awards.

By the next weekend, back at Chawbury from his trip to the States, Miles felt confident the situation could be retrieved from the jaws of disaster. At lunch, he lectured Davina and the children on the importance of cultivating relationships with well-placed individuals, and that through a judicious balance of hard work and discrete networking it was generally possible to achieve everything you wanted. 'Call it a life lesson,' Miles declared, as his family sat around the mahogany dining room table.

But Mollie, who was listening to her father's speech with a disapproving frown, said, 'I don't really get what's so bad about this new house. Other people have to live *somewhere*. And it's quite a long way from us in any case, it wouldn't matter that much.'

Miles regarded Mollie sternly. 'Have you given any thought to this at all? Have you considered what it would do to the value of our house, having a hideous modern mansion—and that's doubtless what Mr Clegg calls it, "a mansion"—directly across the valley? It would halve the value, that's if we could sell it at all. Do you think the kind of people in the market to buy Chawbury would choose to live somewhere with an overgrown *council house* plonked on the horizon? It would be virtually un-sellable. Blighted. We'd effectively be trapped here for life.'

'But you aren't going to move house anyway,' persisted Mollie. 'I'm just saying it wouldn't be such a big thing. I mean, the cottage is there already, and I hardly notice it. That's all I'm saying.'

Miles shook his head 'Peter, what about you? I assume you can see what a total ruddy disaster it would be.'

'Actually, Dad, I agree with Mollie. You're really over-reacting. You always said you'd modernise the cottage yourself, if you bought it.'

'I'm beginning to think my entire family is half-witted. Archie, what about you? And Samantha? You've actually met this Ross Clegg, the Midlands freezer king. Does he strike you as a welcome addition to the Chawbury "community," as Mollie would no doubt phrase it?'

'No way,' said Samantha. 'He's like this really geeky, naff guy? Like someone working in a . . . garage or somewhere? And he's, like, *disabled* or something?' Samantha had developed a tick of ending every sentence on a rising inflection, which Miles hated and thought she'd picked up from too much watching of *Neighbours*. 'He's got this *club foot* thing?'

'You've got to stop him, Dad,' Archie said. 'It'll be such an eyesore if he gets away with it. I reckon it would knock two million off the value of our house.'

'Thank you, Archie,' said Miles. 'Thank God one of my children has a clear brain. As for you, Peter, I want you to conduct some research at the office. In fact, get the whole department on to it. I need a list of every campaigning group for rare mammals, wild flowers . . . all of them . . . *bats, frogs, newts*, I don't know, anything that might be infesting Silas's cottage. And, for heaven's sake, don't hang about. I need it on my desk by Monday afternoon.'

On Monday morning, Miles received the first batch of replies to his letters, none of which reassured him. All were respectful, all sympathetic, all promised to do whatever could be done within the parameters of what was possible. The Lord Lieutenant, who regularly dined with the Strakers at Chawbury, said he was instinctively on Miles's side, and so was Philippa who joined him in sending best wishes to them both, but it must be appreciated that planning regulations did not fall under his remit—'more is the pity!'—but he would do his best to whisper a word into the right ears. Several county councillors replied regretting that Chawbury Manor did not fall inside their wards, and the local councillor inside whose ward Chawbury did fall wrote that if only he had known about all this in advance of the planning decision, he would surely have been able to bring his influence to bear upon the committee. It was generally agreed it is always more difficult to overturn planning consent *after* the event than it would have been before. To Miles's irritation, even Ridley Nairn, his constituency MP, whose electoral brochures and quarterly newsletters were designed free of charge by Straker Communications, and then actually posted through

Straker Communications's mail room, replied that he would do what he could, but hoped Miles would understand he could not openly campaign on behalf of his constituents over every individual planning dispute, especially since Miles's particular area was the least built-up in the constituency. 'We all need to be wary of NIMBYism,' he added self-righteously. At a meeting with his lawyers, Miles explored overturning the planning consent on the grounds that he had never been officially informed about the application, but it turned out Chawbury Manor was slightly too great a distance from Silas's cottage for this to be statutorily required.

A second legal challenge against Silas's niece, Paula, for failing to extract the best price for Silas's family by using an inferior estate agent, was also a non-starter, since Paula was sole beneficiary of her uncle's will.

By the following weekend, Miles was seriously put out. Arriving at Chawbury in the dark on Friday night, he drew back his bedroom curtains the next morning to see a yellow JCB digger on the horizon, and a team of builders laying a temporary access road to the cottage. Later, he thought he spotted a cement mixer and, shortly before lunch, a crane appeared on site.

After lunch, Miles drove Peter and Samantha across the fields in his John Deere Gator, the green six-wheeled open-topped vehicle he used for buzzing about the estate. 'We'll go over for a recce,' Miles said. 'I need to know what's going on up there, I don't trust that man an inch.'

Arriving at the crest of the hill, Miles looked down in dismay. In addition to the JCB, there was a demolition vehicle on site with wrecking ball and chain, clearly intent on flattening the cottage. Several workmen in hard hats were sitting about with mugs of tea, and Miles spotted Ross studying the new house plans. A woman in her early forties hung on to Ross's arm, wearing a beige coat which almost exactly matched her coloured razor-cut hair. Even at this distance, Miles could see her face was suntanned to a shade which didn't look quite natural, and caked in makeup. She looked ridiculously over-groomed to be standing about in a building site, he reckoned.

'*Miles!* Miles! Over here, mate, there's someone I want you to meet.' Ross was beckoning to catch his attention.

Reluctantly, Miles restarted the Gator and edged it down the bank to the cottage. Damn it. He hadn't wanted to speak to Ross. 'Let's get this over with and get out.' he said to Peter and Samantha under his breath.

This time Ross was wearing a chocolate brown leather jacket, with Levis and a pair of Texas-style rodeo boots. Miles now knew his age was forty-seven, though he looked older: a craggy, lined face, short black hair and the limp when he walked. Jangling at his wrist was a narrow copper bracelet, which made Miles shudder. He disliked all jewellery on men, other than a discreet wristwatch and gold cufflinks.

'I'd like you to meet my better half, Dawn,' Ross said, introducing the woman in the beige coat. 'Dawn, this is Miles, our next door neighbour. Well, I say next door, our neighbour from the big place up the valley there. And this is Sam,' he said, turning to Samantha. 'Remember I told you I met a beautiful lady out horse-riding? Well, here she is.' Then, beaming at Peter and grasping his hand, he said, 'Ross . . . Ross and Dawn Clegg . . . we're the crazy idiots trying to turn this heap of old stones into a home. That's if it doesn't bankrupt us first.'

'Peter Straker,' Peter replied. Instinctively warming to Ross's friendly manner, he shook hands with the Cleggs. He sensed his father's disapproval behind him.

'Pleased to meet you,' Dawn said. Her face, beneath the suntan and makeup, was eager and perky. Like her husband, she had a strong Midlands accent. On her fingers were a multitude of gold rings, and her lips were covered with tan-coloured lipstick outlined with brown pencil. She said, 'I do love your house, Peter. One of the reasons we bought this plot, actually, was the thought of waking up to that view every morning. Ross and I saw round a few old places ourselves before buying here, but decided they weren't really for us. Too much upkeep. But a treat to look at.'

Miles considered some caustic put-down about views being a two-way matter, but Ross was saying, 'I know all about you now, Miles, I've been looking you up. When we met last week, I said I know I know that name, but couldn't place it, it was driving me mad, so I did my researches. I'm well impressed too. You're in with all the movers and shakers, so they say.'

Miles experienced several simultaneous emotions. The first was affront that Ross Clegg had been checking up on him, snooping behind his back like a private detective. The second, fleeting disappointment Ross hadn't instantly known who he was in the first place. Thirdly, satisfaction Ross now recognised his elevated status.

'I wouldn't believe everything you read in the newspapers,' Miles replied, in a superior voice.

'You're really quite famous,' Ross went on. 'When I mention your name to people, they've very often heard of you. I've been telling folk you're going to be just across the fields from us. And the kids were very excited when I said you've got kids their age. You know what kids are like about moving to a new place. Our lot don't want to move down here at all. They think southerners are all snobs.'

'Gemma's the worst,' Dawn said. 'She loves it in Droitwich. She turned sixteen last week. Her friends and her school are her world.'

'I'd be the same,' Peter said. 'You don't want to start making new friends at her age.'

'It's all Dad's fault,' Ross said, cheerily. 'I'm not the most popular bloke in our house at the minute, not with Gemma anyhow. We wouldn't be relocating if it wasn't for my job, so Dad's the bogeyman.'

Feeling he'd heard more than enough already about the Clegg family and their foibles, Miles revved the Gator and began to edge away.

'Cheerio then, Miles,' Ross called out.

'See ya later, Miles,' said Dawn.

Miles shuddered as he sped off.

Various new strategies were formulating in his head. But first it was time for Plan B.

It is remarkable how many conservation groups there are in Britain, Miles thought, especially in the area of animal and flora preservation, and how sweeping are their powers. Having carefully studied the document compiled by Peter and the research department, he knew exactly what to do next.

Ensconced at his computer, he composed emails to the Woodland Trust, to the Wildflowers Conservancy Trust, the Bat Conservation Trust and the Invertebrate Conservation Trust. Each of these organisations received a different tip-off that a unique habitat of exceptional scientific and environmental importance was about to be destroyed by developers, threatening a host of endangered species. In one e-mail, it was the horseshoe bat and soprano pipistrelle bat which took centre stage. In another, the red-tipped cudweed—*filago lutescens*—and adder's tongue spearwort. In his message to the Invertebrate Conservation Trust, Miles warned about palmate newts and salamanders which would disappear were the pond at Silas's cottage drained and filled-in. The tithe barn was a favoured roosting place not only of the horseshoe and pipistrelle bat, but of serotine bats, all protected under the Wildlife and Countryside Act of 1981, and liable to a fine of £5,000 *per bat* or six months imprisonment for anyone who displaced them. The meadow around the cottage was the habitat of rare wild flowers and grasses.

By the following Tuesday, Miles was gratified to learn that all work at Silas's cottage had come to an abrupt halt, under a blizzard of compulsory inspection orders. Bat experts and pond-life experts arrived at the hamlet in hordes and were setting up hides and observation posts, and wildflower conservationists had successfully served desist orders on both Ross and his workmen.

That evening in London, at a small dinner he was hosting in honour of the Finance Minister of Abu Dhabi in a private dining room at the Lanesborough Hotel, Miles chuckled to himself. He'd like to see the Freeza King get out of that one.

There were no two ways about it, if you wanted to take on Miles Straker in his own backyard, you'd better know what you were coming up against.

4.

Sitting on the back seat of his dark blue Bristol Continental, Miles speed-read the briefing notes about his biggest and highest-yielding client. His driver, Makepiece, was ploughing through heavy traffic towards the Barbican where Pendletons plc was headquartered.

Although the Pendletons business was handled day to day by a large team of Straker Communications executives, comprising more than forty people, Miles nevertheless made a point of attending quarterly meetings there himself. He knew the importance of giving 'face time' to top clients, and these quarterly sessions, which were known as strategic meetings to distinguish them from the weekly update and monthly review meetings, were by long tradition attended by all four Pendleton brothers, James, Nick, Michael and Otto, who between them controlled 34 percent of the stock.

Miles did not anticipate any great issues at today's meeting. The supermarket group was performing well, with a rising market share, which put it within catch-up distance of Sainsbury's, and only Tesco's was outperforming them in growth and EBITDA. In recent months, they had put further blue water between themselves and Asda, with Morrisons, Safeway and Waitrose ranked behind that.

Glancing at the agenda, Miles saw that only item seven—AOB—Any Other Business—was liable to be controversial. He consulted the slim *aide memoir* he had prepared for that particular item, and which he intended to spring on the meeting as a surprise. He hoped to God the Pendleton brothers would go for the idea, because matters were becoming tedious at Chawbury.

Makepiece pulled up outside Pendleton Plaza, the steel-and-glass building on Long Wall with its lime green logo in the Pendleton corporate branding. Inside the atrium lobby, Miles spotted an advance party of Straker Communications executives watching out for him, including his managing director, Rick Partington, and the various Straker account directors, managers, researchers and coordinators who serviced the Pendletons business. As he entered the lobby, the Strakers team danced attendance, offering extra sets of briefing notes and agendas in case he hadn't brought his own, and handing him the plastic name-badge they had obtained in advance from security. Miles thrust the badge into a suit pocket. As Chairman of Straker Communications, he felt he was slightly beyond pinning plastic badges all over himself.

'Morning, Miles,' said Rick. 'As you can see, we're fully represented today. It's going to be eleven of us and nine of them.' As a matter of policy, Strakers always preferred to outnumber their clients at meetings, believing it made them seem serious and committed. Miles noticed Peter was on the team today, and wished his son in the baggy army surplus coat was as smartly turned out as the rest of the Strakers delegation. He had hoped that, over time, the Strakers culture would rub off on him, and he'd have started presenting himself better, but with Peter it didn't seem to be happening.

They crossed the atrium with its reflecting steel waterfall and concrete tubs trailing with ivy and arrived at a bank of elevators. A pair of enormous paintings by Rothko, comprising squares of maroons and reds, hung opposite the elevator doors with a notice saying they had been loaned by the Pendleton Foundation Trust, part of the extensive collection of contemporary art built up by this generation of Pendletons. In the centre of the atrium was a sculpture of a pregnant woman by Henry Moore.

In the mirror-lined lift, Miles assessed his reflection from every conceivable angle, concluding he looked gratifyingly good for a man of his age; the grey strands in his otherwise jet-black hair adding distinction. He was reflecting, quite literally, on how much better looking he was than the rest of his senior management team when his eyes settled on Peter, and he winced; for here, multiplied to infinity by the mirrored walls, was the tall, lanky, tousled image of his son, *tuned in to a Walkman*. For a moment Miles stared in disbelief, hoping he might be mistaken. Was it actually possible any representative of Straker Communications—let alone his own son—could be listening to a Sony Walkman in the lift, in a *client's lift*, on the way up to an important meeting with the company's biggest account?

Incredulously, he regarded Peter and the plastic headset clamped over his ears. He glared, but the boy was in another world, gazing into space, lips moving with the lyrics. To his father, he appeared so laid-back as to be virtually retarded, his head and shoulders swaying to some internalised beat. Miles glanced about the elevator car, to see which of his subordinates had noticed Peter. If they had, they gave no indication. The other nine Strakers executives were silently watching the digital panel as it charted their progress to the penthouse floor, where the Pendleton family's suites of offices were located.

As the lift doors opened with a ping, Miles strode forward, yanked the headphones from his son's ears, and thrust them into his pocket. 'Don't you *ever* do that again,' he snapped, before stepping out onto the executive carpet with a swagger.

The twenty-fifth floor of Pendleton Plaza more closely resembled a gallery of contemporary art than the headquarters of a chain of supermarkets. Ninety years after their grandfather, Wilfred Pendleton, opened a penny store on the Holloway Road selling everything from pumice stones to scouring powder from a trestle stall, the Pendleton family had reinvented itself as passionate supporters of the visual arts in all their forms. Not only had they amassed extensive private collections of post-war paintings and sculpture, but they endowed public collections, sponsored exhibitions, funded scholarships and purchased pictures for the nation. Miles took vicarious pride in all these benevolent activities, having first suggested them himself, two decades earlier, as a means of burnishing the Pendleton image. It was Miles who had first introduced Jim Pendleton, as he still was in those days, to the idea of buying Hockney and Bridget Riley, and later to upgrade to Bacon and Freud, and sculpture by Giacometti and Moore. It was Miles who encouraged James Pendleton to fund the renovation of the foyer of the English National Ballet, as well as their rehearsal space in Hammersmith, renamed the Pendleton Studios. It was Miles who prompted Nick Pendleton, at the time the supermarket became the first retailer to open an aisle devoted to Indian cookery ingredients, to underwrite the Rajput gallery at the Victoria and Albert Museum, and later to commission Richard Rogers to design the Pendleton Gallery of Contemporary Indian and Asian Art in Bradford. When Michael Pendleton, Group Innovations Director (who introduced chlorine gas preservatives to bags of watercress and mixed leaf salads, thus extending their shelf life by three months), began looking for an appropriate project for his philanthropy, Miles advised him to endow the Michael Pendleton Chair of Biotechnology at Cambridge University. And when Otto Pendleton, youngest and hippest of the clan, developed a passion for experimental theatre and mime, it was Miles and Straker Communications that paved the way for the Otto Centre for the Performing Arts in Camden, to showcase the best of Eastern European improvised drama.

James Pendleton's PA met the Strakers group at the lifts, explaining that 'Lord Pendleton is just finishing up a conference call and will join you in a few minutes. He sends his apologies for keeping you waiting.' They were shown into a large white conference room with steel and white leather chairs; bottles of Pendletons English Natural Spring Mineral Water were arranged down the centre of a bevelled glass conference table, and platters of Pendletons vol-au-vents and mini sandwiches from the chill cabinet range. Mounted on one wall in lime green branding was the new Pendletons slogan, developed through nationwide focus groups by Straker Communications: 'Making every day just a little bit more special.'

Already assembled around the conference table were all the Pendletons team bar James, including Nick, Michael and Otto in shirtsleeves and ties, James's eldest son, Hugh, who had recently entered the business, and a full roster of marketing, logistics, PR and communications executives. Miles bearhugged his way round the family members, complimented Michael on his tortoiseshell spectacles ('very Maurice Saatchi, very elegant') and sat himself next to the empty chair he knew would be James's. One of Miles's maxims was that, at presentations, he should always sit directly on the right-hand of the senior client, giving the subliminal impression that they were, in all senses, joined at the hip. It was a Straker Communications policy that, whenever possible, staff should distribute themselves amongst the clients at meetings, and not to allow a confrontational 'us and them' configuration on two sides of a table.

Miles stretched out in his chair and stared critically at the Pendletons slogan, screwing up his eyes as though seeing it for the first time. 'You know something, Nick,' he said eventually to Nick Pendleton. 'I think that's a very fine slogan we came up with for you. I congratulate you, really I do. It was the brave choice and the right choice.' He tilted his head, as if to appraise it afresh from a different angle; then nodded agreement with his earlier judgement. '*Making every day just a little more special* . . . it says it all, really, doesn't it? *Eight, no, nine short words* . . . encapsulating the Pendletons' lifestyle promise.'

Peter, still smarting from his father's outburst in the lift, felt his stomach clench. If there was one thing he couldn't stand, one thing that made him flush crimson with embarrassment, it was the sight of Miles in full insincere work mode, mouthing platitudes in a room full of people. Gingerly, he looked up from the table at the faces of the others, to gauge their expressions, but none appeared to be grimacing. In fact, they were nodding at everything Miles was saying, plainly delighted to be in the presence of the legendary image guru.

'Well, people seem to quite like it,' Nick Pendleton concurred. 'We've had positive feedback from staff.'

'It tested brilliantly,' Miles went on. 'One of the highest approval ratings we've ever experienced in research.'

Peter rolled his eyes, knowing that last bit wasn't remotely true.

Miles directed his next remark to Michael Pendleton, while still addressing the whole table. 'It was a particularly challenging slogan to get right, actually, which is why I insisted we research it exhaustively in all the regions. It was essential to have every word perfect.'

Peter thought of the endless, pointless focus groups and debriefing sessions he'd attended, none of which Miles had come along to, in which they'd debated *ad nauseam* whether the word 'just', as in 'making every day *just* a little more special', should be included or not, or whether, as an alternative, the words 'for you' should be added on the end—'Making every day a little more special *for you*.'

The Pendletons marketing team favoured the 'for you' option, arguing that it personalised the proposition, while incorporating a call to action, placing the emphasis on *you*—the all important shopper. But forty focus groups from Newcastle to Bristol, conducted with loyal and occasional Pendletons customers, declared otherwise, so the decision was made. Peter felt a wave of depression, remembering the days he'd squandered criss-crossing Britain with the Strakers research department, tuning in to the arbitrary opinions of people who really didn't give a toss either way.

Lord Pendleton joined the meeting, which meant it could now begin in earnest. The eldest of the four brothers, he was the group's Chairman who had driven the rush for growth, transforming Pendletons from a high-class family grocer with fifteen shops to the nationwide behemoth it had become today. Remorseless expansion through acquisition and store openings had put a Pendletons in virtually every high street and retail park in the country. Miles knew it was James he had to win over today, if his scheme was to stand a prayer.

As Miles predicted, there was nothing on the agenda to detain anyone for long, and in well under an hour they reached Any Other Business. People were already zipping away their notes and laptops when Miles spoke. 'Chairman, if I may, there is one thought I wanted to raise under this item. A potential small acquisition which might just merit having someone take a look at.' Miles's delivery was intentionally nonchalant, almost disengaged. Nobody around the table could have had the slightest idea how important this was to him. 'I don't know how familiar you are with a frozen-foods group based in the West Midlands, Freeza Mart? Not one of the more exciting sectors at the moment, I agree, but quite an interesting small business nonetheless with definite growth potential if professionally managed, which I understand it isn't at present. I thought it might be a good fit for the group, either rebranded as Pendletons Freeza Centres in competition with Iceland or merged into the parent brand.'

Lord Pendleton of Longparish asked several pertinent questions about the performance and status of Freeza Mart, all of which Miles was well-briefed to answer, and then Michael Pendleton and his logistics director, Colin Terry, had their own questions about warehousing and distribution hubs.

'The central point about Freeza Mart,' Miles declared, 'is that it's not a well-managed business. The founding partner has taken it to a certain level, but he's way beyond his comfort zone now. They're crying out for professional management, and I know his external investors feel the same. The institutions are sceptical about recent expansion ambitions, which they consider unsound. Now would be the perfect moment to strike. But you'll need to move quickly. I hear Wal-Mart's already sniffing about.'

Miles surveyed the table, knowing it was the *moment critique*. If James decided to pass, then the dreaded Clegg mansion would surely get built and Chawbury valley would be spoiled forever. For three months, the bat, newt and wild flower police had occupied Silas's cottage, cordoning off the hamlet with yellow exclusion tape, but all their bossy efforts had failed to uncover a solitary cudweed, spearwort, bat or salamander, and investigations would shortly be suspended. Miles's last hope lay in persuading the Pendletons to buy Ross's business and chuck him out, terminating his expansion plans and the Clegg mansion in one brilliant stroke. If Pendletons took over Freeza Mart, Ross wouldn't need a house down south and could go straight back to Droitwich with his tail between his legs.

He was passing his gaze from brother to brother, alert for signals, when he caught sight of Peter, staring darkly at him. He had an accusatory expression, as though he'd sussed out his father's plan, and objected on moral grounds. Miles grunted crossly. He found his eldest son exasperating. He appeared to inhabit some parallel world of his own, utterly removed from real life, in which the normal human emotions of cunning, graft and a desire to better oneself played no part at all. He would gladly let him leave Strakers if he thought he had any prospect of finding a job anywhere else. Apart from strumming on an acoustic guitar, Miles couldn't think of anything Peter enjoyed doing at all. The idea of Peter having scruples about his plan infuriated him. For heaven's sake, did he care nothing for Chawbury? Did he have no idea what effort and expense it took, year after year, to maintain the house and garden for the greater glory of the Straker family? Miles glanced over at James's son, Hugh, a nicely presented young man with an intelligent air about him, and wished Peter was more like him.

'My vote goes in favour of pursuing the opportunity,' Lord Pendleton said at last. 'We should do our homework and take it to the next stage, at least. My only reservation is the inevitable one: will we get clearance from the MMC to swallow another competitor? After the hurdles we faced last time, and the prevailing sentiment about monopolies generally, we have to expect a lot of opposition. Miles, this is your area. Is it realistic?'

Miles replied carefully. 'As ever, James, you've gone straight to the heart of the matter. And you're right to be cautious, because we're going to need to handle this one very skilfully. But I do think it's doable, yes. It's just a question of presenting everything in the right way. Why not leave it to me, and we'll see what we come up with?'

It was Miles's point of pride that Straker Communications charged more for their services than any comparable communications agency. This was because, as he explained it, 'we provide the complete package—public relations expertise, lobbying, corporate image enhancement and adjustment, high-level access plus, of course, my personal intervention as required.' Within a few hours of the strategic meeting at Pendletons, Miles appointed a working party to develop media strategy for a hostile takeover of Freeza Mart, and an operations room was set-up at Straker Communications' headquarters in Golden Square. Miles did not, himself, attend any of the subsequent sessions to evaluate the strengths and weaknesses of the target. Instead, he did what Miles did best, which was to lunch a succession of investors, newspaper editors, business editors and politicians, anyone in fact who might be asked for their opinion on the takeover, and subtly remind them what an impressive, philanthropic, forward-thinking group Pendletons was, and how we must never reach a point in this country where entrepreneurship becomes stifled by business-phobic legislation and red tape. To a couple of the city editors from the most important Sunday newspapers, Miles casually predicted further consolidation in the grocery sector. 'There are still a few struggling independents, mostly rather poorly run, which I can't see surviving in current form. They'll have to line up with one of the big boys.' All of these lunches took place at the same table at Mark's Club in Charles Street beneath an oil painting of a King Charles spaniel, which was known to the staff as 'Mr Straker's table' since he ate at it three times a week. One of the reasons Miles had chosen his office in Charles Mews South was its proximity to Mark's Club, and the many potential clients among the high-powered membership of the private dining club.

It was exactly five weeks after Miles embarked upon his softening-up campaign that Pendletons formally approached the Clegg board to take them over. As predicted, Ross duly rejected the offer, and shortly afterwards the approach went hostile. Pendletons plc wrote to all Clegg shareholders offering a premium of 70 pence per share on the price. With Miles's skilful prompting, this was publicly welcomed by several of the larger institutions, and the business sections were suddenly filled with laudatory profiles of Pendletons.

Sitting at home in Droitwich, with the Sunday papers spread out on the pine kitchen table, Ross felt sickened as the tsunami of positive press for Pendletons swept over him. The *Independent-on-Sunday* carried a double-page analysis of the rise and rise of the Pendletons brand, full of graphs and graphics illustrating its immutable progress, and the *Sunday Telegraph* business section carried a rare interview with James Pendleton, pictured rather stiffly at his desk with a Calder mobile behind him.

'Reading what it says here, love,' Ross said to Dawn, 'you'd think it was a done deal already. They're writing about us like we're history. We're like a minnow with this bloody great carp.'

Dawn tried to console him. 'I'm sure that won't happen, Ross. All your investors know what a brilliant job you've done starting up the business. And you're doing so well, opening all these new stores. They're not just going to sell out.'

'I wouldn't bet on it,' Ross replied wearily. 'If the deal makes sense, they'll sell us in ten seconds flat. It's business. You've got to be realistic.' Then he said, 'But I'll still be bloody gutted if it does happen. And I'm not going down without a fight either, I can tell you that.'

It was more than twenty years since Ross had opened his first shop, followed by a second and then, more rapidly, by a further four. After that, he'd kept on expanding, leasing new sites, keeping tight control on overhead and costs. He was also a shrewd picker of staff and a good motivator. One of his boasts was that he seldom, if ever, lost senior managers to competitors. And he was obsessed by efficiencies, forever imposing tougher KPI's—key performance indicators—onto the business, and introducing new training programmes. He often said that the potential for Freeza Mart was exponential. 'In five to ten years we'll have upwards of a hundred shops, we've barely scratched the surface yet.' And now, thanks to Pendletons, he risked losing the lot.

At that moment, the two youngest Clegg children, Gemma and Debbie, came into the kitchen, asking if someone could drive them to Kingfisher retail park to go shopping. 'I really need to go to Topshop and Miss Selfridge,' Gemma said. At sixteen, she was short and pretty, with a mousey bob and freckles, black micro-skirt and red plastic boots. She wandered over to the fridge, took out a raspberry yoghurt and leant against the pine counter to eat it. On the white melamine cupboard doors were blu-tacked school photographs of the girls in their brown cardboard frames.

Ross looked up from the newspapers. 'Are you wearing lipstick, young lady?'

Gemma's hand shot up to cover her mouth. 'Not really, dad. We were just trying something.'

'You can wash it off right now, go on, over at the sink there. You're still too young to be painting yourself with cosmetics.'

'Dad, I'm going to be *seventeen* in a month. Everyone at school's allowed to wear it at weekends.'

'Well, not in this family you're not.'

'Mum wears make-up all the time. Even when she goes swimming, she puts it on.'

'Now don't be silly, Gemma,' said Dawn weakly.

'Yes you do, mum. Admit it. When we went to the leisure centre, you were putting on lipstick in the car. *And* mascara.'

Dawn laughed nervously. 'I wasn't applying it, I was repairing it. Anyway, don't answer your father back, you're getting very lippy, Gemma, I don't like it.' Then she said, 'Give us a few minutes, love, and I'll run you down to the mall. I'm just talking to your father about something important. Run along now, I won't be long. And put some trousers on, I'm not taking you out looking like that, not in that skirt.'

Gemma groaned. 'I'll bet there won't even be any good shops if we move to Hampshire. There won't be anything to do.'

Debbie, aged fifteen, nodded her agreement. 'Yeah, Gemma says they don't have Topshops or New Looks or anything, not even pizzas, in Hampshire or wherever. She says it's going to be *so boring.*'

'Of course they do,' Dawn replied. 'Really, you girls can be very silly sometimes. Anyway, Debbie, you don't even *like* shopping, you're always saying that. And you can have a pony in Hampshire, which you can't here. Now, run along both of you. I'm talking to your dad.'

After they'd gone, Ross said, 'Well, there's someone who'll be happy if we get taken over.' He laughed. 'Gemma and her ruddy Topshop.'

Dawn kissed the top of his head. 'We're not going to get taken over. No way is that going to happen. You haven't spent the last twenty years working your guts out to have it taken from you. You're a fighter, Ross Clegg. Remember when we were just starting out, and that first little office behind Budgeons?'

'I liked that office,' Ross replied, pecking her on the cheek. 'Nice and cosy. Just the four of us in the one room, and you practically sitting on my lap.'

'I was only about five years older then than Gemma is now. That's a funny thought.'

'The sexiest secretary in Droitwich. Remember the red platform boots? I wonder whatever became of them?'

'Since you ask, Gemma's wearing them right now.' And they both roared with laughter.

Ross pushed away the newspapers and stood up. 'Tell you what, if you're running the girls to the shops, could you drop me at the gym on the way? I feel like working off a lot of aggression.'

'You do that,' said Dawn. 'And remember: you fight them, love. It's your company, you started it. No way can Pendletons barge their way in and take it. I'm telling all my friends to boycott their supermarkets, starting tomorrow. I'm going to call them all up and tell them.'

Ross chuckled and patted her bottom. 'You do that, girl. It won't make a blind bit of difference, but it might make us all feel a bit better.'

5.

Pendletons's decision to raise their offer for Cleggs by a further thirty pence was greeted by the press, carefully primed by Miles, as the knockout bid. 'A premium of a pound over the original share price surely reflects full value and more,' wrote *The Times*. 'If Lord Pendleton paid any more for this Droitwich-based cash-and-carry enterprise, he'd have to forgo his expensive Lucian Freud habit for a week or two.'

'I think the job's as good as done,' Miles reported on the telephone to James Pendleton. 'We've pretty much covered all bases now, and there hasn't been a single voice anywhere for Cleggs side. Not one. You probably saw *The Economist* this morning.' *The Economist* had published, in that week's edition, a lengthy analysis of the European supermarket sector, in which Carrefour of France, Tesco and Pendletons of Britain and Auchan in Belgium had been named the four groups to watch. The article referred approvingly to the impending takeover of Freeza Mart.

'And there's an article coming out in Friday's *Evening Standard* Business section I think you might enjoy,' Miles added. 'Nice reading for us, I predict, but not for Ross Clegg.' Miles purred smugly. Some of the unattributable lines he'd fed to the journalist were witheringly rude.

That evening, for the first time in a long while, Miles gave Peter a lift home to Holland Park Square in his office car. Normally Peter found his own way on the tube, but tonight Davina wanted her son back on time for a family dinner, so Miles sent Makepiece over to Golden Square to pick him up and then swing back via Charles Mews South to collect the Chairman. Having asked his son rather cursorily how his day had been, Miles turned to his briefcase and a stash of reports.

As they rounded Marble Arch, Peter said, 'Dad, there's something I've been wanting to ask you.'

Miles reluctantly put down his papers. 'What's that, Peter?'

'About Pendletons and the Freeza Mart takeover thing and all that.'

'Yes?'

'Are we really only doing it to stop Ross Clegg building his house where Silas's cottage was?'

'Absolutely not,' Miles replied firmly. 'We're doing it because it makes sound business logic. Pendletons are seeking ways to expand through acquisition, which they've frequently done in the past so it's nothing new, and the Clegg properties fit that strategy. Our job is to assist the process, make sure it happens as smoothly as possible.'

'But, admit it dad, you never would have suggested it if it wasn't for the cottage. You hadn't even *heard* of Freeza Mart before Ross bought it. All this is just to stop him spoiling the view.'

'Total nonsense,' Miles said. 'You're right Clegg first came onto my radar when he turned up on our doorstep, but that's how business works. You spot an opportunity and seize it. It's not personal. It isn't about me, or about him for that matter. It's about helping Pendletons grow market share in a very competitive sector, by any means we can.'

Peter looked sceptical, which made Miles bristle. Objectively, he could see that his son was good-looking, even handsome, with his long face and floppy brown hair like a rock star. And Miles could appreciate his idealism too, in theory. Miles felt *himself* to be an idealist, working hard every day of his life to make everything around him more *ideal*. He wanted his company to be the ideal solution for every client; he wanted his house—his houses—to be ideally and enviably comfortable; he wanted his holidays to be ideal, taken in ideal places; and most of all he wanted his wife and children to be ideal, to be *seen* to be ideal, actually to *be* ideal. But the idealism of Peter was something else altogether, something disapproving and uncompromising, which introduced a nagging ethical dimension where none was required. Although Miles knew in his heart that Peter had a point, and the takeover had been entirely provoked by Ross's monstrous house plans, he had already rewritten history until Pendletons's expansion programme was the spur, the house merely a happy consequence.

So he said, 'Peter, if I've learned one thing in life, it's this: you make your own luck. Nobody comes along with a big basket of goodies and doles them out, with identical shares for every child in the playground. Things don't work that way. So if you want to take the opportunities life presents you with, I recommend you don't search for the negative in every situation. As for this Clegg business, I'd be grateful if you didn't refer to the cottage like that ever again.'

Just before noon on Friday, when Miles knew the first edition of the *Evening Standard*—the City Prices edition—would be hitting the streets, he dispatched his number three PA to the vendor on the corner of Berkeley Square to buy a copy. The article covering the centre pages of the business section was everything he had hoped and more. From Ross Clegg's point of view, it was devastating. Miles felt a surge of pure, gloating, professional satisfaction that he'd been able to pull it off so brilliantly. Every invented quote 'from a friend,' 'from an industry insider,' 'from a source close to Clegg,' all derived from Miles himself.

To start with, there was a particularly unattractive photograph of Ross, making him look about seventy years old. He had been taken from above, climbing out of a car, evidently having a problem with his leg. He looked frail and incapacitated, far too old to be working, let alone running a public company. Miles was thrilled with the photograph, which his people had sourced from weeks of picture research and provided free of charge to the newspaper.

The article itself was sneering and defamatory. Reading it, you got the impression Freeza Mart was the worst-run business in the country. Anonymous shoppers were quoted on why they'd deserted the stores ('It's a horrible experience going in, the aisles are filthy dirty and the deep freezes solid with stale ice'). Statistics had been corrupted to imply the business was falling through the floor. But the cruellest attacks were reserved for Ross personally. 'Insiders' dismissed him as a 'busted flush,' difficult to work for, vacillating and without vision. An anonymous 'close colleague' complained Ross was seldom seen about the business because of his 'mobility problems.' 'He can't even manage store visits.'

In his elation, Miles called for a glass of champagne and sat at his desk, toasting his sheer cleverness. Afterwards, as he set out for lunch, he asked his secretaries to make three hundred copies of the article, and have them faxed or couriered to every investor and financial journalist, just in case they should miss it.

By the time he arrived home at Chawbury that night, Miles was in terrific spirits. At dinner in the dining room, he bet his family two things. The first: Freeza Mart would fall to Pendletons before Wednesday of the coming week. The second: Silas's cottage (or what was still left standing of it) would be back on the market within two months from today, and Ross's show-home would never get built.

On those Saturday mornings when he wasn't abroad, Miles had an unvarying routine. He liked to drive himself into Stockbridge after breakfast to buy wine at the only decent wine merchant in his part of Hampshire, then go out and play on one of his several trophy tractors and yellow JCBs, or else go riding with Samantha around the Chawbury estate. Today, Davina reminded him they were due to have drinks with the Winstantons at Laverstoke before lunch, so they cut the ride short and returned to the stables in time to change to go out. Nigel and Bean Winstanton lived in a seventeenth-century converted mill two villages along from Chawbury, with the original mill wheel, which Miles privately considered rather naff. But Nigel worked for Lehman Brothers and their parties were always jolly, if slightly undiscriminating, and they had accepted. Bean was a boisterous mid-fifties blonde heavily involved in the pony club and local charities, whom Miles found rather a pain, not least because she picked up every waif and stray and invited them all along to her parties; she seemed to regard—and treat—all her guests equally, which Miles considered disrespectful.

It was nevertheless in high spirits that the Straker family piled into the Mercedes for the short journey to Old Laverstoke Mill. Miles was brimming with goodwill from his media triumph the previous day. When Samantha asked for a raise in her monthly allowance, he instantly said yes. When Archie got into the car holding a slice of marmite toast, which was his breakfast having only just got up, his father barely complained. Nor did he bother to criticise his wife's choice of clothes, or even Peter or Mollie, neither of whom had made nearly enough effort to look smart for the occasion.

They could see from the number of Volvos and BMWs triple-parked outside the mill that it was going to be a large party. Inside, in the beamed hall which had once been a granary, Nigel and Bean were distributing glasses of champagne and elderflower cordial, while their Croatian couple, Stanislav and Vjecke, poured tumblers of Pimms from silver-lipped jugs. Scanning the throng of guests, Miles spotted the Lord Lieutenant and his wife, Johnnie and Philippa Mountleigh, the local MP, Ridley Nairn, and his wife, Suzie, and a large assortment of investment bankers and brokers from Citibank, Merrill Lynch and Goldman Sachs, all in Saturday-casual kit and assembled from their second homes in the county. At Miles's arrival, he became an instant magnet of interest, with half a dozen guests gravitating in his direction, keen to touch base with their glamorous neighbour. Miles positioned himself in the middle of the room, radiating charm and flirting with all comers. His eyes rested on a succession of bankers' wives and female bankers whom he found sexy in their cashmere cardigans, Armani tweed trousers and high-heeled boots, and pondered which might be available for some extramarital dalliance at some point in the future. Their husbands, he noticed, were mostly exhausted, white-faced, bean-counting compliance officers in polo shirts and tweed jackets, or else dressed up like embarrassing late-life adolescents in jeans and expensive bomber jackets.

There must now have been fifty couples inside the mill house, with almost the same number spilling outside on to the lawn. Through the open doors to the garden, Miles could see the young Winstanton children, Toby and Shrimp, circulating with plates of mini-quiches, open smoked salmon sandwiches and bowls of crisps. Davina was crouching down talking to Shrimp, probably about her new school or pony, which momentarily irritated Miles; he found it unbelievable that, in a house full of highly successful, interesting people, all at the top of their professional game, his wife should prefer to chat away to a vacuous eleven-year-old. Astounding really.

Davina, meanwhile, was thinking how refreshing it was to be talking to such a sweet, open little girl, and to have a break from all these pushy adults. It wasn't that she was unused to parties—as the daughter of a diplomat, she sometimes felt she'd spent her entire childhood at one reception or another in overseas embassies— but frequently, as Mrs Miles Straker, she yearned for peace and quiet. The nonstop socialising exhausted her, sucked the life-force from her. She had neither her husband's energy nor his remorseless lust for life. Part of her envied the way Miles was captivated by— and so effortlessly captivated—new people, but part of her despised him for it. As parties went, this one was relatively painless, but she would rather have been at home in her garden, peacefully weeding the bed in front of the orangerie, which she had purposely asked the gardener to leave for her to do.

Samantha completed her second circuit of the garden and decided there was nobody here she was remotely interested in. The men were all over thirty-five, either married or nerds, and she was fed up telling people where she was at school. But at least she was enjoying the lustful glances which followed her around the lawn; her new McQueen jeans plunged so low she had switched to wearing a thong, and she could feel warm shafts of sunshine against her flat stomach.

Peter and Mollie were chatting together on a swing chair on the terrace, well away from the crowd. Mollie had been helping the brother she loved the most with lyrics for a new song; her suggestions weren't helpful, but Peter was carefully writing them down on his pad, pretending they were great. He told Mollie that if the song was ever recorded, he would split the publishing rights equally with her.

Archie had been oiling up to a partner in J.P. Morgan about work experience for himself next holidays, and was now feeling bored, but suddenly perked up. Because heading in his direction was an incredibly sexy girl in the shortest skirt and boots, with exactly the look he always went for: petite and pretty, with short mousey hair. It was the boots that did it for him, red plastic stacks with zips up the sides. The sleaziness of the boots combined with the girl's slightly dopey, sweet and innocent shop-girl face was an instant turn-on, and he began following her around the lawn.

'Darling Miles, I hate to drag you away mid-conversation, but there are some people I *insist* you meet.' Bean Winstanton had taken hold of Miles's arm and was frogmarching him into the garden. Bean held the annoying conviction that her parties were famous for putting people together, and was never satisfied until numerous mismatched couples had been thrust together to their mutual dismay. 'I have an instinct you're going to become *tremendous friends*,' Bean was saying. 'They don't know a single living soul round here poor things. I met them at the garage in Micheldever, we were both filling up our cars. Now . . . here they are, look . . . we were just talking about you two . . .'

And there, almost unrecognisably smart in suit and tie, stood Ross Clegg, with Dawn clinging anxiously to his arm, wearing a big pink hat as though she was at Ascot. Ross's black hair was slicked down at the sides but oddly spikey on top, and Miles wondered whether he was using gel.

Before either could speak, Bean said, 'Now, I want you to *promise* me to remember you first met here in my garden. I'm forever reminding people they first met at Old Laverstoke Mill, introduced by me, and half the time they don't remember. Now, I'm not sure exactly where your new home is going to be, Ross, but I think you're going to be awfully close to the Strakers. Miles, Ross is being frightfully brave and building a *brand-new house* from scratch. I wish we'd done that. We do love it here at the mill, but my God it does get chilly in the winter, we can hardly bear to leave London sometimes, which is awfully naughty of us. Of course we have to because of the horses.'

Ross's face lit up. 'Miles, good to see you. It's alright, Bean, Miles and I have met before. This new place we're doing is down the bottom of his private woods. Dawn, you remember Miles.'

'Yes indeed,' interjected Miles, thrusting out his hand before Mrs Clegg had a chance to kiss him.

Ross said, 'What a great party this is. It's so nice to forget work for a bit. I tell you, I took an awful pasting in one of the rags yesterday. You can see the bruises on my back.'

Miles replied non-committally. 'The press do tend to go over-board, once they get an idea into their heads. Best never speak to them, I suggest.'

'Thanks for the advice, Miles. Coming from someone like your-self, that's valuable stuff. Tell the truth, I'm a beginner when it comes to this press and public relations malarkey. We haven't had much call for it before. All the newspapers have been calling nonstop, but I'm not sure which ones to talk to, and which to avoid.'

'Avoid the lot. A pack of hyenas, most of them.'

'That's what I reckoned. But I did speak to a lady from *The Mail on Sunday* yesterday. I hadn't meant to, but she caught me off-guard after the hatchet-job in the London paper came out. She showed up in the back garden, just as we were setting off to drive down here, and I was in such a filthy mood, I thought, "Right. Ok, bugger this. I'm going to speak out for once." So I poured it all out to her, right there in the garden, I can't even remember half of what I said. And Dawn stood there, shaking her head at me like, "Whoa, Ross, cool it, Ross," but I was on a roll, no stopping me. Now I'm worrying what it was I said to her. She was scribbling it all down in her notebook, scribble, scribble, with this big smile across her face, egging me on. She was alright-looking too, I couldn't help noticing.'

Miles chuckled away at Ross's story, making a mental note to ring the editor of *The Mail on Sunday* after lunch, to ensure they hadn't gone off-message.

Davina caught up with them and was introduced by Ross to Dawn, whom she hadn't previously met. Dawn was soon telling her about all the problems they'd had with the wildflower and bat conservancy people at the cottage, and how it had set the project back months and cost goodness knows what in delays and all the hassle. 'We've had diggers on standby for weeks, waiting to get started. Ross has been marvellous about it, considering the strain he's under from this takeover thing, and then this on top, which we just don't need.'

Unaware of Miles's involvement in the conservancy ploy, Da-vina was full of sympathy, and said they should use the manor whenever they wanted. 'If you want a swim or something—or a hot bath, or if we can ever give you lunch—do just ask. Apart from when the children and their friends are there, nobody uses the pool at all. It seems such an awful waste—all that heating—I'm always begging people to come over. So please, please do.'

Dawn said, 'That's very hospitable of you, Davina. The girls will be thrilled when I tell them. They both love their swimming, Debbie especially. She's our youngest. She's been swimming for her school, and begging us to put in a pool ourselves at the new place, though everything's up in the air at present, until we know about the takeover.'

The women discussed their children, establishing that Dawn had the two girls, Gemma and Debbie, plus an elder boy, Greg, who Dawn said 'is at college down in London, and backpacking around the Far East in his summer vacation, which scares me to death.' Davina said they had Peter 'who works for his father at the moment,' Samantha 'who is mad keen on riding,' Archie and Mollie.

'Oh, Debs loves her horseback riding too,' Dawn said. 'What with her horse riding and swimming, she never stops still for a minute that one.'

'Well, it'll be nice for Samantha to have someone to ride with,' Davina said vaguely, apparently oblivious to the three year age gap, and ten year sophistication gap, between Samantha and Debbie. 'Sam rides at weekends with her father, but during weekdays in the school holidays it's always a bit quiet, and such a performance to keep getting friends over, especially when it means boxing-up. So it'll be lovely having you close-by.'

Davina became increasingly conscious of Miles glaring at her, making signals that he wanted to get away. Once they were out of earshot, he said, 'Tell me I was imagining it, or were you inviting that unspeakable woman to swim in our pool?'

'Actually, I was, yes. They've been having a dreadful time with the rare wildflowers and bats brigade, you can't believe the fuss they've apparently been making, I'm amazed actually. And at the end of it all they haven't found a thing, so it's all been a total waste of time. I feel so sorry for Dawn. She seems very nice, and very keen to learn about the area and know who everyone is.'

'I'll bet she is,' Miles replied. 'She's a ghastly social climber, you can see that a mile off. As for swimming in our pool, I absolutely forbid it. All that make-up would clog the filter.'

Davina sighed. 'I don't know why you're being like this, darling, unless you're still cross about them buying the cottage. Which would be so silly since we didn't need that cottage anyway. We've got quite enough to look after as it is.'

'I repeat, I forbid it. Under no circumstances will the Clegg woman—or any other Cleggs come to that—swim at Chawbury. Is that understood?' Davina didn't reply, so after a moment Miles said, 'Good,' and strode purposefully ahead in the direction of Johnnie Mountleigh.

Archie was closing in on the girl in the red plastic boots. He had been circling her for fifteen minutes, like a leopard on the savannah, appraising his prey. There was no question about it: she was enticingly sexy. His eyes followed her mini-skirt and the firm, tanned legs between boots and thigh. Her short hair was thick and shiny, and there were freckles around her nose. Her lipstick was bright red like a post-box and alluringly cheap-looking. Archie reckoned she'd be easy, he'd never been one for long, drawn-out pursuits.

For most of the party, the girl had been accompanied by a junior version of herself, presumably a younger sister, who trailed around the lawn behind her, occasionally taking a mini-quiche or a sandwich. Neither was drinking anything, Archie noticed, which he took as a bad sign. Once they stopped to talk to a lady in a big pink hat and caked in foundation, who might have been their mother, and a gritty-looking man with a limp, probably their dad.

Now the younger sister peeled away, leaving red-boots on her own, and Archie seized the moment. Accelerating across the lawn, he said, 'Hi, I'm Archie Straker. We haven't met.'

'Oh, hiya Archie,' said the girl. 'I'm Gemma.' Her accent was hard and nasal—'I'm *Jimmer*'—and Archie's first thought was, 'Christ, she's got a *northern accent*.' But he also thought: she's even cuter close up. He liked her pink gums. Around her neck was a little pink locket in the shape of a heart.

'Are you local?' Archie asked.

'Well, we really live between Droitwich and Redditch,' Gemma said.

Archie, who had heard of neither town, nodded noncommittally.

'But we just bought a place down here, well Dad has, so we might be moving,' Gemma went on. 'I don't know exactly.'

Archie was about to discover more when Miles loomed behind him, and said, 'There you are, Archie. We've been looking everywhere for you. Come on, it's time to go, we're already late. It's one-fifteen and we said we'd be home for lunch by now.'

Archie's last sight of Gemma was of her sweet, willing, vacant face smiling up at him. She reminded him of the backwash-girls at his mother's hairdressers, and was precisely his type.

6.

Miles slept badly and got up at seven o'clock to collect the Sunday newspapers from Middleton, which was the first place to have them. If you waited for them to be delivered at home, it could be half-past-ten, even eleven o'clock before the newsagent rolled up in his van, and today there could be no question of delay. He felt troubled as he drove along the winding Hampshire lanes, bordered by rolling chalk downland and flint walls. Straight after lunch yesterday, he'd rung the Editor of *The Mail on Sunday*, using the direct line as he did for all national newspaper editors. The conversation had not been reassuring. Miles had asked about the forthcoming Ross Clegg interview, and whether there was any additional information they could help with from the Pendletons side, but the Editor had been discouraging.

'It's quite a strong piece, actually,' he'd said. 'We're going big with it tomorrow. Clegg comes over very robustly.'

'Well, I hope you haven't allowed it to be one sided,' Miles said. 'We'll be disappointed if it lacks balance. All previous reporting of the takeover has recognised the logic of a Pendletons victory.'

'That's just it. To be honest, Miles, you've done such a fantastic job on Pendletons's behalf, the other side haven't got a word in so far. Which is what makes this piece interesting, it gives the opposing view. I think a lot of readers will have sympathy for some of the stuff he says, too.'

'I still suggest you're very careful. Why not fax the piece over to us, so we can correct and rebut any factual errors?'

'I'm sorry, Miles.'

'I'm not talking about interfering with editorial integrity. Just ensuring it's one hundred percent accurate. Are you saying you're happy to print without checking the facts? I'm offering to protect you from potential litigation, that's all.'

But the editor was obdurate. 'It's been libel read and the lawyers haven't flagged any problems. Ross is having his say, that's all. The small entrepreneur versus the might of the big supermarkets, nothing very new, but he speaks up well for himself, and we're running it as is. Our journalist liked him, so it's a friendly piece, but professional and balanced.'

For the next two hours, Miles had moved into overdrive, searching for different means of getting the article pulled. He had rung the business editor of the paper, threatening to limit future exclusives from other Straker Communications clients if the Clegg interview ran; he rang the group editor-in-chief, who was a regular lunching partner, expressing his concern that an inaccurate and biased article was about to be published, and could he stop it; later, when that failed, he rang the proprietor of the newspaper, Lord Rothermere, who was playing tennis at home in Dorset, and explained how annoyed the Pendleton family would be if the article ran, and reminding him the supermarket spent more than seven million pounds a year on advertising in his newspapers and colour supplements. He added he had it on good authority that Ross Clegg and the female journalist had forged an unhealthily close friendship which went beyond normal professional conduct, and he could see this whole business ending up before the Press Complaints Commission, and this was merely a heads-up before it was too late.

Eventually, Miles had to concede that none of these stratagems had worked this time, which upset him even more, since he hated to pull strings at the highest level and still fail. He knew he never would have bothered if it wasn't for Silas's cottage.

So it was in belligerent mood Miles drew up outside the Spar shop in Middleton to buy the papers. Even entering the run-down premises with its narrow aisles of packet soups and pot noodles, and shelves of cheese dippers and Sunny Delight, filled him with disdain. It amazed him a prosperous county like Hampshire, full of investment bankers and well-paid corporate lawyers, could still support such a poor-persons shop. On the floor in front of the counter were piles of newspapers supervised by a Bengali granny in mittens and housecoat, who was busy inserting random colour magazines into random papers. And there, right before his eyes, was *The Mail on Sunday* with an eye-catching panel printed above the masthead on the front page: 'Exclusive: Freeza Boss Clegg on why he chooses independence. Financial Mail, page 1.'

Miles returned to his car with an armful of papers, pushed back the seat and turned to the business section. The first thing he saw was a big photograph of Ross—an annoyingly good one, this time—and a quote in bold type saying, 'They've tried everything to blacken my name, even claiming I'm a cripple.' Miles shuddered. He was accustomed to consuming media at top speed, and could take the temperature of an article by tasting half a dozen random paragraphs. Often he never read more, having confirmed whether it was a positive or negative piece. Today, he spotted the danger in every line. From the opening paragraph, Ross came across as a blunt, honest, hard-toiling Englishman. The journalist, who clearly fancied the pants off him, banged on about his humble roots—son of a steelworker who lost his job in a plant closure—and how, after a string of casual jobs, Ross had started the tiny business which had grown into Freeza Mart employing 1,300 people. Devastatingly, he described how he'd contracted polio as a boy, through poor sanitation in the terrace where he grew up, and how he'd battled this for years, never letting it beat him, and eventually overcome it, though it had left him with a limp. 'Contrary to certain reports,' Ross was quoted as saying, 'the limp has never affected me in any way at all. I don't think I've taken a day off in twenty years, and I don't know how many other CEOs can say that. But I'll tell you something about my disability if you can call it that: it's a perpetual reminder of what life was like before I found success with the business, and what life is still like for many of our customers. When you live up where I do in the Midlands, surrounded by the people who shop in our stores, and manage on very limited budgets many of them, I can still identify with them. Our customer base is a world away from the Pendletons's customer down south, and even down there, where it's much more prosperous, they only engage with the top end of the market. I don't know how they'd get on up here, not knowing the customers like we do. I remember my old mum coming back from the shops when I was a kid, having not been able to buy something because she was a penny or two short, so we had to go without, and that made a big impression on me, and that's why we're always looking to bring down our prices. If we can knock a few pence off washing powder or a six-pack of beans, I think how chuffed mum would have been. When I look at what Pendletons are charging for everyday items, you think they're having a laugh. A quid for an iceberg lettuce? What planet are you living on, mate? I don't know how they get away with it, half the time.'

Miles drove slowly home to Chawbury, frowning and preoccupied. His instinct for corporate relations, and the likely consequence of every shift in public perception, made him fear the worst.

There was no doubt about it, Ross had pulled off an astoundingly effective PR counter-attack, and Miles had an uneasy feeling the Pendletons takeover bid had just hit the buffers with a shuddering jolt.

7.

t was twelve weeks later that Ross's great building project began in earnest. With the takeover offer withdrawn, Freeza Mart assured of its independence, and the bat and wildflower police reluctantly sounding the all-clear, Ross was impatient to get on.

Every weekend, Miles glared furiously from his terrace through binoculars as work got underway. One Saturday morning, the remainder of Silas's cottage was swept away as though it had never existed. In its place was a muddy hole, corralled by cement mixers and diggers. Soon foundations began to appear, followed by the first storey of bricks; bricks which Miles instantly identified as being too red and too new-looking and entirely inappropriate for the area. He was horrified, too, by the house's footprint; in sheer footage it was three if not four times larger than the cottage it replaced. 'It's going to look like some red brick university. Disgraceful it was ever allowed.'

'Please don't exaggerate, darling,' Davina said. 'It really isn't so bad. And they're planting lots of trees for screening, Dawn told me, we really won't notice it in a couple of years.'

'I can assure you, I'll notice it. I notice it every time I open the damn curtains. I can hardly bear to look in that direction, actually. It's totally spoilt the view, even worse than I imagined. If you can't see it, you must either be blind or wilfully unobservant. I can even see it from the bathroom. I was having a bath this morning and could see those ghastly brick walls on the horizon, it's ruined my morning. Anyway, when do you see Dawn Clegg? She's not been here, has she?'

'She was at Philippa Mountleigh's. At a girls' charity thing to raise money for disabled gun dogs.'

Miles felt grumpy at the thought of Mrs Clegg at the Lord Lieutenant's house. That woman was like broken glass, she got everywhere.

'Then I ran into her in the chemist,' Davina said. 'She's always very friendly. She's offered to help with the Macmillan Hospices.'

'I'll bet she has. That would be right up her street. Won't she just love getting in with all her smart neighbours?'

'Darling, I wish you'd *stop* going on about the Cleggs in this nasty way. You've really got it in for them, it isn't fair. I can't think why you're being like this.'

'If you'll just step over to the window,' Miles replied, holding back the heavily-interlined curtains with their hand-blocked pattern of poppies, 'you'll see precisely why I've got it in for them. Come on, come here, I insist you look.' Davina reluctantly approached the drawing room window, fearing a trap, and Miles gestured triumphantly across the valley. 'What do you think of that, then? Now tell me those aren't the ugliest things you've ever seen. Like something you'd expect to find in Florida.' The object of his derision was a pair of white fibreglass pillars, twenty foot high, the second of which was being winched into position on either side of the front door of the Clegg mansion.

'I agree I probably wouldn't have chosen them,' Davina conceded. 'But *chacun a son gout*. And the trees will hide them.'

'I was coming to those, you can see where they've just planted them, down at the bottom of the field. *Leylandii*! We should have guessed, of all the trees they'd go for them. In five years they'll be sixty foot tall, a ruddy great wall of sickly-green fir. Like living in suburbia.'

Davina slipped away to see how lunch was coming along. She knew her husband when he was like this, there was nothing you could say or do. Better to hide away in the kitchen and talk to dear, sensible Mrs French, who had cooked for the Strakers for four years.

Miles fetched his field glasses from his study and adjusted the focus. He had noticed the first double-glazed plate-glass windows starting to go in, and was thinking how unbelievably naff they looked.

8.

Shortly after the schools broke up for the Christmas holidays, eighteen hundred of England's finest privately educated teenagers began clamouring for tickets to the Macmillan Hospice Ball, colloquially known as the 'Hospers' ball. The Hospers, held annually at the Hammersmith Palais in London, was a notorious snogathon at which every red-blooded fifteen-, sixteen- and seventeen-year-old felt they must be present. For weeks before, from all the poshest boarding schools, pupils were terrorising their mothers to get hold of tickets. Davina Straker had been on the mailing list for ten years, since Peter had first started going to it, so had no difficulty in securing tickets for Archie and Mollie. Peter, of course, was well beyond the Hospers these days, and even Samantha would have been too old for it this year had she been around, and not away in Thailand on her gap year.

Shortly before the ball, the Strakers drove up to London to spend a few days in Holland Park Square for Christmas shopping, dentist visits and parties. It was a particularly hectic time of year for Miles too, who attended as many client Christmas parties as he could squeeze in, often going to three or four in a single evening. His driver, Makepiece, and senior PA, Sara White, planned the most efficient route around London, rationing twenty-five minutes for each event, enabling Miles to connect with all his top clients. Tonight he would put in face-time at the Trent Valley Power 4 U party in Claridges ballroom, the British Regional Airways party in the River Room at the Savoy, Michael Spencer's ICAP cocktails downstairs at George Club and finally dinner at Harry's Bar with Davina and his arms dealer client. As usual, with a long night of client relations stretching ahead, Miles felt exhilarated at the prospect of such condensed, high-powered networking.

Archie, meanwhile, was preparing himself for the Hospers. His bedroom at the Holland Park Square house was right at the top on the sixth floor, opposite Mollie's room, with a shower cubicle shoehorned into a former airing cupboard in-between. First he had taken a shower and washed his hair, then coated it with gel which he smoothed behind his ears in an oily slick; he then changed into his dinner jacket and bow tie and slipped four miniature bottles of vodka into his jacket pocket. The Hospers was a strictly no-alcohol event, with only bottled water and juice on offer, so all Archie's friends turned up with private supplies. In any case, Archie was meeting up with ten mates from his year at school in a pub before the ball, so they should be well tanked-up before they arrived.

Across the corridor, Mollie looked despairing at her clothes, hating them all and wishing she didn't have to go to this horrible party. She had been at the Hospers last year and loathed it. The whole thing had been a total meat market. All round her, wherever she'd looked, people had been getting off with each other—kissing complete strangers, it was so sick—everyone, that is, except her. Nobody had spoken to her all night, let alone asked her for a dance or a snog, which she would have refused in any case unless she really liked and knew the person. What had made it so embarrassing was that half her class from school had been there, all looking amazing, and about five boys each were clustered round them, but nobody gave her a second glance. So she'd stood around pretending she didn't care, wishing she was anywhere else, preferably home in bed. She was sure it would be exactly the same tonight, all over again. She'd told her mother she didn't want to go, but her father insisted, saying everyone went to the Hospers, it was a rite of passage. Morosely, she squeezed into the brown outfit she'd worn at the summer lunch party.

Gemma Clegg, meanwhile, was blow-drying her hair with the complimentary hairdryer in her bathroom at the Thistle Hotel in West Kensington. She was in a state of intense excitement, this being one of her first-ever visits to London, her first time staying at a London hotel and her first big night out. Her mother had heard about the Hospers Ball at hospice committee meetings in Hampshire, and realised Gemma was the only teenager not going. Lots of the other mothers had said what fun it was, and how it was a wonderful way of meeting people, so Dawn bought a ticket and agreed to chaperone her to London. As a great treat, they were sharing a bedroom at the Thistle, which actually had three stars and all kinds of luxurious extras in the room, such as tea and coffee-making facilities, and sachets of sugar and saccharine and mini-cartons of UHT milk laid out on a tray. In the bathroom was free bubble bath and body gel, and a comb and sewing kit which Gemma had already transferred into her washbag.

Scrutinising herself in the mirror for the twentieth time, she still couldn't decide what to wear. Sometimes she liked the velvet skirt and white Zara top, sometimes the purple Miss Selfridge dress with sequins. Each time she'd made a definite, final decision, fresh doubts erupted. She couldn't decide whether the black skirt made her look fat. The white top left three inches of tummy on display, and now she wished she hadn't eaten that mozzarella-and-salami-melt panini on the train. If only she'd brought the orange skirt with her, except it didn't go with the red boots.

Already slightly unsteady after three pints of lager at the Duke of Hamilton up the road from the Hammersmith Palais, Archie arrived at the party. There was an awkward moment at the door when the ball marshals, deployed to exclude drunken teenagers, tried to bar Archie and his friends, but somehow they'd blagged their way through, and now he was in the thick of it. Whenever he looked he saw boys he knew from school—literally dozens of them—and girls he instantly fancied hanging about in little groups, waiting to get picked up. Archie reckoned he could identify the different schools just by looking at them: swotty, butch girls from Wycombe Abbey; pretty, eager ones from Downe House with plenty of midriff on show; posh, arrogant Heathfield babes; leggy, sporty Cheltenham Ladies; grubby, streetwise Godolphin and Latymer girls; sexy, neurotic Paulinas; giggly country-bumpkins from Tudor Hall; then all the various St Mary's dolly-birds, stir-crazy from their convents and horny as hell. That, anyway, was what Archie reckoned as he weaved between hundreds of micro-skirts and glinting braces on white teeth. From the corner of his eye he thought he spotted Mollie skulking miserably behind a pillar, so he turned sharply away. No way was he wasting the Hospers Ball on looking after his weird sister.

Gemma felt out of her depth. It wasn't that she was finding it difficult to talk to people. Loads of boys kept coming up and saying hi, but she wasn't doing well keeping the conversation going. No one had heard of her school, Droitwich Spa High, and they hadn't heard of Droitwich either. They kept thinking she'd said Norwich or Dulwich, wherever they were.

Mollie wanted the room to swallow her up. Surreptitiously glancing at her watch, she realised only an hour and a quarter had passed, nothing like half way, barely a third. She found a concrete staircase beyond the cloakroom which led up to a dark balcony above the dance floor, and as she stared down at the thousands of people dancing and laughing and clutching onto each other, it made her feel so lonely and bereft, she could have wept. On the dance floor, the boys had removed jackets and ties and were leaping about with whoops of wild laughter, holding bottles of water. Many of the girls were dancing together, still in packs, before being picked off one by one by increasingly raucous boys. Mollie had resolved to stay hidden-away up here for the remainder of the party, where nobody could find her, when she heard strange slurping noises close by, like the sound a suction plug makes when covering a bath hole. To her horror she realised she was surrounded by snogging couples, draped across benches or clamped together on the floor, like a class in mouth-to-mouth resuscitation. Flustered with embarrassment, she retreated downstairs, resuming her position behind the pillar.

Archie had already snogged three different girls when he spotted Gemma. He knew he'd seen the face before, but it was the red plastic boots which brought it back: the girl from that drinks party. He didn't think she looked too happy tonight, but she was red-hot-sexy, and this time he'd go for it.

'Hi, I'm Archie. We met at that mill place, with those people, remember?' He wished he could remember the girl's name. Hayleigh or Leah or something.

'Oh yeah, hiya Archie. You having a nice time?'

'There's about a million people I know here, like half my year, so it's totally crazy, you know.'

Gemma, who knew no one, was impressed. She also thought how fit Archie looked in his dinner suit. His hair was slicked back like a singer in a boy band. And he had these amazing silver cuff links on his shirt, like cogs and spanners, really big and chunky, and big accessories were the in-thing this season according to *Glamour* magazine. And she liked the way he was so relaxed, like he was completely used to being at society functions, and had a really cheeky smile.

'Marlboro?' Archie offered a cigarette from a packet.

'Er, I don't really smoke. Well, ok, maybe I will. Thanks.' She extracted a fag and Archie lit it with his lighter. She liked the clicking noise the lighter made, and it's see-through blue plastic casing. Nervously, she drew on the cigarette, hoping she wouldn't cough. It was her third ever fag.

'Want a drink?' Archie clamped his arm around her back, palm pressed to bare skin, and directed her to the bar. 'Cranberry?'

'Er, can I have a water please.'

'No, have cranberry.' Then, to the barman, 'Two cranberries.' He winked at Gemma. 'It disguises the smell—and the taste, if you don't like it.'

Gemma had no idea what he meant.

Clutching the plastic cups, Archie carried them to a distant pillar in a corner near the emergency doors. Around the pillar at breast height was a narrow, circular shelf, covered with overflowing ashtrays and abandoned cups and water bottles. He placed the cups on the shelf amidst the clutter, and tipped vodka into both of them. 'There you go,' he said. 'Drink up, it'll get you in the party mood.'

'Cheers, then,' Gemma said, uncertainly. She took a sip and was surprised it tasted of nothing, just normal cranberry juice. So she took another sip and soon a warm, happy feeling crept over her, and she began to relax and think what an amazing party this was and how envious her friends would be if they could see her. There was nothing like this at home. When she finished the first cup, Archie fetched another and sloshed in more vodka, which she could taste this time because it had formed on the top in a viscous pool, and she'd taken a big gulp before she realised. Archie had his arm draped around her shoulders, and friends of his kept coming up and saying hello to him, and he never introduced her to any of them. Not that she really minded. She liked Archie. Her head felt fuzzy and she leant against him for balance.

From the shelter of a nearby pillar, Mollie watched her brother and the girl. The girl looked extremely tarty, no surprise there, and drunk. Mollie wanted to go over and talk to them but felt wary, in case Archie snubbed her. Archie was weird at parties, sometimes he pretended he didn't know who she was.

Archie and Gemma were on the dance floor, and Gemma was alarmed by how weak her legs felt beneath her. They kept buckling like she was going to fall over, the room was spinning. Archie was boogying round the floor, almost independently of her, like a jokari ball on elastic, sometimes abandoning her to dance with a different girl, then springing back to her again. She didn't know whether she'd been dumped or whether he'd return. He really did seem to know everyone, all the boys and lots of the girls too, who kept coming up and high-fiving or kissing him. Gemma found it disconcerting. But she was also flattered to be dancing with such a popular guy.

They'd been dancing like this for half an hour when, out of the blue, they began snogging. There had been no build-up, no signals, it just happened; one minute they were bopping about freestyle, the next in a clinch with Archie's tongue down her throat. She could smell cigarette smoke on his shirt and in his hair, and his warm hands were creeping about the tops of her legs, and brushing against her tits. The discotheque was playing 'Merry Xmas Everybody' by Slade, one of Gemma's all-time favourite tracks, when Archie said, 'Let's get out of here, shall we? This music stinks.'

'Go where?'

'Leave. Go on somewhere. A nightclub or back to your place or something. You do have somewhere in London?'

'I'm staying at a hotel,' Gemma replied proudly. 'It's really posh, they give you all these free products.'

'Yeah? Which hotel's that?'

'The Thistle.'

Archie made a face. 'Are they good? I hadn't realised. Anyway, can we go there?'

'Well, my mum's meant to be collecting me outside here at midnight. She's up in town too. We're sharing a room.'

Archie looked disappointed. 'That's nearly two hours. We could go to Holland Park Square, I suppose.' He seemed doubtful. 'My parents are out having dinner . . . well, so long as we're quick.' He French-kissed her again, then manoeuvred her past the ball marshals whose job was to keep everyone inside the party until they were collected. 'Just taking my sister outside for some air, she's feeling faint. Won't be a minute.'

On Hammersmith Broadway he hailed a taxi and in what felt like five minutes they had drawn up outside a huge white house in a wide street. From outside, it looked like a hotel, it was that tall, with steps up to a double front door with bay trees in lead planters on either side.

Archie supported her up the steps, while he unlocked the door. The cold December air, coming after the heat of the party, made her nauseous, her head was spinning worse than before. No wonder she was cold; dimly she realised she'd left her coat in the cloakroom at the party.

Archie seemed pleased the burglar alarm was on. 'Good,' he said. 'No one's home. I thought Conception might be in.' Deactivating the code, he guided her into a book-lined room off the hall, with a mahogany desk, sofas and several telephones. 'Dad's study,' Archie said. 'He'd kill us if he knew we were in here.'

He guided Gemma to a sofa and she fell back into deep cushions. Looking around, she had a fleeting impression of fax machines and a computer terminal and framed photographs propped up along bookshelves. Most contained pictures of an older, handsome man whom Gemma remembered from the party at the mill. He must be Archie's dad. In one of those pictures he was standing with another man Gemma thought she recognised, then realised it was John Major, the Prime Minister before Tony Blair. In another, he was with the Queen. There were other people she thought she'd seen before too, but couldn't remember their names.

Archie joined her on the sofa and immediately began kissing her again. It felt very nice to be in this warm room with him, on this comfy settee, and she snogged him keenly back. Her head felt all woozy; she could easily drop off here, Gemma thought, if she shut her eyes.

Archie was lying horizontally on top of her now, and Gemma

wasn't sure she liked that. She kept pushing his hands away from her, as they became more exploratory. But as soon as she moved them, they crept back.

'Don't,' she began. But she was slurring. 'Don't, Archie.'

Archie seemed not to hear. His hands were advancing inside her skirt, higher and higher. 'No, Archie. Stop that.' His fingers were exploring the rim of her Topshop knickers, now she could feel them entwined in her pubic hair. 'No . . .' But he had covered her mouth with his own, kissing her, forcing her head into the cushions.

She tried to push him off but he was too strong, and she didn't want to appear naïve. Maybe everyone did this down in London, maybe it was expected, normal. Now she could feel him fumbling one-handed with his fly buttons, and she became conscious of a new, dangerous presence on the sofa. Archie was tugging at her knickers, tugging them down around her knees, all the time kissing her so hard she couldn't speak. She tried to force her head up, pushing back against him, which seemed only to excite him more. Now he was pushing apart her thighs, and then, shockingly, painfully, he was deep inside her, thrusting away on the sofa.

On and on he went. Distantly, Gemma was aware of a long fax spilling out of the fax machine in an endless coil, and the sound of a car door slamming somewhere outside in the street.

Then, much closer, a key in the front door lock, and a man's voice saying, 'That's odd. The alarm's off. You didn't forget to put it on, Davina?'

Archie heard it too, and looked stricken. As he moved to pull out, he suddenly spurted inside her. A snail's trail of semen was deposited across the sofa cover as he withdrew.

'What the *hell* are you doing in here?' Miles stormed, bursting into his study. 'And who the hell are *you*?'

Archie was pulling up his trousers, jibbering explanations.

'Actually I don't want to hear, I've seen quite enough. What I do want, Archie, is for this young lady, whoever she may be, to be *out* of this house in the next three minutes. And you will never, *never* do you understand, bring any girl back here again. Particularly not into my study. Now, I shall leave you two to get dressed, but I don't expect her to be here when I return.' Then he slammed the door.

'You'd better go,' Archie said. Deflated by ejaculation and chastened by his father's anger, he just wanted her out. Looking at Gemma on the sofa, skirt still high above her waist, Archie was disgusted. What a scrubber. She didn't look as pretty as she had earlier, and he wanted to go to bed, alone, before his parents could get at him.

'You know where you're going, do you?' he asked, opening the front door. Outside, the temperature had dropped to zero, and Gemma shivered without a coat. 'You've got money for a cab, I suppose?'

She shook her head. 'It's . . . in my coat pocket . . . at the ball.'

Archie fished in his trousers and produced a £10 note. 'That should be enough. It's all I've got.'

Gemma looked at him and felt like she was going to cry.

'The best place to find a cab is on Holland Park Avenue,' he said. 'There are usually plenty.' As she stumbled down the limestone front steps, Gemma heard him bolt and chain the door behind her.

Archie crept upstairs. He didn't want to be cross-questioned, not tonight anyway. For one thing, he didn't even know the silly tart's name.

9.

Miles was buying wine in Stockbridge on Saturday morning errands when the next outrage reached him.

He had ordered four cases of claret and two of white burgundy, and was telling the assistant to have it delivered to the Chawbury address, when the man asked, 'Is that to the Manor or the Park, sir?'

'Chawbury Manor. You've been dozens of times before. There is no Chawbury Park.'

'Sorry, sir, we had a delivery for Chawbury Park earlier in the week.'

Miles looked blank, so he went on, 'That new place they're building, that's Chawbury Park. Where the old cottage was.'

Miles's eyes narrowed. 'You're telling me they've changed the name to *Chawbury Park*?'

'A lady and gentlemen were in here, I made a delivery of beers and ciders up there for them. They were having drinks for their builders, to celebrate getting the roof on. I'm sure they said Chawbury Park. I remember thinking that's going to be confusing, with you being Chawbury Manor and so close by.'

By the time he got home, Miles was apoplectic. He shook with indignation. Chawbury Park, indeed! Chawbury *Park*! *Park*! The sheer pretension of it! You couldn't believe it, except you *could*, having met Ross and Dawn. He assumed the 'Park' bit was Dawn's idea. *Park*! How could you call that hideous Barratt Home a 'Park'? The whole county would die laughing. Not that Miles particularly wanted them to hear about it, because he felt it reflected negatively on himself, being provoked in this way. Wouldn't people be slightly laughing at *him*, too, the victim of the Cleggs's one-upmanship?

Quivering with fury, he announced the news to Davina, Archie and Mollie, whom he found reading newspapers in the kitchen. To add insult to injury, Davina and Mollie scarcely seemed to register or care, though Archie instantly got the point.

'They've called their house Chawbury *Park*, dad? That's so weird. *Park* is better than *Manor*, isn't it?'

Miles nodded. 'It goes Palace, Park, Court, Hall, Manor, then Rectory and House . . .' Miles could grade practically anything; he could recite the pecking-order of fashionable London restaurants, Caribbean islands and hotels, advertising agencies ranked by billings, Kensington squares ranked by house-prices . . .

'Are they *allowed* to just change the name? What was it called before?'

Miles shrugged. 'It was only ever "Silas's cottage," far as I know. Or Tumbledown Cottage. Certainly not *Park*!' He stumped off to make a jug of Bloody Mary, muttering, '*Park* indeed. "Chawbury Park" for that ridiculous eyesore. "Chawbury National Car Park" more like.'

Once again, Miles felt outmanouevred, and it wasn't a good feeling.

10.

Samantha Straker, accompanied by her friends Rosie and Hetty, was starting the day as they began every day, having breakfast on the terrace of Surat Thani Guest House on Chaweng beach. It was slightly before midday and they had been staying on Koh Samui for four months, though long ago lost all sense of passing time. As Sam put it, this holiday was turning into the longest uninterrupted veg-out of all time. Before arriving in Thailand, there had been plans to travel round the whole country, including treks in Chiang Mai and Chiang Rai, but all that had been forgotten. Instead, their itinerary consisted of late starts, breakfast-into-lunch at the Surat Thani, then chilling in hammocks under palm trees until nightfall when the island came alive and the video cafés opened. Sometimes they even paddled out into the turquoise blue sea, where you had to walk a hundred yards through rippled sand shallows until it was deep enough to swim, but mostly they sunbathed or had forty-baht massages on the beach.

'It's not like we don't deserve a rest,' Samantha assured her old school friends. 'We were made to slave all last year for exams, so we needn't feel guilty if we don't sightsee every day.'

As a result, in the first fifteen weeks they'd spent in Thailand, they'd visited the floating market in Bangkok, a temple they didn't know the name of on Koh Samui, and that was it. Samantha was proud of her tan, which had turned a rich golden brown. Her only disappointment was the low standard of men travelling in Thailand. It was all student backpackers and Australians. Hetty had had a one-night stand with an Aussie called Rick who she'd hooked up with at the scuba dive shack, but spent the rest of the week avoiding him.

Samantha was picking at a plate of *som tam*—spicy green papaya salad—which was her regular brunch order, when she saw the man eating scrambled eggs on his own. There was something about him that made her stop and look. He certainly wasn't handsome. With his heavy jowls, thinning brown hair and small, darting eyes, he wasn't remotely her normal type, and she flinched at the leather sandals and purple shirt. Nevertheless, he had something. Not charisma exactly, but something approaching it. Compared to most of the travellers hanging out on the beach, he looked purposeful and intriguing.

Samantha noticed him again that evening, eating alone at one of the shacks along the beach, and then again next morning at the Surat Thani. This time he was reading an English newspaper, *The Observer*, which was weird for two reasons: hardly anyone read papers on the beach, especially imported ones which cost a fortune; and Samantha didn't normally see *The Observer* in any case or anyone who read it. According to her father, it was a chippy socialist rag, and they didn't take it at Chawbury. The man was carefully studying every page, including all the columns and political bits. She couldn't tell how old he was, probably about twenty-four.

The following day the girls had planned to go over to Ko Pha-Ngan for a short stay. This long deferred excursion, to the island forty minutes by boat from Koh Samui, was something they'd been meaning to do for weeks. According to the *Lonely Planet*, Ko Pha-Ngan was like Koh Samui had been twenty years ago—before the airport got built, and beach bungalows and video cafés turned the place into a tourist hub—with empty beaches and cheap accommodation and half-price fresh fish. They were hanging about Bo Phut pier waiting for the ticket booth to open when the man appeared again. He was carrying a small, grey backpack and a heavy paperback, an academic textbook it looked like, to do with economics and politics. To Samantha, it looked deathly dull, but she found herself alert.

Predictably late, the ticket booth opened, there was a mad rush for tickets, and the boat prepared to leave. It was smaller than they'd expected, a narrow motorboat, low in the water, painted yellow to the watermark and below that a faded pale green. Thirty or so travellers filed on board, setting up camp on the open deck, marking out their territory with backpacks and rolls of bedding. Samantha watched the man squat against the wall of the engine room, immersed in his book. Even when the boat pulled out of harbour and into open sea, and the quay and warehouses became smaller and smaller behind them, he never once looked up. Samantha increasingly regarded him as a nerd.

Alongside the boat, where the water was disturbed, the sun played tricks in the wake; gold shapes spun beneath the surface, and shoals of fish followed behind them, just below the surface, so they trailed their hands in the sea and tried to catch them. When Rosie thought she'd touched one, and it was slimy and scaly, the shrieking and squealing brought the man to their side of the deck.

'Keep the noise level down, can't you? It's distracting.'

'Distracting from what? Your book?' Samantha looked up at him provocatively. She was resting on her elbows in bikini-top and shorts. 'What are you anyway, a university professor?'

He laughed. 'Not a professor. Studying for a PhD.'

Samantha screwed up her face. It sounded like he was from Birmingham or somewhere. The momentary disappointment was followed by a strange development; an unexpected desire to win his approval. For reasons she couldn't explain, she wanted his respect, to be seen as a person with a brain and not an airhead.

So she said, 'I'm Sam. What subject are you doing?'

'Sociology and Politics. At the LSE. London School of Economics. I'm Greg.'

He loomed above them, awkward at first, uncertain whether to stay or go. So Samantha asked, 'Have you been travelling a long time?'

'It feels that way. Around ten months. Not all here, mostly Cambodia, Laos and Vietnam'.

He talked about visiting the tunnels built by the Vietcong, and the old American embassy in Saigon, from which the last evacuees had left by helicopter. He said his PhD was on the long-term effect of the Vietnam war on the economies of the region 'or what the Yanks left of it, after they'd carpet-bombed it flat.'

When they arrived at Ko Pha-Ngan, it seemed natural Greg should join them for a snack at a harbour-side noodle bar, and afterwards they should travel together up the coast to find accommodation. When the girls approached a taxi, Greg disapproved, insisting they pile into a mini-bus with a dozen others. When he asked what they'd seen on Koh Samui and realised they'd seen nothing, he said, 'Sounds like you could have gone to Torremolinos, if you're not interested in culture.'

Samantha felt rather snubbed.

Greg, meanwhile, was thinking what a very fanciable bird Sam was. She was completely different to the normal women he came across. For a start, she was thinner and more . . . what was the word . . . more classy. Her figure was incredible, her shorts so short it was almost indecent. He considered giving her a lecture on appropriate modesty in the Far East, and what the local women would make of her dressed like that, let alone Thai men. But he also experienced a morale boost, walking down the street with three such beautiful chicks.

He realised they were socially more upmarket than he was, which made him inclined to sneer. He despised spoilt rich girls with their private school educations and sense of entitlement, who didn't know a thing about the real world and took everything for granted. And these girls didn't seem to know anything at all. The one called Rosie had never even heard of the Tet Offensive, and they weren't interested in politics either. He'd mentioned Peter Mandelson, one of his heroes, who'd done so much to make Labour electable, and it meant nothing. Moronic.

But he was also thinking how much he lusted after Sam. Not for her mind, of course, but her body. He watched her long brown legs swaying from side to side as he followed her down the sandy path to the Blue Lagoon Beach Bungalows, and all sorts of grubby fantasies entered his head. Obviously it would be shameful to hook up with a girl like her—he could imagine what his friends at the LSE would say—but who'd ever know? It wasn't like anyone would get to hear about it. And it would be an interesting intellectual experiment, to experience a posh girl. Greg's piggy eyes ogled her smooth brown back, and he drooled.

It was dusk when they checked into the beach bungalows. The three girls shared a cabana, and Greg rented one of his own. He took care, when making his choice, to take a hut as far away from the girls' hut as possible, in case he got lucky; he hoped he might need the privacy. He tipped the contents of his rucksack onto the floor in a heap. Above the bed was a wooden shelf with a wonky anglepoise lamp screwed to it, and he arranged his half dozen fat paperbacks along it, to convey the message he was highly intelligent.

Outside on the bleached white beach was a French couple playing frisbee. No sign of any of the girls. Greg sat on a stool at the beach bar under a coconut umbrella and tried to concentrate on his book. The more he thought about Sam, the more confident he felt of his chances.

Had he known what was going through Sam's mind, he'd have been even more optimistic. Hetty and Rosie were complaining about Greg, whom they found a pain. 'I don't know why he's globbed onto us', Rosie said. 'We've got to lose him.'

'He's so up himself,' Hetty said. 'He's completely obsessed with his own brilliance. Doesn't he realise how boring he is?'

But Samantha, from the shower cubicle, called out, 'Well, I think he's rather a hunk, actually.'

There was a chorus of protest. 'You couldn't. You can't be serious. Not with those sandals. And that voice.'

Rosie tried to impersonate Greg. 'You must have heard of the Tet Offensive . . .' in his flat, whining intonation.

'I think he's quite fit,' Samantha said, squinting into the dark bathroom mirror to apply eyeliner. 'Not for England, obviously. For out here, I mean.' She laughed. 'I've always fancied a bit of rough.'

They drank cocktails on the beach—elaborate rum-and-coconut concoctions with paper umbrellas and fruit—and as the alcohol kicked in and the sun dipped into the ocean, Samantha felt lightheaded. She flirted openly with Greg, called him her 'Commie,' joshed him by saying she fancied William Hague, and that Hague and he had identical voices. 'We could wear matching baseball caps and be William and Ffion.' It was a game made more fun by her friends' disapproval. And she enjoyed Greg's evident unease. His lack of smoothness was part of his appeal, this lumpen northern grockle. Samantha got a kick from tantalising him.

Greg asked them all where they lived, and Hetty replied, 'Half in London, half near Winchester,' and Rosie, 'A bit in London, mostly in West Sussex.' Sam said, 'London and Hampshire. You?'

'You'll never have heard of it. Droitwich. But my folks are relocating down south, near a place called Andover in Hampshire.'

'That's close to where we live,' Samantha said. 'A village called Chawbury.'

Greg looked surprised. 'That's their village too, I think. I'm almost sure that's where they said. Is it a big place, Chawbury?'

'No, tiny. Some cottages, a pub and the church. Do you know which house theirs is?'

'I've not visited. It all happened after I left England. They've bought some old wreck and building a new place on the site.'

Samantha started. 'You don't know its name?'

'Just some cottage at the end of a track, supposedly.'

'Your surname's not Clegg, is it?' Samantha felt queasy.

'How'd you know? Been looking at my passport?'

'Ohmigod, your family are building that revolting house. It's ruining our whole valley.'

'What do you mean *your* valley? You don't *own* a whole valley?'

'Actually we live at Chawbury Manor. And my parents do own the valley, yes.'

'People shouldn't own property,' Greg said. 'Property's theft. Well, land ownership is. Land should be a common resource, not claimed by individuals.'

Samantha stared at Greg. Now she looked at his face, she could see a resemblance. He had Ross Clegg's mouth, the same narrow eyes. She felt weak, thinking what might have happened. She couldn't believe her narrow escape. 'You know what,' she said, addressing Rosie and Hetty and pointedly ignoring Greg, 'I don't particularly like this island. Let's go back to Koh Samui tomorrow. There's more to do there.'

11.

Dawn still found committee meetings at Philippa Mountleigh's house intimidating. She must have attended seven or
eight now, but something could always surprise her, the
other ladies behaved so unpredictably. The Mountleighs' home,
Stockbridge House, was very large and cold, built in a style she'd
learnt was Victorian Gothic, with rendered turrets and a crow's
feet parapet, and stood at the end of a long drive leading directly
off a dual carriageway, with a pair of Gothic lodge cottages. Philippa
was much less smartly dressed than Dawn had expected, considering her husband's position; at the first meeting, Dawn felt quite
awkward, having turned up in a red trouser suit, peach Escada top
and white slingbacks, and found Philippa in tweed skirt and polo-
neck sweater. The other ladies were no smarter, with the exception
of Davina Straker, who always looked nice and tidy. And then Bean
Winstanton appeared in jodhpurs, saying she'd come straight from
riding, and several other ladies wore jeans, including one who
turned out to be Lady something-or-other, though you'd never have
guessed it.

For Dawn, the meetings were a mass of conflicting signals. They
sat around the dining table in an enormous cold room, full of magnificent oil paintings of racehorses and sitting on chairs which had to
be Chippendale, drinking tea out of kitchen mugs. Not even matching mugs, but lots of odd ones with Smilies and mottos on them,
which looked like they'd come free from the garage. Dawn thought
if she'd had all these people coming over to her own place, she'd
have got the best tea service out, and spread a cloth on the table.

Then there was the language. Dawn found it hard to believe.
Some of the ladies used swear words—the worst ones too—as if

they were nothing. At the first meeting, when Philippa announced under agenda item four—Staff Updates—that the Assistant Matron at Alton hospice was retiring, Bean Winstanton had said, 'Thank God for that, that woman's an utter cunt, pardon my French.' Dawn hadn't known where to look. But no one else batted an eyelid. And later, when they were comparing diaries to fix a date for the next meeting, one lady had said, 'Bugger, I can't do a single Friday in January. It's all bloody let shoots.'

Nevertheless, Dawn relished being part of this new, unfamiliar group, and was touched by the friendliness she was shown. A quick learner, she soon picked up on the repertoire of good local hairdressers, cheese shops and butchers the other ladies favoured. After six months, she almost began to feel accepted, and unintentionally to irritate her old Droitwich girlfriends, Vera and Naomi, with accounts of what her smart new Hampshire friends thought about this and that.

The Cleggs were still commuting long-distance between Droitwich and Hampshire, waiting for Chawbury Park to be ready for occupation. Based in the Midlands half the week, Dawn stayed at the pub in Chawbury supervising the architect and chivvying builders. As the project took shape, she thought of other things they might as well do while the builders were on site, so they applied for, and obtained permission for, a floodlit tennis court as well as decorative garden lighting. She was delighted by the cast-iron replica Victorian streetlamps which soon lined the new drive and marked the boundaries of the lawn.

Ross was working harder than ever on his expansion strategy, and Dawn found herself in sole charge of overseeing progress on the house. The heightened public profile of Freeza Mart following their successful rebuff of the Pendletons' takeover, boosted investor interest, and Ross was keen to roll out the programme as rapidly as possible. Often, when Dawn tried to tell him the twists and turns of the building works, Ross smiled encouragingly, having long ago lost the thread of what his wife was saying. He was happy Dawn was happy, because the move south was going to be a big step for the family, and if she was behind it, that was half the battle. It pleased him, too, that Dawn seemed to get on well with Davina Straker, since they were such near neighbours. Ross wasn't sure what he made of Miles, who seemed a bit standoffish, but Davina sounded like a good sort, from the way Dawn spoke of her. Davina promised to come up to the building site and advise on the planting of the new garden, though she explained she was no expert on rock gardens, which Dawn saw as a central focus.

At one committee meeting at Stockbridge House, after Philippa Mountleigh had reviewed the disappointing proceeds of various recent fundraising events including a riding for the disabled rally (£104) and a Spring flower festival at Winchester Cathedral (£317), she emphasised how important it was they 'really go for it with this year's garden party.' In previous years, she reminded the group, 'we have raised almost a thousand pounds, which is excellent, but this year we aim to double that.'

Then, to Dawn's simultaneous anxiety and delight, Philippa turned to her and said, 'Dawn, I was wondering whether you might possibly have time to be one of this year's co-chairwomen jointly with Davina? I though that could work rather well, since you're both in Chawbury. Though we'd perfectly understand if you feel you can't, with your great move and everything.'

Not thinking she could say no to the wife of the Lord Lieutenant of the county, and thrilled by the implied compliment, Dawn immediately accepted, and it was decided the annual garden party should be held at the Strakers' place, Chawbury Manor, with the organisation equally split between the two neighbours.

In the following weeks, Dawn was seldom out of the kitchen at Chawbury Manor, planning everything with Davina. More than 250 people were expected for an afternoon spent admiring the Strakers' garden and traipsing round a range of stalls. Many of these, such as the bring-and-buy and jam and cake stalls, could not be expected to raise more than modest sums. All Davina and Dawn's hopes lay in a better-than-usual raffle and tombola, with really superior prizes, which the two women set about securing with determination.

For Dawn, working alongside Davina was an inspiration. She read the begging letters Davina sent out and learnt from their mixture of charm and firmness. Nobody receiving one of her two-sided missives in her large, confident handwriting could possibly refuse her, especially since her target donors were the hairdressers and shops she patronised so loyally. Soon pledges from all the smartest local tradesmen were flooding in. The delicatessen in Micheldever promised a summer hamper, and the aromatherapist in Odiham a complimentary 45-minute treatment. The riding school offered a dressage lesson for beginners, and the shooting school a clay pigeon session for four guns.

Dawn embarked upon her own offensive, writing to Ross's suppliers asking for gifts. Her letters were faithful adaptations of Davina's, with a word or sentence changed here and there. Ross's PA, Jacqui, was wonderful about forwarding her the right names and addresses, and soon a stream of requests went off to trading estates all over the West Midlands. When a biscuit supplier to Freeza Mart sent twenty tins of sweet digestives and chocolate bourbons, Dawn was ecstatic, and these were followed by a year's supply of tuna and deep-frozen peeled Atlantic prawns, cartons of Arctic Roll, black cherry cheesecake and frozen-profiteroles, and breaded chicken mini-bites. When some of Dawn's successes were reported by Davina at the next committee meeting, Dawn blushed at the public vote-of-thanks and applause from the other ladies.

The time Dawn spent with Davina, bonding through their common purpose, gave her a deeper insight into her near-perfect neighbour. There was no doubt Dawn almost hero-worshipped her, envying her competence and knowledge about practically everything: English flowers (Davina knew them by their proper Latin names, while Dawn could barely identify anything beyond a daffodil or a carnation), her smoothly run house, perfect clothes for every occasion (never over-dressed, never under-dressed), her apparently effortless way of planning every meal a week ahead and instructing her cook, so everything ran like clockwork, even down to which china they'd eat off and which sauces and condiments would be placed on the table.

But Dawn also detected a degree of unhappiness in Davina, a deep-seated fatalism which seemed to be to do with Miles. Although she never even implied as much, Dawn guessed Davina was a little afraid of her husband. The standards she faithfully maintained were Miles' standards, not her own, and when he was expected home at Chawbury Manor she would cancel everything to concentrate on making things perfect for him. She mentioned that, when they were having people over to the house, Miles sometimes commanded her at the very last minute to change all the plates and the tablecloth, if he thought it more appropriate; and Dawn saw the way Davina fretted over the seating plans for their Saturday night dinner parties, which Miles insisted she devise, though he invariably switched them about at the last moment.

As the date of the garden party approached, Dawn's respect for Davina grew and grew. As well as running the house, Davina seemed to be driving miles to one school or another to watch Archie or Mollie in a match or play, and facilitating her husband's restless socialising and ambition. Sometimes, Dawn wondered how she stood it. But Davina never complained, and Dawn realised she simply didn't yet understand the complicated dynamic of the relationship.

A clue—or what she thought might be a clue—came in the final days before the garden party. Davina said she'd been telling Miles about it, and Dawn got the impression she had not previously mentioned the event at all, and been fearful of doing so. The conversation had evidently gone well and Miles announced he would get them some raffle prizes himself.

In no time, Miles came up with a week's holiday for two at a 6-star resort hotel in the West Indies, including Business Class return flights, plus a £5000 voucher for groceries from Pendletons and dinner for six at Le Gavroche restaurant. When Davina told the committee, Dawn thought it might have been her imagination, or was Davina slightly deflated by these astonishing prizes, which undoubtedly eclipsed their own best efforts.

12.

Gemma was seriously alarmed and didn't know what to do. She couldn't tell her dad, who'd go crazy if he got to hear about it, and if she spoke to her mum she was bound to tell dad anyway, which came to the same thing. And it might not be anything anyway, so there was no point going into it all because then it would have been a big fuss about nothing. So she decided to leave it a few days more, or maybe till the end of the week, and pray her period came, which was what she'd been doing for about four months now, or was it longer than that?

She had told nobody what had occurred at Archie's house. Apart from fleeting images which flashed into her head making her shudder and feel hot and sweaty, she never allowed herself to focus on the evening at all. It was an episode which made her feel ashamed and dirty, and so, so stupid. It helped she couldn't remember anything clearly. The next morning, her head had felt like it was cracking open, which her mum had said was a hangover, and she'd sat for nearly an hour in the narrow plastic bathtub at the Thistle hotel, frozen with embarrassment and determined no one should ever know. Her mum had found it all rather a laugh, though she'd pretended to tell her off, and made her drink cups of sugary tea and several bottles of mineral water on the train.

'I hear you had a good time down in London,' her dad had said with a knowing look. 'I hope you've learnt your lesson. We've all done it. But you want to be careful with booze, Gemma. It's lethal stuff if you over-imbibe.'

To make matters worse, she had such complicated feelings about Archie. Of course, she hated him. He'd taken advantage of her—she actually shook, thinking about it—and then just chucked her out when his dad showed up—further shaking at the memory of *that*—it had all been so deeply, horribly, hideously humiliating. She had a brief flashback of Mr Straker peering down at her, her skirt pulled up, and felt breathless with shame. Nobody must ever, ever find out, she would die if they did. She would never go to London again in her life. And if they really did have to move to Hampshire, which she now prayed they didn't, she would never leave the house, so she wouldn't run any risk of seeing Archie.

There again, the idea of seeing him was not entirely repellent, she had to admit that. Although it filled her with panic and a kind of wounded fury, she was also excited. She knew he was good-looking, extremely good-looking, in fact; fit, with a really cute smile. She remembered how he'd looked at her when they were dancing, with his fringe hanging over his face and a fag in his mouth. He was a great dancer. And, later, when all that happened at his parents' place—she shuddered—he must have been her boy-friend, wasn't he? Otherwise they wouldn't have been there. He'd *chosen her*, chosen her from those hundreds of other girls, she was the one he'd taken home to that big posh mansion.

For a fortnight she harboured hopes he might contact her. Each time the phone rang, she started, wondering if it was him. She wasn't sure if he knew her number—she was pretty sure he didn't—so that explained it. On the one occasion she couldn't avoid going down to Chawbury with her mum, she half hoped to find a letter from him on the mat. But there was no letter, though she searched every part of the half-built house. She considered posting a note to the Strak-ers' house, to Chawbury Manor, which she could actually see across the fields, but lost her nerve. When they drove past the entrance to the drive, she ducked her head. Once, her mum had said, 'I've just got to pop over to Davina's for a quick catch-up about the charity func-tion. Want to come with me?'

'I'd rather stay here,' Gemma had said, quickly.

'Come on, you don't want to hang about here on your own, you'll be in the builders' way. Davina's got a lovely kitchen and some of her kids might be around, you never know.'

But Gemma, colouring, was immovable. 'Mum, I just want to stay *here*, ok?'

'You are a strange bunny,' Dawn said. 'One minute you're saying you don't know anyone round here and then you don't want to meet them when you get your chance. Well, please yourself, but don't come complaining about being bored.'

And always, hanging over her, was the business of her period. It wasn't that Gemma exactly considered herself an expert on the subject, but it did worry her it hadn't come for so long. She knew from *Sugar* and *Bliss*, which she used to read all the time, that people did sometimes skip their periods and nothing was amiss, but she didn't remember hearing about it happening three or four times in a row. She didn't feel she could mention it at school because the news would spread like wildfire, like it did when Anais confided in Sarah and Rachel last term about kissing that boy outside the Vue cinema. And she couldn't tell Debbie, of course, because her sister would definitely tell mum, and anyway she just couldn't.

So she told no one, and each morning hoped it would all be alright. And when her mum said, 'Those trousers are looking a bit tight on you, Gemma. And they're only new too,' she blushed crimson.

It was a Monday afternoon at Chawbury and Davina was in her favourite spot in the garden, concealed inside dark green walls of the yew bower, with her paints and easel, deckchair, newspaper and a novel.

If truth be told, Monday was her favourite day of the week, being the day she spent almost entirely alone with no Miles to hector her or boss her about, and very often no children either. Officially, Monday was the day she spent doing the garden and taking care of the housekeeping details that such a large set-up demanded. In truth, she would spend two happy hours on her knees in the flowerbeds, staking and weeding the herbaceous borders, then call it a day. By eleven o'clock she was playing with her watercolours or reading a diverting novel by Joanna Trollope or the *Daily Mail*. If friends rang and tried to make plans to meet up on a Monday, she did her best to resist them, often pretending she'd be up in London which was a white lie. She loved the luxury of spending a lazy day in her garden with a chance to sit still for once, rather than constantly charging about. With Miles around, there was never a single moment of downtime. Even when he was messing about on one of his JCBs, thinning trees or grinding tree stumps, she couldn't relax. At any moment he would be overcome by a sudden social blood sugar low, and crave people to amuse him, restless to start some new project, or critical of some arrangement in the house.

She chose to spend her days in the garden because there, at least, noone could get hold of her. To Miles's irritation she seldom kept her mobile with her, or would leave it turned off for hours at a time. Nor did she look at the computer very often. When she did, the screen was filled with messages from Miles's office, reminding her of one diary date or another.

'For heavens sake, Davina,' Miles would say, 'please respond to your damn messages. We can't run our life if you won't check your emails.'

'I'm sorry, darling,' she'd reply, only half truthfully, 'but I was working in the garden all day. I didn't get into the house once.'

Miles was settled in his favourite window seat, A2, in a First Class cabin on the 8 p.m. flight from JFK to Heathrow Terminal 4.

As usual on a British Airways flight, he was feeling supremely irritable. Cocooned by simpering stewards and stewardesses, and already issued with a glass of Dom Perignon and a menu from which to choose a delicious dinner, Miles felt all his familiar petulance welling up.

For a start, there was the ghastly 'Wellbeing in the Sky' video they made you watch before take-off, surely the most patronising feature ever invented. Miles flinched as a sugary, mellifluent voice encouraged him to relax and take part in a succession of ankle-rotating exercises. Snorting, he turned the screen to the wall, so he could no longer see it, but the naff, soapy soundtrack persisted.

Then the Captain (if there really was such a person these days, weren't these planes all steered by remote control?) began introducing the passengers to the cabin crew over the tannoy. Once again, Miles bridled. He had no earthly interest in knowing the airhostesses' names. It wasn't as if he was going to see them ever again. 'In our World Traveller cabin, we have Janet, Lauraine, Melanie and Stewart . . .' Miles rolled his eyes: Stewart! Another gay Scottish steward, it was unbelievable, the airline was infested with them. 'While in our Club World cabin we have Senior Purser Alan Twigg, assisted by Vicky, Leanne and Duncan . . .' What Miles found so futile was that none of these trolley dollies had even met *each other* before, they were just random people picked for shifts by computer, so why pretend they were some kind of bonhominous team?

On and on flowed the rubbish. Miles flew so frequently he knew every announcement by heart, despite his best efforts not to. Next would come the little speech from the chief airhostess about their primary role being the health and safety of passengers. No it wasn't! Their role was to serve dinner and drinks as quickly as possible. Then there would be the unutterably maddening 'Change for Good' announcement, when customers were urged to donate spare centimes, liras, euros or whatever to Unicef, made in the same syrupy, insincere voice. Each time Miles heard it, it made his spine rigid with annoyance. As if he filled his suit pockets with small change! He couldn't understand why First Class passengers were obliged to listen to it. Yet there was no way of switching it off; it was practically Cambodian.

Once he'd got into a mood, there was no rescuing him. Tonight, everything about the flight annoyed him. The one and only choice of main course he wanted for dinner was already taken. God, it was infuriating. Was it so much to ask from a £6,800 return ticket: one tiny morsel of grilled salmon? He barked at the stewardess who apologised the salmon option had been taken already. He waved away supper, just to make her feel bad, and asked for a bag of peanuts, only to be told they'd been banned because of passengers with nut allergies. Nut allergies! Did she honestly believe First Class passengers had nut allergies or, if they did, that they were too unintelligent to recognise a peanut when they saw one? No, nut allergies were the province of economy passengers. He switched on the movie, only to have it interrupted by the Captain offering to sell duty free and warning about turbulence. (Miles noticed that, however turbulent, the trolley dollies still managed to disturb everyone with their intrusive fragrance offers.)

It was a point of honour for Miles that, whenever the seatbelt sign was switched on, he should stand up and go to the loo. He enjoyed the slight lawlessness of it, and the disapproving look on the cabin crews' faces. He was striding up the aisle looking out for other First Class passengers he might know, such as his numerous CEO clients who used this route, when he did a double take. He had arrived at the washroom at the back of his section when, through the gaping blue curtain into Club World, he spotted a familiar face. Surely that was Ross Clegg sitting there?

Instinctively he turned away, but a voice said, 'Miles? Hiya, it's Ross.'

'Oh, yes, Ross.' Miles hovered at the Club World threshold, peering at all the not-quite-made-it businessmen who couldn't justify flying First. Most of the passengers were asleep on their flatbeds, masks in place, mouths gaping, but Ross was bolt upright, briefcase of papers open on his lap, next to a tray of hardly touched dinner. To his annoyance, Miles saw Ross had grilled salmon.

'Been over in the Big Apple, Miles?' Ross was asking.

Miles flinched at the cliché, and replied, 'A couple of meetings, that's all.'

'Well, don't let me keep you from the toilet,' Ross said. 'I expect we'll be seeing each other on Saturday. The girls have done a grand job co-chairing the party, haven't they? Dawn says Davina's been a star, pulling in the prizes.'

Miles, who hadn't appreciated how involved Dawn was in the garden opening, since Davina had omitted to tell him, looked blank.

'This great shindig on Saturday in aid of the hospice,' Ross said. 'Don't tell me you've forgotten! Dawn's twisted the arms of half our suppliers to contribute gifts. She's practically been living up at the manor, helping Davina get it all together.'

Miles glared in the darkness. Davina hadn't said anything, she'd intentionally deceived him. Hadn't he specifically told her not to get involved with the Cleggs?

An airhostess appeared at his shoulder in maroon and blue blouse. 'Mr Straker? The captain has switched on the seat belt sign. If you wouldn't mind returning to your seat.'

Normally, Miles would have minded very much. He hated being

bossed about. But he was only too glad to escape from Ross. 'I'm impressed you can work out here in the cheap seats,' he said, as he withdrew to his own section.

'Got to be careful with my shareholders' money,' Ross replied. 'See you Saturday at your place then, Miles.'

13.

Still furious with Davina for teaming up with Mrs Clegg, Miles decreed that visitors to the garden party should not enter through the house, but instead walk round the side of the manor, via the garage courtyard where his half dozen tractors and JCBs lived, to reach the lawn where the stalls had been erected.

'It's not like the people coming will be personal friends,' he complained to Davina. 'It's just anyone with fifty pence entry money who fancies a snoop round our property. If the Cleggs have invited half of them, God knows what'll turn up. Criminals casing the joint, I shouldn't be surprised. Or coaches full of check-out-girls from his cash-n-carries. I don't know why you've gone and got yourself involved with these ghastly people when I told you not to.'

Davina began explaining it was Philippa Mountleigh who had suggested the collaboration with Dawn, and invitations had been sent out to the regular hospice mailing list, but Miles wasn't listening. He was already in a furious bate, having experienced the Cleggs' new exterior lighting for the first time the previous night. The horizon had been lit up by a fuzzy orange glow like the perimeter of an airfield or the aftermath of nuclear disaster from dozens of mushroom-shaped bulbs buried in the Cleggs' lawn, or angled at their spindly new trees. For fifteen minutes he'd stood at the bedroom window, fuming, while Davina tried to coax him to bed. Even when they'd redrawn the heavy Colefax curtains, he felt he could see the orange light leaking round the edges, bringing a Halloween chimera to the room.

'How many people are coming to this damn thing anyway? Not more than eighty, I hope.'

'Well, they sent out six hundred letters, but they're not expecting anything like that number,' Davina said hurriedly. 'Last year it was a couple of hundred, I believe.'

'Grief,' said Miles. 'The lawn's going to be bald with all those hoards tramping across it. And we need to keep a sharp eye on the borders, because nobody thinks twice about stealing cuttings from plants. A lot of them bring secateurs specially. Snip, snip, open their handbags, in it goes. I'm telling you, it happens. Ask anyone who opens their house to the public.'

Miles strolled down to the lower lawn, beyond the yew hedge, where two parallel lines of trestles were in the process of being arranged by their respective stallholders. At once his mood lifted, since he spotted several women he considered worth talking to, including Serena Harden with whom he had been conducting an on-off affair for two years. Serena's husband, poor Robin Harden, who never kept a job for longer than a year, was unpacking a selection of scented candles, oven gloves, kneeling cushions for gardeners and traditional Hampshire trugs from a cardboard box, for his wife's country gift stall. In all, there must have been fourteen or sixteen stalls, still in a state of half-dress, but already displaying an array of pretty, charming, faintly manky and unneeded goods, of the kind that could only be given away as duty presents at Christmas time, to cleaning ladies or unloved aunts. Miles had a particular hatred of twee knick-knacks, though Davina loved them and bought them whenever she could, squirreling them away in a special cupboard: nettle and camomile soaps in hemp sleeves, overstuffed lavender bags with seeds already leaking from their seams, slabs of honeycomb and tiny test-tube shaped vases large enough to hold a single rose. Elsewhere, he could see stalls selling embroidered pashminas and nightdresses, and sets of linen tablecloths and napkins machine-stitched with primroses and farmyard chicks. This particular stall was already manned by Philippa Mountleigh and Bean Winstanton, from whom Miles was persuaded to buy a set of six eggcup cosies, each in the shape of a guardsman's bearskin.

Next door, Archie was assisting the Lord Lieutenant at the bottle tombola, on which a bizarre array of random bottles had been set up: Jeroboams of vintage claret next to bottles of Johnnie Walker and Orangina, flagons of Sussex cider, Bulgarian and Chilean chardonnay, bottles of Tabasco and HP sauce, litres of Diet Coke and half-bottles of Sauternes, each festooned with a bow of ribbon around the neck, and a pink or blue cloakroom ticket sellotaped to the label. Miles was irritated to see half a dozen bottles of his best Chateau Canon St Emilion, which Archie cheerfully admitted he'd lifted from the cellar.

'I think you might have asked first,' Miles said, glaring at his son, but not quite wishing to erupt in front of the Lord Lieutenant.

'Buy some tickets, dad. You might win them back. Go on, six for twenty quid.'

Reluctantly, Miles handed over a twenty-pound note, and won the bottle of HP sauce.

The garden was now filling with visitors, all anxious for a glimpse of the Strakers' house. From time to time, Miles allowed Chawbury Manor to be photographed for magazines, as a backdrop for his tightly-controlled self-publicity ventures, and this only fanned local curiosity to see the place in real life. Several years earlier, the interior of the manor had been shown in *House & Garden,* over eight pages, and more recently the garden, in autumn hues, had appeared in *Gardens Illustrated.* Although he was unaware of this, the editors of both magazines had vowed never to get involved with Miles Straker ever again, since he'd made such a nuisance of himself, insisting on approving every layout and caption, and demanding constant small amendments to the text.

Looking at the hoards of strangers pouring through his Linley garden gate and up the herbaceous walk, Miles wasn't sure how comfortable he felt about all this. At his own parties, the guest list was obsessively micro-managed, with every invitation issued with a specific end in mind, the redemption of a social debt or priming of a new business relationship. Today was a free-for-all of riff-raff: nondescript elderly couples with walking sticks and surgical stockings, or even in wheelchairs, leaving track marks on the carefully-mown yew walk; slapheads from the village clutching open cans of Carling from the bottle tombola, nosy old women he thought he recognised from the village shop, all interspersed with the Hampshire smart set in panamas and summer dresses, exclaiming how very lucky we've been with the weather.

He looked round for his children but, apart from Archie, none were anywhere to be seen. Well, they'd better be there somewhere, pulling their weight. Although today wasn't a Miles Straker production, it was still taking place in his garden, and he expected the family to be on duty, conveying the right impression.

Samantha, it so happened, had only recently emerged from her bed and was sitting in the kitchen in her nightdress with a cup of coffee waiting to summon the energy to run a bath. Four weeks after her return from Thailand, she was annoyed her tan was starting to fade and was smothering herself in products to revive it. The prospect of 'this fete or whatever' in the garden didn't exactly fill her with joy, though she supposed she may as well wander down later on, just in case anyone interesting had showed up. Not that she was holding her breath. Since returning to England she'd been unable to shake off the listlessness that had overcome her in Koh Samui. After months of doing nothing, she was finding it difficult to move up a gear. To make matters worse, her dad was pressurising her with questions about what she intended to do next in life, and wanting her to go to university. Sam couldn't think of anything worse. She'd had it up to here with education. All she wanted was to live at the house in London and *be in London*. If she had to get a job, she could surely find something helping out at Asprey or Cartier or somewhere.

Peter, meanwhile, found himself in charge of a White Elephant stall selling plants in plastic tubs, old books, CDs, broken lamps and jigsaw puzzles. His table was positioned at the furthest end of the garden, and it was obvious the merchandise had been donated by neighbours as a cheaper alternative to paying for landfill. It amazed him, looking at this great array of rubbish, that anyone would want to buy anything at all. He had once watched a documentary about life in Soviet Russia, with peasant women trying to scratch a living selling junk from trestles much like this one, but he remembered their stock as being slightly more alluring than his own today. And yet, from time to time, a customer would shuffle up to sift through the boxes of yellowing Nevil Shute and Hammond Innes paperbacks, or the old *Dandy* and *Topper* annuals, and sometimes even buy one for five or ten pence. Or they would ask questions about the plants, wanting Peter to identify them from their droopy stalks. To his shame, he hadn't a clue. They could be anything at all. Foxgloves? Thistles? Marijuana plants? All seemed equally plausible.

At the same time, Peter was enjoying his role as sole-trader. It was rather pleasant to stand outside in the May sunshine, waiting to see who came along and have a nice chat with them. Already, he'd had several conversations with all sorts, and he enjoyed marking-down the prices if people looked like they couldn't really afford them. He'd just sold a pile of children's books with scribbles on their covers for 10p the lot to a young mother, when it should really have been five quid. And he reduced a 1000-piece wooden jigsaw, with three pieces missing, from a pound to 5 pence for a pensioner. Compared to life at Straker Communications where they were encouraged to mark-up everything to clients as steeply as possible, with 30-percent service charges on each and every transaction, this felt so much more ethical and real. It amused him, as he stood waiting for the next customer, to imagine the Straker Communications strategy for the stall, had he become their client. In no time, they'd have been billing a £10,000 a month retainer, and setting up focus groups and viral marketing programmes to triple consumer footfall. What a load of baloney it all was! Often, at meetings, he felt like laughing out loud.

He was standing there, minding the shop, and drinking from a can of cider, when he saw the Cleggs heading in his direction. Dawn was in the lead, knowing her way round the Strakers' garden, which Ross had never visited before, proudly pointing out the herbaceous borders and swimming pool enclosure, and introducing her husband to the ladies on the committee.

'This is Ross, my other half. I told him he had to be here, and not disappear off working on a Saturday morning, which he has a naughty tendency to do.'

'Well, Saturdays are our biggest days,' Ross explained. 'I'm in the cash-and-carry food business, and our customers favour Saturdays since their partners are home to help unload the weekly shop. Anyway,' he went on, beaming at everyone and grasping their hands in his vice-like grip, 'I wouldn't have missed this for anything. Dawn's been on about it for months. And, looking round, I can see all you ladies have done a grand job getting the shoppers out. You're going to have to let me in on your retail strategy.'

As Peter watched them, he saw a straggle of younger Cleggs trailing behind their parents; there was a guy about his own age, quite heavy with small, darting eyes, wearing a Ban Foxhunting t-shirt. Behind him, two teenage girls, both pretty, one running excitedly from stall to stall, the other looking like she'd prefer to be anywhere else in the world but here. She was furtively glancing left and right, with a sense of dread.

Ross and Dawn arrived at the stall, and Ross said, 'Now there's a familiar face. Peter, isn't it? I'm bowled over by your garden. What a grand job you've done on it.'

'It's all my mother. She's nuts about gardening.'

'Your not saying she manages all this on her own?'

'Well, they do have quite a bit of help. But it's all her vision, and she does do a lot of it herself, she's outside everyday when she's down here.'

'It's inspiring. Dawn and I were just saying that, weren't we, Dawn? Hope we can make something of the garden up at our place one day. It's a bit of a prairie right now.' Then he said, 'Maybe I should start by buying some of these plants for sale, if you can help me pick something out.'

'I wish I knew what they were myself. People have donated them, but they don't all have labels and some have fallen off.' He peered doubtfully at a black plastic flowerpot, with a fragile green tendril poking through cracked soil. 'This one might be a tomato plant, I think. Or a sunflower.'

Ross roared with laughter. 'Tell you what, give me that whole tray and I'll plant them all out, and we'll just see what comes up. It'll be fun for the kids to learn a bit about nature, won't it, Gemma?'

'Uhh? What's that Dad?' Gemma slunk up to the stall, peering suspiciously at her father.

'I was telling Peter we're going to plant out these pots and see what grows. It'll be interesting for you to learn where tomatoes come from. You probably think they grow in Styrofoam boxes, don't you?'

'Yeah, Dad. Whatever.'

'This is Gemma—and Debbie,' Ross said, introducing his daughters. 'Gem's our resident shopaholic, and Debs loves her horses.

Horses and pop music. Well, they both love their pop music, typical youngsters.'

'Then you'd better have a rummage through this box of CDs,' Peter said, pushing it over to them. 'Not that there's anything too recent in there.' He fished a couple of random CD cases from the carton: Harry Belafonte and Led Zeppelin. 'This Joan Baez is good though. *Diamonds and Rust.*'

Gemma looked sceptical, but Debbie, who liked the look of this friendly man, asked, 'How much is it?'

'To you? Er, one pence.'

'Really?' Debbie looked thrilled.

'No, make that one pence for three. Go on, pick out two others, three CDs for a penny. You too, Gemma, if you'd like to. Or seven for two pence.'

Soon the girls had a huge stack of CD cases up to their chins, and Dawn was saying, 'Really, you *can't* take all these for just ten pence, it isn't right. Truly, Peter, you must let us give more than that, it's for the charity.' So, in the end, Peter accepted a five-pound note for the lot and they went off gleefully. Debbie glanced back at the handsome man who had been so kind to her.

Greg Clegg drifted between the trestles, sneering to himself about this bourgeois English scene of the worst sort. He had never actually experienced anything like it before, not at first hand, but he had imagined it, and read about it, and now here it was in all its hideous, complacent smugness. The faces of the other people said it all: rich, soft, southern faces of Middle England. Tory faces. Men in blazers with brass buttons and straw hats. Women with plumped-up, wrinkled, kindly, stupid faces that had never experienced a day's hardship. The garden only made him angry; he did not see a labour of love, but an indulgence, and wondered what it took in money and manpower to maintain it to this level. At college, he belonged to a society named the 80:20, which met to debate—to condemn— the indefensible fact that 80 percent of the resources in this country are owned by—*stolen by*—only 20 percent of the population. Although he attended almost all the meetings in the Junior Common Room, he had never previously seen so blatant an example of injustice at close quarters. So he sneered at it all: the yew walk, the flowerbeds with their box hedges and well-mulched herbaceous plants, the enormous flint and brick house which had to be the size of ten normal houses put together. And, of course, Greg had a personal reason to resent everything about Chawbury Manor. Samantha's behaviour in Koh Samui still niggled him, more deeply than he cared to admit. To be given the bum's rush by a privileged, pampered thicko like Sam Straker was more than he could stand. It confirmed every prejudice he'd ever had. He would never forget the way they had dropped him so abruptly—those three la-di-da babes. From the moment Sam had signalled her intention to leave Ko Pha-Ngan and return to Koh Samui, they had withdrawn all semblance of good manners. At supper that night, they had openly mocked him. When he'd mentioned his PhD, they'd yawned openly ('Boring, boring'). When he'd told them about the bus times to the port the next morning, they'd said not to worry, they'd already booked a taxi, which they pointedly didn't invite him to share. His contempt for them—for all this—bordered on the pathological.

To make matters worse, Greg dimly recognised that in his contempt lay an element of envy. Of course, he could not possibly acknowledge it. And yet, each time he pulled up the slated wooden blinds in his new bedroom at Chawbury Park, it was the Manor that commanded the view, arrogantly perched on the brow of the hill. There it was, every morning: right in his face. No doubt the Strakers had inhabited it for hundreds of years, lording it over the peasantry. It wouldn't have surprised him if the Strakers had been implicated in the slave trade; he could easily imagine Samantha's forbears shipping chained Africans to the sugar plantations, without a second thought or a moment's regret. But he was damned if he was going to hide himself away. He had as much right to be here, in this garden, as she did herself, whatever she might believe. For the remainder of his stay in Thailand, he had thought about her incessantly, eaten up with rage and bitterness. Sometimes he entertained visions of exactly what he'd like to do to her (these tended toward the graphically violent and sexual) but other times he imagined her turning up at whichever flea-pit he was staying in, consumed with remorse, admitting his superior intellect and begging to be allowed to do whatever it took to redeem herself. He was unable to think about her without suffering acute sexual agonies. After all these tortures, he didn't relish the idea of seeing Sam again in real life.

He had not mentioned running into Samantha Straker in Thailand to any of his family. When he'd come down to Chawbury for the first time, and Dawn had pointed out the Strakers' house ('my new best mate Davina') across the valley, he'd kept quiet; nor had he said anything when at supper Ross had talked about seeing Miles on the New York flight ('He was sat up in First, needless to say'). As for Chawbury Park itself, Greg suffered anguish over the name, mortified lest anyone at college get wind of it; he would continue to give Droitwich as his address to the university, student grant, rail card and everything else. But secretly he got a bit of a kick out to the family's new, so-much-larger property, and wondered whether it was socially reprehensible to learn how to play tennis.

Having decided the garden party was going better than anticipated, Miles was beginning to enjoy himself. There was something gratifyingly public-spirited about holding the hospice event in his own large garden, with all the county worthy in attendance, thanking him for his hospitality at every turn. Providing it didn't inconvenience him personally, or involve serious outlay of money, Miles was keen to be regarded as a public-spirited citizen, even a benefactor, like his clients the Pendletons. Davina was dressed appropriately for once (he had sent her inside to change) and everyone was saying what a good job she'd done, which reflected well on himself. As a control freak, he had dreaded a failure being put on under his surname, damaging the Straker brand. But, as things were turning out, this was a perfectly inoffensive little jamboree. He did wonder why anyone would go to such efforts to raise barely two grand for charity, when professionally-managed charity galas in London regularly brought in two million plus, but then he wasn't in charge. It pleased him, too, that the Cleggs didn't seem to be anywhere in evidence. Maybe they hadn't actually come.

Davina and Dawn had decided the raffle should be jointly drawn, at precisely three o'clock, by Philippa Mountleigh and a local celebrity, one of the five presenters of *Taskforce Garden South*, a daytime TV makeover programme specialising in transforming Hampshire cottage gardens into gravel-strewn cactus gardens or minimalist potagers. As the person who had found the top raffle prize—the fortnight at the six-star Nelson Bluff resort and spa in

Barbados, with Business Class return flights—Miles was miffed not to have been asked to conduct the draw himself, so instead positioned himself proprietarily next to the shallow stage to watch proceedings. By a few minutes before three, the crowd gathered around the dais was ten deep; there must have been three hundred people craning their necks and nervously fingering their raffle tickets. Bean reported more than 1,500 tickets had been sold as news of the lavish holiday prize filtered round the garden. There was a smattering of applause as the two raffle-drawers appeared on stage and, after a short speech of welcome, began picking tickets from a wicker basket. Soon, triumphant villagers were filing up to collect vouchers entitling them to a manicure at the hairdressers in Odiham, or to carry away value-cartons of Arctic rolls and mini pizzas.

In the throng, Miles now spotted the Cleggs. Slightly to his annoyance, he saw Dawn chatting nineteen-to-the-dozen with Johnnie Mountleigh, the Lord Lieutenant, who furthermore appeared not to mind nearly as much as he ought. One of the teenage daughters looked horribly overweight, which wasn't surprising, since people like that generally had obese children these days, it was the biggest giveaway; he assumed she'd been gorging herself on Ross's trans-fat, no-nutrition, deep-frozen garbage all her life. The younger girl, on the other hand, was surprisingly attractive, if you liked that slightly sharp-featured look.

Gemma, meanwhile, was stricken. She had spotted Archie across the stage, standing next to a tall blonde girl. Her first reaction was devastation: Archie had a new girlfriend. But then her brother, Greg, who was standing alongside her, said, 'Oh fuck, there's Sam,' and told her the blonde girl was Archie's sister, which was a lot better. In her self-absorbed state, it did not occur to Gemma to ask Greg how he knew.

Relieved there was no present rival, Gemma couldn't decide whether to push round and say hello or wait till Archie spotted her, and then whether to give him a big smile or cut him stone dead. She had to admit he looked fit in tight jeans and a pink shirt, her heart was pounding: he was the one. At the same time, she felt hideously self-conscious about her weight. In the last few days she'd felt so fat and heavy, her arms and stomach seemed to be full of fluid, she could hear it sloshing about inside her. No way was he going to fancy her. Then she remembered she loathed him, and it didn't matter.

Standing next to her in his provocative Ban Foxhunting sweatshirt, which he was glad to say had been drawing hostile stares all afternoon, Greg was thinking how much he fancied Sam. She was just so . . . fucking fanciable. Pin-thin, beach-bronzed, blonde hair bleached by sunshine, he was transfixed by her white teeth and air of unwitting haughtiness. Seeing her here, in her own setting, he recognised the preposterousness of ever possessing her. It was unthinkable and yet think about it he did, and the idea was tinglingly appealing. He was still ogling her when she caught his eye and he quickly looked away, instantly regretting it, since he knew she knew he'd seen her. Hot with embarrassment, he tried to focus anywhere but on Sam.

Ninety percent of the raffle tickets had been drawn now, only the star prizes remained. Dinner for six at Le Gavroche went to the reclusive man from the bicycle shop, who immediately began panicking about who he could take with him. The five thousand pound Pendletons supermarket voucher went to the head of North European trading at Goldman Sachs, who couldn't have told you to the nearest five million how rich he was.

Finally, the presenter of *Taskforce Garden South* announced the draw for the top prize, 'The Caribbean holiday worth thirty thousand pounds.' She gave the basket a final shuffle and stir before delving in and announcing, 'Number 497. That's four hundred and ninety seven.'

There was a moment of silence followed by a gasp of surprise, and a voice saying, 'I don't believe it. That's my number.' And Ross, all smiles, was limping up to the stage, brandishing his ticket stub above his head.

14.

The Nelson Bluff resort and spa, following a hundred million dollar refurbishment by its billionaire South African owners, was regarded as the most sumptuous six-star hotel on the island. Celebrated from the thirties to the fifties for its art deco dining room and cocktail bar, much frequented by Noel Coward and the Duke and Duchess of Windsor, it had gently declined over subsequent years before being purchased by Zach Durban's International Leisure and Casino Group, which had razed the old hotel and replaced it with a luxurious campus of high-spec bungalows and multiplex dining options.

When Miles and Davina had been amongst the three hundred A-list guests at the four-day opening event (Straker Communications held the PR and marketing account), Davina had hated the place. Having once stayed there years earlier on holiday with her parents, she could hardly bear how the charming bougainvillea-covered dining veranda had been swept away and replaced by a series of marble hangars serving a choice of Italian, French, sushi, Thai, pan-Asian fusion and Creole food, each more pretentious than the one before. When she'd mentioned this to Miles, in the privacy of their arcticly air-conditioned bungalow, saying she thought Zach Durban had ruined the place, he became paranoid she might say so in public.

'For heavens sake, Davina, we're staying in the *most expensive* hotel in the *world*. Stop being so picky about everything. Do you know what this cabana would normally cost in high season? Ten thousand dollars *per night*, breakfast and tax not included. So enjoy it. And don't you dare look like you're not, Zach's a key client and needs careful handling.'

That same night, at the grand gala dinner, Davina had watched her husband at his most brilliant. While Shirley Bassey and Brian Ferry, both flown in as cabaret, performed from an orchid-fringed pagoda beside the largest of the three hotel swimming pools, Miles had held his end of the top table in his thrall, mesmerising Zach Durban and the numerous socialites and tycoons Miles had imported with anecdotes of the powerful. Placed at the furthest end of an inferior table between the Nelson Bluff's general manager and one of Zach Durban's bodyguards, Davina had studied him at long distance. Once she had felt able to tell when her husband was being sincere and when he was putting on a show for business reasons. She had admired his ability to connect, when he put his mind to it, with just about anyone, at least for short periods over dinner or at a meeting. Once Miles had told her that, even the very next morning after a dinner, he could scarcely remember the night before, or whom he'd spoken to; yet the people seated next to him were invariably charmed by his attention. Over time Davina reached the conclusion that Miles saw conversation primarily as an opportunity for self-affirmation, as he basked in the admiration flowing his way.

She could hear him now, down table, telling Zach a story about having breakfast with Rupert Murdoch and Martin Sorrell at the Connaught, and what Rupert had said, and what Martin had said, and what Conrad Black of the *Daily Telegraph* had said when he'd repeated the conversation verbatim to him over lunch at Mark's Club the same day, and everyone within a ten-yard orbit was transfixed, nodding and laughing. Once, as a shy person, Davina had envied Miles's confidence and energy, because she realised it was his dynamism which enabled their family to live as it did. But sometimes she wondered what it was she'd ever liked about it.

It had been less than a fortnight after the successful launch party for the hotel, which even the normally carping Zach had declared a success, that Straker Communications won the rest of the International Leisure and Casino Group's account, and took on responsibility for hotels and resorts in Macau, Oman, Mauritius, the Maldives and South Africa itself.

Now it enraged Miles to think that, of all possible people at the charity garden party, it should be the dreaded Ross Clegg who'd won the free holiday to Nelson Bluff, and that furthermore he was heading there—entirely thanks to Miles—with his unspeakably common family.

Disembarking from their business class flights from Gatwick to Grantley Adams International airport in Barbados, the Clegg family were in mixed spirits.

Of the five of them, Dawn and Debbie were in the best form, hardly able to believe their good luck. Ever since the raffle three weeks earlier, they'd been elated, telling absolutely everyone. Debs had told every single girl in her class about the 'all-expenses-paid trip to a Caribbean six-star hotel' and became quite annoyed when one of the girls said six-stars didn't exist, it only went up to five stars, so she had brought in the brochure, which did clearly state six stars, and everyone stared in envious silence at the pictures of a glorious white sandy beach, vast marble lobby, personal Jacuzzis, beach boys offering cold towels and grinning black barmen mixing cocktails. Dawn, meanwhile, had been hardly less excited than her daughter. Having initially wondered whether it was right to accept the prize at all, being one of the organisers, she had discussed her reservations with Davina who had firmly dismissed them, saying, 'No, don't be silly, of course you should go, Dawn. You bought the winning ticket, it's all perfectly fair. You *must* go. And, anyway, the hotel is giving it all for free, it's not like it's costing anybody anything.'

Miles, who overheard the conversation and would have loved to withhold the Cleggs' prize, found his wife's attitude extremely annoying.

Dawn's excitement increased with everything she read about the hotel. The Cleggs' prosperity being only recent and embryonic, they had never previously holidayed further afield than Cyprus and Sharm El-Sheikh, so the prospect of the West Indies thrilled her. Furthermore, the Nelson Bluff was the absolutely in-place. An avid reader of *Hello!*, she remembered seeing photographs of the launch party with all sorts of celebrities present, and wished now she'd put her copy aside so she could look at it again. To the best of her memory, Joanna Lumley from *Absolutely Fabulous* had been out there for it, and Shirley Bassey and Aneka Rice, and Tara Palmer

Tomkinson, and all manner of socialites and grand folk. Then there had been a boastful review of the food by Michael Winner in the *Sunday Times*, who'd taken a girlfriend for Easter and bought a two-thousand-pound bottle of wine, and Philippa Mountleigh, who subscribed to *Tatler*, pointed out a glowing hotel review by Victoria Mather who'd praised the goosedown eiderdowns and five-hundred-thread pillowcases, and singled out Amos the beach boy as Hotel Beach Attendant of the Year.

Ross spent the entire flight working. If truth be told, this wasn't an ideal moment for him to be away on holiday, he was right in the middle of a complicated refinancing of his business, with several new investors on the point of deciding whether or not to come in. As he said to his PA, Jacqui, 'this ruddy prize couldn't have come at a worse time. But Dawn and the girls will murder me if we don't go. They're on about it non-stop.' So they laid careful plans for documentation to be faxed out, and he could always phone the office if he had to.

Greg, meanwhile, was torn between the excruciating embarrassment of sitting up front in Business Class, and greedily drinking as many free wines as he could get his mitts on. When a stewardess questioned whether he should really have a seventh mini-bottle, he became belligerent, and Ross had looked up from his briefcase and said, 'Enough, Greg. You're being impolite. And thank you, miss, he's had plenty to drink already.'

Gemma, breathless and panicking, wondered how she could ever get through the next seven days. No way could she wear a swimsuit, let alone a bikini. She had been examining her stomach in the mirror and it was huge, elephantine. By wearing a lot of loose tops, she could hopefully get away with it, but people were starting to give her funny looks, and her parents would guess in five seconds if they saw her tummy. Also, she'd read in *Sugar* that flying after the fifth month of pregnancy could damage the baby. What could she do? Switching on the inflight entertainment screen, she tried to concentrate on the film.

Everyone was blown away by the incredible over-the-top magnificence of the Nelson Bluff. Debbie was so excited she was racing about, saying, 'Dad, Mum, you've *got* to come and see this' and 'Mum, you've got to see the spa, you won't *believe* it.' Everything was so luxurious and so perfect. They'd been met at the airport by a white limousine with tinted windows and air-conditioning so cold it was like being driven about inside a fridge. The windows made the outside as dark as night time, when it was actually the middle of the afternoon, and when the doorman opened the door to let them out at the hotel, they were practically blinded by the fierce sunlight. The hotel's Assistant General Manager, a Swiss-German, greeted them with elaborate ceremony, cold towels and a welcome cocktail called the Nelson Paradise Aloha, made with pineapple and fresh strawberries. 'It is an honour to welcome friends of Mr Miles Straker to the hotel,' he said.

It was the bungalow which astonished them. For a start, it was enormous. 'I think this is about double the size of our first place in Droitwich,' Ross said, as three bellboys delivered their luggage, preceded by the Assistant General Manager and the Hospitality Manager, all eager to ensure the Cleggs' absolute comfort. 'I must apologise that our Executive General Manager, Mr Küppenkülm, is not available to greet you,' said the Swiss-German. 'He will come to meet you tomorrow at your convenience.'

Dawn, who was keen not to appear unaccustomed to all this bowing and scraping, ignored Ross's quip about their first place in Droitwich and concentrated on the tour of the bungalow.

According to Debbie, who was racing ahead exploring, there were ten rooms: 'Three bedrooms, three bathrooms, a lounge, this huge walk-in clothes cupboard as big as a whole room, separate toilet and then, in this little garden, a hot tub which is, like, really boiling. Quick Mum, you've got to see it.'

Two minutes later, Debbie reappeared to announce there were eight TVs in the bungalow. 'I've counted. Including one in the toilet. You've got to come.'

No sooner had the reception committee departed, and the Cleggs were unpacking into cedar-lined closets clearly designed for guests bringing half-a-dozen trunks rather than a single suitcase each, there was a tap at the door. This was Joseph—'Your personal butler'—whose role it emerged was to stick with the Cleggs like a limpet, night and day, during their entire stay, to take care of every whim.

Dawn became quite flustered at the idea of Joseph, not being able to think of anything they needed, until Ross had the idea of asking him to fill the ice bucket on the drinks tray, and Joseph beetled off looking relieved.

'Now, why don't you kids go and check out the pool and the beach, while your mum and I finish unpacking?' Ross said. But Gemma complained of having a stomach ache and didn't feel like swimming today.

As the Cleggs quickly discovered, there were so many choices of things to do and eat at Nelson Bluff, you could spend the day in a muddle of indecision. Unable to adapt to local time from British time, Debbie and Gemma were waking at four in the morning and turning on MTV, which echoed through the bungalow. Ross was, in any case, finding it difficult to sleep, being frozen by air con. Each time he thought he'd turned it off in one part of the bungalow (no easy task, there being a dozen different remote controls for the TVs, DVDs, electric drapes and temperature control), it had come back on in another. It took several days to discover Joseph was re-booting it, each time they stepped outside.

By half-past seven each morning, the Cleggs were the first family waiting outside the buffet breakfast restaurant, having already been awake three hours and starving hungry. Inside, half a dozen chefs in whites and toques were on standby to cook omelettes and bacon. Others were stationed behind ice-beds of exotic cut-up fruit and displays of imported sushi, and trestles covered with sweating German cheeses, salamis, eight different kinds of Danish pastries and Barbadian corn breads. Feeling increasingly nauseous, Gemma forced herself to eat a slice of pineapple. With her customary self-control, Dawn took two Ryvitas and a glass of orange juice. Ross and Greg had the full fry-up, while Debbie tried a little bit of every-thing and left most of it on her plate.

After breakfast each day, they gravitated to one of three enor-mous infinity swimming pools, or sat under straw umbrellas on the beach. Whichever they chose, Joseph soon found them, awaiting his orders for the day. It would be his pleasure, he said, to organise a castaway picnic with vintage claret on a neighbouring sandbank, or a special de-stress seven-steps spa programme lasting an entire day. Increasingly stressed by Joseph's persistent stalking, Dawn felt she was just about ready for the treatment. Ross stepped in, dis-patching Joseph to refill the ice bucket.

One lunchtime, the Executive General Manager of the hotel, Fritz Küppenkülm, came to the table and said, 'I trust you are having an enjoyable stay. I have taken the liberty of faxing Mr Straker, and telling him his guests are enjoying full VIP upgrades.'

When he received the fax at his office, Miles snarled, having never requested any special courtesies for the Cleggs.

By the middle of the week, Dawn had got quite into her stride and was having a blissful time. The hotel was everything she had hoped it would be. As she said to Ross, 'I could easily get used to this.' She loved looking at the other guests in the dining rooms or by the pool, wondering who they were. Some she felt she half recognised—she swore she knew that face—though whether they were on TV or she'd seen them in *Hello!*, she couldn't be certain. She loved the way everyone dressed up to the nines at night—the most lovely gowns came out—not to mention jewellery she'd be nervous to travel with. Her one regret—well, two regrets—was that she hadn't brought more evening clothes with her, and only two swimsuits. Most of the ladies appeared at the pool in a different swimsuit every day, and it was embarrassing wearing the same two in rotation. In the end, Ross told her, 'Go on Dawn, take a look in the hotel boutique and see if they've got anything you like, I'll treat you,' but the cheapest costume cost $650, and she wasn't paying that, even for a designer one.

Dawn was also worried Greg looked scruffy all the time, especially in the La Dolce Vita Italian restaurant in the evening, which was silver service and had a dress code. She'd been on at him all week, but he wouldn't put a tie on, and you could see the headwaiter looking at them. She hoped it didn't get back to Davina he'd shown them up.

And then there was Gemma. Dawn was becoming seriously worried about Gems. She'd been under the weather for weeks, not her normal happy self at all, and so uncommunicative. Of course it was partly her age. You couldn't expect a sixteen-year-old to act the sweet little girl they were accustomed to. But, nonetheless, she missed the old Gemma. And she'd put on quite a bit of weight recently, which she was clearly embarrassed about, poor love, because she wouldn't even wear a swimsuit, just sat about looking hot. Dawn wondered whether all the upheaval of moving house had upset her.

Poor Gems. It would have been better, really, if they'd stayed put in Droitwich, but it was all for Ross's work, which had to come first.

Ross, it so happened, was getting a lot more out of Nelson Bluff than he'd ever expected. Fed-up after two days of frying by the pool, he'd taken to using the hotel gym for a work-out each morning and soon got talking to other guests using the Cybex machines. There was a Glaswegian retail entrepreneur he got on well with, Callum Dunlop, who'd brought the JG SweatMax brand to Britain, and another guy, Brin Watkins, who'd founded and later sold the GrowPoints customer loyalty card programme. Both were evidently very rich men with time on their hands, who quickly got interested in the potential of Ross's Freeza Mart. After four long gym sessions, Ross had found two major new investors who furthermore were giving him a lot of useful advice and contacts. Ross made a mental note to thank Miles next time he saw him, because this Caribbean holiday was going to make a big difference to the business.

Fired up with enthusiasm, Ross had the idea of inviting his new friends, Callum and Brin, to join them for dinner, along with their respective other halves, to toast their new business association. Dawn, who had been surreptitiously eyeing up the immaculate Heather Dunlop by the pool all week, was quite excited by the idea, and the three Clegg children were made to promise to be polite to the guests at dinner, which would take place in the French La Bagatelle d'Or, the most exclusive of all the hotel restaurants. Greg, while signalling his disapproval of his dad's new capitalist cronies, reluctantly agreed to put on a tie for the occasion, and the girls all appeared looking their best in Matalan cocktail dresses. Dawn spent the afternoon at the spa having her hair done plus full manicure and pedicure, and bought a new pair of white evening slingbacks in the boutique, which were difficult to walk in. Ross couldn't help feeling proud of his little family as they set off, bronzed and glowing and enveloped in scent, along the low-lit pathways from their bungalow to the restaurant.

'I bet this is going to be a really plonking evening,' Greg said. 'This tie's strangling my neck, I can hardly *breathe*.'

'That's enough, Greg,' Ross said. 'It's going to be a nice occasion. No one's going to spoil it.'

They rendezvoused for pre-dinner drinks at the Frigate Bar where Dawn initially found herself slightly in awe of Heather Dunlop, who had her hair up on top of her head, which showed off her pendulous pair of pink diamond earrings. And then Brin introduced his new partner, Chantelle, a slinky bottle-blonde half his age who looked like a pole dancer, and turned out to be exactly that, cheerfully declaring she had met Brin at Spearmint Rhino. 'He slipped a fifty-quid note down my thong. We hit it off right away.' Greg couldn't take his eyes off her.

Soon they progressed in to dinner at La Bagatelle d'Or, which turned out to be a large, circular, goldy-beige room, with goldy-beige carpet, goldy-beige tablecloths, goldy-beige chairs and diaphanous goldy-beige net curtains covering every window and totally obscuring the view. At the entrance by the captain's desk was an elaborate arrangement of imported flowers and ferns, and further displays in ornamental urns were strategically placed throughout the room. Heather mentioned that La Bagatelle d'Or was her favourite restaurant at the resort, and that she and Callum ate there most evenings. As usual the air-con was turned up to polar and Debbie wished she'd brought a sweater.

The menu, which ran to sixteen pages, was printed on beige parchment like Egyptian papyrus, bound in purple crocodile, with a minimum of three lines of description for every dish, plus the sommelier's special recommendations for wine to accompany each one. Gemma didn't know where to begin, it was all incomprehensible. She was already feeling nauseous, and the only words she could recognise on the menu were lobster and langoustines, both of which made her feel like throwing up. All she wanted was a bowl of spaghetti or a burger. No, not even that. She didn't want anything.

A French headwaiter appeared in a goldy-beige linen jacket, flanked by two black waiters to announce the specials. He could particularly recommend the grilled lobster, swordfish and scallop kebab, served on a bed of saffron rice with a sauce of sweet sauternes and raspberries. Gemma felt her stomach turn. Suddenly she felt very ill indeed. Her forehead was damp with sweat, even in this icy room. She felt giddy.

Orders were placed and a phalanx of waiters appeared to clear away the decorative place settings in front of them, and replace them with a fresh set to eat off. Meanwhile, the three businessmen were setting the conversational agenda, with Callum and Brin bragging about deals they'd been involved in, and other retail tycoons they were good mates with, and the margin on this High Street business and that. Apart from very expensive wine, which both men had a passion for, all they talked about was retail and how different brands were faring. Dawn got quite muddled as they jumped between Dixons and Comet, Pendletons and Primark. But Ross, she was impressed to see, easily kept his end up.

The dinner went on and on. Everything took forever. The service was slow, formal and servile, with each course appearing under silver cloches to be revealed with a synchronised flourish. Not only were they served the dishes they'd actually ordered but bonus courses—*amuse gueles* and a rich lobster bisque—kept appearing with compliments of the chef. At one point, the chef himself appeared to take a bow. Callum was dominating the table with his views on Philip Green at British Home Stores, and the brilliant way he'd unilaterally imposed extended credit terms on suppliers, from thirty to ninety days. Chantelle the lap dancer tried to strike up a parallel conversation with Debbie about flip-flops, but Brin talked over her about Tie Rack and Debenhams.

It was at this moment Gemma fainted.

She toppled forward, face first, onto her untouched lobster salad, then slid sideways from her chair onto the floor. The goldy-beige carpet was so thick and springy that her collapse was almost soundless.

For a moment she lay there clutching at her napkin, before Ross and Dawn leapt to their feet and the French headwaiter and several other waiters including the sommelier were clustering round, getting in the way, while word was sent to summon the hotel doctor. When Ross called for water for Gemma, the sommelier asked whether she would prefer Vitel, San Pellegrino, Evian or Badoit, so Ross snatched a jug from an adjacent table.

With impressive speed, a Barbadian doctor with battered physician's bag and stethoscope appeared and examined Gemma on the carpet. She had come round, head cradled in Dawn's arms, complexion ghostly white.

The doctor examined her, pressing first her pulse, then abdomen. He frowned, then re-examined her more carefully.

'Don't worry, she's fine. But her blood pressure is a little low for a lady in her condition.'

'Condition?' said Dawn. 'What ever do you mean? What's wrong with my daughter?'

The doctor stretched out his large dry hand. 'You don't know? Then let me be the first to congratulate you. You gonna be a Grandma.'

15.

The bombshell of Gemma's pregnancy, quickly followed by the information that she was five-and-a-half months gone, astounded her family. Dawn blamed herself a thousand times for being so unobservant, wondering what kind of mother she must be. And when it emerged when and by whom the deed had been done, she blamed herself all over again. If she hadn't dragged Gemma to the Hospers Ball, none of this would have happened. It was all her fault! She should *never* have allowed her to go. And what sort of a mother-daughter relationship did she think she had anyway, if her sixteen-year-old couldn't confide in her?

The final twenty-four hours at Nelson's Bluff were mortifying, with visits to the clinic in Bridgetown, and all the trouble Ross had booking an earlier flight home. And then, of course, everyone in the hotel knowing about it. The shame! Although he didn't say anything, you could see the disapproval in the unhappy face of Joseph, their personal butler, as they dispatched him for bucketfuls of ice to keep Gemma cool. God, all Dawn wanted was to check out of the beastly place and get home. She'd had it up to here with luxury living.

On the other hand, she wasn't sure she could cope with a return to Chawbury. Not with the Strakers so nearby across the valley. The prospect of facing Davina made her feel weak. Although it was obvious Archie had behaved atrociously, she still felt some of the responsibility must lie with herself. It was all so embarrassing. And she couldn't think what would happen next. There were so many questions. She'd half wondered whether it would be best for everyone if the baby could be . . . stopped. But after the visit to the clinic, she understood it was far too late, not even legal . . . and there was the reaction of the other children to consider. Debbie seemed totally confused by it all, excitedly telling everyone she was going to be an auntie, and then comforting her sister for hours in the arctic bungalow, curled up round her in bed. Gemma couldn't stop crying poor thing, partly from relief that it had all come out into the open at last.

Dawn kept worrying what the Strakers would say when they got to hear, especially Miles. She had to admit, Miles scared her. She knew he was brilliant and attractive and very successful at what he did, everyone said so, but she didn't find him easy or warm. He acted so superior and she couldn't ever think of anything to say to him, he made her feel stupid. The more she thought about it, the more anxious she became. He wasn't going to be a very nice father-in-law for poor Gemma.

Which opened up another question: would Gemma and Archie get married? They were far too young, surely. Or should they, for the baby's sake? Dawn didn't know what to think. It was all too dreadful. And she was sure this would finish her friendship with Davina too, which she minded about dreadfully

In the end, Ross rang Miles at Chawbury Manor from the hotel, and spoke to both Miles and Davina for a very long time from the phone in the master bedroom. Dawn was sitting on the suitcase rack, listening, and marvelling at how sensible and measured Ross was being. She could hear Miles becoming agitated, then abusive, but Ross didn't rise to it, remaining very calm. Then Davina came on the line and that part of the conversation seemed to go much better. Ross left it that they were flying home overnight from Barbados, and would head straight to Chawbury. They would all talk further once they arrived home.

As soon as Davina put the phone down, Miles went berserk. He marched out onto the terrace and spotted Archie on a quad bike, racing round and round the valley floor. It took fifteen minutes of shouting to catch the bloody idiot's attention, and get him to return to the house. Then Miles let rip. He wasn't so much angry with Archie for rogering a girl, that wasn't the issue, but why the hell hadn't he used a johnnie, and why the Clegg girl for heavens sake? Of all the pretty girls at the dance, why her? Surely Archie could see she was half-witted, just by looking at her. And fat. He'd seen her at the garden party thing, practically obese. Surely Archie could have shown better taste.

An idea now occurred to Miles that maybe Archie wasn't actually the father. Once it had taken hold, he became quite fired up about it. It was perfectly obvious the girl—'Gemma'—he couldn't speak the name without metaphorical sugar tongs—had had endless other boys. 'She's that kind of a girl. Look at the way her mother cakes herself in make-up.' Miles became convinced the Cleggs were trying to entrap Archie. 'What proof do we have the baby's his? None whatever. I tell you we're not accepting this. Not before they provide irrefutable proof, if they can, which I very much doubt. And we mustn't breath a word about it to anyone either. If it got out, it'd be all over Nigel Dempster's column. He'd love this. We need disciplined news management.'

He glared at his children, all of whom had gravitated to the drawing room to see what the shouting was about. 'Mollie, you were at the Hospers Ball that night, weren't you? Did you notice the Clegg girl there? Surrounded by lots of different boys, was she?'

Mollie looked uncomfortable. 'Actually I did see her. She was with Archie all the time.'

Miles sighed. Rapier-witted, and having built his career on anticipating the ramifications of any situation, he kept thinking of further unwelcome consequences. If his son really had fathered a child with Ross Clegg's dopey daughter, would that compromise the future of the Pendletons' account at Straker Communications? Surely it was a conflict of interest, or could be interpreted as such? And how intolerable to have a grandchild at all! He who was barely fifty years old and looked seven years younger!

Mollie said, 'It must be awful for Gemma. I keep thinking how she must be feeling.'

Miles exhaled crossly. 'Believe me, she knew *exactly* what she was doing, that one. I wouldn't waste much sympathy on *her*.'

Another hideous vision swam into Miles's head: the shared grandchild being shuttled to and fro across that valley, between Manor and . . . Park. And the Cleggs using the pretext of the baby to drop in at the house whenever they fancied.

But Peter said, 'Gemma seemed really sweet at the fete thing. She bought CDs from my stall. She's awfully young and naïve. I remember exactly which one she is.'

He gave a sidelong glance at Archie, who was staring guiltily at the floor.

'The other person I'm worried about is poor Dawn,' Davina said. 'It must be frightful for her, so difficult to know what to do. Oh Archie, the trouble you've caused. I think I'm going to write her a letter and drop it in, before they get back, apologising and offering our support in any way we can.'

'You will do *no such thing*,' Miles said. 'I'm serious, we're not offering or admitting a thing, not unless we have to. And don't put anything in writing in case they use it against us.'

Samantha, who had been turning the pages of *Vogue* on the sofa, said, 'Do we know if it's going to be a boy or a girl?'

'For goodness sake, Sam,' Miles said. 'We don't know a *damn thing*, that's the whole point. Other than this stupid tart has placed Archie and this entire family in a very awkward predicament. Archie's the one I'm sorry for. You've got your A Levels coming up this summer and should be knuckling down, not distracted by all this. And university after that.'

'But Archie can't go to university now, can he?' Mollie said. 'He'll need to be looking after his baby. And his wife.'

'His *wife*?' Miles looked thunderstruck. 'The last thing Archie's going to do is *marry* her. The last thing! I'm sure that's what the Cleggs wanted all along, but it's not going to happen.'

16.

The information that the first Freeza Mart in the South of England would shortly be opening in Andover was headline news in the *Andover Daily Echo*. An enthusiastic editorial heralded lower grocery prices for Andover residents, alongside a photograph of 'Chawbury-man Ross Clegg and wife Dawn' standing on the newly-turfed front lawn at Chawbury Park.

The newspaper cutting quickly surfaced in Miles's daily press digest of Straker Communications's clients, and became an agenda item at the next Pendletons strategic review. The 70,000-square-foot Pendletons store in Andover was one of their most profitable and highest-margin outlets, and the prospect of a cut-price Freeza Mart on the doorstep was unwelcome. The Andover branch had in any case always held a special status in the company, being the closest one to Lord and Lady Pendleton's country house. It was the store at which Laetitia Pendleton herself shopped and, as such, seen as a showcase for the group.

'It's important we don't let them gain a foothold in the south,' James Pendleton warned. 'We need to contain them in their Midlands box, so let's put every resource behind maintaining share. Even if that means temporarily forfeiting margin. And of course we need to step up our PR locally. I find I'm starting to read rather a lot about this Ross Clegg character. Has anyone actually met him?'

Miles replied, as airily as possible, 'By extraordinary coincidence, James, he's become a neighbour of ours at Chawbury. He's putting up an awful eyesore, a new-build house, uncomfortably close to us actually. So I've seen him about the place. To be brutally honest, he's not very Hampshire. So I doubt he's going to get much local support longterm.'

Miles carefully avoided mentioning his uncomfortable summit meeting with Ross and Dawn the previous week, when the two sets of prospective grandparents had sat down at the Manor to discuss the increasingly pressing subject of Gemma's baby. In the days following the Cleggs' return from Barbados, Davina had been dropping in on Dawn more regularly than she ever admitted to her husband, making particular efforts to be kind to Gemma, who had taken time off school and was mooching about the house, watching TV on one of the many enormous leather sofas.

Davina's first concern had been for Archie, of course. He was so young and so vague, it seemed ridiculous he could become a father. She still helped him pack his suitcase for school, and nagged him to write thank-you letters. This baby would change his whole life and she couldn't believe he'd been so stupid, so careless. Now he was lurking about, not really speaking, with a hangdog expression. When she tried to discuss it with him, he refused, saying, 'Stop going *on* about it, Mum, get off my back.' Davina adored Archie but, she had to admit, she'd always found him tricky. Too like his father in character. She considered Peter and Mollie her easiest children, being the ones most like herself. The middle two, Samantha and Archie, were pure Miles.

Miles continued to resist liability for the parentage, having his lawyer send a carefully-worded letter to the Cleggs. Eventually, however, after Ross threatened DNA tests, Miles reluctantly conceded the baby was probably Archie's. 'I'm just waiting for Ross to send me a thumping great bill,' he said. 'Money will be the next thing, you wait.' But when they received a brief, professional note from Ross saying that he was, of course, expecting to take care of everything for Gemma's child, and naturally wasn't looking for any financial contribution from the Strakers, Miles felt he was being excluded. 'If Ross thinks he can cut us out, he's got another thing coming. This child is as much ours as theirs. In fact, we're going to have to get very involved over questions of schools and so on, since I can't see the Cleggs having a clue. Davina, we need to get them over to discuss it, sooner the better.'

And so they had met, not without awkwardness, in Miles's study, with Archie banished to the Playstation for the duration of the visit, and Peter, Samantha and Mollie, all down at Chawbury for the weekend, instructed to greet the guests politely and then make themselves scarce. Both Davina and Dawn were dreading the meeting, begging their respective husbands not to fly off the handle. Dawn had actually been physically sick ten minutes before setting off, leaving Gemma and Debbie behind at home. In the car during the short journey up to Chawbury Manor, Dawn implored Ross not to do anything stupid. 'Promise me you won't. Promise you won't loose your rag. Let's try and keep things nice and civilised.'

Ross shrugged. 'I've told you, love, I'm calm as anything. Just so long as Miles doesn't wind me up like he did on the phone in Barbados.'

'*Ross*,' said Dawn, in a warning voice. And then they arrived.

The first half of the meeting went off better than feared, with Davina bringing in a cafetiere of coffee (which felt more appropriate than drinks, under the circumstances) and the two men doing their best to stay calm and reasonable. Dawn said how beautiful the countryside was looking at the moment, and Davina agreed it was her favourite time of year. Eventually they moved on to Gemma. Dawn reported the baby's due date was in the third week of August and that Gemma was planning to give birth in Basingstoke and North Hampshire General Hospital.

'In a private room, I hope. Not NHS,' Miles said.

'Yes, we've decided to push the boat out and go private,' Ross said. 'I want Gemma to have the best care available.'

Miles wished she'd taken better care herself at the Hospers Ball, which was the whole bloody trouble, but said nothing.

Dawn said that, having given it all a lot of thought, she and Ross had decided the best thing would be for the child to be brought up partly as their own. 'Otherwise it'll ruin Gemma's whole life. She's too young to be tied down night and day with a baby. We're not saying she won't look after it, or take responsibility, but we thought we should share the responsibility. And, of course, if Archie wants to play his part, and get to know the little person, he'll always be most welcome. He can come and go at the Park as he pleases.'

'Yes, well, that's something for Archie to decide for himself,' Miles said non-committally. 'He's going to be very occupied with exams for the foreseeable future.'

'It would be nice for Gemma if he gave her a bell some time,'

Ross said. 'Just to say hello and show support. I know she'd appreciate that. She's feeling a bit isolated at the moment. A friendly call would buck her up. Not to apologise or anything, just to touch base.'

Miles began to feel agitated. He was uncomfortable with the direction the conversation was taking. The way the Cleggs were going on, you'd almost have thought it was Archie's fault, all this. So he said, 'I should jolly well think not. Apologise, I mean. Archie's got nothing to apologise for.'

'Well, I'd have thought damn near raping my teenage daughter was something, wouldn't you? You can argue the toss, but that's what happened, give or take.'

'I *strongly resent* that remark,' Miles replied. 'That's not my understanding at all. If your daughter hadn't thrown herself at him. . . .'

Ross felt a muscle twitching in his jaw, which always happened when he became angry. He glared at Miles, hating his stupid, supercilious, arrogant attitude and his stupid, supercilious face. 'Gemma did no such thing. Your son took complete bloody advantage. Plied her with spirits he'd brought into the party, then pressed himself on her. That's exactly what happened.' Ross was seething, fists clenching and unclenching. If there hadn't been ladies present, he'd have stood up and bloody decked Miles, he was that close. 'And if you ever—*ever*, do you understand me—imply anything else, I'll make a formal complaint of rape to the police. I'd have done so already if my wife hadn't talked me out of it.' Ross was perched on the edge of the sofa, poised for a fight. He felt Dawn's restraining hand on his knee.

'Gentlemen, gentlemen,' Dawn said tearfully. 'Let's not get heated. It's the baby we're here to talk about, there's no good casting blame.'

An ugly silence settled on the room.

Davina, peacemaking, said brightly, 'Obviously this is a dreadful situation for all of us. And I agree with Dawn, there's no point trying to cast blame. They're both so young, and what's happened has happened, awful though it is. The important thing is to make sure this new little life is cherished and loved by all of us. I was thinking about this in the middle of the night when I couldn't sleep: much worse things happen all the time in this world. It isn't the end of the world at all, that's the way I see it. And here we are at opposite ends of this lovely valley, all so lucky in so many ways. There are worse starts for a child than to be brought up here at Chawbury, by all of us.'

Miles stared at his wife, incredulous. He had seldom heard her speak at so great a length, and wondered whether it was spontaneous or whether she'd planned it. Either way, he didn't agree with a word she'd spouted. As far as Miles was concerned, it was all a ghastly, excruciating tragedy and that was that. A tragedy for himself, he meant. Being related to the Cleggs.

Through a combination of lucky timing and decisive action, Ross heard that the old Allied Carpets superstore in Andover was up for sale and secured it practically overnight from under the noses of PC World and Halfords. The edge-of-town site could scarcely have been more suitable, with ninety thousand square feet of retail space and plentiful parking. Furthermore, it was directly opposite Pendletons. In fact, Freeza Mart would be separated from Pendletons only by a shallow shrubbery of dusty bushes. Ross knew he couldn't have hoped for a better location for his first venture down south.

Having discussed strategy with his new investors from Nelson Bluff, Callum Dunlop and Brin Wilson, Ross decided on a PR blitz to get the message across that prices at Freeza Mart would be massively lower than anywhere else in Hampshire. 'If you can find any item in our store—not just promotional lines—for less within a thirty mile radius, bring it in and we'll refund the difference twice over,' was his boast. Radio commercials were recorded, using the popular presenters of *Taskforce Garden South*, to blanket Radio Andover. Double-page advertisements were created for the local newspapers, starring Ross himself giving the thumbs up to rock bottom prices.

The culmination of the promotional campaign would be a big launch party, with local dignitaries and celebrities invited, as well as potential customers, featuring a ten-minute trolley-dash of free groceries for shoppers entered into a prize draw.

As the date of the grand opening approached, Ross began to

worry about the launch party and whether it would come up to scratch. Not knowing many people in Hampshire, he was largely reliant on a local PR agency which didn't fill him with much confidence. Their suggestions for celebrities to open the store were a Fourth Division football player and a daytime weathergirl. Nor could they supply many names for the guest list.

The store itself, meanwhile, was rapidly taking shape. Following the no-frills policy of his West Midlands outlets, there was minimum investment in shop fittings, with a pile-it-high, sell-it-cheap philosophy prevailing. Escarpments of beers and beans in twenty-four can packs loomed above the aisles, and the wire trolleys made extra robust to cope with bulk shopping. The plate glass windows were pasted with posters promoting cut-price offers, and tannoys regularly announced spot bargains: 'Value packs of own-brand sweetcorn now on reduction on aisle sixteen.'

Sharing his concerns about the launch event with Dawn and Gemma, now seven months pregnant and horribly uncomfortable, Ross worried no one would turn up. Dawn, however, said she was sure she could rally support, and spent the afternoon calling her old friends from Droitwich, Vera and Naomi, and her new committee friends from the hospice group. Philippa Mountleigh immediately said she'd love to come along to the opening, and promised to try and bring Johnnie, the Lord Lieutenant, as well. 'God I'm looking forward to this store. Our grocery bills come to God-knows-what every week. I'm longing for lower prices.' Bean Winstanton promised to be there too, 'and would it be awful if I brought Nigel, plus Toby and Shrimp, and our lovely Croatians Stanislav and Vjecke? And we have a houseful of guests staying that weekend, tell me if it's all too much.' After that, Dawn rang Davina and explained they were looking for extra people, and Davina immediately said she'd love to come herself, though wasn't sure Miles would be able to ('He's always so busy, I can't speak for him'), and she'd put together a list of other suggestions. In no time, she'd secured a yes from Ridley Nairn, the MP, and his wife, Suzie, and Davina was thinking of ringing James and Laetitia Pendleton to invite them.

'I'm not sure that would be appropriate, really,' Dawn said

doubtfully. 'I mean, Ross's new store is going to be competition for them.'

'Oh, I'm sure the Pendletons won't mind that,' Davina replied. 'They're *such* lovely people. Well, I'll ask Miles's opinion when he gets home.'

They had then talked about poor Gemma and how she was bearing up. Dawn said she was feeling very apprehensive, poor thing, having attended pre-natal classes in Andover and the reality of caring for a new-born was beginning to sink in. Unmentioned between them was the fact that Archie had never once rung her, despite his mother begging him to. Davina didn't say that Archie was, at that moment, staying up in Yorkshire with a bunch of friends from his house at school, attending various local dances.

When Miles arrived home at Chawbury that night from a week's business in Paris and Barcelona, and his wife asked for guest suggestions for Ross's launch party on Thursday week, he went very quiet and thoughtful. And soon afterwards, in the privacy of his study, made several telephone calls to senior executives of Straker Communications and Pendletons plc. Further conversations took place over the weekend, and by midday on Monday invitations had been designed, addressed and posted out. On Tuesday morning, fifteen hundred of Hampshire's smartest residents received a personal invitation from Lord Pendleton of Stockbridge to a classical recital by the Philharmonia Orchestra and reception at the Pendletons store in Andover, in honour of the store's twentieth anniversary. The Pendletons event would directly clash with Ross's opening

The first Ross heard about any of this was when he opened up the local newspaper on Thursday. There, splashed across the front page, was a breathless preview of the great Pendletons gala at which every local dignitary was expected 'including local Member of Parliament Ridley Nairn, the editor of the *Andover Daily Echo* and, it is rumoured, a member of the royal family.' Pendletons, the article continued, 'has been Andover's favourite shopping destination for twenty years and looks set to remain so for many years to come.' In an exclusive announcement to the *Daily Echo*, Pendletons has pledged two hundred and fifty thousand pounds towards a new civic bus shelter and youth-related charities in the area. The

Daily Echo says: "Hats off to Pendletons. Happy Birthday and Many Happy Returns!"'

Ross summoned his PR agency which reported the Pendletons event was certain to eclipse their own, and they were no longer confident the Freeza Mart opening would generate much coverage at all. 'And if they bag a royal, all the celebs will go there instead.'

'Well, we've already got acceptances from quite a few.' Ross said. 'Our MP told Dawn he's definitely coming. And the Lord Lieutenant. We'll just have to work that bit harder, that's all.'

17.

Miles had a golden rule that he never, other than in the most exceptional circumstances, indulged in marital infidelity within a fifty-mile radius of Chawbury. To do so, he reasoned, was disrespectful to Davina. On the same principle, he never took girlfriends upstairs at Holland Park Square, preferring to meet in hotels or, better still, abroad.

The fifty-mile rule was carefully judged, since Chawbury was eighty-five miles from London which meant a long roster of impressive hotels in the Thames Valley were still in-bounds. Clivedon, the old Astor stately home near Taplow, was one of Miles's favourites for assignations, as was Hartwell House near Aylesbury. Davina often commented on the ridiculous number of work conferences he attended, and wondered whether he couldn't sometimes miss one or two.

Generally, however, he chose to meet his mistress of the moment overseas. A long weekend would be tacked on to the end of a business trip, and the lady in question flown out to join him at the Cipriani in Venice or the Villa San Michele in Fiesole. Miles would mention to his PA, Sara White, that 'Mrs so-and-so will be joining me in Venice on Friday,' and the necessary flights and reservations would be taken care of. It was implicitly understood that Mrs Straker should never be appraised of the special arrangements.

Bolstered with self-admiration for his coup in sabotaging Ross's launch event, Miles spent part of the following week in Turin, pitching for the Fiat account. Accompanied by six Straker Communications executives, they made two formal presentations to the Fiat board, but Miles knew that his private dinners with Fiat's Chairman and CEO, which took place in a suite at the Turin Palace

Hotel, were of infinitely greater consequence. His contented mood was enhanced by the prospect of a weekend on Capri with Serena Harden, his on-off mistress.

Serena was the quintessential candidate for a Miles Straker mistress. For a start, she was very attractive. For another, she was flirtatious. Both of these mattered very much to him. But above all she was grateful. Grateful for the treats, for the luxury hotel suites, for the First Class travel, none of which she would otherwise experience, being married to poor Robin Harden.

Miles had worked out, many years earlier, exactly what worked and did not work in a mistress. Single women were definitely a no-no. Statistically the easiest to attract, especially beyond the age of thirty-eight, they were also the most dangerous; demented with baby hormones and fear of life alone, they harboured expectations he could never satisfy. The wives of rich men presented a different challenge, because they were less biddable and less impressed by the *bonne bouches* Miles provided. No, give him for choice the disappointed wife of an unsuccessful man. Give him a woman who felt herself born to better things; who had tasted comfort and luxury early in life, then had them withheld through an ill-judged marriage.

The Honourable Serena Harden, by Miles's criteria, ticked every box. The only daughter of a Suffolk peer, raised in a Jacobean farmhouse without a farm near Ipswich, she had been one of the most lusted-after girls of her generation. Vivacious and effervescent, she had stopped traffic with her long red hair and tight leather trousers, and effortlessly accumulated a succession of dashing boyfriends, including the heir to an Earldom, the scion of a Norfolk cider dynasty and a notoriously handsome commercial property whiz. Amongst the rich and raffish group she played with, she was regarded as a diamond girl. When a date was required for a big night at Annabels, or someone to take to Ascot, you could not do better than Serena Britten-Smith, who could be relied upon to show up looking a million dollars. Furthermore, she was perpetually available for fun: she did not work, or anyway had no job that restricted her social life or made it impossible for her to stay out late at midweek parties. For a while, she was a receptionist at Cluttons, the estate agents; later she worked part-time at a jewellery shop in Walton

Street, and for an interior decorator behind Harrods. She shared a large, grand, second floor flat with three other girls in Cadogan Square, until one by one the other flatmates became engaged and moved on and out.

At the age of thirty, she surprised herself by not being married, since she had taken it for granted she would be by then. At thirty-four, following a two year rollercoaster affair with a commodity trader who whisked her off to St Moritz most weekends, she began to wonder what else was out there. At thirty-five, she'd hooked up with a racing trainer until it became clear he'd never leave his wife. At thirty-seven, starting to panic, she became pregnant by Robin Harden.

Having first met Robin in the company of people she knew to be rich and successful at a dinner at Mortons, she assumed Robin was rich and successful as well. Too late she learnt he attracted bad luck in business like an albatross. Presentably suited, well-spoken, passably handsome, privately educated and with a plausible manner, he had embarked upon a dozen different careers, each ending in failure and disappointment. He had traded bonds, sold equities, become a shipping broker. He had tried his hand at yacht chartering, and at setting up a high-class removals business in central London. He had sold school fees schemes and endowment mortages and attempted to enter the wine trade. At the time he met Serena, he said he was a player in the residential property market, which actually meant renovating a house in Hurlingham, largely single-handedly, for resale.

By the time Serena discovered all this, it was too late. By then, she was already Mrs Robin Harden. Their son, Ollie, was born four months after the wedding. The child inherited the bright red hair of its mother and the perpetually baffled expression of its father.

As a bachelor, Robin had lived in a top floor flat in Redcliffe Square, on which he had bought the remaining six years of a lease. It was in this high-ceilinged flat, full of mahogany chests of drawers, un-ironed shirts and a saucer full of cuff links, that Serena had become pregnant. Married with a child, and needing more space, they had sold the place for next to nothing and bought a house in Hammersmith on a thirty-year mortgage. As Robin stumbled from setback to setback, it became a struggle to keep up repayments; the house remained permanently half-decorated with a kitchen Serena hated, and bathrooms she hated more. Having comforted herself that at least when her old parents died she would come into some money, it was a bitter blow when they left practically nothing, once it had been carved up between the taxman, debts, solicitors' fees and her two brothers. When Robin's short-lived removals business collapsed, they conceded defeat in London and downscaled to Hampshire, to a rented cottage on the Mountleighs' estate.

It was not long after they'd moved in, when Serena was feeling particularly hacked-off with her reduced circumstances, that she met Miles at a drinks party.

Their affair began almost immediately and always on Miles's terms. He invited her to lunch in London, and when she hesitated, saying she didn't really come up to London anymore and the train was too expensive, he'd sent his driver, Makepiece, all the way to collect her from the end of the lane. 'I won't ask him to pick you up from your front door, for obvious reasons,' Miles had said, and in this remark the context of the lunch was defined.

He had already booked a room for the afternoon at the Connaught, which showed generosity and style, but also arrogance. 'How did you know I'd agree to come?' Serena asked him that first afternoon, as they let themselves into the pretty yellow suite.

'I didn't. But I considered it an odds-on bet.'

After that, they met every couple of weeks, whenever Miles said his schedule permitted it. He allowed her to buy clothes at the Bond Street boutiques she favoured, which she later told Robin came from a nearly-new charity shop in Andover. And he encouraged her to pursue her former trade as an interior decorator, to provide cover for their assignations and the pretext to travel away from home. Sometimes on Monday evenings, when Davina wasn't up in London, he took her to the opera and dinner. If they ran into friends, Miles introduced her as 'our near neighbour Serena Harden. You've probably met Serena and Robin at Chawbury with us.' Serena understood she was never to ring Miles at Chawbury or Holland Park Square, only at the office. And their assignations were initiated solely by Miles, never by her.

Having once or twice been unavailable to join her lover when he requested her, pleading a school commitment with Ollie or a prior social one with Robin, Serena had witnessed Miles's petulant displeasure, and having experienced it had no desire to do so again. Now she was permanently at his beck and call.

The invitation—the command—to come to Capri for the weekend had been issued only four days earlier. Serena and Robin had accepted, long ago, a dinner invitation for that Saturday night from their landlords, Johnnie and Philippa Mountleigh, in the big cold dining room at Stockbridge House. Having attended one of these formal dinners at the Mountleighs before, Serena knew how seriously Philippa took them. Not by nature an enthusiastic hostess, Philippa nevertheless regarded it as her moral duty to entertain in the dining room six times a year, especially now with Johnnie doing his bit as Lord Lieutenant, and that the job be properly done. And so eight couples would sit down to dinner, men in dinner jackets, the Victorian silver candelabra would be brought out of the strong room and polished up, Johnnie decanted his best claret, and Philippa, looking down the table at her guests sitting on the wonky Georgian chairs, wished everyone would go home not too late but at least she'd made the effort and given them all a jolly good dinner.

How Serena was going to get out of the Mountleighs' dinner party, which Robin was looking forward to, and what excuse she was going to give for going abroad so abruptly that weekend, she needed to resolve. But the prospect of saying no to Miles was much worse.

Miles arranged for a business class plane ticket to Naples to be waiting for her at Heathrow, being the best class available on this European hop. She had to admit, it still gratified her in a way she knew was silly and immature to be flying in the front of the plane. When she'd been with Roger, the commodities trader, and they'd been flying to Zurich three weekends in four during the skiing season, they'd always flown First. In fact she'd flown First quite a lot before she was married. But with Robin, if they flew at all, which they didn't very often, it was always economy. One of the things she definitely liked about Miles was his generosity over plane tickets.

He was waiting for her at the barrier with a porter ready to carry her luggage. A car was waiting outside the terminal to take them to the port to board the hovercraft over to Capri. Miles barely spoke when she arrived, he seldom did, it was his way. Nor did he embrace her. She asked him, 'How was Turin? You didn't say what you were doing there when you rang.'

'Business meetings.' He shrugged. 'Not my favourite city, Turin.' He sat in brooding in silence in the car to the port, and then for the journey across to Capri.

They arrived at Capri harbour where an open-topped hotel taxi with striped canopy was waiting to take them up the steep hill to Anacapri, and then on to their hotel, the Caesar Augustus, close the summit. Still Miles had barely addressed a word to her.

On previous trips, Serena was mortified when he'd behaved like this, wondering what she'd done to displease him. Despite regarding herself as a tough nut, she was definitely rattled. He was like a television or a piece of computer equipment, normally operating at full capacity, that had lapsed into sleep mode, and a sinister, passive-aggressive mode at that.

The hotel was typical of the places Miles liked: five-stars, civilised and deferential, with large suites, marble bathrooms and long views. The view from the Caesar Augustus was especially magnificent; from the terrace was a panorama of the whole of the bay of Naples with Mount Vesuvius smoking gently on the horizon, and Sorrento and the island of Ischia just visible in the haze. Speed boats and superyachts criss-crossed the bay.

They were shown to their suite and, immediately they were alone, Miles commanded her, as she knew he would, to strip naked and lie face up on the linen bedcover. He made no effort to undress himself, though he unbuckled his watch—a Patek Philippe with leather strap—placing it on the dressing table.

Assessing her critically on the bed, he said, 'Not bad. A pound, two pounds overweight would we say? And your bush needs trimming.'

Very slowly and carefully, he removed his suit trousers and boxers and folded them over a hanger. Then, menacingly erect, he rolled on top of her.

Afterwards he padded into the bathroom, pulled on one of the hotel's towelling robes, combed his hair, and picked up his mobile. 'Find me by the pool in an hour,' he told her. 'I've got calls to make.' They were almost the first words he'd addressed to her since she landed.

Revitalised and freshly alert after sex, Miles settled himself on a sunbed and made four calls in quick succession. The first was to Ridley Nairn, the Member of Parliament whose campaign literature was designed and distributed by Straker Communications. After an exchange of pleasantries about Suzie and Davina, Miles said, 'Reason I'm calling you on a Saturday, Ridley, is a slightly sensitive one. I know you've accepted to attend the Pendletons' Twentieth Anniversary event on Thursday, but I hear you might also be going to Ross Clegg's Freeza Mart launch.'

Ridley replied, yes, he'd intended looking in on both events, since they were so close.

'Be a sensible fellow and give the Freeza Mart thing a miss,' Miles said. 'James Pendleton wouldn't like it if you went, and you know how his lordship can be if he's unhappy. Gets things out of proportion. And he's told me he wants you at his own party from start to finish.'

Ridley sounded uncomfortable, and said something about having promised he'd put his face in at Freeza Mart and how he had an obligation to treat all businesses in the constituency equally.

'Well, it's your decision, of course,' Miles said. 'But I shall have to report back to James. As you know he's a major donor to the Tories. And he was just about to issue Suzie with a Pendletons' gold card too, which entitles you to forty percent off at all their supermarkets . . . I must tell you, Ridley, as your political mentor, I think you're making a mistake. I'd reconsider if I were you.'

Ridley agreed to reconsider.

'Well, ring me later and let me know your decision,' Miles said. 'I'll be speaking to James tomorrow at noon.'

After that, Miles rang the Mountleighs and had a similar conversation with Johnnie. 'As Lord Lieutenant,' Miles told him, 'Lord Pendleton expects to see you at the anniversary party. Confidentially, Princess Margaret's agreed to honour us, so you'll be there all morning in your official capacity in any case. You and Philippa too, of course.'

'Well, I'll have to speak to Philippa. Not now though, she's in a frightful bate. A couple who were meant to be coming to dinner tonight pulled out at the last minute. Invited them months ago too. Bloody rude. You probably know them . . . Serena and Robin Harden.'

Miles sounded vague. 'The redhead with the leather trousers?'

'That's the one. Lives in one of our cottages too. Philippa's gone ballistic.'

After that, Miles rang the Winstantons to say there was a chance Bean might be needed for the line-up to meet Princess Margaret, but he didn't know the precise time, so could she be on standby at Pendletons the whole morning.

After that, he rang Davina to say negotiations at Fiat were dragging on and he doubted he'd now get away before Monday afternoon. 'So while you're all swimming and playing croquet at Chawbury, you can think of me cooped up in this ruddy industrial town in back-to-back meetings.'

Serena joined him at the pool. As usual following their first, always emotionally disengaged, sexual encounter of any trip, she was feeling used. At these moments she questioned what she was even doing here with Miles, and what sort of Faustian pact it was she had entered into. She thought of the lies she'd resorted to, to make it here at all. Philippa had been distinctly cool when she'd rung her with an excuse about confusion over dates, and how she'd long ago promised to meet a potential decorating client with a villa in Italy.

'How come I've never heard about this friend before?' Robin had asked.

'You don't know half my clients,' Serena snapped back. 'If we could afford a house large enough to invite them to, you *would* know them.'

His phone calls completed, Miles's mood brightened. Serena had observed this pattern before: after a period of intense work, like the past few days in Turin, his reserves of energy were temporarily depleted, leaving him introverted and remote. Nothing could shift it except impersonal love-making, followed by more work. And then like sunshine emerging from thunderclouds, the charming, attractive Miles reasserted itself.

Now he was full of self-esteem. As they had baths and changed for dinner, he regaled her with his strategies for sabotaging Ross's party. 'A subtle word here, a little pressure there,' he told her. 'I don't think you'll be seeing Ridley Nairn at the Freeza Mart bash. Or the Mountleighs. And it was a masterstroke wheeling out Princess Margaret. Pendletons have put half a million into the Royal Ballet School. So she owes us a favour.'

They ate outside at the Lucullo restaurant on a candlelit terrace overlooking an inky-black sea. They drank martinis, and then Miles chose a particularly splendid bottle of wine, with each glass feeling more relaxed and expansive. He told Serena about other famous, successful people he'd had breakfast and lunch with since they'd last been together, and what Maurice Saatchi privately thought about the Tories' current electoral prospects, and how the Bernie Ecclestone business had damaged New Labour more deeply than they'd appreciated and how it was the harbinger of further New Labour financial scandals to come. He mentioned he would be in Dubai in October for the opening of Zach Durban's marina and resort, and perhaps Serena would like to accompany him, since the opening clashed with his daughter Mollie's college open day, which Davina was making a ridiculous fuss about and refusing to miss.

At some point during every meal Miles always asked after Serena's unfortunate husband. Ostensibly showing commendable concern for his mistress's spouse, he in fact took ghoulish pleasure in hearing Serena describe how hopeless Robin was, since it contrasted so starkly with his own spectacular success. 'Remind me what he's up to now,' Miles said, savouring a balloon of after-dinner cognac. 'I can't remember whether he's still selling life insurance or renting out gin palaces.'

'Neither, sadly,' Serena replied. 'Both bombed. He's got some new scheme for selling fermented chicken shit and mustard oil as fuel. Apparently it works. Or he thinks it might. He's got in with some guy in the pub, they meet to discuss it every night.'

Miles chuckled indulgently. 'Well, if he needs any help, get him to ring me. John Browne at BP is a friend, I'm sure he'd be happy to give Robin advice, or at least put him in touch with his research people.'

Serena squeezed his hand across the table. Miles was a bastard, of course, but sometimes, on evenings like this, she found him irresistible. The food and wine and the warm, balmy island air helped her forgive his earlier behaviour. Eating on the terrace with its tables of well-groomed Italian guests made her feel glamorous for the first time in months. She thought of what she'd left behind this morning in Hampshire: the two-bedroomed labourer's cottage—Grooms Cottage, where the stablegirls had lived in the days when the Mountleighs still kept horses at Stockbridge House—with its cramped, cold kitchen and dark sitting room. She thought of Ollie tucked up in bed upstairs and felt a twinge of guilt, but not a prolonged one. She justified herself that she always returned from escapades with Miles feeling so much happier— bucked-up—which made her much nicer to Robin. Poor Robin. He would probably be lurking in the kitchen now, eating toast (he could get through a loaf in a sitting, slice after slice, smothered with jam) or maybe his mate from the pub would be at Grooms Cottage for a drink, and they'd be fantasising about the fortune they were going to make from chicken poo petrol.

Miles was telling her more about Ross, 'dreadful little creep with a limp' and how he'd skewered him over the store opening. 'He's going to be a *very lonely man* come Thursday morning. By the time I've finished, he'll be just about the only person at his own opening party.'

Serena said, 'I've heard he's got quite a nice wife and kids, that's what Philippa Mountleigh says. Pretty daughters.'

Miles bristled. 'I wouldn't say any of them are much to write home about. I won't go into it, but take it from me the elder daughter's a manipulative little minx. She's caused a great deal of trouble, that one.'

Then he stood up, and announced with an anticipatory leer that it was bedtime for both of them.

18.

Dawn was dreading the opening party for Ross's new superstore. Partly because she feared it might be a failure, which would be a knock-back for Ross, and partly because she'd secretly love to have been going to the Pendletons' one instead, which everyone was talking about.

For a week now, all she'd heard was Pendletons, Pendletons, Pendletons. Getting a blow dry and her colour done for Ross's party, there were three very smart-looking women in the salon, all going to the Pendletons thing and having their hair done specially. And when they'd stopped at the garage to buy petrol, the man behind the till had said, 'You're looking very dressy, ladies. Off to the big do at Pendletons, are you?'

'No, actually,' Dawn replied. 'We're going to the Clegg's Freeza Mart opening.' She enunciated the word 'Clegg' very clearly, hoping he might notice her name on the credit card and make the connection.

'Don't know about that one,' he replied dully. 'I thought you'd be going to Pendletons. They've got the Queen opening it, so I've heard.'

The more she heard about it, the more Dawn wished she was going. It sounded such a classy affair. Not only this classical orchestra brought specially from London, but a champagne reception which was all going to be photographed for the newspapers, and there was a rumour *Hello!* was sending down a photographer to cover it too. Freeza Mart's own efforts to secure the local newspapers, freesheets and county magazine, *Hampshire Life*, had ended in failure, since all said they'd made agreements to cover Pendletons exclusively, and anyway had nobody spare to send. According to Philippa Mountleigh, who had rung up in a state of total embarrassment, Johnnie could no longer come, being tied up with Lord Lieutenantly duties greeting Princess Margaret. 'I'm supposed to be on duty all day myself too, but I'm going to *sneak out* and come and see your lovely new shop.' Even more annoyingly, the local MP, Ridley Nairn, cried off on a pretext without even the good grace to ring up himself, leaving it to his tax-efficient PA-cum-wife, Suzie.

'Who actually *is* coming to ours then?' Dawn asked despairingly at the final debrief with the public relations people. 'I haven't spent all afternoon at the salon just to party with Ross, you know. We could do that at home at the Park, we've got the space.'

But Ross reassured her at least one hundred and twenty people were confirmed acceptances, including two coaches full of Freeza Mart staff from other branches and head office. 'And there's the minibus Vera's bringing down,' with a dozen mates from the Midlands.

'Well, it'll be nice to see the old gang again,' Dawn said doubtfully, wondering how her old friends would mix with Philippa Mountleigh, if Philippa ever made it, which Dawn now slightly hoped she wouldn't.

'And the band should get the joint jumping,' Ross said. His agency had hired a country music group, fronted by a Dolly Parton look-alike, which they swore was excellent and normally played dancehalls and ice rinks in Portsmouth and Southampton. 'And with luck there'll be some genuine customers. That's what it's all about.' For days, between bouts of intensive training on the new swipe-and-pay checkouts, Freeza Mart staff had been handing out invitations in the High Street, urging people to come along and maybe win a trolley-dash.

'If you ask me,' Ross declared, 'Our event is going to be every bit as good as this Pendletons junket. And once people clock the price deferential, they'll be coming over in droves. Some of the prices at Pendletons, they must be having a laugh. Seventy-nine pence for two hundred millilitre Fruits of the Forest yoghurt? We're doing them for thirty-eight pence, providing you buy a dozen.'

Both events were scheduled to kick-off at eleven a.m., and by ten-to-eleven Dawn, Gemma and Debbie were standing outside the trolley park waiting for Freeza Mart to open its doors. A handful of prospective customers were hanging about, some clutching handbills distributed earlier in the week, entitling them to enter the draw for the trolley-dash. To be precise, there were five punters in the queue: two old women, a single mum with a snotty-nosed toddler, and a gormless young man with a mullet haircut.

'I can see Dad inside,' Debbie said excitedly. Her nose was pressed against the glass doors and she'd spotted Ross making a final inspection of the aisles with the branch manager, who was holding a clipboard.

But Dawn's attention was focused on the far side of the car park where a succession of increasingly smart cars were drawing up outside Pendletons. There was a strip of red carpet across the pavement, which a man was vacuuming in readiness for the royal visit. Dawn couldn't see very clearly, but she thought there were half a dozen waitresses lined up holding trays of champagne. And she spotted a specially cordoned-off area for photographers, packed with cameramen and TV crews filming guests as they arrived. On both sides of the entrance, metal crash barriers had been erected and already five hundred locals were pressing forwards waiting to catch a glimpse of Princess Margaret.

'When are they going to open the doors, Mum? I'm bored.' Debbie was breathing onto the plate glass windows so they misted up, and playing noughts and crosses against herself on the pane. Gemma, feeling horribly bloated, leant against a concrete tub which had been planted out the previous day with geraniums. The queue outside Freeza Mart now reduced from five people to four, the gormless young man having shuffled over to Pendletons, attracted by photographers' flashbulbs.

Inside the store, Ross was furious. The country music band had turned up very late, and furthermore proved to be a transvestite act, a fact of which his PR people had been entirely oblivious, despite having booked them. The five hairy men were now in make-up, changing into Dolly Parton costumes.

Meanwhile, a celebrity weathergirl from BBC Winchester's Daytime Round-up had arrived and was impatient to get on with the ribbon-cutting ceremony, so she could make it over to Pendletons in time for the concert.

'Do you think we should delay another ten minutes, Ross? There isn't much of a crowd yet,' suggested the useless PR person, Lysette.

'Five minutes, no longer,' Ross said. 'We can't keep people hanging about.' He was still hoping the coaches of Freeza Mart employees would turn up; they'd been gridlocked in traffic on the M25.

Across the car park, Dawn could see a reception committee of dignitaries forming up on the red carpet, including the Lord Lieutenant, Ridley Nairn the MP, and a stout gentleman in chains of office, the Mayor of Andover. And now, emerging from inside the store, was Miles with Davina, escorting a very distinguished-looking couple who must be Lord and Lady Pendleton. Lady Pendleton looked very stylish, Dawn thought, though personally she'd have chosen to wear something more eye-catching than a navy blue suit and matching hat.

Her view was now obstructed by two enormous coaches pulling up at the kerb, belching diesel exhaust. It was the Freeza Mart delegation from the Midlands, two hours late and frazzled from the journey, and bursting for the lavatory 'because there were no facilities on board and the driver wouldn't stop for a toilet break, we were that late,' moaned one of Ross's employees. But the injection of an additional seventy people in the queue made a big difference, and Ross breathed a sigh of relief. 'Let them in now,' he told the PR people.

The doors were unlocked and a ribbon stretched across the entrance for the weathergirl to cut and declare the supermarket officially open for business. Ross was handed a microphone, and Gemma and Debbie looked on proudly as their Dad began a speech of welcome, saying how proud he was to have brought Freeza Mart to the town, and how he hoped they would appreciate his low, low prices. He was introducing the weathergirl when an enormous cheer erupted across the car park, and a tall black Daimler with royal insignia drew up at the red carpet. Now four buglers from the Household Cavalry sounded a fanfare as the royal personage stepped out of the car, and an orchestra struck up the national anthem. Everyone outside Freeza Mart immediately turned round to cop a look at her.

Miles, stationed between Laetitia Pendleton and Davina in the receiving line, saw what was happening and smiled. Everything was going perfectly to plan. And there were plenty more surprises to come.

As the tiny figure of Princess Margaret disappeared into the crowd outside Pendletons, the seventy Freeza Mart employees plus thirty or forty members of the public flooded into Ross's store, heading for the trestle table where coffee, drinks and plates of promotional snacks were laid out. Ross was in his element, greeting customers and personally escorting them around the aisles, showing them where the chill cabinets were sited and the glass-fronted freezers full of oven-ready crinkle fries and breaded scampi. The managers of his stores in Telford, Redditch, Coventry and Solihull, some of whom had been working for Ross for ten years or more, all expressed admiration for the new electronic point-of-sale replenishment systems and wondered when their own stores would be similarly upgraded. Dawn was doing her bit, chatting up Ross's executives and his PA, Jacqui, who had inherited Dawn's own role as Ross's secretary when she finally stopped work after Debbie was born. Jacqui was one of the few people Ross had taken into his confidence over Gemma's situation, and she pressed a plastic bag into Dawn's hands containing an elaborately wrapped parcel with silver ribbon. 'Baby clothes,' she mouthed. 'For the little newborn when it arrives.'

Gemma herself was trailing up and down the aisles with Debbie, feeling fatter than ever and trying to avoid her dad's workmates, several of whom were eyeing her bump in a knowing way. She wished she hadn't come, but Dawn wasn't prepared to leave her at home on her own so close to the due date, and anyway she had to support her dad. But she felt so self-conscious, it was excruciating. The joints of her fingers and ankles were swollen and puffy, and if any of her old schoolmates saw her they'd be bound to guess. To make matters worse, she couldn't forget about babies even for a second, because wherever she looked chubby-faced toddlers gurgled down at her from packs of Pampers.

Now the transvestite country music band started up on a stage near the entrance. Ross winced at their appearance, which was shockingly tacky, with the lead singer in a cowgirl fringed jacket, short skirt, fishnets, sequinned Stetson, beauty spot and full moustache; the rest of the band wore cowhide bustiers and buggers grips. Their patter between songs was so vulgar and full of double entendres, it made Dawn blush to her roots. She prayed Philippa Mountleigh wouldn't show up and hear it.

'I thought you said you'd booked this shower before?' Ross snapped at his PR, Lysette.

'Not actually booked them, Ross. But they did come highly recommended by their talent agency.'

Ross groaned as the band launched into a highly camp rendition of 'Stand by Your Man.'

Meanwhile, a hundred yards across the car park, Miles was feeling quietly gratified. Always at his most adept when interacting with royalty, he was ushering Her Royal Highness in the direction of the concert marquee which had been erected behind the loading bay. James Pendleton had already welcomed HRH to the store and would be seated next to her during the concert, so was now hanging back to talk to the lady-in-waiting and to Philippa Mountleigh. Davina was bringing up the rear with Johnnie Mountleigh, and trying to make conversation with the Mayor of Andover who was proving hard work. Half her mind was anyway on her children, whom she hoped had made it to the marquee and were seated before the royal party arrived. Miles would be furious if they were late. Peter was meant to be working in any case, as part of the Straker Communications team co-ordinating the day, and was driving Archie, Samantha and Mollie over from Chawbury in his own car.

As it happened, the Straker children were at that moment circling Andover's one-way system for the second time, having overshot the car park first time round, and finding there was no other way to get back. Peter was panicking, his alarm clock having failed to go off, and then it had taken ages to get Sam and Archie up and out. Only Mollie had been ready on time. Then Sam announced she'd come out in the wrong shoes, and insisted they had to turn back a mile from the house, and then she'd realised she left the pair she wanted at the London house, so had to wear the original ones anyway.

They swerved into the car park with a minute to go, to find every parking bay taken. Desperately following a succession of blue arrows which sent them round in circles, they abandoned Peter's

Golf in a disabled bay and raced to the rear flap of the marquee. As Miles cosseted Princess Margaret into her cushioned seat next to Lord Pendleton, he was annoyed to spot Peter, Samantha, Archie and Mollie disrupting an entire row of guests as they headed for their places. It was monstrous. Miles was inclined to blame Peter, who was meant to be working, for God's sake. And Mollie looked like a *student* in her grungy corduroy smock.

The concert began. Looking around the tent with its lime-green lining in Pendletons's corporate colours, Miles knew he had pulled off a magnificent coup. Less than a fortnight earlier, there had been no concert, no reception, no nothing. And yet here they all were, the cream of Hampshire society, all the movers and shakers; here was the Philharmonia Orchestra with its fabled Hungarian conductor, Milo Magyarovitch, and to crown it all a tame royal, which would wipe Ross Clegg's event clean off the front pages.

The orchestra was playing a particularly gentle passage by Schubert—a pianissimo aria for piano and violin—when Miles became conscious of a distant racket intruding from somewhere outside. At first, he thought it must be a radio, perhaps belonging to a workman. Suddenly, however, it became a whole lot louder. It sounded like a live rock concert carrying in the wind from across the car park. Other guests were starting to notice it too. Miles saw Laetitia look round and Princess Margaret shifting in her seat, an imperious expression on her face.

Unable to spot an usher, Miles tried to catch Peter's eye. It would be easier for him to slip outside and investigate than Miles, seated in the middle of the VIP section. He glared at his son, six rows back. It took Miles several minutes of gesticulating to realise Peter was listening to a Walkman. He could see the headphones buried in that untidy mop of hair. Miles wanted to throttle him. The extraneous beat—rock music, pop music, whatever it was—was all the time becoming more obtrusive. A pained expression appeared on the face of the conductor, Milo Magyarovitch, as he tried to screen it out.

Giving up on Peter, Miles directed his voodoo powers towards his other children, eventually catching Archie's and Mollie's eyes. Mollie had been transported by the Schubert, hardly registering the rival music, but Archie, playing with a Gameboy on his lap, had tuned into it, greatly preferring it to the classical witter. 'Y-M-C-A' they were singing now. 'Y-M-C-A.'

Miles was desperately semaphoring instructions they should go outside right now and kill the music, when the orchestra dried up mid-aria. Milo Magyarovitch, shaking with Mittel European fury, hurled his baton to the floor. 'No, *I cannot perform* like this. It is not possible.' Then he stormed off stage.

'Quite right too,' piped up the Princess, who loved her music and was looking round for a culprit to blame.

The concert prematurely curtailed, guests were directed back inside the supermarket, where a buffet had been set up in the aisles showcasing the pick of Pendletons's most upmarket lines, including Pendletons's premium-cut oak-cured smoked salmon, Pendletons's charcoal-cindered Somerset chevre, and Pendletons's own-brand buffalo mozzarella, from the buffalo herd grazing Nick Pendleton's private Italian estate.

The Princess, her lady-in-waiting, numerous Pendletons, the Lord Lieutenant and Philippa Mountleigh, Ridley and Suzie Nairn, and Miles and Davina were now whisked off to a private dining room, well insulated from the other guests, for a VIP luncheon at which the place setting for Milo Magyarovitch was hastily removed since he was too upset to attend. Realising the event had not gone off as planned, Miles's charm became supercharged as he worked to turn the atmosphere around, and by midway through the main course the Princess was actually laughing, which made the Pendletons relax too, and by the end of lunch the day had somehow redeemed itself from catastrophe to humorous mishap.

Ross was having a grand time. Against all expectations the opening was going off far better than he could have hoped. For one thing, the store was chock a block with customers, and what's more they were shopping, the tills hadn't stopped ringing all morning. Then from midday onwards loads more people began drifting over from the Pendletons bash, having finished the buffet and following the music from the car park. Others spotted the posters in Freeza Mart's windows and couldn't believe they were selling Veuve Clicquot champagne by the case at only £7.99 a bottle, and were loading up their Volvo Estates. Archie, who had downed a whole bottle of Pendletons's house cuvee, shoved his way through the dusty shrubbery which separated Pendletons from Freeza Mart. Following close behind came Peter, fed up with chatting up clients, plus Samantha and Mollie.

With only five minutes to go before the trolley-dash, excitement was running high. Everyone who'd posted a form into the plastic barrel was eligible, and the three winners would have ten minutes to load up a trolley with as much free stuff as they could push. Archie quickly entered, saying if he won he'd head straight for the off-license aisle. And Samantha, who initially turned her nose up at the whole idea, noticed the cosmetics aisle and fancied a trolley-full of Rimmel products. Mollie announced that if she was the winner she'd fill hers with nutritious food and give it out to the homeless.

Ross now observed a disturbing development. A lot of customers seemed to be heading for the exits, all clutching lime green pieces of paper. From what he could see, half his shoppers were melting away, just as the trolley-dash was about to be drawn. He hadn't walked five yards before an attractive blonde in a Pendletons t-shirt accosted him, saying 'Free twenty-five pound Pendeltons voucher. Redeemable only in the next half hour.' Suddenly, wherever he looked, there were attractive girls pressing gift vouchers on his customers. Sprinting to the entrance, Ross took the microphone and announced the trolley-dash.

Dawn was delighted when the first winner turned out to be the single mum with the toddler who'd been queuing outside before they opened. The other two winning tickets were held by Archie and by Philippa Mountleigh, who'd arrived hotfoot from the royal luncheon.

A photographer from the *Andover Daily Echo*, who'd got enough shots of the Princess, wandered over to check out Freeza Mart, and was thrilled by the prospect of the Lord Lieutenant's wife taking part in a trolley dash. Quickly loading his Pentax with fresh film, he knelt by the till for the off.

Ross started the countdown from ten, and everyone joined in. 'Five-four-three-two-one-GO.'

The single mum headed for the frozen pizza aisle and loaded enough supplies to last two months. Archie piled his trolley with twelve different brands of vodka. Philippa Mountleigh, in a lather of indecision, kept saying, 'God this is such fun, I can't believe it. Now, lightbulbs . . . where do they keep lightbulbs? . . . Johnnie's always telling me we need lightbulbs.'

Gemma had been hiding away in the stockroom, but now the pain had got too much and she was searching for her mum. It felt like her stomach was splitting in half, it was definitely contractions, exactly like they'd described at antenatal classes. Bent double in agony, she looked up to find herself face to face with Archie.

'Archie? Have you seen my mum anywhere?'

'Er, hi Gemma. No I haven't . . . but I've won the trolley-dash. Gotta run.'

'Can you find her? I really need to find mum.'

'If I see her, I'll tell her,' Archie called over his shoulder. 'There's only thirty seconds left. I've got sixty bottles of vodka.'

'Gangway! Gangway!' trilled Philippa, as she raced past. 'Anyone know where they keep the dog food?'

Hundreds of shoppers cheered them on, as the winners lumbered to the finish.

'Just room for some beeswax candles,' Philippa said, throwing ten boxes onto the top.

'Five—four—three—two—one,' chanted the crowd as they reached the tills just in time.

In aisle seventeen, Gemma sat on the floor as her contractions became shorter and shorter. She was still sitting there when Dawn found her fifteen minutes later, and summoned the ambulance.

19.

Having finally persuaded her parents to let her leave her snooty all-girls boarding school and go to sixth form college in Andover to study for her A levels instead, Mollie was spending the middle part of each week at Chawbury Manor largely alone, with only the Strakers' housekeeper as chaperone. Peter took a lift up to London every Sunday night with his father for their week of work, Archie was back at boarding school for the Michaelmas term, and Davina reluctantly headed up to Holland Park Square on Tuesday afternoons to accompany Miles to client dinners and cocktail receptions.

For Mollie, after the hustle and bustle and social competitiveness of boarding school, where all anyone talked about was clothes, parties and where their families were going next on holiday, sixth form college felt like a rewardingly real experience. For the first time, she felt people could relate to her for who she was, and not for which designer skirt she had on or who she knew. It had been all right for Samantha, who liked nothing better than to compare the merits of Caribbean islands—St Lucia versus Mustique—and who knew half the people in *Tatler*'s Bystander social pages, but Mollie didn't, and what's more she didn't want to either. It was all so trivial . . . so *nothing*. Mrs French the housekeeper dropped her off each morning at the bus stop on the Micheldever-Andover road, and she caught the bus into town and made her way down Cornmarket and through Friar's Yard pedestrian precinct to the windblown concrete campus that was Mid-Hampshire College for Further Education. From day one, Mollie knew this was the college for her. It was all so inclusive and democratic. Where her former school had at its heart a curved Victorian staircase and walls hung with portraits of former headmistresses and posters announcing dances at Eton and Radley, here it was all ramps for the disabled and posters for world peace and war on famine. For the first time ever she felt exhilaratingly anonymous. No one knew she was Sam's plain younger sister; how many times had people exclaimed, 'I can't *believe* you and Sammie Straker are *sisters*,' with all its too-obvious implication. Nor did anyone know Miles was her dad and, anyway, he wouldn't mean anything to anyone here. At school, quite a few of the girls had kept giggling about him and saying their mothers really fancied him, which made Mollie squirm with embarrassment. She'd hated it when Chawbury Manor had been in that magazine, which so many people had seen, it seemed like showing off. And shameful to read in print they had two full-time gardeners and one part-time gardener, when most people didn't have a garden at all, like those poor people crammed into tower blocks. Most of all, she was excited about being at a college where the terms of reference were so completely different. If you'd stood up at breakfast at school and asked, 'Anyone here been to St Moritz or Val d'Isere?' there would have been a stampede of girls who'd been skiing there, or whose families owned a chalet nearby, or who were planning on becoming chalet cooks in their years off. At Mid-Hampshire College, such a question would have been received with dumb incomprehension. And Mollie loved it that way.

Her first six weeks, it was true, had turned out lonelier than she'd expected. It was proving difficult to make friends, partly because not that many students turned up for lectures or even for tutorial groups. Sometimes even the lecturers didn't show up. And in the cafeteria the other students had friends already, or sat together in ethnic groups she was too shy to try and infiltrate—tables of Koreans, Spaniards and Serbs—so she mostly pushed her tray round the metal counter, collected her food, and sat alone to eat it. Not that everyday was entirely lonely, of course. In economics class, she'd kind of made friends with a bovine Greek girl, but it was difficult to get very far because of her English. And after a history tutorial she'd nearly died when an English boy in her group asked, 'Are you posh or something? Your voice is so weird.' After that she dumbed-down her accent to make it less distinctive.

It turned out, too, that her timetable at college was a lot less full than she was accustomed to at school. On busy days she had only two or three lectures, and occupied the remaining time using the computers in the library (which wasn't that nice in any case, she had to admit, since it wasn't only used by students at the college but all sorts of homeless people came in too, and it sometimes got smelly and didn't feel that safe; though obviously the homeless had a *perfect right* to be there—in fact they were *welcome*), so Mollie spent a lot of time pacing the streets of Andover awaiting her next lecture. Out of boredom, she would wander into Woolworths and buy a cream egg, or into the bakery for a danish pastry. Sometimes when she had a couple of hours to kill, she'd walk across town to Freeza Mart where you could get really cheap fresh soup and pasties at the grub-on-the-run counter. It gave her a wicked thrill spending her money there, because she knew how annoyed Miles would be if he knew. You only had to mention the name Clegg and he went ape. Mollie knew her mum had been to visit Gemma's baby, but Miles never had, and he'd forbidden any of the children to visit her either. Mollie thought it was ridiculous. From what she'd heard and read in the papers, Ross sounded like an amazing guy who'd overcome childhood polio and set-up all these supermarkets selling basic food at fair prices. She really admired people like that, who'd done it all on their own without any advantages, and started something so worthwhile. Furthermore, she was longing to meet her new niece—Archie and Gemma's daughter—even if Archie claimed not to be interested himself. It was lovely, too, that she was a baby girl. According to mum, she was being named Amanda, 'Mandy for short.'

'Mandy, indeed,' Miles had snorted when he heard. 'Like Peter Mandelson. Ghastly!'

On Wednesdays when she had no lectures after midday, she caught an early bus home and often walked the final three miles cross-country from the bus stop on the Micheldever road. It was a particularly pretty stretch of country, passing through gentle downland planted with beech and oak coppices and teaming with pheasants. A local farmer, Matt Marland, ran a shooting syndicate on the land, and in winter the ground was littered with spent cartridges. Miles had several times expressed the wish to one day buy the farm himself for the shooting, should Matt Marland ever sell up. The final part of the route took Mollie along footpaths close to Chawbury Park, before reaching the long valley up to her own house. Having not walked that way for several months, she was at first disorientated by the numerous changes along the way. Previously, the footpath had run directly past old Silas's cottage, cutting between the pond and tithe barn. Now as she trudged along the ancient footpath her way was blocked by the impenetrable boundary netting of an En Tout Cas tennis court, it's sprung green surface glistening in the sunshine. She doubled back to find a route round the tennis court, but a huge expanse of freshly seeded lawn was bordered by wire fencing encircling the entire property. The lower path was blocked by a densely-planted screen of leylandii. Heading in the opposite direction this time, she found herself following the newly-built rear wall of a sauna and solarium annexe, with an overpowering smell of pine wafting from an extractor fan. Eventually she arrived at a wooden gate into a gravelled stable yard, with loose boxes and mounting block and a second gate beyond, leading out towards Chawbury valley. Seeing nobody about, she sneaked across the yard.

She was halfway across when a girl appeared leading a pony, followed by a blonde lady in jeans and riding boots she recognised as Mrs Clegg.

'May I help you?' called out Dawn rather sharply, before recognising the furtive scruffy figure of Mollie. 'Oh, it's you, Mollie. Are you lost?'

Mollie explained she was walking home from college. 'I'm sorry for trespassing.'

Dawn insisted it didn't matter at all, she could cut through the stable yard any time she pleased 'or anywhere else you like in our grounds, you are most welcome.' Mollie noticed how gushing Dawn was, almost as though she was nervous of her. 'I don't think you've met Debbie, she's been out horseback riding on her new mount.' The fact was, since the birth of Gemma's baby, Dawn had been feeling perpetually awkward about the Strakers, not knowing how relations would be in the future with their nearest neighbours. It made her so uncomfortable, she felt quite sick. They had spent so much money and effort in building this house—her dream home— and they were making such nice new friends, and now this. Davina was being lovely about it all, really caring; she'd twice popped over to see Mandy, and called up regularly to hear how she was getting along. Although Davina never mentioned anything, Dawn realised from what she did not say, and from the fact that neither Miles nor any of the kids had been over to visit, that the Strakers were far from happy about the turn of events, and relations were strained. How awkward, how mortifying it all was. And how disappointing. Dawn had so wanted to be friends with the Strakers. She'd like to have invited them over to play tennis on the new court. Before coming to Chawbury, she didn't know them from Adam, but round here they were the bees knees. Everyone talked about and admired the Strakers. When she told anyone where their new home was, people invariably said, 'Ah, Chawbury, you must be near Miles and Davina,' and Dawn replied, 'We're just across the valley. The Manor's one end, and we're at the Park at the other.' Each morning when she drew back the curtains and sat up in bed with her first cup of tea of the day, her view was dominated by Chawbury Manor perched on the hill. Ross was up and gone long ago—he liked to be at his desk before seven—and Dawn had plenty of time to brood over the Strakers. She still felt angry with Archie about everything, but she liked Davina and resented the awkwardness of the situation. As she soaked in the en-suite, she could see the Manor from that window too, and often wondered whether Davina could see the Park from *her* bathroom. That's what made this *froideur* between the two families doubly painful; they couldn't get out of each others' sight.

'Can we offer you a cold drink, Molly? Or a coffee?' Dawn asked her. 'And I've just defrosted a strawberry cheesecake if you'd care for a portion.' Mollie said she'd love that, and then the two girls trailed Dawn into the house. Entering through a side entrance they walked along a wide one-storey corridor, off which Mollie saw the sauna room and solarium with lockers for guests to leave their belongings, then a home-gym with Cybex weights machines and a stepmaster, and finally an enormous deepfreeze room with two matching chest-shaped freezers.

'Yeah, that's Dad's favourite room,' Debbie said, noticing Mollie's interest. 'He tests out all the new product lines for Freeza Mart. Like how long they take to defrost. Take a look if you want.'

Debbie heaved open the lid of one of the freezers. It was packed to the brim with giant bags of deep-frozen croquette potatoes, pizzas, peeled pink prawns, cod in white sauce and several varieties of cheesecake.

'There's . . . so much food,' Mollie said wide-eyed, 'I've never seen so much.'

'The other freezer's fuller, it's all chocolate bars and ice-cream.'

'How come you've stayed so thin, then?' Mollie asked enviously.

'Dunno. Dad and mum are sticks too, and Gemma before she started having Mandy. But have you seen Greg? He's our brother. He's got really lardy. He's twenty-four and Dad says it's the drink that does it.'

They passed through a swing door into one of the biggest kitchens Mollie had ever seen, bigger than the one at Chawbury Manor which was itself large. It was fitted out with everything matching in pearl and grey, not just the units which hung in long rows from all the walls, but the cupboards beneath the work tops, the kitchen table and chairs, a breakfast peninsular and stools, the ovens and hobs, all glistening new and smelling overpoweringly of citrus. Although Mollie was unaware of this, Dawn had seconds earlier wiped down the already impeccable granite counters and freshened the room with a fragrance spray. Sunshine streamed through big panes of glass and French windows leading on to newly-turfed lawn; you could still see the joins between the rolls of grass like stitched-together doormats. The kitchen floor was laid with pearl and grey Amtico tiles, which led through into a living area with wall-to-wall pearl coloured carpet, a giant wide-screen TV and several black leather sofas including an L-shaped black leather corner-unit. Perched on the corner unit was Gemma in her nightdress, gazing into a Moses basket.

'Cheesecake and a coffee, Mollie,' said Dawn. 'Carry them through and relax in the day room. This is where we live, unless we have company.'

It was Dawn's regret that, so far, she and Ross had never once entertained at Chawbury Park, and one of her ambitions was to throw a formal supper party and show off the new lounge and dining room. Thus far, she didn't feel she knew quite enough people to make it possible, though she was close. She was conscious that, had she been able to count on the Strakers coming, it would have been so much easier. With Davina there to support and advise her, it would all have fallen into place. It would have given her the confidence to invite the Mountleighs and some of the other ladies from the committee with their other halves, but without Davina she didn't feel she could pull it off. It was such a shame, because the house had finally come together. The new couches had arrived and the tapestry-backed chairs for the dining room, and Ross had spent half last weekend, bless him, on hands and knees with his drill installing lights in the china cabinet to show off their collection of Wedgwood tea cups. It was upsetting they couldn't show it off to company.

Mollie hurried over to say hello to Gemma and see Mandy, who she'd been longing to meet for so long. The little thing, so sweet and serene, was sound asleep in her basket. Mollie asked Gemma if it was ok to touch her and brushed her hand against Mandy's soft face, and felt warm breath from her nose against her fingertips. She was so adorable, Mollie wanted to cry. Pretty too, just like Gemma, though Mollie reckoned she could detect something of Archie in her eyes and shape of her chin.

'She's beautiful,' Mollie said, staring in wonder at the first small baby she'd really ever seen. She couldn't understand how Archie could bear not to visit her; didn't he realise how lucky he was to have a tiny daughter? She was a miracle.

Mollie sat there eating cheesecake with a fork, gazing at Mandy.

'How's . . . Archie?' Gemma asked, when her mother was out of earshot.

'Er, fine, I think,' Mollie replied. 'He hasn't been around that much.' She didn't say he'd been made Captain of Games at his house at school and Miles had been so pleased he'd sent him a cheque for five hundred pounds.

'Give him my love,' Gemma said heartbreakingly, her eyes filling with tears. Instinctively Mollie hugged her. 'I only want him to see Mandy,' Gemma blurted between sobs. 'He doesn't even have to see me, if he doesn't want to. But he should see Mandy. He's got to visit her, she's so sweet and he is her *dad*.'

Mollie felt terrible, and entirely on Gemma's side. 'I'll try and persuade him,' she promised. 'When I tell him how lovely she is,

I'm sure he'll come. It's just it's all been a bit awkward . . . all this happening . . . and my dad's being weird too.' And Archie's a selfish creep, she felt like adding. 'I can't really exactly explain, Gemma, I'm sorry about everything. It's not your fault, it really isn't, and Mandy's a little angel. I wish she was awake now so I could say hello properly.'

Right on cue Mandy began to stir, and a few seconds later to grizzle. Gemma lifted her from her basket, opened the top of her nightdress and fed her from a swollen breast. Mollie had never seen a baby gulp like that before.

'Really, Gemma,' Dawn said censoriously, returning from the kitchen. 'I don't think it's very nice to do that in front of a guest. I do apologise, Mollie. I'm sure no one would behave like that at the manor.'

Mollie felt it wasn't actually an option, what with her mother being way over the hill at forty-eight or whatever, and neither Samantha nor herself having a baby themselves. So she said, 'It's fine, really. I'm madly in love with Mandy, isn't she so adorable?'

Debbie joined them with more cheesecake and the four women doted on Mandy. 'Say how-do-you-do to Auntie Mollie,' Debbie kept telling Mandy. 'Pleased to meet you Auntie,' she then responded, in pretend baby voice.

Mollie and Debbie soon decided they liked each other rather a lot, and Dawn asked Mollie what Mid-Hampshire College was like, since Debs was thinking about enrolling there herself. 'Now we've decided to make the move south permanent,' Dawn said, 'we've got to find Debs a new school. And get Gemma back into education too.'

'I don't want to go to school,' Gemma said. 'I want to stay home and look after Mandy.'

'Not now,' said Dawn, looking sympathetically at her elder daughter, who had never been a great one for schoolwork in any case. 'It's something we'll have to discuss with your dad, and you know his views. He's a big one for education,' Dawn told Mollie. 'Always has been. We're just going to have to see. As for you, Debs, we need to get you enrolled somewhere quick. And if Mollie says college in Andover's a good option, that could be the answer.'

By the time she departed two hours later, Mollie felt the Cleggs were really nice people and she'd promised to call in again for tea next Wednesday. Gemma let her pick up Mandy and hold her in her arms, and she couldn't get over how warm she was, this tiny doll-like creature, her niece. And then they'd all sat round watching *Bewitched* videos—the Cleggs had every episode in three boxed sets—until it became dark outside, and Dawn dropped Mollie off by car at the top of the drive at Chawbury Manor.

20.

t had been a particularly satisfying few weeks for Ross. You couldn't be complacent, but the Andover store had got off to a cracking start. They were way ahead of budget, and it wasn't like he'd set soft targets either. You only had to walk round the place, as he did several mornings a week, to see it heaving with customers. He felt constantly excited, and vindicated too. All those gainsayers who'd said folks down south didn't care about price, and it was all about providing a poncey retail ambiance, well, they'd been proved wrong, hadn't they? Everyone cares about price. Everyone wants a better deal. Ross had always believed it, and here was the proof.

What's more, his investors were happy. In fact, they were pressing him to roll out new stores even faster than he'd planned, which suited Ross just fine. So long as he had access to capital, he was up for it. He was working with a logistics consultant recommended by Callum and Brin, and they'd been identifying target towns for expansion across the south. Basingstoke was next, then Salisbury and Winchester. Towns dominated by Pendletons were the ones to go for, Ross reckoned.

When he thought of the recent launch event, he flinched. It had been a total cock-up from start to finish, the steepest learning curve. He'd fired the PR agency first thing next morning; next time—if there was a next time—he'd check out the band himself, and it wouldn't be a bunch of drag queens either.

Ironically, the press had been very positive. The *Andover Daily Echo* led with Princess Margaret arriving at Pendletons, of course. But the rest of the page was dominated by a huge photo of Dawn's friend Philippa Mountleigh in the trolley dash, beneath the headline

'Lord Lieutenant's Lady is a trolley dolly.' Philippa was pictured roaring with laughter and gave some very helpful quotes, saying what great value Freeza Mart was and how she couldn't get over the low prices. Furthermore, the local radio station was running items about Freeza Mart non-stop. They'd broadcast an interview with the single mum who'd been one of the trolley-dash winners, and were now asking listeners to phone-in and say how they'd fill their own trolleys, if they'd won. The best answer would get a one-hundred-pound voucher. Ross's one niggling concern over the Andover store was the dirty tricks campaign by Pendletons. First there had been the coincidence of the clashing party date, which had actually worked in their favour in the end. Then those girls handing out Pendletons vouchers inside Freeza Mart, which wasn't ethical. And every Saturday since then Pendletons had put girls in lime-green t-shirts at the entrance to the car park, distributing vouchers and coupons and telling shoppers good food costs less at Pendletons, which was an out-and-out lie. Last week, Dawn had been targeted when she was parking the car, and she'd given them a right earful. Good on Dawn, what a trooper. Not generally one for romantic gestures, he made a point of picking up a dozen roses from the Freeza Mart flower stand (grown in Kenya and air freighted, partially-frozen, direct to Southampton airport) which he thrust at her with a kiss.

For Miles, it was a largely satisfying week, though it started better than it ended. He lured Serena up to London for Monday night and together they'd attended a private view at the newly-opened Tate Modern of rubber sculpture by the Dutch artist Roos van Rinjj, which was being sponsored, at Straker Communications's suggestion, by their client Trent Valley Power 4 U. Miles efficiently networked all four exhibition spaces before taking Serena to dinner and bed at Zach Durban's new London hotel, the Capital Grand Deluxe. Leaving her to make her own way home next morning, he was up and out before seven for a breakfast at Conservative Central Office, at which Paul Tanner was entertaining potential party donors. Miles always found these gatherings valuable, since the kind of men susceptible to bankrolling the party were also susceptible to retaining Straker Communications for strategic advice. On

Tuesday, the satisfying news came through that Strakers had won a chunk of the Fiat account, on highly lucrative terms. Miles reckoned that, if they handled it correctly, there was incremental business to be won there too, and he would evaluate the merit of opening an office in Turin. Davina joined him on Tuesday at Holland Park Square, and irritated him by wondering whether Mollie really was alright on her own down at Chawbury, and how she felt bad leaving her. Miles, exasperated, said, 'For heaven's sake, Davina, she's *not* alone down there. Mrs French is there. And it was Mollie who insisted on quitting her perfectly adequate boarding school to attend this socialist polytechnic or whatever it is, so it's her look out. Now, we're late already. We should have left this house three minutes ago, and you're not even changed . . . What? You *are* changed? I'm sorry, but you *cannot* go to Harry's Bar in that dress. Not with the Chief Executive of Tio Finca sherry. Wear that velvet thing, if you haven't got anything else.'

Thursday morning saw a long-scheduled strategic review at Pendletons. As usual Miles was accompanied by a posse of Straker Communications executives, including his son Peter who at least hadn't brought his Walkman with him this time. From the beginning, Miles detected a slight chill in the atmosphere, coming from the Pendletons side. Not anything drastic, but a heightened anxiety which Miles's antennae picked up immediately. A girl from Strakers presented the press from the anniversary event in Andover, which she claimed was 'worth' more than two million pounds in editorial coverage when the space and TV mentions were monetised at advertising ratecard prices.

'We don't have an issue with the publicity, you did a professional job,' James Pendleton said at last, 'but we do have to face the fact we're losing share to Freeza Mart. The numbers tell their own story.'

He handed over to his Finance Director and the picture was all too clear. Every week since Freeza Mart opened its doors, Pendletons in Andover had seen like-for-like reductions in sales. And, worse, they were deteriorating. Not across all sectors, but in the ones where they competed head-to-head, such as frozen foods, household goods and wines and spirits. Freeza Mart was certainly having an effect. 'In all these categories we've experienced high single-digit or even double-digit revenue reductions,' reported the FD.

'I must say, I'm surprised,' Miles said silkily. 'I've not visited a Freeza Mart personally, but I've heard they're awfully basic. Not like a Pendletons, which Davina uses all the time, in Andover *and* up in London.'

'Well,' James replied, 'that's very generous of you, Miles, and please thank Davina for supporting us, it's much appreciated. But the fact is, Clegg is providing competition. It's unhelpful his Andover store is so close to us geographically. Makes it easier for price comparison, and they're certainly cheaper on many product lines. We have to accept that. Laetitia tells me several friends have started buying their wine there, it's very keenly priced.'

'Surely they won't be able to sustain it,' Miles said. 'They must be trading at a loss?'

'Quite possibly. But it's making people think of them as good value. And I keep reading about expansion plans. Fifteen or twenty new stores. Mostly in towns where we trade rather satisfactorily.'

Miles spent Friday feeling troubled. He did not like it when any Company he represented hit a rough patch. In such situations, businesses re-evaluated their advisors. He had seen it many times; the last, desperate act of a cornered management was to change its communications consultancy. Not that he expected Straker Communications to be replaced by Pendletons. His ties to the family were too strong. Nevertheless, Miles took nothing for granted, not even his friendship with the brothers. Long before he'd arrived home at Chawbury on Friday evening, he was filled with resolve. His mission to undermine Ross must step up a further gear.

He arrived to find Davina in nervous form; more nervous than usual, that is, for she was always anxious on Friday evenings when her husband returned, testy from a week in the office. She had checked the ice bucket was filled with ice, and the double doors onto the terrace from the drawing room were unlocked. When she was at Chawbury on her own, Davina seldom used the terrace doors, preferring the side door from the flower room which was simpler to go in and out of without fuss, but Miles insisted on the big doors, even in winter. He liked to mix a drink, stroll outside and survey the valley . . . *his* valley . . . in which every tree was perfectly shaped by the bi-annual visit of the tree surgeon, and the Test ran clear and unimpeded through his nettle-free meadows. As usual, this evening, he flinched at the horizon, where the Clegg mansion was visible through the bare trees. There were lights on all over the house and he cursed the light pollution.

'Darling, we've had a lovely invitation,' Davina said as matter-of-factly as possible, though her voice wobbled. They were eating supper in the kitchen, which Miles never really approved of, but Mrs French had an evening off and had left a pheasant casserole. Peter, Archie and Samantha were also away that weekend, so only Mollie was present.

'Invitation? From whom?' Miles had never lost his excitement at the prospect of a social engagement.

'Well, it's to Mandy's christening,' Davina said, stumbling over the words. 'Isn't it lovely? Dawn dropped round an invitation. They're having her christened at St Marks. The last weekend in February. We're all going to be here because it's half term.'

Miles stared at his wife. 'They're *what*? They're planning a *Christening*? You have to be joking.' It was simply unbelievable. Why would anyone want to do that, given the circumstances? The last thing they should be doing was drawing attention to themselves.

Davina handed him a card, or rather two cards. The larger one was an embossed Birth Announcement on silvery cardboard with rounded corners, with a pattern of silver ferns and a silver bow. In the middle was a photograph of a particularly ugly baby, or so Miles reckoned, captioned 'Amanda ("Mandy") Grace Clegg.' The Cleggs had evidently sent it out to all their friends. The second, a handwritten postcard from Dawn, confirmed the Christening at St Mark's, Chawbury, during morning service followed by 'drinks and nibbles' at Chawbury Park. 'Your family are all most welcome,' Dawn had written.

Miles's first thought was to chuck them both into the kitchen bin. The last thing he intended to do was stand side by side with Ross in St Mark's—his local church, where Miles read the lesson once a year—publicly acknowledging this unfortunate infant.

'Obviously we're not going,' he said.

'But I'm going, I *have* to,' Mollie said. 'Gemma's asked me to be Mandy's godmother.'

'You most certainly will not. None of us is going. If we do, people will start putting two and two together about Archie. Why else would we be there? It's not as if the Cleggs would ever be personal friends.'

'But I've *agreed*,' Mollie said. 'I said yes to Gemma. *And* to Dawn, Mrs Clegg I mean. I *have* to go, I'm Mandy's godmother.' Mollie's eyes blazed with indignation. 'I *am* going and you can't stop me.'

Miles was a quick thinker. The problem, he could see, was that he simply didn't know what the Cleggs had been telling people about the baby. Specifically, he didn't know what they were saying about its parentage. Were they saying Archie was the father? He damn well hoped not, but were they? If not, what *were* they saying? That the father was unknown? That Mandy was Ross and Dawn's own child? Accustomed to being perfectly briefed in every situation, Miles felt horribly disadvantaged.

During the night, further disturbing thoughts occurred to him. Didn't the identity of the father have to be entered into a register at the church, during the baptism ceremony? The vicar of St Mark's was actually a woman, one of the few female clergymen, and a particularly inappropriate one in Miles's opinion, being left wing. He could easily imagine her announcing the name of the absent father to the entire congregation—Archie Straker. So far, not a hint of scandal had surfaced anywhere, not in any gossip column, nor locally so far as Miles was aware. It occurred to him that, in the interests of news management, it might be advisable to be at the Christening after all to ensure nothing went wrong. So at breakfast the next morning, he announced, 'I have decided we *should* all go to this Christening charade. Just to the service, mind you, not the house afterwards.'

21.

St Mark's and Holy Trinity Church, Chawbury, was widely regarded as the prettiest small church in Hampshire. Originally a Saxon 'shepherds' church,' it had taken its present form in Norman times and been sensitively restored and extended in the seventeenth century. With its Norman tower and font, knapped-flint walls and finely carved Georgian pews, it drew its congregation from well beyond its parish boundaries. People drove ten miles for services at Chawbury, attracted by the pretty setting with swans on the duck pond by the village green and its proximity to the Chawbury Arms, a popular gastro pub.

Miles planned strategy for the Christening with meticulous care, and gathered Team Straker for a last minute briefing. This was over breakfast which all Straker children were commanded to attend. Peter and Archie arrived in dressing gowns with tousled hair, half asleep. Samantha looked gorgeous, having got up early for once to wash and blow-dry her hair and loving the opportunity to get dressed up. Mollie, taking her godmotherly duties very seriously, had bought a new black coat and hat from Principles in Andover and looked like a district nurse.

'This is how we're going to play it today,' Miles addressed the breakfast table. 'Peter, you listening? Archie? Good. Now, in forty minutes time we set off for church. We arrive *twelve* minutes before the service begins, not earlier, not later. We will take up a position all together in the *third pew* on the right hand side. Understood? That's close enough to the font to monitor developments, while not necessarily appearing to be part of them. When we see the Cleggs, we behave courteously but coolly. We don't get involved. With luck, there won't be too many people in church who know us, but we can't count on that. In a way, it's an advantage you're a god-mother, Mollie, because it provides us with an alibi for being there. If asked, we say nothing about Archie of course, but simply mention Mollie's connection to this baby. All clear? Good. Now, you boys, go and get dressed. I'd like to see you in a suit, Archie. And tie, obviously. Then straight after the service ends, no hanging about, into the cars and back here for lunch. I'm sorry, Mollie, but no one's going on to the Clegg mansion.'

They arrived at church and parked the Mercedes on the verge outside. Davina complained it made it difficult for her to get out, since the passenger door was on an angle, but Miles was positioned for a quick getaway afterwards. As they entered the church, Miles acted nonchalant. The Cleggs hadn't yet arrived, which was a relief.

Gradually the pews filled with villagers. Miles recognised several from the garden opening. Norma Tappet, the lady vicar, arrived with her carpet bag full of the paraphernalia for communion, which she plonked down on the altar. With her spiky grey hair and shockingly plain face, Miles considered her a preposterous choice for a Hampshire parish priest, especially in a premium parish like Chawbury. He was looking around, trying to appear disengaged, when he was surprised to see Philippa Mountleigh waving at him and heading over.

'Morning, Philippa. Not your usual church this, is it?'

'I'm here for a Christening,' Philippa replied. 'Dawn Clegg's asked me to be a godmother to little Mandy. Gemma's baby . . . you've probably heard . . .' and she winked in a meaningful way.

Miles flinched. It sounded like Philippa didn't know about Archie, but her presence was uncomfortable.

He surveyed his own pew. Archie, home from school for five days for half term, was staring into space. He'd brushed his hair and looked quite smart in his pinstripe suit. Sam was examining her handbag, wondering if she liked the handle. Peter and Mollie were whispering. Davina looked strained.

There was a commotion in the pew behind, and Miles saw Bean and Nigel Winstanton taking their seats. And then, across the aisle, he spotted Serena and Robin Harden.

The Cleggs arrived and filed into their reserved pew at the front.

Ross was leading the way, followed by Dawn and Gemma fussing over a baby wrapped in a fluffy pink blanket, then the fat son Greg in mauve corduroy shirt and Levis, and the youngest daughter, Debbie, in a hat with a feather. Mollie waved as they passed, which annoyed Miles.

The service began and soon infuriated him further. The hymns were all horribly happy-clappy, including his least favourite, 'Shine, Jesus, Shine.' Then Norma gave a sermon about it being easier for a camel to pass through the eye of a needle than for a rich man to enter the kingdom of heaven, before inviting the congregation to pledge 10 percent of their post-tax income to the church. As if!

Sitting alongside her husband, and picking up on his unease, Davina was doing her best to think holy thoughts. She said a little prayer for her granddaughter—for little Mandy—but it was hard to concentrate. It was just all so awkward. She looked at Archie and felt so sorry for him. Yesterday, he'd spent half the afternoon playing football on the lawn with Peter and Mollie. It was ridiculous really, Archie having a child, he was still a child himself. He was gazing up at the ceiling, miles away, blocking it all out. He was in denial, Davina reckoned.

Mollie moved to sit with the Cleggs, to be closer to Mandy and her new friend Debs, who'd started at college. Peter was quietly amused by the whole unfolding drama, because it had all spun out of his father's control for once. As the eldest son of a control freak, nothing pleased him more than a dash of healthy chaos.

It was time for the baptism, and Norma invited the parents, godparents and families to join her at the font. Miles gave Archie a restraining glance, but he wasn't moving. Mollie, Philippa and the fat boy, Greg, shuffled forwards and assembled with the rest of the Cleggs around the stone basin. Soon the vicar was dipping her finger into the water and tracing the sign of the cross on Mandy's forehead, and the little baby burst out crying at the shock of the cold water. 'I baptise thee in the name of the Father, the Son and the Holy Ghost. Amen.'

'*Forasmuch* as this child hath promised you his *sureties* to renounce the devil and all his works,' proclaimed the vicar. Intentionally she mispronounced the arcane language, because she resented being made to use the traditional prayer book by the parish council. Ross looked equally lost by all the mumbo-jumbo, but Gemma and Mollie, who were now holding Mandy between them and joggling her about, seemed fulfilled and happy. A couple of times Gemma looked rather beseechingly over at Archie, which made Miles stiffen, but either Archie didn't notice or he was ignoring her. Dawn was ridiculously overdressed, Miles reckoned, in a pink suit with lacy panels on the lapels and cuffs, and a pink hat and veil. She wasn't a bad-looking woman beneath the fake tan and make-up, but she hadn't a clue. As for Philippa in her old tweed suit, Miles couldn't imagine how she'd got herself dragged into being a godmother.

They were now into the final hymn, and Miles was almost starting to relax. They'd got away with it. No one in the congregation had given Archie a second look. All they had to do now was get out.

At the end of the service, however, the vicar announced, 'Dawn and Ross—and Gemma too of course—have very kindly invited us all, the worshippers, back to their home for a celebration drink and snacks. It's an open invitation. So I hope to see many of you up at Chawbury Park very shortly.'

Miles grimaced and began shepherding his family towards the exit, but it quickly became apparent all their friends were going on to the Cleggs.

'Surely you're coming, Miles?' Bean exclaimed. 'We've all got to go for twenty minutes. Dawn will be disappointed if we don't.'

'I wish you *would* come,' Philippa said. 'And Mollie *should* be there, my fellow godmother.' She turned to Dawn, who was proceeding gingerly up the aisle towards them, wondering whether she dared say hello to Miles. 'Dawn, I'm telling Miles and Davina they *must* all come back to your house for a drink.'

'That would be nice,' Dawn replied uncertainly. 'I did send them an invitation.'

'I insist you come, Miles,' Bean said. 'After all, it was *me* who first introduced you to Dawn and Ross. You haven't forgotten? At Old Laverstoke Mill, at our party. I said then you were all going to become *tremendous friends*.'

And so, protests pushed aside, the Strakers found themselves swept up in the exodus to Chawbury Park.

With the exception of Davina and Mollie, none of the Strakers had previously visited Chawbury Park, the subject of so much negative conjecture. So it was with considerable curiosity they drove back through Chawbury, past the entrance to their own house then up as far as the Micheldever road before doubling back along the newly tarmaced drive to the Cleggs. The drive, which was unexpectedly long, passed first through a beech copse, then between large paddocks with post-and-rail fencing. Several new trees had been planted, protected by timber frames, and a chestnut mare and pony were visible beneath a shelter. 'Those trees look ridiculously spindly and new,' Miles said. 'Thank God we have decent mature trees at home.'

They pulled up in front of the house where a dozen other cars were already parked, including Serena and Robin Harden's Volvo, Miles was alarmed to see. From this elevation—which was the one that faced up the valley towards Chawbury Manor—the house was unashamedly grand. 'Like JR Ewing's house in *Dallas*,' Miles said with a sneer, as they trooped up to the pillared front door. Curved brick walls extended on both sides, full of overlarge plate glass windows. To their left was a windy expanse of lawn, looking particularly bleak on this winter's day, its perimeter defined by replica Victorian lampposts. As they passed the entrance pillars, Miles tapped one and it was hollow. 'Fibre glass,' he said meaningfully.

They entered a double-height hall with marble chip flagstones off which led the drawing room, from where could be heard the hubbub of a party in progress. The double sweep of a horseshoe-shaped staircase led up to a galleried mezzanine, laid with salmon-coloured carpet. Moments later, Ross appeared to greet them, showing them where to leave their coats and genuinely touched they had come. Having not spoken to Miles since their awkward encounter at the Manor, he made a special effort to make them all feel welcome. He shook Archie by the hand and said very sincerely, 'Good of you to be here, young man. Much appreciated.' Miles found it excruciating.

'Now, what you folks need is a drink,' Ross said. Several bottles of Freeza Mart's house champagne stood open on the hall table and he made sure everyone had a glass ('We've earned this') before leading them through to the drawing room.

Davina's first impression was of overwhelming newness. There was a lingering smell of paint and the pale grey carpet looked like it had just been laid, which was hardly surprising since this was the first time the room had been used. It felt very formal and empty; a pair of gilded French sofas with wooden backs and elaborately carved legs stood on either side of an Adam-style fireplace. The fire itself had evidently never been lit since the bricks behind the grate were unblackened by flames, the fire tongs and shovel shiny and brand new. In a bay window were a pair of tapestry-covered Knoll chairs, neither of which looked like they had ever been sat in. To Miles, the whole effect was a show home. Most tellingly, he thought, was the almost complete absence of any pictures. In the Strakers' own drawing room, there must have been twenty-five different paintings—eighteenth-century oils of ships at sea, watercolours of Venice, small abstract paintings bought at the Royal Academy Summer Show—decades of random collecting to achieve the patina of a proper English home. Here one solitary painting hung above the mantelpiece, of a forest glade. To Miles, it resembled a tea tray, or a thousand-piece jigsaw puzzle of the kind old ladies sat over in care homes. How could Archie have got himself involved with people like this?

Inexplicably, as he surveyed the room, the other guests appeared either not to notice or to mind. They were crowding around the baby, cooing over it, or talking happily together. Philippa was chatting away to Dawn and the vicar, and the Winstantons were making conversation with the fat brother, Greg. Serena, looking very tasty in leather trousers and the red Valentino jacket Miles had bought for her in Capri, was peering at the baby and chatting-up Gemma, which worried him. It was disconcerting to see his mistress and his—whatever Gemma was—his son's illegitimate child's birth-mother, talking together. A dozen nosey-parkers from the village were knocking back Ross's champagne and saying how lovely the new house was. Well, there's no accounting for taste. He couldn't see a soul, other than Philippa and Serena, that he wanted to talk to. He'd liked to have fixed up his next bonking session with Serena, but didn't feel safe doing so in a room full of people.

Greg was talking at cross-purposes with Bean, while glaring hungrily at Samantha from the corner of his eye. Suntanned and luscious from a recent skiing trip, she was distractingly sexy. Naturally she was avoiding him, like he didn't exist, because he wasn't good enough for her. The irony! He wanted to tell her he'd just had his PhD accepted and was now entitled to call himself Doctor. Dr Gregory Clegg. That would make her think twice, surely? Something told him, however, it wouldn't impress her one bit.

Bean was saying something about all these Poles and Croats flooding into the country, and how she'd heard there would soon be a million Eastern Europeans over here. 'There are sixty thousand in Basingstoke already.'

Assuming she was a racist—everyone in Hampshire was racist, Greg reckoned—he launched into a speech about economic migrants and how they had just as much right to be here as white, middleclass bigots.

'I couldn't agree more,' Bean replied, thrilled to find someone who agreed with her on the subject. 'We *adore* our Croat couple. Stanislav and Vjecke are practically *family*. And the Poles who retiled out swimming pool worked like Trojans, the more of them over here the merrier.'

Archie was feeling thoroughly uncomfortable. Obviously he couldn't say hello to Gemma, and he didn't want to see the baby close up, and there was nothing else to do at this party. His mum was being weird too; she kept coming over to see if he was ok, and trying to introduce him to random people from the village. He would have liked to have gone outside to kick a football about on the lawn, or look round the Cleggs' house which seemed cool. He liked their marble hall. It was all much more modern than their own house, he'd spotted an enormous plasma-screen in a room by the kitchen. It annoyed him the way Gemma had kept looking at him in church, and she was doing it again now. She had this really annoying expression, like she wanted to talk to him or something. He had to admit she was quite hot. But so thick. Like . . . hello? Is there anyone at home? Duh!

Dawn was circulating with a plate of chipolatas on sticks, and

Debbie helping hand round breaded scampi and tartare sauce with paper serviettes. Four big pizzas were warming through in the oven and wouldn't be ready for another five minutes, so Dawn hoped people weren't too hungry. Looking round, she thought things were going quite well. It was lovely to see the lounge being used at last. She'd put out coasters and mats on all the tables to protect them. The carpet worried her though, with the pile coming up in tufts, being new. She'd vacuumed it before church but now look at it! She'd like to have asked everyone to remove their shoes at the door.

She had to admit she was nervous, having company in the house for the first time. She wanted everything to be perfect, especially with Philippa and Davina here, not that Philippa's house was anything to write home about. Each time she went over to Stockbridge House for committee meetings, she was quite shocked, it was so untidy; piles of unopened post and dog leads in the hall, and dirty footprints everywhere and threadbare old rugs, she was amazed anyone could live like that, especially people like the Mountleighs with all their pedigree. To steady her nerves she had been at the sherry, just two small glasses to give her confidence, which it had. Suddenly she was feeling quite the lady of the manor. Spotting Miles alone and aloof in the window bay, she decided to approach him.

'It's such a pleasure to host you at the Park at last, Miles,' she said. 'It's taken forever sorting it all out, and I feel terrible we haven't got you over previously. We haven't been able to entertain before now. Other than Mollie's visits, of course, she's become such a friend to the girls, like a third daughter.' Emboldened by sherry, Dawn couldn't stop talking. 'It's so nice Mollie's a godmother to little Mandy, and so appropriate with the girls being such mates as well as the other . . .' she lowered her voice 'the other *circumstance . . .*'

The conversation irritated Miles on so many levels, each new sentence provoking him in a fresh way, that he searched for a suitably damning response. Before he'd found one, however, the lady from Chawbury village stores barged over with her big buck teeth and said, 'I bet I know what *you two* are talking about. You're arguing over who is Lord of the Manor of Chawbury, aren't you?

Most people reckon the Park's bigger than the Manor now. You'll just have to build on some more rooms, Mr Straker.'

Serena was waiting for her chance to catch Miles on his own. They hadn't met up for three weeks and she was feeling horny and ignored. Last time, Miles had dangled a trip to Dubai to the new Zach Durban hotel, but there had been no follow-through, and she feared he might have invited someone else instead. There was always that worry with Miles, she didn't really trust him. Although he had been careful never to make her any promises about the future, she hoped he would eventually leave Davina and she could leave Robin and they could lead a proper life together in the open. She never drove past Chawbury Manor without wondering if it would one day be her home. She had a fantasy that in a year or two, when the youngest Straker child—Mollie, was it?—finished college, Miles would sort things out with Davina and she, Serena, as the second Mrs Miles Straker, could move into the big house with her son, Ollie. Sometimes the fantasy felt so real and imminent she wanted to pack up her things in readiness; other times, she feared it was nothing but a daydream, and dreaded Miles ditching her.

'Miles.'

'Ah, hello Serena. How have you been keeping? How's Robin?' Whenever Miles met his mistress in public, he became archly formal and made a big deal of asking how her husband was, in case they were overheard.

'Fucking useless,' Serena replied. 'Useless at work, useless at fucking.'

Miles smiled smugly. 'I was going to ask what you're doing tomorrow evening? Thought we might have a quiet . . . dinner in London.'

'I'd love to. Where?'

'Call Sara at my office, any time after eleven. She'll have booked somewhere.' Then he said, 'I hope you're as hungry as I am, Serena.'

'Starving.'

'Don't eat before then, will you?'

'I'll tell Robin I've got the curse.'

Later she said, 'I've just met Baby Mandy. She's not yours, is she?'

Miles's blood froze. 'Mine? Whatever made you say that?'

'Just kidding. She looks a bit like you, that's all. Same chin.'

'I don't actually find that amusing, Serena.'

She gave him a strange look. 'Just a joke, Miles. Joke. I didn't really imagine you'd got your rocks off with Gemma Clegg.'

'Well, please *don't* joke. I don't like it. We'd better not talk too long either. People might get suspicious.'

Samantha was wondering what ever could have possessed her. Fancying Greg in Thailand, she meant. Looking at him now, she thought she must have been on something at the time: magic mushrooms or hash cakes, or she'd passively inhaled a cloud of marijuana. He had to be the ugliest, most obnoxious man she'd met. She could hear him scolding the vicar on the malign influence of Christianity through the ages. And now he was arguing with Nigel Winstanton over inheritance tax, saying it should be fixed at 100 percent so everyone began life on a level playing field, and nothing could be passed down. She could see Greg had presence; that was probably it. He seemed so convinced of his own opinions, and stood his ground when Nigel, who was at Lehman Brothers and accustomed to being agreed with, told him he was a naive idealist. But as boyfriend material, Sam rated him zero.

Peter was chatting away to a group of ladies from the church who were involved with the flower rota and Brasso-ing the altar rail. They were all very interested in talking to him, since they knew Mrs French, the Strakers' housekeeper, and loved visiting the garden at the Manor on the occasions it was open for general inspection, though they said they would not themselves like the upkeep on a big place like that. When they asked Peter what he did for a living, he hated replying that he worked in his father's business.

'That's nice dear,' one said. 'Working alongside your dad.' Peter wanted to reply, 'No, you've no idea. It's not nice at all. Each day I spend there, I feel my soul corroding a little more.' He wanted to say he was a . . . what? A deep-sea fisherman, a shepherd, a folk singer . . . Anything but a PR account executive. He'd spent the previous week trying to persuade minor celebrities—or, more accurately, minor celebrities' agents—to get their minor celebrities to show up for five minutes at the launch party of a new watch store in Regent Street, just for long enough to get photographed by the paparazzi on the red carpet, in exchange for which they'd receive a new Arditti oyster solar-powered chronometer with platinum bracelet, something like that anyway. How crass was that? How totally, numbingly pathetic. And the rest of his working life he spent persuading Pendletons shoppers to stay with the brand, and not switch to the cheaper offerings of their host today, Ross Clegg, who Peter had decided he very much liked. Whenever he'd broached the subject of leaving Straker Communications with his father, Miles became furious, telling him he was damned lucky to have a job and he'd never get another one. So, for now, Peter devoted as much time as possible to practicing the guitar and working on his songs about seabirds and Hebridean islands and shingle along the high-water mark on Atlantic beaches.

'You don't remember me, do you?' a teenage girl was asking him.

'Of course I do, Debbie,' he said. 'You bought CDs at my stall at that garden thing. My best customer, in fact.'

'You sold them too cheap. You can't have made much for the charity,' Debbie said.

'You're right there. They were quite annoyed about it. I had to put in a fiver of my own to cheer them up.' He laughed. 'They were mostly scratched anyway. They probably didn't play, half of them.'

'Mine were fine. I like the Joan Baez one.'

'I forgot you bought that. She's a genius, Joan Baez. Up there with Joni Mitchell.'

Debbie was thinking what a nice man Peter was when Ross cut them short, tapping a spoon on a champagne flute. 'Ladies and gentlemen. May I kindly crave your attention for just a few moments for the formalities.'

Ross had been thinking a toast was in order, but appreciated it was all a bit irregular, things being as they were. So he decided to keep it very short, with no speech at all, just a raise-your-glasses to the beautiful Mandy on her special day and life's luck to her. 'Now, is everyone here? Where's young Archie? He should be here. Anyone seen Archie Straker?'

Miles froze again. Why the hell was Ross bringing Archie into it?

'I last saw him watching TV in the kitchen,' Mollie said.

'Well, be a good lass and fetch him, will you? He won't want to miss the toast.'

Everyone stood round waiting for Archie to be fetched, so Ross's speech could go ahead. Miles was sweating inside his suit. Ross wasn't going to let the cat out of the bag, surely?

A minute later, Mollie returned alone. 'He says he's not coming. The film's reached a really good bit, they're about to blow up the bridge.'

'No matter,' said Ross, shrugging. 'I'm sure the movie's more exciting than my toast in any case. Now, ladies and gentlemen, charge your glasses please and drink the health of Mandy Grace Clegg, for a long and happy life.'

'Mandy Grace Clegg,' chanted everyone, raising their glasses.

It was at that moment Miles had his brainwave.

22.

M iles made a point of always being civil to gossip columnists. Many people in his position didn't bother. Once they'd made it, they wouldn't be seen dead saying good evening to the tribe of diary editors and scandal scribes that hung about the fringes of London events. You could not say Miles exactly fraternised with them—he was far too grand for that—nor did he invite them to his private parties. But whenever he ran into them—the haggard stringers from the *Daily Mail*, the *Daily Telegraph* and the *Evening Standard*—he greeted them cordially, and periodically slipped them a story when it suited him to do so.

The following evening, when Serena escaped up to town for their clandestine dinner, he took her first to a cocktail party at the Italian embassy in Belgrave Square in honour of his new client, Fiat. He went because he knew Nigel Dempster, the *Daily Mail*'s chief diarist at the time, would be there, and he needed a word with him. Naturally, it was all done with tremendous subtlety. First, Miles worked the room, greeting the ambassador, greeting the chief executive of Fiat who was in town for the event, introducing his clients to socialites he knew they would be flattered to meet. He reintroduced Serena to Dempster, who remembered her from her previous life as girl about town.

Then Miles said, 'Oh, Nigel. You didn't hear this from me, but here's a possible story for you. Does the name Ross Clegg mean anything? Downmarket supermarket tycoon? That's the one, often in the financial pages. Well, word to the wise, his sixteen-year-old daughter has had an illegitimate child. Big scandal down our way in Hampshire . . .'

Nigel looked like he was taking the bait.

'If I were writing the story myself,' Miles went on, 'I think I'd compare and contrast the parvenu Clegg family, who let me tell you are *loathed* in Hampshire, with the Pendletons, so classy and philanthropic. I'll have my people fax over an updated list of their charitable bequests.'

'Do we know who the dad is? The kid's, I mean?'

'Not a clue. Probably the girl doesn't know herself,' Miles said airily. 'Just some yobbo from the village, probably. No one's come forward.' Miles knew it was a dangerous tactic, reckless even, since if anyone dug too deep on this story Archie might be implicated. But Miles reckoned he could control the situation. And the opportunity to damage Ross was irresistible.

After they left the party, Serena said, 'That was mean of you. Why tell Nigel about the baby? It was really unnecessary. He might put it in his column.'

'That's the point. I want him to.'

'But you were at Ross's yesterday. And your daughter's a godmother, isn't she? I don't get it.'

'Business,' Miles replied. 'If you don't approve, let's not have dinner.'

'No, of course not. It's fine, no problem. Where are we going anyway?'

'The Knightsbridge Towers. I thought we might eat in our suite. Alright with you?'

'Very alright,' Serena said. 'I hoped you might suggest that.'

By long arrangement, Miles and Davina were having lunch that Saturday with James and Laetitia Pendleton at their country house, Longparish Priory. As the crow flew, Longparish Priory was scarcely more than seven miles from Chawbury, and the stretch of the Test which flowed through Miles's meadows also flowed through the Pendletons' estate downstream. Miles often declared that, one day, he would arrive for lunch by canoe, though of course he never would in case his clothes got splashed.

Miles had mixed feelings about their regular lunches and dinners at the Pendletons'. Naturally, it was imperative they be there; if the invitations ever dried up, he would be concerned. It was also a privilege to be asked. James and Laetitia generally invited no more than ten guests at a time when they entertained, mixing grander neighbours with one or two more exciting imports, painters or ballet dancers connected to their artistic endeavours. At previous lunch parties, the Strakers had met Howard Hodgkin, whose work James Pendleton collected, and Darcy Bussell, the ballerina. It was always civilised and low-key, with deliciously understated food. Although Laetitia made a big point of supporting the family firm and buying all her ingredients at Pendletons, her French chef was a genius, and you could not possibly confuse his delicate salmon mousses with the microwaved ready-meals which fed the nation. And, of course, the house in its parkland setting beside the Test was breathtaking. It stood in the heart of that part of Hampshire know as 'Brand Valley,' where the Sainsbury family and the Cadbury family all had houses; a manicured billionaire microculture where, so it seemed, every couple of miles stood another enormous house occupied by very rich people. Being intensely competitive, Miles never visited Longparish Priory without feelings of envy. He adored Chawbury Manor, but after a visit to the Pendletons's, it felt small and unimpressive.

The journey by car from Chawbury to Longparish always took longer than envisaged, since you had to make lengthy detours around the various estates with river frontage. The route took you through pretty flint villages, impeccably maintained by their owners who weekended there. Daffodils were bursting out on the verges, with every hedgerow trimmed, shaped and tamed in the way Miles admired. He slipped a Shirley Bassey CD into the car stereo, a sure sign he was in splendid form. In fact, he had been in splendid form ever since yesterday morning, when the story about the Clegg baby surfaced in Nigel Dempster's column.

Gratifyingly, Nigel had gone for it full hog. It had been the lead item, eight hundred words of it, with a photograph of Ross and a photograph of James and Laetitia with Princess Margaret. Miles knew in advance it was running in Friday's paper, so he'd sent his driver, Makepiece, to pick up an early edition on Thursday at midnight from Charing Cross station, which was the first place to get them, and bring it round to Holland Park Square. He saw at once that the story was perfect. It could hardly have been better if he'd written it himself, which he practically had, with all the additional facts he'd been faxing over.

The hazard of leaking stories to gossip columns was that so many of the diarists had tin ears, but today's offering hit the bull's-eye. It made Gemma sound like the village bike, available for anyone to ride. Freeza Mart was described as 'a downmarket cash-and-carry, unlikely to catch on in upmarket Hampshire.' Dawn was 'a peroxided Northern lass.' The Cleggs' house was likened to 'a footballer's mansion in Cheshire,' and the county was united against them. In short, anyone reading it would be unlikely to enter a Freeza Mart ever again.

Furthermore, the item was wonderfully sycophantic about the Pendletons. Four entire paragraphs were devoted to their charitable activities. There was stuff about the ballet, the museum bequests, research fellowships, all of it. It made Lord and Lady Pendleton sound like latter day saints. It even praised their supermarket food. Miles felt a glow of satisfaction. No one could say he hadn't earned his fee today.

At some point on Friday morning, he rang Davina to check if she'd seen the story. She was down at Chawbury and didn't always open the newspapers, being over-occupied with her garden. Naturally he wasn't going to reveal his own role in the planting of the item, but he wanted her to read it since he felt she was too sympathetic towards Dawn and Ross, and it would be salutary.

Davina, however, had read it already and was horrified. 'So hurtful to poor Dawn, I can't bear it. I rang her straightaway and assured her *nobody* round here thinks about them like that. Nobody I've met anyway. She sounded so upset, poor woman, I drove straight over. Lots of people were ringing up, saying how unnecessary it was. Philippa rang while I was there. And Bean. All that horrid stuff about Gemma and the baby, and who the father is. Do you know, I've a good mind to ring Nigel Dempster and tell him it's Archie. I really am quite tempted.'

'Davina, under no circumstances do that. I forbid you.'

'Well, I won't,' Davina said. 'For Archie's sake, I won't. And Dawn doesn't want it either. She just wants everything to die down. Nothing more in the papers. But it's so hurtful to her. And so mean about Ross's business too. Everything.'

'You're right,' Miles said. 'Goodness only knows how the papers get hold of this rubbish. Its not even as though anyone's that interested. Who's even heard of Ross Clegg? It's a mercy we weren't dragged in ourselves, actually. At least James and Laetitia came out well.'

'Laetitia's horrified too,' Davina said. 'I should have said, she rang earlier and asked for Dawn's telephone number. She said she wanted to apologise to her. You know how she hates that kind of publicity, they're so private, the Pendletons.'

Miles wished he hadn't rung home. The conversation left him feeling almost deflated.

23.

weeping past the Doric gate lodges and up the mile-long drive to the front of the house, Miles felt quite proprietorial. Having visited Longparish Priory several times a year for more than a decade, he regarded himself as rather more than a guest, almost a stakeholder, to use Tony Blair's latest buzzword, in the Pendletons' estate. His eyes approvingly scanned the specimen trees in the park, and the rustic fishing lodge commissioned by Laetitia in the style of a log cabin which could be glimpsed on the riverbank. He thought he could see Hugh—James and Laetitia's eldest son—up to his thighs in waders, casting for trout.

Parking the car, Miles frowned. There were five or six vehicles already lined up outside the house, and he'd pulled up alongside a black Cherokee jeep which looked disturbingly like Ross's car. Peering through the windows, he spotted a Freeza Mart plastic bag on the rear seat. Jesus: the Cleggs weren't going to be here too, were they?

The Pendletons' butler, Lagdon, opened the front door and led them along a wide inner hall hung with remarkable modern paintings: an enormous pair of Hockney swimming pools, a Picasso, several Graham Sutherlands, a small Bacon triptych and, opposite the cloakroom, a Degas of a ballerina.

'Lagdon, we haven't got a Mr and Mrs Clegg having lunch today, have we?'

'They just arrived, Mr Straker,' Lagdon replied. 'I only a moment ago took them through.'

Arriving at the drawing room, the Cleggs' recent arrival was still evident. Lady Pendleton was introducing them around to the other lunch guests, and Dawn was clutching a bunch of chrysanthemums in yellow cellophane as a gift for her hostess. Without missing a beat, Laetitia handed them tactfully to her butler, who returned with them ten minutes later in a blue willow-pattern vase and placed them on a table, next to a cashepot of poinsettias.

Whenever James Pendleton met anyone new for the first time, he was surprisingly diffident. At the office, surrounded by his own people, he was confident and even on occasions peremptory. But in a social situation he was gripped by unexpected shyness, unable to think of anything to say. So it was today, as he struggled to come up with small talk for these strangers, his guests, whom Laetitia had invited only yesterday.

In the end, he said, 'I trust your shops are thriving.'

Slightly awed by the splendour of the house, and meeting for the first time the man who ran and largely owned such a giant competitor, Ross defaulted into the language he used when addressing his shareholders. 'We've been seeing like-for-like revenue growth of between twelve and fourteen percent, and overall growth of closer to forty-five. Retail space is ahead by seventeen percent this fiscal.'

'Wish ours was,' James replied. 'Well done.' And he topped-up Ross's scarcely-touched glass with champagne, which was his stratagem for moving on to the next guest.

Laetitia intercepted the Strakers at the door to the drawing room and softly explained, 'I've asked them because of that *beastly* thing in the *Mail*. So snobbish, I hated it. I don't want them thinking we're all enemies or anything.'

'Marvellous idea, Laetitia,' Miles replied, nodding. 'And a typically thoughtful one too.' He glared over at the Cleggs. Ross was looking stiff and uncomfortable, and Dawn like she had an entire cosmetics department daubed on her face.

'I expect they're friends of yours already,' Laetitia was saying. 'You're all neighbours at Chawbury, aren't you?'

Miles was about to deny anything like friendship with the Cleggs, but Davina said, 'Yes, we've become awfully fond of them. We were all at the christening of their granddaughter last weekend. Our younger daughter is a godmother, which is lovely.'

'We've not met them before,' Laetitia said. 'I know I shouldn't be saying this, and luckily James isn't listening, but I *do like* Ross's new store, the Andover one. Awfully well done. I slipped in the other day and bought something at their bakery. Very fresh and nice. I felt so disloyal afterwards.'

Miles already knew most of the other guests, predictable members of the Hampshire social set. Several worked in private equity, and there was the Chief Executive of a large drinks conglomerate who Miles made a point of lionising since he wanted the account for Straker Communications. There was also an earnest-looking man in spectacles with his earnest-looking wife, who turned out to be the Development Director for a regional ballet company. They referred to James and Laetitia as 'our wonderful benefactors.'

Shortly before lunch, the Pendletons' son Hugh joined them from the river, and Miles found himself, as usual, wishing his own eldest son, Peter, was more like him. Charming, modest, intelligent and nicely presented, Hugh moved around the room chatting up his parents' guests, with no trace of the boredom and cynicism Miles felt he sometimes detected in Peter. It occurred to him that Hugh would make an ideal husband for Samantha one day, and was keen to get the two of them together. Sam was eighteen, Hugh twenty-three, both still slightly young you could argue, but it wasn't clear what Sam was going to do with herself now she'd left school and done her travelling, and an early marriage to the Pendleton boy wouldn't be at all a bad solution.

They moved through to the dining room which had once been the orangerie of the house, with a magnificent barrel ceiling and Georgian planters with full-grown orange and lemon trees. Above the fireplace hung an enormous oil by Lucian Freud of a naked man, his horse-sized genitalia swinging between his legs. As Dawn entered the room, Miles saw her horrified face. Blushing, she quickly averted her eyes. Her mouth was opening and closing in shock, like a bullfrog.

Miles and Ross found themselves in the places of honour, seated on either side of Laetitia. Miles eyed Ross patronisingly, watching him dither over the array of cutlery as the first course, a jellied consommé with chives, which he had evidently never seen in his life before, was served. To confuse him, Miles lifted his knife and fork, as though he was going to eat the jellied soup with them. Ross followed suit, as did Dawn at the opposite end of the table, taking the lead from her husband. As soon as they'd started eating, slicing at the soup with a knife, Miles deftly switched to his spoon. 'Tell me, Laetitia,' he said, ignoring the Cleggs' discomfort, 'Did you enjoy Isolde at Sadlers Wells as much as Davina and I did?'

Ross looked rather lost during Laetitia's reply, so Miles said, 'Ross, we're talking about Baryshnikov's Isolde. Did you and Dawn see it?'

'I'm sorry, I don't know what that is. Is it an opera?'

Miles laughed silkily. 'The new Russian ballet at Sadlers Wells. The Bolshoi. Laetitia's a trustee.'

'The answer's no then, I'm afraid,' Ross said. 'It's all been a bit too full-on lately for shows. Dawn likes to go, though its been a while, I think *Cats* was the last one we got to.'

Miles adored it. He couldn't wait to pass it on. *Cats*, indeed! But Laetitia was saying, 'James loved *Cats* too. We saw it twice. That marvellous feline dancing. Very Twyla Tharp, we felt.'

'Macavity the Mystery Cat . . . They made us learn that poem at school,' Ross said. 'Our elder daughter Gemma, she wanted to become a dancer after seeing that show. On about it for ages.'

'Well, I hope she persevered,' Laetitia replied. 'Has she auditioned for any of the ballet schools?'

'No, no,' said Ross. 'That fad soon passed, she was on to clothes next. Fashion and boys.' His voice trailed away. 'Well, she's a mum now. She's got little Mandy to look after. Our first grandchild.'

'How lucky you are,' Laetitia said. 'James and I are longing for grandchildren. But Hugh, our eldest, is only twenty-three so it'll be a good few years yet, sadly.'

'Has Hugh got an, er, special girlfriend at the moment?' Miles asked, keen to get back into the conversation.

'I'm afraid James keeps him much too busy for that,' Laetitia said. 'He's getting him to work in all the different departments, moving around the company. It's so important he understands it all. And meets lots of people. We're so lucky with our people at Pendletons, some of them stay with us for years and years.' Turning to Ross, she asked, 'Do you have good people in your business?'

'The best. No offence, I'm sure yours are excellent too. But I have been lucky. I often think that. Several of my directors have been with me from the beginning almost. There's my first employee over there look: Dawn. She was the very first—and she's still with me, God help her, twenty-six years later.'

'Congratulations,' said Laetitia. 'I've never actually had a proper job at Pendletons myself, I'm afraid. And I'm much too old and unskilled to get one now, they'd never take me on. But I do sometimes feel I work for them in any case. One does tend to get a bit involved.'

'You certainly do, Laetitia,' Miles pandered. Addressing Ross, he said, 'This amazing lady does so much for the business, it's unbelievable. She's being ridiculously modest. I see you with James at all the corporate events.'

'Only the nicer ones,' corrected Laetitia. 'I feel I'm so lucky, being able to go to these wonderful ballets and operas, and the art exhibitions too of course. We're sponsoring the Turner show at the Tate, did you know that?'

'Actually, I did. We organised it through Strakers,' he reminded her lightly.

'Of course you did, Miles. I'm sorry, I must be going senile.' Then to Ross, 'Miles is a marvel. He helps us with everything, all our charitable things, all the sponsorships, all our publicity. Corporate publicity I mean, of course, not personal publicity. We don't really go in for any of that.'

'Tell me about it,' Ross said ruefully, still feeling burnt by the article in Dempster's column. 'I wouldn't mind if I never saw my name in print again.'

'You should get Miles to advise you. He's the expert,' Laetitia said.

'Oh, I'm afraid not,' Miles said quickly. 'Conflict of interest. Couldn't work for a competitor.'

'Such a pity,' Laetitia said. 'You could help Ross so much. Not that he needs it, his shops are so blissful. I probably shouldn't be saying this, Ross, but I sneaked across to your new store the other day and bought myself a little cheese scone, and it was perfectly delicious!' She placed her hand confidingly on his elbow. 'For goodness sake don't tell James I said that. He gets so cross if the family don't do all their shopping at a Pendletons. They need the customers, you see.' And she laughed prettily.

Across the table, Dawn felt she was struggling, positioned between Lord Pendleton and the development director. She couldn't
think of anything to say to either of them, and they were equally
unforthcoming. She asked the ballet fundraiser about his children,
but he replied they didn't have any, without elaborating, so she
thought she must have put her foot in it. She asked James how he'd
first got into the supermarket business, and he replied that his father had enrolled him the day he left school and he'd never had a
choice. After that, it all dried up. From time to time her eye was
drawn back to the oil painting of the naked man, which she could
hardly avoid since it loomed so large in her line of vision. Each
time she saw it, she shuddered. It was so crude, so vulgar. She
couldn't understand how Lord and Lady Pendleton, who were so
respectable, could bear to look at something like that, especially
while they were eating.

'Don't you like it?' James was asking her.

'Delicious,' Dawn replied. 'I just couldn't finish it all, it's so rich.'
She had in fact been trying to conceal her almost untouched *sauce
hollandaise* underneath the cutlery on her plate.

'I meant the Freud, the painting. You looked dubious.'

'Well, I must confess, it isn't exactly my kind of thing. But it is
very . . . ,' she searched for an appropriate adjective, '*striking.*'

'A lot of people find Lucian too raw. But I like that about him.
It's a powerful piece. I first started collecting him twenty years ago.
It was . . . easier back then.'

'So you have other ones too?' Dawn asked, aghast at the thought.

'We've been very fortunate,' James said. 'I was able to buy seven
or eight direct from his studio, well before he'd gained his current
reputation. We've added a few more from the Marlborough Gallery since then.'

Dawn observed, 'It's very *modern.*'

'Do you collect yourself?' James asked. He seemed genuinely
interested, and Dawn decided he was a kindly man.

'You couldn't say collect exactly. Just things we've picked up
here and there that caught our eye. On holiday mostly.'

'That's the best way to collect,' James assured her. 'Only buy
things you like yourself, and which make a connection.'

'That's what we do,' Dawn said. 'We found this lovely papyrus in Sharm el-Sheik, with all the old hieroglyphics and Pharaohs on it. And we bought a lovely oil painting of the boats in the harbour at Antibes. I never look at it without remembering that holiday, it brings it all back.'

'It sounds like you're approaching it entirely correctly,' James said. 'Follow your own eye and don't deviate. Sometimes I'm afraid I disappoint our curator by not buying the pieces he'd like me to. He tells me we ought to be filling certain gaps in the collection, but if I don't admire the work, I won't. There has to be a coherent eye or it doesn't make any sense.'

Dawn was digesting the fact that Lord Pendleton had a curator, especially to help him buy his pictures, when everyone started scraping back their chairs and standing up, and lunch was over. Moments later, Laetitia was bearing down on them. 'I *do* hope James has been looking after you properly,' she said. Then, to James, 'Darling, I've been having *such* an interesting conversation with Ross. He and Dawn are great fans of Andrew Lloyd Weber's musicals. I thought we might try and persuade them to come and see *Phantom* with us in Basingstoke. At the summer festival.'

'Marvellous idea,' said James. 'They're very underrated, musicals. I love them myself.'

24.

Arriving home at Holland Park Square as early as possible after work, Peter would let himself out through the garden door at the back of the house into the communal garden, and find a quiet place to practise his guitar. Second only to Ladbroke Square Gardens, the three enclosed acres of Holland Park Square was the largest communal garden in West London. It was also the best-maintained and, as Miles liked to inform visitors, the garden with the highest annual service charge to support the three full-time gardeners who tended the various shrubberies, lawns and the famous Holland Park Square rock garden with its collection of alpine ferns. It was a garden full of hidden bowers and glades, each with its own bench inscribed in memory of some long-dead resident. It was here Peter hid himself away to strum at his acoustic guitar. If the wind was in the right direction, you could hardly hear the traffic at all and almost believe you were in the depth of the countryside, rather than one of the city's most desirable residential neighbourhoods.

In the eleven years the Strakers had lived at Number 32 Holland Park Square, Miles had enjoyed the heady sensation of having bought very wisely indeed. At the time he'd purchased the house, from Robert de Vass of Knight Frank, it had felt expensive at £720,000. A decade later, the same narrow cream-stucco six-story semi-detached mansions were changing hands at five million pounds, and ramping up in value at the rate of half a million a year, powered by an unending influx of American, French and Italian investment bankers and private equity shysters. Now, of course, Miles kicked himself for not having extended himself further by buying an even larger house on the south side of the square, where the prices were half again higher. In particular, there was a pair of stucco palazzos he could see directly across the garden from his bathroom window, which were said to be valued at almost eight million pounds each. They had the added prestige of pillared porticos on both elevations, on the street side and the garden side, and it irked Miles that properties existed on his communal garden that were superior to his own.

None of these considerations entered Peter's tousled head, however, as he sheltered behind laburnum bushes working on a song about crofters on the isle of Jura and the contentment they found around the dying embers of a peat fire. His songs, which Samantha considered very samey, had a melancholy beauty. Mist, seabirds and brooding love were their constant themes.

It was Peter's challenge each evening to arrive home unobserved. This was not always easy. While he struggled back from Golden Square on the Central Line, Miles was driven home from Charles Street Mews by Makepiece, cutting fifteen minutes from the journey. On the occasions he spotted his son arriving home at the same time as himself, Miles expressed surprise. 'Don't you have something to go to this evening? Isn't there some client event you should be at?' Miles himself seemed always to be setting off to one client dinner or another.

Then there was Conception, their Holland Park Square Filipina maid.

'Is my idle son home yet, Conception?' Miles would ask.

'I think he go backside in garden, Mr Straker,' Conception replied, massively blowing his cover.

Minutes later, Miles would hound him down in the shrubbery, declaring, 'Here you are. Put down that ruddy instrument and come with me to the Pendletons' drinks. Come on, you're meant to be one of their account men, aren't you? You won't do any good skulking out here in the bushes.'

Learning from experience, Peter gravitated deeper into the hinterland of the garden. He incubated a fantasy in which his songs were recorded by a major label and he became the new Neil Young or James Taylor, only less overtly commercial. He believed that if only the whole world was exposed to his lyrics and music he could make a difference, and escape the purgatory of working for Straker Communications and his father for his entire life.

Samantha hadn't set eyes on a single member of her family for five days in a row. Their hours no longer coincided. These days, she seldom returned from nightclubs before three or four o'clock in the morning, which was three hours before Miles left for his breakfast meetings and five before Peter set off on the tube for Golden Square. Archie was away at Bristol University and Mollie went into college every day from Chawbury. Which left Sam, gloriously unsupervised, recuperating by day in her bedroom at the top of Holland Park Square, in preparation for the next night's fun.

Ostensibly in London to find some kind of job, her efforts in this direction were cursory. She was intending to send letters to the HR department of Sotheby's, Christie's, Condé Nast, the Admirable Crichton party planners, Louis Vuitton, Harrods, Tiffany and several other organisations where she wouldn't object to working, but these letters had not yet got themselves written, and somehow the notion of fulltime employment with *hours* became less appealing the longer she did nothing about it. In fact, she couldn't see how it would even be logistically possible to fit in a job, given how little time she already had just coping with all the things she needed to do. Such as remembering to drop her clothes into the laundry basket so they could be washed and ironed by Conception, and shopping for new clothes whenever she forgot, and making arrangements for each night with so many people, like whose flat they where all going to meet up in first, and whether to go to L'Equipe Anglaise behind Selfridges or Chinawhite, or even Tramp if someone could get them in.

Blessed with a fabulous figure, long blonde hair, instinctive sexiness and a strong sense of entitlement, Sam felt immediately comfortable in her new persona as proto 'it' girl. School had never held much interest for her, nor had travelling, beyond the soporific comfort of sunshine. But now, here in London, shuttling between nightclubs in an endless succession of black cabs as a fully assimilated member of a young, rich, attractive subculture, she felt fulfilled. It was amazing how many people she already knew, and counted as good friends, that she hadn't even heard of four months earlier. Her mobile rang incessantly. She was greeted by name by the barmen at half a dozen clubs, and was waved straight inside by the clipboard gatekeepers. She was named by *Tatler* in their annual list as one of the 500 most desirable teenagers in Britain, in a write-up which began 'Straker Communications heiress Sammy Straker, 19, is one trust fund babe who knows how to party big. Woo her with her favourite Moscow Mule at Po-Na-Na and watch her shake her booty at nearby 151 on the Kings Road.' When he saw the piece, Miles experienced a surge of paternal pride, loving the idea of his daughter as a leading socialite, as well as the flattering name-check for his company. So he agreed, with only token complaint, to pay off her overdraft and raise her allowance to better reflect her new circumstances.

As Sam explained it, she lived a life of incredible economy in any case, since so many of her drinks, club entry fees and taxis were taken care of by others. 'I probably only have to pay for one drink in ten,' she said. 'You're getting away with murder, Dad, you've no idea. Margaritas are twelve quid each at most places.' And Miles, who was perfectly happy to be wound round his beautiful daughter's finger, took her clothes shopping at Joseph and paid another two thousand pounds into her account when she told him she was short.

During this initial period of her initiation to the party circuit, Sam was pleased enough to hang out with anyone at all. Her circle was composed of school friends and their brothers, all more or less her own age. If they ate out, which they seldom did, it was at pizzerias or creperies where the bill didn't exceed ten pounds per person. In these early days she regarded boys aged twenty-five, let alone thirty, as impossibly old. Over time, however, she found herself taken up by a more sophisticated group, older and richer, who took her instead to Italian and French restaurants like L'Incontro, Sale Pepe and above all San Lorenzo, and money was no longer a consideration.

These new friendships came with strings attached. Samantha understood instinctively that she was expected to put out in return for dinner, or anyway in return for a second dinner, and this she did without a second thought, with neither moral nor emotional hesitation. She regarded sex as the natural conclusion to a fun evening, a favour lightly conferred, costing nothing, and likely to validate not imperil a new acquaintanceship. In her first year in London, she slept in fourteen different beds in bachelor flats across four boroughs: Chelsea and Kensington (8), Fulham (3), Westminster (2, both Pimlico) and Barnes (once only, far too far). Few of these liaisons endured for longer than a few weeks, nor were they intended to. Sam discovered she enjoyed and was good at sex, but her boredom threshold was low, and there was seldom much regret in moving on. Her new boyfriends drove powerful cars and took her to watch polo at Windsor and racing at Goodwood. One, who was her oldest admirer so far being 46 (a fact she decided to conceal from her parents) was a notorious philanderer working in commercial property. One evening, after a boisterous dinner at Morton's in Berkeley Square, they had gone on to Annabel's. It was the first time Sam had been inside, and she liked the place immediately, recognising it as a grown-up nightclub, a step up from the ones she usually went to.

The property whiz, who evidently came to Annabel's all the time, led her to a table next to the dance floor and ordered champagne. The bottle was being opened when he said, 'Good God. There's an old flame of mine, the redhead. Scrubber with the big tits. She married Robin Harden. Robin Hard-on, we called him. But that's not Robin she's with tonight, oy oy.'

Samantha looked for a redhead, and recognised her at once. It was Serena, their Hampshire neighbour. A split-second later she saw the man she was with: her father. Miles had one arm draped round Serena's bare shoulders and was smoking a cigar. His eyes, lustfully focused on Serena's cleavage, looked ready to pop from their sockets.

25.

wo years almost to the day following the opening of Andover Freeza Mart, Ross was persuaded to take his business fully public on the Footsie.

His financial svengalis, Callum and Brin, were convinced the timing was right, with a surplus of institutional cash looking for a home. Furthermore, the business had been growing at such speed, with eighteen new stores opened in as many months, they were keen to play down their investment. Ross, too, could see the sense in it, even though a part of him resisted the idea of being quoted on the main stock exchange with all the hassle and accountability that implied. His newest stores in Romsey, Haslemere, Farnborough and Sevenoaks, fitted out to a higher design spec, had been instantly successful, performing way ahead of forecast. Anecdotally, Ross had heard the folks at Safeway and even Sainsburys were taking him seriously as a competitor for the first time. And when he interviewed a potential new marketing director, who came from Pendletons, the guy told him his bosses were 'obsessed' by Freeza Mart and monitoring prices against their own on a daily basis. Ross found it hard to believe, but it was flattering nonetheless.

He broke the news of the flotation to Dawn on the evening before he informed his senior staff. Dawn was initially nonplussed, not understanding what it meant for them. But after he'd sunk a couple of cold beers, and then a couple of glasses of wine, Ross told her the stockbrokers were placing an initial valuation on the business of £320 million, of which the Clegg family owned thirty percent. They would realise £35 million of their stock at flotation, and still retain a big chunk of the equity. Dawn looked astounded, she'd had no idea. 'Not bad, is it love, when you think where we started out, in that little one-room office,' Ross said.

After that, they spent a long celebratory evening reminiscing about the early days of the business, and the problems they'd had borrowing from the bank and managing cashflow, and some of the lovely people who'd worked for them at the very beginning. Ross said he intended to award shares from his personal stake not only to the directors and senior managers, but also a few hundred shares each to every single person on the payroll, full time and part time. 'It won't make much odds to us, and it'll make a big difference to them,' he said. Then Dawn cried, partly at Ross's generosity and partly at the emotion of all the money that was coming their way.

One early consequence of the flotation process was that Ross had to spend a great deal more time in London. He had underestimated the sheer number of meetings he'd need to attend with lawyers and brokers, and the presentations to fund managers who quizzed him on every aspect of the business. At first he found these formal presentations with his financial director intimidating, and found himself becoming aggressive when investors second-guessed his assumptions. 'I've had it up to here with these jumped-up city slickers,' he told Dawn. 'They think they know everything but they don't know jack-shit, most of them.' Much of the time, his blunt Midlands persona played surprisingly well. He might not have been as slick or smooth as the investor relations professionals representing Sainsburys or Pendletons, but his honesty shone through.

With twelve- to fourteen-hour schedules sucking up to institutions, not to mention trying to stay on top of the business which felt more neglected with every passing week, Ross could no longer get home to Chawbury each evening. Instead, he began renting a two-bedroomed terraced cottage in a street behind Waterloo, a former railwayman's cottage which reminded him of the terrace in which he'd grown up. He couldn't get over the rent, which was £350 a week. 'We paid four shillings and sixpence for a place exactly like this one when I was a kid,' he told people. 'The landlord came round each Friday to collect and you were in trouble if you

Nicholas Coleridge

missed a payment.' But the Roupell Street cottage suited him, being functional and efficient, and within walking distance of the new Freeza Mart corporate headquarters at One Riverwharf. That was another consequence of going public: transferring the registered headquarters from Droitwich down to London, along with key corporate staff. Ross had severe misgivings about that, because he worried the company might forget its roots and lose touch with their customers. 'We've got a new rule in this office,' he addressed the team from a jumble of packing cases and files. 'Every one of us takes the train up to the Midlands once a month for store visits. It doesn't matter who we are: FD, company secretary, marketing—*especially* marketing—all of us, we spend a full day checking out our shops, checking the competition, listening to customers. There's a lot of fancy places with fancy prices to match down here in town, and I don't want anyone getting seduced by it. Its not real life down here. It's all bollocks, London, most of it, and don't you forget it. The day Freeza Mart starts heading downhill is the day we start believing all the London bollocks. Got that everyone?'

As for absorbing any London bollocks himself, Ross simply didn't have the time. He was treated to dinner at the River Room at the Savoy on a couple of occasions by his new advisors, but generally he microwaved his own supper in Roupell Street. His PA, Jacqui, who reluctantly agreed to relocate with him but was already missing Droitwich, sent him home with cold-bags of Freeza Mart products to fill the freezer. Sometimes he bought a KFC or burger on the walk home, and ate it in the street to avoid stinking out the cottage.

He rang home every evening to chat to Dawn and the kids, and discovered he missed them much more than he'd expected. He missed little Mandy too, who felt more like a third daughter than a first grandchild. Gemma was trying her best, bless her, to be a good mum but it was hard on her, she wasn't even eighteen yet. For the moment, Chawbury was the best place for her, sharing the care of Mandy with Dawn, but in the long run they'd have to decide what to do. She couldn't stop at Chawbury for the rest of her life. She'd quit school when she fell pregnant and lost touch with most of her mates; the move to Hampshire hadn't helped either. She was getting awfully lonely with just her mother, Debbie and the baby for company. Dawn and Ross discussed it and reckoned that in a year or so Gemma should enroll at college or even get a job—locally or up in town—and enjoy a bit of freedom again.

In one respect only, Ross felt disappointed by his new life. He had hoped, in spending more time in town, to get closer to Greg. The fact was, he'd had a tricky relationship with his only son for as long as he could remember, for ten years at least. It was hard to say exactly why, but they rubbed each other up the wrong way. Whenever Greg came down to Chawbury, as often as not they argued. They argued about everything from politics (Greg was way to the left of his father, though Ross still considered himself a socialist) to the way he spoke to his mother (he was routinely supercilious to Dawn). What irked Ross most was the dismissive attitude Greg showed towards Freeza Mart. He went out of his way to denigrate his dad's business, saying what eyesores the stores were and how disgusting the food. Or he banged on about them being capitalist institutions, designed to rip-off working class customers. 'All food outlets should be nationalised, along with the distribution chain,' Greg proclaimed. Since Ross was proud of being a fair employer, and had recently signed off on a corporate mission statement which put permanently low prices as a core competence, he was stupidly annoyed by Greg's crassness. He knew he shouldn't be, but he was.

He set himself the objective of using his time in London to get closer to his son; he would meet him on neutral ground, or better still on Greg's own territory. Several times Ross left messages to set up drinks or supper. He suggested meeting up in pubs in Holborn or the Strand, close to Greg's halls of residence, and they'd find a place for a bite to eat afterwards. Greg, however, was slow in replying, often claiming not to have received the message, saying his answer-phone was playing up. And when Ross did get hold of him, he was evasive. When, eventually, they fixed a date, Greg rolled up forty minutes late saying he only had time for a quick drink, not supper, because he needed to work on his PhD. Ross had to work hard to control his temper.

They met for a drink in a noisy wine bar called All Bar One in Aldwych and Ross told his son about the impending flotation of Freeza Mart, without mentioning his own share valuation. Greg was instantly hostile. 'You've really sold out, haven't you?' he said when Ross finished. 'What's it feel like, Dad, to abandon your last vestige of self-respect?'

'Actually, Greg, it feels good. Getting a full listing gives us access to a lot more capital, which means we can grow the business faster. We're planning on opening another fifty, maybe a hundred stores in the next three years if we can get the right locations. We should be in a position to bring good food to a lot more people for less. I'd have thought you'd have approved. We might start up overseas too. There's big opportunities in the new Eastern Bloc countries. Poland, the Czech Republic, maybe Slovenia.'

'You're an empire builder, Dad. A retail colonialist. Think about it. And what it means.'

Ross did his best to part on good terms, but it still niggled away at him a week later. He hated admitting this, but he didn't like Greg much at all.

26.

Miles read the announcement about the Freeza Mart flotation on the flight to Dubai. He and Serena had settled into adjacent First Class seats on the Emirates 747 when the stewards handed out newspapers. And there in the Lex column was the five-paragraph item: the Droitwich-based cash-and-carry retailer was seeking full public listing, underwritten by Nomura, at a target market cap of £320 million. Freeza Mart founder and CEO, Ross Clegg, 49, would see his personal stake valued at £105 million. Accordingly to the *Financial Times*, Clegg, who had homes in the West Midlands and in Hampshire, was a low-key workaholic and long-term supporter of Birmingham City football club. He was married to Dawn, 'who is involved in local charities,' with a son and two daughters.

Miles read the item twice, then turned to the news pages where the story was reported in greater detail. For a moment he couldn't focus on the words, having been knocked sideways by a wave of envy. So intense was it, so debilitating, he was unable to function. The steward offered a tray of champagne and he took two glasses, bolting them both. Then, semi-anaesthetised against the pain of the words, he forced himself to read about the remarkable Freeza Mart success story which had seen expansion from a single outlet to sixty-two in nineteen years, and was now rapidly gaining ground across the prosperous South of England. According to a spokesman for the British Retail Consortium, Freeza Mart was trading particularly strongly against Pendletons, the £8 billion high-end supermarket chain.

He felt sick. The news entirely ruined the flight. Every bit of pleasure he would otherwise have derived from his senatorial First Class seat and unlimited Dom Perignon and caviar was instantly curdled. He felt a hideous gnawing in the pit of his stomach, and waves of hot anger coursing up and down his arms. One hundred and five million pounds! Normally Miles was instinctively respectful of anyone who made serious capital, but in the case of Ross it was obscene. Repellent even. He couldn't imagine what people like the Cleggs would do with so much cash; it wasn't as though they owned racehorses or collected art, or even had private school fees to pay or a decent garden to maintain. He tried to watch a movie to take his mind off it, but the film about a million dollar bank robbery only made him think of Ross, who'd just become a hundred times richer than the thief in the film. Fresh humiliations occurred to him all the time: he was no longer the richest man in Chawbury. He wasn't even baby Mandy's richest grandfather. It was intolerable!

They landed at Dubai's International Airport where a white stretch limo had been sent by the Zach Durban organisation to deliver them to the resort. At one hundred storeys, it was the tallest new hotel in the Gulf with an Olympic-sized swimming pool and three helipads on the roof, and a thousand-berth marina at sea level.

A team of sixteen Straker Communications staff were already installed at the hotel, overseeing the three-day launch celebrations. Tonight, there was a gala dinner on the rooftop for 600 guests; tomorrow a convoy of Land Cruisers would drive the same guests into the desert for sand skiing and quad biking, followed by a lavish brunch at an oasis. They would later be airlifted back to the helipads by a flight of Durban Corporation helicopters.

Miles had personally approved every detail of the programme, as well as the one hundred and eighty British guests flown in for the opening, plus the several hundred others imported from Hong Kong, Singapore and South Africa. The British contingent comprised a press-friendly mixture of celebrity chefs, television newscasters, Members of Parliament and championship golf and motor racing stars. Following his usual principle of double-networking, he had also included several key clients from other Straker accounts, such as the chief executive of Trent Valley Power 4 U and his wife and kids, and marketing bosses from the sherry company and from Pendletons. Having also included his constituency MP, Ridley Nairn, and wife, Suzie, on the trip, Miles was being doubly cautious about Serena, arranging for his mistress to be given a single room of her own, further along the corridor from his suite.

Normally Miles would have been in his element. His people had done a good job with the organisation, Zach was satisfied, there were unrivalled networking opportunities at every turn and, furthermore, Serena was on-message. Thrilled to have escaped from her husband and son for a few days, she was prepared to go along with any subterfuge Miles deemed necessary. Miles, however, was far from content. The image of Ross kept playing on his mind. Bumping across the desert in a Land Cruiser he could think of nothing else; making love to Serena, he first lost momentum, then his erection as Ross's grotesque windfall seeped into his head.

To make matters worse, other guests on the trip kept mentioning it too.

'I say, your neighbour Ross Clegg's doing awfully well, according to the newspapers,' Ridley Nairn said. 'Do you think he'd be a good prospect for our local Tory Patrons Club?'

'I believe he votes socialist,' Miles replied.

'Really? Well, perhaps all the filthy lucre will change his mind.'

Later, Suzie Nairn said, 'I wish you hadn't told us not to go to Ross Clegg's shop opening in Andover, Miles. Everyone's saying he's enormous fun and very bright.'

'I wouldn't say so. Let me put it this way, he isn't exactly someone you'd choose to go on holiday with.'

'But God he's done well,' Suzie persisted. 'Apparently he's made *millions* from all his horrid frozen food.'

To add insult to injury, Serena was flicking through the channels on one of the four plasma TVs in Miles's suite and there was Ross being interviewed for the business slot on BBC World. He didn't come across particularly confidently, but there was something solid and self-deprecating about him that was impressive.

'So, what are you going to do with all the money then, Ross?' asked the interviewer. 'Any big plans for a celebration?'

'Sorry to disappoint you, but it won't change anything,' Ross replied. 'It's only on paper in any case. And I have outside shareholders to worry about, there'll be no time for playing silly buggers.'

27.

During the months leading up to the flotation, and for the first five months after it all went through without a hitch, Dawn gave the money hardly a second thought. Ross seldom referred to it, nor altered his routine in any way, and they never felt tempted to behave like one of those lottery winners you saw on TV, firing off champagne corks and buying sports cars. Dawn did, however, enjoy the comforting glow that having £35 million sitting on deposit in the bank inevitably brings, and the knowledge they had double that again in Freeza Mart shares. She fell into the habit of checking the share prices each morning in the newspaper and it was exciting to see it moving up and up, by a few pence every week. In the first six months as a Footsie-traded stock, Freeza Mart increased by 72p. Dawn couldn't work out what that meant to her and Ross personally, but she knew it was a lot.

To have become suddenly so wealthy, Dawn found hard to take in. It was too abstract an amount of money. If someone had handed her fifty thousand pounds in cash, she'd have found it easier to visualise and felt a lot richer. One weekend, Ross casually mentioned he'd paid off the mortgage on Chawbury Park and they no longer owed a penny to anyone. At around the same time, he announced he was going to buy a new flat for his mother up in Salford, round the corner from her present place, and he'd like to do something for Dawn's parents too, if she thought they'd like that. 'A cruise or a holiday or something. Maybe you could mention it to them, Dawn. We must put it to them in the right way, we don't want to cause offence.'

As the months passed and she became more accustomed to it all, Dawn began to think of improvements she would like to make to their home. Ross was so stretched all the time these days, it was

hard to talk to him properly; he still did his store visits every Saturday, driving all over the country, and often had to leave again
straight after Sunday lunch for a meeting up in town or to catch a
plane somewhere abroad. So it was largely left to Dawn to choose
the new swimming pool and oversee the contractors from a company named Blue Marine Pools and Leisure whose catalogue she
was sent through the post. Unable to decide between dozens of
designs in every shape and size, she eventually sat down with
Gemma and Debbie and they went for a lotus-shaped liner pool
with a pattern of stencilled dolphins on the bottom, which was
constantly refilled by an ornamental waterfall at the deep end.
They chose to site it directly outside the kitchen window, so whoever was standing at the sink could see what was going on in the
pool. With Mandy growing up at the speed she was—her second
birthday was looming—it would be safer as well as convenient.

The contractors from Blue Marine Pools and Leisure, having
given so many assurances about their efficiency and high standards, turned out to be shysters. Initially turning up with a lorry-
load of Poles, who dug a deep hole and trenches for pipe-work, they
then all but disappeared. Dawn spent hours tracking down the
foreman on his mobile, and listening to empty promises. Different
sets of subcontractors came and went, leaving their tasks half-
done. Boilers and filtration equipment never arrived. Dawn was
distraught. It worried her, too, that the muddy hole was closer to
the kitchen wall than she'd envisaged, but the foreman told her not
to worry since the coping stores and paving would make it look different when they were laid.

Probably the pool would never have been completed at all if
Ross hadn't taken control and got Freeza Mart's in-house legal
team to issue a blizzard of heavy letters. No letter was capable of
shifting the hole, however, which had certainly been dug eight feet
too near to the kitchen. For ever afterwards, the pool lapped almost up to the kitchen door; you could step straight off the pedal-
bin and into the water. Gemma and Debbie said they didn't care at
all, in fact they preferred it, because people could hand you Cokes
and snacks while you were swimming and you didn't need to get
out. But Dawn blamed herself for the disaster, and vowed never
again to allow a project to slip away from her control.

Her second project, which was an all-weather ménage for the horses, she managed meticulously, doing several months of homework and research before even contacting any contractors. She visited several different examples all over Hampshire, and was particularly impressed by the ménage Lady Pendleton had installed at Longparish Priory when the youngest Pendletons had got seriously into their riding. Like everything Laetitia did, it was in perfect taste with a hornbeam hedge around the fenced arena and a stable block with clock tower and mounting block. Dawn decided to model her own ménage as closely as possible on Laetitia's, though she did seek her permission first. 'Of course you can. Copy anything you like,' Laetitia said. 'I'd be flattered. In fact, I'm sure we have the plans put away somewhere, so you can work straight from them if that would be helpful.'

When Miles spotted work starting on the ménage, coming so soon after the ghastly swimming pool which he couldn't actually see from Chawbury Manor because it was on the other side of the house, but he'd heard all about from Mollie ('Dolphins indeed!'), he swiftly rang the council to see if they'd got planning consent and to his irritation found they had.

'Its awfully predictable,' he remarked to James Pendleton next time they met. 'The Cleggs are building for Britain at Chawbury, it's a non-stop spending spree. Ever since Ross floated the business. They've put in this unbelievably naff pool like a country club in Surrey. And now there's a fancy riding ring going in, can you believe?'

'Ah yes, I think Laetitia's been helping Dawn with that, giving her some advice.'

'I thought she must have been,' Miles said, quickly changing tack. 'It's all being beautifully done.'

Although the Pendletons and the Cleggs had by no means become close friends, or anything like it, Laetitia followed up on her promise to invite them to the Basingstoke summer festival, where they watched a performance of *Joseph and the Amazing Technicolour Dreamcoat* followed by supper in the festival restaurant. It had been a pleasant evening, with both couples enjoying the performance and Laetitia feeling they'd done their bit in supporting the local arts community, as well as showing friendship to their new neighbours. Laetitia understood that she and Dawn would never be entirely on the same wavelength, but she liked her brassiness and pluck and obvious desire to learn new things. James, who wasn't generally comfortable with new people, got on with her well too, and of course Ross and James had plenty to talk about, even though they both did their best to stay off the subject of retail. 'Now you two, *enough*,' Laetitia said once, when she felt the shop talk stepping up a bit. 'Let's talk about something we can *all* join in, shall we?'

In the car on the way home, James commented to his wife, 'That man's very smart. I rather wish he was working for *us*, not as a competitor.'

'Maybe you should make him an offer, darling?' Laetitia said. 'Or buy his company and bring him in to Pendletons.'

'I would too, if I thought there was a chance he'd accept. But he's not a chap who'd be easy to place, not in a mature business like ours. Too much of an entrepreneur: but he knows what he's doing, that's clear.'

Later that same summer, Ross and Dawn received a second invitation from the Pendletons, this time to buy tickets for a country house opera benefit of *The Magic Flute* to be held against the backdrop of the ruins of a Palladian country house. Ross was not remotely interested in going, and thought the seats at seventy-five pounds each were way over the top, but Dawn wanted to support it because Laetitia had been so kind to them. So they sent off for their expensive tickets and, several Saturday nights later, found themselves joining a picnic of six local couples around the boot of James Pendleton's Bentley.

Ross found the performance very trying. It wasn't his kind of thing at all, and he found himself quickly drifting off, revisiting the business plan for Freeza Mart's expansion into Holland. Dawn, on the other hand, adored everything about her first opera: the lovely costumes, the elegant music and setting, it all struck her as very refined and gracious. And James Pendleton was such a gentleman; in both intervals he explained to her what was going on in the plot, all the twists and turns, and showed her where a digest of the story was printed in the programme. So she really did feel, by the end of the evening, that she'd found a new interest and could easily get into this whole culture thing, if she only knew more about it.

Debbie Clegg's arrival at Mid-Hampshire College for Further Education made a decisive difference to Mollie's life there. For a start, it provided her with a permanent friend to have lunch with in the cafeteria and hang out with between lectures. Furthermore, Debbie was much better than Mollie at making friends around college, friends who became part of Mollie's circle too. It may partly have been their respective choice of courses which made things easier for Debbie. Mollie had combined her A level programme with a social studies and educational diploma, which was a foundation course for teacher training. It was a course which attracted an earnest crowd of wannabe academics and social workers, whom even Mollie conceded were heavy going. Debbie, however, was enrolled on a vocational course in Hospitality and Catering Management, where her classmates were would-be chefs and hoteliers and a lot more fun in every way.

Mollie and Debbie fell into a routine of catching the bus together into Andover each morning, unless Dawn was willing to drive them in, which she very often did. On those mornings, Mollie would be ready and looking out for the Cleggs in the kitchen at the manor which overlooked the front door, and hurry out as soon as she saw the black Cherokee coming up the drive. Mollie was aware from various derogatory things she'd heard Miles say that the Cleggs had recently come into money. Debbie never breathed a word about it, and Mollie wondered if she even knew. Certainly in the college café, both girls were as parsimonious as every other student, carefully paying for their own coffees and couscous.

Mollie found it fascinating, as she got to know Debbie better, how different she was in character to her older sister. Mollie had come to like Gemma a lot, and often visited her and baby Mandy on the way home from college, but had long ago realised Gemma was no brain-box. With her sweet, trusting face and passion for high street fashion and celebrity magazines, she was affectionate and ditsy. So far as Mollie could tell, all she did all day was play with Mandy in the living room end of the kitchen, always with the television on in the background. Gemma was a devotee of soaps and reality programmes, regularly texting to vote on *Pop Idol* and *I'm a Celebrity*, which Mollie considered a ridiculous waste of money. In summer, Gemma swam in the new pool outside the kitchen window, but otherwise seldom left the house. Mollie noticed she still frequently asked how Archie was, and seemed downcast when told he'd gone to university in Bristol.

Debbie, by contrast, reminded Mollie of Ross. She had her father's compact and wiry frame, though you had to say she was pretty too. Unlike Gemma or Dawn, she had no interest in make-up or boys; athletic and sporty, she still rode every weekend and most evenings in summer. She also played netball twice a week for Mid-Hampshire College and went kayaking with the college canoe club. All this was a revelation to Mollie, who hadn't realised you could do sport at the college at all.

Despite her multitude of extra-curricular activities, Mollie also saw what a conscientious student Debbie was. At a college at which almost no pressure was placed on anyone to deliver any assignment on time, or even to produce it at all, she was never late with project work. She was impressively well organised with the course notes for her various modules meticulously ordered in multi-coloured files. And she seemed genuinely enthusiastic about her studies, announcing she wanted to work in a hotel when she graduated, and absorbed by the lectures on portion control, food hygiene and bar management. As the first summer vacation loomed, Debbie said she had written off to several luxury hotels asking for an unpaid holiday job. 'They probably won't bother replying, but I may as well try.'

Mollie was impressed, and also a little jealous since she'd talked about getting a holiday job herself, but Miles had vetoed the idea when he realised it would mean her missing the annual family holiday in Porto Ercole.

'Have you told your parents about your job?' Mollie asked.

'That's if I even get one,' Debbie said, 'which I most probably wont. But yeah, I have. Dad said no problem, go for it. Mum wasn't so keen, but she doesn't like the idea of me working in hotels, period. She says its menial.'

'My dad put the kybosh on me doing a holiday job at all. He's so weird like that. He rents this villa in Italy every August and we all have to go, there's no choice, we *have* to be there the whole time.'

'I heard Mum talking about your holiday,' Debbie said. 'Your mum was telling my mum about it and she was really envious. She was on at Dad about it for hours, about how the Strakers go abroad on this big family holiday every year, and how we never go any-where. She wanted Dad to rent a place too, she got all these bro-chures of places in Spain and Greece and was going through them. But Dad's not interested. He's too busy with all the new stores they're doing. They had this big barney about it. Mum was saying, 'What's the point of making all this money, Ross, if we never doing anything with it?'

28.

Each time Dawn saw Laetitia she hero-worshipped her a little more. And since Laetitia had invited her to join a group of ladies committed to bringing cultural events to Hampshire state schools, Dawn had the opportunity to study her on a regular basis.

Once a month, a select committee of women congregated at Longparish Priory to discuss which opera or ballet companies, poets or theatre groups might be invited to perform in inner-city secondary schools in Basingstoke and Southampton, where pupils might otherwise never be exposed to the higher performing arts. It was an initiative about which Laetitia was determinedly passionate, seeing it as her personal vehicle for 'giving back,' as she put it. 'If we can inspire *one single pupil* to consider a career in the creative arts, we will have more than justified our efforts,' she liked to say. Although her initiative was, by intention, kept totally separate from the many cultural programmes sponsored corporately by Pendletons, Laetitia was nevertheless shrewd about inviting many of the same artists, already supported by a Pendletons bursary, to perform *pro bono* for her culturally-deprived school kids.

Dawn was thrilled when Laetitia asked her to join the group, and struck by how different it was from her other charitable committee meetings at Stockbridge House. Laetitia's group was at once more intense and more elegant. At Philippa Mountleigh's house, the cheerful and profane county women regularly arrived late for meetings, or needed to leave early, and devoted much of their time to local gossip and eating Philippa's chocolate digestive and ginger nut biscuits. At Laetitia's meetings, which were held in the library at Longparish Priory with pads and pencils laid out in readiness, none of the committee would have dared arrive late, nor stray from the businesslike agenda. Invariably charming and self-effacing in everyday life, Laetitia became rather serious when chairing her committee. And the members themselves, comprising a mixture of smart neighbours and worthy representatives of county education and arts trusts, would not have risked introducing a flicker of levity. At the conclusion of each meeting the Pendletons' butler, Lagdon, always appeared with a tray of glasses of champagne and a jug of elderflower cordial, and elaborate canapés made by the Pendletons' chef. None of the committee felt it quite appropriate at midday in midweek when they had to drive themselves home to choose a glass of champagne, so each took a glass of elderflower. Dawn, longing for champagne, found it torture. Nor did she feel she could take more than one of the exquisite canapés, so most of the tiny foie gras on fried bread squares and miniature *oeufs en gelés* went back to the kitchen uneaten.

The meetings gave her a chance to study the house, which fascinated her more and more. There was a serenity and perfection to Longparish Priory and Dawn noticed everything, and tried to work out what it was that made it feel so gracious. For a start, there were flowers everywhere, in the hall, in the library, in the drawing room, that was surely part of it; six or more cachepots and vases on every surface of orchids and lilies, and bowls of hyacinths and silver jugs filled with white roses. The entire house was infused with the scent of flowers. And everything was so clean, without a speck of dust or a glass ring on any surface. And the modern paintings, some of which Dawn was gradually coming round to, were beautifully framed and lit. Until now, she had preferred elaborate frames around pictures, old fashioned and fancy and gilded bright gold, but here the mounts and frames were simple and unfussy. Another thing she noticed were the little sculptures everywhere on the tables and bookcases. There were some really modern ones made out of bronze, but also Greek and Roman statues of heads, and even some *without* heads, all mingled together. It was quite effective, she decided, though she didn't know what Ross would make of it, he hated bric-a-brac.

Everything at the Pendletons' was so nicely done; even if it was just her and Laetitia sat there for a coffee, a tray was brought in with a cloth on it and a percolator and china coffee cups, and little jugs of cream and milk—you got given the choice—and little silver bowls of sugar cubes, brown sugar crystals and sachets of sugar substitute on a saucer (Laetitia never took sugar). And upstairs in Laetitia's bathroom there were six bottles of Floris on a glass shelf and the whole room was so pretty and fresh, with a lovely rose fabric on a little chair, all smelling of rose geranium bath essence. Where Laetitia and James kept their shampoos and toothpastes and the usual bathroom gunge, Dawn had no idea. She thought of her own master bathroom with its half-used Silvikrin and Pantene bottles, and the big plastic toothmugs full of old toothbrushes, and Ross's roll-on deodorants and aftershaves all over the place, and it felt like a different planet.

Arriving home after each meeting, she found herself increasingly dissatisfied with Chawbury Park. Seeing it now through what she thought of as Laetitia's eyes, she knew she'd have done the place differently if she was doing it again today. Even the features she'd been particularly pleased with, such as the pearl grey and silver-veined kitchen worktops and the carpets they'd chosen for some of the rooms—all the rooms in fact—now seemed not quite right. She would like to have invited James and Laetitia over for a meal, but felt uneasy about what Laetitia would make of their place. One morning, waking abruptly, she found she'd been dreaming about the Pendletons perched on the black leather settee in the day room, eating supper from a tray with the TV on, and the thought of it made her cringe.

The next time she was up visiting Davina, she found herself starting to look at the Manor more critically too. She noticed the many similarities between Davina's style of decorating and Laetitia's style, for instance the wide floorboards covered by old rugs, and the flagstoned hallway with its big, worn slabs. When she had first visited the Strakers, she'd considered the flagstones cold and gloomy, and would have covered them over completely with fitted carpets had it been her own place. Growing up in Solihull, the idea of fitted wall-to-wall carpets underfoot had been the ultimate luxury, and in their previous home in Droitwich she had finally achieved that ambition. But now she found herself regretting the fitted carpets at Chawbury Park, and even the marble floor in their hall.

At the same time she felt the Strakers' house, which had hitherto struck her as impossibly posh with its glazed-chintz curtains and settee covers and paintings everywhere, was less perfect than she'd remembered. The ceiling in the drawing room in which she and Ross had had their distressing encounter with Miles and Davina, after Archie had got poor Gemma pregnant, appeared to have lowered by a couple of feet, and the walls moved closer together. In fact, Chawbury Manor seemed to have shrunk. And the bookshelves in Miles's study were full of leatherbound sets by Charles Dickens and Sir Walter Scott, which didn't look like they'd ever been read, whereas the Pendletons' floor-to-ceiling bookcases were filled with novels, biographies and the stout white spines of art volumes.

When she attempted to explain some of this to Ross, and how she wished now they'd laid flagstones in the hall rather than marble, he became quite annoyed. 'Well, you chose marble. That's what you said you wanted, love, and it cost an arm and a leg. And very nice it is too. No way are we ripping it all up, so you can forget about that.'

Dawn loved and admired her husband dearly, but sometimes he was exasperating. He was so stubborn and work-obsessed, he didn't see things half the time; it was all work, work, work, Freeza Mart, Freeza Mart, Freeza Mart. Recently she'd realised there was so much more to life, and Ross just didn't get it.

Driving back from Longparish Priory with Strauss's *Der Rosenkavalier* at full blast on the CD (Dawn was educating herself on opera, mugging up on the ones the committee was bringing to inner city schools), she had a brainwave. The business of the decoration of Chawbury Park, and the various mistakes she'd made, was getting to her, and Ross was completely unsympathetic. If she so much as mentioned changing anything at all, he was instantly opposed, claiming to like everything exactly as it was and refusing to alter a single thing.

Dawn's brainwave was that she wouldn't bother saying anything to Ross, she'd just go for it and get the job done anyway. She was sure he'd be chuffed when it was finished. And it wasn't as if they couldn't afford it. Furthermore, she knew exactly the person to help her: Serena Harden, who she'd heard was desperate for decorating jobs, and people said was very professional in her approach.

So it was that only a few days later Serena and Dawn were cloistered together at the kitchen table at Chawbury Park, having inspected every room in the house, upstairs and down, and found themselves getting on like a house on fire. Already Dawn's head was buzzing with good ideas Serena had suggested, and she was encouraged by how simple Serena made everything sound. Nor did Serena reckon it need all be ruinously expensive; for instance flagstones could be laid straight on top of the marble, without taking the marble up, and floorboards battened over the concrete skree in the living room. She agreed with Dawn they should do away with slatted wooden binds in the bedrooms and order proper curtains, for which Serena would get started on sourcing fabric samples. She recommended taking Dawn up to town to the Design Centre at Chelsea Harbour, where all the top fabric suppliers had shops-within-shops, and they could probably make all their decisions in a couple of days, once they knew what they were looking for. When Serena questioned her new client about her taste, all Dawn could think to say was that she liked the way Davina Straker and Laetitia Pendleton did their homes and she'd like hers as much like theirs as possible please.

After the coffees, they went outdoors and walked round the outside of the house, where Serena had thoughts on how the windows might be improved. She was particularly helpful about the velux windows in the roof and the plate glass panorama windows onto the lawn, which had been the devil to install and required eight workmen. She had an idea that traditional sash windows could be built off-site and simply slotted in, with minimum fuss or reconstruction.

Dawn led her to the pergola at the end of the lawn, which was her favourite place to sit with a white wine, since it offered views up the entire valley. Serena was very interested to see the Strakers' house from this particular angle. Naturally she was careful not to overpraise it to her new client, whom she'd quickly sussed had the potential to keep her in work for months and months, if not years. She had liked Dawn from the first moment they'd met, but seeing her today, in this new relationship, she realised she lacked confidence, and was jaw-droppingly unsophisticated. As such—and having a very rich husband—she promised to be a welcome client indeed.

'That's Chawbury Manor up there on the hill,' Dawn said, noticing Serena's line of vision. 'I think you met our friends the Strakers at Mandy's baptism.'

Serena agreed that she had indeed met the Strakers.

'Davina's become a very close personal friend,' Dawn couldn't resist saying, anxious to impress her smart new decorator. 'I'm in and out of the manor all day long.'

The turn of the conversation began to make Serena feel uncomfortable, since she knew Miles's opinion of the Cleggs. In fact, she had been wondering how to tell him she was working for Dawn, and whether she even needed to. It embarrassed her, too, that she'd been there when Miles had placed the derogatory story with Nigel Dempster about Gemma's baby.

'Davina's such a lovely lady,' Dawn went on. 'We co-chaired a garden function at the manor last year, you know. And then there's Miles, such a brilliant man, everyone says.' She looked briefly troubled. 'Well, I can't say I know Miles as well as I know Davina. I find him a little bit difficult, to tell the truth.'

Serena, who had her own reasons to agree, smiled noncommittally. 'All men are tricky, some of the time.'

'Tell me about it,' agreed Dawn, who was already worried about Ross's reaction to her covert house makeover, before it had even begun.

29.

aving obtained his Doctorate from the London School of Economics, Greg considered what he might do next. His first thought had been a career as an academic, which he was well placed to pursue, having obtained a First in his degree course and kudos for his PhD. His analysis of the Vietnamese economy in the decades following the war of 1963–75 was enthusiastically received by his tutors for its depth of research and pervasive anti-American sentiment, and he could certainly have found tenure at half a dozen universities had he wished. Greg was certainly tempted. He called on contacts at Birmingham Aston University and at Leeds, both of whom encouraged him to put his name forward. Something, however, made him hesitate; he saw too easily how an academic career might unfold—the scholarly papers and, if he was lucky, a book meanly published by a university publishing house, and the lectures and tutorials with students who were seldom enthralled by the subject they had chosen.

He toyed with entering the research department of an investment bank, and actually called on the Human Resources department at Goldman Sachs (you could not call it an interview since he had not formally applied, but the fearsomely smart Dutch woman he talked to was not discouraging, saying his research credentials in South East Asia could well be useful to them). However, when she mentioned the starting compensation would be in the region of £55,000, which was almost triple the starting salary for an academic, Greg backed off, refusing to sell out and become a cog in the wheel of an über-capitalist organisation.

He moved into a flat in Hammersmith with two ex-college mates, and took a part-time part-paid job at the local Labour headquarters on Greyhound Road, stuffing mailers into envelopes and helping establish a website for the borough council Labour group. Despite identifying his co-workers in the office as both incompetent and insufficiently committed, he nevertheless became absorbed by the political manoeuvring around the constituency party and council, in what was an intensely marginal seat. During the dark days of Thatcherism, Fulham and Hammersmith had been won by the Tories, though they had been swept out during the glorious 1997 counter-revolution by New Labour. The council, however, remained under Tory control by a majority of three seats. Greg considered this a scandal of gerrymandering, since it was only the prosperous wards around Parson's Green and the newly gentrified streets off Hammersmith Grove and Brook Green which had swung it for the Conservatives; in the past, these brick terraces would have been solidly occupied by the working class they'd been built for, Labour voters all, and it was the capitalist pressure of rising house prices that had skewed the demographic mix of the neighbourhood; that, anyway, was the gist of Greg's nightly harangues to his co-workers in the pub at the end of Greyhound Road. Greg had the answer to everything, being able to spot a big business or media conspiracy a mile off.

As far as his family was concerned, Greg was content to keep them at arm's length. Ross did his best to stay in touch, regularly ringing his son from the car on Saturday mornings when he was driving between store visits. In fact, these calls were a source of tension between them. Ross would listen to the ringing tone in the flat, leaving it to ring on and on until it was grumpily answered by a half-asleep flatmate. 'You *couldn't* still be in bed,' Ross would tell Greg. 'I've been up five hours already. I'm on the dual-carriageway between Chester and Stoke.'

Which was all it took to set them off: almost by reflex, Greg would mutter disparagingly about profit-driven capitalism, and Ross become testy, and the conversation would be riven with antagonism. When Greg first left the LSE, Ross invited his son to live with him in Roupell Street—there was a second bedroom and it would save on rent. Greg declined and it irked Ross at the time, who couldn't see the sense. Now he felt relieved. On the infrequent weekends when Greg consented to come down to Chawbury, there was generally a flare-up between father and son, or between Greg and Dawn, or sometimes all three: Greg had an ability to make both parents feel prickly. He could not visit Chawbury Park without criticising its size and amenities. Noticing Ross had installed a home car wash with power spray and several different settings, he was sarcastic: 'I see you don't have time to use a bucket and sponge.' And he was fierce about the swimming pool, with all the oil and chemicals it took to maintain it.

But the largest part of his contempt was reserved for the Strakers on the hill. He knew Miles was an influential Tory ('One of their inner circle of spin doctors, not that they're a patch on our lot') and made a point of glaring up the valley at the manor, and grimacing.

The fact that his parents' own house was 1,700 square feet larger than the Strakers' place was just one of the inconvenient crosses he had to bear in life.

Mollie left Mid-Hampshire College at the end of her course announcing she wished to become a schoolteacher. Specifically, she wanted to teach in the state sector helping kids from disadvantaged backgrounds, and she had already sussed out the various teacher training colleges which would be her next step.

Miles was instinctively opposed to his younger daughter's choice, having long-held opinions about the quality of comprehensive teachers who were perpetually off sick and refused to supervise sport, even assuming there were any playing fields left after dynamic New Labour had sold them all off. ('New' Labour was another phrase he never used without metaphorical inverted commas.) On the other hand, he had agreed to join a Tory think tank on education, with a brief to bolster manifesto policy, and it occurred to him that having a daughter actually working at the sharp end, out in the field, would boost his credentials. And so he did not discourage her, and even agreed to pay her share of the rent on the flat she planned to take with three other trainee teachers in Olympia, which Miles chose to call West Hammersmith since it sounded better. If truth be told, it rather suited Miles to have Mollie safely billeted in a student flat in Olympia, and not parked in Holland Park Square with him, where she would doubtless have been more underfoot than her elder sister whom Miles scarcely clapped eyes on from one week to the next. Recently, on a Monday evening, when Davina was safely down at Chawbury, and Conception out at some Catholic church service at St Francis of Assisi in Pottery Lane, and Samantha God knows where with the beau of the moment, Miles had done something he'd never previously risked, namely making love with Serena in the Holland Park Square house in his and Davina's own bed. Afterwards he regretted his recklessness, because it had crossed a line. But Serena had become available to join him at late notice for dinner in London and, afterwards, feeling suddenly horny, he had rung Claridges to see if they had a room, and then the Berkeley, and drawn a double blank. Both hotels were full to capacity for Chelsea Flower Show week. Feeling uncomfortable ringing hotel after hotel from the back of the car, with Makepiece driving them and no doubt listening to every word, and Serena resting her hand on his cock through his trousers, Miles had said, 'Just drop us at Holland Park Square please, Makepiece. Mrs Harden will get a taxi home later, so don't bother waiting round.' Thus they had ended up in the marital bed in the bedroom with three sash windows overlooking the communal garden, which was something Miles had vowed never to allow to happen. Straight after he'd come, he'd wanted to ring a cab and kick her out, already worrying how he'd be able to extricate her in the morning; he had a breakfast meeting to go to, and Conception was up and about by eight in any case. One of her first duties was to arrange the morning newspapers on the hall table. For someone ostensibly so holy, Miles considered Conception a beady little gossip, who might easily consider it her duty to report any overnight guest to Davina. His discomfort increased further when Serena insisted on having a leisurely bath in the marital bathroom next morning, making free with Davina's toiletries and giant loofah.

'I've wanted to do that for so long,' she said, as Miles stood over her, urging her to hurry up.

'Do what?'

'Sleep with you all night in a proper bed. Not a hotel one, I mean. It feels different, much nicer.'

'Yes, well, if you could just keep moving Serena, I have a breakfast to go to.'

'You don't have to wait for me. I can see myself out.'

'No, better if we leave together. And we need to be out of here in five minutes.' He was thinking about the double hazard of Conception lurking in the hall, and Makepiece parked outside the front door. He felt like a prisoner in his own home.

But Serena would not be hurried. Stretching out in Floris-scented water, she said, 'I do like those houses across the garden. With the pediments and pillars. They look wider than the others in the square.'

'They are. One of them was lived in by the speculator who built the square in the first place. Its all flats now. The other one's a refuge for battered women or something, they're not allowed into the garden.'

'How mean. Why ever not?'

'God, Serena, you sound exactly like my daughter Mollie. She's always banging on about them too. Anyway, out of that bath. I mean it, we really do have to go.'

Mollie knew that, in teaching, she had found her true vocation. She found it extraordinarily fulfilling, in a way that nothing had come close to before. All the theoretical side—to do with children's human rights and best practice in the classroom—interested her greatly, and she only wished her own teachers had adhered to the new legislation on the mental bullying of minors and appropriate teacher-pupil interaction. However, it was the practical side of teaching which she found most rewarding. As part of the training programme, she was attached to an ethnically-diverse comprehensive close to her flat where she assisted in the classroom two afternoons a week. On her first afternoon, the head teacher told her they had pupils of twenty-eight different ethnic origins, who spoke thirty-three different languages at home, and that English was the first language of only a third of the intake. It was a school categorised as 'failing' by a recent Ofsted report. When Miles heard which one it was, he gleefully informed her, having had it checked up on, that it was the worst sink comprehensive in West London. 'If I were you, Mollie, I'd carry a gun. You can be damn sure most of your pupils do.'

Undeniably there were serious discipline problems—knives, drugs, endemic truancy, violence against staff, Mollie learnt more about the evils of the real world in her first six weeks of teaching that in her whole previous life—but this only made the challenge, and the satisfaction when she felt she had made a difference, all the greater. Of course, you could not expect miracles. She measured her achievement in small things: the Albanian pupil who had arrived at school without a word of English three months earlier, who learnt to count from one to twenty; the aggressive bipolar Maltese boy, unable to socialise with other kids, who worked in a team to help create a wall collage using special blunted scissors; the painfully introverted Bengali girl who sang a little song at Diwali at the front of class.

For Mollie, the home lives of her pupils were a revelation, or rather, in so many cases, the absence of any settled home life. Alternatively despondent and exasperated by what she saw, she veered between determination to help more and realism about the futility of doing so. She had been unprepared for the depth and prevalence of poverty. Having been brought up hearing her father rail against dependency culture, and how the impetus to work had been removed by state handouts, the indignity of poverty shocked her. She began to view the city through new eyes; she had seldom previously noticed the numerous charity shops which occupied the cheaper locations, or the pound stores where everything on the shelves was priced at a quid, or the gimcrack supermarket chains—CostCutters and PennySavers—where the parents of her pupils shopped. There was an enormous new Pendletons behind the Olympia Exhibition Centre, where Mollie out of habit did her own weekly shop, but she never ran into any of her school kids in the aisles, even though they lived all around. When Freeza Mart opened a Hammersmith store in King Street, she transferred her loyalty there instead.

As summer approached, she had an idea of hiring a coach and taking a bunch of children, and their parents as well if they wanted to come, to Chawbury for the day for a picnic. She mentioned it to her mother and Davina thought it was a lovely idea, but did wonder what Miles would think and whether he'd approve. In the end, Mollie didn't even bother asking. She could easily imagine his sarcastic comments about slum children tearing about the garden and, on reflection, Mollie wasn't sure she really wanted the other teachers to know about her home life.

30.

The man Samantha had been seeing off and on for the past four months, who did not advertise himself as her boyfriend but with whom she made love whenever he bought her dinner, was spending the weekend in Dorset with a bunch of old mates but had not invited Sam to join him. That was the nature of their relationship: they shared beds but few friends, they shared fun times but did not envisage those fun times leading to anything more enduring. The man, Nigel, who traded commodities such as sugar and sunflower oil for a big American company based at the Royal Exchange, was forty-two years old and Sam had met him through her previous man, Peter, the one who worked in commercial property and first took her to Annabel's, who was one of Nigel's best mates.

Faced with the prospect of a weekend with nothing planned, Sam considered going home to Chawbury. She had not actually been to Hampshire for three months at least, probably four, and it was tempting. Her bedroom at Chawbury Manor was comfortable and frilly, full of the pop posters and gymkhana rosettes of her childhood, and she would be able to sleep until lunchtime; there would be three delicious meals in the dining room (four if she arrived on Friday evening) with drinks and wine and everything done for her; furthermore, and not unimportantly, the weekend would be absolutely cost-free, especially if she took a lift down with Peter in his car. Recently she was skint. She was so overdrawn she could barely withdraw cab money from an ATM. The last time she'd tried it had flagged up 'Insufficient Funds' and refused to pay out. Another attraction of returning home would be the chance of a top-up from her father, if she caught him in the right mood. If she agreed to go out riding with him, that was generally the opportunity, when he was feeling most squirarchical and indulgent.

Against this, Samantha had two reasons for reluctance to return home. The first was the question of her employment. One the rare occasions she passed Miles on the stairs at Holland Park Square, he commented on her lack of a job and asked what she was doing about getting one. He had threatened to find her one himself, either at Straker Communications or with one of their clients, if she didn't find something herself and sharpish. The whole concept of work was a pain. She had actually gone to see some old bat at Harvey Nichols, who was located in a personnel office above the restaurants on the top floor, and been given a form to fill out about her qualifications and experience. The interview hadn't gone too well, Sam felt, and the pay didn't seem much considering you had to be there from 8:30 a.m. until 6 p.m. and only got 20 days holiday a year. It hardly seemed worth it.

The pace of her social life became ever more frantic. She went out five or six nights a week, seldom returning home until the small hours if she returned at all. Recently she'd spent quite a bit of time over at Nigel's place in Ennismore Mews South. She was capable of occupying her days without effort or activity yet considered herself overstretched. She could take a hot bath and make it last from lunch to teatime. She spent fifteen minutes brushing her teeth twice every day, and almost as long brushing her hair. Her make-up routine, before she went out for the evening, was also very time-consuming, though she hardly needed to bother, being naturally beautiful. Her figure was amazing, with perfect posture and a good bum from years of riding. She had a perpetual shine about her, except in the mornings when she could scarcely function. Her mind was capable of drifting off when people were talking to her; she gave the impression, however, of listening intently, and this was extremely flattering to men. Both Nigel and Peter loved the way she listened to their business problems.

Samantha's second hesitation about a weekend at Chawbury also concerned her father. She had never alluded to seeing him at Annabel's draped over Serena Harden; nor had Miles referred to it, though Sam thought he must have spotted her. She had spent the remainder of dinner that evening ducking her head, and soon afterwards Miles had directed Serena to the Buddha room at the other end of the club. In the ensuing months, Sam wondered about the state of her parents' marriage. Having never previously given it a moment's consideration, she began to notice his frequent trips overseas and the many weekends spent away from home. And Conception had twice mentioned that her father was not expected in London on a particular Monday night, when Davina had clearly said he would be coming up. All this made her watchful. Had she known for sure Miles was unfaithful, she would not have blamed him but her mother, for choosing to live in the country and spending too much time gardening and painting.

Her relationship with her siblings was similarly estranged. Peter always struck her as weird in any case, and their paths did not cross in London; they inhabited parallel universes. When Miles criticised his elder son for being disengaged at Straker Communications, and not attending enough client events in the evenings, Samantha took her father's side. 'God, Peter, *I'd* go to your parties if they invited me. You're so lucky.'

'You're welcome, Sam. There's a fiesta of Spanish tapas and sherry in the Regent Arcade tonight, if you want to go along. I'm supposed to be there. And a cocktail party to launch pan-Asian Gourmet Week at Zach Durban's hotel.'

With an insatiable appetite for socialising, Sam found Peter's reluctance pitiful. Similarly, whenever Mollie came round to Holland Park Square, which she didn't often, Sam sensed her disapproval and was annoyed by it. What grounds did Mollie have for patronising her? She looked at her younger sister and felt pity and embarrassment. She made so little of herself, her clothes were terrible and so was her hair. When Mollie spoke breathlessly about her teaching job and tried to engage Sam with tales of the Albanian and Bengali kids she was so absorbed by, Sam felt a shutter of indifference coming down. Mollie's dispatches meant nothing to her, nor was she interested. The only one of her siblings she had time for was Archie, and he was away at Bristol. Archie was a laugh. Last time he'd been home at Chawbury, he'd brought three friends back from university including some girl he was clearly shagging. It was great he'd put all that hassle about Gemma Clegg and the baby behind him. Girls like Gemma should be shot.

In the end, it was the prospect of spending the weekend with Peter and Mollie, both of whom would apparently be at Chawbury too, which made Sam decide to remain in London, on her own, in Holland Park Square. So she announced she had a party to go to, and that was that. Miles was slightly put out, since there were things he wished to discuss with her, but of all people he understood the importance of putting parties before family.

Having taken a stand about staying up in London to attend a party which did not exist, Sam felt rather deflated and at a loose end. She rang her usual gang of friends but, for one reason or another, all were busy or away. She dialled an ex-boyfriend but his phone was answered by a strange female and she rang off. She left messages on answering machines but nobody called back. Fleetingly she imagined the scene at Chawbury Manor, with the family bathed and changed and assembled for drinks before dinner in the drawing room, and began to regret not being down there herself. Revisiting her address book for names she'd rejected calling first time round, she rang a guy she'd met out clubbing, Gaz Paul, and he said, 'Yeah, sure, come over, there's a crowd of people here.' In the background she heard laughter and music.

She took a cab to an address in Drayton Gardens, a flat in a mansion block on a thoroughfare of Victorian houses. Gaz let her in and there were eight or nine people sprawled about on sofas or on the floor. There were bottles of wine everywhere, all empty, and saucers as ashtrays. 'The booze has run out,' Gaz said, 'but at least there's plenty of weed.' A reefer was passed in her direction and she took a long drag; she liked the sensation, which made her mellow and relaxed. After the frenetic hours she'd spent looking for social stimulation, it felt good to be chilling out at Gaz's place, not doing anything, just hanging. It was a cooler scene than she was accustomed to, which made her self-conscious. When cocaine appeared, she tried that too. All of a sudden, she felt courageous and full of energy which was a revelation.

Before she went home at 3:30 a.m., Gaz said, 'Hey, Sam, you hoovered up that coke, babe, I was watching you.'

'It was. . . . great.'

'Yeah, you liked it, babe. When you need more, you know where to come.'

31.

Ross became accustomed to returning home after a week in London and finding some dramatic alteration to his house. The first surprise had been flouncy silk curtains across the four big windows in the hall, with a verdant pattern of purple verbena and pink carnations, with pelmets and braided fringes and tasselled cords.

'What the Dickens are these doing, Dawn?' he asked. 'I thought we had blinds in the entrance hall.'

Gingerly, Dawn admitted what she had not previously told him, that Serena was helping redecorate—or rather 'updating'—some of the rooms. 'Just a few touches to make it more liveable.'

'I liked it well enough before. And we only just moved in, never mind "updating."'

But Dawn assured him it was all necessary. 'I just don't think we got it all quite right first time round. Serena thinks that too.'

'I'll bet she does,' Ross said. 'Is she helping out as a favour, or are we paying her for her services?'

'Ross, she's a *professional lady*, of course we're paying her. But she only keeps the difference between retail and wholesale, which she gets as a decorator, so it doesn't cost us much at all. Only her time.'

A couple of weekends later, elaborate new curtains appeared at the drawing room windows, along with new sofas and armchairs, making the room feel fuller.

'It's like a ruddy furniture shop in here,' Ross said. 'I feel I'm in DFS. And what's happened to our picture? The one above the fireplace of the forest?'

'Serena didn't think it went with the new sofa covers. It wasn't a very nice painting anyway.'

'You liked it when you chose it. Debenhams in the Bull Ring, I remember us buying it. And where did this new one appear from, whatever it's of? Three Kit-Kats on a saucer, it looks like.'

Dawn smiled patiently. 'It's an abstract, Ross. It's not meant to be *of* anything.'

It was when their old House of Fraser bed with leather head-board—a bed Ross had always particularly liked and found comfortable, and in which their two younger children had been conceived—was removed without warning and replaced by a silk-draped four-poster with yellow ruched silk canopy, that Ross finally flipped.

'I *cannot* sleep in that thing. No way. It's like something what's-her-name, Sleeping Beauty, and Prince Charming would kip down on. If anyone thought I slept in something like that, I'd be a laughing stock. Get it out of here. And bring back our old one.'

Dawn looked pained. 'It's already been carried upstairs to Greg's room. I though it would be nice for him having a bigger bed at his age.'

'Well, fetch it back please. And Greg doesn't need a bigger bed, he scarcely ever comes here. He hasn't visited for months. I can't remember when he was last down.'

'He says he's very occupied with all his politics,' Dawn said. 'I called him up Wednesday, but he said he was too busy to speak for long.'

'I wish he'd find himself a job. A proper paid one, I mean. It's all very fine this messing about at the Labour Club, but he needs to get stuck in to something.'

Hurt by her husband's negative reaction to the new decorations, and wondering what to do with the four-poster if Ross refused to sleep in it, Dawn was inclined to support Greg for once. 'If you gave him a job at Freeza Mart that would solve it. Surely there's something he can do at your office?'

'Dawn, you are speaking about one of the most obtuse, anti-business young guys in the country. Why would I want him working in my company?'

'Well, I think you're very mean. James and Laetitia's son Hugo works for his dad at Pendletons and is doing very well there apparently. They're training him up.'

'If I thought Greg had the slightest interest, never mind aptitude, I'd be only too willing to give him a shot. But he doesn't. To hear him talk, he'd like to shut down all the supermarkets, ours included, not work for one.'

Dawn sighed. Ross was very difficult, he was such a stick-in-the-mud. As she saw it, they had so many opportunities opening up to them now as a couple—to live nicely and enjoy the rewards—but he didn't seem bothered. He just wanted to keep his head down, slogging away. It was particularly disappointing since Dawn had another ambitious plan, which she'd not yet dared tell Ross about because she knew he'd be negative. But she was determined to get her way on this one. She'd already started looking into it.

It was when Samantha began dating Dick Gunn, the eighteen-stone group chief executive of private equity investors the Gunn Partnership, who was only two years younger than her father, that Miles and Davina started worrying.

Davina instinctively felt the thirty-two-year age gap was much too big, and wished Sam spent time with friends closer to her own age. She hadn't met Dick Gunn, but his photograph regularly appeared in the newspapers, and she couldn't see anything beyond his big blubbery face, full lips and the brutally wide pinstripes of his suits. Sam hadn't even told them she was seeing him; Miles spotted a paragraph about it in the *Evening Standard* Londoner's Diary—'Gunn's silver bullet'—with a picture of them together at some party. Sam looked like a waif in tight white jeans and sequinned top, enveloped by Gunn's enormous bearhug.

At that time, it was impossible to open the financial pages without reading about the Gunn Partnership. Backed by Dutch and Qatari money, they specialised in acquiring underperforming public companies, taking them private, slashing staff and overhead, inserting their own puppet managements, then refloating the businesses a few years later, always at a massive premium. In the past fifteen years, Gunn's jowly features had been seen toasting the acquisition of web-offset printing companies, office rental businesses, employment agencies, a motorcycle factory, a budget hotel and tavern chain, and a high street fashion retailer. In his many interviews he was invariably described as a 'larger than life character.' The photograph most commonly used showed him, massively obese, gnawing at a cold chicken leg in the members carpark at Ascot, during a picnic alongside his silver Bristol.

Miles, it so happened, had twice become indirectly embroiled with Dick, when the Gunn Partnership targeted businesses retained by Straker Communications. Miles had been involved in the defence strategy for his clients, lobbying PMs and ministers and fabricating anti-Gunn stories for the business press. It had, in fact, been Miles who had sourced the photograph taken in the Ascot carpark, intended to project an image of a greedy, self-indulgent corporate raider. It disappointed him when both his clients succumbed to the takeovers, since he'd lost two good accounts as a result.

The idea that his beautiful twenty-year-old daughter was virtually shacked up with the fat asset stripper first irritated and then, as time went by and they were still together, enraged him. What the hell did she see in him? Dick Gunn looked older than Miles himself, a lot older in fact. The thought of this gross businessman copulating with Samantha played on his mind. 'Is my daughter home, Conception?' he asked his Filippina maid each morning, as he left the house.

Conception looked uncomfortable. 'I'm not sure Mr Straker. I think maybe she don't come home just yet.'

Then Miles would explode, and spend the day finding fault with his secretaries and with every aspect of his business.

One weekend he practically commanded Samantha to come down to Chawbury, so he could see her and speak to her, and with reluctance she consented. But the weekend was not a success. Miles found her elusive, hardly leaving her bedroom except for meals, and unwilling to be drawn on the subject of Gunn.

'So, Sam,' he said at dinner, 'tell us about your new young man. The one we keep seeing you with in the newspapers.'

Sam shrugged and replied, 'He's fine.'

'You don't think he's too young for you, then? Your toyboy?'

She didn't reply.

'Well, you don't sound very keen on him. Come on, we'd like to hear about him. Your brothers and sisters are interested, and so are your mother and I.'

It was a rare weekend when all four Straker children were present, home from their universities and jobs.

'Are we going to be allowed to meet him? You can invite him here to Chawbury, with some other young friends. Make a weekend of it. A young weekend. Everyone bring sleeping bags. Boys in one room, girls in another. I'll be patrolling all night, of course.'

'Leave it, dad. It's not funny.'

'Aah, the girl *can* talk. Now you've regained the power of speech, Samantha, come on, your parents would like to hear about your suitor. Perfectly normal, natural request. You're not embarrassed about him, are you? Give us the lowdown. What's he look like? Is he very handsome, this Mr Gunn? Has he got a car? Has he taken you to meet his parents? Assuming they're still alive, that is?'

'Dad, stop it, please.'

'No, I won't stop it. And since you seem not to want to tell us anything about him, perhaps you'd like to hear my views on the subject. Which are that it's utterly disgusting. Revolting. He must be a pervert, a great big man in his fifties, preying on a twenty-year-old. It's beauty and the beast. I don't know how you can bear it. Shut your eyes and think of England, I suppose.'

Davina shook her head at her husband, warning him to stop.

'No, Davina, I'm sorry but I am going to say this. I wouldn't be a responsible parent if I didn't. And I don't approve, Samantha. I thoroughly disapprove. And I don't want you to go on seeing Mr Gunn.' He drew a cigar from his pocket and snipped off the end. 'Do you understand me? You're to end this right now.'

'For God's sake, Dad. Stop being pompous.'

'I am *not* being pompous. This is basic morality. And I absolutely mean what I say. You don't have a job and who's supporting you? Your father is, thank you very much. And if you persist in seeing this ridiculous fellow, I'm going to *stop* paying. Lover boy can support you instead, do you understand me?' Then, turning to his other children, he asked, 'What do you lot think, then? You've all gone very quiet. Are you happy about your sister hanging round with a man almost three times her age. Does it strike you as seemly, Mollie?'

'Well, I don't actually think you should judge anyone by their age. We shouldn't be ageist.' Mollie could see her father ready to explode, so quickly added, 'But he doesn't sound like a very nice or kind person, from what I've read about him.'

Miles grimaced. You could trust Mollie to see everything the wrong way round. 'Archie?'

'Yeah, well. I haven't actually met the guy, Dad. But basically he does sound like a bit of an old fart.'

'Peter?'

Peter shrugged. 'I think it's up to Sam.'

Miles scowled. 'Well, let me make this crystal clear. Far as I'm concerned, it's going to stop and stop now. And I'm perfectly serious about what will happen if it does not.'

But even as he issued the ultimatum, a devious new plan was forming in his mind.

32.

For eighteen weeks, and without breathing a word about it to Ross, Dawn had been travelling up to London every Wednesday by train, accompanied by Serena. Arriving at Waterloo, they would take a taxi across town to rendezvous with one of the several estate agents that had become her new friends, meeting on doorsteps to be let in and shown round. Generally, they would visit four properties in the morning, then have a quick lunch at one of the restaurants Serena recommended, before catching an afternoon train back to Micheldever.

Dawn regarded these clandestine trips as amongst the happiest and most enlightening she'd experienced. Travelling with Serena was a revelation. Previously, Dawn had always felt an outsider in London. As she confessed, 'I hardly know the place, I couldn't find Harrods if you paid me. To be honest, I find it quite scary in town.' With Serena as her guide, however, everything felt easy and unthreatening. It was like visiting a different city. With Ross, she'd travelled down from Droitwich for the rugby, and visited the stores along Oxford Street, and her impression was always of too many people, too much traffic, fumes and rudeness. When they'd taken Gemma and Debbie to see *Les Miserables*, they'd had supper afterwards at an Angus Steak House and been disappointed by how unglamorous it was in the fabled West End. Serena took her to neighbourhoods she'd never visited before, Chelsea and Kensington, Holland Park and Notting Hill, full of interesting shops and tranquil streets, and big white houses she wouldn't mind living in herself. It was after one of the fabric-seeking expeditions to choose curtains for the living room windows, when they were rewarding their efforts with a salad and glass of champagne at Joe's Café in

Sloane Street, that Dawn said, 'I really could imagine keeping a place up in town, Serena. A proper one, I mean, not Ross's little pied à terre. It's all very well and good being stuck down in Chawbury, and I do enjoy the countryside, but I don't know what I'm going to do with myself all day when the girls leave home and get their own places.'

'Maybe you *should* buy somewhere in London,' Serena said. The prospect of decorating a second house for the Cleggs held obvious appeal, and the work at Chawbury Park could not be spun out much longer.

'Ross would never agree. He's negative like that.'

'It couldn't hurt if you looked at a few places though, could it? Just to see what's out there, get a feel for the market.'

Dawn was dubious. 'He's a lovely man, my husband, but so tight with his pennies. And a big place in town would cost buckets, wouldn't it?'

'The market *is* a bit crazy at the moment. But that's what makes London property such a great investment. It keeps on going up and up. And it's not going to stop.'

So it was decided that Serena would contact some estate agents she knew, and she and Dawn would start getting their eye in. They agreed there was no point mentioning anything to Ross, not yet anyway, not before they found somewhere perfect with investment potential. Dawn was keen to concentrate the search on the new, prestigious parts of town she'd recently discovered, and favoured a white stucco house over anything redbrick. As she explained to Serena, it was important to have good entertaining space with sufficient room to give a proper supper party. Though she did not say so out loud, she already imagined James and Laetitia coming over one evening for a meal, something she still felt insecure about risking at Chawbury Park.

Dawn was immediately impressed by the estate agents, and a little intimidated by them too. They were all such complete . . . gentlemen. Tall, pinstriped and endlessly deferential, they stood back to allow her to enter every room ahead of themselves, and tantalised her with stories about the next-door neighbours at each property they viewed. '*Entre nous*, Mrs Clegg, we sold Number 14 to a very senior commercial silk. And the house on your other side we sold to the manager of the Spice Girls.' And unlike Ross they agreed with her on everything, and congratulated her on her shrewdness in seeking a London property. 'You're getting in at exactly the right time,' they told her. 'Prices are seriously on the rise, but there's still plenty of headroom, a long way still to go. But you don't want to hang about,' they warned. 'A lot of our new instructions are being sold even before they reach the market. There's a lot of Russian and Hong Kong money around.'

The more properties Dawn viewed, the more confident she felt about what she was seeking. She soon realised the majority of London houses are built to identical five-storey configurations, with narrow double-living rooms on the first floor and a warren of small bedrooms on the two or three floors above, with bathroom extensions on the half landings. It didn't matter whether you were in South Kensington or Belgravia, all were essentially the same. If you wanted generous reception space—and this Dawn desired above everything—you had to go for something a lot dearer. Initially, she was horrified by the prices. She had envisaged paying up to a million—a *million* pounds, could she really be a lady looking at million pound properties?—but soon realised even two million bought you very little. By the third visit, they were viewing houses priced at 2.4 and then 2.7 million ('You can always put in a cheeky offer,' said the estate agents. 'Though obviously it's rather a sellers' market at present, owing to the shortage of good properties in the 2.5 to 3 million bracket.')

By the sixth week they had nudged up yet further, and were looking at places with three to four million price tags. Having viewed a spectacular white mansion in Phillimore Gardens, just out of curiosity, for which the Belgian vendors were asking five million, it was impossible to readjust downwards; the houses in Edwardes Square and Kensington Square suddenly felt narrow and cramped by comparison, and Dawn couldn't imagine herself showing Laetitia up such mean staircases to the first floor living room, since they would be unable to walk two abreast.

She shared her misgivings with Serena, who was wonderfully reassuring. They were sitting in the bar of the Berkeley hotel, having just viewed a heavily-gilded up-and-up house in Wilton Crescent, and Dawn felt suddenly confused and overwhelmed by the hunt. Both their principal estate agents, Robert de Vass and Nigel Shuttlebuck, had been so endlessly patient, and shown them round so many gracious homes, Dawn felt it was becoming embarrassing she hadn't chosen anywhere. In fact, she felt she ought to be buying a place from *both* of them, she couldn't bear that they'd put in so much time if they didn't make a sale. And then there was Ross. It was uncomfortable going behind his back. She could hear him now, his voice in her head: 'You've been looking at houses costing *how much*? Six million quid? Are you quite mad, lass?'

But then, emboldened by a second kir royale, she reflected: Is six million so very much money? When we're worth over a hundred. Not for the first time, she recognised Ross's limitations. He was such a decent, hardworking, caring man, but he hadn't adjusted to their altered circumstances. Left to himself, Dawn guessed he might never adapt at all, continuing to live in the same house, in exactly the same way as they had before they came into money. What a waste it would be: to have made all this lovely cash and do nothing with it. No, Dawn recognised it was her duty to raise his sights.

Shepherded by Serena, the quest now focused only on homes of more than 6,000 square feet, which alone could provide the desired reception space. With Robert or Nigel (and sometimes both together, since they had joint instructions on many of the largest properties), Dawn inspected stucco palaces in the Little Boltons, Tregunter Road, Dawson Place, Old Church Street, Chelsea Square, Palace Gardens Terrace and numerous others until all blurred into a single entity of tall corniced ceilings, designer kitchens and basement staff accommodation. 'I really don't think we could go quite as high as eight million,' she heard herself apologising to Nigel, after viewing the former Croatian consulate off Chester Square.

'Totally understood, Mrs Clegg,' Nigel replied. 'I believe this one's under offer in any case to a Mainland Chinese family.'

Just as she was despairing of ever finding anywhere, Robert took them to view a house in Holland Park. 'I have to warn you, Mrs Clegg, this one needs a lot of TLC. It's still partitioned up into studios at the moment, but it's freehold and offered with vacant possession. It's being disposed of by a charitable trust.'

From the moment they drew up outside the pedimented façade, with its pillared front door set into the middle of a double-fronted stucco-faced mansion, Dawn had a good feeling about the place. However when after much fumbling Robert managed to unlock the stuck door, and they had stepped into a wide dilapidated hall, she almost lost her nerve, instantly deterred by the sagging ceilings and pervading smell of damp and urine.

'It's been used until recently as a refuge for battered women,' Robert said. 'You've got to view it as virgin canvas. Wonderful opportunity. I can't remember when I last saw an unrenovated house of this size in Holland Park. And, of course, the condition is fully reflected in the asking price.'

Had Serena not been on hand to talk up the potential, and point out the various original features such as the fan-light above the front door and some badly graffitied marble mantelpieces at both ends of the thirty foot drawing room, Dawn would surely never have given the place serious consideration; the task was too daunting, the condition too far gone. She was particularly put off by three stained mattresses leaning against the wall in the master bedroom, cracked sinks in the corner of every room and the unpleasant smell wafting up from a disconnected lavatory. As they clambered higher to the third and fourth storeys, the staircase lights, controlled by a plastic timer, suddenly went off, plunging them into darkness. But Serena said, 'Look at the views from up here across the communal garden, Dawn. Stunning. It's one of the best-kept ones too, Holland Park Square.'

At that moment, as they were gazing onto the lawn and shrubberies from a top-floor window, Dawn said, 'It can't be. That looks like Miles Straker down there.' She peered at the tall, handsome figure striding along the path. 'It *is* him. And Davina too, look.' She could clearly see her dear friend trailing behind Miles. 'I must say hello.'

She hastened down to the first floor drawing room, where Robert yanked open a jammed French window.

'Miles, Davina, *coo-ee*. I'm up *here-ere*.'

Miles glanced up to see the eager face of Dawn, waving at him from the balcony of the hostel for battered women. Ross had always struck him as a rough diamond, but it was unforeseen that Dawn should have ended up there. Then he spotted the pinstriped figure of Robert de Vass of Knight Frank standing beside her, and a nervous-looking Serena lurking behind them both.

'Dawny, what a surprise,' Davina was calling up to her. 'What *are* you doing there?'

'Viewing the property . . . we're thinking of buying a place in town.'

'But that's *wonderful*,' Davina replied. 'You've got to get that one. It's the nicest on the whole garden. It would be *lovely* having you so close.'

Miles felt a wave of white envy sweep across him, followed by sheer horror. This was surely not happening. Tell him it was impossible. Ross and Dawn could not, repeat not, become their neighbours for a second time.

33.

t was a point of pride for Miles that every August the Strakers took a month-long family holiday in Italy. 'One small thing I've learnt in life,' he liked to tell people, 'is the importance of completely switching off once a year. I find it takes me ten days for the internal machine to wind down, when one's been running it as hard as I do. And you return to work buzzing with energy and new ideas.'

He then added, 'Of course I take all my ruddy gizmos with me, so I'm never out of communication with the office. In fact, I find I often end up working harder than ever on the terrace at the villa. Fewer distractions.'

At a company in which a two-week-maximum rule was strictly applied to staff holidays, it was Miles's privilege, as chairman and chief executive, to broadcast the benefits of taking a full month.

For seven consecutive summers, the Strakers had rented the same terracotta-painted farmhouse overlooking the sea close to Porto Ercole. It stood halfway up a hillside above a rocky cove, two bays along from the five-star Il Pellicano hotel, which for Miles was a good part of the attraction since he liked to play tennis on the courts at the resort, and sometimes to eat there as a change from dining at the villa. The villa itself, with its wide bougainvillea-fringed terrace, nine bedrooms and rustic olive press converted into an outside dining room, was the luxurious property of the Conte and Contessa Manfredi and Irene Rusculli, aristocratic Romans who were able to maintain their seaside home for the entire year upon the August rental from the Strakers.

Having leased the house for so many summers, Miles had come to regard it almost proprietorially, along with the Italian cook and housekeeper, and the two ladies who came up from the town on Vespas to change the beds and deal with the laundry, and the surly Sicilian, Fabulo ('If only he was!') who tended to the swimming pool and olive grove on the hillside above them. 'If I ever sat down and worked out what I've paid the Ruscullis over the years to take this place, I'm sure we could have *bought* it twice over,' he liked to declare to the stream of Straker Communications clients who came to the villa for lunch, or sometimes to stay, over the course of the holiday. 'I think of this place as our third home.'

Despite his many boasts about taking a full month's vacation, which flattered his status and powers of delegation ('I think they ought to be able to rub along without me at the office for twenty-eight days'), the fact was that Miles valued his August as a time for enhanced networking. 'If you're going to be anywhere near Porto Ercole, you must come and see us,' he told the managing director of Trent Valley Power 4 U. Hearing that the chief executive of Eazi-print would be on a family holiday near Amalfi, he'd say, 'That's no distance at all, Martin. I insist you bring, er, Ros and the children over to us for lunch.' Other weeks were set aside for the entertainment of politicians. Their constituency MP, Ridley Nairn, generally flew down for a few days with Suzie, as did the party Deputy Chairman Paul Tanner and his third wife, Brigitte. As a matter of record, Paul had been a frequent houseguest at the villa with his second wife, Hetta, but this was no longer referred to. On one memorable occasion, James and Laetitia arrived for lunch by chartered yacht, which they'd moored out in the bay, and that visit had been a triumph of civility and corporate bonding. Miles was confident that, should they ever challenge it, he would have no trouble justifying the villa as an entirely legitimate business expense to the Inland Revenue.

Settling into the master bedroom with its infinite views of the deep blue Aeolian Sea, Miles could hear the sounds of his family moving into their respective bedrooms around the villa. Instantly he was made irritable, because all four children had been annoying him in different ways before they'd even left England. For several weeks, Archie had been asking whether he really needed to be in Italy for the entire month, since he'd been invited to Corfu and to Rock by friends and really wanted to go there instead. Miles considered Archie extraordinarily ungrateful, considering how expensive the villa was, and no way was he forking out for air tickets for him to buzz off to Corfu. Anyway, he considered Archie indispensable when clients came over, being both handsome and sociable.

Peter, of course, could only get two weeks holiday from his job, so would only be with them for the first part of the holiday, and he too had been half-hearted about coming. He mentioned a tentative plan to go travelling to Cape Wrath in Scotland and maybe crossing over to the Orkneys. Miles vetoed that idea at birth, telling Peter he was certainly required in Porto Ercole. 'Zach Durban and his Mauritian girlfriend might be driving over from Florence for lunch, so you're on duty.'

Mollie, meanwhile, annoyed him by arriving at the airport with two plastic bags full of school textbooks, which she said she had to read and note for next term. All had dull academic front covers and looked unsuitable for poolside reading. In Miles's world view, daughters on holiday should be draped across sunloungers wearing pretty micro-bikinis, smelling of sunscreen and reading chick-lit. Mollie, he suspected, had brought no pretty bikinis with her, just an old swimsuit, and was intending to defile the poolside scene with sociology textbooks and yellow post-it stickers.

Normally, he could at least rely on Samantha to enhance the holiday mood. In past summers she'd arrived with several Heathfield friends, and these luscious, lithe-limbed girls had looked gorgeously decorative, sunbathing and lightening their hair with lemon juice, and chattering away pleasingly at meals. This summer, it had been a struggle to get Sam out to Italy at all. She declared, very late in the day, that she'd be spending August with Dick Gunn on his new motor yacht, *Gunnslinger II,* cruising the Med from St Tropez to Sardinia. Miles had been instantly opposed, resenting the idea of Dick owning a yacht when he didn't have one himself, and wanting Sam at the villa, most attractive of his offspring.

In the end, after a furious paternal ultimatum and lots of behind-the-scenes diplomacy from Davina, Sam consented to join the family holiday, but a deal had been struck. Dick Gunn and party would sail over to the villa in the third week of August for lunch, and meet the Straker parents for the first time. Miles made a big thing of resenting the intrusion ('Are you sure your young blade will be able to manage the steps up from the beach?') but secretly he was pleased. For his own reasons, he wanted to meet Dick and this was the ideal opportunity.

Meanwhile, Samantha had arrived at Gatwick late and grumpy, having been dropped off at the terminal building by Dick's driver. She spent the flight hiding behind *Tatler* and muttering how boring the holiday was going to be with no friends to talk to.

It was true that, for the first time, the Strakers had not encouraged their children to bring friends along. In past years, they had been allowed to bring two or three each, though generally it had been Archie and Samantha who'd invited the most. Peter and Mollie never seemed to have any available friends, or friends that could afford the airfare.

This year, however, Mollie surprised them by saying she wanted to invite along Debbie Clegg.

When Davina told Miles, he exploded. 'No way. Absolutely not. We are *not* having any Cleggs on holiday. I forbid it.'

Davina reasoned with him. 'It would be so nice for Mollie to have a friend. She didn't last year. And Debbie's a very sweet, bright girl.'

'I'm sorry, I'm not discussing this. It's not negotiable. Davina, this holiday in Italy is my *only proper* holiday of the year, I am not having it polluted by Cleggs. For God's sake, don't we see enough of that damn family? I can't look out of the window *at either of our houses* without being reminded of them. They're bloody well everywhere. I'm surprised you're even suggesting it, you know how cross I am they've bought in Holland Park Square. If I'd realised that boarding house was on the market, I'd have bought it myself. They're like *stalkers,* these people. I've half a mind to refer them to the police.'

'Darling, you really are being rather silly. Dawn didn't even *know* we live on the square. She was as surprised as we were.'

'Of course she knew. We've been there for years, for heaven's sake. Just as we'd been at Chawbury for years before they turned up there.'

'Well, actually, they didn't know. You've never allowed me to invite them to the London house. It's so embarrassing, they've never actually been to *either* of our houses, not to a lunch or dinner party, because you won't let me.'

'Nor *will* they come. Not after the way their daughter behaved with Archie. What was her name? Sharon? Donna? Gemma, that's it. We don't want them *anywhere near us*, none of them. Which is why this friend of Mollie's isn't welcome on holiday. You're going to have to explain to Mollie she isn't suitable, that's all there is to it.'

Davina was accustomed to extreme and unreasonable outbursts from her husband. They had always been a staple of their marriage. She had learnt when to acquiesce, knowing the moment would pass, and when it was important to take a stand. Today, she said, 'Miles, I'm sorry, but actually I'm not going to tell Mollie that, or anything like it. I refuse. Debbie's a lovely girl. Mollie rides with her all the time, and Dawn has been endlessly kind to Mollie. Always having her over when I'm up in London helping you, going with you to all those ghastly parties you so love. I couldn't possibly tell Mollie that Debbie isn't welcome in Italy. I can't and I won't. And if you try to make me, or try to disinvite her yourself, I'm not coming on the holiday myself. And that really *is* final.'

The only compromise they could come up with was that no childrens' friends would be invited this summer. Miles let it be known he was stepping-up his business entertaining, and regrettably there would be no space for anyone else at the villa, including Debbie Clegg.

Miles was seated at the marble-topped breakfast table on the terrace, all alone, feeling irritable. Despite the perfection of the holiday scene, he frequently felt dissatisfied in the mornings, and this summer was worse than usual.

He surveyed his surroundings—the tall Cyprus trees framing a view of the blue sea—and the surprisingly cold swimming pool, shaded by firs, at the far end of the garden. It irritated him he was sitting here in solitary splendour with nobody to talk to, since his wife was taking a long bath and the children fast asleep, and would doubtless remain so for several hours more. This business of nobody getting up in the mornings was getting to him. Neither Archie nor Sam were seen before lunchtime, and Peter seldom appeared before eleven. The only one who surfaced at a halfway decent hour was Mollie, and that was hardly a consolation. In fact, he hoped Mollie *wouldn't* appear, until after he'd finished breakfast at any rate.

There was something lugubrious about the whole breakfast procedure. When he arrived on the terrace, as he did every morning at nine o'clock, he found a dozen slices of melon cut into narrow strips, arranged on a plate beneath a muslin cloche. Next to it were two wicker baskets of hard Italian bread and rusk-like biscuits, some in wrappers. A yellow and blue ceramic platter was crowded with pots of jams, honeys and lime preserves, the same pots every day, their surfaces pitted with the bodies of dead wasps which had somehow crawled inside. Each morning it annoyed him that there was no sign of Maria or Immacula, cook and housekeeper, so he had to find them in the kitchen to announce his arrival for breakfast, and ask for a cup of coffee. This took forever to arrive, twenty to thirty minutes, while Maria boiled up milk and dealt with the process of grinding coffee beans. Was it too much to ask that a cafetiere of hot coffee be awaiting him on the breakfast table, every morning at nine? He had discussed this—frequently—with Davina, whose role it was to liaise with the domestic retinue, but she seemed incapable of effecting it, explaining the Ruscullis liked it done this way.

It annoyed Miles his Italian was not better. The fact was his languages were poor. Davina, however, spoke rather good Italian. As a child, she had partly grown up in the embassy compound in Addis Ababa, when her father was posted as a diplomat to Ethiopia, and most of the indoor staff there had spoken Italian. Consequently, it was Davina who undertook the necessary conversations, not just with Maria and Immacula about menus and housekeeping details, but restaurant bookings, boat charters, car hire and everything else. Miles resented the loss of control, and felt that his wife, given her command of the language, frequently failed to achieve what was required.

He brooded at the table, drumming his fingers, waiting for Maria to bring the coffee. Needles had dropped from the umbrella pines during the night on to the surface of the swimming pool, and he wished Fabulo was there, scooping them out with his net. Where *was* Fabulo? Didn't he begin work at eight? And what time had the older children arrived back from that nightclub, he thought he'd heard car doors slamming at three o'clock in the morning, and a Vespa backfiring. This summer, Peter, Sam and Archie had taken to going out after dinner, down to Porto Ercole or further afield, taking the second car Davina insisted they needed, or the moped or both. So they rolled back in the small hours, waking the whole house and then lay in bed recovering next day.

Alongside his plate lay his cell phone, an additional source of irritation. Probably the only serious drawback to the villa was the telecom signal, which didn't reach the breakfast table. If he wanted to speak to the office, he must either use the landline or stroll to the end of the garden, beyond the swimming pool, where the signal was strongest. He glared at the impotent device, blaming Davina. Had he not asked her, summer after summer, to contact the Ruscullis and insist they install a booster?

As usual, he longed for an English newspaper. These could be obtained from a kiosk in Porto Ercole, but did not arrive until noon and were anyway a day late. An *International Herald Tribune* was brought up for him by the cleaning ladies, but this did not appear until ten o'clock, and anyway he found the *IHT* unsatisfactory. The girls in his office compiled and faxed a daily digest of the British newspapers, but London was an hour behind and it would not be ready for a while yet.

All these petty irritations compounded to sour Miles's morning, as he sat at the table spreading hard bread with apricot jam.

Mollie arrived on the terrace, weighed down with books. She placed a stack on the breakfast table, and Miles flinched at their spines: psychotherapy textbooks written by lefty whingers. Why couldn't Mollie teach a proper subject like history? It was one of Miles's bugbears that traditional English history—kings and queens, dates of battles and so forth—was barely included in the state sector curriculum. At the education committee on which he sat, he championed a return to 'real' history: 'Alfred burning the cakes, King Canute, the British Empire which wasn't all bad by any means. Not the ruddy Corn Laws and Tolpuddle Martyrs and Victorian chimneysweeps every time.'

'Morning, Dad. Did you sleep ok?' There was always a wariness in Mollie's conversation with her father. Miles was wondering why his daughter wore black or brown t-shirts on holiday, on a beautiful sunny day.

'I *was* sleeping ok, until I was woken by confounded car doors slamming. You weren't out nightclubbing with the others?'

'No, I needed to be up early. I'm blocking out next term's coursework.'

'No sign of your brothers and sister, I assume?'

Mollie shrugged. 'They won't be up for hours. Peter might be though. He said he'd give me a guitar lesson this morning.'

Miles grimaced. Peter's guitar was another curse of the holiday. Each afternoon, when trying to take a siesta in his bedroom, he could hear Peter in the garden below, strumming away. Or, worse, singing. Yesterday at the end of lunch, Davina had actually encouraged him, and they'd all had to endure a dirge about Cornish herring fishermen. It annoyed Miles the way Peter rolled his eyes upwards when he sang, a gesture of sincerity.

With nobody except Mollie about, and no guests staying, Miles found mornings at the villa a challenge. Easily bored, needing perpetual stimulation, time weighed heavily. He considered walking down the 240 cliffside steps to the jetty, for a dip in the sea, but couldn't face the climb back up afterwards. How the Ruscullis could live here without a lift, he didn't know; if this was his own place, he'd have installed one. He considered swimming in the cold pool, but knew the proximity of Mollie and her textbooks would spoil the experience. Instead, he carried his cell phone to the far end of the garden, where he made his calls, ringing first Serena, then the office.

Following the exposure of her treachery with Dawn, his relationship with Serena had deteriorated. Miles found the thought of her helping his sworn enemies, behind his back, difficult to forgive, and he was inclined to blame Serena for introducing them to Holland Park Square too. For several weeks he refused to speak to her, and their affair was in abeyance. But recently, driven by boredom of the family holiday, Miles resumed ringing her again. Serena was full of remorse, and frisky on the phone.

'Tell you what, darling,' Miles said. 'If I come up with a pretext for being in Rome for a night or two next week, can you be there? I need a break from the joys of family life.'

She accepted like a shot.

'Splendid. I'll have the girls organise transport.'

The remainder of the morning he spent speaking to the office, having every piece of post and every invitation read out to him, and dictating long, aggressive memos to his people. Then he said, 'Oh, I may need to head over to Rome for a couple of nights for a client thing. Next Monday and Tuesday. Book a suite at the Russie. And Mrs Harden will be joining me. Facilitate it, please.'

Davina delayed coming outside for as long as possible. First she would take a long bath, which was out of character but helped fill in the morning. Then she liked to discuss menus with Maria and Immacula in the kitchen, and practise her Italian with them. If Peter was down, she'd have a cup of coffee with him in the drawing room with its terrazzo floor, which was cooler than sitting outside, and hear what was on his mind. Since he'd begun the job at Straker Communications, which she knew he hated, Davina felt she was losing touch with her eldest, favourite son, so it was an opportunity to chat about folk music and ecology and his other enthusiasms. If they heard Miles ('Maria! We need ice') they both jumped.

Although she came along dutifully every summer, Davina was not a fan of their Italian villa holidays. Given the choice, she would prefer to have been home in her garden. But she recognised how important it was to Miles, and did her best to entertain the stream of corporate visitors. The heat of Italy in August, even by the sea, didn't suit her; she missed the overcast skies of Chawbury, and these holidays were far, far too long. A week would have been plenty. The prospect of a further twenty unbroken days with Miles, with all his pent-up energy and expectations, filled her with dread. So when he casually mentioned that he needed to show his face at a client conference in Rome next week, she considered it a merciful reprieve.

Shaken awake by his mother at a quarter-to-one with a message that lunch was in twenty minutes and his father would be angry if he was late down, Archie stumbled into the shower. He was badly hung-over and queasy. Had he really got into a sambuca drinking contest with that Italian bloke? He groaned.

The thought of lunch turned his stomach. Why did he even have to come to lunch at all? He wasn't hungry, and it wasn't as if any guests were coming, it was just family. He pulled open a shutter but the sun was too bright, so he closed it again. Dripping water from the shower, he dropped his wet towel in a heap on the floor and looked round for some clothes. Finding nothing to hand, he put his pyjama bottoms back on, with the t-shirt he'd worn last night to go clubbing.

You had to hand it to the Italians, they did know how to party. This new club they'd discovered, the Strada, about an hour beyond Porto Ercole, was fantastic, much better than the Club Jolly where they used to go. It was like an open-air discotheque inside a bamboo stockade, right next to the autostrada, full of crazy people. It didn't matter he couldn't speak one word of Italian, the music was so loud, nobody realised. And some of the women there were wild. You could tell they were well up for it.

The only pain about the clubs was having to go with Sam and Peter, who never wanted to stay that late. By two o'clock, they became killjoys and started agitating to go. Peter was always like that anyway, so no surprise there, but even Sam was being boring these days. She hardly danced anymore, because of being in a relationship with Dick Gunn, and she seemed spaced out all the time. Archie hadn't met Dick yet but had seen his picture, the fat-arsed tosser.

Screwing up his eyes, he stumbled outside to the loggia, where bowls of different pastas and salads were laid out on a table, and platters of mozzarella, prosciutto and parmesan.

'Anyone seen my shades?' he asked croakily.

'I think you left them on the table at the Strada,' Sam said. 'That's where I last saw them.'

Archie cursed.

'Good *morning*, Archibald,' Miles said, with heavy irony. 'Is there a special reason you're still wearing your pyjamas? Would you mind putting on some clothes for lunch? And change that shirt too. Its got something slopped down it.'

Archie rolled his eyes and wandered back inside. This whole stupid holiday was a waste of space. If he hadn't lost his mobile phone, and if he'd remembered to bring the charger with him, he'd have called his mates in Rock to find out what was happening. They'd probably have moved on to Polzeath by now in any case. It was just *so ridiculous* he was made to be here. He hated his dad somethimes, his whole family in fact.

Miles held very strong views about restaurants which filled Davina with dismay, since it was her job to satisfy them.

Every second evening, he insisted they eat out as a family, generally at one of the harbour-side restaurants in Porto Ercole. His requirement, which Davina was expected to facilitate, was that they should drive down to the town in two cars, buy the English newspapers, then first have a drink at a bar. The only bars acceptable to him were the three smart canopied ones on wooden pontoons, jutting out over the harbour. It was impossible to make reservations at these places, which were frequently crowded, but Miles became testy if Davina couldn't secure one of the best waterside tables, large enough to spread the newspapers out on.

'This is intolerable, Davina,' he would rage, if asked to wait for a table for a single moment. 'Tell the waiter we come here all the time. He *knows us* for Christ sake.'

Miles became especially exasperated if they had clients in tow, as they did tonight, having been joined by the Managing Director of British Regional Airways, Bradley Pike, his wife, Carole, and silent, sunburned kids Owen and Keeleigh, who had driven down from Portofino. Bradley was an important client of Straker Communications, and Miles was intent on impressing and patronising him, in equal measure, to keep him keen.

Running his gaze critically over his family, he felt that, on balance, they were conveying the right image tonight. Archie looked clean and smart in white chinos and a blue shirt with unfrayed cuffs, and turning on the charm with Mrs Pike, and Samantha had pulled out all the stops in a floaty white sundress, which he knew Dick Gunn had bought her at Chloé. Bradley couldn't take his eyes off her breasts, which was all to the good. Peter still dressed like a student unfortunately, and Mollie resembled a trainee comprehensive school teacher . . . which she was.

A waiter delivered Bellinis and Bloody Marys and bowls of olives, nuts and crisps, and Miles devoted his attention to flattering Bradley while impressing him with his more famous clients. 'James and Laetitia Pendleton sailed over for lunch on their yacht,' he told him. 'They moored in our bay, which was tremendous fun.'

'I see Pendletons are getting quite a run for their money from this Freeza Mart guy,' Bradley said, hoovering up a fistful of crisps. 'He's doing some smart new things, there's a story in to-day's *FT*.'

Having only just bought the newspapers, Miles hadn't read it yet. He made a mental note to ring the office and bawl them out for missing it in the daily digest. Opening the paper, he spotted the piece at once: 'Freeza Mart's Clegg announces pure-play logistics company.' There was an accompanying photograph of Ross standing outside an enormous warehouse like an aircraft hanger, giving a cheery thumbs up.

Miles scanned the article with rising irritation. Ross's new company was offering distribution and logistics services to all retailers, including direct competitors, from a new 400,000 square foot facility in Coventry. Asda, Proctor & Gamble, Sara Lee food and Nestlé were reported to have signed up as clients. The new business would begin as a subsidiary of Freeza Mart but was expected to float as a stand-alone business within three years.

'We're confident this is the largest state-of-the-art warehouse facility in the West Midlands,' Ross was quoted as saying. 'With next-generation IT capabilities already up and running, we can provide third party clients with a fully integrated logistics solution.'

Miles felt a dark cloud had drifted across the sun, making the warm Italian evening bleak and chilly. God how he despised Ross Clegg. His plan to undermine him was assuming a new urgency, and the sooner Dick Gunn arrived the better.

Stretching out on a white sunbed on the balcony of his suite at the Hotel Russie, Miles felt the rush of elation which always came when given a reprieve from his family.

Through the open door to the bedroom, he could hear Serena taking a shower in the adjacent bathroom, following their reunion lovemaking session. Having got all that out of his system, Miles was looking forward to a civilised dinner outside in the hotel courtyard, and an opportunity to berate Serena some more about her clients, Dawn and Ross.

Seeing Serena with fresh eyes following the eight-week hiatus in their affair, he was reminded how greatly he still desired her. It did not put him off that, for the first time ever, he noticed a strand of grey in her magnificent red mane of hair.

'Do I spot a grey hair?' he asked her, peering critically at her scalp.

Dismayed and panicking he might drop her, Serena blushed crimson. 'How awful, I must do something about that.' She wondered if there was a hotel salon for an emergency colour-job.

Miles smiled. It gave him a delightful sensation of superiority to have wrong footed her. In the same way it pleased him that his mistress had a useless husband in Robin, he enjoyed commenting on her little imperfections. He preferred his women in a state of perpetual anxiety. It gave him the upper hand.

Objectively, he recognised Serena would not make a suitable or satisfactory wife for him, and he had no intention ever of leaving Davina for her. Once, on a long flight, he had listed the pros and cons of both women, awarding marks out of five under different categories: homemaker, reliability, loyalty, bed, taste, appearance and public image. He used a similar system for ranking his executives at work, and found it illuminating. In ranking Serena versus Davina, Davina came out ahead in every category except bed. In the 'appearance' category, they tied; Serena being obviously a lot sexier, but Davina more elegant, if he nagged her. He suspected, too, that if he ever made Serena his wife, she would quickly become less compliant with his ring on her finger.

In his more philosophical moments, Miles acknowledged (to himself, never to her) how dependent he was upon Davina and how the rhythm of their marriage largely suited him, even in this its tepid mature phase. She was non-judgemental, and did not impede him in his career. In fact, she could be regarded as an asset, since she accompanied him to business dinners, when pushed into it, and organised the annual summer lunch party at Chawbury, if adequately supervised. Certainly she did a good job on the garden and he felt able to delegate almost total responsibility in this department to her. Above anything, Miles valued the illusion of being happily married. Working in an industry in which few of his peers had been able to sustain their marriages for longer than ten years, he considered it a USP of Brand Straker that he and Davina were still together, with four industrious and well-adjusted children. Only three days earlier, Bradley and Carole Pike had been fulsome in their praise for them, commenting on how polite and delightful they had been during their visit. 'You must be awfully proud of them,' Bradley had said. 'Carole and I were just saying what a grand job you've done with your parenting.'

Serena joined him on the balcony wearing a short black leather dress, with zips and buckles and a studded leather belt.

'So,' said Serena. 'How's the duty holiday been so far?' She resented Miles spending a month in the bosom of his family. He frequently assured her his marriage to Davina was over, certainly in that way, but she didn't know whether or not to believe him.

Miles shrugged. 'I've been working to keep busy. A lot of client entertaining. You? How are *your* special clients?' He peered at her, tilting his head, to emphasise which clients he referred to.

'Dawn, you mean? Fine, I think. I haven't seen that much of her.' She blushed, having in fact been in almost constant communication, choosing a kitchen company for Holland Park Square and joining her for site meetings with the architect. Following the surveyor's report, they were now looking at a total gut job, with every inch of pipework and wiring replaced, as well as all the windows and most of the floorboards and joists.

'I hope you've thought seriously about what I said. About stopping working for the Cleggs.'

Serena shifted uncomfortably. She hoped Miles had forgotten that conversation.

'I told you, they're my biggest clients, I can't just dump them. I need the money. And I don't know why it bugs you so much, it's not like I ever discuss you with them.'

'I should hope not. If anyone ever found out about our . . . situation . . . it would have to end immediately. I've made that clear.'

'I'm only giving them some decorating help, it's not like they're my best friends.'

'I don't understand how you can bear to work for them. Ross Clegg's a peasant, you've nothing in common. That ghastly house he built, like something in Weybridge. Worse, actually. As for his wife—Dawn—what's that television programme Samantha's always glued to? *Desperate Housewives*. That just about sums Dawn up. I couldn't get over the way they'd done their Chawbury house, the one time I saw it.'

'It looks better now,' Serena found herself saying. 'Everything's been redone.'

'Precisely. Ross makes some money with his turkey twizzlers, whatever they're called, throws up that monstrosity, then blows another fortune putting it right with a decorator. Proves my point. No taste, no clue about anything. And I find it incredible, and rather disloyal, you have allowed yourself to become some sort of glorified lady-in-waiting at their beck and call, choosing their curtains, choosing their *houses* for them for heaven's sake, when you *know* I hold them in contempt. And to crown it all you find them a house on *my own London square*, directly opposite mine.'

'Miles, I told you, that was nothing to do with me. The estate agent showed it to her.'

'You could have put her off. You knew I wouldn't want them anywhere near us.'

They went down to dinner where Serena did her best to lift his spirits, regaling him with gossip about mutual friends and flattering him about his business success. She liked to believe Miles's filthy mood was bought on by being cooped up with Davina on holiday, and she only needed time to smooth him out. She understood his competitiveness with Ross, and it was a problem for her, though she reckoned she could handle it. Still imagining herself marrying Miles at some future point, she would do nothing to jeopardise that. But the Cleggs were far and away her most lucrative clients, and she couldn't lightly walk away from them. Besides, a little harmless rivalry couldn't hurt. Although she did not say so, she had come to have a lot of respect for Ross, and even found him quite attractive in a strange way. He lacked vanity and paid her bills on time, both rare attributes in Serena's world.

So when Miles reverted to the subject of the Cleggs at the end of dinner, reminding her he didn't much enjoy spending his money on dressing their personal decorator, and maybe he wouldn't bother if she carried on like this, she intentionally provoked him. 'You realise Ross and Dawn are spending the best part of a million quid on doing their London house, when you tot it all up?'

Miles regarded her darkly. 'All I can suggest, Serena, is that I'd get your fees paid up-front if I were you. I'm not going into details, but you may find your benefactors have rather less to throw around, a few months from now.'

Serena looked startled. 'Whatever do you mean?'

'I'm not saying any more. But keep the name Dick Gunn in mind, that's as far as I'm prepared to go.'

'Samantha's lover, you mean? *That* Dick Gunn?'

Miles flinched at the word 'lover.' 'Sam's friend, yes, that one. You know my opinion on that, and it's got nothing to do with this other business. But be warned.'

'Oh, come on. You can't leave me on tenterhooks. If you know something, tell me.'

Miles shook his head. 'My lips are sealed. Now one last drink and it's bedtime.'

Samantha sat at the open window of her bedroom at the villa, smoking a joint and staring, somewhat hazily, at the silver sea below. She knew it had been risky bringing gear through customs, but no one had even asked her to open her hand luggage, let alone her sponge bag. She'd been scared shitless queuing at the X-ray machine, but the lady behind the screen hadn't given her bag a second glance. Gaz told her it'd be cool, and he'd been right.

There had been a second scary moment just before boarding the aircraft. They'd all been waiting in the first class lounge, courtesy of Miles's Gold Executive Club card, and when they'd filed down the gantry there'd been this security guy with an alsation which started sniffing at her case. Luckily she'd been able to shuffle past, reading *Tatler*.

She knew she'd never have got through the holiday without her secret stash. Every afternoon she came upstairs to smoke, or something stronger when she needed it, and boy did she need it, marooned here with her family for weeks and weeks. From somewhere below in the loggia she could hear Peter playing the guitar and singing one of his depressing songs. She could see Mollie by the pool under an umbrella, nose in a schoolbook, which struck Sam

as just totally bizarre behaviour. And her Dad, back from his conference in Rome, glued to a mobile as usual, in swimming trunks,
shirt and straw hat.

Through the haze of smoke and her befuddled brain, she saw
yachts and Sunseekers coming and going on the horizon, and wondered whether one of them was Dick. She couldn't exactly remember which day he was meant to be coming, though her Mum had it
written in the diary. At this precise moment, she couldn't visualise
Dick clearly at all. She'd tried calling him a couple of times on the
boat, but it was complicated with sat-phones, you couldn't use a
normal mobile unless they were in port. She hoped he'd arrive
soon, since she was planning on joining the yacht and sailing off
with him, not that she'd told anyone that. She hoped her Dad
would behave himself when Dick came and wouldn't be ridiculous,
as he usually was.

Peter had asked her last night at supper, 'When's your boyfriend
showing up?' It had taken her a second or two to realise who he
meant. She didn't really think of Dick as her boyfriend, even though
she virtually lived in his flat in Eaton Square, and she supposed she
was his girlfriend in every way, even though she didn't like to dwell
too deeply about some aspects of it. What really worked with Dick
was he left for his office at six thirty, five whole hours before she
even woke up. And he generally left a wodge of banknotes on the
dressing table for spending money.

Despite his numerous misgivings about Dick, such as his age, his
great wealth, his big yacht and the fact that he was sleeping with
his favourite daughter thirty years his junior, Miles was determined
the visit should be a success.

Consequently he was up and about an hour earlier than usual,
double-checking the jetty was free of slime and ready to receive
visitors, that the garden was perfectly tidy, the swimming pool perfectly clean, and the lunch appropriately magnificent to receive their
high-profile guest. It had irritated Miles that, shortly before setting off on holiday, the London *Evening Standard* had produced its
annual magazine supplement entitled, 'The 1000 Most Influential
People in London.' Although self-evidently an arbitrary production
in every way, it nevertheless annoyed him to find himself listed only

at Number 169 ('smooth-as-butter spin-doctor to the Great and Good . . .') while Dick Gunn was at Number 107 ('Roly-poly Private Equity Tsar with a finger in every pie'). Almost as irritating, Ross Clegg had made his first ever appearance at Number 973 ('Gritty supermarket boss opening 25 London superstores this year, with a new £10 million home in Holland Park . . .'). Well, that might be Ross's one and only appearance on the list, Miles thought grimly.

Shortly before midday, the enormous Gunn motor yacht, *Gunnslinger II*, glided into the bay beneath the villa and dropped anchor. Seen from above where the Strakers were keeping watch from the terrace, the yacht seemed almost obscenely large, with two expanses of wooden deck and three tiers of windows, including the portholes of the crew accommodation at the waterline, and a pair of speedboats suspended above the stern from davits.

'Oh God, look, they've got jet skis too,' Archie said. 'Those amazing new sort, which go twice as fast. Wicked.'

'Is that a Jacuzzi on the top deck?' Miles said, sounding pained. 'That really is rather gross.'

Samantha, who envisaged spending a lot of time in the Jacuzzi in the coming week, ignored the jibe.

The crew were preparing the tenders to ferry the Gunn party to the jetty, and Davina, counting the number of people transferring into inflatable boats, said anxiously, 'There's an awful lot of them. I hope we've enough lunch for everyone.'

As the Strakers descended the cliff steps to greet their guests, Miles surveyed the Gunn party, which seemed to consist of at least fifteen people. Dick himself was clearly visible, his vast gut bursting over a pair of knee length Villequebrun swimming trunks, with a pattern of red and white starfish and shells. He was bare chested but wore a safari hat and reflecting sunglasses. Two members of crew helped him in and out of the rib, which lowered noticeably in the water when he stepped in. As the boats neared the jetty, and Dick began the complicated business of clambering up the metal steps, you saw he had a holster round his waist containing a brace of mobile phones.

Arriving on dry land, he lumbered over to Samantha and enveloped her in a bear hug. 'Whoa, you're looking juicy, sex goddess.'

Sam giggled. 'Don't call me that.'

'Why not? It's what you are. We've needed you on board, there's been a serious shortage of acceptable skirt.'

The rest of the Gunn party was forming up on the jetty. Several seemed to be mini-me versions of Dick, with fat stomachs and Villequebrun swimwear, and turned out to work with him in private equity. There were several women too, predominantly blondes, in leopard print swimsuits and bikinis. Also in tow were a couple of small children, a boy and a girl, introduced as Dick's kids by an ex-wife. Most of the visitors appeared to know Sam, greeting her with kisses and hugs.

Miles began to feel irritable as this procession of strangers gave all their attention to Samantha, while ignoring him. Normally Miles was the first focus of attention at any gathering, and he resented being sidelined. In particular, he would have expected some respect from Dick who, having greeted Sam, became involved in protracted discussion with his yacht's Captain, then picked up a phone call. By the time they'd climbed back up to the villa, Dick was sweating, and Miles feeling testy.

Chairs had been set out in a semi-circle on the terrace for drinks, and Maria and Immacula prepared plates of crostini and bruschetta which Archie and Mollie handed round. Peter, assisted by a surly Fabulo, was in charge of dispensing Bellinis and wine.

Dick plonked himself in a chair in the centre of the circle, surrounded on both sides by his acolytes, so Miles and Davina were relegated to the perimeter, which annoyed Miles even more. He reminded himself to remain calm; he needed Dick on side.

Picking up a chair and moving it closer to the principal guest, he asked Dick, 'So how's summer been on board?'

'Sybaritic. Done sweet FA except drink and eat with this bunch of reprobates,' Dick replied, indicating his posse of mates. Still shirtless, his hairless chest fell in small bunches of fat, like half-inflated balloons; in order to sit down, he yanked up his swimming trunks above the knees, revealing swollen, fatty kneecaps. 'We did manage one interesting deal. We've bought out Third Capita, the business relocation people, and are going to try and do something with that basket case.'

'How long have you had the yacht?'

'The current one? This is its second summer on the water. It took forever to build. I had to sue the shipyard in Hamburg, threaten to. It goes well though. A few niggles, nothing major. Bathrooms too small, that's been the biggest fuck-up. I'm suing the designer.' Then, turning his back on Miles, he called out, 'Hey, Sammy, over here, darlin', and sit on my lap.'

Sam perched on his fat knees, and Dick said, 'Go on, jiggle about a bit, sweetheart. Give us a knee trembler.' The Gunn acolytes cheered her along.

'The last time we had lunch guests arrive here by yacht was the Pendletons,' Miles said. 'James and Laetitia.' He didn't want Dick to think they were unaccustomed to visits from yacht owners, and the Pendletons were many times richer than Gunn.

'They charter, don't they, the Pendletons? It's not their own yacht. I'm particular like that, I prefer my own spec.'

Miles had a hideous premonition of what life would be like with Dick as his son-in-law. Until that moment, he had never given a minute's consideration to what he expected in Samantha's future husband, since it still seemed impossibly far off; but, instinctively, he had hoped for some bright, well-spoken, keen young man, full of respect for his successful father-in-law. Instead, he was faced with this gross asset-stripper, who was all but stripping Sam of her assets in front of him.

Lunch was called in the loggia, and they took their places at the long wooden table. Miles took care to position himself next to Dick, awaiting the optimum moment for the conversation he needed to have. On Miles's other side was a nut-brown blonde in a leopard-skin bikini. Close-up, her skin showed signs of advanced skin damage, with wrinkles and sunspots.

'I've been hearing about your cruise,' Miles said to her. 'Are you an old friend of Dick's?'

'Yeah, I'm Sybilla, Dick and I were together for four years,' the girl replied. 'On and off.'

'I see.'

'I was two before Sam,' she said matter-of-factly, compressing a handful of Parma ham in her fingertips.

Surveying the dynamics of the lunch party, Miles wasn't sure it was going well. The Gunn visitors and Straker family seemed alarmingly unintegrated, each group sticking to its own. Davina was working hard on her neighbour, Dick's corporate lawyer, and Peter was talking to Dick's six-year-old daughter, but elsewhere it all felt distinctly sticky. The Gunn group, accustomed to high living on the yacht, seemed dissatisfied with the food and company, and were talking noisily amongst themselves. A man in a Hawaiian shirt said, 'Where's the fucking caviar? This is the first meal in a month with no caviar.' Bridling, Miles noticed Dick's hand resting on the crutch of Sam's bikini. The moment had come. 'Tell you what,' he said, turning to Dick. 'You're in the market for takeover prospects, I might have an idea for you.'

Dick looked interested.

'Freeza Mart,' Miles continued. 'Worth a serious look. Growing exponentially, but doing so despite weak management. That's Pendletons's internal analysis, in any case.'

'This is Ross wasisname's show, right?'

'That's it. Clegg. Perfectly nice guy, but no genius. Lives locally to us in Hampshire. Anyway, point is, if you got in there, took the business private, ditched Ross and inserted first-rate management, you could clean up.'

'Isn't Ross any good, then? I heard he was.'

'God, no. Less than useless. Devotes most of his time to personal self-promotion. Obsessed with his own PR.'

'Really?' Dick's eyes narrowed.

'You must have seen him in the *Evening Standard* guide the other day. The 1000 Most Powerful Poseurs, some nonsense like that. He adores that kind of thing, laps it up.'

'You could be right,' Dick replied, 'but I'm not convinced there's enough cost to take out. We took a look at the grocery sector recently, and my research people reported Freeza Mart was one of the most tightly managed.'

'I'm surprised. Ross has been buying ten-million-pound houses for himself like there's no tomorrow.'

'That may be so. But we'd need to believe we could enhance margins by five to six points or it's not worth doing.' He pronged several pieces of prosciutto and mozzarella on a fork, and crammed them into his mouth. 'In fact, if we were going to take a run at the grocers, we'd more likely go after Sainsbury's or Pendletons. There's more fat on both of them . . . art in the boardroom, all that crap.'

Miles's heart fell. Across Dick's fat knees, he could see Dick's fat fingers probing the bottom of Sam's bikini, and his daughter's long brown legs extending endlessly under the table. Now Dick was whispering something into Sam's ear, and she smiled eagerly. Then, before pudding and coffee could be served, Dick stood up, scraping back his chair.

'Ok, team,' he announced to the table. 'Team Gunnslinger—back on board. We need to leave right away if we're going to make Capri by dinner. The table's booked for nine thirty.' Then, turning to Miles, he said, 'That was great, old man. I like your place. I might buy somewhere round here myself. Sam's joining me on the boat if you don't mind, I've sent her to collect her stuff, not that she needs bring much.'

'I'm afraid that's not possible,' Miles said firmly. 'Samantha's on a family holiday, and I have her return air ticket from Rome to London.'

'Not an issue. She can fly back in my plane with me, there's plenty of room. It's only me and the kids using it.'

34.

For two hours every Thursday morning, though it felt much longer, Ross endured the visits to his office of his presentational coach, Megan Miller of Megan Miller Associates. It had been Freeza Mart's corporate PR company that first recommended the appointment of a presentational coach, and directed him to Megan. Ross initially resisted the idea vehemently, saying he didn't need or want any fancy-pants consultants telling how to dress and speak, and anyway he didn't have the time, and he'd prefer to be judged on his company results than his party manners. But following a couple of challenging interviews in the business sections of the Sunday newspapers, when he didn't feel he'd got his message across clearly enough, and found he was battling against a lot of negative spin from competitors, Ross changed his mind.

'Ok,' he said. 'I'll give it a try. But if they tell me to start wearing a pink bow tie and aftershave or dressing from some poncey gents outfitters, I'm chucking it in right away.'

Not long afterwards, he had his initial appraisal with Megan. A one-time newsreader with Granada television, who still made periodic appearances on screen, Ross was immediately impressed by her, and by her sexy tortoiseshell glasses. Megan explained her role would encompass everything from media training for TV and print interviews, to helping Ross position himself as a coherent brand.

'And what's that supposed to mean then,' Ross asked, sceptically.

'It's all about building up a story around you,' Megan said. 'Right now, I don't know much about you at all, nor do the public. You're basically an unknown quantity.'

'That's just how I like it,' Ross said. 'Our customers aren't interested in Ross Clegg. They want to know our tuna and sweetcorn are consistently less dear than Pendletons's tuna and sweetcorn, and our household essentials cost less than the same product at Asda.'

'Wrong,' replied Megan. 'Well, you're absolutely right about value, of course, and that's what you do best. I can't help you with that, it's the meat and potatoes of your business. But you're mistaken if you think shoppers aren't interested in you. Or, anyway, that they wouldn't be interested if they knew who you were. People know who owns Topshop, right? They know—or some of them do—the guy who runs Marks & Spencer, he's always in the papers. And everyone knows Richard Branson.'

Ross made a face. 'Listen, Megan, let me make one thing clear. I don't want to be Richard Branson, thank you very much, or anything like him.'

Megan laughed. 'Point taken. I won't morph you into Branson. Shame. I was about to tell you to grow a beard and get bigger teeth. Just kidding.' Then she turned serious. 'I don't actually want you to change at all, I want you to be yourself. That's once we've agreed what yourself *is*. My job is to talk to Ross Clegg about Ross Clegg, establish his character—the bits that tell a story, and work it up into something. Give you some definition for your media profile It's an editing process. Focusing on the essence of the man.'

Ross shrugged. 'Well I've got to warn you, Megan, you've not got a lot to work with. I'm not a particularly fascinating bloke, you know. I didn't row for England or win a gold medal in the Olympics or anything, before coming into this business.'

'What *did* you do then?'

'Nothing. That's just it. This is all I've done. I set up Freeza Mart when I was twenty-four years old, that was the first store in Droitwich. It was only small—tiny compared to the superstores we're putting up today. Fifteen hundred square feet. You could have fitted ninety of them inside our new Paddington Basin store, and fortty-nine into the new Selly Oak one.'

'How long was it before you opened your second branch then?'

'The second store? Two years. That was in Redditch. We'd have done it quicker if it wasn't for Dawn having our first kid. That's Greg. He was almost born on the shop floor, literally. Dawn was serving a customer and filling their plastic bags—it was all plastic shopping bags then, before we got into this eco business—and suddenly the baby started coming. I had to shut up store, into the car, and we just made it to the hospital. Another ten minutes and I'd have been delivering him myself in the car park, we were that close.'

'So your wife worked with you at Freeza Mart?'

'Dawn was our first employee. Not that the business could afford to pay her anything, it couldn't pay either of us, come to that. We lived off the food that was past its sell-by. I shouldn't say that, should I, not in an interview. The health and safety people will be down on us.'

'Actually, I think you *should* say it. It's a good story. Use it next time.' She made a note in her pad. 'Were either of your parents in retail?'

'Retail! Well, they wouldn't have used that word for a start. They'd not have known what it meant. My mum helped out at the local haberdashers, when they were busy, and my nan worked there too, but my father was a steel man, in the old Dudley works for twenty years until they shut it down. I often wonder what he'd say if he saw some of the new Freeza Mart stores. It's a shame he's not still around. I can hear him now: 'Forty different varieties of yoghurt?' I'm sure he never ate a yoghurt in his life. The choice today, people take it for granted. We've got 70,000 product lines in Paddington. Three hundred and sixty different cheeses. In our first shop, we only sold cheddar and Dutch Edam—the one with the red waxy rind, remember that? And cheddar slices, pre-cut with plastic leaves in between. They were very popular, people put them in sandwiches in their lunchbox. That's something else you don't see, lunchboxes. People prefer to buy a sandwich from our grub-on-the-run bakery.'

'I have to ask about the limp.' Megan said. 'Sorry. But people do ask. Polio, wasn't it? I think I read that somewhere.'

So Ross told her about his childhood affliction and the three years of hospital visits and blood tests it had taken before he was finally diagnosed free of it, and how it had prevented him from playing any sport. 'Not as a youngster. I had to stand by and watch my mates but could never join in, it was a very frustrating time. I was determined to beat it. There was this gym in the community centre with weight machines—they were still quite a novelty back then—and I worked on my upper body strength. Since my legs weren't strong, I reckoned I'd work on the top half. Which is why, to this day, I have this over-developed torso—don't worry, I'm not about to show you—and then these stick-like legs, one of them anyway.'

'Can you manage any sports? You look fit.'

'No squash, no jogging, nothing like that. But I swim regularly. And don't laugh, Dawn's been getting me into the horseback riding. Our younger daughter, Debbie, she's always been mad keen, and Dawn rides out most days, when she's able to. And recently I've been giving it a go. Just hacking out, nothing too clever. I hadn't appreciated what good exercise it is. The first few times I was so stiff I could barely walk afterwards.'

'That's down in Hampshire somewhere, right?'

'We built a place in Chawbury. Small village, nobody's heard of it. I needed to relocate south when we expanded the business out of the West Midlands.'

'Chawbury? Doesn't Miles Straker have a place there? I went to a big lunch a few summers ago. I've done media training for some of his clients.'

'That's right. Miles and Davina. They live across the valley from our place. Dawn sees more of them than I do, and our daughters are good mates.' Ross looked thoughtful, and Megan sensed that there might be more he wasn't saying. Then he went on, 'By coincidence, we recently bought a place up in town, which is right across from them too. Over in West London.' He shrugged. 'I'd probably not have bought the place; it was Dawn's idea. She'd seen this house—far too big for us really—and I was dead set against.'

'So she talked you round?'

'Right. Kept telling me what a grand investment it was, on and on about it. Until I caved in. I asked a couple of my larger investors, Callum Dunlop and Brin Watkins, what they reckoned, and they were positive too. So now we're in the middle of this big renovation project costing an arm and a leg, on top of everything else, with the new Coventry warehouse still bedding down.'

Ross's PA knocked at the door. 'Sorry to interrupt, but your twelve o'clock is here.'

Megan stood up to leave. 'Thank you for being so forthcoming.'

'You see. I was right, wasn't I? There's nothing interesting to say about me.'

'Actually, Ross, quite the reverse. There's plenty. Classic triumph over adversity stuff, the public responds well to that.'

'I don't know. I don't feel comfortable about it. What worries me, if you put your head above the parapet . . .'

'It might get shot off?'

'Exactly. I'd sooner keep my head down working. I don't really like seeing my name in print.'

'I saw you made it onto the *Evening Standard* Power List.'

'That's what I mean. I hated that. Especially the mention of the London house and what I was supposed to have paid for it.'

Megan smiled. 'Half my clients pay me to increase their profile. They love appearing on lists like that.'

'Me, I hate it. It makes me squirm. I hated our people inside the business reading it.'

'Then you'd better start getting used to it,' Megan said. 'The way your business is growing, it isn't going to stop anytime soon.'

35.

reg Clegg's adoption as Labour candidate for the Kings-town ward of the Hammersmith and Fulham council was a triumph of political manoeuvring and bad faith. At the outset, Greg's chances of selection seemed negligible; there were at least three others with greater claims than he. One, the deputy headmaster of a local comprehensive school, had served the party faithfully for fifteen years. Another, a pillar of the borough proba-tion department, was the live-in partner of the local party secretary. The third, being a Jamaican-born female trades union convenor at the Royal Mail, had obvious credentials of her own. Greg's appli-cation was welcomed as evidence of his future ambition but scarcely taken seriously by the selection committee. In the first round of in-terviews, he was ranked third or fourth by each of the six council-lors on the panel, having struck them as too young and supercilious. Several commented they had found him obnoxious in his replies to their questions.

As the selection process moved to the second round, however, two candidates surprised everyone by withdrawing their names. It was very unexpected and rumours circulated about dirty tricks. Greg said he suspected a smear campaign by the Tories. Whatever the reason, the deputy head and the Jamaican union convenor dropped out, leaving only Greg and the probation services supervi-sor, Gaynor Barnes. Gaynor's selection looked like a shoe-in until the local newspaper, the *Hammersmith and Fulham Courier*, following an anonymous tip-off, ran a front-page story exposing an alleged expenses scam in her department. This was vehemently denied by all involved, and no incriminating evidence was ever produced, but the publicity alone was enough to make a full investigation inevitable, and it was of course impossible for Gaynor to seek public office until this was concluded. And so, with no other candidates left, the committee had no option than to select Greg as the youngest ever candidate for the safe Labour ward.

His selection was a source of surprise and pride to Ross and Dawn, who both immediately promised to canvas for him in the council elections, six months away. Greg consented to spend a rare weekend at Chawbury where toasts were proposed by his parents and Ross made a nice speech predicting a glorious future in politics.

'Uncle Greg might become prime minister,' Gemma said to Mandy, who was perched on her lap. 'He's going to be Tony Blair.'

'I hope you realise what you're taking on, Greg,' Ross said at one point. 'It's quite a commitment being a councillor. Folk expect you to help them jump the housing queue or get a new bathroom put in.'

Greg rolled his eyes. 'I won't be involved in any of that. I'll leave that to social services, thank you.'

'You'll be surprised by the size of your post bag. You'll have to set aside quite a bit of time to deal with it all.'

'Listen, I'm not getting dragged down by the small stuff. I'm interested in the big issues—planning, policy and resources, the environment.'

'It'll be helpful having you in planning,' Ross said, laughing. 'We've been having no end of trouble with Hammersmith and Fulham over our North End Road superstore. You'll be able to sort it for me.'

'I don't actually approve of the big supermarkets growing share in the borough, Ross.' Greg had recently stopped calling his father 'dad' and switched to his given name. 'You're squeezing out the small shopkeepers.'

'Bollocks. Anyway, what about consumer choice? We're much cheaper. People appreciate affordable food. You should welcome us.'

'Ross, this is *real politique* we're talking here. Small shopkeepers have votes. You don't. And you're environmentally undesirable.'

'How so? Freeza Mart has a darned good environmental record. Could be even better of course, but we're working on it.'

'Please,' Greg said, rolling his eyes. 'You're all as bad as each other. Pendletons, Freeza Mart, Asda. I tell you, I'd like to see the whole lot driven out of the borough. We're already a nuclear-free zone. I'd like to see us become a capitalism-free zone too.'

Debbie was eleven hours into a double shift, with only a twenty-minute break for a bite to eat, and feeling ragged. Not that she was complaining. Even after seven months, she never forgot how fortunate she was to have obtained a traineeship at such an amazing place. With a Michelin star, a semi-celebrity chef and a state of design hydrospa, the Buckingham Park Hotel between High Wycombe and Stoke Poges was a dream position. She knew she was absorbing so much, and it was great to see all the hotel management theory she'd learnt at college being put into practice by such a professional team.

Of course, she had started at the very bottom, doing everything from chambermaiding to waitressing in the hotel restaurants. The first week she'd been assigned shifts in the formal restaurant, Wycombe's, which had been awarded the coveted Michelin star, and been terrified she'd get something wrong: that she'd hand round the elaborate bread basket, with its ten different varieties of olive and corn breads, the wrong way, or make a mistake pouring the wine. Wycombe's was renowned for its cellar and many guests came specifically to enjoy particularly rare bottles, carefully considered by the Belgian sommelier, Ricard, a stickler for protocol. The dining room was so grand and formal, with its heavy curtains and damask wallpaper and framed citations and awards on every pillar, that most guests were intimidated into total silence, or whispered to their friends in anxious undertones. The food itself was gloriously elaborate, featuring duck foie gras in aspic with a fanned lobster tail on top, or medallions of venison in a reduced partridge and Madeira source. Debbie was excited to be serving it, though privately she didn't much care for the taste.

The complexity of running a five-star hotel fascinated her, especially since the Buckingham Park had so many facilities. In addition to the gourmet restaurant, there was a coffee shop known as Le Coffee Shop, popular at lunchtime with parties of local ladies, the spa with its own healthy eating menu, an 18-hole golf course and club house, and a thriving banqueting business for weddings, conferences and dinner dances. The hotel had a licence for wedding ceremonies in the original Georgian morning room, with receptions afterwards in a semi-permanent marquee on the lawn. Debbie found herself constantly occupied, regularly assigned to three different functions in a single day, pouring coffees, clearing plates, handing round trays of canapés and showing guests to their rooms. In her first two months she developed muscles in her right arm from lugging suitcases up to guest suites.

Partly because she didn't complain about doing late shifts, Debbie was often assigned on busy evenings to front desk reception, which gave her a chance to learn about the computerised billing system. One of her tasks, whenever anyone was checking out, was to dial the chambermaid for that floor and ask her to check whether they'd pilfered the towelling robes from the bathroom. It was surprising how many respectable people made off with bathrobes, bathmats and even blankets and electric hairdryers. Toiletries, of course, were expected to disappear, and allowed for.

Debbie was behind reception one Thursday evening, hair in a bun as required, and wearing her name badge—'Deborah'—when a distinguished-looking couple arrived at the front desk. It was clear from their body language they were in a filthy mood. Out of context, it took Debbie a moment to place them.

'You've got a reservation for me,' said the man, peremptorily. He did not focus on her face while speaking to her.

'Name, sir?'

'Straker.' He blew crossly, as if all this bureaucracy was already too much for him. His companion had dark copper hair and black leather trousers.

'Here you are, sir,' Debbie said, tapping at her computer terminal. 'We've got a lovely suite for you today, the Dashwood suite. If I could just have your signature here sir, and if I could just take an imprint of your preferred credit card.'

Miles made a cursory scribbled autograph, then said, 'I can't believe you need a credit card. We've stayed here before. You don't seriously believe we'll leave without paying.'

'I'm afraid it's the rules, Mr Straker. If you don't mind.'

'Actually, I do mind. In fact, I've a bloody good mind not to check in at all. Jesus Christ, my company held a conference here recently for a hundred people. Where's the manager? I'd like to speak to him please?'

'I'll try and locate him, Mr Straker.'

'No, never mind that, I don't want to hang about waiting for him. Have our bags sent straight up to the room, we're going to have a drink in the bar. And get someone to park my car. I've left it outside.' He dropped his keys on the desk. 'The traffic was crawling, it took *two hours* to get here. It states one hour from London in your literature, which comes close to fraud.' With that Miles and Serena turned away.

Left alone behind reception, Debbie attempted to track down a bellboy to carry the cases and someone to shift the car. Before she'd found them, there was the sound of hooting from outside: Miles's new Jensen was blocking the drop-off point, and vehicles queuing up behind. Shrugging, she picked up the keys and went outside.

The Straker Jensen was the swankiest car she had ever seen. Dark metallic blue with tan leather seats and a tan leather steering wheel, the interior smelt like a new pair of shoes. Gingerly, she inserted the key and the walnut dashboard lit up like the cockpit of a plane and a Jamie Cullum jazz CD began playing. The bucket seat was pushed so far back her feet could barely reach the pedals. She was searching for the handbrake, which didn't seem to exist, and the off button for the music which she couldn't find either, when the cars behind began honking her to get a move on.

Clutching at random levers to release the brake, the car jerked forward before instantly stalling. Restarting the engine, she proceeded in a series of jolts and lurches along the asphalt drive to the visitors' car park. By the time she got there, and had inched the Jensen into a numbered parking slot, she was sweating.

Stretching back in the seat, she let out a sigh of relief. She wondered what the car was worth and whether she was insured to drive it, and what Miles would have said if she'd wrapped it round a bollard, which she almost had. It was typical he hadn't recognised her. She had actually only met him twice in her life, at that garden opening at the manor and at Mandy's christening, but nobody ever recognised her in her hotel uniform: it made you anonymous.

In the walnut tray between the seats she spotted a bottle of scent, Poison by Dior, evidently Serena's, and rewarded herself with a little spritz. It was shocking Miles would arrive so blatantly at a hotel with Serena, and Debbie felt mortified for Davina and wondered whether she knew. Mollie would be devastated too, and must never find out. If Mollie had any knowledge of her dad's mistress, she'd never breathed a word.

Debbie was getting out of the car when she spotted the file on the back seat, with the Freeza Mart logo on the cover. It was a clear plastic sheaf with photocopies of newspaper cuttings and a lot of papers and reports, with coloured stickers protruding from them. Having first checked she wasn't being observed, Debbie took the file to the front and sifted through it.

There were numerous articles about her dad, some from newspapers, others from trade magazines like the *Grocer* and *Retail News*, with paragraphs marked in yellow highlighter. And notes in the margins: 'Stock options far too generous—speak institutional investors' and 'Growth projections unsustainable—shareholder value?'

For some reason, Debbie found it troubling. She couldn't explain exactly why, but the sight of so many cuttings about her father struck her as dangerous, even hostile. It was silly really, since Mollie was her best friend, but she didn't like Miles Straker, and didn't trust him either.

Mollie had a dream, which had begun with a casual conversation in her mum's kitchen.

She hadn't been home to Chawbury for several weeks but had been given, along with the rest of the teaching staff, two days off as 'marking leave,' so had headed down to Hampshire for a good rest. After the comparative squalor of the shared flat in Olympia (not that she was complaining: she felt perpetually guilty about how civilised her own place was, compared to the homes of many of her pupils), Mollie found it wonderfully relaxing to hang out in the warm family kitchen, with just her mum there (Miles was at a work conference at a hotel near Stoke Poges) and a lentil and marrow casserole (Mollie had recently turned vegetarian) and have a really good heart to heart.

Unlike Miles, Davina was a good listener, and could actually remember the names of the pupils they'd talked about from one visit to the next, so they discussed Omar the dyspraxic Tunisian boy, and sweet little Benazir who'd been betrothed at the age of six and would shortly be returning to Karachi to live with the in-laws she'd never met, and Kio from Lagos who'd never seen his father. All had been taken on by Mollie for remedial reading classes and quickly become the focus for her boundless compassion. She had only to recount their life-stories to become quite tearful, for the injustices of the world weighed heavily upon her. When Miles was around, he confused and belittled her with macro-generalisations about the underclass and their pre-programmed imperfections ('Fact: if you confiscated all the capital in the world and gave everyone—all six billion of us—fifty thousand dollars each as a fresh start, a totally level playing field, within five years the world would have re-attained its status quo; and nothing you could do to stop it. The Bill Gateses and Warren Buffets would have made it all back again. Ditto the Pendletons. And, dare I say it, the Strakers. And your tragic little Omars, Kios and Benazirs and whoevers would be right back at square one. That's why Communism failed utterly as a phi-losophy. *Redistribution doesn't work*. You can help people to a certain point—and *should* help them too, which is why I keep on encouraging Pendletons to fund all these scholarships. It's all very fine these caring-sharing sentiments, and teaching your school kids about the obligations of citizenship and suchlike, but ultimately you're not going to make a blind bit of difference.')

With Davina, it was so much more reasonable and relaxed. They sat at the kitchen table and ate their supper, and it was low-key and sympathetic. Sometimes Mollie sensed a deep sadness in her mother, but couldn't tell whether it was to do with the conversation they'd just been having or something else, and didn't feel she could ask. When she enquired about her week, Davina said only, 'Oh, darling, it was very nice really. I spent a couple of nights in London with your father, supporting him at his things, and the rest of the time down here in the garden. We're starting a new composting system.'

The telephone rang during supper and Davina, answering, said, 'That was Dawny. She's dropping back some flooring samples she borrowed, from when we re-did the barn.'

'I haven't seen Dawn for ages. How is she? I used to spend so much time over there.'

'Flourishing, I think. Frantically busy. I don't envy her doing up that great big London house they've bought, but she seems to be thriving on it. She's so organised these days.'

'I buy soup from Ross's shop every day,' Mollie said. 'From the big new one near school. Freeza Mart's organic squash and pumpkin soup. We had a supper party at the flat, and everyone thought it was home made.'

'Tell Dawn that when she gets here. Ross will be so pleased to hear you like it. But don't tell your father, you know how he can be.'

'He'd go ape,' Mollie said, laughing. 'I bought my lunch at the Freeza Mart bakery almost every day at college, but never told him. He thought I went to Pendletons.'

A few minutes later they heard the sound of Dawn's car outside on the gravel, and she joined them in the kitchen.

'This is all very nice and cosy,' she declared. 'And how lovely to see you, Mollie.' She placed the wooden floor samples on the kitchen table, along with printed fliers for a performance of *La Bohème* which was to be put on at a notorious sink-comprehensive in Portsmouth. 'Do come along if you'd like to. Lady Pendleton's worried not enough of the pupils will show up on the night and we can't have empty seats when the orchestra have donated their time.'

Davina put on the kettle and made coffee and herb tea, and Dawn, who was in no hurry to leave, being all on her own at the Park, told them her news and caught up with Mollie's. She had always had a soft spot for Debbie and Gemma's friend, considering Mollie the nicest of the Straker kids and the only one she found it easy to talk to. So they chatted about the horses and Dawn's plan to buy a new one for dressage ('Don't tell Ross, if you see him, he'd have a fit. He thinks we've quite enough horses already') and how the building project in Holland Park Square was coming along ('Serena, my decorator, and I are putting double vanities in the master bathroom, which Ross thinks a dreadful extravagance, but I said to him, "Ross, I'm forty-seven years old. I'm not sharing a basin with your toothbrush a day longer"').

She said Gemma had taken Mandy up to Droitwich for a few days, to show her off to her old schoolmates, which was virtually the first time she'd left Chawbury Park since Mandy was born, which would be a nice change for her, and good that she was finally spreading her wings a bit. There was always a slight awkwardness when Mandy entered the conversation, despite Davina and Dawn's best efforts; by the same token, Davina seldom mentioned her younger son in front of Dawn: Archie remained a perpetual spectre at the feast, expunged from the family run-down. Dawn told them how well Debbie was doing at her hotel ('Though I do worry about her. She was exhausted, poor love, last time she came home. All she could do was sleep and sleep. I *wish* she'd do something else, its no life for her . . . but she won't listen') and how Greg was 'so caught up in all his politics we scarcely clap eyes on him from one month to the next.' She said he'd upset Ross who'd offered him some Freeza Mart Chablis and own-brand samosas and all-day-party snacks and dips for a political husting at the Labour Club, but Greg turned him down flat, saying the voters wouldn't appreciate the gesture. 'They're chalk and cheese, those two,' Dawn said. 'Greg winds Ross up every time, knows just how to do it. Niggle, niggle, niggle and they're fighting like cats in a sack.'

'Not that our lot ever squabble,' said Davina, turning to Mollie. 'You and your siblings never exchange a cross word.'

'As if! You should have seen us last summer in Italy, Dawn,' Mollie said. 'Peter and Archie were unbelievable, much worse than my worst school kids. They bickered all day about *everything*, like whose turn it was to drive the speedboat and who'd lost the car keys. You wanted to bang their heads together.'

'And how's that beautiful Samantha?' Dawn asked. 'Every magazine I pick up, she's in it. Gemma gets *OK!* at home, and there's a lovely photo of her in the new one. She's like a model.'

'That's what she wants to be,' Mollie said. 'How sad is that? Not using your brain, just standing there like a dumb blonde posing all day.'

'Now, now,' said Davina. 'You're all very different and that's what makes it interesting.' Then, turning to Dawn, she said, 'We *hope* Sam's alright. She seemed a bit withdrawn over the summer, and we haven't seen enough of her lately. She's got very involved with this boyfriend of hers, who Miles doesn't approve of, so it's all a bit tricky. He's quite a lot older, and we do worry.'

'Well, I wasn't going to mention anything,' Dawn said prissily, 'But I did see a picture of him. A slightly larger gentleman?'

'He's *gross*,' Mollie said. 'Not wishing to be fattist or anything. He visited us in Italy in this huge yacht which must emit about fifty million tons of carbon.'

Then Dawn talked some more about the committee she sat on with Laetitia Pendleton, and how the opera and theatre programmes were so well received in the schools. 'We took a delightful *Much Ado* to a primary school in Farnborough recently. Anyway, watching their little faces I couldn't tell how much they were taking in, Shakespeare's quite challenging for the best of us, but Laetitia says it all sinks in somehow, even if its . . . what's the word? . . . *subliminal*. I was sitting with James Pendleton, who's such a dear man, and he explained the plot to me as we went along.'

Listening to her, Mollie had a brainwave. 'Dawn, do your opera people only do schools round here, or would they ever consider a London performance, do you think? You see, I was just thinking how great it would be if they came to my school.'

'Well, I don't exactly know, I'd have to ask Lady Pendleton,' Dawn said doubtfully. 'So far it's always been in our area, but I could ask her. I'm meeting her for a coffee next week.'

'Please *do* ask her, it would be brilliant. It could be a life-changing experience for my kids. I'm sure none of them has ever seen an opera in their lives, they'd be so excited. And we've got the space for it. The old gym hall's been turned into a multimedia studio space.'

'I'll put it to Lady Pendleton over coffee. The family are friendly with your father in any case, so I'm sure she'd want to help if she possibly can.'

Mollie thanked Dawn profusely, though the fact that Miles might be a factor in the decision deflated her. Sometimes Mollie felt that, no matter what she tried to do in life, the long shadow of her dad always fell across her.

36.

Sam didn't know which was fading quicker: her suntan or her illusions about Dick.

Her rescue from the Italian villa had been gloriously liberating despite, or perhaps partly because of, the breach it had opened up with Miles. He had been furious, hating his authority being publicly challenged. And life on *Gunnslinger II* suited Sam perfectly, being aimless and luxurious in equal measure. They had cruised down the coast as far as Ischia, stopping only for dinners at a succession of harbour-side restaurants, and waited on hand and foot by Dick's eleven-man crew, including an on-board masseur and Pilates teacher. She spent hours every day in the Jacuzzi in a contented haze, watching the coastline drift by. Her transfer on board also gave her access to fresh supplies of grass and cocaine, Dick's guests being well provided for, and her position as Dick's squeeze-of-the-moment gave her honoured status with crew and guests alike. She had only to clap her hands, or extend a long brown leg from the hot tub, and someone rushed over with cocktail, towel or fluffy bathrobe.

If she was honest, the sole aspect of the cruise she didn't relish was the time she spent alone with Dick in their cabin. Despite his limitless mental energy, which drove him to make and remake half a dozen deals at a time, buying and divesting himself of businesses, he was correspondingly lacking in physical energy in the bedroom. Grotesquely obese, he found it difficult to complete sexual intercourse, huffing and puffing on top of her for four minutes maximum before rolling off and asking to be finished off manually. The fact was, Dick seldom initiated sex with Sam. As with previous girlfriends, once he had had them half a dozen times and established them as part of his retinue, he lost interest. When he felt horny, which normally only happened in the early mornings following boisterous alcohol-enhanced celebration of some deal, he would roll over towards Sam with his semi-erect cock rubbing up against her warm back, and invite her to take care of it, like bleeding an airlock on a radiator. Within minutes of coming, his penis shrivelled to a tiny walnut-sized knob nestling in the under-hang of his belly. Sam couldn't help feeling the name Dick was singularly inappropriate. The only time he showed her affection was in public, when he liked her to sit on his lap, or knead his back on the massage platform with her fingers. She found it repellent the way her hands sunk into the lardy folds of his back fat.

Back in London, the afterglow of the holiday overtaken by the sterility of life in Dick's Eaton Square apartment, Sam idly wondered what to do next with her life. The prospect of marriage and becoming Mrs Dick Gunn, with all that implied, was not something she was prepared completely to rule out. While recognising it was less than ideal, and scarcely conformed to the fairytale ending she once envisaged for herself, her character did not run to affirmative action. She lived by the day, content to take things as they came. And what was coming now was breakfast on a tray, delivered by Dick's Thai housekeeper, consisting of yoghurt with wheatgerm, a cup of strong coffee and sliced fruit. After a long bath and the daily ritual of washing, conditioning and drying her hair, Sam considered ringing her mother who, it being a Friday, would be down at Chawbury. But something stopped her: the inevitable hassle of being told Miles was still angry with her, and the promise Davina would try to extract to ring him and make things up, was more than she could quite face, any more than she wanted to commit to a country weekend at home.

She was setting out for a trot round the shops along Elizabeth Street when she heard the phone ring, and Lila, the Thai maid, saying she would fetch her. Gingerly she took the handset. 'Hello?'

'Darling? It's your mother.'

'Oh, hi Mum. I was about to call you.' She spoke warily.

'Look, I'm not ringing about the holiday. You know how your father can be, and he is still rather upset, but I'm sure it can all be sorted out. I'm ringing to remind you it's the big garden lunch party at Chawbury this weekend. You haven't forgotten? We're expecting you to be there, your father especially.'

Sam made a face. She had forgotten all about it. It was the last thing she needed.

'Is Dick asked?'

'I'm afraid not. I'm awfully sorry, Sam, it just wouldn't work this year.'

Samantha knew how stubborn Miles was, and how annoyed Dick would be if she sloped off to Chawbury without him. It wasn't as if Dick would actually want to go himself, but recently he had become oppressively possessive, demanding to know where she was all the time, and unhappy if she was unavailable for him at a minute's notice. He expected to be able to ask his PA to get her on the line and be instantly put through. If she turned her mobile off while having a massage or some other treatment, she would find half a dozen missed calls and urgent messages to ring when she switched it on again, and further messages at the flat. She found herself habitually lying about where she was and what she'd been doing. Even if she said she'd been having lunch with old school friends, Dick was disapproving, hating her to have any other life. When she went round to Gaz's for supplies, which happened more and more, she pretended she'd been at the hairdressers.

Caught in the crossfire between Dick and Miles, Sam knew she had no choice but to support Dick.

'Sorry, Mum, I can't make it this weekend. I'm doing something.'

'Oh dear, are you *sure* you can't?' Davina sounded worried. 'Isn't it something you can change? Your father will be so upset if you're not there, you know how he is about that lunch.'

'I'm sorry.'

'Oh, goodness. Well, if you can't come you can't come, I suppose. But it's not going to go down well.'

37.

Resplendent in a new lightweight summer suit, pale blue cotton shirt, dark blue silk tie and a sleek pair of sunglasses, Miles stood on the terrace surveying the lunch party preparations. Waiters and waitresses from Gourmand Solutions were delivering glassware to the twenty-five round tables in the marquee, and further glasses for cocktails and champagne were set-up on tables outside the orangerie for the pre-lunch reception. There were still too many clouds scudding across the sky for Miles's liking, but the forecast promised sunshine by noon so drinks in the garden remained a possibility. He certainly hoped so, since his brigade of gardeners had been working for weeks to produce perfect herbaceous borders for the 250 guests to admire. Miles's eyes scanned the horizon and, as usual, flinched at Ross's house. From this elevation you could see the rooftops of the entire mansion, as well as the outhouses and stables. Leylandii had grown to sufficient height to shield part of the tennis court, but you could spot the ornamental lampposts on the lawn. According to Davina, Ross had started taking shooting lessons which was obviously risible, and Miles was listening out for the blam-blam of clay pigeons. If he started blasting off in the valley, Miles would report him to the council.

Davina had been making a ridiculous fuss about wanting to invite the Cleggs to the lunch, and Miles had once again put his foot down.

'It's *so embarrassing*,' Davina said. 'What am I meant to say to Dawn? She's probably my best friend, one of them anyway, and she must know about the lunch. She must think it's so odd—and so hurtful—not to be included when they live so close.'

'This is a business event. It isn't appropriate.'

'You've invited all our other friends. They're all coming. The Mountleighs and the Nairns. And Nigel and Bean. And James and Laetitia. Laetitia sees Dawn all the time, they've become very close.'

'Well, I'm sorry. I don't want the Cleggs and that's all there is to it. They wouldn't fit in.'

'They'd actually be an asset. Everyone likes Ross, he's so easy, and I'm sure he knows plenty of your clients already. He'd get on like a house on fire with those airline people, the ones who came over in Italy, Bradley and Carole.'

'I'm sorry. The Cleggs are not invited. That's final.' Having closed the subject, Miles felt rather pleased with himself. He believed it was important for the man of the house to take a stand.

This year, apart from the Cleggs, there had been the irksome business of Samantha and Dick to contend with, and Miles was in a bate at the thought of his daughter defying him by boycotting the lunch. His first act had been to ring his bank and cancel the monthly allowance he still paid into her account. His second had been to inform Carmelita that Samantha was no longer welcome in Holland Park Square. If Dick wanted to carry on with his daughter, he could pay for the privilege, Miles would no longer subsidise it. He was still feeling sore that Dick had declined to mount a takeover of Freeza Mart. It seemed the least he could do, given his situation with Samantha.

The guests began to arrive and Miles, Davina, Peter, Archie and Mollie took up their position on the terrace to receive them, with the famous long view of Chawbury valley behind. A line of waitresses stood with outstretched trays of drinks, to sustain guests until they reached the longer bar by the orangerie. Miles was greeting the most prominent visitors with his customary warmth, gripping and embracing the managing directors of Eaziprint and Trent Valley Power 4 U. 'I think you've met my wife Davina—of course you have—and these are three of my reprobate children . . . Peter works with me at Straker Communications, poor chap . . . Sadly Samantha can't be here today, got herself a better invitation, ha ha . . .' All the time he was looking out for James and Laetitia—the Pendletons business accounting for forty-two percent of his annual revenues—at whose arrival he would dissolve the receiving line and escort Laetitia down to the lawn for pre-lunch drinks.

Paul and Brigitte Tanner rolled onto the terrace, Paul full of swagger now that Iain Duncan Smith was installed as Conservative leader. 'Never mind what the newspapers are writing. They'd be bound to take cheap pot-shots. But inside the party morale is high. We've got a grown-up, experienced leader again, and it's playing well on the doorsteps. The tide's finally turning.'

'God it's all looking immaculate here, Miles,' he went on, staring down the valley. 'Impeccable.' Then he said, 'I'm not sure I've ever noticed that other house before. Was it always there? I don't remember seeing it.' He peered at the rooftops of the Clegg mansion.

'Perfectly vile, isn't it? Should never have been allowed. We're furious about it.'

'Whose is it? I can see a tennis court . . . and a ménage, isn't it? All the toys.'

'Chap named Clegg. Moved down from Birmingham. Runs supermarkets.'

'Not *Ross* Clegg? That's a coincidence. We were talking about him yesterday as a potential party donor, but no one knew him. Is he going to be here for lunch?'

'No, he certainly isn't.'

'Pity. Tell you what, I might trouble you for a phone number. He's done awfully well I hear, and might be able to help us.'

Miles was still feeling irritable when Nigel and Bean bustled into view, Bean full of noisy exclamations about the beauty of the garden. 'The phlox by the front door are thriving, I see. Well done. Our soil's too alkaline, such a sadness.' Then turning to Davina, she said, 'Darling, *promise* you won't let me leave before I've spoken to Dawn Clegg. I want to ask if we can use their fields for the Pony Club gymkhana.'

'I'd love to, but very sadly they're not coming.'

'Oh, dammit. I've been meaning to speak to her, I was sure they'd be here.'

It was ten minutes before one, and Miles was beginning to wonder what had become of the Pendletons, when they finally turned up, full of apologies, explaining that a man from the Royal Academy in London had arrived very late to look at their Lucian Freuds for a forthcoming retrospective. Laetitia was carrying an envelope which she said contained tickets and car passes for a production of *Der Rosenkavalier* to which she and James were taking Ross and Dawn the following weekend. 'I guessed they'd be here, since you're all part of the Chawbury mafia. I keep telling people, "All the brilliant people live in Chawbury. They must put something in the water."'

Miles, aghast, replied, 'Actually, Laetitia, Ross and Dawn couldn't make it this year. I think they said they're abroad.'

'Goodness how sad. We do enjoy them. But *what* a party you're giving us as usual. Everything so pretty.' And with that they moved into lunch.

Surveying the marquee, Miles felt everything was going as well as could be hoped. The waitresses from Gourmand Solutions were bringing out the first course of pate de foie and toasted brioche with a marmalade of onion and quince jelly, and the tables of guests all looked appropriately animated. He spotted Serena and Robin at table four and acknowledged her with a discrete nod of his head.

This year he had doubled the size of the top table to accommodate as many of his most important clients as possible, though the table was carefully segregated with the Pendletons, Mountleighs, Tanners, Nairns, Zach Durbans, Sir Korma Gupta and Strakers insulated at one end, and less elevated guests well away at the other. Peter, Archie and Mollie were allocated to tables composed of secondary VIPs and marketing people, who would nevertheless appreciate the presence of a Straker. Archie looked like he was doing well, making the Corporate Communications Director of Trent Valley Power 4 U laugh, but Peter was struggling, and Mollie looked way out of her depth. Once again, Miles cursed the absence of Samantha. It would have been helpful having a gorgeous daughter here, to lift the scene.

The plates from the first course were being cleared away, when the roar of an engine turning over began drifting up the valley, followed by the clatter of rotor blades.

'Good heavens, whatever's that?' Miles said to Laetitia, apologetically.

Then, slowly and steadily, a helicopter ascended from the Cleggs' lawn and hovered above the house at the end of the valley. It was small, black and very sleek, with a glass bubble of a cockpit, and a black and gold fuselage.

'We all know who *that* is,' Laetitia announced. 'Dawn was telling me yesterday Ross has just bought one.'

'That helicopter belongs to the *Cleggs*?' Miles stared at it, stupefied with envy.

'He's been taking lessons for months. Didn't you know? He spent a fortnight at that marvellous place in Utah doing an intensive course. And now he's got his certificate.'

The helicopter accelerated a thousand yards up the valley—over *Miles's land*—then rose up above the horse chestnut trees and disappeared from view. All Miles could think was that the marquee must have been wonderfully visible from up there, and hoped Ross felt snubbed.

Laetitia was saying, 'He's going to find it invaluable. He'll wonder how he ever managed without one. He'll be able to visit lots of his stores in a day, and of course it'll be a godsend for travelling to and fro from this amazing Coventry warehouse he's built.'

'Ah, yes,' said Miles. 'The so-called logistics centre. I gather it's a terrible flop.'

'How interesting you should say that. You must tell James. You see, I know Pendletons are planning on using it for some of their own distribution. James has heard wonderful reports.'

38.

Miles was spoiling for a scrap, and knew who he was going to take it out on. The image of Ross's helicopter rising above the valley replayed in his head, until the entire afternoon was reduced to that single devastating moment. To make matters worse, all his guests had been excited by it and spoke of little else, impressed by Ross and his ability to fly himself. 'They're such an asset to the area, Ross and Dawn,' Laetitia declared. 'Completely unpretentious and natural.'

Miles felt obliged to agree, though he couldn't see what was unpretentious about owning a helicopter.

At last, the final lunch guests were expelled from the house, leaving only the caterers packing up plates and wine glasses. Without telling anyone, Miles slipped into his Jensen and drove in the direction of the Mountleighs. Two miles before their drive, he turned off onto a rough track leading between wheat fields to a deserted farmyard. Here, shielded by cowsheds and a grain dryer, was the secluded meeting point he used for rendezvous with Serena. When they hooked up for their illicit hotel jaunts, it was here in the farmyard Serena parked her Ford Fiesta and transferred into Miles's sports car. If they needed to talk, it was a simple matter for Serena to dodge in here, on her way to and from the shops.

As he swept into the farm yard, Miles saw Serena had arrived before him. Good: he had hoped from the tone of his voice she'd have got the message and jumped to it.

'Serena, get in this car.' He was peremptory. 'We're going for a drive.'

He pulled onto the dual carriageway and accelerated at full throttle. In a four-mile stretch of road he shot through two Gatso speed cameras, activating flashes in his rear mirror. Long ago, he had arranged for his cars to be registered at the Paris offices of Straker Communications, where all speeding letters were ignored. It was one of Miles's precepts that speed limits did not apply to people like himself.

'This has gone on long enough,' he said to Serena. 'It's got to stop.'

Imagining he meant their affair, she replied, 'I don't see why. Nobody's found out, have they?'

'I mean the business with the Cleggs. You working for them.'

'Oh no, Miles, not this again. We've discussed this so many times.'

'The discussion's over. I forbid it, and that's final. I insist you tell them you can't work for them, not at Chawbury, not in Holland Park Square. Is that understood?'

'Miles, you're being so silly . . .'

'Serena, read my lips: You are resigning from those jobs. Now. Today. I want you to ring Dawn—or Ross, I don't care which— from this car, on your mobile, in front of me. I'm not prepared to tolerate prevarication.'

'But Miles . . . the job's two thirds done. I can't just walk out. But I promise not to take on anything else.'

'You're not listening. I've asked you to call them.' Jerking the steering wheel, he swerved between two articulated lorries into a lay-by and switched off the ignition.

'Miles, you realise this is ridiculous. All of it. This perpetual rivalry with Ross.'

'It's *not* rivalry. How dare you call it rivalry? I hardly see myself in competition with the limping price-cutter, thank you very much.'

'Yes, you are. That's why you're being like this. It was the helicopter.'

'Rubbish. Anyway, the choice is yours. The phone's right there. I'm sure you know the number. Come on, I'm waiting.'

Attempting to diffuse the atmosphere, she draped her arm around his shoulder and stroked his hair, but Miles shook her off. 'I'm waiting.'

'Because they've bought a bigger house than you in London. The house and the helicopter. That's what this is all about.'

'I'm waiting.'

'Well, wait as long as you like. I'm not making the call.'

'Get out then. Go on, get out of this car.'

She hesitated, so he leant across her and opened the passenger door from inside. 'Make the call or get out.'

She stepped out into the lay-by, saying, 'You're pathetic. You do realise that.'

'Thank you,' said Miles. 'It was nice knowing you too. Please close the door behind you.' Then he accelerated across the pot-holed tarmac and back onto the road.

Serena stood in the lay-by, buffeted by the tailwind of passing traffic, and wondered what to do. Her car was parked in the farm-yard eight miles away, and she wasn't sure how she'd explain it to Robin, if she rang him to collect her. She felt desolate at the quarrel and furious with Miles; she'd had it with his arrogance and deter-mined to end the whole thing. At the same time, the prospect of life with Robin, without the treats and adventures Miles provided, was wretched. At the end of the lay-by was a food van selling snacks and drinks, and she picked her way along and bought a cup of tea.

She was standing there, feeling miserable, when a black Chero-kee jeep pulled up in front of her. 'Serena? It *is* you. I thought so. I spotted you as I drove past and said, "That's our Serena."' Ross was beaming at her through the open window. 'Not your usual style of place is it, the roadside caff? Not where you take Dawn anyway.'

Ross said he was driving back to Chawbury from Coventry, hav-ing collected his car, and did she need a lift anywhere. 'What have you done with your wheels, Serena? You never hitched here?'

Soon she was heading in the direction of her car in the comfort of Ross's jeep, and as usual thinking what an attractive and straight-forward guy he was, so different from Miles's tricksiness. Slowly, she found herself telling him something about the quarrel with Miles, and how he had abandoned her in the lay-by. She realised their affair was horribly implicit in the story, and felt embarrassed about that.

'I never realised you and Miles were such mates,' Ross said dip-lomatically. 'That had somehow passed me by.'

'He didn't want anyone knowing. Nobody does.'

'Poor Davina,' said Ross. 'Sorry, I didn't mean that as a criticism of you, love. It's only that Davina and Dawn are so friendly, that's all.' Then he asked, 'What were you and Miles barneying about anyway, if you don't mind me asking?'

Serena laughed. 'About *you* mostly.' She stared out of the window.

Ross looked surprised. 'About *me*? Why?'

'He's jealous of you, not that he admits it.'

'You're kidding me.'

'Be careful of him,' Serena said. Then she told him how annoyed Miles was when the Cleggs bought their house on Holland Park Square, which was bigger than his own.

'I'm gobsmacked,' Ross said. 'There's no other word for it.' He seemed genuinely surprised, and Serena found his naivety attractive.

'You've no idea how obsessed he is about you. I've had dinners where all he's done is talk about you.' She began to cry. 'It's not surprising he's jealous,' Serena sniffed, 'because you've done so well, Ross. Everyone says so.'

'Nice of you to say so,' Ross replied. 'Mostly it just feels like slog and grind.'

Her arm brushed against the back of his neck and his hair was short and bristly, like stroking a clothes brush, quite different from Miles's silky mane. 'I've always admired you, Ross. You know that, don't you?'

Ross felt an unexpected surge of sexual frisson. The fact was, it was several years since he'd felt anything very strong for Dawn. What with his punishing work schedule, early starts and late hours, and Dawn being so occupied with her horses, builders and committees, Ross sometimes felt their lives had diverged. Serena was the sort of woman he's always considered out of his league. But here she was, crying all over him.

They arrived at the farmyard where Serena had left her car. Serena said, 'Ross, I sometimes need to be in London on Monday nights. I know Dawn is usually still in Chawbury on Mondays. So if you ever need company . . .' Her hand pressed on his thigh, he felt her warm breath on his cheek.

'You know something,' he said at last. 'I think we'd best not.

Dawn and me, we go back a long, long way.' And with that, he opened the car door and walked round to the passenger side and let her out.

Serena gave him a lingering look, full of implicit sexuality, and said, 'Sure I can't change your mind?'

'Quite sure, love. Sorry.'

As he drove off, he said, 'Dammit, dammit,' loudly under his breath. And that night, unable to sleep, he stared up the valley at the lights from the Strakers' house and tried to come to terms with everything Serena had told him.

39.

arly that February, and little more than eight months behind
schedule, Ross and Dawn's new home in Holland Park Square
was ready for occupation. Having known it as a wreck for so
long, and remembering the walls stripped back to their brickwork
and the basement floors exposed to bare earth, Dawn could hardly
believe the speed with which the final stages came together. Under
Serena's direction, carpets were laid over a weekend, and curtains
and sofas appeared from the curtain-makers and upholsterers and
were delivered to their designated rooms. Tall bookcases had been
built off-site and now arrived in bubble wrap, and stood like giant
bare sentry boxes on either side of the study fireplace. It worried
Dawn they had so few books to fill the shelves, so she placed the
telephone on one shelf, and well-spaced ornaments on another, and
some of the free estate agents magazines that fell through the letter
box on another. She made a mental note to go to an art bookshop
at the earliest opportunity and buy a lot of white-spined art volumes like James and Laetita had, to fill them up.

Once everything was installed, Dawn was delighted by the effect. The house was everything she had wished for, and she had to
pinch herself to believe it was really hers. With Serena's eye, it looked
more like the Pendletons's home than their own. Gazing around at
the subtle sofa covers and cushions, the abstract paintings Serena
had helped buy in Cork Street, and the elegant bronze statues dotted
on every surface, she perched herself on the edge of a sofa so as not
to crease it, and emitted a sigh of contentment. Now, at last, her
grown-up life could begin. At last, she had a home in which to receive friends, and the people she envisaged becoming her friends in
the future. She had a vision of herself as patron of the arts, receiv-

ing fellow connoisseurs in this room. And, above anything, she could repay James and Laetitia for all their hospitality. She had frequently promised Laetitia they would be the first guests through the front door.

Ross moved into the new house from Roupell Street, crossing London with his knocked-about suitcases and sports bags, which Dawn felt looked very shabby plonked down in the new hall. Having invested so much time and thought to create her perfect home, she recoiled at any intrusion of real life, such as Ross's paste-encrusted toothbrush and toiletries on the pristine vanity units. Greg came for supper in the new kitchen and declared it 'obscene' such an enormous mansion should be lived in by only a few part-time inhabitants, his parents and siblings. 'It's too big to be a private home. The local authority should take it over as a refuge for abused women or something,' he said, blithely unaware of its former use. Dawn decided not to mention Gemma wouldn't actually be living with them at the house, having elected to take over Roupell Street after her dad moved out. As Mandy approached her fourth birthday, it seemed the right moment for Gemma to resume life and move up to town. Gemma hoped to find a job, having taken a typing and computer skills sandwich course. Ross and Dawn both felt it was time she got her teeth stuck into something; she was still so young, and couldn't live down in Chawbury as a single mum forever. Dawn also realised her own ambitious life plans would hardly be enhanced by having Gemma and Mandy underfoot, much as she loved them, so the idea of retaining Roupell Street as Gemma's London base made every kind of sense.

Dick had been in Zurich for three days working on a deal, and rang to say he would be flying to New York that evening. He would drop in to Eaton Square around three o'clock to switch suitcases and hoped Sam would be there since he needed a word. He then asked to be put through to Lila, the Thai maid, to brief her on his packing requirements.

Sam was doubly put out by the call. She felt grumpy with Dick. For one thing, he had been travelling for weeks and she was bored and lonely alone at the flat, and feeling ignored. He was such an enormous figure that life felt flat in his absences. Moreover, she had intended to go round to Gaz's place that afternoon and hang out there, but now she had to wait home for Dick. She switched on the television—God, she watched a lot of television these days—and Lila brought in a percolator of coffee on a tray.

At ten past four there was a commotion in the hall, with Dick's driver carrying his luggage and briefcases from the lift, and Dick exploding into the drawing room in a double-breasted overcoat with further attaché cases in each hand. 'Je-*sus*,' he said. 'There was a fucking queue to land at Northolt. We had to circle for twenty-five minutes. Might as well fly commercial.'

Sam was stirring herself to greet him when she noticed the other woman slipping into the room, looking awkward and embarrassed. She was older than Sam, maybe thirty-two, and carrying what looked like the new Fendi handbag, the one Sam herself coveted.

Sam looked at her quizzically, then at Dick.

'Ah, yes. This is Delphine. Delphine, this is Samantha Straker, who I've told you about.'

Delphine smiled and held on to Dick's arm. Sam noticed the driver had left two pieces of Delphine's logo-embossed luggage by the door.

'Dick, is there something I should know?'

Dick lit up a small cigar. 'I do need a word actually, Sam. Delphine, would you mind giving us a moment, darling? Need a bit of privacy with Sam, if you don't mind.' He watched her leave, waiting until the door closed behind her.

'Thing is, Sam, to put it bluntly, it's time for a bit of a changing of the guard. Hope you understand, sure you do, being a grown-up girl. But, you see, Dephine and I . . . no easy way to say this frankly, but we've become a bit of an item over the past couple of weeks, which presents us with rather a problem with our own situation. Past situation, I should say.'

'You and Delphine?'

'She's a spunky lady, used to be married to a good mate of mine in fact. Known her for years, not like now of course.'

'So . . . you're saying we're over?'

'Well, only in that way, darlin'. Can't run two birds in tandem, not right. Unbreakable rule. But hope you'll come and stay on the boat next summer as usual. Always fun on the boat. Crew will be awfully disappointed if you aren't there.'

Sam felt numb at the speed of it all; one minute she was Dick Gunn's woman, the next she wasn't.

'Tell you what,' Dick said. 'Don't feel under pressure to clear out today or tomorrow. No gun to your head, forgive the pun. I've told Lila you're moving on and she's going to take care of your packing, everything like that, so no need to bother about anything. I'm away till the end of the week, so take your time, you can stay until Thursday.'

Mollie just stood there, unable to respond to the compliments coming from all sides. She felt only relief it was over and nothing had gone wrong. Her headmaster was shaking her by the hand saying what a grand job she'd done, and so was the local community outreach officer. Across the room she spotted Laetitia and Dawn and she had to go over and thank them, since it was all due to them the performance had happened at all. And of course she had to go backstage and thank the performers, who had donated their time and talent. So many people had been sceptical about the initiative, predicting *La Traviata* would go way above the audience's head, but the kids loved it. You could see it in their faces. Only a minority had been disruptive, and you had to expect that. Verdi was a challenging new experience for them all.

It had required so much effort to pull it off, but Mollie now knew it had been worth it. She'd had several meetings with Laetitia, then with the Pendletons's sponsorship people who had generously put up most of the funding, and meetings with the local education authority some of whom had questioned whether opera wasn't too elitist for a multi-cultural audience. But Mollie stood her ground. She had sat in the front row tonight with two little Ghanaian kids on either side of her, and watched their rapt attention at every aria. Her one regret was that her parents hadn't been able to make it. Miles had promised to try his best, but a client dinner shifted at the last minute and he'd had to go to Mosimann's with some big cheeses from Fiat, and insisted Davina accompany him.

A reporter and photographer from the local paper were covering the event for the *Olympia Guardian*, and Mollie was embarrassed when they asked to take her picture. Having worked flat-out until curtain-up shifting chairs and benches into the hall, and helping backstage making coffee and snacks for the performers, she hadn't had a moment to smarten herself up and knew she looked a fright.

She was posing in a line-up with her headmaster, plus the community outreach officer and the deputy director of development for the ENO, when an overweight man in tinted glasses barged his way into the picture. For a moment, Mollie couldn't place him, though she was sure she'd seen him before somewhere. Having positioned himself in the centre of the group, he beamed at the photographer, waiting for him to take the picture. When the reporter approached them with her notebook to check their names, the man said, 'Greg Clegg. Chair of the Labour Arts and Leisure Panel, Hammersmith and Fulham Council.'

'Greg?' said Mollie. 'It's me, Mollie. Mollie Straker. Remember? Your neighbour in Chawbury.'

Greg looked at her, surprised. 'What on earth are *you* doing here?'

'I teach here. At the school. And I got the opera to come here for the show.'

'Ah yes,' replied Greg, addressing himself to the reporter. 'Initiatives like tonight are a key plank of our Bringing Culture to the Community outreach programme. A Labour-endorsed initiative to prioritise the performing arts in inner-city areas of special need.'

The reporter was writing it all down in her notebook, nodding encouragement.

'For too long,' Greg went on, 'what might be termed "the higher arts" have been kept as the elitist preserve of the very rich, under successive Tory arts policies. Now, at grass roots community level, Labour is committed to the democratisation of so-called culture, making it accessible to everyone irrespective of creed or colour.'

The reporter was still nodding away.

'Under a Labour authority,' he proclaimed, 'culture has no price barrier to entry.'

'And Pendletons were really generous and sponsored it all,' said Mollie, feeling she should acknowledge Laetitia's help.

'Yes,' said Greg, 'another of our New Labour initiatives: working in partnership with business in the community. Within the context of our overall framework, of course.' He then retrieved from his wallet a business card with the red rose of Labour termoprinted on the top, and thrust it into the reporter's hand. 'Feel free to call if you need further information. I'm a close personal friend of your editor, by the way.'

After the reporter had left, Greg said, 'I hadn't realised you're employed by the local authority, Mollie. I can't believe your dad approves of you working in the state sector.'

Mollie laughed. 'You're right. He thought I was mad when I told him. He'd rather I was teaching at some private school in Kensington. But it wouldn't be nearly so satisfying.'

'So you like it down here with us plebs?'

'The kids I teach are great. It's very fulfilling. I really feel I'm making a difference.' She started telling him about some of the children in her class and how concerned she was that, by the time they turned twelve or thirteen, there was so much peer-pressure to get into drugs and gangs and joy-riding in stolen cars. 'Some of the estates, they're incubators for crime.'

Halfway through her speech Mollie felt she was losing Greg's attention, because his eyes were roaming the sports hall, so she said, 'I'm sorry, I'm being boring. Dad's always saying I bang on too much.'

'Not at all,' Greg replied, pulling himself back. 'I'm impressed. I wouldn't have expected social responsibility from a Straker somehow. I thought you lived in an ivory tower.'

'Certainly not,' said Mollie. 'Well, I guess some of my family do. Anyway, it's been nice seeing you again. I didn't realise you're on the council.'

Greg was affronted. 'I'm surprised you haven't seen my literature. There's a flier that goes to everyone in the ward. Saying what I've achieved for the community.'

'I'm sorry, I'll look out for it.'

'Listen, give me your address and I'll get someone to post you the recent ones. I'd like to. And give me your phone number.' It occurred to Greg there might be some advantage in cultivating Miles

Straker's daughter. He didn't yet know what it might be, but sensed she was a socialist sympathiser and perhaps this could be used against the Conservatives at some point in the future.

Besides, he rather liked the idea of having an in to the perfect family at Chawbury Manor, and making an ally of Samantha's kid sister.

There was something guileless and idealistic about Mollie which, in his cynical way, he found attractive.

40.

jected from the Gunn apartment in Eaton Square, and banished from Holland Park Square on the orders of her dad, Samantha was suddenly homeless. Lila, the Thai maid, packed her suitcases with care and tissue paper, and now Sam was standing on the steps of Dick's white stucco building wondering where the hell to tell the taxi driver to take her.

In the end, she rang Gaz and he said, 'Yeah, sure, come over to Draycott Gardens, that's cool babe, no problem.' So in less than fifteen minutes she had occupied the little back bedroom and dumped her stuff. It was the perfect place to crash and Gaz was great about it, asking only a hundred quid a week for rent and letting her run a tab for gear. 'Pay me when you've got the cash,' he said. 'Now, what can I give you, babe?'

For six weeks, Sam barely left the flat. There was so much happening there, people coming and going, the phone ringing off the hook, time passed in a blur. Nobody got up before midday at the earliest, and most days her breakfast consisted of dry Ricicles or Frosties (there was seldom any milk) and a glass of open wine from last night. In the afternoons, she smoked dope or took cocaine against the backdrop of daytime TV. Sometimes Gaz handed her cash to buy bread and coffee at Cullen's on the Fulham Road, but mostly she just hung indoors. Most nights there were a dozen or more people over, dossing on sofas or cushions on the floor. More than once, Sam wondered whether she should ring her mum and tell her where she was, but it would be too much hassle going into the split with Dick. Much of the time she was too out-of-it to talk coherently, in any case. So she existed in limbo in a semi-permanent daze and had no wish to change a thing as the days ran into one another.

After a couple of months, Gaz said, 'Hey, Sam, you know you owe me over three grand, babe? £3,400 to be precise.'

'Is it that much? I didn't realise.' She felt rising panic.

'You've been going for it babe. Hoovering up the nice stuff.'

'I'm sorry. I'll pay you back soon.'

'How about today, babe? I need cash, I owe people myself.'

Sam was stricken. The last three times she'd tried to withdraw money from the ATM, she'd been rejected. Nothing seemed to be flowing into her account, she didn't know why, and she didn't like to call her dad. How she missed those wodges of cash Dick left out for her. Right now, she hadn't even enough money to get her hair cut, or buy stuff from the chemist.

'Gaz, I'll get the money soon, promise. Soon as I can. It might have to be a week or two . . .'

'Can't your dad lend it? I thought you were meant to be a fucking heiress or something?'

Sam shrugged.

'Listen, I do need that cash. I'm being pressed for it myself. You do *have* the money, don't you?'

'I'm fairly sure I can get it. I think so,' she said uncertainly.

'Because if it's a problem, I know how you could make some. Easy money. Like, people make thousands a week. And you've got the looks for it, they'd snap you up.'

Sam looked blank, so Gaz said he'd make a call for her, and arrange for her to meet up with some people he was friendly with.

It was Miles's Sunday night routine to leave Chawbury Manor after an early supper and drive up to London with whichever children had been staying for the weekend. This Sunday only Peter was home, so shortly before 9 p.m. they loaded their bags, Miles's two briefcases and Peter's acoustic guitar and set off for the big smoke.

Turning left at the end of the drive in the direction of Micheldever, they were approaching the new electric gates to Chawbury Park when Ross's black jeep pulled out ahead of them. Inside, they could see the back of Ross's and Dawn's heads.

Instantly competitive, Miles waited for a straight stretch before pulling out and overtaking. As he passed he hooted and gave a little wave. It felt good to be putting empty road between himself and the Cleggs.

Forty miles up the M3 he stopped for petrol at Fleet Service Station. As usual, he felt mildly exhilarated by the enormous volume of fuel his Jensen consumed, especially as it was paid for by his company. The dial was approaching ninety pounds when the Cleggs' Cherokee drew up at the next pump.

'Hiya, Miles,' Ross said, reaching for the diesel nozzle and withdrawing it from its holster. 'I've just had all the vehicles switched to diesel. Lower emissions.'

'Have you really,' Miles replied flatly, signalling lack of interest.

'I'll email you over the data,' Ross replied. 'There's a website with an emissions calculator. Nothing complicated. Even I can understand it.' Since his conversation with Serena, and Debbie telling him something about a file on Freeza Mart in Miles's car, Ross was wary of him, but resolved not to show it. You know what they say: stick close to your friends and closer to your enemies.

'Ah,' said Miles, heading inside to pay. He joined what looked like the shortest queue and waited in line. Service stations were places he instinctively despised, with their plastic fittings, moronic cashiers and complete lack of insulation from ordinary people. He gazed in pained dismay at his fellow customer and the repellent snacks they were piling into their baskets: the phallic pepperoni sausages, bonus-sized Yorkies, pasties and pies. It annoyed him there was no Fast Track line, like at the airport, for people prepared to pay a bit more.

His irritation grew when he noticed Ross's queue was moving faster than his own. Ross was, in fact, now slightly ahead of him, with just one person between him and the cashier, whereas there were two in Miles's queue. Ahead, some gormless punter was asking advice from the cashier about motor oil, and now—*intolerable*—discussing Nectar points.

Ross had paid and was walking back past him down the line. 'See you, Miles. I'll email you over the address of that website.'

Back on the motorway, Miles did his best to make up ground; he was determined to overtake the Cleggs' jeep and reach Holland Park Square before them. All the way into London, he was scanning the road ahead.

As they turned off Holland Villas Avenue, however, and up towards their square, they passed Ross unloading suitcases into the Clegg mansion. Dawn was crossing the pavement with a pile of clothes in dry cleaning bags across her arm. Spotting Miles, she gave a friendly little wave.

Miles snarled. What was it about these damn Cleggs? He couldn't get away from them. Wherever he went, in Chawbury, in London, at the ruddy *garage* for Christ sake, there they always were, turning up like bad pennies, following him about . . . aping him . . . bugging his entire family.

If things continued like this, he'd go insane.

Without mentioning it to anyone—and certainly noone at home—Peter was working on a bunch of new songs. Although by nature self-deprecating and easily discouraged by his own efforts, he felt these were his best so far. For the first time, he'd escaped from the influence of Neil Young and Joni Mitchell and was starting to find a voice of his own. His constant themes, more subtle and universal in the new work, were of escape: escape from the rat race, escape from the vanity and conceit of city life to something simpler and more authentic. He sang about quitting his job for a sandbar in the Caribbean, living off coconuts and fresh fish harvested from the sea. In another song, 'The Cormorant's Cry,' he evangelised life in a crofter's cottage on the island of Stroma, where strong winds blew away the poison of urban existence.

Sitting at his computer at Straker Communications, pretending to be writing a press release about Pendletons's new extra virgin cranberry juice, Peter burnished his lyrics. Having saved enough money to rent studio time and pay a couple of session musicians, he laid down seven tracks to semi-professional standards, and was thrilled when the sound guy at the studio said he was genuinely impressed by the result. 'You should send these off to record companies.' And so, over the next few weeks, Peter burned the tracks onto CDs and couriered them from Straker Communications's mailroom to all the big labels plus several independents. When he told Mollie, swearing her to secrecy, she filled him with optimism, saying she was sure they'd love them and everyone would be fighting to sign him up.

At work, Peter was still assigned as a client executive on the

Pendletons and Zach Durban accounts, and could not insulate himself from the growing anxiety at Pendletons. The mood at review meetings shifted from vibrant triumphalism to pessimism and blame-apportioning. Pendletons's market share slipped for the fourth quarter in succession, and every part of the business was suddenly under review, with new shop-fits, buying policies and accounting standards being adopted to boost results. Already, Pendletons's long-standing advertising agency, Barnes, Fleischman, Dwork, Fleischman, had been subjected to an open account pitch, and Straker Communications could not expect to avoid scrutiny if things continued in this way. Always at his best under pressure, Miles conducted himself with senatorial confidence, lunching and dining the Pendleton family at every opportunity, and initiating numerous research programmes aimed at pinpointing the problems.

Twenty thousand Pendletons customers were cross-questioned in supermarket aisles by market researchers with clipboards, and the same number of competitor customers quizzed about their shopping habits. The results were unequivocal: more and more loyal Pendletons shoppers were defecting to Freeza Mart.

What made everything doubly awkward for Miles was that Freeza Mart continued to get excellent PR, despite doing almost nothing to court it. Where Pendletons employed the forty-person Straker Communications team, Ross took calls from the press himself. After a couple more sessions with Megan Miller on interview technique, he'd perfected the knack of giving user-friendly sound bites that connected with his customer base. Increasingly, eco issues had risen up the agenda, and Miles, despite instinctive scepticism about the whole business, encouraged Pendletons to sponsor a Rainforest in Peril exhibition at the Museum of Mankind. To his fury, the sponsorship brought virtually no positive coverage to the supermarket, and Straker Communications was obliged to falsify their post-mortem report to the client. Ross, meanwhile, announced he was so ashamed at spotting Freeza Mart plastic bags stuck on hedgerows in country lanes he was banning the lot, just like that, and would use only recycled brown paper ones from now on. This was reported everywhere and his approval rating soared. Radio Four listeners put him in at number eight in their annual *Today* programme Man of the Year poll.

Miles's behaviour inside the firm became increasingly exacting and autocratic. Executives were removed from the Pendletons account for the slightest perceived failing, and several sacked. Peter reckoned only his family connection saved him from the same fate. It mortified him when his father savaged colleagues unjustly in front of a room full of people, and they felt too fearful of their jobs to answer back. And he contrasted the never-satisfied Miles of the office with the super-smooth Miles who took clients to the smartest restaurants.

Each evening he hastened home to Holland Park Square, hoping to find a letter from a record company. But six weeks after dispatching the CDs, he'd heard nothing whatever.

41.

Mollie read the article in the *Olympia Guardian* and tried not to feel disappointed. The important thing was the opera was written-up in the newspaper and the journalist was so positive about it all. Obviously it was a bit hurtful she hadn't been mentioned herself, and they'd cut her out of the photograph too. On second thoughts, that was probably no bad thing: she'd never been photogenic.

She did feel a twinge of irritation though, seeing Greg Clegg's picture so big. And most of the quotes came from Greg too. In fact, anybody reading it would think the opera had been his own idea. About half the story was devoted to Labour's Bringing Culture to the Community programme, and it didn't mention Pendletons's sponsorship, which was mortifyingly embarrassing.

Mollie heard her flatmates returning from work (Tina was another teacher, Kerry a sports therapist) and they both read the newspaper and were outraged on Mollie's behalf. 'How dare they? I can't *believe* this. They haven't given you any credit.'

Mollie insisted she didn't mind. 'It's not like I was doing it for the glory.'

'But who *is* this guy?' Kerry asked, affronted. 'He's muscled in on everything.'

'Actually he's OK, I think,' Mollie said. 'He lives near us in the country.'

'He needs to get into shape. He's carrying a lot of weight. Look at those chins.'

Later that same evening, Mollie's mobile rang when she was marking coursework.

'Is that Mollie Straker? Greg here. Greg Clegg from Hammersmith and Fulham Labour Party. We met the other night.'

'Yes, of course. Hi, Greg. I've just been looking at your picture.'

'In the local *Guardian*? I'm surprised you see that rag. I don't know why they dragged me into that opera report. It should have been *you*.'

'It doesn't matter. You're on the Council, you're more newsworthy.'

'Well, yes. I suppose I am a bit of a local celebrity. But I'm uncomfortable with personal publicity, I try to avoid it.'

'It sounds brilliant what you're doing with arts in the community.'

'Sometimes it feels like an impossible task, trying to change the culture. Not to mention years of Tory under-funding. But it's something I'm passionate about.' Then he said, 'It's the reason I'm calling you, I need to pick your brains. We're embarking on a ground-up review of social care provision, it'd be helpful to have your input . . .'

'I'd be happy to,' she replied, instantly excited. 'But I'm sure there are more qualified people than me to talk to.'

'That's just it. I need to speak to someone at the coalface, with first-hand experience of day-to-day issues. The other night you were telling me stuff about our immigrant communities . . .'

'Well, OK, if you really think I could help. When do you want to meet up?'

'Tomorrow? Supper? You know the Turkish place behind Barons Court tube?'

With Serena off the scene, this time very likely for good, Miles was feeling horribly oversexed and frustrated. Several times his fingers hovered above the keypad, deciding whether to ring her, but he was stubborn and disinclined to make the first move. Furthermore, he wouldn't take Serena back until she capitulated. Once she'd convinced him she'd dumped the Cleggs as clients, then and only then would he contemplate forgiveness. He did not doubt Serena would come running back. He imagined her sitting by the phone in her chilly farm cottage, with poor Robin Harden and the unfortunate kid, kicking herself for crossing him, and he hoped she'd learnt her lesson.

He gave lunch to Zach Durban who was passing through town,

and reported on his strategy to have Zach's Nelson Bluff hotel voted Best Caribbean Resort in the upcoming *Condé Nast Traveller* Readers' Awards, and his Dubai spa hotel named winner in the Emirates category. Straker Communications staff had covertly bought up half the newsstand copies with entry forms inside, and were busy filling these out in a variety of different handwritings and pens. Zach declared himself well pleased, and discussed appointing the agency to promote his new ski lodge in Vail, Colorado.

After lunch, Miles joined his MD Rick Partington and a posse of executives for a new business pitch to represent the Kingdom of Brunei. They met with a group of bluff former British army officers and royal advisers in a conference room in the basement of the Lanesborough Hotel. A solitary Brunei courtier, possibly a cousin of the Sultan, sat in shrivelled silence in their midst. Miles left most of the presentation to his people but intervened at the end, promising his personal involvement at every turn if they were afforded the great honour of assisting the Kingdom, and dropping the names of several big cheeses in industry and government. He left the meeting feeling confident of success, knowing his own intervention had been decisive. In the short car journey back to his office, he reminded his team that personal contacts are everything in this industry and none of them were worth their salaries unless they upped their game. Turning on a bright recent recruit to their graduate scheme, he said, 'Martin, I heard you say earlier you'd been at the cinema last night with your girlfriend. Mind telling us what you think you achieved by that? Sitting in darkness staring up at a screen? End of the evening, who've you met? Useful new contacts, clients, I mean? Woman behind the popcorn counter? Big deal. You should be out and about in fashionable restaurants, attending public lectures, cocktails. For the next four weeks I want a list on my desk every Monday morning: who you've met, why and how they could benefit us. I can't prop up this business all on my own, you know.'

By teatime, cocooned in his office, he experienced a violent randiness and went onto the website he most trusted in these situations. Mayfairbabes.com never let him down, with an ever-changing roster of escort girls from across the world. Scrolling the heavily-airbrushed pictures of the Mayfair babes on offer, he dialled the contact number.

'Good afternoon, I'm looking at your website and wondering whether Danielle or Yana might be available for ten p.m. tonight. An outcall. Ninety minutes.'

He gave the address of Zach Durban's London hotel, the Capital Grand Deluxe, where he had permanent access to a suite.

'Name?' said the receptionist. She might as well have asked, 'Alias?'

'Er, *Ross*,' replied Miles, relishing the mischief. 'My name's Ross.'

'I'm pleasantly surprised. Really, I didn't expect you to be like this.'

'Like what?'

'So sincere and idealistic. And *getting it*.' Greg was eyeballing her over the mezze, uncomfortably intense, almost like he was placing her under hypnosis. He lent across the formica tabletop, invading her personal space, and Mollie didn't know whether to feel intimidated or flattered. It was peculiar.

The whole evening was peculiar in fact, starting with the fact she was sitting here at all with Greg in this restaurant. Well, more of a café actually, six tables behind a Turkish takeaway with a big doner kebab on a spit in the steamed-up window and a counter where people queued to place orders. Beyond the counter were tables, metal legs bolted to the vinyl floor so you couldn't shift them back or forwards; which was a pity, since she'd like to have retreated a few inches further from Greg.

At the same time, there was something forceful about him she found impressive. Unlike most people she knew, who were apathetic or totally oblivious to the realities of the world she worked in, Greg actually wanted to do something about it. And furthermore he seemed to know how to set about it, and how things worked in local government. He talked about the local education authority in such a dismissive way, unlike her headmaster who was terrorised by them, saying, 'Listen, if they won't or can't change, we'll have to change *them*. Simple as that. We have the statutory powers and they're going to have to get with the programme.' He was similarly derisive about social services, implying they were entirely answerable to him, and he would brook no obstruction. 'I asked them for the ethnic split on Greek Cypriot and Turkish Cypriot families across the borough, and they said they don't have that information. It's not good enough. They're asleep on the job.'

As the meal progressed, Mollie attempted to introduce the subject of her experiences in the classroom, and explain the incremental steps by which she'd helped—or hoped she had helped—her most disadvantaged pupils, for whom English was often not even a second language. Greg nodded away, but she sensed he wasn't engaged, which was strange since that was the whole point of the supper. The times she felt he was most alert was when he cross-questioned her about her family. He seemed surprisingly curious about Sam. Mollie hadn't realised they even knew each other, and she had to admit she hadn't seen her for a while. 'She hardly ever rings up. I think she's living with her fat boyfriend.' Then, blushing, because Greg was a bit overweight himself—not that she was fattist or anything—she hurriedly said, 'Not that it matters, of course. It's just that Sam's sort of drifted away from the family. Dad doesn't approve of Dick—Sam's man—which doesn't help.'

'It must be difficult having a father like yours. I'm interested how you handle it, ethically I mean.'

'What do you mean?'

'Oh, you know, his support for questionable regimes, capitalism, consumerism. His entire job: it's being paid to lie. You'd have to feel ashamed, acting as spokesman for arms dealers and Pendletons and that dodgy billionaire with the *de-luxe* hotels. I visited one of his hotels once with my folks—we'd won a free trip—and the place stank, nothing but rich people frying on sunbeds.'

'It isn't just lying,' Mollie said, defending her dad, even though she half agreed with Greg's analysis. 'It's more giving advice to the clients, helping them handle the media.'

'Alright, not lying. Spinning then. You could argue it amounts to the same thing. It's all about helping big business crush the little guy while pretending to be doing him a favour. Take Pendletons. Take Freeza Mart for that matter. What do you think they pay their checkout staff per hour?'

Mollie knew the answer to this, since the mothers of several of her pupils had part-time jobs on the tills.

'Precisely,' said Greg. Four pounds eighty. And what did so-called Lord Pendleton take home last year, including dividends? Best part of thirty million quid. Is that fair? Is it equitable? I don't think so. But do we read about it? No, because guys like your dad are paid squillions to keep it out of the newspapers. If people found out there'd be a revolution. Not that I'm advocating revolution, there are other forms of affirmative action open to us, through legislation and progressive taxation. That's what I entered politics for, to create a fairer society.' He stared at her, eyes blazing with self-righteousness, challenging her to disagree.

Mollie, it so happened, did agree with him, and found his speech inspiring and slightly shaming, to hear the part her father played in the cycle of oppression. Greg put it all so damningly. She felt she ought to apologise, realising everything her family enjoyed—the two big houses, their private education and comforts—were rewards garnered from the oppression of others.

'I feel ashamed, I've never thought of it that way before.'

'Don't be too hard on yourself,' Greg said. 'They've gone to great lengths to ensure you *don't* think of it that way. That's part of the conspiracy. Prevent the proletariat from having access to knowledge, keep them acquiescent through ignorance. Why do you think the Tories wilfully underfunded the state education system for so long? It was government policy, made in Cabinet, not that it was allowed to be minuted of course. No incriminating fingerprints. But it was policy: the preservation of an underclass to buy cheap food from Tory-funding supermarkets, to be given the "choice"— "choice," what a clever, pernicious concept that is, worthy of Goebbels at his finest—between "independent" energy providers, all owned by profit-driven utility companies. I could go on.'

Mollie stared in earnest admiration, feeling for the first time in her life she'd met someone of real moral worth, and wanting above anything to earn his respect. 'Will you make big changes? The Labour government, I mean, now you're in power?'

'Well, we hope to,' he replied. 'We've started off quite cautiously, because everything we inherited—the economy, the infrastructure— was in such bad state through decades of neglect. But we're going to step it up, get more radical, we just can't tell anyone yet. Come the third and fourth terms we'll be renationalising the railways, the utilities, banks, supermarkets. The whole supply chain, in fact. It'll be bad news for people like the Pendletons—Ross too—but that's tough.'

42.

ight months out of university and Archie knew he should be finding a job. Miles was pressing him to join Straker Communications but it felt too predicable, nor did he want his dad breathing down his neck. From what Peter told him, it was a pretty futile existence doing PR in any case, writing press releases and sucking up to clients, not that Peter was a good judge. It crossed Archie's mind that, were he to join the family business, he'd quickly overtake his elder brother. But, for now, he'd rather have his freedom.

He was living in Holland Park Square in his old bedroom; from the window he could see right across the communal garden and into the Cleggs' place. From the bathroom you got an even better view, directly into the first-floor drawing room but also down into the kitchen in the basement. Quite often, while taking a shower, he saw Dawn pottering about unloading the dishwasher, or Dawn and Ross having supper at the table in the alcove. The kitchen looked really modern and flash, much cooler than their own kitchen which was traditional and old fashioned.

Archie started off thinking he'd like to be a futures trader, and met up with a few old college contacts who were doing it already, but it didn't actually sound that great the more he heard about it, and you had to poll up unfeasibly early miles away in the city. Instead, he took a temporary sales job at the Lexus showroom on the Old Brompton Road, and later helped out on the door at a mate's nightclub in South Ken, Thurloes, which was crawling with cool chicks and guys he knew from school. His job was to stand behind the velvet rope checking names on a clipboard, saying who could come in and who couldn't. Not that he consulted the list much, you could tell by looking who was suitable. Then, around two am, the door would be locked with everyone inside, and Archie went in to join the party. There was an incredible cocktail you could order, which cost like a hundred quid, consisting of champagne, rum, vodka, Grand Marnier, coconut water and eight straws, and you sat in a booth hoovering it up. Four sucks and you were bladdered. At such moments, the idea of a nine-to-five job was a joke.

It surprised him, while preparing to go out each evening, how often the Cleggs entertained in their new house. It seemed like every fortnight they had some big event going on, generally a supper with all the food laid out in the kitchen and loads of hired waiters and waitresses handing round. The four sash windows in the drawing room would be lit up and you could see about sixty people milling about or sitting on sofas, or sometimes coming outside onto the balcony to smoke. Trained by Miles to despise the Cleggs, and assured they were social pariahs, Archie was surprised by how classy some of the guests looked.

When he mentioned this to his father, Miles replied, 'I can assure you, Archie, the Cleggs largely mix with the frozen food set. If there really is such a thing.'

But Archie wasn't convinced and even wondered whether Miles entirely believed it himself.

It was around his fourth month working on the door at Thurloes, on a heaving Thursday night, that Archie encountered a familiar face across the velvet rope. At first he was aware only of a pretty girl in a sea of similar faces, all petitioning him to get in. Archie relished his power over life and death, able to grant entry to one group on a whim, while rejecting another, with no right of appeal. This particular group of girls, he decided, were distinctly borderline. Too bland, too unfashionable, above all *too keen*. Their expressions were all wrong: it really *mattered* to them whether they got in. At Thurloes, you were more likely to succeed with a blasé show of indifference. Archie was saying, 'Sorry ladies, we're full up tonight,' when the prettiest one said, 'Archie, don't you recognise me? It's me, Gemma. Gemma Clegg.'

He did a doubletake and turned crimson. God, this was embarrassing. He could see it was her now: that perky little face. Fit too, he'd forgotten how fit, quite tasty in fact. You could certainly say that.

'Er, nice to see you, Gemma.' He kissed her uncertainly on one cheek. 'You alright?'

'I'm good. Living up in town now.'

'Across the garden from us?' Even referring to Holland Park Square made him shifty, it being the venue for their ill-starred shag.

'No, that's my parents' place. Mandy and I are living in Dad's old house in Waterloo.'

The mention of Mandy filled Archie with further embarrassment, having not clapped eyes on his daughter since the Christening four and a half years earlier.

'Er, that's great,' he replied weakly, looking round in case anyone had overheard anything. 'Er, if you want to go on in, that's fine.'

'Thanks,' said Gemma, smiling at him in a way he found sexy, as she and her friends filed through the velvet rope.

Later, with the doors locked and Archie able to relinquish his post, the first people he spotted on the tiny dancefloor were Gemma and her mates. Gemma was remarkably cute, having shed her coat and wearing a thin white tee, perky little breasts bouncing up and down to the music. A guy Archie knew was dancing with her, looking dead keen, which brought out the competitive spirit. God, Archie reckoned, if anyone had the right to first crack at Gemma it was *him*. After all, he'd been there first.

So he muscled onto the dance floor, cut in on the mother of his child, and found her pleasantly receptive. A good dancer too; he was mesmerised by the outline of two enticing nipples through her cotton top as she bopped about the floor. She had the sweet, uncorrupted, childlike face Archie always found alluring. Watching her, he found it unbelievable she could have given birth to a baby, since his idea of women who'd been through childbirth was of sagging stomachs and sloppy breasts.

After they'd been dancing for a long time, they sat in a booth and ordered cocktails and beers, and talked about the tedium of Chawbury and what a great place London was, while avoiding any reference to the living bond between them. But, just as she was leaving, Gemma blurted, 'If you ever want to visit Mandy, it's OK, you know? She's five, quite a big girl now.'

Archie shrugged. 'Yeah, maybe I'll do that some day.'

'You should. She's adorable. You needn't say who you are if you don't want to.' She entered a phone number into his mobile and handed it back. 'It's been nice catching up, Archie.'

'Yeah, sure.' He smiled at her for the first time all night, and Gemma thought: he's still the most handsome boy I've met by miles.

Flat broke, and conscious she had exhausted the goodwill of her landlord unless she paid him something soon, Sam was ready to consider anything. At Gaz's suggestion, she took the tube to Baker Street and found the mansion block apartment at the top end of Gloucester Place, north of the Marylebone Road, the address of which he had given her. The door was opened by a raven-haired woman in her mid forties named Pat, sunbed-brown and English, who led her into a back kitchen and introduced her to Mike. Mike was a few years younger than Pat, stocky in a leather jacket, with an accent that sounded Essex. He was smoking a cigarette over a plate of fried food.

'Coffee,' said Mike, and Pat put the kettle on. On the kitchen table lay five or six mobile phones and several cartons of fags. The kitchen reeked of cigarettes.

Pat looked at Sam appraisingly, seemed pleased with what she saw, and said, 'How much do you know about the agency?'

'Not much at all really.'

'Well, we only book English girls. We specialise in that, that's what our clients come to us for. No Asians, no exotics, no EEs.'

'EEs?'

'Eastern Europeans. They have their own agencies, run by their own people. Best to steer clear.'

Sam sensed Mike staring at her hungrily, which made her uncomfortable.

'How much experience do you have?' Pat asked.

'I . . . haven't done anything like this before. But . . . I've had some boyfriends.'

Pat cackled. 'I assumed that, darling. You've got a valid passport?'

'Yes.' She sounded surprised, so Pat said, 'Quite a lot of our business is overseas. Europe mostly: Brussels, Paris, Bruges, they're the main ones. International businessmen wanting overnighters. So you have to be prepared to travel at short notice.'

'That'd be fine, I think.' Sam thought: it would actually be better, doing it abroad, less tacky, less chance of anyone knowing.

'Is there anything you *won't* do in the bedroom?'

'I'm . . . I'm not sure. I don't think so. What sort of things do you mean?'

Pat handed her a card like a short menu with various sexual activities written on it, several in acronyms, largely meaningless to Sam: OWO, GFE, CIM.

'I . . . I'm sorry, I don't know what all these stand for exactly.'

'She's awfully posh, isn't she?' Pat said to Mike, approvingly. 'I think we know a few people who are going to be very happy bunnies.' Then, to Sam, 'You're discreet, I assume? That's very important. You may meet clients you recognise from television or sports. Not a word to anyone, including the other girls. You're ok with threesomes, I take it?'

Sam mumbled something about having never tried.

'Sheltered, isn't she?' Pat said, cackling again. 'Go on, Mike, you're on now, you lazy slob.' Then she said, 'Mike's going to give you your test, check everything's working and in the right places. Right, Mike? Use the room at the back, I've shut the cat in the front one. It's scratching itself demented *and* the furniture. Fleas must've come back.'

Mike pushed his chair slowly back from the table, and directed Samantha to the little back bedroom with the pink candlewick bedspread and the towel.

Archie surprised himself by ringing Gemma. He was sitting at a pavement table outside the Café Rouge, drinking cappuccino and editing the address book on his phone, when he spotted her number. Seconds later he'd pressed Call.

He heard the ringtone—ring once, ring twice—and remembered how cute she was. How long was it since she showed up at the club? A week maybe. He'd thought about her quite a few times since, wondering if she'd come again. He'd been keeping a look out.

The number went to voicemail, her sweet, eager tone: 'Hello, you've reached Gemma and Mandy. I'm afraid we're away from our phone at present, but if you leave a message for us, we'll call you back as soon as we can. Byeeeeee!'

'Hi, this is Archie. I'm calling for no reason. Ring me if you want, it's not important, no problem.'

Thirty seconds later Gemma was on the line. 'Hi, Archie. I'm *so sorry* I couldn't get to the phone, I'm in Freeza Mart with Mandy, I couldn't find my mobile in my handbag.'

'Yeah, well, I was just calling you. Like you said.'

'It's lovely to hear you. Do you want to come over? For tea, or I can get some wine?'

He consented to visit her the next day at four o'clock in Roupell Street, half wondering what the hell he thought he was doing. That night, at supper with his parents in Holland Park Square, Miles was having a go at the Cleggs as usual. He had taken exception to their new garden furniture in the private patch behind their house on the communal garden: a table, benches and chairs in a too-new, too-bright cherry wood.

'It'll quickly fade,' Davina said. 'Wood always looks like that when it's new. By next summer you won't be able to tell.'

Miles looked sceptical. 'I hope it doesn't mean they'll be sitting outside all the time. Knowing Ross, he'll have one of those gas-fired barbecues out there next, flipping beef burgers with his cronies. Where've you put those garden by-laws? Barbecues are banned, aren't they? Certainly should be.'

'Darling, I'm not even going to answer,' Davina said. 'You know perfectly well they're lovely neighbours. And Ross hardly even uses the garden, I've only seen him out there a couple of times all year.'

'That doesn't come as any surprise,' Miles declared. 'People like the Cleggs never go in for fresh air. It makes you wonder why they bother having a country place at all. They don't go on walks, don't get involved in country pursuits. They sit in front of a giant TV screen and could be anywhere!'

'Now you really *are* being silly. Dawn rides every day at Chawbury, and Debbie their youngest was eventing to county standard. She still rides when she's home, though she's working very hard at her hotel so she's away most of the time.'

'Debbie indeed,' said Miles. 'She's the one who got Archie into trouble that time isn't she?' Turning to Archie, he said, 'Wasn't she called Debbie? The tart who threw herself at you?'

'No, it was . . . her sister,' Archie replied, not wanting to become embroiled.

'Plump girl. I think I've seen her in the garden tottering about on stilettos.'

Archie made no reply, knowing he would be visiting her the following afternoon, and surprised by how much he was looking forward to it.

Debbie was in a serious quandary, and they'd allowed her only until the end of the week to decide. She had to call Hans-Peder at six p.m. French time, which was five p.m. English time, to say whether or not she was accepting the position, which would be a major life-changing step into a strange country. What made it so difficult was that she still loved her current job and didn't want to let anyone down. The staff at the Buckingham Park had become like second family and the management had given her so many her new responsibilities and opportunities. She doubted many hotels would have allowed a trainee, with barely eighteen months experience, to oversee events in the banqueting suite, from liaising with the clients to ensuring everything ran perfectly on the day. Almost single-handedly, she'd organised an incentive conference, a clay pigeon shooting competition with dinner for Buckinghamshire Mercedes-Benz dealerships, and a luncheon club for two hundred local ladies, which involved pre-lunch cocktails and canapés in the conservatory followed by a three-course meal and *petits fours* in the Stoke Poges Suite.

It was all her own fault she was in this predicament, of course. She'd spotted the advertisement in *Caterer and Hotelkeeper* and, in a moment of blind ambition, sent off her CV, never imagining she'd hear anything back. Applying for a job at the Hotel Meurice in Paris was like flying to the moon, it just wasn't going to happen. She'd looked the place up in several guides before firing off her letter, and it seemed incredible: right in the middle of the Rue de Rivoli, opposite the Louvre and the Jardins de Tuileries, it was more like a palace than a hotel, with frescoed ceilings in the public rooms, marble floors and gilded pillars. She couldn't imagine what it would be like to work there—scary, probably—but it would be an incredible experience, and a great thing to have on your CV, to be able to say you'd worked at the six-star Meurice.

Before she could think better of it, she'd composed her application on Buckingham Park Hotel letterhead. Later, she'd walked down into the village to the post box.

For four weeks she heard nothing and had practically forgotten about it, when she received the letter inviting her to a preliminary interview in London. The assistant general manager of the Meurice, accompanied by someone from HR, would be meeting candidates at the Strand Palace Hotel. Feeling awfully guilty in case any of her workmates should find out, Debbie took the coach up to town on her day off, brushing up her GCSE French from a phrasebook on the way. To her relief, the interview was conducted in English anyway, though they did ask about her French speaking skills and she was able to exchange a few confident sentences. She felt she'd got on rather well with her interviewers, especially the assistant general manager, Hans-Peder Herrmann, who turned out not to be French at all but Swiss, from Lausanne. Consequently, she'd been slightly disappointed to hear nothing from them for a further three weeks. Then the phone call came asking her back for a second interview, at the worst possible moment, since she was down to do a double shift that afternoon, but somehow she'd switched things about and made it to the meeting. This time she had been told to bring her passport with her, and she quickly got the impression she was part of a very short shortlist. By the end of the interview, Hans-Peder had offered her a job as a junior trainee manager on a salary slightly below what she was paid already, and told her to let him know by Friday night.

During the journey back to High Wycombe she alternated between elation—she'd been offered a *management position* in *Paris* at the *Hotel Meurice*—and a terrible foreboding at the prospect of telling anyone at the Buckingham Park. Worse, she didn't know if she even wanted to go. She worried she'd be lonely in a foreign city where she knew nobody, and she knew she would miss her family.

On the evening before she had to make up her mind, she rang her Dad and had a really long heart-to-heart. Afterwards, she felt a lot better, and saw things a lot more clearly. He was amazing like that, he always gave the impression of having all the time in the world for you, and his advice was so sensible.

So, just before the deadline, she hid herself away in a vacant hotel bedroom, took a deep breath and rang the number she'd been given in Paris. Having made her decision, she knew it was the right one, and felt quite lightheaded. Five minutes afterwards, she told her sister on the phone, 'Guess what Gemma? I'm going to live in Paris.'

43.

Your table's confirmed at George Club for eight thirty this evening,' reported Sara White, Miles's senior PA, as he returned from lunch, 'and Lord Pendleton's office has emailed over details for the shoot this Saturday.'

Shooting at Longparish Priory was one of the great treats of Miles's life. James invited him as his guest every year and it was always a day to savour. Every aspect of the shoot was perfection: by general consent, the drives at Longparish Priory were among the prettiest in England, with high beech woods above steep grassy banks providing famously challenging sport. It had been James's father, David Pendleton, a mad keen shot, who had bought the estate and pumped fortunes into it to turn it into one of the great Hampshire sporting estates. His eldest son had never been nearly so keen, but kept the shoot running out of respect to the memory of his father, and because it was there, and because he could easily afford to do so. There were six fulltime keepers at Longparish Priory and, on shoot days, more beaters than at any other shoot in the county: Miles liked to comment it resembled the classic scene in *Zulu* where the savages appear on the ridge, when James Pendleton's beaters emerged at the completion of a drive.

Not only was the shooting first rate, but so was the networking. In his modest, haphazard way, Lord Pendleton knew everybody and the other guns frequently included the great and the good, though there was no pattern to this. One time it would mostly be neighbours shooting, or one or other of the Pendleton brothers, or James's son Hugh and his friends; another day, your fellow guns would be bigwigs from Lazards, General Electric or Vodafone, and sometimes royals or shadow cabinet ministers. Miles knew many of them already, but others he didn't, and he regarded the Pendleton shoot as a valuable source of new contacts. He told his executives he'd won more business over shooting lunches at Longparish Priory than by any other means.

Settling himself in front of his computer, he opened the email his PA had forwarded to his screen. What interested him was the list of other guns. Scrolling down the message, he smiled: this was going to be one of the better days, plenty of good people coming. Then he stopped dead: no, it was unbearable. *Ross Clegg was shooting this Saturday.*

With leaden heart, Miles drove over from Chawbury to Longparish with his shotguns in the boot of the Jensen. Of course, he knew Ross had been taking shooting lessons, but assumed he was still on clays. It hadn't entered his head he might surface at a proper gentlemens' shoot. Accelerating through the Doric lodge gates and up the mile-long drive past Laetitia's rustic fishing lodge, Miles was in a seriously filthy mood. Passing the front of the house, he took the fork in the drive to the cobbled stable yard with its clock tower and garages where the guns gathered for the day. Already half a dozen Mercedeses and Range Rovers were parked up with men in plus-fours assembling their shotguns and filling up cartridge bags; loaders with grizzled grey beards were congregating with the pickers-up and gundogs. Normally, Miles relished this picturesque English sight, but today it was undermined by the presence of Ross clambering awkwardly from his jeep and limping over to greet his host.

As Miles parked, he heard someone say in a joshing voice, 'Morning, Ross. So you didn't come in your chopper today then?'

Ross laughed. 'I don't think James would ask me again if I had! I'd have scared off all his birds.'

This was the first time Miles had encountered Ross in his shooting kit, and his instinct was to mock. He looked him up and down, taking everything in: the perfectly pressed shooting suit which looked like it had never been worn, the woollen shooting stockings with their too-perfect orange garters, the brand new mud-free boots. And then the guns: a shiny new pair of Purdeys, with freshly engraved plates.

'Hello Miles,' Ross said. 'Nice to see the Chawbury contingent out in force.' Was it Miles's imagination, or was Ross more reserved in his greeting than usual? There was something wary about him.

'You're looking very ... dapper,' Miles said. 'Is it shop-new, all that kit?' He looked around, pleased several of the other guns were listening, including James Pendleton. 'Hope you haven't left the price tags on.'

'First outing for the lot, head to toe,' Ross replied cheerfully. 'I feel like a kid at a new school wearing my new uniform.' Sticking out his hand, he introduced himself to the other guns. 'Ross Clegg. I've got to warn you fellows, this is my first time. First time at a proper shoot. So when I make a complete horlicks of it, I'm relying on you to put me right. I warned James when he kindly invited me, I don't know anything about how these shoot days work.'

Immediately everyone promised their help, and the Chief Executive of Allwheat Cereals, who was a large supplier to Pendletons and whom Miles was keen to schmooze, told Ross he'd only been shooting for a year himself, and regarded himself as another novice so they could stick together.

In due course, Lord Pendleton invited the guns to draw for their pegs, and Ross drew number four in the middle of the line, which irritated Miles since it was the best position on the first drive, while he had drawn the end stand so was stuck out on the side. James gave a short speech about safety being paramount and not going for ground game, and then they all gravitated towards the Land Rovers lined up for them. Despite his best efforts, Miles was directed into the same vehicle as Ross, so they would be travelling together between drives all day. Miles clambered into the front passenger seat, Ross sat behind with the loaders.

The first drive, which Miles knew from previous days, was known as Home Farm Hill and renowned for being difficult. Even experienced guns found it challenging. The birds were pushed by the beaters from two small woods towards a dense patch of gorse on the top of a steep bank. For twenty minutes, hardly a bird would fly out, before suddenly exploding in a great mass, two hundred pheasants and partridges at high altitude. Normally Miles approached Home Farm Hill rather gingerly; delighted when he was seen to shoot well, frustrated when he wasn't. His duff position today placed him on the margins of the firing line, but at least he'd have a good view of Ross, out of his depth.

It was a bright, chilly morning, Miles's favourite shooting weather, with clear blue sky and a watery winter sun doing its best. From his vantage point halfway up the bank he had a fine view of the other guns taking up their positions. Ross was limping to his peg, accompanied by his loader for the day, Barry, an instructor at the Mid Hampshire Shooting Ground. Miles knew Barry well, and anticipated exchanging conspiratorial jokes about Mr Clegg's performance later in the day.

Ross stood at the ready at the bottom of the hill, peering up at the skyline for any signs of life. Apart from a light breeze in the trees, and the occasional snuffle from a gundog, they waited in stillness and silence. This for Miles was always a privileged moment, the calm before the storm, an opportunity to reflect on the beauty of the English landscape at its best, by which he meant prinked and pampered by generations of benign private ownership. He surveyed the frozen fields, the noble leafless trees, the muted tweeds of the shooting party, and thought how much he deserved to be there—a favoured, regular guest of Lord Pendleton.

The line of beaters was getting closer now, you could hear their calls and the thrashing at undergrowth. 'Won't be long now, sir,' murmured his loader, Chris. 'Here comes one over now.' A lone cock pheasant rose high into the air at the altitude of the tallest beech tree, and cruised towards the guns.

Miles smirked, this was perfect: it was heading directly over Ross. All eyes were upon him. He watched while Ross raised the gun to his shoulder. Barry the loader appeared to be telling him something, and Ross adjusted his aim. There was a single shot and the bird dropped to the ground, hitting it with a thud.

'Now that, sir, is what I call a very good shot,' said Chris, Miles's loader. 'That's Mr Clegg isn't it, the gentleman from Freeza Mart?'

'Er, probably yes.'

'I recommend his cherry cheesecake,' Chris said. 'We have that a lot at home.'

At that moment a flurry of birds rose up all at once, and the guns were banging away as they soared overhead. Two came above Miles and he shot one, missed one, with two barrels.

'I was watching Mr Clegg,' said Chris, when the action died down. 'Looked like he got eight birds with ten cartridges. High ones too.'

A second, even larger flight now broke cover, eighty pheasants at least and some tiny French partridge. This time, none came over Miles so he watched the action below. Ross had adopted a ridiculous half-crouching position like some red Indian tracker with his barrels flailing about in the sky. But he was shockingly accurate. Miles saw him take a left and a right, swap guns, then immediately hit a third. By the time the horn sounded to signal the end of the drive, Miles was spitting.

In the Land Rover to the second drive, Miles pretended to be unaware how well Ross had shot, and said nothing, but the loaders were full of congratulations.

'Beginners luck, nothing more,' said Ross modestly. 'I can tell you, there's a definite knack to this lark. Different to clays.'

But at the second drive Ross again shot well, while Miles found himself to be off-form. By lunch-time, when they were joined by Laetitia and some of the other wives at the barn on Longparish Down that the Pendletons had converted for shooting lunches, Ross was the hero of the hour. Dawn, who had spent the morning with Laetitia at the big house occupied on charity matters, was warmly congratulated for being married to a crack shot.

'You have to come out after lunch and stand with him,' they told her. 'Your husband's incredible. This *can't* be his first time.'

The food at the Pendletons shoot, chosen and supervised by Laetitia, was famously generous, as was the wine. James, almost teetotal himself, went to endless trouble to provide only the finest clarets for his guests. Under ordinary circumstances Miles relished the lunch recess, considering it the heart of the day, but today it was another burden to be borne. The sight of Ross, embraced by the other guns and now sharing his predictions for the economy to a receptive audience, was intolerable. His mood hardly improved when Laetitia and Dawn cornered him after lunch, and reported what a marvellous job Mollie had done with the inner-city schools opera performance. 'You've got a little star there,' Dawn said. 'What a pity neither you nor Davina could make it, you'd have been so proud.'

'Yes, well, I'm afraid some of us have livings to earn,' replied Miles, and then regretted saying it, because it sounded impolite to Laetitia when he had intended only a snub to Dawn.

Feeling the liverish after-effects of three large glasses of claret, Miles staggered to the Land Rovers for the afternoon drive. The last drive was always a short one since the light was going, and the guns were ranged up along two sides of a wood, full of oaks and elms of great antiquity. From his middle peg, Miles had a fine view of the other positions in both directions. Ross re-adopted his crouching stance, legs bent at the knee; like a weightlifter waiting to take the strain, Miles decided. Far above them in the treetops, black rooks tumbled and cawed at the sinking sun.

The beaters had advanced two thirds of the way through the wood now, striking at tree trunks and sweeping the air with flags. Solitary pheasants were breaking out for open country to a crackle of gunfire. Twenty metres into the wood, swooping on majestic tawny wings from its roost in a hollow tree, came a large owl, heading in the direction of Ross.

In an instant, Miles had an idea. 'Cock bird *over*,' he hollered, as the protected owl emerged from the wood.

A single shot from Ross brought it down, and the other guns looked on in dismay. Miles felt the eyes of his loader boring into his back, but ignored him and slowly shook his head. 'The trouble with shooting these days,' he declared at last, 'is that some of the people taking it up don't have the *slightest idea*.'

44.

avina and Dawn had joined a weekly ladies' exercise group held in the communal garden of Holland Park Square, and fallen into a routine of having coffee together afterwards. Sometimes they would head for Davina's cosy kitchen, sometimes to Dawn's larger, more impersonal one. Sitting around in exercise pants, sweatshirts and trainers, waiting for their metabolisms to normalise with the aid of a cafetiere of coffee and a digestive biscuit, they talked openly about their children and more guardedly about their husbands. Both women were aware that eachothers' men could be handfuls on occasion.

Dawn, in particular, was concerned about Davina, who behind a stoical front frequently seemed downhearted. 'All my birds have flown the nest,' she would say. 'Not one of them wanted to come home this weekend, the house feels so empty and pointless really.'

'But Miles was with you? Isn't it nice spending time together for a change? Being able to talk?'

Davina laughed ruefully. 'He was physically there, yes, and he came through for meals, but most of the time he shut himself away in his study working. He's very uncommunicative at the moment, I keep worrying I've done something to upset him, which is ridiculous because we all tread round him on eggshells. The only time he cheered up was Saturday night when we went over to the Mountleighs' for dinner.'

'They didn't invite *us*,' said Dawn, sounding peeved. Lately, Davina had noticed how social Dawn had become, and quick to take offence when excluded from any gathering, large or small.

'It was only a few old locals,' Davina reassured her, 'Robin and Serena Harden and Nigel and Bean.'

'Do you trust Serena?' Dawn asked suddenly.

'Serena? Yes, of course. Why?'

Dawn made a face. 'I don't know. It's probably nothing. Just something about her, like she's a bit forward around men.'

'Really? I'll pay more attention. I've always thought of her as a bit sad. They're frightfully hard up. Miles has never liked her much either, now you mention it. Whenever I've suggested getting them over to dinner, he's said no, unless it's a big party.' Davina blushed, because Miles also excluded the Cleggs. It was another topic the friends never broached, along with the old Archie-Gemma situation.

'Not that I'm worried. Ross works too hard for anything like that. Getting him to do anything at the moment is like pulling teeth. I've been on at him about a weekend in Paris to visit Debs at her hotel, but it's hard pinning him down. I had quite a go at Jacqui his PA about it: Give me back my man. I'm putting a stop to weekend business engagements. Between store visits and the shooting, we've no Saturdays left.'

'Miles is the same. He's travelling four weekends out of five this month. If I complain he says, 'Come with me,' but I don't think he means it. He says he'd be out at meetings all day and I'm not a great one for shopping. So thank heavens for the garden to keep me busy.'

'Perhaps you *should* accompany him,' Dawn said, rather prissily. 'It's helpful for an important man to have his other half with him. Laetitia accompanies James to all his work functions, she's the one who memorises the names of his managers and their ladies. I've been trying to learn them myself at Freeza Mart, but it's such a big concern these days, and some of the wives look so alike. All those awful haircuts.' Dawn's own awful haircut was now such a distant memory, having been reshaped by ever-more-fashionable metropolitan scissors, that she no longer acknowledged it had ever existed. Similarly, Davina noticed whenever Dawn was introduced to anyone new whom she wished to impress, she implied Chawbury Park and Hampshire was their lifelong home and the old Droitwich years had been erased. Davina kept this observation firmly to herself, since she was extremely fond of Dawn, and she knew Miles would use it against the Cleggs, if she said anything.

'I know what I meant to say,' said Davina. 'Mollie *adored* her supper with Greg, she said he was sweet to her, when he's so important on the council and everything.'

Dawn looked surprised. 'I didn't know they'd had supper. He never tells us anything.'

'Oh yes, he invited her to a lovely Middle Eastern restaurant, she said. Wanted to talk about local schools and get Mollie's views. She says Greg's awfully impressive, sorting out the whole borough.'

'He takes it very seriously. It's a bit much, the way he lectures us. He came over recently and was on and on about this house: how it's too big, the central heating's too high, you'd think we were terrible people the way he goes on. Drives Ross up the wall.'

'Well, he's got a fan in Mollie. Her headmaster was very impressed that she'd had supper with him. They're all slightly in awe of Greg because he sits on the education committee.'

'It was very kind of Mollie to help. In fact it's rather encouraging, because Greg never seems to have any lady friends, not ones he mentions anyway. It's all politics, politics in unpleasant smelly pubs. I hope he looked after her nicely and didn't just talk politics all the time.'

'He sounded lovely, from what Mollie was saying. He made a big impression on her. It was Greg says this, Greg says that.' Davina could have added, but didn't, that it had driven Miles mad, hearing so much about Greg Clegg.

'What is it about my children and that frightful family?' he'd complained to Davina afterwards.

It was in a spirit of adventure that Archie abandoned his comfort zone on the north bank of the Thames and took a cab to the address Gemma had texted to him across Waterloo Bridge. Roupell Street turned out to be a Victorian terrace of flat-fronted railwaymen's cottages, long since confiscated from their intended inhabitants, now the gentrified preserve of professionals and young families.

He pressed the chime and heard a voice, 'Hang on, just coming,' and there was Gemma in jeans and a white tee-shirt, hair freshly washed and smelling of shampoo. Sheltering shyly behind her on the doorstep with a thumb stuck in her mouth was the cutest little girl Archie had seen in ages, a mini-me version of her mum, with big blue eyes staring up at him and the same mousey-coloured hair.

'This is Mummy's friend Archie, Mandy. Say "how do you do Archie," sweetheart, it's nice to be polite.'

'How do you do Arch . . .' mouthed Mandy in an almost inaudible whisper.

They entered into a sitting room which was very neat and rather empty, with a pair of cane-sided sofas and a television sitting on a cloth-covered table. A Disney cartoon of *Aladdin* was playing and Gemma said, 'We can't watch videos when we've got a *visitor*, can we?'

Mandy looked crestfallen, and when Gemma moved to switch it off she developed a trembly lip.

So Archie said, 'Oh do leave it on, why don't you? It doesn't bother me. Anyway I love Aladdin. It's just coming to the good bit when he snogs Princess Jasmine.'

'You seem to know it very well,' Gemma said.

'We've got this one at home, I watch it in bed all the time. I'm too lazy to fetch another vid from downstairs. There you go you see, Mandy, he's *kissing* her. It's deep tongues . . .'

Gemma giggled. 'Don't say that. It'll put her off for life.'

Just then, Mandy covered her eyes with her small pink hands and said, 'Yuck, I don't like that princess. She's *nasty*.'

'Ah, jealousy, jealousy,' said Archie. Then, to Gemma, 'She's definitely jealous, I think she fancies Aladdin. You do, don't you Mandy? Admit it. Are you going to *marry* Prince Aladdin when you grow up? Is he going to be your husband, is he?'

Mandy stared at him very seriously, trying to work out if he was teasing her.

'Maybe,' she whispered at last.

'So you're going to be Mrs Aladdin! Can I come to your wedding? Will you invite me?'

'No,' She replied defiantly, and Gemma looked worried in case she'd caused offence.

'Oh, come on, *please* let me,' said Archie. 'I'll bring you a wedding present, a really nice one. Not a saucepan or a dishcloth, I promise. What would you like for a wedding present then? Sweets? Ice cream?'

'Sweeties.' Mandy wrapped her legs round each other in shyness.

'Alright then, I'll bring you sweeties, a big bag for you and Aladdin to share on your magic carpet. How's that then?'

Gemma watched the exchange, thrilled Mandy and her dad had such instant rapport. 'You're really good with her, Arch,' she said. 'How do you know about talking to kids then?'

'I work in a club, don't I? Half the chicks who come in, they're not nearly so bright as Mandy. I'm telling you, they couldn't follow the plot of *Aladdin*, "Eer, who's this wicked Vizier geezer then? Duh, I don't get it."'

'You're terrible, Archie. And I haven't even offered you anything, what am I thinking? I've got lapsang, Earl Grey, Freeza Mart blend, herb and fruit ones if you prefer?'

'Freeza Mart, please. No, bugger that, what about that wine you mentioned? You said there'd be wine. I'll have a big mug of that, please.'

He trailed her into a small back kitchen, with views over a yard with washing hanging out on a droopy line. A plastic pedal car and plastic sandpit covered by a plastic lid were just visible, protruding from under the weight of bed sheets and laundry.

'Sorry about the washing,' Gemma said. 'I'd meant to bring it in before you got here, but it got rained on.'

'I like it,' said Archie. 'Especially the bra display. These are your B-cups, I take it, dangling on the end?'

Gemma coloured. 'Sorry about that.'

'Why sorry? Normally I spend ages on the Internet searching for excitements like them. When I'm fed up with *Aladdin*.'

Gemma opened a bottle of Freeza Mart's Californian cabernet sauvignon with a screw top, which was currently sweeping the country, being priced as a promotional loss-leader at £2.15 to lure punters from Pendletons and Tesco.

'I love that wine,' Archie said. 'Such a steal. They were blind tasting it on one of the afternoon food shows, and this ditsy wine expert, can't remember her name now, thought it was the twenty-quid one.'

'Dad drinks it at home. They were going to sell it in proper bottles with corks, but dad said go for screw tops because corks put some people off. They think it's too posh.'

'Yeah, well I prefer screw tops myself. Quicker. No arsing about with corkscrews.' He knocked back the wine in two gulps, then said, 'How about the other half, Gems? And in a bigger glass this time. You don't get enough taste in these incey-wincey ones. And, go on, have one yourself. I hate boozing alone. Tell you what, how about we take the bottle through and catch the end of *Aladdin*? Prince Aleee,' he sang, 'Wonderful me . . . Come on, and bring those pretzels. I love Freeza Mart cheese pretzels. Much nicer than Pendletons pretzels but don't tell my old man I said that.'

They sat side by side on the little sofa, watching the film with Mandy perched on Gemma's lap, while Archie kept the wine flowing. At some point he fetched a second bottle from the fridge and they got stuck into that too. 'So what do you do with yourself all day then, out here in the badlands of Sarf Lundun?'

'Depends what day it is. Mandy does playschool three mornings, so I have to drop her off and collect her again at twelve, which doesn't leave much time in-between, cos I like to stay with her 'til I know she's settled. And then I fix lunch back here, and in the afternoon sometimes we go for a little walk down to Vauxhall market or to the playground, not that it's a very nice playground because there's gangs of teenagers hanging about in hoodies, so we do watch quite a few videos, I must be honest. You love your videos, don't you sweetheart?' said Gemma, hugging her daughter. But Mandy was too absorbed to reply.

'Doesn't sound too riveting so far,' said Archie. 'So when does the partying go on?'

'I wish.'

'But seriously. You can't have a nice place like this all for yourself and not throw parties. This place should be Party Central. I'd kill for somewhere like this. I'm banned from using our house, Dad totally overreacted after these gatecrashers turned up, and Carmelita our maid's like a Stasi spy, she's completely untrustworthy and tells him the smallest thing.'

'Even if I did have a party, I don't know that many people in town to ask. Just a couple of school friends—you met them outside the club, Rachel and Becky—and my sister Debs comes over too, but she's working in Paris so she's not around much. Maybe I'll meet more people when I find a job. That's what I'm hoping. I'm meant to be looking for one, but it's got to be part-time because of Mandy, so it's not easy.'

'That's tough. About the job, I mean. And being on your own all day. Must get boring.'

Gemma shrugged. 'I'm used to it, I'm not complaining. Mandy's company enough most of the time. The past five years I've hardly seen anyone, just Mum and Dad. And Debbie before she began at her hotels. And Mollie sometimes. She comes to visit Mandy, she's been a lovely godmother to her. How is Mollie, by the way?'

'Obsessed with teaching asylum seekers how to read and write English, so they can defraud the benefits system when they leave school. No I didn't say that, it's grossly racist, I should be ashamed, I should be *arrested*. Please don't report me to the authorities, Gemma, I'll do anything, anything, pour you another glass of wine, you need a top up . . .'

'No more wine. I've had plenty. I wont be able to put Mandy to bed.'

'Now there's a thought,' said Archie. 'Put Mandy to bed. Why don't you just do that? Then the grown-ups can do grown-up things together undisturbed.' He held her with a quizzical, flirtatious gaze. 'We, Gemma, have a lot of catching-up to do, you realise? Five years in Chawbury cooped up with your mum and dad? Doesn't bear thinking about, you must have been climbing the fucking walls.'

Leaning behind Mandy across the back of the sofa, he kissed her on the mouth, and was encouraged when she kissed him back.

'Well, hurry up then, put the sprog in her cot or whatever. It must be well past her bedtime. Off you go. I'm rewinding *Aladdin*, I missed the beginning.'

45.

amantha was on the early-afternoon Eurostar from Waterloo to the Gard du Nord. Above her on the rack was the leather Mulberry bag Dick gave her once as a present, containing her wash-bag with the tricks of her trade, condoms, lube, her make-up, a change of clothes for tomorrow and a nightdress. She wondered whether she wasn't being ridiculous, packing a nightie?

Pat from the agency had been particular about not bringing a big suitcase. 'Nothing you can't carry yourself. You don't want to attract the attention of hotel porters.'

This being Sam's first overseas overnighter, Pat had written the instructions step by step: train to Paris, wait in line for a cab to the hotel in the Rue de Rivoli, through the front revolving door, straight through the lobby to the rear bank of elevators—look confident, like you know where you're going, no eye contact with anyone—take the lift to the third floor, follow signs to Suite 302. The only other instruction of consequence was: get the money straight up. The gentleman was paying £1200 for an overnighter, payable in cash in advance. Not that Pat was expecting problems, he was a long-standing customer of the agency. Nevertheless, soon as Sam arrived at the suite she was to text Pat in London to confirm.

Not for the first time, Sam wondered what she thought she was doing. The train was packed with businessmen on their way to meetings, speaking into cellphones and working on laptops. It occurred to her any one of these men could be her client tonight, and the idea was shocking, but also intriguing. There were two guys sitting there, borderline three, who maybe wouldn't be so bad to go with. She guessed they were French. But the majority were middle-aged blokes, balding and overweight, wearing dreadful suits and shoes, and the idea of doing it with them was repellent. If you visualised them with their clothes off, you felt sick. Sam consoled herself that at least her punter, whoever he turned out to be, was rich, because suites at the Hotel Meurice didn't come cheap. And neither did she. She was proud when Pat and Mike priced her at the very top agency rate—more than double what some of the other girls got—because she was classy and new. 'There's going to be a lot of interest in you when word gets round.'

Sam stared at her reflection in the window while the black French countryside rolled past outside, and wondered if there was any way people could tell. Did she look different now? Was there some debauched, giveaway expression in her eyes—a licentiousness, or a hardness—that hadn't been there a month earlier? Not that she could tell. She still wore the same clothes, no basques or leopard-prints. Pam advised her to keep it that way: 'Men like it, lady on the outside, tart under the knickers.' The only thing that was different, objectively, was she'd been able to repay Gaz a third of his loan, and she'd bought herself the Chloé bag she'd been wanting too. Well, now Dick wasn't around to get it for her, nor her dad, she had to pay for her own treats. Girl power!

She tried to work out what she'd earned so far, after the agency's 40 percent. The weird thing was, she could scarcely remember how many punters she'd had, and it wasn't even like there'd been that many. Pat's agency wasn't a knocking shop, it wasn't a *walk up*. That would be truly degrading, a procession of different men coming and going all day long. No, she was something entirely different. A high-class escort, paid as much for her companionship as anything that might subsequently arise between two consenting adults. That's how they worded it on the website at least. Sam thought of the website and flinched. That was the part that worried her most, having her picture up on the internet. She insisted that they pixelated her face, of course, so you couldn't recognise her, even though Pat warned her it would cost her some business as a result.

Sam had spent ages scrutinising herself on the site, wondering whether or not she was identifiable. She didn't believe so, even in the close-up shots and the kinky ones in boots and black knickers. She'd had this recurring nightmare of someone she knew recognising her and it somehow getting back to her parents, and everyone in Chawbury finding out. Or her old schoolteachers.

She paged through her pocket diary, day by day, remembering from coded prompts where she'd worked and what she'd earned each time. The guy at the Royal Lancaster Hotel had been the first paying punter—a bit cheap in that tiny room—and the Greek guy at the Inter-Con was a disgusting perv, and turned nasty when she said no to a couple of things. At the Four Seasons she'd got lost looking for the lifts and one of the managers asked if she needed any help, and which guest was she visiting, and she was sure he'd sussed her. It was weird the way the appointments blurred until she had no distinct recollection of each. In a sense, they were all very similar. And coke blunted the experience in any case.

Tonight she reckoned would be her fourteenth, and the highest paying, being an overnighter. At the rate she was going, she'd have cleared the debt in another month or two, providing she didn't blow too much on clothes and shoes. She might take a quick look in the Christian Louboutin boutique tomorrow morning, if there was time before the train.

Thinking about it, Samantha felt almost proud of herself, for clearing her debt all on her own. And she didn't reckon she was doing anything very wrong, people were so ridiculous the fuss they made, trying to stigmatise it. As Sam saw it, she wasn't doing much she hadn't done a thousand times with Dick, Nigel, Peter or any of her boyfriends. Except now she was paid directly for her services, rather than indirectly.

Debbie had been on action stations all day, helping cope with the emergency. Basically, it was every hotelier's nightmare. The Meurice was already running at over 90 percent occupancy, owing to all the trade fairs going on in Paris, and barely had an empty room in the place. Then one of the ministers of the Congo, who'd been occupying half a floor of the hotel with his family and bodyguards for three weeks, and who was supposed to be checking out before noon today, suddenly announced he was staying another week. Meanwhile, the Crown Prince of Morocco was waiting to move in with an entourage, and been promised the suites inhabited by the Africans. The Elysee Palace was pressurising Debbie's bosses not to expel the Congonese, for diplomatic considerations, and everyone was in a panic wondering how to shift things about.

Debbie was relishing the drama, particularly when the Africans ordered their armed security to seal off their corridor, so the chambermaids couldn't strip the rooms of their bedding. And the Moroccan chief of protocol threatened to sue if the Crown Prince didn't get his regular suite, and spoke about switching the booking and all future bookings to Le Bristol. Debbie adored the high-level diplomacy, which had certainly never gone on at the Buckingham Park Hotel, and felt this was the hospitality business at its most elevated. She was learning things at the Meurice that took her experience to a new level.

Everything about the place was ritzier: the toiletries in the guest bathrooms were Acqua di Parma; the floral displays were unbelievable, not only in the lobby and dining rooms but on every floor outside the lifts where scarcely anyone even noticed them; and all the breakfast pastries were freshly baked by the sous chef on the premises. All these luxurious touches thrilled her. One of her first jobs when she joined the hotel was to place a special card on each breakfast trolley, before they were delivered by room service, informing guests what the weather was like outside, to save them the bother of looking out of the window; she ticked a symbol of an umbrella, a blazing sun, or a sun half hidden behind a cloud.

She was relaxing for an instant in the office behind the cashier, where they prepared the bills and conducted the credit checks, when she thought she spotted a familiar face striding across the lobby. The very pretty girl with long blonde hair—surely it was Samantha Straker? She hadn't seen her in ages, but she was sure it was her.

Debbie thought she'd say hello later on, and check she was being properly looked after.

Sam was following the brief precisely, and so far things were going just fine. She'd got a taxi at the station with hardly any queue and there hadn't been much traffic across Paris, so she'd arrived outside the Meurice forty minutes early. She killed time in a brasserie up the street with a coffee and a glass of wine, waiting for seven o'clock.

Nobody looked twice as she crossed the marble lobby in her stilettos, click, clack, click, clack, looking neither left nor right, exactly like she was a guest staying there. She waited for the lift, cool as a cucumber, though she did feel conspicuous when some scarfaced African guys got in too. She hoped her client wasn't one of them.

The lift doors pinged open on the third floor, and she was the only person to get out. Good. A signboard directed her to the suite.

She walked along what seemed like a thousand yards of patterned carpet, turning left, turning right, past the doors of other bedrooms. Some had Privacy Please notices hanging from the doorhandles. She passed a couple of abandoned service wagons heaped with dirty plates and stemmed roses in vases.

At the end of the corridor was a pair of cream double doors. Suite 302. It looked reassuringly grand. For a moment she stood outside, gathering herself. Then took a deep breath and pressed the bell.

She could hear movement beyond the doors, first distantly, then closer. There was the rattle of a chain being unhooked. She saw the handle turn and the door starting to open.

They locked eyes at exactly the same moment.

Miles was standing in the doorway in a white towelling hotel robe, his face frozen. 'Samantha? What on earth . . . ?'

But she was bolting down the corridor. She ran down three flights of stairs, past reception, out into the Rue de Rivoli and didn't stop running until she could run no further.

Debbie, who watched her tear through the lobby, wondered why she could possibly be in such a hurry.

46.

Mollie couldn't remember a more exciting invitation. In fact, she had woken up the next morning wondering if she'd dreamt it, and had to replay the message on her mobile. And, yes, there was Greg's flat Midlands voice asking if she'd like to accompany him to the Labour Party conference in Blackpool, where he was a delegate. Mollie felt immensely flattered he would think of her, that he considered her worthy, when she was so ignorant about politics. Well, she would educate herself in the next two weeks, read all the newspapers, she couldn't look a fool.

Her friendship with Greg had all been slightly peculiar so far, now she thought about it. He wasn't the easiest person to get along with, you never knew where you stood with him. Since supper at the kebab place, he'd taken to calling her quite a bit, which was amazing, but he was stilted on the phone, with long silences which made her uncomfortable, and she couldn't always think of clever enough things to say. He made her feel dumb. And sometimes he was crushing, saying, "Would the daughter of Miles Straker ever deign to have supper at a Greek taverna with me? Or is that beneath your usual standards?" Mollie wished he wouldn't go on like that, when she was a primary school teacher in Olympia and not some spoilt trustafarian.

They'd had supper four times, twice with some of his political friends. Mollie had also visited him at the Town Hall and been shown into the visitors' gallery at the Chamber, while the council were in session, and watched Greg make a brilliant speech—he really knew how to use words—which was so damning about the Tories' record of care provision for the elderly that the Conservative councillor kept trying to butt in, saying it was all rubbish, but

Greg stood his ground, really going for him in his clever, belittling way. Mollie almost felt sorry for the Conservative man, who reminded her of the pharmacist behind the prescription counter at Boots in Andover. Greg in full flow was mesmerising, she couldn't take her eyes off him, the words issued from his mouth without a single hesitation, completely different to when they were talking on the phone or over supper. This made Mollie think it must be her fault their conversation was such hard work, and resolved to try harder.

Once, he had asked her round to his flat to stuff envelopes for a mail-drop to voters. Mollie was fascinated to see his place, which was totally different to what she'd been imagining. She already knew, because he'd told her, that he rented a council flat on the Guinness estate, in one of six identical mansion blocks next to the Hammersmith flyover. In fact, you could practically see into Greg's windows from the raised section of the M4, and it had been so noisy when he moved in he'd had double glazing installed by the council. Outside, the Guinness estate was depressingly run down and felt unsafe. The lift was broken and the stairwell filled with rubbish. Mollie was relieved to reach Greg's front door unscathed from a fourth floor walkway open to the elements. Inside, however, all was immaculate. She didn't think she'd ever entered such a tidy flat. The walls along the corridor were lined with black ash bookcases, some filled with books, others with political pamphlets and fliers, perfectly aligned. The sitting room, with its view of the motorway thundering past, contained a black leather-and-chrome sofa, a black leather Eames chair and an immense Bang and Olufsen music centre, four decks high, blinking and winking with lights and dials. A black Perspex business card holder contained cards for 'Dr Greg Clegg,' Labour Steering Group Executive Member, with a mugshot of Greg looking dreadfully serious. Propped on a wooden shelf above a Victorian gas fire stood a framed poster urging the ratepayers of Hammersmith and Fulham to Vote for Clegg in the Kingstown ward.

'What an incredible flat,' Mollie said, impressed by how slick it all was. A couple of years earlier she'd visited one of her Serbian pupils on this same estate, and their flat was full of broken-down furniture, cooking smells and black-eyed kids.

'Yeah, it works for me. And cheap. Affordable housing has to be a priority. Thatcher sold off half the national housing stock. In many societies she'd be facing criminal prosecution.'

As Mollie sat at Greg's desk with its fat black filofax and tub of sharpened black pencils, filling envelopes with pamphlets boosting the achievements of the Labour-controlled council, she felt a rare contentment and a feeling that, for once in her life, she was making a modest difference on a wider stage. By nature, she felt comfortable helping in small, personal ways—coaxing a dyslexic child with their reading, or boosting a shy child's confidence—but there was something satisfying about assisting Greg with his politics. She hoped he might invite her round to help again sometime.

And then came the invitation to Blackpool, which was thrilling and terrifying at the same time. When she rang to accept, Greg was very cool about it and just said, 'I'm glad you can make it. I'll book rooms at a boarding house, that's if you don't object. It won't be up to your usual standards.' He said they'd travel up by train and stay two days. 'I don't imagine you've been up North before,' he added, mockingly. 'It's very different.'

'Of course I have,' Mollie replied crossly. But, in truth, she'd only been to Scotland with her family to stay at Gleneagles.

As the Blackpool expedition loomed closer, she became apprehensive. She was buying the *Times* and the *Guardian* each morning and concentrating on the political bits, and took to watching *Newsnight*. It reassured her, and made her proud, to learn about the resources New Labour was putting behind education. At grass roots in the classroom it never felt like the government was doing much, but probably it would all begin to come through soon, which would be a wonderful boost for the children. She mentioned to her mother she was going to the conference with Greg, and Davina was delighted for her, saying how interesting it would be to watch Tony Blair's speech, but they agreed it would be better not to say anything to Miles.

Although she knew this was ridiculously trivial, Mollie began to fret about what she should wear. She didn't know how smart you were supposed to be for the keynote speeches and also in the evening. She seemed to remember Cherie Blair always looked very dressy, and the female Cabinet ministers like Patricia Hewitt and

Tessa Jowell and the other ones, not to mention Blair's Babes (God she hated that expression, so derogatory and patronising; typical *Daily Mail*, she refused to open that newspaper). Her wardrobe of ankle-length denim skirts and brown corduroy smocks, perfect for school, didn't feel quite right for the Blackpool Winter Gardens. One Saturday she slipped into Marks & Spencer and tried on a red suit, but thought she looked a fright, like a hi-de-hi redcoat from Butlins. In the end she settled on a fitted grey suit—slightly nondescript, she had to admit—which she'd jolly up with a red silk scarf tied round her neck.

On the train up, Greg wasn't especially friendly, Mollie felt, almost offhand, spending the journey studying his conference notes and agenda. Once he said, 'Fetch us a coffee, Mollie. Black, one sugar,' and when she returned from queuing in the buffet carriage, barely thanked her. But she did appreciate how hard he was working, and considered it a privilege to assist. When they arrived in Blackpool, he cheered up, and was actually very amusing when they found the boarding house. 'Breakfast is served in the parlour from 7.30 to 8.15,' announced their landlady, a blue-haired Blackpool scold. 'If you're late, you'll go without. And no refunds given, so don't ask.' Greg had a large cold bedroom with a bow window on the first floor; Mollie was up at the top in a room so tiny you couldn't open the wardrobe. And there was a teasmade-cum-radio on a bedside shelf protruding above the pillow, on which she kept knocking her head.

Mollie changed into her conference outfit and went downstairs. Greg looked her up and down disapprovingly. 'Heavens, Moll.'

'Sorry, is it all wrong? I wasn't sure . . .'

'You look like a rent-a-car lady. Hertz or Avis.'

Mollie blushed. 'I can change if you think it's inappropriate.'

'Forget it. We've got to go, I want to catch Ken Livingstone's speech.'

They walked through a quarter of a mile of residential streets, then along the tacky seafront to the Winter Gardens. At registration, Greg handed her her guest pass and they headed inside, pushing past the demonstrators protesting against foxhunting and supermarkets. One of the demonstrators thrust a flier into Mollie's hand, calling for the nationalisation of Pendletons and Freeza Mart.

Inside the conference building, Mollie was almost overwhelmed by the sheer press of people. There were stands for every organisation and pressure group, from the Institute of Directors and Confederation of British Industry to the Carbon Trust and Action on Poverty League. All the different regions of Britain had stands, with their development boards promoting their areas for inward investment, as well as charities like Oxfam and Save the Children and a group of scary-looking anarchists from the Workers Revolutionary Party handing out newspapers. Whenever she stopped at a stall to collect literature, Greg became impatient and said, 'Come on, Moll. Get a move on or we'll miss Ken's speech.' Mollie was excited when they passed the deputy prime minister, John Prescott, looking incredibly important being ushered along with his wife towards the hall, and later the Home Secretary Jack Straw, who was smaller than she'd expected from watching him on *Newsnight*. As they shoved their way through the crowds, she was impressed when several people greeted Greg, high-fiving or slapping him on the back; he seemed very well regarded in these circles.

'Who was that?' she asked, when he'd finished speaking to a fat man with an Access All Areas pass on a chain round his neck.

'A member of the Party Executive. MP in Tyne-on-Weir. Very influential, great bloke.'

In the hall, Greg ran into more people he knew, this time fellow councillors from Hammersmith, who asked them to sit with them.

'Can't, sorry. We've got places saved up front,' Greg replied.

'I didn't know we've got reserved seats,' Mollie said, when they were out of earshot. 'How come?'

'We don't. I didn't want to sit with them. Petit bourgeois tossers.'

Ken Livingstone was brilliant, Mollie thought. He was an amazing orator and so inspiring, it was fantastic he was back inside the Labour party where he ought to be, because he was doing so much for London as its mayor. Whatever he said, Mollie found herself nodding in agreement: the emphasis on multi-culturalism, his attack on the Tories' racist attitude towards the Islamic communities, bus lanes, cycle lanes, punitive new taxes on 4-by-4 owners, his progressive policies to sort out London's transport for the twenty-first century, reinvesting in the tube system, public firework displays, backing community-based small enterprises by Afro-Caribbean and Bengali immigrants, Diwali festivities . . . all spoke directly to Mollie's kind heart. She imagined each and every one of these initiatives being received with joy by her schoolchildren and their parents, and shared the excitement. Ken Livingstone was the People's Mayor.

'Wasn't he wonderful?' she said afterwards, when the applause died away.

'He's a tosser,' Greg replied. 'He's sold out. Their private-public funding schemes stink.'

For the rest of the afternoon there were dozens of short speeches by men wearing red rosettes, some a bit waffly and disappointing Mollie had to admit, and she slipped away to visit the stands. These she found much more interesting, especially the environmental ones, and soon accumulated a stack of literature about wind turbines and carbon emissions. She felt tempted to post the carbon ones to her dad anonymously, since it was terrible he still drove a high-polluting Jensen. She could hardly bear to ride in it. At the Save the Rhino stand she was so moved by the photographs of dead animals with their horns sawn off by poachers that she made an enormous donation, almost all her remaining cash. The charity worker, having taken nothing all day, was so grateful he presented her with a badge in the shape of a rhino, which Mollie decided to send to her goddaughter Mandy.

At supper, however, Greg was most put out when she had to confess she'd spent all her money, and could he lend her some for her meal? 'You gave sixty bloody quid to wild animals?' he said, incredulous. 'You Strakers don't live in the real world, do you?' Mollie felt tears of humiliation welling up.

'Tell you what,' said Greg. 'I'll pay for supper, and you can do the lodgings on your credit card. Then we'll be quits.'

47.

Samantha was filled with shame and self-disgust. Ten days had gone by since that hideous moment at the Hotel Meurice and she couldn't get it out of her head. If anything, it had got worse. The vision of her father in the bathrobe opening the door to her, made her freeze with horror. It said something about Sam that she was infinitely more censorious about her own role in the drama—the callgirl—than about Miles, the punter. It was unbearable, unforgivable, how could she ever have sunk so low? She realised two things immediately. The first was that she couldn't continue working as an escort, not possibly, she could see now how sordid, how soul-destroying it was, she must have been crazy to get involved. She resigned the same day and insisted her picture be removed from the website. Annoyingly, it was still up there ten days later, and she was furiously texting Pat to have it taken down. The second was that obviously she could never see her father again in her life; and so, by extension, she must cut herself off from her family. The thought of being in the same room as Miles made her blood run cold.

To make matters worse, she had nowhere to live, or very soon wouldn't, once Gaz found out she'd stopped working. For now, she still pretended she had bookings, and left the flat for a couple of hours at a time ostensibly on outcalls but in fact to wander around the shops. He'd find out soon enough when she couldn't pay him, and kick her out for sure. She still owed more than two grand, and Christ knows where that would come from.

After ten days of confiding in no one, in a lather of shame and indecision, she decided to ring Peter. She and her elder brother had never been close, and in normal circumstances she would never have sought his advice on anything. But by process of elimination he was the only family member she could trust to be discrete. Archie, the obvious candidate, being the most similar to herself in character, was incapable of keeping a secret for five minutes, and if she told him it would be broadcast all over London. Mollie was a prude, she'd never understand. Her mother . . . well she could hardly confide this particular episode in her mother. Which left Peter; handsome, unworldly Peter. She found him exasperating sometimes, like his brain wasn't fully in register. But in her present predicament the prospect of confiding in someone non-judgemental was appealing. So she called him at Straker Communications and told him she needed to meet urgently. She had another reason for choosing Peter too: he was the only one of her siblings liable to have money. Congenitally un-extravagant, coveting nothing in any shop, Peter actually saved from his salary which was unheard of. Sam thought she might be able to borrow the cash to pay off Gaz.

They met at Starbucks on Beak Street, close to Peter's office, which Sam immediately realised was a bad choice since the place was teaming with people and she felt they could be overheard at the window counter. Peter, however, was unconcerned. In fact, Sam was struck by how carefree he was, like all the heaviness that generally enveloped him had blown away. No sooner had he collected the coffees plus two chocolate muffins for himself (Sam didn't do muffins), than he produced the print-out of an email from his pocket. 'Read this.'

Sam looked at it. It took her a moment to work out what it was, since the message was quite short, much of the email being devoted to long corporate legal disclaimers from the sender's business. But she saw it came from a record company, Black Cat Wardoursound Music; specifically from an A&R executive enthusing about Peter's demo CD. The message said, 'everyone here really loves it, including the marketing folks,' and saying they were interested in signing him. 'The tracks you've sent aren't enough to make an album, so we're keen to know what other material you have. Otherwise you'll have to write some more.'

'This is amazing,' Sam said. 'When did it come?'

'Last week. I didn't believe it at first, I thought it must be a wind-up by the guys at work.'

'And it isn't?'

'I rang Jasper, the guy who emailed. And he took me for drinks at Soho House.'

'You at Soho House? That's deeply cool, Peter.'

He laughed. 'I know, I felt slightly out of place. But some Straker Communications people came over and said hi, so it worked out quite well, because now Jasper thinks I'm a regular and it helped my cred.'

'And he really likes your music?'

'Seems to. Says he does. I'm embarrassed to tell you, they exaggerate so much these music people, it's all hyperbole. But the fact is . . . they want to sign me. Give me a recording contract. Not a huge one, obviously. I mean, not like Robbie Williams. But enough to live on for a year if I'm careful, to work on my song writing.'

'That's *fantastic*. Have you been celebrating? Does everyone know?'

Peter looked anxious. 'Actually, no. I'm a bit worried about that, telling Dad. I don't think he's going to be too happy when I tell him I'm quitting my job.'

The mention of Miles made Sam anxious too. 'You should probably just get it over with.'

'That's what I reckoned. I tried to see him yesterday, but he wasn't available. Flying back from Brunei, I think they said. But he's there today, I checked again with his office.'

'Well, good luck. And for God's sake don't say you've seen *me*. That's very important, OK? You haven't seen me.'

'Really? Why's that?'

'Just something that happened . . . I . . . don't know if I want to talk about it.' And then, shoulders crumbling, Sam collapsed.

'What is it, Sam? Come on, you can tell me.' Peter tried to comfort his sister, leaning awkwardly along the Starbucks counter and placing his arm around her shoulders. 'Whatever it is Sam, it can't be that bad.' He guessed it had something to do with a boyfriend. Peter found Sam's taste in men execrable, one buffoon after another. As for the most recent one, Dick Gunn, he was monstrous with his great fat stomach and floating gin palace. Peter hoped he wasn't going to have to commiserate with Sam about Dick, because he didn't think he could be very convincing.

And then it all tumbled out: the drugs, the debts . . . then the escorting . . . Sam felt herself blushing from head to toe when she
owned up to that . . . and finally the encounter with Miles at the
Hotel Meurice. The words would hardly come out when she reached
that part. 'The door opened and there was . . . *Dad*,' she whispered.

'Oh my God,' was all Peter could say when she finished. 'Oh my
God.' Then he said, 'You poor, poor thing, Sam. I *wish* you'd come
to me earlier, before you got into all that. I'd have helped you, I'd
have given you money.'

Sam was crying, white faced in the coffee shop. 'I feel so disgusting, so seedy. I've screwed up my life.'

'No, you haven't. You've got yourself in a hole, that's all. You
can get out of it. And let me start by giving you the cash to pay off
this drug pusher. Though I've a good mind to go round there and
smash his face in. How *dare* he set you up as a hooker? I'll kill the
bastard.'

'Don't blame Gaz. He's been a mate, he's OK. But if you could
lend me the cash, I can get him off my back. I'll pay you back,
promise. It's a loan.'

'Have it. I never spend it anyway. It's not like there's anything I
want to buy.'

'You're amazing, Peter. Really. And I can trust you, can't I, never
to repeat what I told you? Not *ever*. Promise.'

'Promise.' He hugged her. 'Now, come on, we'll go to an ATM.
Several in fact. I can only withdraw two hundred pounds a day. So
we may need to do this over a few days. But I want you to pay off
that creep by the end of next week. Then we'll figure out where you
live next. I don't think you should stay in Draycott Gardens.'

'You've been so lovely, Peter. I feel better now, just by talking. I
knew you were the person to tell, you've such great judgement.'

'I don't know about that,' Peter said. 'We'll see if Dad agrees with
you, when I quit. Somehow I don't think he's going to like it much.'

Miles was cloistered in his office in Charles Mews South when
Peter rolled up at six pm for his appointment.

Any visitor to the corporate offices of Straker Communications
pressed a brass bell set into a discrete brass bell plate, and the
Georgian front door was opened by Miles's driver, Makepiece,

who doubled as gatekeeper when he wasn't driving or hand-washing the Jensen or the office Mercedes with bucket and sponge further up the mews. From the Regency hall, with its leather-upholstered footman's chair and real coal fire in winter, visitors were collected by Miles's number three PA, who would lead them upstairs to the first floor and into the outer office where the number two and number one PAs could be found organising Miles's complex life. At this precise moment, Peter observed, they were engaged in securing a particular table for dinner at Harry's Bar, and a particular first class window seat on a BA flight to Beijing. The atmosphere in the outer office was always one of barely disguised anxiety, as Miles's exacting expectations were impressed upon a less fastidious world.

Eventually, Sara White, Miles's senior PA, told Peter, 'I think it's alright to go in now. He's finished his call.' So Peter opened a heavy mahogany door and entered the inner lair, where the great corporate affairs specialist sat in splendour, surrounded by marble busts, photographs of Chawbury Manor and various awards won by his agency over the years.

'Ah, Peter,' he said, looking him up and down. 'Trainers with a suit. Very dotcom. I hope you weren't dressed like that in the office.'

'No, I changed. I'm walking home.'

'Good. And I hope you're arriving with positive news about Pendletons. I've been reading negative pieces all week. And a puff about Freeza Mart in the *FT*.'

'Actually that's not why I've come over, Dad. I need to tell you something.' He felt awkward under his father's beady gaze. 'In fact, I'm resigning. I've . . . got another job, well, not a job exactly, but something very good's happened.'

'It had better be very good indeed to make it worth leaving Straker's. What is it?'

'I've been offered a recording contract by an indie label. They're paying me an advance to write music. It'll come out as an album.'

Miles's first reaction, on hearing either good or bad news about any of his children, was to evaluate how it might be interpreted by the world at large in relation to himself. Would it enhance or diminish his personal reputation? So when Archie was selling cars in the Lexus showroom he felt mildly disadvantaged, having a son who was a car dealer. Conversely, he felt good telling people Archie was employed at Thurloes ('that frightful dive where the royal princes go'), believing it made him trendier by association. Similarly, he had enjoyed saying Samantha was at Heathfield, but not that Mollie was at Mid-Hampshire College or later at teacher training college. In fact, he'd seldom found he could mention Mollie to anyone.

With Peter, he digested the idea of having a pop star for a son. 'How much is the contract for?'

'Twelve thousand,' Peter replied proudly. 'Not paid all at once though. It comes in instalments.'

'Practically nothing. So what'll you live on?'

'Well, the advance. It should be enough. They've given me a year to lay down ten tracks.'

'Twelve thousand to last a year? You'll be lucky. Twelve thousand is two return flights to Beijing.'

'I'll be fine,' Peter replied.

'That's what you say. And what happens when this bottomless twelve thousand runs out? Which it will, sooner than you imagine. What then? Am I meant to hold your job open for you, for when you come creeping back with nothing to show for it? That what you're expecting?'

'Actually, no. I'm giving my notice and that's the end of it. If the music doesn't work out, I'll find something else. But it might do well. The record company's optimistic.'

'Though evidently not *that* optimistic, given the smallness of your advance. You're really prepared to walk out of this highly successful company—your family company—to write folk ditties? Speaking as one of the few people fortunate enough to have heard your songs, I think that's a brave decision, Peter. And probably a rash one.'

'Well, I've decided. If I don't give it a try, I'll spend my whole life regretting it, wondering if I could have made it. At least I'll have given it a shot.'

'You'll be poor, Peter. You realise that? Because if you walk out of Straker Communications, you can kiss goodbye to inheriting any of it. I'm not giving it away to people who don't value it, who haven't played their part in building the asset.' Miles was working himself into a massive strop. 'No, you'll be poor. You'll never make a success of anything, you never have. In fact, I'm not sure I'm going to allow you the dignity of resigning. No one resigns from Straker Communications, least of all family. So you're *fired*, Peter. You've been dismissed. An internal email will be issued to that effect tomorrow morning . . . Pendletons have been dissatisfied with your performance for a while now. It's placed them in an awkward position, because they don't like to come out and complain about my son, but they've made it perfectly clear. Zach Durban feels the same. He doesn't rate you either. So you're fired, Peter. You needn't go back to the office. If you do, they won't let you in. Security will be informed. And you needn't think you can stay in Holland Park Square either. Don't imagine you'll be living there, strumming your guitar in the communal garden, scaring the children and pigeons. You're banned from the house. And from Chawbury. No doubt your record company can find you a suitable place to doss down. Or you can rent a hotel room with your famous advance. See how long that lasts, eh? I don't think you'll find a very comfortable room for that, if you need it for a year.'

Peter stared at his father with level gaze. For the first time in his life, he felt ready to stand up to him.

'Probably I won't be able to afford a suite at the Meurice,' he said. 'You're probably right about that. Not with all the extras on the bill.' He looked at him meaningfully, saw Miles flinch, turned on his heel and walked out.

48.

Miles arrived home at Holland Park Square feeling testy. The more he thought about it, the more angry he became about Peter. Loyalty, he told himself, was one quality he placed above all others, and Peter had shown himself wholly disloyal in quitting his job. Especially now, when he knew how important the Pendletons and Zach Durban accounts were to the company, and any disruption of account personnel was destabilising for the client. Furthermore, he didn't know what to make of Peter's jibe about the Hotel Meurice. Had Samantha told him something, or was it coincidence? Miles suspected the second, but it had been an uncomfortable moment. Well, with no job and nowhere to live, Peter would soon learn his lesson.

Pouring a large vodka and tonic in his study by the front door, he wandered down to the kitchen. He found Davina sitting at the table with Mollie deep in conversation, which stopped when he entered. Mollie looked particularly unglamorous in a cycling jacket with fluorescent safety strips all over it, and a raw complexion from excess bicycling. On her feet were big galumphing boots with rubber heels.

'Hi, Dad,' said Mollie, 'I've come for supper.'

'Bit of a cold night for a barbeque, isn't it?' he replied. 'Davina, are we really eating outside?'

'No, of course not. Whatever made you ask that?'

'Mollie's attire. She's dressed for outdoors. You look like a traffic policeman, Mollie. Can't you remove that extraordinary jacket inside the house?'

On the nights she was up in London, Davina brought with her from Chawbury various pre-prepared dishes made by Mrs French, fish pies and chicken stews which were quick to reheat and could easily be frozen if not required. One of the challenges of living with Miles was that he didn't decide until the very last minute whether he would be in or out for dinner, and yet expected to be fed, and fed well, when at home. Davina's solution was the pies and stews she or Conception could serve at thirty minutes notice, accompanied by vegetables from the Chawbury vegetable garden or from Kenya via Pendletons, whichever was more in season. Miles, endlessly contrary, was seldom happy. 'If I'm given one more fish pie, I'm going to go mad,' he'd say. 'I had a very large lunch at the Ritz, I don't *need* this stodgy food in the evening. Can't we just have a simple slice of Parma ham and a piece of cheese?' On other nights, he'd say, 'For heaven's sake, Davina, I had lunch at my desk, a tiny box of sushi. Can't *somebody*—you, Conception, Mrs French, someone from this vast and expensive retinue of domestic staff you insist upon—prepare me some hot food? Is it really so much to ask?' All these conflicting demands made Davina apprehensive, feeling she could never do anything right.

'So what have you been up to since I last saw you, Mollie? Everything alright at the immigrants' reception camp? Sorry, state-funded education system.'

'It's good. We're starting on the new citizenship classes they've brought in. Teaching the kids about the benefits and obligations of being British.'

Miles rolled his eyes. 'That's all we need. Teaching them about benefits and how to claim them, I expect. How to sign on.'

'It's not that. It's about taking pride in being British. The freedoms we have here, going right back to Magna Carta. Some of the children don't know about them. They come from countries with less developed constitutions. Alan Milburn gave an amazing speech at the conference . . .'

'Which conference? The Labour one? How come you were watching television in the middle of the afternoon?'

'Actually, I was *there*,' Mollie replied, instantly regretting it, because she hadn't meant to tell him.

'You were in Blackpool? Why? And with whom, may I ask? Since when did my daughter start hanging out at socialist conventions?'

The cat out of the bag, Mollie found herself confessing about her trip with Greg, and what an inspiring time it had been hearing

Tony Blair and Ken Livingstone and all their new schemes to improve the country and the world. As she spoke, she became aware of her father's face turning to thunder.

'And I suppose you knew about this, Davina?' he asked when she'd finished. 'Did you know Mollie was going to Blackpool with the fat Trotskyist Clegg boy? Tell me.'

'Actually, darling, I did know, yes. Mollie did tell me. And I decided not to mention it because I thought you might react in this silly way.'

'Ah, I see. So it's a conspiracy? A conspiracy by mother and daughter against me? So that's how you spend your time when I'm at work, hatching schemes to stop me knowing what's going on in my children's lives?' Then another thought struck him. 'I suppose you knew about Peter, too? He came to see me at my office, to tell me he's leaving to become the new Bob Dylan. Did you know about that?'

'Actually I did. He's so excited, I've never seen him so happy. I told him he should tell you the news himself.'

'And I told him exactly what I thought of it. Don't you worry, I left him in no doubt about that. I've told him he's a bloody fool, and banned him from living in this house. Either house. So you can tell Conception to pack up his stuff. And don't forget the guitar, he'll be needing that. For busking in the tube probably.'

Then, turning on Davina, he said, 'If you ask me, this whole family is going off the rails and you, Davina, aren't helping. I will *not* have secrets kept from me. One after another, the children have been sneaking around behind my back. I'm talking to *you*, Mollie. You will never again attend a socialist jamboree without my express permission, is that understood? Think what would have happened if the press had got hold of it, they'd have had a field day. Miles Straker's daughter turns New Labour. Samantha's another one I'm not happy with at the moment. That's why she's banned from our house, houses. I hope you're respecting that, Davina? I don't want to discover she's been coming round here, or you've been giving her money. So now two of our children are banned, Peter *and* Samantha. And I won't hesitate to extend that to you, Mollie, if you continue in this way. The only one of my children I'm reasonably satisfied with is Archie. Archie is the only one of you with a brain in his head. That's because he takes after me.'

* * *

It was at twenty past three in the morning, that same night, that Davina made the momentous decision to leave her husband.

The argument at supper replayed in her head, and the more she pondered it the more indefensible Miles's behaviour seemed. One by one he had fallen out with the children, always without cause, Davina felt, until two had been banished from the house, a third, Mollie, was crushed by his constant sarcasm, and even Archie was around very seldom these days. He hadn't slept at Holland Park Square more than two nights in the past fortnight, and when she asked where he'd been, he was evasive. For the first time, Davina saw how pointless her life had become. Of course, she had recognised for a long time that her marriage was far from ideal. She had become accustomed to Miles's mental bullying and chilly perfectionism. All this she put up with for the sake of the children, and because she found consolation in her garden and watercolours.

But now she felt a line had been crossed. In alienating the children, he made their life together meaningless. What was the point of these ridiculous big houses with all their bedrooms, if they were to be empty? What was the point of the time and energy she put in to supporting Miles at his work things, if their family life was so dysfunctional? Davina had never especially admired Miles's business, which she saw as shallow and superficial, but she recognised the satisfaction it gave him and the money it brought in to support the family. So she had done her best to be there at his side, whenever he'd asked, especially in the early days when he regularly took her with him to business conferences. Recently, there had been less of that. Miles said he preferred going alone to conferences without the distraction of a wife.

She contrasted the gentle contentment of her parents' marriage— and as a diplomat's wife her mother had supported her father just as she supported Miles—with the hectic discontent of her own. She tried to remember what it was that had first attracted her to Miles, all those years ago, and realised it was the energy, the ambition, the brittle cleverness and fastidiousness . . . all the same qualities that now repelled her. She remembered him before he was successful— though, even then, you knew he was going to be successful—and the relentless way he had pursued her, sending flowers to her flat, inviting her to dinner night after night, collecting her in the Aston Martin he'd borrowed from a Piccadilly showroom. In those days, it was understood that Davina was a bit of a catch, the beautiful diplomat's daughter with porcelain skin, and Miles the-young-man-on-the-make lucky to catch her. It was years, of course, since anyone thought of them in those terms. Miles was the star now, Davina his non-working garden-loving wife.

Often, she was afraid of her husband. Not physically afraid, but afraid of his caustic tongue, of his criticism when she failed to meet his standards. Had she always been? She felt she probably had, though she'd have phrased it differently in those early days. She'd have considered herself 'in awe' of him.

Now, looking back over her marriage, she could see that awe had transformed first into anxiety, then timid dependency, so that everything they did in their lives—every decision—became Miles's decision and his alone. Their choice of homes, holidays, the schools the children went to, all had been Miles's decisions. If she wanted to buy a painting for the house, Miles had to see it first, to decide if he approved; if he wanted to buy one himself, he bought it. Half the paintings at Chawbury and Holland Park Square had been chosen by Miles alone and, though she was too loyal to say so, many were not good choices. Even the clothes she wore were scrutinised and vetoed by him.

Having made her decision to leave him, Davina wondered what to do next. She could hear him snoring through the wall in the dressing room, to which he'd withdrawn to sulk following their argument. The prospect of life without Miles made her feel afraid; afraid of his reaction, and afraid for her future. Having been permitted to take so few decisions during their marriage, she began to worry whether she even knew how.

Archie had as good as moved in to Roupell Street. Not officially, of course, but little by little his stuff migrated south across the river. After that first afternoon when he'd had Gemma on the sitting room floor, he'd taken to heading over to her gaff straight from the club, in the early hours. The first couple of times he'd leant against the bell and thumped on the door until she came down to let him in. After that, she gave him a key. The arrangement suited Archie very nicely. For a start, it was free sex on tap. And he had to admit, Gemma was surprisingly hot. This he attributed to five years of being cooped up in Chawbury like a nun in a convent, she was gagging for it. He found it rather a turn-on the way that, when Mandy was awake, Gemma was like this perfect, angelic mother, making jigsaw puzzles with her daughter on the floor, but later, when Mandy was down for her rest, she turned into this eager, melting sex babe. No question, she was fit. With her big blue eyes, above-average legs and baby-soft skin, Archie reckoned she was a definite 8, maybe even an 8.5. Only her plump ankles let her down.

Life in Roupell Street suited him too, in ways he couldn't have anticipated. For a start there was no Carmelita on his case all day, badgering him to get up before lunchtime because she wanted to do his room, or vacuuming right outside and thumping the nozzle against his door, waking him when he needed his sleep. Gemma never disturbed him in the mornings. He'd let himself in at three or four a.m., climb into her bed, shake her awake if he fancied some of it, then doss down until mid afternoon. She was great too at delivering brunch in bed on a tray, and his clothes from Thurloes were put through the wash and ironed, and his jacket hung up by the bathroom window to air the fag smells out. As far as service was concerned, he had no complaints.

Obviously he couldn't tell anyone at home he was seeing Gemma, and certainly not Miles. Archie had no illusions how he'd react if he found out, and there were ever present dangers of a leak. His mum and Gemma's mum did yoga together, and were always bumping into each other in Chawbury, so Gemma had to be sworn to secrecy, which she didn't like, but agreed when Archie insisted. Ever since he'd reappeared in her life, Gemma had felt perpetually joyful, reunited with Mandy's dad, seeing herself at last at the heart of a proper little family. In all those years as a single mother in Chawbury she'd hoped against hope Archie would come back; slowly that hope diminished, then died. But now—a miracle. She longed to broadcast the news, to tell everyone, all her friends that she and Archie were an item and furthermore—guess what?—he was Mandy's dad all along. She didn't get why he needed to be so secretive, but she daren't risk jeopardising what they had.

* * *

Davina took a deep breath and, telling nobody, called on a firm of divorce lawyers in Lincolns' Inn Fields. All the way there in the taxi she felt uneasy, in case anyone should see her. She had emphasised when she rang up that this was only an exploratory meeting, she hadn't decided anything, and it all had to remain completely confidential. 'Of course, Mrs Straker, that's perfectly normal and understood, Mrs Straker.' Davina wished they didn't keep using her name, it made her anxious.

In the event, she met up with a sympathetic female divorce solicitor, along with a keen young trainee taking notes, who put her under no pressure but asked a lot of questions about how long they'd been married and how many children they had, and where they lived and whether they were domiciled in the UK. The solicitor, Angela Strawbetter, seemed more than satisfied by the information, nodding at the seven bedroom house with staff accommodation in Holland Park Square, and Chawbury Manor in Hampshire with its sixty acres of paddocks and parkland, swimming pool and tennis court. When Davina mentioned her husband was chairman and chief executive of a PR and corporate image consultancy, Angela nodded knowingly, having already carried out a 'conflict search' on the Strakers, following Davina's initial call.

'You won't tell anyone I've been to see you,' Davina said nervously. 'He'd be furious if he knew I was here.'

Angela was reassuring and asked more questions, such as what were the grounds for the divorce ('not that you need grounds these days, marital breakdown is quite enough but unreasonable behaviour is even better'). Then she asked which schools the children had attended, how much domestic help they kept in both houses, any animals? 'Three horses and a pony,' Davina replied. And would Mrs Straker say she'd supported her husband in creating his business, had she attended business dinners and functions with him over the years? Had she given up a career? Did she have any wealth at the time of the marriage?

'Well, yes,' Davina replied uncertainly. 'He does sometimes take me to lovely dinners with his clients. But I can't really say I've done much to build up the company. That was all Miles.'

'Oh, you mustn't dismiss the part you played in making it possible, Mrs Straker,' said Angela. 'If you hadn't been there managing the houses and running round after him and taking responsibility for the children, he couldn't have done it at all, could he?' Then she asked, 'Are all your assets in joint names, do you know, and do you have joint or separate bank accounts?'

'Separate. Well, we have a joint one for domestic bills and all the everyday stuff, and for my clothes and hairdressing etcetera, not that I'm extravagant about that sort of thing, it doesn't really interest me actually. If I wasn't with Miles, I'd spend even less. And Miles has his own bank accounts too, I think. To be absolutely honest, I don't know. He's always looked after the money side, that's always been his area.'

'If you do decide to go ahead, we can take care of all that for you. The crucial thing is to establish the size of the family pot. The statement of assets is fairly standard: property, investments, pensions and so on.'

'I want to make it clear I wouldn't want to ask Miles for too much,' Davina said. 'It was him who made all the money. A little flat or a cottage somewhere, that's all I need. Somewhere with a couple of spare bedrooms so the children can come and visit.'

Angela smiled a patronising smile. 'You'd be surprised, Mrs Straker, by how many of the wives say that when they first come and see me. The nice wives that is, not the grabby ones. And I can tell you're one of the nice ones. But I always advise them not to settle too easily. After all, you only have one chance, and you never know what might happen in the future, do you? If you don't take sufficient from the marriage you may find yourself severely disadvantaged, if you don't have a comparable lifestyle to the father. If your husband remains in Holland Park and Chawbury Manor, and you end up in some pokey cottage, it's unlikely your children will gravitate towards you with their friends in the holidays. Those are the things to think about. I always ask my clients to think very long term, like what happens when you want to entertain your grandchildren.' Then she said, 'So if you do decide to proceed, let me know, we'd be delighted to represent you, and we'll hold your hand all the way. And of course we'll need to explain our standard terms and conditions and schedule of payments, so you always know exactly where you are with your planning.'

49.

You see the rocks on the headland? That's Strathy Point,' Peter told her. 'And the islands on the horizon, you can just make them out? The Orkneys. Beyond that, nothing but sea till you hit Norway.'

Peter collected Sam from Wick airport and was driving her along the top of Scotland, following the single track coast road to the whitewashed crofter's cottage he'd leased to write music. He had chosen it as the remotest place in which he could find a short let in mainland Britain, nine miles from the nearest shop, in a hamlet of stone dwellings overlooking the wild Atlantic. The cottage stood a little apart from the others, elevated on a bank above the road. From the windows the view was only of sand dunes sprouting with sea kale and steel grey ocean beyond.

'Yes, I'd say this was fairly . . . isolated. I think you can say that,' Sam said, as Peter bumped the car onto the grassy parking place beside the croft.

'If you're hoping for nightclubs, you're going to be disappointed. The nearest is probably in Scrabster, forty miles. And you wouldn't like it, so don't ask.'

Sam laughed. 'I'm so over with all that. I wouldn't care if I never went to another club in my life. I don't want to see anyone, speak to anyone.'

'Just as well. Because there's nobody here, not that I've met at least. And did I warn you, your mobile won't work, no signal? The nearest place is three miles away up a hill.'

'Believe me, Peter, I'm not intending to call anyone.' She thought of all the people she was avoiding—Gaz, Dick, her mother, Miles above all—and blanched. 'I want to disappear off radar. And sleep. Sleep for weeks and weeks.'

'I'll try not to disturb you with my music. I've been leading quite a selfish existence, getting up early and writing till the afternoon, trying to. Outdoors, if the weather's nice. It changes so quickly here, one minute bright sunshine, the next it's tipping down, you have to keep going in and out. I sit on that bench looking out to sea. It's right underneath your window, I think, so I'd better shift it.'

'Don't do that. I'd like to hear. I like your songs.'

'That's not what you said in Italy. You were always complaining.'

'Yeah, well, that was then. I had lots of stupid opinions then. Lot of good they did me.'

Peter took her bags into the unlocked cottage ('No one locks round here. Nothing to steal and no one to steal it') and put the kettle on. The place was small and basic, two rooms on the ground floor, a sitting room and bedroom, plus a lean-to kitchen and bathroom extension at the back, and a second bedroom in the eaves reached by steep wooden stairs. The walls inside the croft were lined in pitch pine, so it felt like a sauna, Sam thought. Peter had stuck posters up of seabirds and made a display of shells and stones from the beach and the bleached skull of a sheep.

'So . . . this is it. Your hideaway. It's so nice you've let me come, Peter. I thought maybe you'd changed your mind when you didn't call.'

'I hadn't listened to my messages. Sorry about that. Zero bars of reception. Then I climbed the mountain behind us and it burst into life near the summit. All your messages telling me to ring you. I wish you could see where I was calling from—by this deep black loch—the bleakest, most spectacular place. We can walk up there one day if you like.'

'Maybe not, if you don't mind.' She made a face. 'Please remember my recent backstory, big brother. Kept woman, escort girl. I don't think I can become hillwalker and outwards bound freak overnight. It's going to take a while.'

Peter laid a fire of driftwood from the beach, and they sat on the floor by the hearth staring into the flames. 'You know what this place reminds me of?' Sam said. 'It just came to me. It's like that old cottage across our valley, Silas Trow's cottage, before the Cleggs came along and bulldozed it.'

'Maybe that's why I took it. Subconsciously, I mean. I always loved Silas's cottage. I had this fantasy about moving in and getting away from everyone, the family. Dad mainly, I guess.'

'That's so weird, that was my fantasy too. Except I wanted to live there with some tall handsome lover. Someone like Dad, in those days.' She looked rueful. 'Obviously the idea has lost some of its appeal lately . . .' Then she said, 'Do you remember the first time we met the Cleggs, or was it the second time? We drove over in the Gator, and Ross and Dawn were checking the place out with their builders. And Dad was so unfriendly to them.'

'As were you, Sam, I seem to think. No one had heard of Ross then. It wasn't that long ago either. Six or seven years? And now he's famous. They're even using him in the new Freeza Mart TV commercials.'

'Was I really unfriendly? How embarrassing. I think I might have been quite snobbish back then.'

'And now you're not?'

'Let me tell you, working as an escort you can forget it. You have to make it with whoever shows up. And they're mostly loads less tasty than Ross.'

'I always felt we behaved appallingly to the Cleggs over that whole thing. Our family, I mean. Whenever I see the Cleggs or hear about them, I'm ashamed. It's like we're in denial about the baby. Mandy, I mean. I sound like Dad talking about "the baby," he never says her name. That's if he refers to her at all.'

'Does Archie ever see Mandy? I haven't asked him about her for ages.'

Peter shrugged. 'I don't think so. He acts like it never happened. But that was Dad's strategy. Total *omerta*. The subject that could never be mentioned.'

'Well, now there's another one. Something else that'll never be mentioned. Me. And him. And Paris.'

'I wonder if Mum suspects? I've been thinking about that and can't tell. Whether she turns a blind eye. I mean, if he's using hookers all the time—sorry, escorts. Your agency said he was one of their top customers, didn't they? It's so weird. He always presents himself as so perfect, with this perfect life where nothing goes wrong and all of us, the family, are like this perfect idealised family unit. That's the image he likes everyone to see. But all the time he's lusting after call girls—sorry, escorts—or envying people like the Pendletons. Or Ross, come to that.'

'Lust and Envy. They're meant to be two of the deadly sins, aren't they? Not that I can remember any of the others.'

'Pride. Greed . . . Christ, they could all be about Dad. And Wrath. That's another, I think. You should have heard him at the office when anything went wrong.'

'What about Sloth? I'm fairly sure Sloth is one, but you couldn't say Dad's lazy. No way.'

Peter laughed. 'No, Sloth's me. That's what he thinks anyway, he's always saying, "you lazy bugger, Peter."'

'So that's Lust, Envy, Pride, Greed, Anger—I mean Wrath, whatever. They're all definitely Dad. Plus Sloth . . . that's only six. There must be one more.'

'Gluttony. I wouldn't say that's Dad either, not in the greedy pig sense. He's not fat.'

And then, both together, they cried out, 'Greg!' and fell about laughing.

'That's it then,' said Peter. 'All the deadly sins reside in Chawbury.' He put on a voice: 'Welcome to the valley of deadly sins, staring Miles Straker as the lustful, envious, proud, greedy squire . . .'

'I've never told anyone this before,' Sam said after a while. 'But a few years ago I was in Annabel's and Dad was there with a woman, with his arm wrapped round her. I'm sure they were having an affair, it looked like they were. And he spotted me and moved tables. He was incredibly cool about it though, didn't look guilty at all. It made me wonder if I'd imagined it.'

'What was she like? The woman?'

'Actually you know her. Serena Harden. They live over by the Mountleighs. They always come to Dad's big lunch parties in the summer.'

'I know the one. The redhead, quite sexy-looking.'

'Quite tarty-looking.'

'Poor Mum, I feel so sorry for her. Do you think someone should tell her?'

'Christ, no. I'd kill you if you did. When I told you about Paris, it was a secret. You promised.'

'She wouldn't need to know that bit. But surely she should know about Dad's girlfriends, mistresses, whatever. You'd want to, wouldn't you, if you were in her shoes?'

'Would I? Not sure. Perhaps I'd rather stay in blissful ignorance. Anyway, I can hardly come on all moral, can I? Probably most of the guys I saw were married or had partners. Half wore wedding rings. They didn't even bother taking them off.'

'They must've thought they'd died and gone to heaven when you showed up.'

'Why?'

'Because you're stunning, Samantha. You look better now than ever. All the drugs and . . . that other stuff, it doesn't show or anything. You could never tell.'

'I've lost weight,' she said. 'The drugs do that. But thank you for the compliment. Much appreciated. My self-esteem's in a bad place, it needs all the boosting it can get.'

'I'll remember that. Three compliments a day after meals, to boost your esteem system. And exercise. That's part of the treatment programme too. Come on, we should walk on the beach. It's quite blowy, bring a coat. But it clears your head. And we could do with some of that, us Strakers. And afterwards I'm going to work on my music.'

For six weeks, Sam lay in bed every day until two in the afternoon. Some mornings she slept, others she dozed in her room beneath the eaves, listening to the drag of the waves and Peter strumming his guitar outside. She found it oddly comforting, the folk chords on the wind and Peter's mellow voice. She heard him working on a song about a whale washed up on the beach by the tide, and there was a haunting beauty about it she found moving. His latest songs, however, were angry and intense. One was called 'The Secret Trapped Inside' and you didn't need to be a genius to know what inspired it.

For lunch, Peter liked to roast chickens, and she could smell the aroma drifting up from the kitchen. 'Is it my imagination,' she asked after four consecutive days of roast chicken, 'or is this all we ever eat?'

'Uh? Oh, chicken you mean? Yeah, well, it's easy. It cooks itself while I'm writing. I bought twelve frozen ones at the Co-op in Wick when I collected you.'

'Would you mind if we had something else sometimes? I'm only thinking, it might begin to lose its novelty if we have roast chicken every single day.'

'Uh, sure,' said Peter. 'Whatever you think.'

After that, Sam took over the cooking and they drove round the Kyle of Tongue to Durness every few days to stock up on provisions. Sam found a stall on the harbour where you could buy fish—mackerel and sea salmon—direct from the fishing boats. And then, in the granite town square, one of the new Freeza Mart Expresses Ross had been opening in smaller towns all over the country, with a delicatessen and proper cheese counter.

In the afternoons they took long walks along the beach or through the plantations behind the croft, each day at Peter's prompting walking a little further, and Sam felt herself become fitter and more grounded, as her traumatic encounter at the Hotel Meurice began to lose some of its paralysing rawness. As they walked, they chewed over everything: Miles, his mistress and callgirl habit, their mother and how she could put up with it (Sam was censorious, considering Davina too acquiescent; Peter protective of the mother he adored), Archie and Mandy and how awful it was he never saw his daughter and, above all, whether Sam could ever face Miles again or whether she'd avoid him forever. Having not talked properly with her elder brother for years and years, Samantha was surprised by how helpful she found it and how sensible and compassionate he was. What she hitherto dismissed as vagueness, and compared so unfavourably with her super-confident boyfriends, she now recognised as heightened sensitivity and maturity. She was constantly surprised by his range of knowledge, by his ability to identify birds of prey, by the stories he told her about the windblown Sutherland coast. And she was struck by, and learnt from, Peter's measured attitude towards Miles, never bitter, while hinting at a deep well of fury. Several times he referred to the ritual humiliations of every-day life at Straker Communications, and the personal humiliations he endured for so long. 'For ages I thought it was my own fault for disappointing him—and I was always disappointing him, whatever I did was never good enough, never quite right. Then one day I re-alised he was impossible to please. I wasn't *him*, you see. I would never be, and never *could* be, Miles Straker. The great Miles Straker. However hard I worked, however much I improved at the job, it wouldn't make a blind bit of difference. Because I'd still never be him. And he'd always need to point that out. Add to that, of course,' he said, suddenly laughing, 'that whole Public Relations business is such a crock of shit. I mean, you couldn't take it seri-ously. All those meetings, the balls people spoke with a straight face, the posturing, you sat there with your mouth hanging open half the time. So now you get why I was no bloody good at it. Hope-less. Dad was right about that, at least. And every morning I cele-brate that I'm not going back. Not ever. I'll never darken their door again. No more press releases, no "positioning" conferences, no try-ing to place positive profiles about Zach Durban. God that man's a reptile, by the way. If there wasn't some big overblown puff profile about him three times a month in the newspapers, he whinged and whinged. As for Mrs Durban she adores Dad, naturally. He kept promising to get her on the cover of *Tatler*, as if. We got her on the cover of some rubbish Mayfair estate agents magazine instead.' He rolled his eyes. 'But I'm trying to forget all that, bury the memory. That's a sparrowhawk by the way, in case you're wondering. Up there, no, much higher, that's a *seagull* you're looking at. Higher, hovering above the Scots pines.'

Sometimes in the Durness post office, Peter bought postcards to send to his mother or to Mollie: his preference was for nondescript views of the town showing the war memorial and harbour wall, or cartoon postcards of gregarious Jocks in kilts and sporrans with Loch Ness sea monsters wearing Tam O'Shanters. 'I've told Mollie you're staying at the cottage, and how I intend to get you up Ben Aulty one day. That's the hill I keep going on about, the one with the loch.'

'You'll be lucky. Though in actual fact, the idea isn't quite as im-possible now as it was. I'm not saying yes, but I'm not ruling it out.'

'I'll tell Mollie it's a maybe. And do you want to add a message to her yourself? There's space.'

Sam took the card and wondered what to write. She barely knew Mollie, she felt, and was guilty about that. She knew she'd been a bitch to her sister, or anyway had disregarded her, having nothing in common. Now, of course, she appreciated Mollie was rather admirable in her own way. Nor had she previously realised how close Peter was to her. From what he said, they regularly had supper together, usually round at Mollie's Olympia flat. He knew her flatmates too. Sam realised she'd never even seen Mollie's flat or had any idea whom she shared with. In the end she just wrote, 'I hope being a schoolteacher is going well. Scotland is beautiful.'

It was during her eighth or ninth week staying with Peter that Sam agreed to climb Ben Aulty.

'You sure?' Peter said. 'It's four hours to the top. No actual climbing, but it's quite testing.'

Sam bought boots in Durness and a blue cagoule, which she considered the most hideous garment she'd ever put on.

'You'll be grateful for it when it pours. Which it probably will,' Peter said.

They tramped up through the plantation, then followed a stone track which cut across a mile of low heathery hills towards a higher range beyond. As time went by, the heather and bracken were strewn with boulders and immense slabs of flat rock, and the sheep which had grazed on the lower hills were prevented from venturing higher by wire stock fences.

Peter was carrying a shepherd's crook and once brought it down sharply on the earth. 'A viper. Got it in one. I hate doing it but they eat the birds eggs.'

Towards the crest of the second hill, when she'd hoped they must be near the summit, Sam realised a third, steeper one lay ahead, and began to regret coming. She was impressed by how fit Peter was, when she'd never considered him sporty. They were picking their way across an interminable flat area of bogland on the perimeter of the loch, when both their mobiles bleeped and rang at the same time. 'That's exactly what happened last time,' Peter said. 'Same place. The signal locks on.'

Texts and voice messages began downloading in rapid succession. 'Here they come,' Peter said. 'Two texts from Mum and three, no four from Mollie . . .' He started opening them and gasped in shock. 'Sam, listen to this. Good God. Mollie's getting married! She says she's engaged to Greg Clegg. And, wait a minute, here's a text from Mum confirming it. I'm speechless.'

Samantha was scrolling her way through her own texts. 'I've got one from Archie saying the same thing. It's incredible. Did you have any idea, Peter?'

'None. I mean, she mentioned she'd seen Greg and they'd had supper. But she didn't give the slightest hint. Not that they were going out. And she's so young. How old's Mollie now?'

'Twenty-one? Tweny-two? Four years younger than me. Twenty-two then.'

'And she's marrying *Greg*? I mean, I don't know him that well, so I don't want to be negative . . . And he's quite a bit older.'

Samantha was stunned. She thought of Greg in Thailand and how she'd almost fallen for him herself, on the island of Koh Pha-Ngan. She'd spent the intervening years avoiding him. And suddenly he was going to be her brother-in-law.

'I don't know what to say. It's gobsmacking,' Sam said.

'I wonder what Mum thinks about it,' Peter said. 'She doesn't say in her text.'

'I wonder what Dad thinks, more like,' said Sam. 'Not that we need ask. He's going to go fucking ape.'

50.

Mercifully, as Miles declared more than once, it being his official public position on the matter, Mollie and Greg wanted their wedding to be extremely private, with only immediate family and a handful of very old friends attending. As far as he was concerned, the smaller the better, and at least he wasn't expected to shell out for a big reception.

Ironically, he had always rather looked forward to throwing a big wedding for a daughter. He'd envisaged a top-of-the-range marquee on the lawn at Chawbury, a dinner dance for five or six hundred people, family friends and clients judiciously blended, and a nicely turned speech from the father of the bride. But in these daydreams the bride in question had always been Samantha, not Mollie, and the bridegroom emphatically not Greg.

The announcement was so unexpected, so disagreeable, it had taken a day or two to take it in. Miles had just landed in New York, and was waiting by the carousel for his luggage at JFK, when Mollie rang his mobile to break the good news. He had to call Davina to confirm it wasn't a joke. Greg Clegg! Of all potential husbands in the world, why had she picked *him*? Miles was inclined to blame Davina, who had allowed Mollie to go to Blackpool with Greg in the first place, which set the whole unfortunate business going. If Davina had put a stop to it then, as he would have done himself, it never would have got off the starting blocks. It annoyed him she didn't accept responsibility or apologise. She'd been behaving most strangely lately.

Following the engagement, Davina insisted they invite Molly, Greg and the Cleggs over for celebration drinks, and Miles reluctantly agreed providing it take place in London, not Chawbury, which he believed made it somehow less intimate. So one evening when Miles was back from New York, Ross and Dawn strolled across the communal garden from their own house, Mollie and Greg came up from Hammersmith, and Archie made a rare appearance to make up the numbers. The seven of them stood stiffly around in the Strakers' drawing room, regretting the fact that so many of their other children couldn't be there. Peter and Samantha were both away, Miles said airily, not having a clue where either of them was. Ross explained Debbie was working in a five-star hotel in Paris, and Gemma was putting Mandy to bed in Roupell Street and hadn't been able to get a baby-sitter. Just as well, thought Miles; an encounter between Gemma and Archie could have been awkward.

Mollie, plainly, was ecstatic about her engagement. She bubbled over with happiness, telling everyone how Greg proposed in a pub near the National Film Theatre where they'd been watching a South American film. The children at school had made a card which she brought along to show everyone, with a crude crayon of a bride and groom, and bits of tinsel glued on, signed by the whole class. 'Isn't it so sweet?' Mollie said, passing it round. Davina wondered whether it was her imagination or was Mollie more excited about everything than Greg, who seemed rather withdrawn and unanimated. When she asked, 'Have you had any thoughts yet about a church? And what about setting a date?' Greg replied, 'I'm leaving all that to Mollie. I've told her it can be whenever she likes, except during council or mayoral elections.'

On the Clegg side, the person who was most delighted was Dawn, who never stopped saying how she couldn't have hoped for a nicer daughter-in-law than Mollie, Debbie's best friend. She raised her glass to her again and again, remembering how Mollie used to come over to Chawbury Park for riding lessons, and what a lovely girl she'd always been, and how no one ever imagined she'd end up part of the family. 'It must be fate,' she declared. 'I'm a great believer in fate, and if we hadn't bought that little cottage in the woods which became the Park, we'd probably never have met and none of this would have happened.'

Ross didn't appear quite as elated as his wife, and gave Miles a couple of hard sidelong glances, but did his best to get into the party spirit. When Miles showed no sign of proposing a toast to the couple, Ross did so himself, saying how pleased he was to welcome Mollie as a daughter-in-law ('And how old does that make me feel? Having a daughter-in-law?') and how he hoped he might be allowed to provide Freeza Mart champagne at the wedding breakfast, unless Pendletons had got in there first.

Watching Greg's face during this little speech, Miles noticed a disdainful sneer on his lips at the mention of Freeza Mart and Pendletons, and a general antipathy towards Ross which surprised him. He hadn't realised there was bad blood between the Cleggs. As for Greg himself, he seemed to have dropped a lot of weight recently. He was dressing differently too, less scruffy. Miles wouldn't have chosen the single-breasted grey suit himself, and the red tie was ghastly, but the overall effect was a definite step up. Very New Labour.

It was during the engagement drinks that Mollie told everyone they only wanted a small wedding. 'Probably a civil ceremony at the Town Hall. And we can have our reception there too. Forty people maximum.'

All things considered, Miles regarded this as a good result.

The new Hammersmith and Fulham Town Hall, with its Speer-like architecture and acres of echoing, marble-encrusted Thirties corridors, struck Miles as a rum place in which to hold a wedding. But the happy couple had been set on it from the start, and managed to secure a special discount because of Greg being a councillor, so who was he to interfere?

Greg and Mollie were married by a registrar in a council chamber known as the Mayor's Parlour or Mayor's Robing Room, Miles couldn't remember which, with the names of past dignitaries chiselled into the stone walls. As he commented afterwards, it had been a bit like marrying on a conveyor belt, with the previous wedding party fifteen minutes ahead of them—a jocular Nigerian and his English bride—and a bunch of Poles following along behind. Miles assumed most of them were marrying for passports, in any case. You couldn't say the Straker-Clegg wedding was the most fashionable of all time, but they looked more presentable than anyone else getting married that day at the Town Hall.

Mollie wasn't wearing a wedding dress of course, it being a registry job, but looked surprisingly nice in a cream suit and matching
hat. Greg was dressed identically to the evening of the engagement
drinks, in the same grey suit and red tie. He had shaved more closely
than usual in honour of his wedding, and had razor nicks on his
neck stemmed with flecks of cotton wool. Both Miles and Ross
wore morning suits, and Davina and Dawn looked their best too,
Davina in a smart new black and white Caroline Charles outfit, and
Dawn in electric-green Ben de Lisi with a feathered beret. As for
the rest of the congregation, they comprised of an uneasy mixture
of family members, Mollie's flatmates and fellow schoolteachers,
and a dozen Labour councillors and party activists who were friends
of the bridegroom. Just as the ceremony was about to start, James
and Laetitia Pendleton turned up, to Miles's horror, having not invited them himself but there as guests of the Cleggs. Both were
impeccably smart, as if going to a society wedding at St Margaret's,
Westminster, and not remotely phased by the corporation surroundings of the Town Hall. Grouped around Mollie were her five
little flower girls. Four of them were pupils from her class, dressed
in the brightly-coloured multi-cultural outfits Mollie had made for
them herself at her sewing machine, and which reflected the ethnic
origins of her Turkish, Moroccan, Kosovan and Vietnamese atten-
dants. The fifth bridesmaid was Mandy, Mollie's goddaughter.

Davina and Dawn stood side by side feeling proud, and relieved
that the ceremony was at last underway. Although they never compared notes, both women had felt the strain as the day approached.
You couldn't disguise the fact that it was all rather awkward. Miles,
needless to say, was no help, endlessly complaining about the arrangements and this unwelcome alliance with the Cleggs. Because
of the engagement, Davina hadn't felt she could pursue her divorce
plans and put them on hold. She could hardly do anything else, she
decided, with a family wedding looming. But once it was over, she
was pressing the destruct button.

There was no question about it, it was all very stressful. She
didn't relish the prospect of Archie and Gemma being in the same
room together, especially as Gemma was bringing Mandy. She felt
ashamed that Archie hadn't seen her since her Christening, which
Davina reckoned was at least five years ago. She felt tense at the

thought of them meeting. She was thrilled to see Peter and Samantha. Both had flown down from Scotland the previous night and booked into a hotel, still being banned from Holland Park Square. Davina, of course, knew they'd been staying in Peter's cottage, having received regular postcards she hid from Miles. It made her happy her two older children had become friends, which they never had been in the past. But she resented the turmoil Miles brought upon the family; she hated the schism. It was all so unnecessary, so wrong.

Peter and Sam had turned up at the ceremony with minutes to go, Samantha looking breathtaking in a red hat and jewellery she'd bought at Accessorize at the airport. Blooming from fresh air and exercise, she looked like a model. Her skin was flawless and she'd slept-out the weeks of tiredness so the dark circles under her eyes had disappeared. Davina hadn't seen her so pretty and healthy for years. An odd thing, she noticed, was that Miles and Sam didn't say hello to each other. Sam seemed to be avoiding her father. It was disconcerting. She had hoped the Dick Gunn quarrel was behind them now, especially since Sam and Dick were no longer together.

Peter looked well too, Davina thought, seeing her eldest son for the first time in five months. Like Sam, he was fit and sunburnt from being outside all day. It suited him. He seemed more confident too. The months in Scotland, working on something creative he enjoyed, had transformed him.

The registrar was concluding the civil ceremony and informing the bride and groom they were now a legal entity in the eyes of the State, and then everyone filed out of one door in the direction of the reception, while the Poles and their entourage filed in from the other.

'What a *lovely* service, darling,' Davina said to Mollie. 'I loved the lady registrar, such a jolly person.'

'I'm glad you liked it,' Mollie replied. 'I did too. I felt so much joy and love surrounding us, everyone wishing us well.' Then she said, 'I hope the food's going to be ok. I was up till midnight with Tina and Kerry, my flatmates, making it. Well, we made a lot of it anyway. Some we bought at Freeza Mart, but don't tell Greg, he doesn't approve.'

They arrived at a community function room where the food had been laid out on trestles, with cutlery rolled up inside red paper napkins and bottles of wine, champagne and beer. Not Freeza Mart champagne, Miles noticed, but a brand he hadn't previously seen, which looked very cheap. He was helping himself to a glass, sniffing it suspiciously, when a very pretty, efficient-looking young woman in a hat approached him and said, 'I hope you had a pleasant stay at the Meurice recently, Mr Straker?'

Miles almost dropped his glass.

'I'm Debbie Clegg. Deputy Assistant Manager at the hotel. You're one of our regular guests, I believe?'

'Er, yes. I do stay there quite often.'

'I thought so,' said Debbie. 'You're one of our special VIPs. They always give you a corner suite on the third floor. Anyway, sorry to bother you. I just wanted to introduce myself.' And she handed him her business card.

Surveying the reception, Miles couldn't help feeling it was a thoroughly third-rate affair. It was a maxim in his business that, when arranging any event for their clients, it had to meet three distinct criteria: excellent location, excellent food and wine, and 'A' grade guests. Today's party missed on all counts. The room, for a start, was unutterably squalid: stacks of plastic chairs piled up in the corner, and around the walls felt-covered partitions displaying vintage photographs of the borough, under the heading, 'Hammersmith at the turn of the Century.' The food, displayed on ceramic platters and laid out buffet-style, looked inedible, numerous brown-coloured dishes, rice and aubergine salads, curries, couscous and falafel beans, trays of naan bread and vegetarian pizza. A metal baking dish contained an Iranian delicacy of lamb and saffron rice, which Mollie said had been brought along by the mother of one of her pupils as a gift. Alongside these hot dishes was a selection of cold snacks and dips, some still in their Freeza Mart plastic boxes, including salmon pinwheel roulades, scotch eggs, and salad and vegetable crudités with Thousand Island dressing.

And then, of course, there were the other guests. Miles cringed at the thought of James and Laetitia being made to rub shoulders with this unprepossessing shower. He could have killed Ross and Dawn for inviting them, it was so obviously inappropriate. He could see them now, talking to Mollie's flatmate Kerry, the sports therapist, and couldn't imagine they'd find much common ground. Greg's Labour friends were getting into the beers and piling up their plates with carbohydrates. The parents of the flower girls, the Turks and Kosovans and the rest of them, were sitting round the edge of the room on benches, surrounded by Adidas bags and plastic holdalls, playing no part in the proceedings and looking like disorientated arrivals at an internment camp.

Greg and Mollie stood side by side, fielding the stream of compliments from well wishers. Dawn's friends from Droitwich, Vera and Naomi, were telling them they'd sent an Argos voucher as a joint wedding gift, since there were bound to be lots of household things they needed. And Laetitia mentioned she and James were sending a little painting she hoped they'd like, by a talented young artist shown by the Waddington Gallery.

Greg looked at his wife—the new Mrs Clegg—and felt he'd done well. It was time he married, and he needed a wife to get through any selection committee for a constituency. One of the drawbacks of the Labour Party was its working class morality, especially in the safe seats up north. Other than Peter Mandelson, he couldn't think of a single Labour Member of Parliament without a wife or partner. And Mollie would be a good constituency wife. She'd demonstrated that already with her leafleting and canvassing. At moments like this, Greg could feel a lot of affection for Mollie. He appreciated her unconditional support. Every leader needs a follower. He could boss her about, send her on missions. And he liked the way she was a schoolteacher, that was a further advantage; a partner working at the sharp end in the state education system was a definite plus in New Labour.

There was another, less honourable, reason Greg had married Mollie. Turning Miss Straker into Mrs Clegg was one small victory for class revolution, reversing the usual order of things. It was rather satisfying having the daughter of a Tory grandee as your wife, at your permanent beck and call.

Mollie and Greg made it clear they didn't want any speeches at the wedding, nor would there be a wedding cake, but Ross felt there had to be a toast to the couple, it was traditional, and people were asking. On the other hand, Miles was the father of the bride, and Ross didn't want to step on any toes. 'I don't mind which one of us does it,' Ross said. 'But someone should propose their health, don't you think?'

Miles was wondering which was the lesser of two evils, to speak himself or allow Ross to take the limelight, when Dawn's friend Vera, evidently slightly drunk, came up and joined them. 'This has been a lovely occasion, Ross,' she told him. 'I thought you'd have forgotten about us, you've become so famous now, you've done so well.' Miles recoiled as she invaded their space with her over the top pleasantries.

'It's lovely you're here, Vera. We couldn't have had a family wedding without you,' Ross said.

'I do all my shopping at Freeza Mart, you know, I wouldn't go anywhere else.'

'Thank you, Vera. Much appreciated.'

'I've been talking to the Lord too, Lord Pendleton. He seems like a nice man. We've been yattering away for hours.'

'That's grand, Vera.'

'Wait till I tell everyone I met you and Lord Pendleton. People aren't going to believe it. Two celebrities. And you are a celebrity, you know, Ross. I love you on that advert on the telly. I say "Look everyone. That's our Ross."'

'Thanks, Vera. And have you met Mollie's dad, Miles Straker? Miles, this is Vera, who used to live next door to us in Droitwich.'

But Vera couldn't have cared less about Miles. 'I've a good mind to ask for your autograph, Ross. And the Lord's. Otherwise people won't believe it.'

Miles decided that, for the sake of his self-esteem, he must make the speech and re-establish himself as top dog. So he tapped a spoon against the side of his glass and called for silence. Slowly the room came to order, gathering around him. Mollie came and stood next to her father, dragging Greg behind her, and the little bridesmaids reformed on the floor at their feet. Davina was standing next to Peter, and Dawn between Ross and the Pendletons, and the Labour councillors carried their beers from the bar, and Mollie's flatmates and the schoolteachers carried their glasses of wine.

Miles stood at the centre of the circle looking handsome, confident and rich, waiting for absolute silence before beginning. He had decided to make a short but unimpeachably charming speech, which rose to the occasion, but at the same time signalled that the occasion fell somewhat short of the occasions he usually attended. He was puffing himself up in readiness, when Mandy the bridesmaid's little voice rose into the room. 'That's my mummy,' she said, pointing to Gemma. 'And that man's Archie, her boyfriend. Archie stays in our house every single night. And he sleeps in *Mummy's bed.*'

An audible gasp went up round the room, and Miles, who could see everyone's faces, didn't know who was more astounded, Ross, Dawn, Davina, Peter, Samantha, Debbie, the bride and groom or Gemma and Archie themselves, both of whom looked aghast and hideously guilty.

51.

By the following weekend Miles's fury with Archie had lost none of its heat. If anything, it had increased. That his favourite son—the son he regarded as most like himself—had got back together with the gormless Clegg girl, left him lost for words. It was the duplicity that shocked him most. If Archie had been man enough to admit what he'd been up to, maybe he'd have understood. Though, frankly, there must be hundreds of prettier girls only too willing to be rogered by Archie, which was what this was all about. Sex! Miles had no problem with Archie wanting sex. God knows, he was his father's son. But with Gemma! Clearly the sly little minx had seduced him back by offering it up on a plate. And Archie had fallen for it, the bloody idiot.

Seeking to lift his mood, he drove into Stockbridge to buy wine. He didn't need any wine, the cellars at Chawbury Manor were full to the rafters with the stuff, but he knew the purchase of excellent claret—claret shipped in proper wooden cases—did wonders for the human spirit, as did the respectful conversation of his wine merchant. He placed his order and was discussing delivery when the wine shop man said, 'And what about Matt Marland's shoot then? I never thought that day would come, Matt selling up at West Farm.'

'I hadn't heard.' Miles felt uncomfortably alert.

'It's all the talk round here. No one thought it would happen, Matt lives for his shooting. But farming's not what it was, with all the subsidies coming to an end, and Mr Clegg offered him such a price. He said he'd have been mad not to take it.'

Miles listened in disbelief. Could this really be happening a second time? How often had he discussed buying Matt Marland's farm? Never with Matt, it was true, because a sale had seemed inconceivable. Matt ran a thriving shooting syndicate with a long waiting list.

'So Ross made him an offer he couldn't refuse?'

'Five thousand pounds an acre. That's what people are saying. And there's four hundred acres, all the way up to the road. Two million quid. And extra for the cottages. He's keeping on both gamekeepers with a pay rise for their loyalty.'

Miles shook his head. 'More money than sense, it sounds like.'

'A very nice gentleman, Mr Clegg. Comes in here a lot, likes to buy his wine here. I asked him, "Wouldn't you do better getting it at your own place, Freeza Mart, if you don't mind my asking?" Their prices are lower than ours, they've more muscle with the suppliers. But Mr Clegg said he prefers buying it here, because he gets the advice and the service. Very pleasant, Mr Clegg, I've a lot of time for him.'

Driving back to Chawbury, Miles felt wave after wave of envy breaking over him, a tsunami of raw covetousness. Why was life so unjust? Of course he understood exactly why Ross had bought West Farm. It marched with his own property—with Silas's tumble-down cottage—and protected him from encroaching development. And the shooting was surprisingly high quality for a farm shoot. That was why Miles had wanted it himself. In his life plan, he had envisaged inviting James Pendleton to shoot there, and putting the gamekeepers onto the Straker Communications payroll.

Now the shoot belonged to Ross, and James would doubtless be shooting there with him instead.

Davina spent the Monday alone at her desk at Chawbury, composing a letter to her husband. It underwent many drafts before she felt satisfied, with each word carefully considered. The earlier drafts were much too long, she decided, running to six sides of handwriting, giving too many reasons for her decision. In the end she kept it short and factual: she had decided to leave him, and would in due course be seeking a divorce. She had been thinking about this for a long time, and not taken the decision lightly. Now the children were grown up she felt it was possible, even though she realised it would be unsettling for the family for a time. But she had reached the conclusion it was the right thing for both of them. Finally, she acknowledged the many happy times they'd spent together over the years, and how proud she was of their children 'who will always be a great bond between us.' As a long P.S., she added, 'There is no hurry for us to decide anything. You will want to know there is no one else involved. Let's try and keep everything as civilised as possible, out of respect for each other and for the sake of the children. And please try not to be too cross.'

Having arrived at the version she felt was as good as it was ever going to be, she made a fair copy and put it in an envelope. The process of composition had been draining and, looking at the time, she was amazed to see it was already four o'clock in the afternoon—she'd been at her desk for six hours. She went into the kitchen to put the kettle on and found Mrs French wiping down worktops. 'You look exhausted, Mrs Straker. What *have* you been doing?'

On a whim, Davina told her her decision. She was going to have to hear sometime, everyone was, and she felt the need to start the process. 'I'm afraid it's going to mean a lot of change,' Davina said. 'I don't know where I'll end up living. Or what will happen to this house. I'll miss the garden dreadfully . . .' She suddenly felt heartbreakingly sad about it all.

She set off for a long walk along the valley, only turning back when she reached the leylandii screen at the bottom of the Cleggs' garden. The lights were all out at Chawbury Park; Dawn was spending all her time up in London these days, only coming down at weekends. Dawn was someone else she ought to tell, Davina realised; not just because she was a dear friend, but they were family as well now through Mollie and Greg, not to mention the Archie and Gemma situation. There were so many people who were going to have to be told, the prospect exhausted her; all their old friends and neighbours discussing them, talking about them, taking sides. She'd detest all that, the gossip, she'd have nothing to do with it. Whatever she felt about Miles, she would never demean herself by being disloyal about him. Whether Miles would be equally magnanimous, she wasn't sure. In fact, she dreaded him opening the letter and wondered if she was mad to be taking such a drastic step.

Twice during the walk she almost decided to call the whole thing off. The letter was not yet posted, it wasn't too late. Strolling home in the twilight, she thought how pretty the manor looked on the brow of the hill, and how cosy with the windows lit up, and the thought of leaving that beloved house and garden filled her with dismay. And wasn't it unfair on the children to break up the family? And where would they all spend Christmases and Easters with separated parents? And how especially sad for Mollie and Greg, so early into their own marriage.

But then Davina reflected on Miles, and all her suppressed anger rose up again. The past couple of months, during the lead-up and aftermath of Mollie's wedding, had been especially bad. Miles had been a nightmare. He had spent the weekends raging against Archie, against Ross and Dawn, against Gemma. It hadn't helped that Ross bought that shoot, which was clearly a big factor in it all. Miles could be so immature. He wouldn't refer to Ross by name, only as 'the owl murderer.' He couldn't go out to dinner locally without regaling everyone with the story of the owl. And then it found its way into one of the newspapers. Miles insisted he'd had nothing to do with it, but Davina wasn't sure she believed him. And he was being ridiculous about Gemma, too. She was a perfectly nice girl, she'd looked sweet at the wedding reception, and so polite. But Miles referred to her as 'the scrubber.'

In the end, it was his attitude to the children that made the marriage untenable. One by one, he'd fallen out with them all. Apart from at the wedding, she hadn't seen Peter for six months, or Samantha either; if she so much as mentioned their names in front of her husband, he became tetchy. Mollie was as good as ostracised by marrying Greg—Miles insisted he wouldn't have Greg to stay in the house—and now Archie had fallen from grace too. If she wanted to speak to her own children, she had to wait until Miles was out to use the telephone. During the wedding, Gemma sweetly invited her over to her little house in Vauxhall to play with Mandy—her only grandchild—but if she told Miles he'd try and stop her going, so she'd have to sneak off behind his back, which was perfectly ridiculous. No, she had to end the marriage, she had to be brave, her mind was made up. She fetched the letter from her desk, addressed it to Miles at his office marked 'strictly private,' and drove to the village to put it in the box. The errand completed, she took a deep breath and poured herself a glass of wine from an open bottle in the fridge.

It was only the next morning Davina remembered she hadn't told her solicitor about the letter and wondered if she should have. So she rang Lincolns' Inn Fields and spoke to Angela, who was very reassuring and supportive, but slightly put out that she hadn't kept a photocopy. 'From today on, every letter, every phone call, every conversation must be copied, logged and minuted. Ideally tape recorded if you feel comfortable about that. I'm opening a file for you and I need you to be scrupulous about telling us everything. If I'm not here myself, talk to my colleague Tristram whom I think you met.'

'You're being so kind,' Davina said gratefully. 'I'm so sorry about all this. I know I'm being a perfect nuisance.'

'Nonsense,' said Angela. 'You're taking the first important step in the second part of your life. And you mustn't hesitate to ring about anything, however trivial. Because in a divorce, nothing is trivial, the devil's in the detail. As soon as you hear anything from your husband, any reaction to your letter, ring me.'

Miles, it so happened, had been at a breakfast briefing at the offices of Trent Valley Power 4 U, where they were announcing an exciting diversification into the online gaming industry. The rationale, as Miles helped formulate, was that TVP4U's 5.7 million customers would be offered, at great convenience to themselves, the opportunity to play internet blackjack and poker on the utility giant's website, with prize money (and of course any losses) added to or subtracted from their quarterly direct debit.

Returning to Charles Mews South, he found Davina's letter sitting on a pile of today's invitations on his desk. Assuming it wasn't important (Davina was forever forwarding requests for work experience and internships for neighbours' children) he did not open it immediately. Eventually getting round to it, he was astonished by its content and the measured manner in which it was written. Evidently Davina was very cross about something and he wondered if she might somehow have found out about the Samantha misunderstanding in Paris. He certainly hoped not. If she had, he reckoned it would take a diamond bracelet to patch things up, not that Davina particularly desired jewellery. A specimen tree for the garden then.

He considered ringing her, but decided against. Better to let her stew in her own juice for a while, they were going out to dinner together tonight with clients in any case. Later he read the letter a second time. Something about its tone had been niggling away at him, as though it were written with calculated deliberation rather than in the heat of anger. He lifted the phone to ring Chawbury, changed his mind and dialled Angela Strawbetter at Freshfields instead, just in case. He'd always heard she was the best.

It came as a shock to learn, when put through to Angela, that regrettably she couldn't represent him since she was already engaged by another party in the matter.

'What? *Davina's* rung you? You can't be serious. When?'

'I'm sorry, Mr Straker, but that's all I can say without speaking first to my client.'

'Well, I'm sorry, but you can tell your client that *I'm* not bloody paying your bills. I hope she realises that. And I hope you do too. Davina doesn't have money of her own, you know. Not a bean. And if you start sending *me* her bills, you can bloody whistle for it.'

'I'm going to say goodbye, Mr Straker. It isn't appropriate for us to speak directly in this way.' He heard the click of the receiver being put down on him.

Now Miles was really mad. How *dare* Davina start ringing divorce lawyers without his permission? Had she the first idea what they charged? Hundreds of pounds an hour. It wouldn't surprise him if she hadn't even enquired about fees, she was like that. And, worse, there was the publicity. All the big divorce firms leaked like sieves, they all had hotlines to the gossip columns. If it got into the papers they were having marital problems, he'd bloody kill Davina. Clients didn't like seeing their confidential advisors all over the newspapers, not in that context anyway.

By lunchtime, he had engaged his own divorce lawyer, a silver-tongued rottweiler who regularly represented rock stars and royals. 'I don't for one moment think this will come to anything,' Miles briefed him. 'My wife's probably having her period. Or the change of life. Or feeling depressed because the children have grown-up and left home and it's dawning on her how little she's achieved in her life. But as a precaution, I want you on standby. If we hear a squeak out of her, I want you to scare the living daylights out of her with a ten-page letter. Knock her sideways. Tell her she won't get a cent and I'll be demanding custody of the children. And keeping both houses—which are mine anyway—so she'll have nowhere to live.'

The rottweiler made encouraging noises, but pointed out that it might present problems to give her nothing at all. 'And what ages are your children, Mr Straker?'

'God knows. Twenty-two or something up to . . . Peter's thirty I think. Not that you'd guess. No job and no prospects either.'

'Child custody won't realistically be a factor then, Mr Straker. But you can depend on us to represent you . . . vigorously. That's what we're known for at these chambers. We never forget who it was who created the family's wealth in the first place.'

With lawyers retained by both sides and eager to lock horns, it was surprising how rapidly everything began to move. Davina found the process mortifying, though Miles considered it worse for himself than for his wife, since he had more to lose.

His starting position—that Davina should buzz off without a penny or a bed to sleep in—quickly became untenable, his lawyer explaining that, in any ultimate settlement, the judge would take into account the behaviour of both parties in the interim. So with much complaining and ill will, he agreed to move out of Holland Park Square and rent a London apartment for himself. Davina would make her (temporary) home in Holland Park, while Miles kept possession of Chawbury Manor. In the long run, Miles intended keeping both his homes. If necessary he could rent Davina a small cottage in somewhere like Dorset, where you could get them cheap.

He had chosen to hold on to Chawbury rather than Holland Park Square for two reasons. The first was simple spite. He realised Davina was more attached to their country house than their town one, and she would miss her garden. Well, that'll teach her, was Miles's attitude. Secondly, the greater part of his self-esteem was tied up in his ownership of Chawbury, nor did he want to loose access to it for his annual client lunch party. And so—grudgingly, reluctantly, and with many self-righteous outbursts against the in-justice of the law—he instructed Davina through his lawyers to pack up his clothes and personal possessions and various paintings from Holland Park Square, and have them delivered to the first-floor flat in Mount Street which was to become his new weekday base.

The Mount Street flat suited Miles surprisingly well and, with the help of his three assistants and Makepiece, his driver, who hung up his pictures, was soon made habitable. From his windows the view was of the Connaught Hotel, and there was twenty-four-hour porterage downstairs which made deliveries straightforward. At his insistence, Carmelita the maid came round four mornings a week from Holland Park to keep the place tidy, make his bed and wash up his coffee cup. Aside from coffee, Miles did not cook or eat in the flat, preferring the Connaught and Scotts.

At first, the life of a late-life bachelor suited him very nicely. The removal of Davina from the scene made him realise how superflu-ous she had been for so long. He could not honestly say that, in material terms, his life was disadvantaged in any way without her. It was liberating not to have to inform her of his plans, or to find her clothes strewn over a bedroom chair or her toiletries cluttering up the bathroom. Between his secretaries, Carmelita and Mrs French, it was a simple task to run Mount Street and Chawbury Manor, and Miles began to think Davina had shot herself in the foot by walking out on him. As he attested in one of his many le-gal depositions about their marriage, Davina's contribution to the running of the households was precisely nil. 'She spent her days dabbling in watercolours and confusing my gardeners with her in-structions,' he asserted.

Davina, meanwhile, felt perpetually anguished about her change of circumstance. Not wanting to discuss it with her friends, she saw almost nobody, apart from the children and Dawn. Dawn was the only friend she took into her confidence, and after their weekly yoga Dawn would always ask how Davina was feeling. True to her word, Davina tried hard not to complain about Miles beyond the general inference that their marriage had become unhappy. Dawn, for her part, was unrestrained in her prying, desperate to learn what precisely had gone wrong. Davina made Dawn promise to tell no one about the separation, even Ross, and it was a measure of Dawn's loyalty to her friend that she resisted telling him for almost a week. When she did eventually tell him, Ross commented, 'Well, it was the women, wasn't it? Davina must have got fed up with all the other women.'

Dawn was astonished. 'Miles had *mistresses*? I've never heard that before.'

'You must of. He's famous for it. He was seeing Serena—*your* Serena, the decorator—for years and years apparently.'

Dawn was so tantalised by this piece of gossip she couldn't decide whether or not it was appropriate to pass it on to Davina. She didn't want to be the one to upset her dear friend and neighbour; on the other hand, Davina probably knew about it already, and if she didn't she surely *ought* to know, it might be relevant to the divorce. So, with trepidation, she did tell her what she'd heard. She was surprised when Davina seemed to take it calmly in her stride. Though privately, Davina was mortified.

As a matter of fact, Davina did not feel comfortable picking over her failed marriage with Dawn, particularly since she constantly raised the financial aspects of the divorce. She was far too keen to hear what Davina was expecting in any settlement, and what Miles's 'total wealth' might be. 'This house must be worth seven million at least,' Dawn said, sitting at Davina's kitchen table and gazing about her. 'And Chawbury Manor has to be worth four. Five on a good day.'

'I've really no idea,' Davina replied vaguely. 'I haven't thought about it.'

'And Miles's business must be making a mint too,' Dawn went on. 'Ross says it would fetch a multiple of eight times earnings in a trade sale.'

For Davina, her priority lay in visiting or telephoning the children, and doing her best to reassure them she was alright, and that everything would continue to be alright in the future. She saw a great deal of Mollie, who was sweet to her and regularly came round for kitchen supper while Greg was out doing his politics. Since their marriage, his search for a safe Labour parliamentary seat had accelerated, and many of their weekends were spent up in the Midlands and the north of England making contact with constituency officials. Davina also spent several evenings in Roupell Street visiting Archie, Gemma and Mandy. One of the more obvious dividends of her separation from Miles was that she could now see her granddaughter whenever she liked, and invite her and Gemma over to Holland Park for tea and walks in the park. Mandy loved feeding the squirrels in Holland Park and playing in the playground which was so much nicer than the Vauxhall playground. Archie was still working on the door at Thurloes so was frequently out when Davina visited Roupell Street, which meant she got to know Gemma better, and discovered she liked her very much. She was a natural mother with plenty of common sense; a lot more than Archie, if truth be told.

The preliminary sparring over the divorce ground on, and each time she received a letter from the lawyers she felt quite sick. Miles's solicitors kept issuing manipulative diatribes, pages and pages long, which left her belittled and depressed. How could he allow them to write things he knew to be untrue? Her replies, at her insistence, started off conciliatory, attempting to defuse the escalating venom. But, over time, Davina found herself acquiescing to Angela's argument that they should match fire with fire, until the replies sent in her name achieved a similar tone of violent injury and theatrical outrage as those sent in the name of Miles.

After several months, both parties were issued with forms for the full disclosure of their assets, which ran to many pages. Davina found herself making a list of all her clothes and jewellery, including the few pieces inherited from her mother, with an estimate of the value of every item. Compelled to list her equities, investments, pensions and cash deposits, as well as the value of any UK or overseas properties held in her own name, she realised her net assets amounted to virtually nothing. Miles, meanwhile, was drawing up his own list. Unable to decide whether to transfer most of his money offshore, out of reach of Davina, or whether to list the whole lot and thus make himself look big in the eyes of his lawyers, he decided to wire three million pounds to a bank in Switzerland but disclose the rest.

As the months passed, Miles had to admit that running Chawbury Manor at arms length was more difficult than he first believed.

There was an almost endless list of inconsequential chores to be undertaken, not all of which could be dealt with by Sara and the girls at the office. Maddeningly, Mrs French expected to be talked to on a regular basis, with menus to be discussed and dozens of small domestic queries. Miles considered himself far too busy to sit down in the kitchen with his housekeeper and debate hoover bags and food for the next weekend. Couldn't she think of them herself? After all, she'd worked at Chawbury for years, she surely knew by now what he liked eating. But he soon discovered Mrs French could not be relied upon to serve meals in the manner Miles expected, or on the correct tableware. When he attempted to give Saturday night dinner parties for their neighbours, continuing life as before, and invited Ridley and Susie Nairn, Johnnie and Philippa Mountleigh and Nigel and Bean Winstanton, he found peculiar navy blue paper napkins set on the table, and the wrong wine glasses and supermarket cheeses still in their plastic wrappings on the cheeseboard. It was extremely frustrating. The obvious solution, which was to brief Mrs French on what he wanted, was not something he was prepared to do.

Similarly, the house seemed to become less civilised week by week. Nobody any longer unbolted the French doors onto the terrace before his return. The wrong lights were switched on in the drawing room. Fires were left un-laid or laid in the wrong way with fircones (which he detested) instead of kindling. In his bathroom, unpleasant purple soaps appeared on the bathrack smelling of violets and disinfectant. Lilies and orchids, once so pretty in cachepots around the house, and tended by Davina in the Chawbury greenhouse, were replaced by supermarket sprays from Freeza Mart. The downstairs cloakroom ran out of lavatory paper and was replenished with peach quilted toilet roll. Exasperated, he sacked Mrs French and told Sara to interview replacement housekeepers.

The indoor shortcomings of Mrs French were only part of the problem. Each weekend, Miles encountered displeasing evidence of slackness in the garden too. After heavy storms, fallen branches and twigs were left lying on the lawn by his gardeners, instead of being immediately gathered up and burned. The greenhouses became untidy and borders inadequately weeded. Gutters overflowed with leaves. He spent a great deal of time trying to amuse himself with his boys' toys, riding around the estate on his yellow JCB excavator or zipping about on his new John Deere utility tractor. Then a problem emerged with the Chawbury burglar alarm which kept going off for no reason and may have been an electrical fault. When Miles told Sara to speak to the utility company, Trent Valley Power 4 U, and get them to sort things out with the alarm people, she reported that the call centre refused to talk to her and could only speak to the named bill payer because of data protection. Furious, Miles was held in a queue by the call centre, then routed through to Bangalore where 'customer services' was apparently based these days. When he explained he was a personal friend of Trent Valley Power 4 U's chief executive 'who regularly lunches with me', the Indian functionary had never heard of him nor of Mark's Club.

Privately, Miles began to concede Davina may have done more at Chawbury than he'd given her credit for.

52.

Through his contacts at the town hall, Greg was able to jump the housing queue and secure a new, much larger council property in a street behind Hammersmith Grove. Originally earmarked for a multi-generational family of Romanian gypsies recently arrived in the UK, Greg pressed the case that as newlyweds with frontline occupations in teaching and politics their need was greater, so he and Mollie moved out of their respective flats and into the Georgian terrace opposite a petrol station. With the aid of local authority grants Greg was so adept at securing, they soon had the place painted from top to bottom, a new gas boiler and hot water system installed, and the loft insulated free of charge by the ratepayer.

Mollie was delighted with their new home and set about making it as welcoming and comfortable as she could. Although it slightly embarrassed her they had so many empty bedrooms, she secretly hoped they might over time fill them all with happy children. Meanwhile, she planned on inviting several of her pupils from school for sleepovers, if their parents agreed and once the local education authority had completed the necessary checks.

The one small blot on her happiness was Greg's rigid attitude to the decorating. She had taken it for granted the furniture from both their flats would be brought to Sudan Road, and the new house reflect a mixture of both their tastes. Greg, however, had other ideas. He insisted only his own furniture—the black leather sofas and Eames chair—be placed in the double sitting room downstairs, and only his own art and memorabilia be displayed on the sitting room walls. When Mollie plugged in one of her ceramic lamps with the starfish pattern, Greg moved it to an upstairs bedroom. When she arranged her framed family photographs on a table in the sitting room, including one of her parents on a wooden bench at Chawbury, Greg snapped, 'Those can't stay there, it'd give completely the wrong idea.' It soon became clear there were to be two separate zones in the house—the public area which became a virtual recreation of Greg's old bachelor flat, and the upstairs floors where Mollie was grudgingly permitted to display her colourful rugs, bedcovers and lamps. A room at the top of the house was allocated to her as a study, where she positioned her desk in front of the window and had a place of her own to do her marking, and to pin up paintings by her pupils.

No sooner was the house ready to receive visitors than Greg began to entertain. These gatherings, he explained to Mollie, could not be seen primarily as social in intention, and were certainly not frivolous 'parties.' Guests were invited strictly for political considerations, being colleagues from the Council, Labour apparatchiks from Millbank and from the Institute for Public Policy Research, left-leaning journalists and increasingly Members of Parliament and their advisors. When Mollie suggested she include some of her fellow schoolteachers and old flatmates, or her brother Peter when he was in town to see his record company, Greg refused. 'I don't think that would be *at all appropriate*,' he said.

For the forty or so guests who did show up at these monthly suppers, Mollie had mixed reactions. Some were unquestionably good and well-meaning citizens with all the right progressive ideas, and the fact they were here in her house, eating her food, made her feel virtuous, and reminded her what a fine, idealistic man it was she had married. At these moments, she could see he was right to exclude her staff room colleagues, because they wouldn't have been sufficiently serious or committed to the cause. She did secretly admit, however, that some of Greg's new friends were dreadfully pleased with themselves, and she couldn't say for certain she liked them. It irritated her, too, that the young researchers from Labour Party headquarters, who worked for something called the 'Instant rebuttal team,' never remembered meeting her before even though they'd been introduced three or four times. She realised she wasn't that interesting—not in their terms anyway, with all their talk of 'Tony' and 'Peter' and 'Alastair'—but nonetheless, it was annoying. So, over time, she rather gave up trying to make conversation with them, and concentrated on replenishing the food and emptying ashtrays.

'Well, the offer stands if you want to take it up. You think about it, young man, and let me know.' Ross had called round at Roupell Street to talk to Archie, having been put up to it by Dawn.

Archie, for his part, didn't know what to think. The prospect of working for Gemma's dad at Freeza Mart didn't exactly turn him on. 'What'd I be doing? Stacking shelves?'

'We'd start you off as a trainee in the marketing department, probably. That's in the same building as me on Southbank. Ten minutes walk from here, which is why I bought this property in the first place.'

Archie looked sceptical. Working somewhere like Freeza Mart was simply not something he'd considered. It wasn't the sort of job people did; the people he knew, in any case. He imagined it would be pretty deadly, and you'd be working with grockles. And it wouldn't be a great reply when anyone asked what you did. Like if some juicy bird comes up at a party, and you had to admit, 'I'm a trainee at Freeza Mart.' She isn't exactly going to leap into the sack.

On the other hand, Archie realised he had to find something to do. He still had the bouncer job at Thurloes, but it didn't pay well, and without the allowance from his dad he was perpetually skint. It was so pathetic of Miles cutting him off and not even telling him. The first he'd known about it was when he was badly overdrawn. In fact, if it wasn't for Gemma doing three days a week temping at Freeza Mart as junior PA to the ops director, they'd be stony broke.

So this job offer from Ross came at a good moment, and the money wasn't terrible either. £26,500 a year. You weren't exactly going to get rich on it, but it was more than he took home from the club.

He knew Gemma wanted him to accept, but then she would. Anything her dad said she thought was brilliant. It was annoying, the way she hero worshipped him. There'd been a glowing profile of Ross in one of the Sunday supplements saying how clever he was and how the new Freeza Mart in California were performing well, and Gemma had cut it out and stuck it on the fridge. Archie felt undermined. Gemma was meant to be totally obsessed with *him*—Archie—wasn't she? Not her dad.

There again, Ross did seem like quite a decent bloke, you couldn't really say he wasn't. He'd always been civil towards him and never brought up that business after the Hospers Ball, when he easily could have done. Under the circumstances, you could say it was quite magnanimous of him to be offering him a job. Over the weekend, he rang his mum and asked her advice, and Davina said she was sure he should take it. In fact, Davina already knew about the job from Dawn, who had first suggested the idea after a yoga session.

'Won't Dad go ape?'

'Probably your father won't be very pleased,' Davina conceded. 'But I don't think you should worry too much about that. It sounds like a perfect first job for you, and nice it's so close to Gemma's house, you'll be able to walk to work together.'

The more he thought about it, Archie felt it would be a good way of getting his own back on Miles, working for Freeza Mart would annoy him so much.

So, after two formality interviews with the Freeza Mart HR department and with his future head of department, Archie became the 17,272nd employee of his not-quite-father-in-law's company.

Archie was surprised, and privately pleased, to discover he was rather good at marketing. He had a natural talent for it, which was hardly surprising being Miles Straker's son, not that Archie attributed his ability to genetics. Whatever the reason, he quickly absorbed the syndicated research and reams of demographic and quantative data which was the lifeblood of the department. He found it oddly satisfying to be able to compare the Waitrose customer base with, say, the Sainsbury's customer, and pinpoint the dozens of small idiosyncrasies between them. Freeza Mart's Director of Customer Development, Barry Shipley, who'd come over from Pendletons, and his deputy, Gill Sweet, who'd previously been at Superdrug, were big advocates of qualitative research and one of Archie's first tasks was to tabulate responses to 50,000 questionnaires, some conducted face to face, others online, in which Freeza Mart customers were interrogated on their attitude to carbon emissions, destination shopping, plastic packaging and organic versus farmed salmon. A parallel survey invited customers to rank twenty attributes of the supermarket in order of importance. Top came 'value for money,' followed by 'shorter queues at check-out.' Only slightly behind, in third place, came 'Ross Clegg' himself, who scored highly under 'honesty,' 'down to earth' and 'understands ordinary families like us.'

Having never previously worked in an office environment, Archie was half enthralled, half repelled by it. He detested the labyrinth of low-level partitions in which everyone sat with their computers and cuddly toy mascots and photographs of their kids and pets pinned up. He was tempted to stick up a picture of Gemma nude in the bath, or the one he'd taken of her on the furry sitting room rug acting out a *Playboy* centrefold. But maybe it wouldn't go down too well, Gemma being the boss's daughter. His co-workers, he reckoned, were sad sacks. With a few notable exceptions, he regarded them as braindead. In the mornings, they ate bowls of cereal at their desks, before tapping moronically on their keyboards all day; at lunchtime they made pot noodles with boiling water from the kettle, or shopped for groceries at Freeza Mart Metro using their staff discount cards. On the other hand, there were consolations to office life. There were several definite honeys working in Direct Response on the eleventh floor, and Archie liked to wander up and hang out by the water cooler, chatting them up. Competition was non-existent, so they were always receptive. And, he had to admit, it certainly wasn't a disadvantage having Ross as his mentor. Even though he seldom mentioned the connection, everyone seemed to know he was shacked-up with Ross's daughter, and indulged him as a result. If he was late completing a piece of work, he never got bollocked, and he was included in meetings he might otherwise not have been.

When Sharon Turner, who had been in the department four years and was senior to Archie, announced she was leaving to go travelling, Archie got promoted into her job ahead of six other candidates and inherited her office, a glass-walled pod with a door and nine carpet tiles, the size of a telephone kiosk.

53.

The sudden death of Laetitia Pendleton in such distressing circumstance made front-page news in every national newspaper. Although prior to the accident she was virtually unknown to the wider public, the fact she was married to 'billionaire grocer Lord Pendleton,' combined with the particularly ironic cause of death, meant she achieved overnight fame, provoking acres of comment from columnists and obituarists alike.

On Day One came the bald facts of the tragedy. Lady Pendleton was shopping in her local Andover branch of the family supermarket when she had slipped on a spillage of concentrated orange juice, cracked her head in an aisle, was concussed, rushed to hospital and never regained consciousness. Despite the best efforts of doctors and neurosurgeons in intensive care, she died seven hours later of a massive brain haemorrhage. A photograph of Lady Pendleton taken six years earlier with Princess Margaret at the anniversary concert was reproduced on several front pages, along with the information that her husband, James, was head of the 'eight billion supermarket clan.'

By Day Two, the talents of Straker Communications had been brought into play, and fulsome obituaries appeared in the broadsheets acknowledging Laetitia's contributions to the cultural community and membership of numerous boards for the visual and performing arts. In every obituary the Pendletons were described as 'fiercely private' and it was emphasised how many of the family's bursaries and philanthropic bequests were made on the assurance of complete anonymity. Several museum directors and curators, in the United States as well as in Britain, remembered how unpretentious Laetitia had been, and the story was much repeated about how she had queued patiently for three hours with the general public to get into the hit BritArt Sensation show at the Royal Academy, when at least eight key pieces were loaned by James and Laetitia themselves; a single telephone call would have enabled her to jump the queue.

By Day Three, the macabrely comic aspects of her death moved to the fore, and articles of dubious taste began to appear in the papers. The *Daily Express* conducted a consumer test on the relative slipperiness of various orange juices, from Tropicana and Mr Juicy to Sunny Delight and Pendletons's own brand concentrate. It emerged that a stack of cartons, being transported to the shelves from the stockroom on a caged trolley, had collided with a freezer unit, causing the fatal spillage. The *Daily Mail* ran no fewer than five items on the tragedy, including columns by Allison Pearson and Amanda Platell, gossip from Ephraim Hardcastle and an op-ed piece on the advisability or otherwise of wealthy, titled women doing their own grocery shopping.

By Day Four, the health sections got in on the act, questioning how beneficial orange juice was in a balanced diet. The *Evening Standard* ran a scare piece suggesting Vitamin C could give you stomach cramps if ingested in too large quantities.

On Days Five and Six, *The Times* and *Daily Telegraph* ran competing two-part serials on the 'Reluctant Billionaires,' the Pendleton family, complete with family trees showing how everyone was related, and archive photographs from family weddings. Hugh Pendleton, James's son, was tipped as a future chairman or chief executive.

By Sunday, despite Miles's strenuous efforts, the story took an unwelcome turn with several city commentators taking Laetitia's death as the impetus for a wider survey of Pendletons's prospects, and concluding it had lost ground to Freeza Mart. 'Both in international expansion and dotcom, Ross Clegg has opened up a decisive lead over the third generation, family-owned grocer. How long investors and pension funds will allow this to continue, without questioning the present family management, is anyone's guess. 'Would Pendletons benefit from professional outside management?' posed the weekend *Financial Times*.

Reading all this unhelpful rubbish in the newspapers, all alone at Chawbury, Miles rang half a dozen of his top executives and gave them an ear-bashing. 'Pendletons remains twice the size of Freeza Mart in revenues, and forty percent ahead in profits. Why aren't I reading this anywhere?' All in all, it was a bad week for Pendletons and Miles felt thoroughly fed up about it.

Laetitia's funeral was a private affair for family and a few old friends, held in the village church in Longparish. Had Miles had his way, it would have been vastly bigger and more public in one of the thousand-capacity social London churches, with the great and good strongly in evidence, plus influential politicians, institutional investors, business editors and selected Pendletons supermarket staff. Miles had an idea of busing in managers and checkout staff from all over the country, as proof of the esteem in which the Pendleton family was held. He thought it would be a timely reminder of the power and patronage of the controlling family, as well as free publicity for the supermarket. He was sure the television evening news could be persuaded to cover it, if they got it right.

But James, grief-stricken and racked with guilt that the accident should have happened in one of his own stores, refused to contemplate anything of the sort: 'I'm not having it turned into a circus.' So the opportunity was missed and Miles felt he was asked to do his job with one hand tied behind his back.

Instead, there were no more than a hundred mourners in the little Saxon church; the widower standing at the door between his son Hugh and his Pendleton brothers, Nick, Michael and Otto, greeting friends and neighbours as well as representatives from some of Laetitia's museums, galleries and charities. Davina, at Miles's insistence, travelled down with him from London, since Miles hadn't yet informed James they'd split up, and felt it was important to put on a show of unity. A second vehicle from Straker Communications followed in convoy, containing Rick Partington the MD and half a dozen key account personnel on the Pendletons' business. It was important to be seen to show support at this difficult time.

Occupying his reserved seat in the second pew, immediately behind the family, Miles looked round the church to see who else was there, and to ensure as many mourners are possible noticed his premium placement. Disconcertingly, almost the first people he spotted were Ross and Dawn, in the third pew across the aisle. Ross looked grim and sober in a dark overcoat with a Remembrance Day poppy in his buttonhole. Dawn, caramel coloured from the sunlamp, wore a flamboyant black hat with feather and veil, and gave James a fleeting smile of sympathy when their eyes met, before reverting to her sad funeral face. It always surprised Miles how well Laetitia and Dawn had got on, when they had nothing in common. Dawn had been pushy where Laetitia was concerned, and he reckoned Laetitia was simply too kind to rebuff her.

As the service was about to start, and the pallbearers were forming up outside to carry the coffin into the church, Miles noticed Serena and Robin slipping into a back pew. Serena looked very tasty, he thought, with her porcelain white skin and red hair pinned up under a black hat. Like Dracula's niece.

For a brief moment, they locked eyes, and Serena tilted her head quizzically. Miles wondered whether the time hadn't come to re-kindle that particular liaison.

Debbie's new job opportunity came out of the blue. She hadn't applied for it, or even thought about moving, as she'd only been at the Meurice for eighteen months. But when the offer came, she knew she had to go for it. It was irresistible, and completely different to a big city hotel, so she'd be learning an entirely new set of skills.

The overture came from the assistant manager of her previous hotel, the Buckingham Park at Stoke Poges, whom she had always liked. Paul had recently been offered the promotion of a lifetime, to become launch general manager of a new Zach Durban hotel in the Maldives, and he wanted Debbie to join him as his food and beverage director. As he explained it, the Grand Maldives Retreat and Spa wasn't going to be a five-star place, or even a six-star, but was aiming to become the archipelago's first seven-star resort. Durban's International Leisure and Casino Group was investing $250 million in the development, had already purchased a mile-long island in a coral attol and embarked on building forty luxury bungalows, each with private pool, as well as ten cabanas on stilts in the bay. The only means of reaching the resort would be by a fleet of hotel helicopters from Male, which would land on a pontoon in the sea. Concealed in the middle of the island, amidst copious undergrowth, would be Zach Durban's trademark 'Cuisines of the

World' restaurants, serving everything from Chinese to Russian specialities, Chinese and Russians being forseen as the dominant guest nationality.

Everything about the assignment thrilled Debbie. She couldn't think of any hotel she'd rather work at next. For one thing, it represented an enormous promotion for her, and a massive vote of confidence from Paul. Secondly, to be part of a start-up was every hotelier's dream. She'd be picking her whole team virtually from scratch, waiters and barmen, chefs and front-of-house; she'd need to hire over 150 people, Paul told her. A few staff could be transferred from other Zach Durban properties around the region, and some she'd headhunt from rival luxury resorts, but the majority would have to be trained from scratch. That was the part Debbie looked forward to the most. She would have to conduct interviews throughout the Maldives, pick a hundred or so novices on the basis of instinct, ship them over to the sandbar with their families and within six months turn them into top class staff at a seven-star resort. It wasn't going to be easy, but she relished the challenge.

There was a third reason, too, she was excited, though she knew it wasn't a noble one. She longed for sunshine. All her life she'd had a thing about the sun, she found it mood altering. And all her life she'd lived under grey skies, in Droitwich, Hampshire, Berkshire and now, even in Paris, the weather was depressing half the time. When she prepared the weather cards for the breakfast trays, she noticed how seldom she ticked the sunny symbol.

Paris had been a priceless opportunity, she'd learnt so much; you couldn't regret living in a city like Paris. But it had frequently been lonely, especially at the beginning. She had spent more time than she cared to remember sitting in those grand, formal parks on her afternoons off, watching the world go by, knowing nobody, killing time until her next shift. The second year had been better because her French improved until she was almost fluent, and then she'd met a guy, one of her opposite numbers at the Plaza Athénée. He was Danish and completed the hotel training course at Lausanne, which Debbie always wished she'd done herself. They'd spent four months together, much of it in bed, pulling every favour at their respective hotels to ensure their shifts and nights off coincided. But eventually they discovered they didn't have so much in common after all, and

Debbie ended it three months ago. That was another reason to leave Paris: a fresh beginning.

Taking a deep breath, she handed in her notice at the Meurice, having been promised a contract by International Leisure and Casino Group (ILCG). Paul rang her twice a week to update her on progress, and Debbie spent her evenings on her laptop making lists and timelines of everything she'd need to do. It was going to be a massively full-on assignment.

Paul told her to expect a call from the hotel's PR agency, which he said was preparing a press release to go out to the travel industry and media. 'They just need some CV background, the hotels you've worked at before, that kind of thing. There'll be biogs of the key appointments, so when you get the call, that's what it's about.'

Debbie was duly rung by a pleasant-sounding girl from Straker Communications, who wrote down her details and promised to send her a copy when it was ready. 'I'd love that,' Debbie said. 'I'm going to send it on to my dad. I've never been in a press release before, this is my first one.'

It surprised her when her new employment contract didn't arrive by the end of the week, nor the press release. It was odd, because they'd definitely said she'd receive the contract by Tuesday. She was about to ring Paul when he rang her himself, sounding embarrassed.

'This is so weird, Debs. I don't know what to say, but have you done something to upset a high-up in Zach Durban's company?'

'I've never met anyone from it. At least I don't think so. Why?'

'Because they've put a block on hiring you. I've been having a major row about it for three days, but they won't budge. I'm really sorry.'

'But *why* Paul? Didn't they say why?'

'That's the strangest thing, I haven't managed to speak to anyone who knows the reason. They just say it was someone very high up, they don't know the name. An edict came from head office.'

'I don't believe this. You really mean I've lost the job? I mean, I've already resigned from here.'

'I'm sorry Debbie. I can't understand what's gone wrong, I'm still trying to find out.'

'Thanks Paul. It's not your fault, I'm not blaming you. But if you do discover, let me know, won't you?'

She put down the phone, feeling utterly defeated. How could this have happened? Who would do something like this to her?

Archie had barely completed his six-month trial period before earning a second promotion. His self-assurance and glibness were spotted by Freeza Mart's Corporate and Investor Relations department, and he was offered a position as number four in the team, liaising with institutional shareholders and managing corporate PR. Instead of slaving among the densely-populated pods and hutches of the lower storeys, Archie found himself on the thickly-carpeted corporate floor, barely a dozen doors along from Ross's own office, and sharing the same executive washroom. Settling into his big shared space with its drinks fridge and plasma TV, Archie felt things were definitely looking up. The money was better too and so was his expense account. It took him no time to adapt to his new life of taking investors to lunch at Christopher's Bar and Grill or One Aldwych, or any of the expensive places he favoured across the bridge from his office. The corporate culture at Freeza Mart normally frowned on expense claims, or anything beyond no-frills budget travel, but this rule did not apply to Corporate Relations who lived high on the hog.

The success of the department was measured by its ability to manage investor expectations and the shareprice. At lunch after lunch, Archie found himself speiling the Freeza Mart growth statistics, with half a million square feet of new retail space scheduled to open each quarter, nine new superstores and a farmers market concept being rolled out in city centres. At the same time, Freeza Mart was considering a Spanish supermarket acquisition, their first venture into Continental Europe. Archie noticed a procession of small, moustached execs parading in and out of Ross's office, 'reeking of garlic,' as he told Gemma.

One of Ross's business maxims was an insistence on transparency with shareholders at all times. If they were in danger of missing a growth target or disappointing analysts' expectations, he made a point of telling them 'the earlier the better, I'd sooner surprise them with a slightly better than expected result than catch them unawares with bad news.' Archie found this straight dealing a liability. His instinct was to put an optimistic spin on everything and watch the shareprice jump. At the same time, he became expert at talking competitors' shareprices down, with a bearish word here and a downbeat market rumour there. Over lunch he would let slip, as though by accident, that he'd heard Tesco was trading down year on year, or that Pendletons was about to be refused an important planning consent for a new store. It gave him a kick to watch his lunchdate dump millions of shares later in the afternoon.

Knowing how deeply Miles was engaged in boosting Pendletons's shareprice, Archie derived special satisfaction from talking it down. When the price dropped below five pounds for the first time in four years, on rumours of a profit warning, Archie could imagine his father's fury, and was tempted to ring him up and tease him. But they hadn't spoken for months, not since he moved in with Gemma. According to Davina, Miles regarded Archie's job at Freeza Mart as an act of treachery. 'Perhaps you should give him a ring some time,' Davina suggested. 'I'm sure he'd like to hear from you.' But Archie wasn't so sure. Instead, he got his kicks from undermining Pendletons's stock.

A bonus of working in corporate relations was the extra status it gave him around the building, especially with the honeys in Direct Response on the eleventh floor. It amused him to take a detour between their tightly-packed desks, and enjoy the admiring glances that followed him. Or he'd sway up to the water cooler, reeking of wine from his expensive lunch, and chat them up.

One afternoon he noticed a pretty new face he'd not seen before, though she did look vaguely familiar, he didn't know why. She had shoulder-length brown hair and was dressed in a fitted black suit. Early twenties, Archie reckoned.

'So, what's a babe like you doing in a place like this, then?' he said, patting her on the bottom.

'Working for Dad for a month. I'm between jobs.'

'We should have a drink one evening. I bet you like cocktails.'

The girl looked at him oddly, then said, 'You don't recognise me, do you? It's Debbie. You live with my *sister*. *Gemma*, remember?'

'Oh fuck,' said Archie. 'And double fuck. Look, just forget I said that. It was only a joke. Don't say anything to Gemma.'

54.

'm so glad I came up here. I should have done it ages ago when you first asked, but it always feels like it's so difficult to get away.' Hugh Pendleton and Peter were tramping along the beach beneath the cottage, scrunching over bladderwrack and sea lace, enveloped by the bleak emptiness of it all. Even after all these months, Peter couldn't contemplate the view without shivers up his spine.

'The past few months have been knackering,' Hugh said. 'First the shock of Mum dying and all that business, the press and everything, and trying to take care of Dad who took it quite badly. And then all sorts of challenges at work, one after another, non-stop crisis management. For the last couple of days I've been away at a so-called blue sky conference at a hotel in Crawley. A hundred senior managers, with keynote speeches and incentive coaches and break-out sessions, almost all of it a complete waste of time. You can't imagine.'

'Actually, I *can* imagine. You were staying at the Crawley Fairlawns Convention Hotel?'

'How on earth did you know that?'

'You've still got the hotel name tag pinned on your jacket.'

Hugh groaned and pulled it off. 'Anyway, now I'm actually here it feels like a million miles away. Another world. I'm so envious of you living here all the time. Writing songs on the beach. I'd love to do that. Not that I can write music, but the principle.'

'You could though, couldn't you? Quit the rat race, I mean. I'm sure you don't need the money. Sorry, that sounds rude.'

'Fair point. And probably true I suppose. But in our family you have to work. Everyone does. Dad, all my uncles, even my mother never stopped working at her charities and ballets. If I announced I was giving up, there'd be such disapproval. Particularly if it was me, because I'm meant to be the big white hope of the next genera-tion, the next chairman-but-three after all my uncles have had their turns. But you've seen the zero responsibility I'm given . . . you've seen me at enough meetings, taking the notes, pouring the coffee, learning by example from my elders. In our family you get to take your first solo business decision when you're about fifty, and only then if half your cousins sign off on it too.'

'I thought you liked your job? You always give that impression.'

'Well, I don't particularly. I try to, of course, I'm not so bad at it either, though it gets quite frustrating sitting there watching my family screw up. Actually that's an exaggeration. We're still making a lot of money. But every year we lose a bit more share to competi-tors, and our margins erode while everyone else's grow. And we've been too cautious overseas, so everyone's got in ahead of us. I've been pushing them for years to go into California, but we never did and now Ross Clegg's in there doing a brilliant job.'

'Ross is still public enemy number one, I take it?'

'That's what your father was lecturing us about yesterday. I should have told you, he was speaking at the Conference. The open-ing keynote speech: Keeping Pendletons ahead in the PR war. He was scathing about Ross. Said he'd lost interest in his business, shoots pheasants midweek through the shooting season. If only it were true. Wishful thinking by your dad, I fear.'

'Did you talk to him?'

'Sure. He only came down for his speech, he didn't stay at the hotel, but we talked about Mum—and about you. I said I was com-ing up here after the Conference.'

'You did? He doesn't even know I'm in Scotland.'

'He does now. Sorry if I've let the cat out of the bag, I didn't re-alise. Anyway, he sent you his regards, sort of.'

'I bet he was dissing my music. He usually does.'

'Well, he did mention something about caterwauling. And rec-ommended I bring earplugs. But he's always like that, isn't he? It's his style.'

'I guess. It gets pretty wearing when you live with it, especially when it's aimed at you all the time.' Then Peter asked, 'How was he looking? You heard he and Mum have split? I talked to her yesterday—she sends you her love, by the way. She said Dad's being hell over the divorce. Playing hardball, won't agree a thing. She sounded quite down.'

'Miles looked the same as ever. He's so slick, your old man. You have to admire it, even when you know he's spouting bullshit. Dad says the same. He says Miles inspires confidence, he's worth it for that alone. You want him on side.'

'Dad loves your parents. His best clients and most distinguished neighbours. But you know that. All through our childhood he kept banging on about the Pendletons. You were always presented as these perfect beings, like the royal family or something. When I joined Dad's company and was assigned to the Pendletons account, I was determined not to like you. But here we are.'

'Well, those review meetings we used to go to have deteriorated since you left. I felt you were the one kindred spirit in the room. Now there isn't one. Your successor is very heavy going. He's so stressed out about the positive PR Ross keeps getting, he's practically frothing at the mouth.'

They reached the headland where beach gave over to jagged rocks, and looked back at the cottage, just visible a mile and a half away. A thin plume of smoke rose from the chimney.

'Wonders will never cease. Looks like Sam's remembered to keep the fire going. She generally lets it burn out,' Peter said. 'It's a girl thing.'

'She's been staying up here for ages, hasn't she?' Hugh asked.

'Four months. Kicking her bad habits. It's worked out really well having her here. I wasn't sure it would. We were never that close before. Now we're all part of the Straker diaspora, expelled from Camelot by Dad.'

'He's a long shadow in your lives, I can tell that.'

'You're not kidding.'

'With us, my mother was always the stronger one. That surprises some people, but it's true. She took all the decisions. Dad's quite lost without her, though people are being kind, inviting him for meals and stuff. But he's very lonely. I'll tell you who's being particularly nice and that's Ross's wife, Dawn. They play tennis quite a bit. And she goes to art exhibitions with him.'

'I didn't know Dawn's interested in art. I've only been to their house a couple of times, but I don't remember seeing any.'

'Well, she is now. She's a collector. Dad was telling me. He says she's got a good eye for contemporary British, she's become very knowledgeable.'

'She's my sister Mollie's mother-in-law, as you know. I need hardly tell you how that went down with my dad.'

Hugh laughed. 'Having heard him on the subject of Ross yesterday, I can imagine.' Then he said, 'Come on Peter, I want to hear your new songs. I insist. Sam says they're brilliant.'

Alone at Chawbury on a Saturday afternoon, Miles brooded in his study. With no Davina and no children, the house was spookily quiet. Furthermore, he felt the place deteriorating around him. The replacements for Mrs French, lined up and interviewed by Sara White, his PA, had one after another proved themselves useless. In recent months there had been a fat housekeeper from Andover, followed by two unsatisfactory English couples and now a New Zealand girl. None had a clue how a house like Chawbury Manor should run, or the standards to be striven for. From his desk, Miles could see glass rings on a polished tabletop from tumblers placed there the previous weekend, clear evidence of carelessness. And arriving down late on Friday night, tired after a long week, he found a duvet—a *duvet*!—on his bed, when the master bedroom was always made up with sheets and blankets. He had lain awake half the night fuming, feeling like a child or a Scandinavian, interpreting the duvet as a calculated insult from Stefanie the Kiwi housekeeper.

These weekends at Chawbury, once his revenge against the world that living well was supposed to guarantee, became week by week more squalid. No one any longer seemed capable of keeping the larder adequately stocked, or of noticing when supplies of mint jelly, redcurrant, Tabasco, Angostura bitters, goats' cheese, Clamato juice, cheeselets or other basic household provisions ran low. He spent his life asking for things that weren't there because *nobody was thinking*. For the first time, the house felt cold and felt fusty. Piles of post lay unopened and unsorted on the piano, including bills from utility companies, mail order catalogues in plastic shrink wrap for country outfitters and spring bulb nurseries, invoices from local tradesmen, junk mail, begging letters from the church, postcards from neighbours in indecipherable handwriting asking him to lunch or for drinks. Previously it had been Davina's role to sift through all this, drawing his attention to the more alluring invitations only. Sweeping the pile into a carrier bag, he took it to the office and dumped it on his assistants. But even with their input, it took most of a morning to dispatch.

Outdoors, the situation was critical. Wherever he looked, he found evidence of neglect. Slates slipped from the roof but nobody noticed. Ivy snaked its insidious way up treetrunks, but did his gardeners do anything about it? No, they did not. The edging around flowerbeds became blurred and overgrown. Was he expected to micro-manage everyone every minute of every day? Did nobody appreciate the pressure he was under, not only from a roster of important and demanding clients, but from an avaricious soon-to-be-ex-wife employing bloodsuckers as lawyers, four deeply disappointing and delinquent children, the Tory party which seemed to expect him to work for their benefit without even proper expenses chargeable, and a crazy ex-mistress acting like a prima donna at the very moment her big chance came along. During his second weekend in sole charge at Chawbury he had rung Serena and summoned her over at Sunday teatime. For years she had put pressure on him for a rendezvous at the manor, but he had honourably denied her while Davina remained in residence. But now Davina was history. Miles took it for granted Serena would come straight over for a session on the marital bed. Instead, she was all of a sudden full of scruples, withholding favours until her long-term position was clarified. Long-term position! Her long-term position was the same as it had always been—on all fours doggie-style. In the bedroom as in life, Miles had an aversion to women on top.

The unreliability of local tradespeople astounded him. Without Davina perpetually on their case, Chawbury Manor became virtually untenable. The simplest things such as getting a water metre read, a septic tank emptied, the dangerous bough of a tree lopped by experts, all involved hours of negotiation and long-range supervision. He commissioned the local tree surgeon, Ed Badger, to tidy the crown of an oak, but after fourteen weeks nothing had happened. Commanding his secretaries to harass him every hour on the hour until the job was completed, he was affronted when Badger resigned the work, saying he didn't appreciate being pushed around. He had more than enough work already from Mr Clegg.

After six months with no Davina, Miles would gladly have paid £40,000 a year for her services as a project manager.

55.

ncouraged by his record company, Black Cat Wardoursound, Peter was booked to play three London gigs at venues in Hammersmith, Brixton and Putney. The idea was to try out the new material in front of a live audience and begin the process of generating positive word of mouth. Black Cat's A&R team hoped to bring along well-disposed stringers from the music press, and Peter would also be working for the first time with backing musicians to fill out the sound. As the dates of the concerts came closer, and he worked on his lyrics at the cottage, the prospect of returning to London became scary; he'd spent so long in self-imposed exile, the big city felt threatening.

Then there was the question of what he'd wear to perform on stage. It wasn't something he'd given a moment's thought to, until Sam started making out it was a big deal.

'Just my normal stuff, I guess,' Peter said, shrugging. 'Jeans and a sweater.'

'*Not* a hairy woolly sweater,' Sam replied, horrified. 'You're playing a cool London gig, not going mackerel fishing. For Christ's sake Peter, your image is vital. We've got to really consider this.'

And so, over the remaining weeks, Sam appointed herself personal stylist to the artiste, scouring the various charity shops in Durness and, having rejected everything, searching on the internet from the Durness cybercafé. Parcels of leather waistcoats and beanie hats began arriving at the cottage, and each evening Sam caused Peter endless embarrassment by making him try everything on, and hunch over his guitar in the new gear to see what worked.

Then there was the question of the guest list. A part of Peter would have been happy for nobody to show, and to play to an empty hall. But the promoters said he could have sixty comp tickets if he gave them names for the door, so he came up with a list of former Straker Communications colleagues to invite, plus Hugh Pendleton and several old schoolfriends.

'And don't forget the family,' Sam said. 'I know Mum wants to come, she keeps asking about the dates. And Mollie says she and Greg want to.'

'You think so? I can't exactly imagine Greg there.'

'Well, Mollie would like him invited, even if he doesn't make it. And Archie and Gemma, of course.' Then, tentatively, she asked, 'And what will you do about Dad?'

'I've been wondering about that. Not sure. He'd never come, and if he did he'd hate it. It's just so not his thing. And we haven't been in touch for eight months, longer probably. What do you think I should do?'

'Not invite him.'

'I was thinking of maybe forwarding him the publicity e-mail, with the dates and venues, and leaving it at that. If he wants to come, he can pay at the door. Unless you'd rather I didn't? I don't want you to feel uncomfortable, Sam. But he won't show up in any case.'

Sam said, 'If he does, I won't speak to him, I'll turn round and walk off. Don't worry about me. I'm practically over it anyway. I only have nightmares once or twice a week.'

They flew down to London three days ahead of the first concert and stayed with Davina in Holland Park Square. The atmosphere in the house had changed a lot, Sam sensed it the minute she stepped in; like an unloaded weapon or dismantled bomb it no longer felt so threatening. Several of the larger, more important paintings had disappeared from the walls, taken to Mount Street by Miles, but every surface was still filled with vases of flowers. Having always thought of their London garden as vast, Peter was struck by how much smaller it seemed after the endless vistas of Caithness. He was thrilled to see his mother and relieved to find her calmer than he'd expected, despite the pressure of the divorce. But London struck him as a detestable place: dirty and squalid and claustrophobic. The sooner he could get back to the cottage, the better.

The opening gig was booked at The Blind Fiddler on King Street, Hammersmith, in an upstairs room above the pub. Peter was to be the second of two acts, following the cult singer Plavka, with his set scheduled for 10:40 p.m. All afternoon he'd been rehearsing with his back-up band and ironing out technical problems at the sound check. Not having performed with session musicians before, several of whom had supported famous headline acts in the past, he felt bashful about what they thought of his songs. But then the bass guitarist, Rattan, said he really liked the whale song and Peter's confidence returned.

By half-past ten there must have been eighty people in the room. Peter was leaning against the bar with Mollie and Sam, drinking Bud from the bottle, while the soundmen assembled the set. According to a publicist from Black Cat Wardoursound, someone had turned up from NME.com who might post a review, and a guy from *Time Out* had tickets waiting on the door. Peter was greeting old friends from Straker Communications who'd supported him by turning up, as well as Hugh Pendleton who'd brought along three mates to swell the crowd. Mollie reported Greg was hoping to drop by later when his council meeting ended, and just before he went on stage, Peter spotted his mother arriving with Dawn, along with Archie, Gemma and Debbie.

Afterwards, he was surprised by how quickly it all went. He performed nine songs but it only felt like he'd been up on stage for ten minutes. It helped that, with the lights, he couldn't see much of the audience beyond the people packed right up at the front. But he sensed their support, and was bucked by the response to some of the new tracks like 'Cormorant's Cry' and 'The Secret Trapped Inside.' At one point he noticed both Clegg girls grooving away, getting really into it, and Sam lip-syncing the lyrics she'd heard so many times. At the end of the set, he felt dazed and drained as friends and family, and people from the record company, as well as people he'd never clapped eyes on before, came up to congratulate him. Even Greg said well done, pointing out that The Blind Fiddler was supported by a bursary introduced under a Labour initiative.

He was touched when Debbie, whom he scarcely knew, came up and said how great he'd been and how moving some of the songs were. 'You're as good as Joan Baez.'

'Hardly. And how come you're a Baez fan?'

'You won't remember, but you sold me one of her CDs at a fete in your garden. I was about fourteen at the time. I've been a fan ever since.'

'I remember now. At my junk stall. Well, I'm glad you like Joan. She's a goddess.'

'You're pretty good yourself. When your record comes out, I'm definitely going to get it.'

Peter was packing up his stuff and wondering where Sam was for his lift home, when she appeared looking spooked. 'You realise he was here, don't you?'

'Who was?'

'Dad. Just before the end, there he was, standing at the back. I suddenly spotted him in his overcoat, the velvet collar one. All on his own, staring at the stage.'

'He can't have liked it much, he didn't say anything.'

'He left before the end, I was watching him. He just stood there, like he was checking everything out. And then left. It's the first time I've seen him since the Paris thing. It felt really creepy. I followed him downstairs, making sure he didn't see me. Makepiece was waiting outside and he just got into his car and was driven away.'

56.

awn's friendship with James Pendleton, incubated in the desolate vacuum of his loss, deepened with each passing week. Dawn felt genuinely sorry for this diffident, cultured man, so clearly bereft without Laetitia on whom he had relied completely. Alone, he was scarcely capable of functioning. As Dawn discovered, he had few friends, either male or female, anyway of the sort he felt comfortable about ringing. It had been Laetitia who always made their arrangements, who had filled the house with neighbours at the weekends and invited the procession of museum directors and curators to lunch and dinner. It was Laetitia who booked tickets for the theatre and decided which exhibitions they would visit at London galleries. James admitted to Dawn he had never rung up a single neighbour in twenty years, and she had to show him the page in the newspapers where art exhibitions are listed. Devastated in his loneliness, Lord Pendleton continued to move as he always had between his London home in Cadogan Square and his country home at the weekend but, without the intervention of Dawn, would probably have spent every evening in front of the television, eating supper off a tray.

It was Dawn who, little by little, coaxed him back into the world and rekindled his interest in life. Initially there had been the odd game of tennis at Queens Club, or at the weekends when she drove over to Longparish Priory, or James came over to Chawbury to play doubles with whomever was around. Because of his leg, Ross had never been able to play serious tennis, but Debbie was a good player, and Gemma and Archie came down for weekends with Mandy. Then Dawn began escorting James to private views at the Whitechapel Gallery and the White Cube in Hoxton, as well as to important private views at the Tate. Ross was away on business such a lot at the moment, with Freeza Mart's expansion into California and the new superstores in Thailand and Taiwan, that it suited everyone. Ross detested art exhibitions in any case. It annoyed Dawn, on the rare occasions she made him come to anything cultural with her, the way he looked bored and dubious and just stood around wanting to leave. Recently, through James, Dawn had become interested in installation art, and it made her cross that Ross was always so negative, saying his retail display people could knock up something similar in a couple of hours. So, all in all, it was a godsend to enjoy her artistic pursuits with James, who was open to every new development and trend in contemporary art, and grateful to have someone to go with. Furthermore, she knew she was learning so much. To walk round a show at the Serpentine Gallery with him was like a one-to-one tutorial by a university professor, he was that knowledgeable on every period and school of art. And, of course, it made it extra special that many of the artworks they saw together actually belonged to James, having been loaned by the Pendleton Trust. Dawn couldn't help feeling privileged when she was included with James at development board lunches at the Tate, where she was sat next to all sorts of prominent people. It was embarrassing when, once or twice, the namecard at her place at table said 'Lady Pendleton'. The first time it happened she'd been mortified; the second, she took it more in her stride. When a party photograph of them appeared in *OK!* magazine, captioned 'Lord and Lady Pendleton of Pendletons supermarket,' she was relieved Ross wasn't a reader of *OK!*, but it made her think. Constantly conscious of how lucky she was to be going on all these wonderful treats courtesy of James, she was also aware of her own contribution to the success of their expeditions. It was Dawn who decided which shows he would find interesting, and who liaised with James's office to secure tickets and special passes. And she knew he enjoyed teaching her how to appreciate certain artists, and that her constant presence as his walker enhanced his enjoyment. As Dawn said more than once, 'We make a very good team.'

Initially, she was entirely open with Ross about these outings with James. She was comforting a family friend in his bereavement, and certainly Ross saw no mischief in it. In fact, he found it flattering

that the legendary Lord Pendleton should have become a close personal friend of theirs. And, of course, it let him off the hook that
Dawn now had someone to see all those art shows with. He felt he
owed James a big drink.

Over time, she didn't quite know why, Dawn found herself saying rather less about their jaunts. When Ross returned from eight
days in California, followed by a side trip to Hawaii to size-up a
retail acquisition, and asked what she'd been up to while he'd been
away, she felt uncomfortable admitting she'd spent every single
evening with Lord Pendleton, even though it was all entirely innocent.

Samantha was sitting alone at one of the pavement tables outside
Tootsies on Holland Park Avenue, five minutes from the house, having a cappuccino and a fag, when she became aware of being watched.
A lady kept staring at her, glancing away, then staring again. Whenever Sam caught her eye, she turned away, pretending she wasn't
looking. She was a woman in her late forties, Sam reckoned, slightly
plump. It was kind of annoying.

After fifteen minutes of this, Sam was seriously considering saying something when the lady came over and handed her a business
card. It said she was Marketing Manager of Freeza Mart plc and
looked very official, with a wodge of phone numbers and email addresses.

'Sorry to approach you like this, but I was wondering if you're a
model?'

'A model? Er, no.'

'So you don't have an agency or representation? You do live in
London?'

'Mostly up in Scotland at the moment. But I'm sometimes down
here. Why?'

'We're looking for potential models to appear in a campaign
we're putting together. For Freeza Mart superstores. We're bringing out a fashion range and the concept is to use only "real" women
in the advertising, which is why I needed to check you're not a professional.'

'No, I'm not.'

'That's great. Obviously we need "real" women who *could* have become models but aren't. And your look might really work for us. Obviously the casting director and photographer will need to see you. Would you be available to come along to a casting at all?'

'Depends when it is.'

'Thursday and Friday morning. The studio's in Covent Garden.'

Sam shrugged. 'If you tell me where to come, I'll try.'

'And there's a fee of a hundred pounds for showing up,' the lady added.

57.

Dawn's decision to leave Ross, to end her marriage, to quit both the homes into which she had poured so much time and love, and to move into James's houses, was not one she took lightly. Rather, it crept up on her, over many months of soul-searching. Having spent her entire adult life with Ross, and been through so much together, it was difficult to imagine life without him. And there was the reaction of the children to consider. She knew how unhappy they'd be about it, the girls especially. But they were all grown-up now and increasingly settled into their own lives. If ever there was a time to do something for herself, the time was surely now.

She told herself it was a long, long time since she and Ross had been truly happy. Their marriage had been drifting for years, they were no longer the same people they'd been when they'd met; she found it difficult to remember what they *had* been like in those far off days in Droitwich. She had read that people develop in life at different speeds, and felt that in many respects she had outgrown Ross, had left him behind. Of course, you had to admire the success he had made of Freeza Mart, and she did not underestimate the sacrifices she'd made for his career, relocating down south and seldom complaining about his business trips. Ross was a workaholic and the strain this placed on their marriage could not be overstated. But, beyond that, she saw herself as having grown as a person, intellectually, artistically, at a faster rate than Ross, until they no longer had much in common. Whole areas of her new life were closed to him. When she tried to describe exhibitions she'd visited, his eyes glazed over. When she filled their Holland Park house with her art world friends, he looked out of his depth, so she preferred to hold supper parties when he was overseas. On the infrequent occasions they had dinner alone together, they talked at cross purposes, she about art, he about the challenges of taking Freeza Mart into emerging markets. She convinced herself they had simply grown apart, as happened to thousands of couples their age, it was a very sad fact of life. Probably Ross felt the same way, if he was honest about it.

And, of course, she adored James, adored and mothered him. He was such an interesting, unusual man, as different from Ross as chalk and cheese. And he was so self-effacing, almost to a fault. He never pushed himself forwards. Left to himself, he would have sat at the worst table in a restaurant rather than announce himself as Lord Pendleton, one of the richest men in the land. But when she saw him in conversation with his curator, discussing some addition to his collection, or sitting with his financial people reviewing the performance of his different share portfolios, Dawn was filled with respect for his shrewdness and knowledge. And he was always so courteous and thoughtful. When he shyly gave her a small oil painting by Patrick Heron for her birthday, she felt deeply moved.

Instinctively she understood that James would never take their relationship to the next level unless she seized the initiative. He was too much the gentleman to make any move on a married woman, on any woman come to that. Laetitia once told Dawn that it was she who had suggested to James they become engaged, 'otherwise I'd have been waiting forever.' Dawn was sure it would be the same today, and she sensed he would be equally receptive to an overture.

One evening, with a deep breath, she talked about the state of her marriage to Ross for the first time, and how it was to all intents and purposes over. 'It's a very sad situation,' she said, 'but we're different people with different interests.' From here, it was a small step to declare how much James had opened up her eyes to the world, and how he had brought out a whole new side to her character that she could never share with her husband. She explained how, for the first time, she felt she'd become her own person, and not an appendage to Ross. James, visibly embarrassed by so much emotion and self-revelation, could only nod sympathetically, and agree how much more in common Dawn had with him. Forty-five minutes later, he had passively agreed it made sense she should become his second wife.

It was an indication of their naivety that neither James nor Dawn had any inkling of the public scandal they were about to bring down upon themselves. Dawn informed Ross one Saturday afternoon that she had decided to leave him, and promptly did so ninety minutes later, driving over to Longparish Priory in her car. Having had not the slightest premonition anything was wrong, Ross watched her go in stunned disbelief; it did not help that he was badly jet-lagged from a seventeen-hour flight from Taipei via Singapore. None of the children being home that weekend, he sat alone in the kitchen, digesting the fact that his wife had asked for a divorce to marry Lord Pendleton. It was the craziest thing.

For a week he told no one, not the children, not anyone at work. It felt strange returning to the big white London house to find no Dawn. He still half expected her to return any day, he didn't seriously believe she could stay with James Pendleton, it was a ridiculous idea. Although never a man to read magazine articles or novels about relationships, he had nevertheless heard about midlife crises, and this is what he assumed was happening with Dawn. He knew he hadn't been paying her much attention lately, he could see that now, though you couldn't always choose your workload at any particular moment. He left several messages on her mobile, but if she was picking them up she didn't return his calls. He couldn't bring himself to ring the Pendletons' home.

Then, on the eighth day, fate forced all their hands. A story appeared in the Richard Kay column in the *Daily Mail*, saying Dawn had left the Freeza Mart tycoon for the recently widowed Lord Pendleton and moved into his house. A spokesperson for Pendletons declined to comment, but Dawn herself was quoted confirming the situation and requesting privacy 'at this very difficult time.' The item was headlined: 'Supermarket Wars: Mrs Freeza Mart checks out for Pendletons.' The story was full of puns: Ross had been frozen out, Dawn was headed for fresh aisles, billionaire Lord Pendleton had wooed and won his rival's trolley dolly. Ross, who did not read the *Mail,* only became aware of it when the girls in his office, looking hideously embarrassed, pointed it out; he'd heard them whispering outside for twenty minutes deliberating on whether they should. Then Gemma rang up in hysterics, having seen it, and Ross left another furious message on Dawn's mobile insisting she call him without delay, before telling first Debbie, then Greg. Dawn finally called him at midday, sounding uncharacteristically subdued, saying how upset James was about the story, as she was herself, and how James had just informed his son Hugh as well as the Pendleton brothers. She added that Miles Straker was taking personal charge of the public relations strategy, and was very put out not to have been briefed about it in advance. He had ordered all participants not to speak to the press under any circumstances, including Ross, and she hoped he'd respect that. 'I'll speak to whom I bloody well please,' Ross retorted. 'It wasn't *me* who got us into this mess, it was you, love. So you can tell Miles exactly where he can put his advice.' But then he added, 'Not that I'm planning on speaking to any journalists. It's nobody's damn business but ours.'

Afterwards, he felt almost more annoyed with Miles for muscling in than he did about losing Dawn to James Pendleton.

Samantha turned up for the initial casting in Covent Garden, and again the next day at the studio of a photographer in Clerkenwell. On the first day there had been several hundred 'real' women candidates of all shapes, sizes and skin colours, but at the second look-see there'd been only a couple of dozen. Polaroids were taken, then digital shots against a white paper colorama, and the photographer, his assistants, several people from the Freeza Mart marketing department and their advertising agency crowded around a computer screen to see the results. Sam's must have come out ok, because at the end of the afternoon they asked if she'd be available for a full dummy shoot the following day, for which she'd be paid £600. And could she potentially be available to come into the office next Tuesday to meet the marketing director and some of the board.

And so it was she found herself arriving at Freeza Mart House with the, by now, six other remaining 'real' women. They were being escorted across the lobby towards a bank of elevators by a marketing assistant, when she came face to face with Archie.

'What the hell are *you* doing here, Sam? Joining a harem?' Archie stared approvingly at the blonde, brunette, Asian and Afro-Caribbean women who embodied the diversity of Freeza Mart customers.

Sam explained her mission and her brother nodded. 'Yeah, I heard about this. It's going to be a blatant rip-off of the Dove commercials. Using fat ugly dogs instead of proper models.'

'Thanks, Archie. That makes me feel great.'

'Sorry, not you obviously. But generally. And even you are a bit over the hill for a normal model.'

'Archie, *enough.*'

They were herded into a meeting room on the ninth floor with views over the Thames, given coffee and name badges, and a woman called Jo briefed them on the concept for the campaign. As Archie had intimated, the idea was to give an illusion of random British women, in all their glorious variety and imperfection, wearing items from the inaugural Freeza Mart fashion range. Group photographs of Freeza Mart females would appear on thousands of billboards around the country, as well as across double-page advertisements in magazines. There would also be a sixty-second television commercial presenting the women as multi-cultural 'girlfriends' in different real life situations, such as shopping together in Freeza Mart, watching sports or attending a hen party. Furthermore, it was explained, the women weren't expected to act as models for a single campaign, but become long term 'brand ambassadors,' giving interviews and endorsements and possibly cutting ribbons at store openings once they'd been successfully implanted in the public's consciousness. 'The agency envisages each of you developing as a distinct personality with your own style attributes,' Jo said. 'A bit like the Spice Girls did. I hope you're all comfortable with the concept.' Afterwards, the creative director of the advertising agency gave a long speech repeating what Jo had already said, and then Jo and her boss, Matt, wrapped up by summarising everything.

During the speeches, Sam noticed several senior guys in suits being ushered into the room, including Ross, who stood at the back while marketing assistants fetched coffee for him. These were evidently the Board, arriving to check out the 'real' women. Sam thought Ross looked rather drawn and tired, which was hardly surprising. She'd heard about Dawn leaving him.

Ross limped over to greet Sam when the presentation ended. 'So it *is* you, Samantha. I noticed your name on the list and wondered. I hope you're going to take part.'

'Well, I haven't actually been chosen yet. And it's come out of the blue. I've never done modelling before.'

'You'll be perfect. At least that's what my people tell me. I don't get to choose the models myself, sadly. You lot here today are the final choices, if you're up for it.'

'God, that's amazing. Do we get paid, do you know?'

'A ruddy fortune. We're going to have to sell millions of garments just to cover the model fees. I was complaining to our marketing folks about that. But you should do it, Sam. It'll make you famous. Like those birds in the Marks & Spencer commercials.'

Sam laughed. 'As if.'

'Well, it'll make your dad proud, anyway.'

Sam nodded, knowing it certainly wouldn't.

58.

Behind a gritty carapace of normality, and an insistence it was business as usual, Ross was desperately unhappy. He missed Dawn's presence far more than he'd ever have imagined. Their houses felt absurdly large and empty without her there, and he responded by throwing himself deeper and deeper into work, arriving earlier at the office, staying later, filling his weekends with store visits and overseas trips. By helicopter, he was able in a single Saturday to visit eight different Freeza Marts as far apart as Swansea, Exeter and Gateshead. He would pilot himself from city to city, landing in a specially-cleared area of car park or, if this was impractical, at a local airfield to be met by the Freeza Mart area rep. Although he tried not to allow his personal problems to affect his demeanour at work, his colleagues, and particularly his PAs, noticed him become less communicative and more short-tempered. Arriving at the office by six am, he insisted the trading reports for the previous day be waiting on his desk, and he reviewed them territory by territory, store by store, emailing questions and comments direct to managers before most were awake. A manager in Telford would receive 'Cleggmail,' as these came to be known, enquiring why sales of washing powder or a particular brand of cheese cracker had fallen short of forecast, or why sales of fuel at a Freeza Mart forecourt were growing at a slower rate than at a neighbouring Tesco forecourt. He became daily more obsessed by market share and particularly, it was observed, by Freeza Mart's market share versus the market share of Pendletons. In those areas where Pendletons still outperformed Freeza Mart, Ross instigated aggressive promotion wars on everyday items, with discounted loss leaders. When Dawn had been resident at Chawbury, he'd had a rule of never catching a flight at weekends before Sunday evening, but now his secretaries were encouraged to put him on any flight they wished, because his weekends were no longer sacrosanct. With all this frenetic displacement activity, Ross tried to numb his sadness about Dawn.

His health deteriorated but he scarcely noticed, and either ignored the symptoms or took Paracetamol. And the pains in his legs returned, to a level he hadn't experienced for many years. He would work incessantly, almost without stopping, for six weeks on end, then collapse, polaxed, and be forced to take a day off work.

Unaccustomed to spending time alone, he took to having supper with Gemma and Archie at the cottage in Roupell Street, arriving with a bag full of Freeza Mart ready meals. Gemma was only too glad to see more of her dad, and for Ross to see more of Mandy, and encouraged him to drop round whenever he liked. Of the three children, Gemma took her parents' separation the hardest and Archie became quite bored with Gemma banging on about it. 'I wouldn't say it's *that* terrible,' Archie said. 'Your mother has only run off with a multi-billionaire. He's number eleven in the *Sunday Times* Rich List, you know.'

Debbie was also sweetly supportive of Ross, ringing him daily to check he was alright. Her temporary job at Freeza Mart headquarters evolved into something permanent in the property division, where she was busy learning about commercial leases and buy-backs which turned out to be a lot more interesting than she'd envisaged. Ross had recently decided the group should buy up as many brownfield sites as possible, even on the edge of towns where they already owned superstores, to prevent rivals from gaining a foothold. And they were gearing up to bid for grocery concessions at motorway service stations; a lot of Debbie's time was spent monitoring footfall at Moto and BP convenience stores, estimating how Freeza Mart could grow those businesses. One of Debbie's happiest days was spent travelling with her dad, just the two of them in the helicopter, from Chawbury to a service station near Warwick to check out potential. Afterwards, they had a cup of coffee in a Travelodge and Ross said, 'If we win the grocery concession, the hotel comes too. Perhaps you could run a hotel chain for us, Debs. You're the expert. We could build up a Freeza Mart hospitality brand.'

As for Greg, he scarcely ever rang Ross, but Mollie did, inviting him over for supper in Sudan Road. Ross had quickly become fond of his daughter-in-law, whom he considered impossibly nice to be a daughter of Miles Straker, but evenings at the house were never wholly satisfactory. Greg seldom missed the opportunity to lecture Ross on something—carbon emissions or some progressive new taxation on business Labour was about to introduce—and it always riled him. How Mollie put up with it, he didn't know. Greg announced he thought he might have found a safe Labour seat to fight at the next General Election, a constituency near his birthplace in Droitwich. 'I'm being sponsored by Millbank,' he told his dad. 'They're keen to fast-track me into Parliament. Gordon's people are fixing it.'

Outside his immediate family, Ross noticed how few people made any reference to his marital difficulties. At work, even his closest colleagues avoided any allusion, not wanting to intrude on the Boss's private life; at Chawbury, the phone hardly rang, their neighbours worried about putting their foot in it. Of their friends, the only one who made contact was Serena who left a message on BT callminder: 'Look, Ross, I saw all that stuff in the *Mail*. I don't know how accurate it is—probably complete balls—but if you're around this weekend and want to come over for supper, give us a bell. It'll just be Nigel and me and Ollie in the kitchen, totally casual.' Grateful for the company, Ross took her up on the offer and felt loads better for it. Serena produced a chicken casserole from the Aga and mashed potatoes, and he sank several glasses of Rioja and the world began to feel a better place. It was his first visit to the Hardens' cottage, he hadn't appreciated quite how modest it was or how tight they were for money. Nigel hadn't had a proper job for six years and, aside from Serena's intermittent fees as a decorator, they lived on air. Nigel's most recent venture, selling water coolers to friends for their kitchens, had disappointed expectations, and he was now selling school fee schemes on commission. After supper, the four of them sat in a row on the sofa and watched an Indiana Jones video, with a duvet over their knees for cosiness and warmth. Ollie had seen the movie so many times he knew the dialogue by heart and spoke along in sync. He was a very nice kid, Ross decided.

Visits to Serena's cottage soon became Ross's sole weekend re-
spite from work. He drove over to watch sport on Sky with Ollie
and Nigel, or DVDs with Serena, and when the weather improved
to play swingball and badminton with Ollie in the back garden.
The normality of these visits helped keep him sane, he was eter-
nally grateful for them and for the fact Serena never questioned
him about the Dawn situation unless he first brought it up himself.
Since the turbulent afternoon when he'd discovered her in the lay-by
and delivered her back to her car, Serena had never made any further overture to him. He sensed, however, that her life with Nigel
was unhappy.

Once, on a hot summer's afternoon when he'd gone inside to
fetch a drink, the telephone in the Hardens' cottage started ringing
and Ross picked it up.

'Serena?' a man's voice asked.

'Serena's outside on the patio. Who shall I say is calling?'

The caller cut himself off.

Afterwards, Ross thought he'd recognised the voice as Miles. It
was oddly unsettling.

Alone at Chawbury for the weekend, as so often these days, Miles
concluded women are unfathomable. Certainly one woman in particular, and that was Serena.

He had been ringing her several times a week, leaving messages
on her mobile and also on the landline. Sometimes she returned his
calls, but generally not, and always with excuses for not meeting
up. It was almost as if she was giving him the brush-off.

In his confidence and arrogance, Miles found it impossible to
credit. Logically, it made no sense. There she was, barely a penny to
her name, living in a poky grooms' cottage on the Mountleighs'
charity, with a loser of a husband and no prospects. And here was
he, suddenly available, rich and attractive with everything going
for him, and she was refusing to bite. Either she'd lost her marbles
or there was someone else sniffing around. Last time he'd called, a
man had picked up the phone and it wasn't Nigel. What's more,
Miles had a suspicion about who it had been.

Prowling crossly around the Manor, his pleasure in the place
was further undermined with each passing weekend. Stefani the

New Zealand housekeeper had been given her marching orders but her replacement was, if anything, worse. This time they'd gone for an English one, Angie, a single mother with toddler in tow. The toddler, Bethany, trailed round the house behind her mum while she did her housework, covering every surface with sticky little fingers and had already broken two porcelain snuff boxes. Only that morning, Miles stepped out of bed and trod on a piece of Lego in his bare feet, clearly dropped by Bethany. The food Angie served up was inedible. When Miles complained, she said she wasn't accustomed to cooking from fresh and couldn't she provide Freeza Mart ready meals, since he was on his own.

Increasingly, he found himself brooding over Dawn's coup in bagging Lord Pendleton, which had to be the least expected, least welcome development. Miles couldn't fathom what James saw in her, and disliked his subservient role in handling their PR in the newspapers. Already he had endured several long telephone conversations with Dawn, listening to her complaints about press intrusion and counselling her about what and what not to say. He made several calls on her behalf to editors to pull derogatory features they'd been planning about her, when secretly he'd have loved them to run. God, he could have told them a thing or two about Dawn, the calculating social mountaineer.

Was it really possible James would go through with it and marry her? Surely he'd come to his senses. Miles longed to tell it to him straight, to pull no punches, but on the couple of occasions he'd been limbering up to do so, something in James's manner made him back off. Instead, he found himself obliged to make himself pleasant to Dawn and pretend he was delighted about everything. James made it clear he wanted Dawn to accompany him to every social function as if she was already his wife, and requested Straker Communications ensure she was included by name on every invitation. When the Queen toured the Chelsea Flower Show and visited the woodland garden sponsored by Pendletons plc, it was Dawn who greeted Her Majesty with Lord Pendleton and escorted her and the Duke of Edinburgh around the plot.

It occurred to Miles that if anyone was going to become the next Lady Pendleton, Davina would have been a far more appropriate candidate. In fact, in many ways, it would have been the perfect solution, cementing his ties with James for all time and, of course, solving the problem of a divorce settlement. If she'd left him for a Pendleton, there would surely be no question of a pay-off.

Not for the first time, Miles felt his wife had badly let him down.

59.

'Davina? Miles.'

Her husband's voice down the telephone made her jump. She had hardly exchanged one word with him in months.

'I think I left my dress studs in Holland Park Square,' Miles said. 'I need them tonight for a dinner. I'm coming round to collect them.'

Davina felt a rush of panic. She'd been painting at her easel in the kitchen: a view from the window of the communal garden. 'Ok . . . when were you thinking of coming exactly?'

She could hear Miles consulting his chauffeur, Makepiece, in the background. 'We should be there in fifteen minutes, traffic permitting,' he told her.

Davina looked round the kitchen in dismay. The place wasn't in any state to receive him. Normally, she'd have spent several hours preparing for her husband's return, most of the day in fact. She scanned the room, seeing today's and yesterday's *Daily Mail* open on the table, plates from lunch uncleared, a coffee cup draining by the sink. Next to the back door an umbrella was propped against the wall, and a pair of her outdoor shoes on the mat. Miles hated shoes not put away in their proper places.

All her familiar feelings of rising panic came to her. Oh God, the hall! None of the lights were switched on upstairs, and there were several more pairs of shoes underneath the hall table. And then she noticed her hands covered with paint and she'd never be able to scrub it off before he got there.

She began madly rushing about the house, but then, just as abruptly, stopped. No, this was too much. There were separated, this was *her* house, *her* home. She didn't need to worry any more.

She exhaled, caught her reflection in a mirror and almost laughed at her audacity and bravery. She was damned if she was tidying up for him. Instead she put the kettle on, ran a comb through her hair and felt, for the first time, that she was a free woman.

The doorbell rang and before she could answer it she heard a key in the lock. Miles had kept his key to the front door. He entered the hall, noticed the jumble of shoes on the floor, the lack of lights, switched on a lamp and sniffed. The house smelt beautiful, of fresh flowers and furniture polish. Not musty like Chawbury. It smelt how Chawbury used to smell, before.

Davina called up, 'I'm downstairs in the kitchen. The kettle's just boiled. Have you time for a cup of tea?'

'Er, maybe. I'll find the studs first.'

He went upstairs to his old dressing room. It was a lot less tidy than it used to be, with Davina's clothes and old magazines and books lying around, and she had hung up some of her own new watercolours in the spaces where he'd removed their better paintings to Mount Street. The watercolours looked quite good there, he had to admit. In their bedroom there was another jug of spring flowers.

Retrieving his studs, he went downstairs to the kitchen. Davina's appearance startled him. She was wearing a painting smock covered in paint splats, and the kitchen was disturbingly messy. He noticed her hands which were a disgrace, like she'd been fingerpainting. He straightened up a picture on the wall above the fireplace. Davina looked younger than he remembered. Scruffy, certainly, but definitely younger. And annoyingly carefree.

Davina was feeling suddenly nervous, alone with her husband for the first time since Laetitia's funeral. She kept thinking of the vile letters they'd been sending each other through their respective solicitors, and the wounding, unjust things he'd said about her. She wondered whether she should kiss him hello, and decided best not.

Instead, she said, 'I've made you Earl Grey. I hope that's still what you like?'

'Actually I don't think I've got time,' Miles replied, sounding uncommonly flustered. 'I need to be changed and at the Dorchester in under an hour.'

He had seen more than enough already.

60.

Are you happy darling? You'd tell me if you weren't?' Dawn was mixing James a drink in the first-floor drawing room of their Cadogan Square flat.

'Very happy. No complaints whatever,' replied her lover, wincing slightly at being asked such a direct and personal question. A low evening sun sent bright shafts through the nine sash windows and onto forty impeccably hung oil paintings. Dawn lowered the blinds to protect the Bacons, Hodgkins and Frank Stellas. This wonderful room, laterally converted across three first-floor apartments, sometimes seemed more like an art gallery than a home, and came with awesome responsibilities. Hardly a day went by without an overseas curator, art historian or expert from an auction house requesting to see the pictures, and Dawn quickly learnt to be selective or they'd never have got any one-on-one time together at all.

Sitting in his favourite chair, watching Dawn realign the magazines and auction catalogues on the coffee table, James felt he was a fortunate man indeed. Little by little, his grief over Laetitia had abated, and he knew this owed everything to Dawn. Her arrival miraculously put an end to the disruption and desolation of his wife's death. He still missed Laetitia deeply but, if he were honest, there had lately been a blurring between the old and new regimes. It could almost be said to be business as usual. Looking at her now, it could have been Laetitia sitting there. They dressed very similarly and Dawn was sipping a Dubonnet and soda which had been Laetitia's own favourite drink. She even smelt like Laetita, wearing the same scent, and lit the same rose-fragranced candles in the bathroom. James was no expert, but he could almost swear Dawn's hair colour had turned more like his wife's.

And, of course, it was wonderful having someone to organise his life again and keep in touch with his office. Dawn was awfully good at it, just as Laetitia had been, handling those awkward conversations with chefs and gardeners that James dreaded. Dawn was more formal with staff than Laetitia, James noticed, saying, 'Lord Pendleton wants you to do such-and-such,' and 'Lord Pendleton would like you to bring the car round to the front immediately,' which was laying it on a bit thick, but she'd learn. The previous weekend when they'd been flying out to Venice for the Biennale, Dawn had become stressed in the queue to check-in and complained when some economy passengers were looked after ahead of them. 'Excuse *me*,' Dawn had said. '*Lord* Pendleton and I are travelling in *first*. I think we have priority.' James calmed her down and apologised to everyone, but it embarrassed him. Next weekend they were off to Salzburg for the music.

Dawn's passion for classical music grew all the time, and she already talked about continuing Laetitia's charity work bringing cultural events to inner-city schools. She was planning on holding her first committee meeting in the library at Longparish Priory at some time in the autumn.

James was impressed by her single-minded fervour for the higher things in life. Just occasionally, he wished she could be less inflexible about it all. When he asked to see the musical *Billy Elliot* as his birthday treat, Dawn was discouraging and took him to the Royal Festival Hall to listen to Mozart instead.

In Greg's opinion, the democratic process was getting way out of hand. He had been as good as told by his mates at Millbank the seat was his for the asking, but this was the third weekend of the selection process and it was dragging on and on, with no end in sight. He was fed up being cross-questioned by self-important Droitwich borough councillors, who seemed to expect him to be impressed by them and banged *ad infinitum* about local politics, as if he cared. He wanted to say, 'For fuck's sake, *Tony* and *Gordon* want me to have this seat. What is your problem, comrades? It's going to happen, so stop pissing about.'

He was fed up staying at the bed and breakfast run by the constituency agent's sister. They'd been given the same bedroom three

Saturdays in a row and Greg had come to despise the pink acrylic bedcover, the corn dolly in the fireplace, the paper-thin walls and two different patterned wallpapers on opposite walls. Not to mention the breakfast ritual with a choice of tinned juices, pineapple or tomato, followed by Ricicles or Freeza Mart Flakes and finally the heaving Full English. Greg would have moved to the big Edwardian hotel on the main square which looked a lot plusher, but Mollie thought it'd be impolite and prejudice his chances with the committee.

Mollie, needless to say, hadn't put a foot wrong all through the process. Whenever Greg threatened to say something cutting—like when the Mayor banged on about what a diamond bloke John Prescott was, and how he'd always had this sneaking respect for Mrs Thatcher despite him being a lifelong Labour man—Mollie headed him off and made things ok. To his amazement, Mollie genuinely seemed to connect with these people and chatted away about their kids, local schools and hospitals. The delivery of state education and health were two of Greg's buzztopics—he'd helped develop party policy on 'the knowledge economy' going forward—but that didn't mean he wanted to hear how Mandy and Darren were coping with their GCSEs or about the waiting list for hernia ops in Droitwich General Hospital.

As he'd predicted before their wedding, Mollie's job as a state sector teacher was playing brilliantly with the committee. One of them was a headteacher herself, and Greg quickly antagonised the contrary old bat, but Mollie was winning her round with staff-room banalities and agreeing with her how Ofsted's league tables (one of Greg's pet enthusiasms) were demoralising under-resourced schools. When the chair of the committee asked him a difficult question about his experience of 'disenfranchised local kids, you coming from London and having no kids yourself,' it was Mollie who had chimed in, reminding the committee Greg had been born and raised in the West Midlands and how both Greg and she came from broken families, their parents having split up, so they could easily empathise with people in similar situations. And then Greg, who seldom mentioned his connection to Ross or Freeza Mart, gave an emotional speech about his dad's commitment to providing cheap food for decent hardworking socialist families, and how he'd persuade Freeza Mart to pay for the refurbishment of the local swimming baths if he was given the opportunity to represent the constituency. At the end of the session everyone applauded and Mollie said afterwards how brilliant he'd been, and told him she loved being married to such an inspirational idealist.

On the train back to London, having secured the nomination and celebrating with wine in the buffet carriage, Mollie felt wonderfully fulfilled and happy, and amorously suggested to the prospective Member of Parliament for Droitwich and Redditch they should consider starting a family of their own.

'No way,' Greg replied. 'I've got a constituency to nurse now. I'm going to need your total support every weekend meeting the voters. We won't have any time for kids.'

61.

This may sound strange,' Dawn told Serena as they sat together on the terrace at Longparish Priory drinking midmorning coffee, 'but I already feel I've lived here for years. I feel so *settled*. Though there's so much that wants doing. I've been telling James, there's so much untapped potential for the estate.'

Serena was fascinated to see her friend for almost the first time in eight months. Dawn did, indeed, look fully at ease in her new life as the *de facto* chatelaine of the Pendleton seat. Where once she had been awed by her predecessor and by the unattainable perfection of everything she undertook, Dawn now regarded Laetitia and her legacy with less tolerance. As she became more familiar with the set-up, she identified guest bedrooms, and particularly bathrooms, that urgently needed updating, and found herself surprised Laetitia had let things slide. Serena was already working with Dawn on several new schemes.

'If you could bring us a little more warm milk, Lagdon,' Dawn instructed her butler. 'And Mrs Harden might like to be offered an Elizabeth Shaw mint.'

'No chocolates, I mustn't,' Serena said quickly. 'I'm watching my weight.'

'One does have to be vigilant,' Dawn agreed. 'James has put on a little weight too. I blame myself, I've been feeding him up. So I've told chef to exclude cream from every dish.'

'This view . . . and the garden . . . it's heaven,' Serena said, taking in the immaculate borders and parkland beyond, gently sloping to the banks of the Test. Every tree was perfectly formed like illustrations in a children's encyclopedia. Artfully placed between the horse chestnut trees she could see the stone doughnuts of a Henry Moore and the pitted bronze torso of an Elizabeth Frink.

'Oh, don't look too carefully,' Dawn implored. 'It all needs sorting out. I've told James, though he still needs persuading, he's quite a sentimental old thing in some ways. But I've had several top garden designers over and they agree with me. We're going to strip out all the beds this autumn and start again. And take them organic. I gave James an article about Prince Charles to read and all his wonderful ideas. My long-term plan is to take the whole estate organic.'

'And James agrees?'

'Oh, he doesn't know yet. But they've always supported organic at his family supermarkets, so we should do it here too. I've already told the head gardener to take the vegetable garden organic.'

'And what news of the children?' Serena asked.

Dawn looked momentarily uncomfortable. 'Well, it hasn't been easy,' she said. 'I freely admit that. Gemma's taken it very hard. It probably just needs time, that's what I keep telling myself. She's been down here to visit with Archie and Mandy, she knows she's got a standing invitation. But I know she wishes Ross and I were still together.'

'And how about the others? Debbie and Greg?'

'Oh, Debs is fine about it now, I think. She wasn't at first, of course. She's working for Ross. I hear she's doing very well, though obviously I haven't heard Ross's view. We don't speak much these days. I don't know if you've seen him at all?'

'Oh, once or twice, here and there,' Serena replied vaguely. She decided to play down Ross's frequent visits to the cottage in case Dawn thought she was taking his side. 'He seems fine. Working very hard.'

'He's always worked hard. That was part of the problem. Work always took priority.'

'And what about Greg and his politics? I heard he found a seat.'

'Yes, he's going to be an elected Member of Parliament after the next General Election.'

'A constituency somewhere up in the West Midlands, isn't it?'

'Droitwich and Redditch. Where Ross's family came from originally. Well, it's quite an achievement for him, I must say. Though I
wish he wasn't standing for Labour.'

'Really? I thought you supported them yourself?'

'Oh, no,' Dawn replied quickly. 'It was Ross who was for Labour, I'm a lifelong Conservative. James donates a great deal of
money to the party every year. Privately, of course. Pendletons plc
supports all the parties equally, they have to be even-handed.'

'All the same, it'll be exciting having a son in Parliament. He
might introduce you to Tony Blair.'

'That's what I said to Greg. James has met Tony several times, of
course, being a Captain of Industry. I can't wait to meet him. I can't
help rather liking him, even though he's Labour and has that awful
pushy wife. But Greg doesn't have much time for Tony Blair, he's
keener on Gordon Brown. He wants him to take over, and Mollie
does too which surprises me.'

'How is Mollie? She used to be such an awkward unhappy thing,
her father was always beastly to her. But now she's got away from
Miles, I've heard she's blossomed.'

'She and Greg came down for Sunday lunch recently.' Dawn
looked mildly anxious at the memory. 'Greg was being very tricky
all day, getting at James about every little thing. Thank heavens
Mollie was there too. And Hugh. They got on like a house on fire,
which was lovely and rather saved the situation.'

Peter could hardly believe he was finally holding the CD in his
hand: an actual, finished, pressed CD of *The Cormorant's Cry* in its
plastic jewel case, with the printed sleeve and lyrics inside the box.
The record company had couriered four copies to Scotland and a
Fedex van driven sixty miles to deliver it. He removed the disc
from the case and slipped it into his laptop and, what's more, it
played. The opening track, 'Keeping it Real,' echoed around the sitting room . . . 'The lobster farmer with his creel . . . in wind and
rain, he keeps it real.'

He played the album right through, then in euphoria rang Davina and told her, then tried Sam, Archie and Mollie. Sam was
down in London on a Freeza Mart shoot, so no change there, she
seemed to spend every third week in London these days. Her mo-

bile went straight to voicemail so he left a message. Archie was out at a meeting, so he tried Gemma and talked to her for ages and she said she'd order a CD on Amazon right away. The more he'd got to know Gemma the more he liked her, and he hoped Archie was being kind to her; somehow, he doubted it. Finally he tried Mollie on her mobile who picked up on the third ring and said she was attending an inter-school sports event near Droitwich, meeting Greg's voters, as she put it. Greg was in Hammersmith at a policy forum, so she was flying the flag on his behalf.

'Is it ok? Being up there on your own, I mean?'

'Fine. I'm getting used to it, and I've met some nice people. I didn't know this part of England before, so it's interesting. Different to Hampshire.'

He told her about the CD arriving and she was sweetly overjoyed. 'I've got a rock star for a brother. The kids at school are going to be so impressed. It'll do wonders for my cred.'

'Oh yeah? Rock star's pushing it a bit. It'll probably sell about twenty copies.'

'No, it won't. I'm buying thirty-four for starters. One for every kid in my class. Plus a copy for us, of course. Actually, maybe I should buy one for every voter in the constituency, or do you think they'd say it was bribery. What do you reckon?'

'It might jeopardise Greg's chances . . . if they hated the music.'

'Of course they won't, it's great. Remember Italy? I was the one who always said you'd make it. You're the new James Blunt.'

'Thanks, Mollie. I do *not* want to be the new James Blunt, thanks very much. Nick Drake maybe, but not James Blunt.'

'What's wrong with the new Peter Straker?'

'Nothing. Except it's Pete Straker now. That's what they've called me on the CD. Pete sounds more real, apparently. It was my record company's idea.'

'Pete then. It'll take some getting used to, Peter. I mean Pete.'

Peter laughed. 'I think *you're* still allowed to call me Peter. It's just my stage name, as it were.'

'Greg'll be pleased anyway. He's always banging on about how the Strakers are too posh and we've got posh names. I have to call myself Moll up here, which I hate.'

'He makes you do that?'

'And I'm not allowed to say we're from Hampshire. That's too posh as well. We say Hammersmith or Shepherds Bush. And of course we never mention Chawbury—Chawbury Manor or Chawbury Park. Or Dad working for the Tories.'

'Your husband's a clown, you know that.'

'He's not actually. He's doing it all for good reason. He wants to be an MP so he can change things, make things better for ordinary people.'

Peter grunted.

'He really does,' Mollie insisted. 'I know what he's like, he's really sincere about it. It's like you with your music. You're both idealists, just in different ways.'

62.

Almost everyone at Freeza Mart House knew something was going on, but very few were in on the secret. Those that were paced the corridors with mysterious smug expressions designed to prove they were part of the magic inner circle. Delegations of investment bankers, M&A specialists and corporate lawyers got out of the lifts on the corporate floor, from where they were collected and ushered into Ross's presence. Ross himself arrived earlier and earlier at the office and stayed later, regularly leaving not much before midnight. The night watchman in the underground car park complained he'd never known such comings and goings, and he couldn't concentrate on his television for people expecting him to open and close the security gates.

Debbie, who had been told nothing, was aware only of a sharply increased demand for property leaseback reports and projections, which must be completed to ever shorter deadlines. When she asked her dad what was up, Ross shrugged and said, 'Sorry love, I can't comment. If anything's happening, you'll find out soon enough.' Archie, as number three now in Investor Relations and Corporate Communications, was one of only a dozen executives in on the plan, and felt daily more self-important. When Gemma asked why he was getting home so late, and peered at him suspiciously, he said, 'Sorry Gems, my lips are sealed. Your dad will kill me if I breathe a word.'

As weeks passed and the plan progressed, higher and higher levels of security were put in place. Meetings with bankers no longer took place at Freeza Mart, but at safehouses in Mayfair or in hotel conference rooms, the more anonymous the better, at the Millenium

Hotel in Grosvenor Square or in a suite at the Carlton Tower. It was recommended Ross's office be swept for bugs in advance of the announcement, and this process be repeated on a regular basis. The press releases and communiqués Archie worked on with his department, and with the advisors from Goldman Sachs, were not allowed to be printed off the system, and enhanced firewalls and security codes were installed by an external IT company that specialised in counterespionage.

At the centre of everything was Ross, presiding over every meeting, micro-managing each detail, challenging every assumption and step of the plan. Goldman Sachs had their senior retail managing director leading the team, supported by a scarily bright vice president, three associates all with MBAs and two analysts fresh out of university. Within two weeks they'd generated Excel spreadsheets, thousands of pages long, tabulating both the Freeza Mart and Pendletons businesses, with every store and lease as well as cashflow and overhead. They were now working on a computer module to demonstrate how an amalgamated business, with combined revenue but much lower overheads, would be so compelling. 'We have to anticipate *everything*,' Ross told his executive group at their daily strategy update. 'However they react, whatever they say or do, we must have thought of it first and got all our ducks lined up in a row. Remember, we're barely forty percent their size, in revenues anyway, and their advisors will be every bit as smart as our own. They're going to resist us every step of the way. The only way we're going to pull this thing off is by being that bit smarter and not screwing up.'

As an exercise designed to sharpen their perception of enemy tactics, four Goldman bankers devised a shadow defence strategy for the target, including every piece of mud they might conceivably throw at Freeza Mart. 'Make no mistake, it's going to get dirty,' Ross predicted. At the same time, he detailed Archie's Communications team to compile briefings on every member of the target's board of directors, including all non-execs and advisors, but concentrating on the four Pendleton brothers and their families. 'I'm giving you guys a week to pull it together,' Ross told them. 'Then I want every last detail: strengths, weaknesses, whatever you can find. Political leanings, friends in high places, journalists and business editors likely to take one side or another, pro or anti. Anything in fact, the good as well as bad. Got that?'

Archie nodded.

'Grand. You can present your findings next Friday at eight thirty a.m.'

After everyone had left his office, Ross opened the bottom drawer of his desk and retrieved the leather-framed photograph he knew was inside. It was an A3 colour picture of Dawn taken out riding at Chawbury. For years, the picture had sat on the window sill in his office, but after she'd left him he'd put it away in the drawer.

Looking at it, he felt a furious desire to get even.

James Pendleton may have stolen his wife, but now he was going to steal James's family company.

The Cormorant's Cry had been out for six weeks but, as Peter gloomily told Sam, you wouldn't really know it was out at all. It had made no waves. Nor was it available in any record shops so far as he could tell. There was no record outlet in Durness, so he'd driven over to Scrabster, then down to Wick, in the hope of seeing his CD on sale, but the supermarkets sold only the top twenty and mindless compilations, and he'd returned to the cottage feeling downhearted. To make matters worse, Mollie and Gemma both went into HMV and Virgin Megastores in London and couldn't find a copy either, and Mollie said there weren't any in WHSmith or Tesco in Droitwich.

He pestered the record company, but the sales department stopped taking his calls. Phoebe in publicity said she'd asked around but couldn't get anyone interested in writing anything. The CD had been sent out for review but, so far, nothing had materialised. 'All the space is going to Coldplay,' reported Phoebe. 'And Westlife are reforming.' So far as anyone knew, not one track from the album had been played on any radio station. It was desperately disappointing.

'I might as well not have bothered,' Peter told his sisters. 'It's not like I was expecting to be number one or anything, I'm not naïve. But I did hope it'd get *played* at least a bit, and get some reviews. It's sunk without trace.'

'Probably just needs time,' Mollie said, trying to cheer him up. 'The people who've bought it are bound to love it, and they'll be playing it all the time, and their friends will hear it and want it too. It'll be a word of mouth thing.'

'I wish I thought you were right. The thing is, you can't buy it anywhere, it isn't *for sale*, it's not in any shops. So no one can buy it even if they wanted to, which they won't because they've never heard of it, because it's not on any playlists. That's the truth.'

'It must be in *some* record shops, surely.'

'Maybe one in the Portobello Road. Probably on a barrow.'

Mollie sighed. 'That's so annoying for you, and so stupid, it's such a brilliant record. I'm playing it all the time in the car. And the kids in my class like it too. I told you I gave them all copies.'

'I'm amazed you could find any. Where did you?'

'Well, actually, direct from the record company. I went round to their office and bought them there. They said that would be easiest.'

'You see.'

'Well, try not to get depressed. I love the album. So does Sam. She's got it on her iPod.'

Peter laughed. 'It's probably the only thing you two have in common—saying you like my music. It's very sweet. Thanks, Mollie.'

63.

The news of Freeza Mart's hostile takeover bid for Pendletons electrified the financial markets. At 8.00 a.m. precisely the offer was announced in the stock market and the offer document posted, an immense wodge of paper with laminated covers, 140 pages long including 36 pages of appendices. The takeover was the lead story on the lunchtime television news across all channels, and the headline in that afternoon's *Evening Standard* with a front page photograph of Ross taken on the roof of Freeza Mart House, and a photograph of James being collected from outside his flat in Cadogan Square by his chauffeur. Ross looked marvellously confident in his picture, with the skyscape of London unfolding behind him. James looked harassed by the press attention, as though he'd been caught on the hop, which indeed he had been, having had not the slightest forewarning. He had, in fact, intended to spend the morning with his curator, assessing whether or not to bid for various paintings at the forthcoming Sotheby's Contemporary sale in New York.

Dawn was being driven up from Hampshire when the story broke, and remained blissfully unaware for the whole journey being immersed in classical music. She had set herself the task of listening to the complete works of all the great composers, concerto by concerto, so there would be no gaps in her cultural education. They were driving round Chiswick roundabout when she spotted the *Evening Standard* poster on a garage forecourt: 'Freeza Mart in Pendletons takeover drama.' At first, she assumed it was Pendletons taking over Freeza Mart, rather than the other way round, and felt cross with James that he hadn't told her. But when she read the story, she was aghast. How could Ross possibly make such a fool of himself? And he might have warned her, because this was going to be very awkward for her personally. At noon, she read, the Board of Pendletons had announced its rejection of the offer.

By the evening, *Newsnight* had put together a twenty minute segment about the bid, heavily biased towards Freeza Mart in the opinion of Dawn who watched it with James and Hugh in the book-lined study where the television lived. The whole angle of the report was anti-Pendletons, saying they'd missed out on growth opportunities and lacked a strong management team. A helicopter had hovered above several of the Pendleton family's homes, including Longparish Priory, filming the magnificence of their houses, and Dawn could actually see herself sitting on the terrace in her sunhat, reading a newspaper, so the film must have been made several days ago. Ross was interviewed in his office explaining why he'd decided to make the bid, and how he'd enhance shareholder value. 'I'm sorry to say they've taken their eye off the ball at Pendletons. They've been asleep at the wheel, and have developed no digital strategy.' The tone of the interview with Ross was laudatory, and he was allowed to speak unchallenged about his revenue growth and market share gains. Watching his father peering at the screen, Hugh saw James flinch again and again, hating their business results being interrogated and criticised so publicly, and hating his home, and the homes of his brothers, being paraded across the television. For James it had been a hideously uncomfortable day in every way. Ross had rung him out of courtesy to inform him about the bid, but James didn't feel he'd handled the conversation well, still feeling awkward about the Dawn situation. When one of their advisors had spoken about a 'dawn raid,' James's first thought was of his wife. And then his telephone had started ringing and never stopped, with rival bankers calling to offer their services, which James considered opportunism at its worst, and all his brothers ringing constantly, and the press asking for a reaction. And then there were all his non-execs wanting to muscle in and give their advice, and talking about their corporate and fiduciary responsibilities, and frankly he just wished they'd all go away.

After the *Newsnight* film, several 'industry experts' were brought on for a debate, including a dreary representative from the British

Retail Consortium and two city editors from the newspapers. Almost all of them seemed broadly supportive of Ross's bid even though, as the man from the *Financial Times* pointed out, it would be a 'David and Goliath' fight, with David picking on a giant twice his size. 'Logic dictates Freeza Mart shouldn't be able to pull this one off,' he said. 'But I don't know that logic will be the deciding factor.'

The moment the item ended, the phone rang and it was Miles. 'That was a *disgrace*, a travesty,' he stormed. 'The first thing I shall be doing is putting in a formal complaint to Ofcom. The BBC have contravened their charter obligation for impartiality. I don't know who's working their PR, but they've pulled a blinder. That footage of your house, James, it can only have come from Ross's side, they must have handed it to the TV people. Outrageous. To overfly a private house belonging to someone like yourself . . . totally irresponsible. Don't worry, we shall be filing a formal complaint to the Press Complaints Commission about that.'

'I wouldn't bother complaining about the house being filmed,' James began.

'I'm sorry, but I *do* bother. I notice we weren't shown Ross's enormous house, that blot on the landscape at the end of my valley.' Then, suddenly remembering Dawn had helped commission the place, he backed off and said, 'Well, the whole programme was a farce but don't worry, James, we've already put a rebuttal team in place. I've got sixteen people working round the clock at Straker Communications and we're drafting more in as we speak. Believe me, they won't be getting a free ride from here on. The fightback has started. We've already begun work with Deutsche Bank on the defence document. We've got fourteen days to produce it and it's going to be very feisty, don't you worry. I've spoken personally to six of the thirteen national newspaper editors and three proprietors so far. And over the next few days we'll be putting quite a few people right about Ross Clegg. He's not going to be looking so pleased with himself when it all starts coming out, I can assure you.'

Amidst all the drama, everyday business still had to go on, as Ross constantly reminded his managers. Distracted as he was by interviews on the *Today* programme, video conferences with fund managers and institutions, and constant demands for quotes from the newspaper business sections, he still tried to put in five hours a day of 'proper work,' as he described it, keeping on top of sales and epos data and meeting with the Freeza Mart logistics team. But he recognised that by far the most important two hours was the 8am 'morning prayers,' the daily war cabinet with his advisors and inner circle. Each meeting opened with a briefing from Investor Relations and Corporate Communications, who presented a digest of the morning's newspapers and radio and television comment. Each item was categorised as friendly, unhelpful or neutral. So far, friendly pieces outweighed hostile ones by five to one, though Archie and his bosses did not expect this to last. 'Straker Communications are being very proactive,' they reported. 'They're fixing up interviews all over the place. Even family members who *never* speak to the press are being touted around town, like Michael Pendleton and even Otto. You're going to see a mass of pro-Pendleton propaganda coming out in the next few weeks.'

After that, the group was updated on investor sentiment. Freeza Mart's bankers, accompanied by Ross himself or by Ross's finance director, Heather Smail, were touring as many institutions as would agree to see them, making their case for the takeover and talking up the efficiencies and enhanced purchasing muscle it would bring. It was part of Freeza Mart's argument that Pendletons had fallen behind in its IT development and lacked precision in stock control and logistics. 'They have some of the best retail sites in the country,' Ross repeated again and again, 'but they're not capitalising on the advantage. An integrated business could add four or five percentage points to the operating margin. And the first thing we'll do is sell and leaseback all the property, the whole damn portfolio, every store, Pendletons's head office, the lot, releasing hundreds of millions in shareholder value.'

In one area only, Ross was unwilling to go for the jugular. His PR team—and Archie in particular—urged him to attack the Pendleton family personally. 'They're sitting targets,' Archie argued in a presentation on the subject. For almost an hour, he gave a Power-Point briefing on each of the Pendleton brothers, their respective inherited shareholdings, homes all over the world, art collections, racehorses, and collections of high performance and classic cars.

Photographs had been sourced of yachts bobbing in the marinas of Cannes and Sardinia, evidence of their unfitness to run a major supermarket group, and even of their wives and partners. Ross flinched when a photograph of Dawn flashed up onto the screen. 'That's enough, Archie,' he said. 'I'm sorry, but I don't want to go down this route. I know James Pendleton personally and he's a decent bloke, I won't say anything different. And I don't want any-one on our team being disrespectful about them either.'

'But, Ross,' Archie persisted. 'We've got this whole strategy worked out. It's going to be, like, this northern self-made hero on the one hand, versus all these effete toffs and pooftahs blowing gazil-lions on modern art. Which would you rather buy your loo paper from?'

'Forget it. No way am I approving that. And, for the record, I don't actually come from the north country, I'm from the West Midlands. And before you say 'same thing,' you might like to take a look at a map and figure out where our great industrial cities are located.'

'Ross, I'm telling you, it's a great PR angle.'

'No. And that's my final word. If we can't make our arguments and win this thing without resorting to personal abuse, I'd rather not win and carry on as we are. Understood?'

Archie nodded sullenly, but seemed unconvinced.

At midday, Ross joined his marketing people in the ninth floor meeting room where a photocall and press day had been set up for the media to interact with Freeza Mart's brand ambassadors. The seven girls including Sam had become famous almost overnight, following the launch of the first multi-platform campaign. Wher-ever you looked, their faces loomed down at you from billboards. The media buying agency had snapped up half the sites on the ap-proach roads in to Central London, including ten on the Cromwell Road opposite Tesco, to push the new fashion range. Half a dozen West End tube stations, including Oxford Street, were temporarily 'owned' by Freeza Mart, with every platform and escalator plas-tered with their posters. Glasgow and Newcastle undergrounds received the same treatment. All the bus sides in Manchester, Leeds and Birmingham were covered with them too. Archie was massively excited by the campaign, telling everyone, 'the blonde with small tits is my sister,' though he complained when a sixty-sheet billboard went up in Roupell Street bang opposite their cottage. 'I can't even shag my girlfriend without seeing my sister's big face through the window.'

Magazines like *Glamour* and *Marie Claire* carried eight-page promotions pushing the FM brand and ran contests to win key pieces from the first collection. But it was probably the television commercial which most quickly captured the public's imagination, with its saucy catchphrase, 'I'm a Freeza kinda girl . . . just kiddin',' with a knowing backwards glance over the shoulder.

Whenever Sam walked down the street, teenagers pursued her shouting, 'just kiddin'.' It was an enormous relief to escape back to Scotland where the campaign hadn't penetrated.

Today, however, she was back in town for the photocall and press day, and as usual it all seemed a bit unreal, sitting on stage with the six other girls, answering random questions from the media.

'Hey, Sam, what's your favourite piece from the collection?'

'Er, probably the button-front sundress for six pounds . . . but it's all nice actually.'

'Sam, are you girls really all best friends, or is it just for show?'

'We get on great together. We always have a good laugh on shoots.'

She spotted Ross standing at the back surrounded by his PR people including Archie, and Debbie who'd come down from her own floor to watch. Ross smiled at her and gave a thumbs-up. He looked tired but full of energy still, clearly running on adrenalin. It would be several more weeks before the takeover was decided. Few of the big institutions had come out one way or the other so far, and Pendletons were due to issue their defence document in the coming few days.

After forty minutes of questions, Sam's attention began to wander. She'd been listening to Peter's music on her iPod on the flight down, and couldn't get it out of her head. It was stuck there in a loop. Even now, having heard it for so many months, she found many of the tracks addictive. It should have been a big hit, Sam reckoned.

Afterwards, standing by the table for coffee and a Danish, and chatting to Ross, Archie and Debbie, she gave Debbie a listen to her iPod.

'It's *fantastic*,' Debbie said after a bit. 'Really, really amazing. And I'm not just saying that because it's Peter.' She went very quiet, then said, 'Dad, I've had an idea. Can I drop by and talk to you about it later on?'

64.

iles felt personally affronted. Each time he saw a picture of Ross, which at the moment was several dozen times a week since you couldn't open a newspaper without confronting his cocky face, he erupted. 'This impertinent, mendacious, opportunist bid,' was how he described it over lunches and dinners. His rota of meals with politicians, regulators and opinion formers reached new heights, at which he briefed against the proposed merger, citing consumer choice, abuse of monopoly position, corporate governance issues, spurious diversity issues and anything else he could come up with that might strike a chord. If all else failed, he fell back on 'character issues,' implying Ross was unstable ('His wife, Dawn, recently walked out on him, and I'm afraid an awful lot of bad stuff is going to come out') and contrasting him with the public-spirited, philanthropic Pendletons. Most of the people he lobbied never entered a Freeza Mart from one year to the next, so he painted a picture of filthy aisles and food past its sell-by date ('They've been fined more than once') and 'one of the worst corporate responsibility records in the country.'

But, most of all, Miles felt afraid for his own business. If Ross prevailed, and Straker Communications lost the Pendletons account, it would leave a gaping hole in his results. Not only was Pendletons his most profitable account, it was also one of the most prestigious and acted as a magnet for other wins too. For more than twenty years the fortunes of Straker Communications had been inextricably intertwined with Pendletons plc. In his vainer, madder moments he saw himself as the fifth Pendleton brother, so closely did he identify with the family. That all this might come to an end thanks to Ross Clegg was something terrible to contemplate, and he would resist it by every means at his disposal.

It did not help that he kept seeing giant posters of Samantha aiding and abetting the opposition. Between his office in Mayfair and Pendletons's Barbican headquarters, he passed no fewer than nine super-sized billboards starring his daughter in cheap clothes. One of his new lines of attack, unleashed over his lunches, was that Freeza Mart manufactured its fashion range using sweatshops and child labour. There was no proof of this, but Miles wouldn't put anything past Ross. He had recently dispatched an investigator and photographer to China and Sri Lanka to sniff about.

As for Sam, he admitted she looked very fetching on the posters and, under normal circumstances, and a different client, he might have been quite proud of her. But modelling for Ross was an act of treachery. To have a daughter prepared to demean herself in this way was something he found personally abhorrent.

Meanwhile, the public relations strategy he devised for the Pendletons became subtler and more sophisticated. He realised the qualities he most admired in the Pendletons—their impressive houses and money—were the same qualities most liable to condemn them. And so he organised articles that saluted their artistic philanthropy (The Saturday *Telegraph* magazine published a piece about six sculptors and carpenters who had benefited from Pendleton bursaries) and sought to suppress anything that hinted at their wealth. At the same time, he organised for journalists to be flown above Chawbury Park and photograph Ross's huge home from the sky. Newspapers were supplied with pictures of Ross in shooting clothes carrying a sleeved shotgun and cartridge bag, to imply he was a greater toff than any Pendleton. The photographs duly appeared and doubtless did some damage, but Miles understood that investor sentiment was continuing to shift towards Ross. If he was to avert catastrophe, he must raise his game.

Peter and Sam stood in the cheese and dairy aisle of Freeza Mart in Scrabster, allowing the music to waft over them. It was unbelievably exciting. Sam looked round at the other customers, seeking a reaction, but they continued loading up their trolleys, seemingly oblivious to *The Cormorants Cry* broadcast over the in-store tannoy.

Peter's voice sounded wonderfully mellow as the lyrics reverberated around the superstore.

'Well, Debbie wasn't exaggerating then,' Peter said. 'They really are playing it.'

'And, just think, it's playing in all the other Freeza Marts too, at this exact moment. According to Debbie, four million people will have heard it by Sunday night.'

Peter laughed. 'All that time I was writing songs, I imagined them being played on the radio, not in a supermarket. But you know something, I like it. It feels good.'

They had driven along the coast road from the cottage to the recently-opened Freeza Mart, the largest superstore in Scrabster, a cavernous shed right by the ferry port overlooking the North Sea. Seagulls wheeled and shrieked on the quay outside. 'Ten o'clock is when they ought to begin playing it,' Debbie had said. 'Depends how good local compliance is, but a head office directive has gone out to all stores. They're supposed to play it five times a day, the whole album, for a week. Call me if it doesn't happen. In fact, call me anyway. I'd love to know.'

'It's just so kind of Debbie,' Peter said, as he'd been saying every day since she'd come up with the idea. 'I really owe her one.'

'I told you, she loves the music. I mean, really loves it. I couldn't get my iPod back, I had to pull it off her head.'

'And nice of Ross, too.'

'Oh, he likes it as well. Debs played it to him in his office, when she was selling him the idea. He thinks it's great. If this works, they might do it with other new records, it's like a test.'

Peter's voice, singing 'The Secret Trapped Inside,' echoed around household products.

At checkout, paying for their groceries, Sam said to the cashier, 'This music's really great. What is it, do you know?'

'You're the third person this morning to ask,' she replied. 'He's a new one on me—Pete Straker, that's the name. It's on promotion in the music and DVD section, if you're interested.'

'You should sell them next to the till,' Sam said.

Miles set up three lunches in a row and was looking forward to none of them. It was an indication of how pessimistic he'd become recently that he had to resort to such desperate measures. The Pend-leton brothers seemed sanguine, but the people who surrounded them—their managers and loved ones—were starting to panic and to point the finger of blame at Straker Communications for failing to get their message across. The defence document, upon which so much hope was pinned, had been tepidly received, despite its tren-chant language. 'Reject Freeza Mart's Offer,' urged the Board, speaking of this 'unsolicited and unwelcome offer which substan-tially undervalues your company.' It went on to praise Pendletons's 'strong management team with a clear and focused strategy, excep-tional growth prospects, outstanding track record and financial per-formance and global leadership in attractive markets. The Board therefore has no hesitation in advising shareholders to reject the offer.' Miles had hoped the defence document would stop Ross dead in his tracks, but the momentum behind him was alarming. Only this morning, Dawn called Miles at his office agitated at having watched Ross on GMTV's breakfast business news 'spouting com-plete rubbish about how well he's doing, and all the ditzy inter-viewer did was nod her big head agreeing with him.' Worse, two of Ross's most high profile supporters, Brin Watkins and Callum Dun-lop, both came out strongly for him on a Bloomberg investor fo-rum, saying they'd built up positions in Pendletons which they planned to vote behind the takeover.

At his regular backs-to-the-wall banquette table at Mark's Club, Miles bought lunch for Dick Gunn and was already regretting sit-ting alongside rather than opposite him, since the space was uncom-fortably tight. In the intervening years since he'd last encountered Dick, during the Italian holiday when he'd kidnapped Samantha on his yacht *Gunnslinger II*, Dick had become even richer and more obese. The City pages were full of his exploits, adopting aggressive investment positions in a national garden centre chain, house-builder and roadside recovery service, before disposing of them again at high premiums. Miles had scarcely forgiven him for the seduction of his daughter, but needs must. Today, having ordered a dozen blue-shelled gulls eggs as a pre-starter, and made appropriately ad-miring remarks about the Gunn Partnership, Miles raised the pros-pect of Dick buying Pendletons stock. 'If you acquired, say, 4 or 5 percent of the company, and announced you'd be voting with the family to stay independent because you believe greater shareholder value will be created that way, that would be a highly satisfactory development.'

'I'm sure it would. For the Pendleton family. What's in it for me?'

'Ah,' replied Miles. 'Obviously I'll need to discuss that with James and the brothers. This is merely an exploratory chat, to gauge whether there's any interest on your side. But I don't think it would be exceeding my authority to promise a seat on the Pendletons board. And I think our friends in Whitehall might see their way to some . . . public recognition, given your remarkable contribution to the fitness of British industry over the past two decades.'

'What are you saying here? I'll get a knighthood if I back Pendletons?'

'I'm sure I said nothing of the sort,' Miles replied silkily. 'That would be most improper. But if you choose to read that implication into what we have discussed, that is entirely a matter for you.'

'I'll consider it,' said Dick. 'Five percent of the company, you say. What'll that set me back? Half a billion quid?' He shrugged. 'It's do-able. But do I give enough of a fuck to bother? That's the question.'

Greg Clegg was not, of course, the sort of man Miles would have considered lunching at Mark's Club, so instead arranged to take his son-in-law to an Italian restaurant named Don Barrollo in Hammersmith High Street. It occupied a basement beneath a bicycle shop.

Greg arrived by account cab from his council office two streets away and took in the restaurant. 'Not your usual style of place, is it, Miles?' he said. 'I hope the credit crunch isn't affecting your expense account?'

'Happily not. We're entirely unscathed. I thought it might be more convenient for you, if we met in your part of town.'

'So you're not hiding me away then? I reckoned you might be embarrassed to be seen out with a socialist.'

Miles replied with an affected laugh. 'Quite the opposite. I have several very distinguished Labour peers as clients. Though, if the polls are to be believed, we'll have a change of government before long. It doesn't look so good for your friend Gordon.'

Greg gave a knowing little sneer. 'I think you'll find rumours of our demise are greatly exaggerated. There's a lot of difference between mid-term council elections and a freak by-election, and a General Election. Our focus groups show the wheels are already coming off the Cameron bus. People won't vote for a toff, not in a General Election.'

They ordered their food and Miles chose a Bulgarian red with Greg in mind, and enquired after Mollie. 'Fine, I think,' Greg replied. 'Teaching today at her school, of course. Then she's taking the train up to the constituency to attend a swimming gala. I can't make it unfortunately. Diary clash.'

'As a matter of fact, politics is one of the things I want to talk to you about, Greg. That and this great standoff between your father and James Pendleton, currently enriching so many investment bankers to their great delight.'

'My views on supermarkets are a matter of record. They're all as bad as eachother, one giant con, hiking prices while pretending to slash them. There's a case to be made for nationalising the lot.'

'Nevertheless, one side or the other is going to prevail in this takeover. May I take it you're rooting for Ross?' Miles asked leadingly, allowing the question to hang in the air.

'I told you, I really don't care. There's nothing to choose between them.'

'The reason I ask is, I've got a proposition to put to you. Rather an unusual one, and I'd be grateful if you heard me through before saying anything or interrupting.'

Greg shrugged.

'The thing is, Greg, I've always had a lot of time for you. I respect your integrity, which actually very closely matches the position of the modern Conservative Party, though it may surprise you to hear that. We've made a lot of progress under Dave and the others, and I think can genuinely lay claim these days to the ethical and environmental high ground. Which is where you come in. And I'm speaking now with two hats on—first as your father-in-law who naturally wishes you to reach your full potential in politics and public service. Secondly, as an occasional advisor, mentor, *eminence grise*, call me what you like, to the new Tory Party—a party I've to some small extent helped shape behind the scenes—which is anxious to attract all the talent it can in a big tent, non-tribal way. In some respects, you are the perfect new Tory candidate—idealistic and sceptical at the same time, exactly what we need. Your own man. So I thought I'd mention to you our local Member of Parliament for Mid-Hampshire, Ridley Nairn, will be standing down before the next election after twenty years in the House, and if you put your name forward I'm fairly certain you'll be successful. Particularly with my personal backing. Which I'd be only too happy to offer, both as my son-in-law and as a local man who's lived in the constituency for much of his life.'

Greg gave Miles a long appraising look, wondering whether this could be a trap.

'I'm absolutely serious, Greg. I've sounded out Paul Tanner, one of the party deputy chairmen, and he's given it his blessing. I'm assured you'll go straight onto the A List of approved candidates without having to jump through any hoops.'

'Well, this comes as a surprise,' Greg replied. 'It isn't something I've ever considered.' In this, he was being mildly disingenuous, since he had been worrying rather a lot about his prospects of winning the Droitwich and Redditch seat, with a majority of only 3,800, which would require only a 5 percent swing to the Tories to be overturned.

'And wouldn't the local selection committee have a fit if I'd defected over to you lot from Labour?'

'Ah,' replied Miles. 'I don't think we need worry overmuch about them. And it will be easy enough for you to demonstrate your independence of mind. If you speak out for Pendletons against your father in the matter of this takeover, that'll clinch it. James Pendleton is revered in the constituency. With so much goodwill behind you, you can't fail.'

Miles's third and final lunch was with Archie whom he hadn't spoken to for over a year. His son, unlike his son-in-law, was deemed worthy of the full Mark's Club treatment, and Miles appraised Archie critically as he swaggered into the upstairs bar with its deep sofas and Regency furniture. Tall, handsome and evidently fit, Miles liked what he saw, though the suit looked disconcertingly cheap and off-the-peg (it was part of the new Freeza Mart Hommes Plus menswear range) and the haircut too cocky.

'That isn't *gel* in your hair?'

'It keeps it in place, Dad. Got to look the part for business, you know.'

'Makes you look like Ross Clegg. He wears Brylcreem, used to. Ghastly.'

After that, Miles did his best to be affable to Archie, bathing him in charm and asking how his job was going and even, through gritted teeth, asking after Gemma.

'She's OK.'

'And you're still shacked up together behind Waterloo station? You'd have thought Ross would buy her somewhere more salubrious, with all the money he's made. Glass of champagne before lunch?'

Later, they went downstairs to the dining room where Miles insisted his son choose the richest and most expensive dishes on the menu, and ordered unusually good wine. 'This is my clever son,' he told the Polish waitresses in their white pinafores. 'I think we'll have to make him a member here soon, don't you?'

'Oh yes, Mr Straker. And can I offer you anything from the dessert trolley today? We have strawberry millefeuille, a very nice chocolate cake, some fresh raspberries very nice.'

'I must tell you,' Miles told Archie over the coffee, 'I'm proud of the job you're doing at work. I'm impressed.'

Archie was touched by the unexpected compliment. His relationship with his father had once been close, and he disliked their estrangement. Frequently, during domestic weekends cooped up in Roupell Street with Gemma and Mandy, he wondered what the hell he was doing there, when he'd much rather have been home at Chawbury.

'Thanks, Dad. I'm really getting into this whole corporate PR thing. It's interesting.'

'You've got a talent for it, which I suppose shouldn't really surprise us for obvious reasons . . .' Miles made an immodest bow of his head. 'I keep being told you're a natural.'

'Really? Thanks a lot!'

'Not many people get it, you know. Your brother never got it, not even after three years, didn't have a feel for it. Either you have it or you don't. Peter didn't, you obviously do.'

Archie was massively buoyed up by this flattery which, combined with the wine and the hushed gravitas of the dining room and fawning flunkies, made him feel privileged.

'The thing that concerns me, the fly in the ointment so to speak,' Miles continued, 'is you're on the wrong team, Archie. I mean over this Pendletons business, this ill-advised Freeza Mart adventure, barbarians at the gates of Paradise. You're on the wrong side. Batting against your family. I don't want to make too much of it, but Pendletons has been Strakers' biggest client for years, almost from the beginning. Everything we have as a family—Chawbury Manor, Holland Park Square, the people who look after us, our holidays, horses—it all derives, good part of it, from Pendletons's fees. Which is why it concerns me having you working for the enemy. After all, in the end, Straker Communications is going to come to you. After I'm gone, I mean, and I can't go on forever. It's going to be your inheritance, that's what I've always intended. So we need to be damned careful we don't damage the business in the meantime.'

Archie stared at his father, taking in what he'd said. 'You really mean I'd take over Strakers?'

'Certainly. Who else? I didn't spend my life building this thing up to see it leave the family. We've got plenty of good people inside the business, but they're managers not wealth creators. There's nobody I see as my successor. Whereas you've demonstrated a natural aptitude, working outside the family business. I can't pretend I'm happy you're working for the insufferable Clegg. To be honest, I'd be happy never to hear his name or see his face ever again. But I'm also proud of you for doing well there. It can't be a barrel of laughs working for a man like that, but you've stuck it out and full marks to you. And now you're ready to join the family business.'

'You think I should join now?'

'Why not? I don't mean start at the bottom like Peter—for all the good it did him—I mean join as a senior account director, step up to the Board next year, perhaps take over as MD the year after that. We'll kick Rick Partington upstairs as deputy chairman. I envisage you running the whole shooting match in three to four years.'

Archie looked at his father, to figure out whether he was kidding.

'Another reason we need to get you bedded down at Strakers sooner rather than later is Chawbury,' Miles said. 'What I mean is, the sooner you assume proper, senior responsibility in the company, the sooner you can be paid enough to enable you to run the house. Obviously Peter's never going to be able to afford to, not a hope. Mollie doesn't approve of big houses and Samantha's way off the rails. So you're going to have to step up to the plate and take over Chawbury too.'

Archie wondered whether he was dreaming. To inherit Chawbury—to have it ahead of Peter. Suddenly life's path was gloriously clear: Chairman of Straker Communications, Master of Chawbury Manor, sole heir to his dad.

'God, amazing. I'd love to join, yes please.'

'Well, I'm glad,' Miles replied. 'I thought you'd make the sensible decision. So all we need to finesse are the details, such as what and how to announce your appointment, and the setting of your renumeration.' He paused. 'Also, of course, now you're transferring your allegiance to the Pendletons' camp, it will be useful to hear everything they're saying over at Freeza Mart. All their strategies and so forth.'

For a moment, Archie looked uncomfortable.

'I think it's the least we can expect,' Miles said. 'Given what we've just been discussing.'

65.

t was four days after the record went on sale at Freeza Mart that
Peter took the call.

Debbie rang his mobile while he was driving into Durness, on a
stretch of road where there was actually a signal, and he almost
crashed the car at what she said. 'Peter? It's Debs. I've just seen the
early EPOS data and thought you'd like to hear how your record's
selling. It's amazing. We've shifted nearly 18,000 copies.'

'*How* many?'

'Eighteen thousand. Well, 17,657 to be precise. That's up until
ten p.m. last night. It averages out at about 25 CDs per store. Your
record company's reprinting. We've just ordered a further thirty
thousand.'

'God. That's quite good isn't it?'

'It's *massive*. Like, one of the five fastest-moving CDs. Customers are hearing it in the stores and snapping it up. And it's selling
everywhere, right across the country.'

'Christ, Debbie. You sure about this? You couldn't have got it
wrong?'

'I told you, I've seen the EPOS. The data comes direct from
checkout. And Dad's seen it too, he just called me. He says to say
well done.'

'Well, I'm stunned. I wasn't expecting anything like this. I need a
cigarette.'

'You better get yourself straight down to London. I mean it.'

'London? Uh, why's that?'

'Because *The Cormorant's Cry* is going to chart this week. It's
going to come in at number four or five, we reckon. And everyone's

going to want to interview you. So get yourself onto the first flight down, Peter. You're *famous*.'

Dawn was on her third site visit with the architects and the plan was starting to take shape. Having rejected both Home Farm and the watermill as being too close to the big house, they'd settled on a medieval barn on the western boundary of the estate, with good access to the dual carriageway. It was here Dawn planned on locating her new pet project: the Longparish Organic farm shop.

It had not been lost on the soon-to-be-new-Lady Pendleton that all the best, most modern-thinking country estates these days possessed a personal farm shop, and she could not think why Laetitia had refrained from starting one. She could not open the pages of a magazine without seeing photographs of this smart lady or that posing infront of their cheese counter or with a wicker trug of homegrown vegetables. If truth be told, Dawn was finding life with James Pendleton slightly less glamorous and high profile than she'd anticipated, since he was perfectly content staying home in the evenings, and reluctant to go out as frequently as she'd have liked herself. And since this terrible takeover thing began their routine had been disrupted, with business meetings and conference calls at all hours and James constantly on the phone to his brothers. Dawn could have murdered Ross. She suspected he'd dreamt up the whole thing to upset her. She found it personally mortifying that Ross was behaving like this towards the Pendletons, when James and Laetitia had welcomed them into their home and taken them to the theatre as personal friends. It made her uncomfortable in front of James's brothers and their wives that it was her ex who was causing all this trouble. It wasn't helpful when she was still trying to *integrate* herself into the family.

Then, of course, there was Miles ringing at all hours. She knew Miles didn't approve of her, not that he'd ever said so; whenever they met he was perfectly charming and solicitous, but she sensed his insincerity and didn't trust him. When James stupidly mentioned her Longparish Organics idea, which she hadn't wanted him to talk about yet, Miles was all over her offering his services on the publicity. Dawn still kept in intermittent touch with Davina, though it was all quite awkward what with Miles working for James. She'd most recently run into Davina at a little birthday supper party for Gemma in Roupell Street, which she felt she had to drop in on, even though she didn't really like returning to Ross's railwayman's cottage and even felt awkward telling James's driver that this was the right place. Gemma invited both her siblings and their significant others, so Greg and Mollie were there, and Debbie, plus Archie of course, and Davina who was playing on the floor with Mandy. Dawn hadn't stayed long. Gemma and Debbie had been on excellent form, but she thought both Greg and Archie seemed preoccupied.

Davina, too, appeared under the weather. Dawn hesitated to ask how the divorce was going, especially in company with Archie and Mollie both there, but she did get her chance, and Davina groaned and said it was all so slow and expensive, and Miles was dragging his feet over everything, so it went on and on.

'Tell me about it,' Dawn replied. 'Ross and I have been separated for eighteen months, and have hardly started the process. And I'm not even asking him for half his wealth in alimony since James is much richer in his own right.'

'It hardly seems worth it, any of it,' Davina said. 'All this disruption and unhappiness. Sometimes I think we'd have done better staying together, and just put up with eachother.'

'I could *never* have stayed with Ross,' Dawn replied. 'James and I are so much better suited. We have our art and music in common, you see. And we each have our own little businesses to think about—James with his supermarkets and me with my little farmshop.'

As it happened, Dawn's ambition for her farmshop was growing every week. Having originally conceived it as a utilitarian outlet for surplus produce from the vegetable garden and fruit frames, her visits to rival farmshops inspired her to greater heights, and her architect saw new potential at every turn. The old, collapsing milking sheds next to the medieval barn had potential as a gourmet café, and the Victorian threshing sheds could be opened up into another light-filled space selling plants, bulbs and garden tools. Already, Dawn was working with some very clever consultants in London developing Longparish Organic shampoos and conditioners made from nettles, elderflower and apple blossom harvested on the estate. The more she thought about it, the more excited she became. She had an idea for a contemporary sculpture park in the meadows behind the barn, with talented young sculptors from all over the county—in fact the country—showcasing their work, and the estate becoming a magnet for exciting new design, with resident sculptors, painters and carpenters inhabiting James's cottages. As she told everyone, good design meant everything to her, and she was delighted to be invited to become a Trustee of the Institute of Contemporary Arts on the Mall. It annoyed her that, in the many feature articles coming out about Ross at the moment, they always used a photograph of Chawbury Park taken from the bottom of the garden, showing the Victorian lampposts and the ornamental iron gates she'd ordered from the local blacksmith. Both made her cringe these days, and she hoped nobody thought she had anything to do with them.

Greg spent four days thinking about Miles's overture over lunch, considering it from every possible perspective. That is to say, he analysed how it might advantage him personally, balancing benefit against risk.

Although in his regular quotes to the *Droitwich Advertiser,* and in his television soundbites for Midlands Today, he remained implacably confident about prospects for the Labour Government, and spoke of a fourth and even fifth term of compassionate, progressive socialism for decent hardworking families, Greg was in fact increasingly panic-struck. The latest polls were alarming, even those published in Labour-supporting papers, and results from recent by-elections seemed to back these up. If his constituency followed the national trend, he wouldn't have a hope of winning the seat, through no fault of his own. The local government elections in the West Midlands saw a wipe-out for Labour, with most of the councils turning from red to blue. And during his rare forays on the doorsteps, and at the 'listening' surgeries he convened in church halls, the voters were increasingly hostile towards him and towards the whole Labour project. Proletariat who complained about democracy didn't deserve to have it.

He considered taking Mollie into his confidence—after all, Miles was her dad—but hesitated. The trouble with Mollie was she didn't think like a politician, she was too idealist. Under normal circumstances, this was an advantage. Greg could explain to her the party's intellectual position on any topic—on eradicating child poverty, for instance, or Gordon and Ed Balls's pet tax credits for the low paid—and Mollie bought into it and regurgitated it in her own words at the school gates, which Greg had to admit she was very good at. The flip side was that once she'd got an idea into her head it was difficult to shift. She didn't seem to appreciate that *realpolitik* contained a degree of expediency, and party policy needed to reflect this. In recent months, Greg and Mollie had argued over the tax arrangements for non-doms, Iraq and the new state schools 'academy' projects, with Mollie taking unrealistically ethical positions each time. Greg doubted she'd be too keen on his plan to switch to the Tories.

Secretly, he met with Miles a second time at the flat in Mount Street. Later, with mounting secrecy, he met other leading Tories from party headquarters who quizzed him on his motives for defecting, and peered at him like an alien species in a lab. Finally, he met Paul Tanner, recently elevated to party Chairman, who was well briefed on Greg's career in local politics and seemed more than willing to embrace him into the party. 'Miles has been telling me a lot of good things about you,' Paul said. 'And our communications people are excited about the idea of you coming over.'

'I'm glad,' said Greg.

'What would you say has been the decisive factor in your decision?'

'Oh, my belief in the small state, your ambitious programmes for health and education reform with greater local autonomy. And your support for small enterprise versus the multi-nationals. I mean, I'm strongly against further consolidation in big business, in favour of consumer choice.'

'Quite,' replied Paul.

Archie had never arrived at the office so early. Normally, he found it a struggle to roll in before 9.45, so the 8.00 a.m 'morning prayers' almost finished him off. Today, he startled the commissionaires by getting in at 5.30 a.m. Tucked into his wallet was the checklist he'd drawn up with Miles over a drink at the Mount Street flat the previous evening. It was alarmingly long, and Archie knew he'd need to work fast to make copies of everything before anyone else arrived.

It didn't help that he had never previously used the photocopier. Ordinarily, he considered himself far too grand to do his own photocopying and delegated it to one of four departmental gofers. But now he was on his own. The photocopier stood in a glass-walled pod along the corridor, and he felt uncomfortably exposed as he snuck inside with the big stash of documents camouflaged within a pile of newspapers. It worried him the photocopier seemed to be broken, with no sign of life, until he noticed the plug was switched off at the wall. Slowly the great grey machine purred and rattled into life. Archie placed the first of the strategy documents onto the glass plate and was dismayed when it came out blank. He turned it over and had more luck.

Over the next ninety minutes he copied the lot: the four ring-bound dossiers, minutes of all the 'war cabinets,' PR strategy, investor contact notes with Freeza Mart's internal assessment of how likely they were to vote their shares behind the takeover, the highly sensitive plan for integrating the two businesses if they were successful, including the proposed new organisation chart and reporting lines. Every detail of the deal structure was copied, and every memorandum from Freeza Mart's investment bankers. As the pages rolled off the copier and into the sorting tray, Archie slipped them inside his briefcase.

He was on the final document when he heard a rapping on the glass wall. Glancing up guiltily, he saw Ross.

'You're in bright and early, Archie.'

'Er, yes. Lots to do at the moment. Thought I'd make an early start.'

'Well done, lad. You saw this morning's papers? The news about Dick Gunn?'

'Um, no, I haven't got to the papers yet.'

'Front page of the *Financial Times*. The Gunn Partnership's bought a stake in Pendletons. Quite a big one, actually. And he's come out for them.'

'Really? That's a pain.'

'A setback, certainly. We need to plan our reaction, put out a release. He's a sharp operator, Gunn, by all accounts. I've not met the guy.'

'He used to shag my sister,' Archie replied. 'Not that that's a very exclusive club.'

Mollie was sitting in the staff room at school in front of the lunchtime television news. Her hands half covered her face, because she couldn't bring herself to watch it full on, it was too upsetting. Her discomfort was enhanced by the presence of several of her fellow teachers, all left wing, clustered disapprovingly around the screen.

The story about Greg switching parties was the lead item on a slow news day. Mollie could see her husband now, standing alongside David Cameron, George Osborne and the Conservative party chairman, Paul Tanner, on St Stephen's Green outside the Houses of Parliament, giving a news conference. Greg had a big blue rosette pinned to his suit and was wearing a blue tie for the first time in his life.

The newsreader was saying Greg had been selected as prospective Conservative candidate for the safe Tory seat of Mid-Hampshire, following the retirement of long-serving Monday Club backbencher Ridley Nairn. Everyone was slapping Greg on the back, and he was smirking smugly into the television cameras. Mollie couldn't bear the thought of all her new friends up in Droitwich watching this, who had been so welcoming to them and so kind.

Greg had only broken the news of his defection to her at breakfast time that day. At first, Mollie thought it was a joke, he was winding her up. 'That's right, Greg. I can just see you in a pinstripe suit and top hat, a Tory toff.'

'They're not like that these days, Mollie. You should get with the programme. We're an all-inclusive, multi-cultural political force for the third millennium.'

'You *are* joking, aren't you? Please tell me you are?'

Then they'd had a blazing row which left Mollie bewildered and crying, and Greg stormed off to a breakfast briefing with the Conservative communications department. Since then, they hadn't exchanged a word.

And now here he was on TV, being lauded as a hero for his traitorous behaviour. A voiceover was predicting a General Election in six to nine months time, and it was suggested Greg might be only the first of several talented young Labour politicians to switch sides.

'I am honoured to join a party which reflects my political philosophy of helping the underdog. I deeply regret that my former party has sold out, and no longer represents the ordinary decent disadvantaged working people of this country. Consequently I have resigned my membership of the Labour Party and joined Dave's new Conservatives.'

There was a crescendo of cheering from the small crowd of Tory apparatchiks ranged up in the background, and Greg continued, 'I shall fight to champion the cause of a fairer, more equal Britain.'

'Mr Clegg . . . Mr Clegg,' called out the political editors. 'Where do you stand on your father Ross Clegg's takeover battle against Pendletons?'

'I'm sorry, I don't want to get drawn into that,' replied Greg. 'But as ever I am on the side of the consumer and individual choice against the growing power of big business conglomerates. For this reason, I hold a different opinion to my father. I support an independent Pendletons.'

66.

Miles felt wonderfully self-satisfied for the first time in weeks. The fact was, he was playing a blinder and was nothing less than an utter genius.

If anyone had earned his fees tenfold in the past forty-eight hours, it was him. In fact, he now reckoned his handsome retainer from Pendletons was woefully inadequate, and he intended getting it raised significantly in the euphoria of victory.

That Pendletons would prevail was no longer in doubt. Miles felt perfectly confident on this point, the change of sentiment had been as profound as it was sudden. And all credit to himself, the master strategist. It was at moments like these that Miles could see how seriously good he was, and only hoped others recognised it too. In every field of endeavour there is one towering figure who stands head and shoulders above the rest, and in the field of public relations that man was Miles Straker.

This morning's newspapers, spread out on his desk in Charles Mews South, were testament to his ability. Eight news stories, seven columns of opinion, four leader articles, three op-ed comment pieces, not one of them favourable to Ross. Not one! Miles would love to have been a fly on the wall at today's morning conference at Freeza Mart House, and had instructed Archie to call him the minute he came out. He guessed it would be a long meeting, with so much bad news to digest. Sometimes the only recourse is to sit back and gloat.

Everything had come together, as only a brilliantly conceived plan can. The announcement of Dick Gunn's strategic investment had taken the markets by surprise, and his public backing of Pendletons's management made a number of windy fund managers have second thoughts. If a buccaneer like Gunn was putting his reputation and cash behind the status quo, perhaps that was the smart thing to do; you never wanted to bet against Gunn, he tended to call these things right. Not that it had been easy persuading James Pendleton to put Gunn on the Board, and the honours people in Whitehall had been violently opposed until Miles arranged some attractive half-term family holidays at Zach Durban's hotels. But it had been a strategic masterstroke, and kick-started the whole Pendletons resurgence.

Archie's daily bag of goodies was helping enormously too, even more than Miles had anticipated. To have the entire Freeza Mart game plan at his fingertips . . . it was glorious. It was all here . . . Ross's scribbled notes to his communications people, his bankers' assumptions and spreadsheets and, best of all, the maximum price they were prepared to pay. At present, their bid valued the business at just under 11.5 billion pounds, but Miles now knew they were prepared to go up to 12 billion, but not beyond. Furthermore, he could see exactly how the financing was structured, and which banks around the world were in on it. Already, he had briefed Pendletons's own bankers, without revealing how he had come by the information, and they were exerting pressure on several institutions. Archie was relaying everything, every change of strategy, every conversation. The benefit to Pendletons was incalculable.

And then, of course, there was his inspired masterstroke over Greg. Not entirely palatable, of course, having to consort with pondlife like his son-in-law who made you want to hold your nose, but it was working triumphantly. All the newspapers were running stories about Greg's attack on Ross, and Freeza Mart increasingly coming over as the ugly face of capitalism. Ross had looked rattled last night on *Newsnight*, blathering on about Freeza Mart's environmental and corporate responsibility programmes. The interviewer gave him a hard time which Ross clearly hadn't expected, and he fluffed his lines more than once.

It was a feature of Miles's character that when things were going well in his working life he felt a corresponding surge of bravado in his personal life. All of a sudden he felt all his old recklessness and smoothness returning. On his way back from lunch, he commanded Makepiece to draw up outside his wine merchant in St James's where he ordered ten cases of very expensive claret on the Straker Communications account; afterwards, he commissioned three new suits and a velvet collared overcoat from his tailor in Mount Street. Later that same afternoon he briefed his PAs that the annual Chawbury Manor client lunch party would be resumed, and that they would be organising it all, in conjunction with Nico Ballantyne of Gourmand Solutions. To round off a highly satisfactory day, he arranged for a nubile and very young hooker to join him in Mount Street for an overnighter. It was the first time he'd used the agency since the regrettable encounter with Samantha at the Hotel Meurice.

Having declared his intention of reviving the Chawbury lunch party, it occurred to him he needed to repair relations with his children in advance of the event. A hallmark of the party had always been the illusion it was a 'family' celebration, and many thank you notes from his corporates explicitly referred to the attractiveness and politeness of his offspring. With no Davina there, it was doubly imperative to reassemble the children.

As Miles was quick to recognise, the job was already partly done. Archie, the prodigal son, was back in the fold and so, of course, was Mollie. As the wife of the prospective Member of Parliament, Miles expected to see a good deal of his younger daughter in the coming months, and he would need to make sure she got help with her wardrobe. It was one thing dressing like a batty social worker when you are the wife of a Labour candidate for a Midlands seat, but this was Hampshire. She'd need an appropriate frock for the lunch party.

Which left Peter and Samantha. Miles didn't know what to make of his elder son at the moment, except that it was all rather pathetic. How he filled his days in the Siberian wastes of northern Scotland where nobody lived, Miles couldn't imagine; apart from deer stalking and mackerel fishing, nothing went on there at all. In the past couple of weeks, people had been mentioning Peter's CD, saying it was rather good, but Miles assumed they were just being kind. He'd spotted a short interview with him in T2 of *The Times*, but the trouble with the pop industry is that, unless you're Mick Jagger or someone, there was no money in it. Nevertheless, he instructed Sara White, his senior PA, to track down Peter's telephone number and tell him it was a three-line whip for the Chawbury lunch. It would look odd if Peter wasn't present.

As for Samantha, she was an altogether more complicated proposition. The bottom line was: Miles needed her at the lunch. For a start, she was his most attractive child. Secondly, she was the only one who could be said to be reasonably famous and successful. Wherever he went—and he found this intensely annoying—people told him they loved Sam's cringe-making Freeza Mart commercials ('I'm a Freeza kinda girl') and billboards were still up on every street corner. If she wasn't at the lunch party, people would wonder why. And then, of course, she was his favourite, always had been, always would be. He had adored his blonde, classy, gorgeous elder daughter, before she went off the rails.

Against this, he found it difficult to overlook the mess she'd got herself in. To have a daughter who'd worked as a call girl was something he should never have had to contend with. If it ever got out, it would be mortifying for him. Her taste in men was appalling but with hindsight she could have done a lot worse for herself than marrying Dick Gunn. She was foolish not to have snapped him up while she'd had the chance.

In his current mood, however, Miles found himself looking more benignly upon his elder daughter, and resolved to extend the hand of forgiveness before the invitations went out.

Finally, there was the abiding Serena question. Miles found it genuinely baffling, and was surprised by how irritated it made him. Had Serena been the wife of a great nobleman or hedge fund tycoon, he'd have understood. But she had told him countless times how unhappy she was with Robin, and how desperate for an exit.

The good thing about giving a large party at home is that it provides you with a deadline for getting your house in order. Miles decided it would be rather satisfying to have Serena at his side by the time the guests arrived at Chawbury Manor.

Mollie didn't know what to do or who to confide in, and in the end she called on her mother in Holland Park Square.

She found Davina in the kitchen doing yoga with a couple of neighbours and the table pushed back. Since Dawn departed the square for her upgrade with James Pendleton, Davina had lost her yoga buddy and found substitutes. These days, she devoted much of her time to the traditional divorcee pastimes of yoga, pilates, weight training and working out in Kensington Gardens with a personal fitness coach. Twice a week she did remedial reading at Mollie's school, teaching the alphabet to struggling immigrants.

All this aerobic exercise and honing had altered her mother's body shape, Mollie noticed. Still sweetly beautiful, she looked five years younger and more confident than she had when living with Miles. Her figure had a leaner, more urban definition. She'd finally lost her 'victim' face too, Mollie decided.

After the yoga session, Davina made coffee and she and Mollie sat outside in the little patch of private paved garden which gave on to the larger communal space. Recently, Davina had filled it with dozens of terracotta flowerpots bursting with jasmine, clematis and tobacco plants which filled the air with their sweet musky fragrance.

'Well, you know my dilemma,' Mollie said. 'I've been thinking and thinking, and I just don't know what I'm supposed to do, or what to say when people ask. I haven't slept properly for days worrying about everything.'

'And what does Greg say, when you talk to him about it?'

'That's the trouble, he won't discuss it, not really. It's just "I've switched political parties," so what? Big deal. It's like it's got nothing to do with me, like my opinion doesn't count. He doesn't seem to realise it's bizarre, being Labour one day and Tory the next. He used to be virulent about them, the Tories I mean. I've been listening to him for months saying what rubbish they are, how he despises everything they stand for. And now, overnight, it's like "Dave this" and "Dave that" and how we're twenty-three points ahead in the polls.'

Davina looked at her daughter, with her indignant, snappy eyes, and realised it was the first time for ages she'd seen her really angry. Since marrying Greg, Mollie had often seemed too much in his thrall, appeasing and subservient. But today she blazed with fury.

'You know the most annoying thing? Well, one of the most annoying? I've spent two years of my life up in Droitwich, helping Greg nurse the constituency, weekend after weekend we've been up there, and sometimes midweek too, and you know what? I've enjoyed it. I really like the people, I've made loads of friends. Not just political ones, but teachers at the schools, people we've met out canvassing, local businessmen, hospital nurses—all sorts, really genuine people. And it's so embarrassing, worse than embarrassing, it's like we've kicked them in the teeth. I tried explaining it to Greg, but he couldn't care less. He looked at me like I was mad. He just said, 'Droitwich and Redditch will go blue next time anyway. They're swing seats. No way will Labour hold them.' He doesn't care about our supporters. I keep thinking of new ones, like the Mayor's sister, and the wife of the constituency chairman, Bev, I don't even dare ring her up in case she won't speak to me. I'll have to, of course.'

'Maybe Greg's right,' Davina said. 'Have you considered that? That he can do more good inside the Conservative party than in Labour? It does rather look like they won't win next time round, and you can't achieve much in opposition. That's what your father used to say.'

'I wish I could believe that was the reason,' Mollie said. 'I don't know what to think about Greg anymore. Not at the moment, anyway.'

But she did know: as an idealist, Mollie was outraged by his cynicism, by his lack of commitment, his vaunting ambition and opportunism. His political betrayal was far worse to her than if he'd had an affair with another woman, because her feelings of love and respect for her husband were inextricably connected to the pure flame of idealism she had always believed he had at his core. When he behaved rudely or carelessly towards her, or imposed upon her (as he did so frequently) or was disrespectful and dismissive, Mollie excused his behaviour, because she understood he was engaged on a higher, altruistic mission for the betterment of all mankind. How then could she reconcile herself to this casual treachery? It was as if everything he'd said previously about his commitment to socialism had been an out and out lie. The scales had fallen from her eyes.

It did not help, either, that she had come to find him physically repulsive. This was not something she had felt able to admit, even to herself, though she had been aware of a mounting reluctance to touch him, or to get too close to those blubbery lips and sweating face. It had been the sight of him on television, at one step's remove, that brought it home to her: that he made her flesh creep.

'Your father, at least, must be pleased,' Davina said. 'He was never happy having a Labour son-in-law. Personally, I thought it was rather good for him. But he's going to like it much better having Greg in the party.'

'I know. In fact, I think Dad must have had a hand in it. Greg hasn't said anything, but it was one of the first things I thought. I mean, Mid-Hampshire, our own constituency.'

Davina smiled. 'You know your father as well as I do, he adores plotting and planning. I can't believe it happened without his involvement. Haven't you talked to him?'

Mollie shook her head. 'There was a message on the phone from his office, saying he's arranging for someone to take me shopping for clothes. A "personal shopper," whatever that is. For all the Conservative events he thinks I'll be going to.'

'Typical Miles. He was always trying to get me to see one of those.'

'I can just imagine myself in a powder blue suit with power shoulders, like an airhostess. And lots of flowery frocks. And big hats. The new Mrs Ridley Nairn.'

'And what about Greg? The Tory faithful of Hampshire are going to be a bit of a culture shock for him. They're lovely people, but it is all a bit stuffy. I hope he realises. He was scarcely ever down at Chawbury before.'

'He's describing himself now as Hampshire born and bred, the local candidate. I heard him talking to the *Andover Daily Echo* on the phone, saying he spent all his teenage years there, and comes back as often as he can.'

'You'll have to find a cottage in the constituency, I suppose, unless you can stay with your father. Or with Ross, of course.'

'Yes,' Mollie replied, without much enthusiasm. 'I'm sure that's what we'll do. Something like that.'

But, at that moment, an audacious and subversive idea was forming at the back of her mind.

Debbie was midway through a two-hour board meeting at Freeza Mart House when the Post-it note was brought in to her.

It was a particularly important meeting for which she had been preparing for several weeks, with six members of the Executive

Board present, including her father, at the conclusion of which she hoped they'd finally make the decision to go ahead. If Debbie was to become MD of a new hospitality division, which was what she desired above anything else, then this meeting had to go brilliantly.

There had been so many different versions of the presentation over the past few weeks, and so many versions of the business plan, her abiding fear was that an old version would somehow get bound up in the Board packs by accident, or a redundant version get cached in her laptop which was linked to the plasma screen. The version she was presenting today was version seventeen. 'So here goes,' she hissed to her number two, Justin Briggs.

It was far worse presenting to your dad, Debbie had decided, than anything else on earth. It wasn't like she was frightened of him or anything, it was just that he was so observant and clever. If a single market share chart was wrong in any way, or didn't tie in with the financials at the back, he'd be certain to notice. That was the sort of brain he had. If he saw a number once, he never forgot it.

Debbie felt she'd been working on this presentation for months. In fact, it had been seven weeks but it felt much longer. Like everything these days, it all depended on what happened with the Pendletons takeover. The whole of Debbie's proposition pre-supposed a significantly enlarged company, which was what made it so tricky to put together since you couldn't get your hands on the Pendletons books and had to do it all by guesswork. Anyway, today's presentation focused on the twenty-seven hotels located on Pendletons's properties—mostly in service stations—plus the four hotels on existing Freeza Mart properties, and the nine new ones they hoped to take over in the coming months. This would make a total of forty hotels, mostly Travelodges and similar budget accommodation, which could be pulled together under a new FM Sleep hospitality brand. Debbie was massively excited but also nervous. The project was so huge, she felt slightly daunted. And the research reports based on dozens of focus groups conducted across the country, which Ross had already seen, were inconclusive, in Debbie's opinion. For instance, 72 percent of haulage drivers said they didn't particularly like their present budget accommodation and were open to change. But few were willing to pay more than £17 per room night. Debbie had spent weeks reviewing choices of soaps and toiletries for the en-suites, and seeking to upgrade meal choices in the all-day coffee shops. The economics of this project were entirely different to everything she'd done before. For a start, the forty hostelries had an average of 150 rooms each, 6,000 room nights every night of the year. Her idea of placing a posy of roses or sweet peas on each dressing table was a non-starter; it would cost millions and, anyway, the focus groups didn't give a damn.

She had reached the most innovative part of the presentation about her DVD library concept, when the post-it was passed to her.

'God,' she said. 'I'm sorry, I'm so excited by this I just have to tell you. Pete Straker's record has gone to number one. That's the CD we've been playing in Freeza Mart, we've been pushing it. And now it's top of the charts.'

There was a round of applause in the meeting room, Debbie clapping loudest of all.

Davina felt she couldn't escape this takeover business which just seemed to drag on and on. Even though she had no personal involvement whatever, and didn't normally have much interest in financial shenanigans, it intruded on her life from every side. For a start, the newspapers were full of it, not just the business sections but news and features pages too. Today, *The Times* had a big interview with Ross, laying out his plans and responding to some of the negative stories circulating about him. 'Some of the stuff going round, I don't know where they get it,' he was quoted as saying.

Davina thought she could make a pretty good guess, and felt sorry for Ross. Having been married to Miles for twenty-seven years, she knew exactly how he operated.

And then, in today's *Daily Mail,* was an extraordinary double page article about Dawn 'the lady love of two warring supermarket tycoons.' Poor Dawn. She had agreed to the interview to promote her Longparish Organics farm shop, but they'd scarcely mentioned it in the piece. Instead, it was all about why she'd chucked Ross, and what it was like living in a stately home with Lord Pendleton. Davina couldn't believe her friend had said half the things attributed to her, it didn't sound like Dawn and was toe-curlingly embarrassing. 'My husband likes to see the table formally laid for dinner every night, regardless of whether or not we have invited guests coming over. And if the silver isn't properly polished or there's a chipped wine goblet, woe betide the servants. The only thing we ever disagree on,' she went on, 'is over our sweets. I enjoy dainty puddings—though I have to be careful about my weight—but Lord Pendleton likes his savouries and cheeses. Men do love their cheeses.'

Later in the article, Dawn refuted the accusation that her new relationship involved a move upmarket. 'I wish people would stop making spiteful, ignorant comments. I've lived in spacious mansions all my life, there's nothing new about it. We were very comfortable at Chawbury Park and previously I was fortunate enough to live in one of the most prestigious homes in Droitwich.'

Well, Davina reflected, Dawn couldn't say she hadn't warned her. When she'd asked her advice, Davina had told her friend, 'Don't touch it with a bargepole.'

'That's what Miles said too,' Dawn had replied. 'I don't know why you're all being so negative. I told Miles, "I'm passionate about my little farm shop. This is a golden opportunity, I can't pass it up."'

Davina knew that Archie was also working on the takeover, which kept him at his desk from dawn to long after dusk, according to Gemma. She said she barely saw him, he was working so hard. From what Davina had read in the papers, things seemed to be going rather against Freeza Mart. At the beginning, everyone had been pro-Ross and saying what a good job he'd done. But lately there'd been lots of criticism, suggesting his clothing range was manufactured in sweatshops, and some of his supermarkets were dirty and employed illegal asylum seekers. Davina didn't know whether the sweatshops bit was true, but she shopped at Freeza Mart Metro in Holland Park Avenue and it was always lovely and clean with an excellent flower stall inside.

What with one thing and another, her loyalties were totally divided. Archie and Samantha both worked for Freeza Mart, so of course she wanted them to do well, and she'd always liked Ross, right from the beginning. And Peter owed so much to Freeza Mart over his CD. Even this morning, when she'd dropped into the Holland Park branch for milk and orange juice on the way back from her jog, they'd been playing *The Cormorant's Cry* over the loudspeakers. Davina felt so proud, she wanted to tell everyone she was Peter's mother.

At the same time she felt dreadfully sorry for James Pendleton, who'd been a dear friend for years, it seemed terribly unfair if he ended up losing all his supermarkets. In Davina's opinion, they seemed very well run and always full of lovely fresh produce, and she couldn't see that the Pendletons deserved to have their family business taken from them. Ross surely had plenty to occupy himself with already, without Pendletons too. Privately, she thought there might be something in what they were saying in the press, that Ross was only going after it to get his own back at Dawn. How strange it was. Dawn was a sweet person and a loyal friend, but she wasn't exactly Helen of Troy. Extraordinary she could inspire all this chaos.

And as for Greg coming out so publicly against his father and speaking up for Pendletons, Davina didn't understand it. She'd seen Greg twice on the television news, and heard him again on the *Today* programme this morning insisting Freeza Mart was too big already and any merger should be blocked by the DTI and OFT. Mollie was rooting for Freeza Mart, because she said their food was less expensive, and this was another bone of contention between her and Greg. Davina was seriously concerned about the state of her daughter and son-in-law's marriage. Mollie remained horrified by his political conversion and Davina didn't know where it would end. She'd rung Miles that morning about it, because she was so worried, and it was the first time they'd spoken in three months. Hearing his voice brought him vividly back to her, both for better and for worse. She'd forgotten how charming he could be, how full of conviction and self-belief. She could feel his energy coursing down the telephone line.

'Things are going splendidly this end,' he assured her. 'No way is Ross Clegg going to win this, not now. The city's gone cold on him. I was speaking to Alistair Darling this morning and he agrees with me. Pendletons is a great British brand. It's rock solid.'

Davina told Miles her concerns about Mollie and Greg, and wondered whether there was anything either of them could or should do to help. But Miles couldn't see a problem.

'Don't worry about Mollie, she'll make a perfectly sound Tory politician's wife, once she's got the uniform together. In fact, you could help her with that, Davina. That'd be the most useful thing you could do, take her clothes shopping. As for Greg, there was no point sticking with Labour, they're a busted flush.'

After the conversation, Davina felt unexpectedly low, she didn't know why. She felt flat and dispirited, as if she'd been unplugged from a source of energy.

Sometimes, her days had lately seemed rather empty and short on incident, and she wasn't sure she liked it as much as she'd expected. Marriage to Miles had been exhausting, unrelenting, she had felt herself trapped on a treadmill which never let up, constantly pushed to look her best, be ready on time, make conversation with people she didn't give a fig for. For years, part of her had longed for a smaller life without two big houses to look after, parties to organise, dinners every weekend. Now she'd got what she'd wished for, she felt a little lost. Her new life was calm and almost free of stress, but lacked jags of excitement. The people she saw— her yoga friends, the other teachers at school where she did her remedial reading—were kind and pleasant, but unambitious and happy with their little lives. Slow lane folk, as Miles called them. They lived in a different world to the one Miles and Davina had inhabited for so long. Angela Strawbetter from Freshfields rang her several times a month, cajoling her to sign the next round of documents on the road to divorce, but Davina found herself dragging her feet.

If she was honest, she was slightly missing her former life.

67.

t was part of Miles's annual routine to take a table at the Grocers and Retailers Ball, held each June in the Great Room of the Grosvenor House Hotel. This gruesome industry function, a charity fundraiser in aid of a hospice and sheltered housing for needy retired shop assistants, was not something Miles normally anticipated with enthusiasm. It was not an event that drew the elevated social crowd he loved, the majority of tables being occupied by executives from the larger supermarkets and department stores. Nevertheless, Straker Communications felt an obligation to be there, to support the industry, to network and entertain executives from Pendletons and other relevant clients.

Tonight, however, Miles was rather in the mood for it all. The past two days had seen further excellent news for Pendletons, with a comment piece in today's *Financial Times* questioning the business rationale behind the proposed takeover, and two Scottish pension funds coming out publicly against the Freeza Mart plan. Miles knew Freeza Mart had taken several tables at the ball, and that Ross himself was certain to be there. It would be satisfying to see him at close quarters, when he must be feeling wrongfooted and despondent.

Drawing up outside the hotel entrance in Park Lane, Miles saw the evening promised to be as ghastly as ever. Shockingly ugly women were tottering through the doors on white stilettos, with huge fat bottoms and wobbly arms, spaghetti straps and raw, sunburned backs from Spanish and Greek holidays. The men were if anything worse, and he flinched at the moustaches, white tuxedos, stick-up evening collars, red bow ties and impossibly naff, spiky, gelled haircuts. At events like these, Miles viewed himself as a god-like creature from a higher planet, dignifying proceedings with his presence.

His first act, on entering the area where the champagne reception was in full swing, was to confirm the location of the Straker Communications table on the table plan. To his satisfaction, it was dead centre in the Great Room where he expected it to be. He had once fired a PA when a Straker table had been disadvantageously positioned. Freeza Mart's top table was right alongside his own, which meant a ringside view of Ross. Pendletons had brought five tables of guests tonight and there were tables for Tesco, Matalan, Sainsburys, Waitrose, Debenhams, House of Fraser, River Island, the Arcadia group and all the rest.

A toastmaster in red tailcoat announced dinner was served and the vast herd of guests began their slow migration down the horseshoe staircase into the Great Room. Miles found his guests milling around the table and they all took their places. As well as Rick Partington, the Strakers' MD, Miles had invited two of their more presentable account directors and two senior Pendletons executives, plus Paul and Brigitte Tanner, Greg and Mollie, and a business journalist from *The Times*.

They had no sooner sat down than the Freeza Mart party arrived at the adjacent table. There was Ross in his dinner jacket, copper bracelet jangling at his wrist, though he wore a proper bow tie these days, Miles noticed. He scrutinised Ross's face for signs of stress, but couldn't spot any. Annoyingly, he looked rather cool and relaxed as he directed his guests to their seats. Both his business mentors, Callum Dunlop and Brin Williams, were at the table with their women, and Miles identified Freeza Mart's finance director, Heather Smail, and a couple of their non-execs. Then Archie turned up with Gemma, which took him by surprise since he hadn't expected it, and finally, sitting on Ross's right, Samantha in a silver beaded evening dress split to the knee.

Dinner was predictably detestable, Miles felt, with the gala food he left ostentatiously untouched: a glutinous salmon and leek roulade, rubbery breast of duck with Dauphinoise potatoes, some preposterous pudding involving blackcurrant ice-cream inside a basket of spun barley sugar. He devoted himself to telling the *Times* journalist how he confidently expected Freeza Mart's bid to collapse within the fortnight, and how he'd make himself look clever if he wrote that in his next column. 'I think you'll agree,' he told the journalist, 'that if Ross can't even convince his own son the takeover's a smart idea, then he's going to struggle to convince anyone else.' Across the table, Greg loosened the waistband of his trousers. He was conscious of being the centre of attention in the room tonight, the man of the moment. He had been invited to appear on *Question Time* and relished the prospect. For the first time in his life he felt he was receiving proper respect as a statesman. From time to time he glanced surreptitiously at his father at the next table, taking care not to catch his eye. Ross had rung him after his defection to the Tories, and again after his remarks about the takeover, but Greg hadn't taken the calls, nor rung him back. It was a nice feeling having the upper hand for a change.

He glanced stealthily at Samantha too, wondering what she thought of his recent prominence. He assumed even someone as uninformed about the world as Sam could hardly have failed to know about it; his face had been on the front of every newspaper as well as on TV. He wondered if she now regretted the way she'd behaved towards him in Thailand; he doubted she'd be so dismissive these days, when he was shortly to become her Member of Parliament. There was no question about it, Sam was a great-looking bird, much better looking than Mollie, he'd definitely married the wrong sister in the looks department. Generally, he was disappointed in Mollie who had scarcely congratulated him on winning the constituency nomination and was still banging on about those losers up in Droitwich. Move on, babe. Some people were their own worst enemies.

Dinner was followed by a loo break and then an auction.

'Good evening, ladies and gentlemen,' announced a smooth-looking auctioneer, loaned by Sotheby's for the event. 'Now, we have a long list of very special lots to get through and I can see some very generous individuals in the room tonight, so I want you all to have your cheque books open. There are a number of highly attractive young ladies on standby, ready to take your names and, haha, your money when you are successful . . . so let's move straight on to Lot One, which is one week's stay at a Center Parcs of your choice for a family of four people, including complimentary upgrade and food and beverage vouchers to the value of £250 redeemable in any of the resorts' many restaurants and cafes. Now, for a lot of this quality, who will kick off the bidding at one thousand pounds? One thousand pounds . . . come on, this is cheap at the price . . . worth double that at least . . . thank you, sir . . . yes, you sir.' A Primark executive raised his arm. 'And now we have twelve hundred . . . fourteen hundred . . . sixteen hundred pounds . . . against you, sir . . . thank you sir . . . we have two thousand pounds now, two thousand pounds . . .'

The auction ground on from lot to lot. With only a handful of guests willing to take part, few dared raise their heads, still less their hands, lest they were accidentally mistaken for bidders. Men stared down at their pudding plates, or shook their heads in warning at their wives as holidays and cars were sold at stratospheric premiums. A Lexus went for forty thousand pounds to a Mancunian mall owner, a VIP day at Alton Towers for six people for fifteen thousand, and a villa holiday in Sardinia with use of a boat and eighteen holes of golf for thirty-six thousand, drawing gasps of excitement.

'Lot twenty,' said the auctioneer, 'is the chance to win dinner à deux with a very lovely model, the face of Freeza Mart, who we all recognise from television and posters across the country. If Samantha Straker could join me up here on stage . . .'

Ross rose to his feet and gallantly pulled back Sam's chair, and she walked up the steps to the stage. Mollie thought she'd never seen her sister looking more beautiful than that night in the silver dress. But she also looked shy and vulnerable, as if she wished she hadn't agreed to be a prize.

'This is a lot I'm sure every red-blooded man in the room will kill for,' said the smoothy auctioneer. 'So who will make me an opening bid of, let's say, five thousand pounds? Do I have five thousand anyone? Thank you sir . . .' There was a thicket of raised hands. 'Ten thousand . . . twelve . . . fifteen . . . twenty . . .'

At twenty thousand the bidding lost momentum, and the auctioneer was about to bring down the hammer when Ross stuck up his hand.

'Ah, thirty thousand . . . thank you Ross Clegg. Any advance on thirty thousand pounds? I now have thirty thousand, thirty thousand from the Chief Executive of Freeza Mart, to have dinner with his own supermodel . . .'

Miles was indignant. He glared across the room at Ross and felt pure hatred. No way, absolutely no way, was that man buying dinner with Sam. So he raised a languid hand, gold cufflinks glinting, and the auctioneer said, 'Forty thousand. We have a new bidder on table thirty-three.'

Ross looked at Miles in surprise, shrugged and raised his arm. 'We have fifty thousand from Ross Clegg. Fifty thousand pounds.'

Miles swallowed, then nodded. 'We have sixty thousand. A bid, unless I'm mistaken, from Samantha's father, Miles Straker. A bit of fatherly interest here. Dinner with his daughter for sixty thousand pounds.'

A gust of laughter rose from the room. This was fun: boss versus father. People were craning their necks to catch sight of the two adversaries. The better informed appreciated the additional dimension: that Miles, chief spin doctor for Pendletons, was entering a public head-to-head with Ross.

Looking down from the stage, Samantha suddenly felt sick. She could see her dad at the centre of his table in his perfectly cut dinner jacket, perfect white silk shirt, perfectly tied bow tie, relishing the attention. He looked almost obscenely smooth, hair swept back, cuff links glinting. The idea of having dinner alone with him filled her with dread.

She stared plaintively at Ross who seemed to understand and, after a terrifying delay, stuck his hand up. 'We have seventy thousand pounds,' said the auctioneer. 'Thank you very much sir. That's *seventy thousand pounds* for this very worthy charity from Ross Clegg.'

All eyes were on Miles. He could feel the whole room staring at him. He looked at Ross and felt . . . contempt. He thought of Ross's hideous house ruining his view, he thought of the shoot bought from under his nose, he thought of Ross buying his daughter at this auction. He could not concede, his pride would not allow it.

He raised his hand from the table with a curt nod of assent.

'We have *eighty thousand pounds*,' announced the auctioneer and the room exploded into applause.

Now it was Ross's turn. Total silence descended on the Great Room, an anticipatory hush.

Sam stared at her boss imploringly. But Ross shook his head. 'I'm out,' he said. 'I fold.'

Now the room rose to its feet, aware they'd just witnessed something rather incredible, and Miles adopted his special expression of triumphant modesty that he reserved for occasions like this one. Sweet revenge!

'Sold for eighty thousand pounds . . . dinner with this stunning young lady . . . bought by her father, Mr Miles Straker.'

The auctioneer beamed out at the crowd, his job well done.

Then Sam dissolved into tears on the stage as her long brown legs gave way beneath her.

68.

Sam caught the midday flight up to Wick, desperate to put as much distance between herself and London as possible. After the auction, Miles had loomed over her at Ross's table and said, 'I'm very much looking forward to our dinner, Samantha. We have some catching up to do.' And there had been a malicious, prurient look in his eyes she'd found creepy. Miles then shifted his attention to Ross. 'We've been reading a great deal about you recently, Ross. Can't get away from you, frankly.'

'Well, don't read too closely,' Ross replied. 'It hasn't been that friendly just recently.'

'Well, it wouldn't be. You've overreached yourself. Big mistake. But we all learn from our mistakes, do we not, Samantha? At least we would be well advised to.' Then he had glared at her meaningfully.

On the journey to the airport her mobile rang twice, and each time the number for Miles's office had flashed onto the screen. She hadn't picked up, but let it go to voicemail. Later she'd listened to her messages. The first was from Sara White: 'Hello, this is a message for Samantha. This is Sara from your father's office. He has asked me to confirm you are coming to his lunch party at Chawbury Manor. Please call me at the office.' The second said, 'This is a message for Samantha Straker from Anya in Miles Straker's office. He has asked me to fix up a date for the dinner with you he bought at auction last night. Please ring me at your earliest convenience with your schedule.'

Sam shuddered. There was no way, absolutely no way, she was going to be having that dinner, trapped in a restaurant alone with her dad.

Peter had said, 'Get on the first plane. I'll drive over and meet you.'

'Shouldn't you be doing something more important? Like signing autographs or whatever?'

'Forget that. No one knows me from Adam up here. Actually that's not true. I did get asked for an autograph yesterday in Durness, by a kid in the carpark. It was quite weird.'

'Get used to it. How long have you been in the charts? Six weeks?'

'Er, nine. But sinking like a stone now.'

'They're still playing it everywhere. You've been Number One.'

When they stopped for petrol at a garage on the way back from Wick airport, there was a display of *The Cormorant's Cry* alongside the till and a cardboard cutout of Peter's head. Not that the cashier noticed when he paid. They were driving along the coast road when a wall of bright sunshine swept across the bay, illuminating the tops of the waves and turning the sea a deep, alluring blue. 'Thank God I'm here,' Sam said. 'I always feel nobody can get at me here. I have to tell you about last night . . .'

She was halfway through her description of the auction when Peter's mobile leapt into life, announcing a voice message. 'I'd better listen to it, probably the record company, they keep stalking me.'

'Hello, is that Peter? This is Sara from your father's office. He's asked me to confirm you'll be at the Chawbury Manor lunch on Sunday week. And he's asked me to say he hopes you'll be wearing a suit. Kindly confirm you received this message.'

'Jesus,' Peter said. 'I've been dodging that lunch for weeks but she won't let it go. I'm getting three messages a day about it.'

'Me too.'

At that moment, Sam's mobile began ringing and she glanced down at the screen. 'Them again.' She pushed the button to switch it off.

For three days they sat outside the cottage in the sunshine, doing nothing but talking fitfully about Miles. Peter strummed at his guitar and built a fire out of driftwood over which they grilled fish. Sam became increasingly despondent as the prospect of the dinner weighed upon her. 'How can I possibly have dinner with him on my own?' she asked over and over. 'It'd be hideous. I think he's quite evil, he has to control everything. He's even got my old boyfriend, Dick Gunn, on his side in this takeover thing, Ross told me that last night. I bet Dad only did that to freak me out.'

They walked to the furthest end of the beach where it became headland, and their mobiles leapt simultaneously into life. 'More voicemail,' Peter said. 'Any bets?' Both messages were from Miles's office. There was also a second message on Peter's phone, this time from Mollie, asking him to ring back as soon as possible.

'Mollie? It's Peter.'

'Hi Peter. Look, I need to know, are you going to this lunch thing at Chawbury? I was wondering if you'd be there. And Sam. I don't know where she is.'

'Right here. You can talk to her. But we're both undecided. We'd love not to, but we're under big pressure.'

'Please *do* come,' Mollie said. 'I can't tell you why yet, but I'd love you to be there. Something's probably going to be announced and I want you to see Dad's face.'

Archie had found the perfect place from which to communicate with Miles. If he took the lift up to the top floor of Freeza Mart House, there was a fire exit outside onto an area of flat roof where the water tanks and machinery rooms were. Nobody ever ventured out there other than an occasional maintenance man, so he would shelter behind the tank room with a birds eye view across the Thames, and speak to Miles on his mobile. He rang him twice a day, immediately after the war cabinet finished at ten o'clock, and again at close of play. If anything came up after that he felt his father might be interested in, he would slip out of the kitchen door into the back yard of Roupell Street and call him from there, having first checked Gemma was reading Mandy a bedtime story and safely out of earshot, at the front of the house.

As the takeover ground into its ninth week and matters looked ever gloomy for the predator, Ross worked harder. Although now privately conceding there was a chance they might not succeed, he remained resolutely confident in the media, refusing to give an inch. He spent his days touring those financial institutions which had not yet declared for one side or the other, spreading his mantra of greater efficiency and enhanced margins. Other days he flew up to Edinburgh to lobby the Scottish institutions, or to Zurich where two Swiss-based hedge funds had taken strategic positions in Pendletons plc.

It concerned Ross that, wherever he went, he was met by a level of scepticism he had never previously encountered. Often, this turned out to be based on misinformation freshly fed to investors by the other side, and it took all his efforts to put them right. It was peculiar and disturbing, almost as though people knew his schedule in advance, and which investors he'd be calling on next. Similarly, any small setback had a way of leaking into the financial diaries. And several of his key decisions about the shape of the merged business, including sensitive personnel deployments, were splashed across *The Times*, causing endless embarrassment.

On the rare evenings he didn't work late, Ross often headed round for kitchen supper in Roupell Street. He found it therapeutic spending downtime with his daughter and granddaughter, talking about anything and everything except the takeover battle. And if he felt the need to discuss work, Archie was fully in the loop so was a useful sounding board. Over time, Ross had come to have a lot of respect for Archie, who was always well informed and sharp as a pin. At weekends, if he thought he could justify a few hours away, Ross piloted the helicopter down to Chawbury for a night at home to check everything was OK with the place. If truth be told, he found it rather joyless being there on his own, so he generally drove over to Serena's for a meal and a friendly face.

One evening in Roupell Street, after a particularly challenging day when a pension fund previously thought to be supportive of the takeover had suddenly gone wobbly, he felt knackered. It was as much as he could do to eat the bowl of pasta Gemma placed in front of him and sink a big glass of red wine. Gradually, however, he revived enough to tell Archie about his difficult ride, and how he was afraid another investor had moved over to Pendletons's side.

Not long afterwards, while going for a pee, Ross was surprised to hear furtive talking in the backyard, through the cloakroom window. The voice had been Archie's, and was repeating, word for word, the conversation they'd just been having together in the kitchen, plus details from that afternoon's strategy meeting.

He listened until he was in no doubt at all about whom Archie had been speaking to. Suddenly, a great deal was explained. Once again, Miles Straker was the cause of his problems. 'That fuckhead,' Ross cursed, shaking with a hatred and fury he didn't even know himself capable of. Well, two can play at that game, he thought grimly. At that moment, he had only one thought: revenge. Whatever it took, he would win this great standoff with Pendletons, and do his damnedest to ruin Miles in the process. Without challenging Archie, but with a very stern expression on his face, Ross said goodbye and headed out into the night.

69.

Striding purposefully across the terrace in his new summer suit, Miles surveyed the activity of the lunch party preparations. Nico Ballantyne of Gourmand Solutions was briefing a phalanx of forty young waiters and waitresses in the marquee, while the florists put finishing touches to the table centres. The garden, he was pleased to see, had finally achieved the standard of near-perfection he demanded, having been tended over the past ten days by contractors brought in specially for the job. The glass panes of the orangerie sparkled in the sunshine, as did the hundreds of champagne and cocktail glasses set out in rows. The yew hedges were newly sheared with precision.

The overall effect, Miles smugly concluded, was every bit as glorious as it had been in any previous year, better if anything. Which only went to show how little difference Davina had made in the past, and how superfluous to the arrangements. When he thought of the fuss she used to make! And yet he had effortlessly arranged the entire thing himself assisted only by his three PAs and Nico Ballantyne and his five-woman events team. He could see Sara White and the other girls now, bustling about with clipboards, double checking the final details.

There was no two ways about it: this year's Chawbury Manor summer lunch party would be the largest and most glamorous of them all. The list of acceptances far exceeded that of previous years, both in numbers and quality. Most of his senior clients were coming, all the big hitters, as well as several prospective ones. One thing he'd learnt over the years was that nothing encourages a prospective client more than the sight of significant competitors in a social context. Eleven Footsie 100 chairmen had accepted, plus seven chief executives. Furthermore, two national newspaper editors were expected (one bringing his wife, the other his PA), three City editors and five Tory shadow cabinet ministers. This year, Miles had decided not to invite any socialists, who suddenly seemed past their sell-by date. Once a Conservative government was safely installed in Westminster, Miles looked forward to the knighthood he felt he so richly deserved. Recently, it had begun to annoy him at large dinners to see his placecard still read 'Mr' when so many of his clients were ennobled, often at his own instigation.

The weather being sunny for once, Miles decreed that two sides of the marquee be left open on the garden and valley side, so a breeze could circulate and guests better enjoy the views. As usual, he glanced up the valley towards Ross's house—the *Park*!—to see how obtrusive it looked. The night before, when Greg and Mollie had arrived in time for supper, he'd fulminated against the house, and Mollie annoyed him by claiming not to notice it. 'The trees have grown, you can scarcely see it now.'

'Believe me, I can see it alright,' Miles had replied. 'I never *stop* seeing it. One would have to be blind not to. What about you, Greg? What does the prospective Member of Parliament for Mid-Hampshire think? Can you see it?'

And Greg, to Miles's satisfaction, replied he could most certainly see it, and he was surprised it had ever been given planning permission in the first place.

Soon afterwards, Archie and Gemma had rolled up in the black BMW which was Archie's company car, and which Miles, for the sake of his cover, made a big thing about denigrating. 'I don't know I even want that thing parked on my gravel. Not in front of the house. Take it round the back, please. Ghastly Freeza Mart vehicle.'

'What do you reckon, Archie?' he soon asked him, apropos the view. 'We've been discussing what we think of Ross's monstrosity these days, your boss's show home. Mollie claims she doesn't notice it. But Greg agrees with *me*. What about you? Proud to work for the kind of man who puts up a house like that, are you?'

Archie replied he'd always considered it a very ugly house, and Gemma, who had grown up at Chawbury Park, felt horribly uncomfortable and said nothing. Sitting on the terrace beneath a big white umbrella and sipping the glass of champagne Miles had handed to her, she remembered the anguished years when she'd first been in love with Archie and was carrying his baby and couldn't tell anyone about it. And how she used to stare up at the manor on the hill, where she now sat, and wonder whether she'd ever see Archie again. And all these years later she was finally here, for the very first time as a houseguest, not actually married to Archie but at least as his publicly acknowledged partner, with Mandy asleep upstairs, and this was as close to a happy normal life as she'd ever come in Chawbury. She knew she should be blissfully happy, but for some reason she was not. She watched Archie talking to his father and, she couldn't say why, but she didn't trust him. For several weeks now he'd been behaving very strangely, and she didn't like it.

Miles spent the best part of three weeks deliberating over the seating plan for his lunch. With so many VIPs to place, it was exceptionally complicated, since it was easy to cause offence. In the end, he decided to create three top tables of twenty people each, one presided over by himself, one by Archie and a third by Greg. Peter, he decided, was not up to the job and would doubtless arrive looking like a homeless person. Peter was driving down with Samantha on Sunday morning from Heathrow, having rejected the invitation to spend Saturday night at Chawbury.

Miles's one and only serious issue was with Serena, who had never even replied to the lunch party invitation, let alone responded to his amorous overtures. Well, it was her loss. Some people will always miss the train in life.

Shortly before noon, when the first guests were scheduled to arrive, Miles made a final inspection of the tent with Nico Ballantyne. This year, the plates were all to be different shades of Tory blue glass, upon which the first course of mixed organic salad leaves and organic quail eggs, all from Dawn's Longparish Organics shop, would be artfully displayed. In front of each place setting was a printed menu card with an engraving of Chawbury Manor.

Miles reviewed his table to check the name cards were all in their correct places. Dawn would sit on his right. On his left, Suzie Nairn, wife of the retiring MP. Also at his table: James Pendleton, as well as the two most senior shadow cabinet ministers, three chairmen, one Sunday newspaper editor and the Lord Lieutenant of Hampshire Johnnie Mountleigh with Philippa. It looked pretty good, Miles reckoned. He was particularly pleased that James and Dawn were going to be there today, since he expected the takeover to be imminently abandoned, so wanted to be as publicly associated with the outcome as possible. The supply of inside information he'd been receiving from Archie in the past five days certainly suggested that Freeza Mart was about to roll over and concede defeat.

At midday he took up his position on the terrace. Archie and Gemma were both in place beside him on the greeting line, looking presentable and smart. Gemma was quite a pretty little thing, he had decided, provided she didn't open her mouth. Greg was also there, sweating in a beige linen suit, but no Mollie, late as usual. Nor had Peter and Samantha arrived yet, which was unforgivable since they'd promised to get there in plenty of time. As the first guests were ushered onto the terrace, Mollie surfaced in a baggy corduroy smock. But her face flushed pink and she looked excited. 'Sorry,' she mouthed. 'I've been on the phone.' Miles thought it odd that two of the five people on the receiving line at his party were children of Ross Clegg. He wondered what people would think, and whether it might be misinterpreted.

For the next ninety minutes, Miles was absorbed with the receiving of his guests. With no Davina at his side, he found himself overcompensating for the omission with an even greater show of hospitality than usual, grasping hands and hugging his clients and neighbours with gusto. Dick Gunn rolled up with a new young girlfriend who looked no older than seventeen, and both Nick and Michael Pendleton arrived with their respective wives. With each new arrival, he said, 'And have you met Greg and Mollie yet? Greg is going to be our new Member of Parliament. His wife, of course, is my younger daughter.' And then people would assure Greg how delighted they were to meet him, and how he could certainly rely on their vote. Mollie felt increasingly sickened by all these wealthy neighbours with their red faces and Panama hats, all sucking up to Greg, who was lapping up the attention. She guessed this lot would have voted for a chimpanzee if it was put up as the Conservative candidate and wore a blue rosette. She thought of Greg's previous constituents in Droitwich, and how much more real they were.

Well, the secret would be out soon enough and the thought of it terrified her.

James and Dawn arrived with Hugh, and Miles noticed how confident Dawn looked. She was wearing a very large, chic, expensive-looking bleached straw sunhat, with a white fitted linen trouser suit. Her sole piece of jewellery was a modern ring comprising of a huge uncut diamond wrapped in gold. Her skin, once permanently brown from the sunbed, was these days almost wanly pale, and her make-up, if she wore any at all, undetectable. 'You are *so sweet* to invite us,' Dawn declared in a gracious, lady-of-the-manorish voice. 'Goodness, look at all these people. What an amusing group you've put together.'

Dawn and Miles both privately remembered this was her first ever invitation to Chawbury Manor, in all the years they had lived so close by, and Miles felt briefly uneasy. Dawn was thinking about the ghastly evening when she and Ross had called on the Strakers after Gemma turned out to be pregnant with Archie's baby. She shuddered. She had never actually gone into any of that business with James—it just seemed unnecessary to tell him, it was so long ago—and she hoped he would never hear about it.

Having got past the receiving line, and said hello to his soon-to-be step-children Greg and Gemma, James became suddenly shy and introverted, as often happened at large parties. Dawn was accustomed to this now, so directed him to a quiet area of the terrace where there were no other people, and allowed him time to gather himself. This was a little trick Laetitia had told her long ago, at a time when it was inconceivable she would ever become Lady Pendleton herself. In a while she would see if she could spot any of their old friends, and bring them over in turn to talk to James.

Looking down the valley, James said, 'This is a beautiful piece of country. Lovely trees. Shame about that house across the valley, though. Ruins the view.' Dawn decided not to mention it was her old house, which she had helped design.

Lunch was announced and Miles's PAs and the assistants from Gourmand Solutions circled the terrace coaxing guests towards the marquee. Miles felt everything was going brilliantly, he was elated. He had just been informed that one hundred percent of the VIPs had turned up—there were no no-shows at all—which just went to show what a hot ticket the Chawbury lunch had become. He spotted Peter and Samantha slipping into the throng, disgracefully late but at least they'd arrived. Sam looked sexy in a yellow Freeza Mart sundress, Peter off-message in denim jeans with holes.

Miles took his place at the top table between Dawn and Suzie, and surveyed the tent. Every seat at every table was filled, everyone appeared to be happy. Lines of waitresses were emerging from the field kitchen with the first courses, the quail egg salad from Longparish Organics. Miles congratulated himself on that particular stroke of genius, which would create a sense of obligation in Dawn. Elsewhere in the tent he could see his political VIPs and neighbours, all seemingly with full wine glasses. It surprised him to spot a line of guests forming up at an outlying table, the table where Peter was nominally in charge. Six or seven people at a time were queuing up, with new ones taking their places as others departed. He couldn't imagine what it was all about.

Beckoning a waitress, he asked, 'What's going on at table twenty-six? Is there a problem?'

Her eyes lit up. 'It's Pete Straker. The rock star. People are getting autographs.'

'Are they indeed?' Miles replied in a disapproving voice.

'He's a really nice guy,' said the waitress. 'Really friendly and normal. It's so amazing he's here, being in the same marquee as Pete Straker.'

It was while the plates from the first course were being cleared away that Miles's BlackBerry vibrated in his suit pocket. Automatically, he removed it and clicked on the Google Alert. Expecting some item about himself, he frowned to see it was about Mollie. 'Mollie Clegg to stand as Labour candidate for Droitwich and Redditch,' read the breaking news. 'Following the defection of her husband, Greg Clegg, from the Labour party to Conservatives to stand as candidate for the safe Tory seat of Mid-Hampshire, his wife Mollie has been named official Labour candidate for the West Midlands constituency he was formerly contesting.'

Miles peered at the tiny screen in disbelief. This had to be some kind of joke, surely. He sought out Mollie and spotted her at the next table. Their eyes met and Mollie blushed. In an instant, he knew it was true and the shock was unbearable. To have a daughter as a

Labour candidate, he felt consumed by shame. Everywhere he looked he could see important people who'd soon hear about it. The damage to himself would be incalculable.

A text pinged onto his mobile, rapidly followed by a second. The first read: 'Have u comment re yr daughter's defection 2 Labour? Plse call, Times Newspapers.' The second: 'Need 2 speak soonst abt family politics rift. Daily Mail.'

Turning in his direction, Dawn said, 'I've been meaning to thank you, Miles. I know you had a hand in getting Greg his seat. One feels much happier having him as a proper Conservative. James is delighted about it too.'

It was during the main course of half a wild lobster, new potatoes and mayonnaise and frisée lettuce, that his mobile began vibrating.

'Forgive me, Dawn,' he said, leaning away from the table to pick up.

It was the chief business reporter of *The Independent*; not one of the grandee City editors Miles included in his golden circle, but a man with a reputation for getting hold of scoops. In the past, he had caused problems for clients of Straker Communications.

'Is that Miles? Sorry to trouble you on your weekend, but I wanted your reaction to this Pendletons–Freeza Mart development?'

'Actually, this isn't very convenient, I'm hosting a large lunch party for three hundred people at the moment. Lord Pendleton's here with me, as a matter of fact. And I don't know about any developments either.'

'Oh, I thought you would. There's a rumour going round that eighty percent of the institutions have declared for Ross Clegg. That's what the market's saying. It'll be officially announced when they open tomorrow morning.'

'I don't think that's remotely likely,' Miles replied airily. 'Our own information's suggesting the precise opposite. Sentiment is strongly behind Pendletons.'

'Well, that's not what we're hearing. We're reporting it's all over bar the shouting.'

Miles longed to whip out his mobile and put in some calls but felt impossibly constrained. Most of the City editors he'd have rung were here in the tent anyway, and he could hardly go from table to table asking if they'd heard anything. Nor did it help having the Pendletons seated so close by, and he didn't want to disturb them with a no doubt erroneous rumour. So he did his best to act natural, making polite conversation with Dawn while feeling slightly sick inside. It couldn't possibly be true, he reassured himself, it was out of the question. For the past fortnight Archie had been passing on statistics which showed how badly things were going inside the Ross camp, and how close to the wire they were

A flurry of texts pinged onto his mobile, and the vibrating drone of the BlackBerry downloading message after message, including Google Alerts with links to blogs. Half refered to Mollie; the rest to the Freeza Mart rumour, all predicting the takeover would go through on Monday.

Wiping his forehead with a napkin, Miles became conscious of the distant drone of machinery. At first, he thought it must be a tractor working in a nearby field, but it became rapidly louder and seemed to be coming from above. At that moment, the black and gold fuselage of Ross's helicopter swooped low across the marquee, hovered above the lawn and tipped in the direction of the guests. Inside the bubble cockpit he could clearly see Ross, laughing and giving a cheery thumbs-up.

The down-draft from the chopper, now hovering less than four feet above the lawn, blew the flowers and plants in the herbaceous borders almost horizontal, and petals were strewn like confetti in the breeze. Even more infuriatingly, many of the guests were now standing up in excitement at the sight of the helicopter, leaving their tables and clustering round the open flaps of the marquee for a better view. 'That's Ross Clegg,' people exclaimed. 'He looks very happy about something.'

Ross was staring round the interior of the tent, as if searching for someone in particular. From the cockpit he spotted Archie and Gemma, then at an adjacent table Greg. Then he saw James Pendleton, virtually the only person left in the marquee concentrating on his lunch, and Dawn—still legally Ross's wife—sitting opposite him. Then, at last, he spotted Miles. Miles was glaring out at the helicopter, eyes bulging with fury.

For a split second they held eye contact and then Ross, very deliberately, raised the middle finger of his right hand in an obscene gesture. Then he accelerated into the air and headed off down the valley.

It was at this precise moment Miles snapped. It was the moment that thirty-five years of coiled ambition and achievement, of his quest for respect and perfection, finally fell apart. He surveyed the top table, he surveyed the tent, taking in his guests, his children—Mollie the socialist candidate, Samantha the callgirl, Peter the so-called pop star, Archie . . . even Archie had let him down in the end—and felt only hot rage and humiliation. Ross had given him the finger! Ross Clegg of Chawbury *Park* in the county of Hampshire, with his damned helicopter (which Miles so wanted himself), with his bigger, more expensive house in Holland Park Square, with his grander country address, with the *shoot* Miles himself coveted, all of it. And now it seemed he had stolen Pendletons too, and with it Miles's oldest, most important, most lucrative client.

Without a word Miles left the tent, weaving his way through the tables of guests which passed in a blur on each side of him. He walked up the yew walk like a man in a trance in the direction of the house, before turning into the cobbled yard where he kept his collection of tractors and JCBs. The keys to the vehicles hung on a special keyboard in an outhouse, meticulously labelled. Stepping up into the cabin of a yellow JCB excavator with hammer attachement, he turned the key and began his trundling progress across the yard. Eventually he reached the wall of beech hedges and the track down to the valley floor. Still in a trance, he stared through tunnel eyes at the valley ahead. Slowly he crossed the ornamental bridge over the Test, then out into open parkland. Half a mile ahead, at the crest of the hill, he could see the upper storey and rooftops of Chawbury Park.

At the halfway point of the valley, he turned as he always did to gaze back at the manor. He found himself unable to focus, seeing only the outline of his house and the big white tent alongside it. Cocooned inside the cabin, his brain swirled with insanity and revenge.

Arriving at the wall of leylandii trees on the boundary of Ross's property, he crashed through them, toppling several trunks with chain-tracked wheels. Twenty yards ahead was the Italian gazebo in which Dawn had loved to sit with her glass of Chablis on a summer's evening, and he flattened that too. On and on he rumbled, striking out a lamppost as he passed with the JCB hammer arm, like the tail of a dinosaur loose in a big city. Now he was crossing the wilderness of Ross's lawn, heading towards the house. He spotted the helipad across the drive, with the reviled helicopter parked dead centre on the letter H. Dropping into bottom gear for maximum thrust, he drove directly into it, knocking it over and flattening the fuselage, then reversing back over it. Now he turned again towards the house. The hollow fibreglass pillars by the entrance disintegrated at first push. 'Ha!' Miles muttered grimly to himself. 'Ha!' He was steering the JCB up the steps of Chawbury Park, smashing through the front door and into what Dawn had called 'the reception hall' and demolishing the horseshoe staircase, when he saw Ross sprinting through from the kitchen, alerted by the noise.

'What the fuck . . .' Ross shouted. 'Miles, for Christ's sake . . .'

But Miles was experiencing a sharp tightening in his chest which quickly travelled to his neck, shoulder blades and arms. He felt nauseous and dizzy, and had the distinct feeling he was about to die. Then he collapsed across the steering wheel of the still-moving vehicle.

He was still there when the ambulance arrived from Basingstoke and North Hampshire General Hospital, and the paramedics worked to restart his heart before carrying him away on a stretcher.

70.

Miles spent eight days and nights in intensive care, followed by a further seven weeks in hospital before his doctors would consider discharging him. His consultant told Davina that he had never before encountered such high or reactive blood pressure, and he was surprised Miles hadn't suffered a heart attack much earlier, his levels of stress being almost off the scale.

Davina travelled down to Basingstoke as soon as she heard about the heart attack, and spent virtually the next two months at his hospital bedside. It was Davina who liaised with the doctors and with the medical insurance people, and who organised the rota for the children's hospital visits. It was Davina, too, who rang Ross and told him how horrified she was about what had happened, and apologised profusely, and said she thought Miles must have had some kind of clinical brainstorm, something must have flipped in his head. She promised they'd pay for every repair to his house, of course, and only hoped Ross wouldn't prosecute.

The newspaper coverage was mortifying too, and had to be kept from Miles as he began to recover. The *Daily Mail* had a field day describing the well-connected multi-millionaire spin-doctor and Tory grandee who'd bulldozed Ross Clegg's mansion, 'causing an estimated million pounds worth of damage.' There had been photographs of both houses at opposite ends of the valley—the Manor and the Park—and pictures of Miles and Davina, and pictures of Ross and Dawn, and pictures of Dawn with James, and lists of all the high-profile guests who'd witnessed the vandalism from the marquee. Had Miles been allowed to read it, he'd certainly have had a second heart attack.

Davina decided it made sense for her to move back into Chawbury Manor, into a spare bedroom, as a base for her daily visits to the hospital. The surviving gardeners and help at Chawbury were delighted by her return, feeling appreciated again for the first time in more than a year, and Davina was able to reassure them after the shock of what came to be known as 'the incident' which had left them shaken and fearful for their jobs. Soon, much of the old routine was re-established at the house, and Davina made a point of inviting the children to stay every weekend or whenever else they came down to visit their father. It was a good feeling having them all home again, in their old bedrooms, and hanging out as a family in the kitchen. As far as Davina was concerned, all Miles's family feuds and banishments were abandoned. He was hardly in a position to object, in his present enfeebled state.

The children found it all very difficult. The incident had shocked them, and Sam and Mollie in particular were mortified by the memory of their father in the JCB crushing Ross's helicopter, clearly visible from the terrace and watched by the 300 guests. Now they were shocked by Miles's appearance in hospital, grey-faced and propped up on pillows. Sometimes he scarcely seemed to recognise them, or was too tired to talk. When he did speak, his voice was husky and his breathing laboured. It was hard to connect this sad befuddled figure, hooked up to a saline drip and heart monitors, with the Miles of old.

Davina was glad to have the children there with her, Peter especially, because there were big decisions to be made about Straker Communications. Several of the largest clients, such as Trent Valley Power 4 U and Eaziprint, had immediately sacked their agency after the incident, and of course they'd lost the Pendletons account too following Ross's successful takeover. Revenues plunged by 70 percent and Rick Partington, Strakers' MD, warned of further account losses to come. Hundreds of staff had to be let go, three floors in Golden Square stood empty, and it was difficult to envisage what future the business could have. New clients were unlikely to appoint a public relations consultancy whose crazy chairman had bulldozed Ross Clegg's house. Strakers was a tarnished brand.

After months of indecision, Davina agreed it made sense to dispose of the rump of the business for whatever they could get for it, and soon afterwards it was absorbed into one of Sir Martin Sorrell's WPP subsidiaries.

Davina made other important decisions too, the first of which was to call off the divorce. She felt uncomfortable about leaving Miles in his present condition. It was one thing to leave a rich, vain, feuding, unfaithful control freak; another to leave the pitiful convalescent in the hospital bed. After weeks of negotiation with Ross's insurance underwriters, agreement was reached on compensation for the damage Miles had caused to Chawbury Park and to the helicopter; Davina heard Ross had intervened personally with the insurance company and been very helpful behind the scenes in reducing the Strakers' contribution. Nevertheless, with Straker Communications out of business and a sizeable compensation bill, Peter and his mother recognised the necessity of cutting back, and they put the Holland Park Square house on the market. Despite the credit crunch, it sold in a matter of weeks for a very good price, and the Strakers would be able to continue living comfortably at Chawbury Manor without problem or anxiety. On the advice of his doctors, they decided to say nothing about the sale to Miles at this point, in case the stress should trigger a relapse. He had been back home at Chawbury for several months now, but suffered a series of minor strokes which affected the muscles in his legs and his face, and it was becoming clear he might never make more than a partial recovery. Certainly all thought of any return to work was out of the question. He spent much of his time these days sitting in a favourite armchair in his study, looking at the newspapers or, more usually, the television. His concentration deteriorated noticeably, and he often dozed off in front of the screen. When the children came to visit, he was docile and benign, but sometimes confused about who was who and what jobs they all did. Both Samantha and Mollie were endlessly patient with him and even moved into the house for a period to help their mother look after him, despite Mollie having her seat in Droitwich and Redditch to nurse as well.

Old friends like the Mountleighs, the Winstantons and the Nairns rallied round, shrugging off the terrible publicity of the incident, though it soon became clear that Miles wasn't really any longer up to dinner parties. On the rare occasions he was coaxed out, his speech was slurred from the stroke and he was hard work for the people seated either side of him. Everyone commented on what a complete saint Davina was, the way she cared for him so unselfishly. After Nigel Winstanton lost his job at Lehman Brothers, when the whole thing went belly-up during the credit crunch, he regularly drove over to Chawbury bringing a good bottle of wine, and sat with Miles in front of the racing on television all afternoon, getting quietly sozzled. When the weather became warmer again, Miles often sat outside on a deck chair watching Davina work in the garden. He seldom so much as glanced at the horizon and the gaping facade of Chawbury Park, unoccupied and shored-up by scaffolding.

Ross had so much on his plate following the takeover that repairing the house had to be a low priority. The surveyors' report said much of it was now structurally unsound, Miles having damaged several supporting walls, so it was going to require serious thought. His combined new supermarket group was second in size only to Tesco, and his workload punishing as he sought to integrate the two businesses as well as selling and leasing back all of the Pendletons store sites and properties, and disposing of the Pendletons headquarters building behind the Barbican. 'We won this takeover by the skin of our teeth,' he told his Board, 'now we owe it to our investors to make it work.' The only person Ross felt seriously sore about was Archie. He found his betrayal of trust unforgivable, and fired him without regret. Nor did it upset him when, soon afterwards, Gemma called an end to her affair and told Archie to leave Roupell Street. No way could she go on living with someone who'd spied on her dad.

As for Miles, Ross only ever referred to him as 'that madman.' 'I'll never forget the sight of him crashing through my house in this bloody great JCB. The bloke's round the twist, there's nothing else to say about him.' Whatever downtime Ross could manage, he spent with Serena who played an increasingly pivotal role in his life. In due course, she left Robin altogether and moved in to Holland Park Square and it was tacitly understood they would marry as soon as they were legally free to do so. Ross had always got on well with Serena's boy, Ollie, and the new arrangement promised to be as painless as these situations ever can be. Both Serena and her son settled quickly into the enormous stucco mansion and, since Serena had made most of the important decorating decisions herself in the first place, very little needed altering for the incoming regime.

In due course, they discussed the idea of finding somewhere in the country for weekends and holidays. Neither felt comfortable at the prospect of living at Chawbury Park, which anyway remained uninhabitable. Serena also felt it was much too close to Miles, an old association she wished to forget. Eventually, Ross bought a Jacobean manor house in Warwickshire, within easy reach of his Coventry warehouse, which had the added appeal of closely resembling the Jacobean farmhouse in which Serena had grown up as a child.

Dawn and James married quietly at Chelsea Registry Office, with Hugh, Gemma and Debbie as the only witnesses, and honeymooned in St Lucia which James found much too hot for his taste. Initially very hurt by the hostile takeover of his family's business, there was at least consolation in having almost a billion pounds in cash in the bank, as did all his brothers. He found it disorientating at first having no office to go in to, and no structure to his days, but he soon became used to it and actually enjoyed leading a quieter life, adding to his picture and sculpture collection. Dawn, in any case, did more than enough for both of them. The combination of her energy and vision for Longparish Organics, bankrolled by her husband's money, meant that her ventures took off at impressive speed. The farm shop on the estate quickly became a magnet for well-heeled locals and did extraordinary business, despite its astronomical prices. Punnets of organic strawberries and raspberries sold out at ten pounds each, and the Longparish range of reproduction antique and contemporary garden furniture soon required a dozen full-time craftsmen in the workshop. In due course, she opened a vast and deeply chic showroom for the furniture in London, in Sidney Street, as well as the Longparish Organics delis in Notting Hill and Marylebone High Street. Everyone agreed Lady Pendleton had taken Longparish Priory to new levels of comfort and good taste, with the help of decorators flown in from New

York and Milan. She threw herself into every kind of cultural philanthropy, and very few museum or art gallery extensions were completed without the names James and Dawn Pendleton being chiselled into the sandstone wall commemorating the benefactors. Every December, on the Saturday before Christmas, the Pendletons gave a large cocktail party at Longparish Priory for all their friends and Hampshire neighbours, and never neglected to include Miles and Davina on the invitation list, and whichever Straker children were at home that weekend.

Peter, of course, was a household name these days and seldom in Chawbury. Following the worldwide success of *The Cormorant's Cry*—a top-five album in the Billboard charts in the States as well as all over Europe—he bought a farmhouse and fifteen thousand acres of hillside in Caithness, and a house on the beach in Mustique. The second album has been a long time in the making, but Sam, who has heard several of the songs says it is as good, if not better, than the first.

Samantha has been kept on as a face of Freeza Mart fashion and otherwise lives quietly in the country, attending NA meetings and doing a lot of riding. For the first year after her father's heart attack and strokes, she stayed down at Chawbury to help her mother, but recently has fallen in love with a handsome racing trainer at Lambourne and spends a lot of time over there. Davina is very hopeful it might lead to something. Meanwhile, the racing trainer is having an incredible time in bed, doing things he'd only previously read about.

Mollie's political career started to take off, and she was often heard on the radio in her capacity as junior shadow Minister for Education. She won the Droitwich and Redditch seat by the thinnest of majorities, though the swing against Labour in the constituency was well below the national average, entirely thanks to her personal popularity. She was delighted when both Davina and Peter made the effort to come up to the Midlands to canvas for her. Peter, in particular, was a big draw with the voters, being a celebrity. As a Member of Parliament, Mollie was exceptionally hardworking and effective in the constituency, showing up at every event and championing local hospitals and schools. Her sincerity and competence were quickly noticed within the shrunken Labour Party, who deployed her as a voter-friendly spokesperson in numerous situations. Her marriage to Greg was quietly dissolved, but she kept her new love interest firmly to herself.

As for Archie, he returned home to Chawbury the least frequently of all the children, never quite finding the energy or impetus to leave his dissolute new existence in London. Having been dumped by Gemma and by Freeza Mart, he reverted to his old doorman's role at Thurloes before gravitating to other, seedier nightclubs. Eventually he found the financial backing to open a club of his own off Leicester Square, drawing a very young teenage crowd, which is said to be doing rather well. He leads an entirely nocturnal life, bloated with alcohol and pasty-faced from lack of sunlight and fresh air, but always with a younger girl on his arm. Gemma told him he could visit Mandy whenever he liked, but he is lazy about it and seldom does.

Gemma took several months to adjust to life after Archie, but there could be no question of staying with him once she learnt how treacherously he'd behaved towards her dad. Slowly the tentacles of her enduring obsession loosened their grip, and she threw herself into her part-time job at Freeza Mart as well as caring for Mandy, who was dismayed when Archie left Roupell Street so abruptly. She had adored Mummy's naughty boyfriend who made her laugh. A year or so after the takeover went through, Gemma met one of Ross's regional managers at an office social, and fell in love. A year later she and Mike married and moved up to Worcestershire, to a house in Droitwich less than half a mile from the house Gemma had lived in as a child. It felt good to be back. Hampshire and London were all very fine, but she felt more at home in the West Midlands, and she hoped Mandy would one day go to her old school, Droitwich Spa High. Many of her school friends were still living in the area, with families of their own, and she and Mike liked to think they'd stay put for the rest of their lives. Almost the only person Gemma ever sees these days from her Chawbury years is Mollie, their local MP and Mandy's godmother, who comes over all the time and is as friendly as ever. If Mollie ever mentioned Archie's name in conversation, Gemma didn't even blush, the spell was well and truly broken long ago. And, of course, it was great to see Mollie's new partner on his frequent visits to the area.

Mollie and Hugh Pendleton quietly got together eighteen months after she left Greg. It is the happiest of romances, with both of them leading their own lives and spending time together whenever their schedules permit. Hugh used part of his considerable inheritance to start an ecological hedge fund, investing only in green and ethical ventures, which is said to be booming. One day, he and Mollie might get round to getting married, but there's no hurry, it isn't even on the horizon at the moment.

Debbie continued to thrive at Freeza Mart as Managing Director of the hospitality division, overseeing almost sixty budget hotels. All the old Pendletons's service station lodges were successfully rebranded FM Sleep, and Debbie has been looking closely at several competitor chains, weighing the benefits of taking them over too. She found she relished the mass-market end of the hotel industry, and never regretted not going to work at that splashy resort in the Maldives. It still annoyed her like hell when she discovered Miles Straker had caused her job offer to be withdrawn out of spite, but it no longer rankled, it had been a lucky escape really. She was thrilled when her mother called at one of her revamped motorway lodges with Lord Pendleton, who said he thought she'd done a tremendous job. 'It looks a great deal better than it did when *we* managed it,' he said. Debbie also retained responsibility for choosing the new pop releases to play in the supermarkets. There were now so many stores, including the 700 Pendletons ones, that Debbie has become an influential figure, endlessly courted by the record companies pushing their talent. It tickled her to be included in a *New Musical Express* list of the 50 most powerful people in the music industry, capable of making or breaking new bands with her selections. As Debbie said, 'I don't know the first thing about rock music. I just have the same taste as our customers.'

Of all the Chawbury diaspora, the most tragic was Greg. It was a hugely public humiliation losing the Mid-Hampshire seat to the Liberal Democrats at the General Election, with an 18 percent swing against the national trend. The explanation was all too clear: voter mutiny against an unpopular and obnoxious candidate. Even loyal lifelong Tories either abstained or voted Lib Dem as tales of

Greg's arrogance swept the constituency. Many people were openly critical of Miles for imposing him on them in the first place. Having heard the crushing result from the chief returning officer on Election night, Greg gave a long, bitter and partly incoherent speech from the platform, blaming his defeat on his party workers, the constituency Secretary, the local media, Miles, Ross, Lord Pendleton and anyone else who came to mind. It was all excruciatingly embarrassing. Afterwards, he got straight into his car and drove up to London, never to return. These days, he makes a living writing weekly columns for the *New Statesman* and the *Sunday Mirror*, full of bile and contempt for both the government and the opposition, as well as for business and commerce, the education system, the Establishment, the green movement and many other pet hates. He seldom missed an opportunity to slag off his ex-wife in print, and also to attack Ross. Mollie in particular found this very hurtful, but Hugh told her to just ignore it. 'Everyone else does.'

What with his workload at Freeza Mart and the renovation of the Jacobean manor, Ross was in no hurry to decide what to do about Chawbury Park. For three years it just stood there, held up by scaffolding, and increasingly a magnet for vandals on motorcycles. For a time, Ross thought it would be easier simply to put it up for sale in its present condition and get shot of it. But he enjoyed bringing parties of mates to the pheasant shoot over Matt Marland's old land. In the end, he decided to demolish the rest of Chawbury Park, leaving only the stable yard and garages standing, which he converted into a dining room for shooting lunches. Everything else was flattened. Only a few outbuildings and garden walls gave any clue that a sizeable house had once existed on the site.

Ross arranged for plantations of native English trees to be established on the old paddocks and lawns, in tens of thousands of grow tubes, and for shallow ponds to be dug as habitats for newts and salamanders. In time, horseshoe bats took up residence in the ruins of the old sauna and gym complex where they roosted undisturbed from one year to the next. When he was interviewed by the *Sunday Times* following his knighthood for services to retail in the Queen's Birthday Honours list, and was asked what he thought his greatest achievement had been, Ross immediately said his nature reserve at Chawbury Park. 'Long after all the rest of it's gone and forgotten, all the stores, warehouses, merchandise, all of it, I like to think the trees I've planted will still be standing, the oaks and whatnot, and the ponds for endangered species. That's something I'm proud of, for sure. That and my wife and the kids, and my stepson Ollie, of course.'